THE BOOK OF
FANTASY

THE BOOK OF
FANTASY

Edited by
JORGE LUIS
BORGES
SILVINA OCAMPO
A. BIOY CASARES

INTRODUCED BY URSULA K. LE GUIN

VIKING

INDEXED IN SSI 89-93

VIKING

Published by the Penguin Group
Viking Penguin Inc., 40 West 23rd Street, New York, New York 10010, U.S.A.
Penguin Books Ltd, 27 Wrights Lane, London W8 5TZ, England
Penguin Books Australia Ltd, Ringwood, Victoria, Australia
Penguin Books Canada Ltd, 2801 John Street, Markham, Ontario, Canada L3R 1B4
Penguin Books (N.Z.) Ltd, 182–190 Wairau Road, Auckland 10, New Zealand

Penguin Books Ltd, Registered Offices:
Harmondsworth, Middlesex, England

First published in 1988 by Viking Penguin Inc.
Published simultaneously in Great Britain by Xanadu Publications Limited

10 9 8 7 6 5 4 3 2 1

Library of Congress Cataloging in Publication Data
Antología de la literatura fantástica. English.
  The book of fantasy.
  Translation of: Antología de la literatura fantástica.
  Includes bio-bibliographies.
  1. Fantastic literature. I. Borges, Jorge Luis,
1899–1986. II. Ocampo, Silvina. III. Bioy Casares,
Adolfo. IV. Title.
PN6071.F25A5513 1988   808.83′876   88–40100
ISBN 0–670–82393–7

Printed in Great Britain by Richard Clay (The Chaucer Press) Ltd, Bungay, Suffolk
Set in Garamond
Designed by Richard Glyn Jones

CONTENTS

Introduction by URSULA K. LE GUIN   9

Sennin RYUNOSUKE AKUTAGAWA   13

A Woman Alone with Her Soul
    THOMAS BAILEY ALDRICH   16

Ben-Tobith LEONID ANDREYEV   17

The Phantom Basket JOHN AUBREY   20

The Drowned Giant J. G. BALLARD   21

Enoch Soames MAX BEERBOHM   28

The Tail of the Sphinx AMBROSE BIERCE   48

The Squid in Its Own Ink ADOLFO BIOY CASARES   49

Guilty Eyes AH'MED ECH CHIRUANI   57

Anything You Want! . . . LÉON BLOY   58

Tlön, Uqbar, Orbis Tertius JORGE LUIS BORGES   61

Odin JORGE LUIS BORGES and DELIA INGENIEROS   73

The Golden Kite, The Silver Wind RAY BRADBURY   73

The Man Who Collected the First of September, 1973
    TOR ÅGE BRINGSVAERD   77

The Careless Rabbi MARTIN BUBER   81

The Tale and the Poet Sir Richard Burton   81

Fate is a Fool ARTURO CANCELA and
    PILAR DE LUSARRETA   82

An Actual Authentic Ghost THOMAS CARLYLE   92

The Red King's Dream LEWIS CARROLL   92

The Tree of Pride G. K. CHESTERTON   94

The Tower of Babel G. K. CHESTERTON   95

The Dream of the Butterfly CHUANG TZU   95

The Look of Death JEAN COCTEAU   96

House Taken Over JULIO CORTÁZAR   96

Being Dust SANTIAGO DABOVE   100

A Parable of Gluttony ALEXANDRA DAVID-NEEL   104

The Persecution of the Master
   ALEXANDRA DAVID-NEEL   105

The Idle City LORD DUNSANY   106

Tantalia MACEDONIO FERNANDEZ   110

Eternal Life J. G. FRAZER   114

A Secure Home ELENA GARRO   115

The Man Who Did Not Believe in Miracles
   HERBERT A. GILES   123

Earth's Holocaust NATHANIEL HAWTHORNE   124

Ending for a Ghost Story I. A. IRELAND   137

The Monkey's Paw W. W. JACOBS   138

What is a Ghost? JAMES JOYCE   145

May Goulding JAMES JOYCE   146

The Wizard Passed Over DON JUAN MANUEL   147

Josephine the Singer, or The Mouse Folk FRANZ KAFKA   149

Before the Law FRANZ KAFKA   160

The Return of Imray RUDYARD KIPLING   162

The Horses of Abdera LEOPOLDO LUGONES   170

The Ceremony ARTHUR MACHEN   175

The Riddle WALTER DE LA MARE   177

Who Knows? GUY DE MAUPASSANT   180

The Shadow of the Players EDWIN MORGAN   190

The Cat H. A. MURENA   190

The Story of the Foxes NIU CHIAO   192

The Atonement SILVINA OCAMPO   193

The Man Who Belonged to Me GIOVANNI PAPINI   202

Rani CARLOS PERALTA   208

The Blind Spot BARRY PEROWNE   213

The Wolf PETRONIUS   222

The Bust MANUEL PEYROU   224

The Cask of Amontillado EDGAR ALLAN POE   229

The Tiger of Chao-Ch'Eng P'U SUNG LING   234

How We Arrived at the Island of Tools
   FRANÇOIS RABELAIS   236

The Music on the Hill 'SAKI' (H. H. MUNRO)   237

Where Their Fire is Not Quenched MAY SINCLAIR   241

The Cloth Which Weaves Itself W. W. SKEAT   256

Universal History OLAF STAPLEDON   257

A Theologian in Death EMANUEL SWEDENBORG   257

The Encounter FROM THE T'ANG DYNASTY   259

The Three Hermits LEO TOLSTOY   260

Macario B. TRAVEN   265

The Infinite Dream of Pao-Yu TSAO HSUEH-CHIN   291

The Mirror to Wind-and-Moon TSAO HSEUH-CHIN   292

The Desire To Be a Man VILLIERS DE L'ISLE ADAM   294

Memmon, or Human Wisdom VOLTAIRE   300

The Man Who Liked Dickens EVELYN WAUGH   304

Pomegranate Seed EDITH WHARTON   315

Lukundoo EDWARD LUCAS WHITE   336

The Donguys JUAN RUDOLFO WILCOCK   346

Lord Arthur Savile's Crime OSCAR WILDE   353

The Sorcerer of the White Lotus Lodge
  RICHARD WILHELM   376

The Celestial Stag   G. WILLOUGHBY-MEADE   377

Saved by the Book   G. WILLOUGHBY-MEADE   377

The Reanimated Englishman
  MARY WOLLSTONECRAFT SHELLEY   378

The Sentence   WU CH'ENG EN   379

The Sorcerers   WILLIAM BUTLER YEATS   380

Fragment   JOSÉ ZORILLA   382

SOURCES AND ACKNOWLEDGEMENTS   383

Introduction

by Ursula K. Le Guin

There are two books which I look upon as esteemed and cherished great-aunts or grandmothers, wise and mild though sometimes rather dark of counsel, to be turned to when the judgment hesitates for want of material to form itself upon. One of these books provides facts, of a peculiar sort. The other does not. The *I Ching* or Book of Changes is the visionary elder who has outlived fact, the Ancestor so old she speaks a different tongue. Her counsel is sometimes appallingly clear, sometimes very obscure indeed. 'The little fox crossing the river wets its tail,' she says, smiling faintly, or, 'A dragon appears in the field,' or, 'Biting upon dried gristly meat . . .' One retires to ponder long upon such advice. The other Auntie is younger, and speaks English—indeed, she speaks more English than anybody else. She offers fewer dragons and much more dried gristly meat. And yet the *Oxford English Dictionary*, or *A New English Dictionary on Historical Principles*, is also a Book of Changes. Most wonderful in its transmutations, it is not a Book of Sand, yet is inexhaustible; not an Aleph, yet all we can ever say is there, if we can but find it.

'Auntie!' I say (magnifying glass in hand, because my edition, the Compact Auntie, is compressed into two volumes of terrifyingly small print)—'Auntie! please tell me about *fantasy*, because I want to talk about *The Book of Fantasy*, but I am not sure what I am talking about.'

'Fantasy, or Phantasy,' replies Auntie, clearing her throat, 'is from the Greek φαντασία, lit. "a making visible."' She explains that φαντασία, is related to φαντάζειν, 'to make visible,' or in Late Greek , 'to imagine, have visions,' and to φαντειν, 'to show.' And she summarizes the older uses of the word in English: an appearance, a phantom, the mental process of sensuous perception, the faculty of imagination, a false notion, caprice, or whim. Then, though she eschews the casting of yarrow stalks or coins polished with sweet oil, being after all an Englishwoman, she begins to tell the Changes: the mutations of a word moving through the minds of people moving through the centuries. She shows how a word that to the Schoolmen of the late Middle Ages meant 'the mental apprehension of an object of perception,' that is, the mind's very act of linking itself to the phenomenal world, came in time to signify just the reverse—an hallucination, or a phantasm, or the habit of deluding oneself. After which, doubling back on its tracks like a hare, the word *fantasy* was used to mean the imagination, 'the process, the faculty, or the result of forming mental representations of things not actually present.' This definition seems very close to the Scholastic sense of *fantasy*, but leads, of course, in quite the opposite direction—going so far in that direction, these days, as often to imply that the representation is extravagant, or visionary, or merely fanciful. (*Fancy* is *fantasy*'s own daughter, via elision of the penult; while *fantastic* is a sister-word with a family of her own.)

9

So *fantasy* remains ambiguous; it stands between the false, the foolish, the delusory, the shallows of the mind, and the mind's deep connection with the real. On this threshold sometimes it faces one way, masked and beribboned, frivolous, an escapist; then it turns, and we glimpse as it turns the face of an angel, bright truthful messenger, arisen Urizen.

Since the *Oxford English Dictionary* was compiled, the tracks of the word *fantasy* have been complicated still further by the comings and goings of psychologists. The technical uses in psychology of *fantasy* and *phantasy* have deeply influenced our sense and use of the word; and they have also given us the handy verb *to fantasize*. But Auntie does not acknowledge the existence of that word. Into the Supplement, through the back door, she admits only *fantasist;* and she defines the newcomer, politely but with, I think, a faint curl of the lip, as 'one who "weaves" fantasies.' One might think that a fantasist was one who fantasizes, but it is not so. Currently, one who fantasizes is understood either to be daydreaming, or to be using the imagination therapeutically as a means of discovering reasons Reason does not know, discovering oneself to oneself. A fantasist is one who writes a fantasy for others. But the element of discovery is there, too.

Auntie's use of 'weave' may be taken as either patronizing or quaint, for writers don't often say nowadays that they 'weave' their works, but bluntly that they write them. Fantasists earlier in the century, in the days of victorious Realism, were often aplogetic about what they did, offering it as something less than 'real' fiction—mere fancywork, bobble-fringing to literature. More fantasists are rightly less modest now that what they do is generally recognized as literature, or at least as a genre of literature, or at least as a genre of subliterature, or at least as a commercial product. For *fantasies* are rife and many-colored on the bookstalls. The head of the fabled Unicorn is laid upon the lap of Mammon, and the offering is acceptable to Mammon. Fantasy, in fact, has become quite a business.

But when one night in Buenos Aires in 1937 three friends sat talking together about fantastic literature, it was not yet a business. Nor was it even known as fantastic literature, when one night in a villa in Geneva in 1818 three friends sat talking together, telling one another ghost stories. They were Mary Shelley, her husband Percy, and Lord Byron—and Claire Clairmont was probably with them, and the strange young Dr Polidori—and they told awful tales, and Mary Shelley was frightened. 'We will each,' cried Byron, 'write a ghost story!' So Mary went away and thought about it, fruitlessly, until a few nights later she dreamed a nightmare in which a 'pale student' used strange arts and machineries to arouse from unlife the 'hideous phantasm of a man.' And so, alone of the friends, she wrote her ghost story, *Frankenstein: or, A Modern Prometheus*, which I think is the first great modern fantasy. There are no ghosts in it; but fantasy, as the Dictionary showed us, is often seen as ghoulie-mongering. Because ghosts inhabit, or haunt, one part of the vast domain of fantastic literature, both oral and written, people familiar with that corner of it call the whole thing Ghost Stories, or Horror Tales; just as others call it Fairyland after the part of it they know or love best, and others call it Science Fiction, and others call it Stuff and Nonsense. But the nameless being given life by Dr Frankenstein's, or Mary Shelley's, arts and machineries is neither ghost nor fairy, and science-fictional only in intent; stuff and nonsense he is not. He is a creature of fantasy, archetypal, deathless. Once raised he will not sleep again, for his pain will not let him sleep, the unanswered moral questions that woke with him will not let him rest in peace. When there began to be money in the fantasy business, plenty of money was made out of him in Hollywood, but even that did not kill him. If his story were not too long for this anthology, it might well be here; very likely it was mentioned on that night in 1937 in Buenos Aires, when Jorge Luis Borges, Adolfo Bioy Casares, and Silvina Ocampo fell to talking—so Casares tells us—'about fantastic literature . . . discussing the stories which seemed best to us. One of us suggested that if we put together the fragments of the same type we had listed in our notebooks, we would have a good book. As a result we drew up this book . . . simply a compilation of stories from fantastic literature which seemed to us to be the best.'

So that, charmingly, is how *The Book of Fantasy* came to be, fifty years ago. Three friends talking. No plans, no definitions, no business, except the intention of 'having a good book.' Of course, in the making of such a book by such makers, certain definitions were implied by inclusion, and by exclusion other definitions were ignored; so one will find, perhaps for the first time, horror and ghosts and fairy and science-fiction stories all together within the covers of *The Book of Fantasy;* while any bigot wishing to certify himself as such by dismissing it as all stuff and nonsense is tacitly permitted to do so. The four lines in the book by Chuang Tzu should suffice to make him think twice, permanently.

It is an idiosyncratic selection, and completely eclectic. Some of the stories will be familiar to anyone who reads, others are exotic discoveries. A very well-known piece such as 'The Cask of Amontillado' seems less predictable, set among works and fragments from the Orient and South America and distant centuries, by Kafka, Swedenborg, Cortázar, Agutagawa, Niu Chiao; its own essential strangeness is restored to it. There is some weighting towards writers, especially English writers, of the late nineteenth and early twentieth centuries, which reflects, I imagine, the taste of the anthologizers and perhaps particularly that of Borges, who was himself a member and direct inheritor of the international tradition of fantasy which included Kipling and Chesterton.

Perhaps I should not say 'tradition,' since it has no name as such and little recognition in critical circles, and is distinguished in college English departments mainly by being ignored; but I believe that there is a company of fantasists that Borges belonged to even as he transcended it, and which he honored even as he transformed it. As he included these older writers in *The Book of Fantasy*, it may be read truly as his 'notebook' of sources and affiliations and elective affinities. Some chosen, such as Bloy or Andreyev, may seem rather heavyhanded now, but others are treasurable. The Dunsany story, for instance, is not only very beautiful, as the early poetry of Yeats is beautiful, but is also, fascinatingly, a kind of miniature or concave-mirror of the anthology itself. The book is full of such reflections and interconnections. Beerbohm's familiar tale of

'Enoch Soames,' read here, seems to involve and concern other writings and writers in the book; so that I now believe that when people gather in the Reading Room of the British Library on June 3rd, 1997, to wait for poor Enoch's phantom and watch him discover his *Fungoids*, still ignored by critics and professors and the heartless public, still buried ignominious in the Catalogue,—I believe that among those watching there will be other phantoms; and among those, perhaps, Borges. For he will see then, not as through a glass, darkly.

If in the 1890s fantasy appeared to be a kind of literary fungus-growth, if in the 1920s it was still perceived as secondary, if in the 1980s it has been degraded by commercial exploitation, it may well seem quite safe and proper to the critics to ignore it. And yet I think that our narrative fiction has been going slowly and vaguely and massively, not in the wash and slap of fad and fashion but as a deep current, for years, in one direction, and that that direction is the way of fantasy.

An American fiction writer now may yearn toward the pure veracity of Sarah Orne Jewett or Dreiser's *Sister Carrie*, as an English writer, such as Margaret Drabble, may look back with longing to the fine solidities of Bennett; but the limited and rationally perceived societies in which those books were written, and their shared language, are lost. Our society—global, multilingual, enormously irrational—can perhaps describe itself only in the global, intuitional language of fantasy.

So it may be that the central ethical dilemma of our age, the use or non-use of annihilating power, was posed most cogently in fictional terms by the purest of fantasists. Tolkien began *The Lord of the Rings* in 1937 and finished it about ten years later. During those years, Frodo withheld his hand from the Ring of Power, but the nations did not.

So it is that Italo Calvino's *Invisible Cities* serves many of us as a better guidebook to our world than any Michelin or Fodor's.

So it is that the most revealing and accurate descriptions of our daily life in contemporary fiction may be shot through with strangeness, or displaced in time, or set upon imaginary planets, or dissolved into the phantasmagoria of drugs or of psychosis, or may rise from the mundane suddenly into the visionary and as simply descend from it again.

So it is that the 'magical realists' of South America are read for their entire truthfulness to the way things are, and have lent their name as perhaps the most fitting to the kind of fiction most characteristic of our times.

And so it is that Jorge Luis Borges's own poems and stories, his reflections, his libraries, labyrinths, forking paths, and amphisbaenae, his books of tigers, of rivers, of sand, of mysteries, of changes, have been and will be honored by so many readers for so long: because they are beautiful, because they are nourishing, because they do supremely well what poems and stories do, fulfilling the most ancient, urgent function of words, just as the *I Ching* and the *Dictionary* do: to form for us 'mental representations of things not actually present,' so that we can form a judgment of what world we live in and where we might be going in it.

URSULA K. LE GUIN, 1987

Sennin*

Ryunosuke Akutagawa *(1892-1927), Japanese writer. Before taking his own life, he calmly explained the reasons which brought him to this decision and compiled a list of historical suicides, in which he included Christ. His works include* Grotesque and Curious Tales, The Three Treasures, Kappa, Rashomon, Japanese Short Stories. *He translated the works of Robert Browning into Japanese.*

My dear young readers, I am stopping in Osaka now, so I will tell you a story connected with this town.

Once upon a time there came to the town of Osaka a certain man who wanted to be a domestic servant. I do not know his real name, they only remember him by the common servant's name of Gonsuké, for he was, after all, a servant of all work.

Now this man—we'll call him Gonsuké, too—entered a 'WE CAN GET YOU ANY JOB' office and said to the clerk in charge, who was puffing at his long bamboo pipe:

'Please, Mr Clerk, I wish to become a sennin. Would you kindly find me a family where I could learn the secret while working as a servant?'

The clerk remained speechless for a while as if astonished at his client's tall order.

'Didn't you hear me, Mr Clerk?' said Gonsuké, 'I wish to become a *sennin*. Will you find me a family where I could learn the secret while working as a servant?'

'We're very sorry to disappoint you,' the clerk drawled, beginning to puff again at his forgotten pipe, 'but not once in our long business career have we undertaken to find a situation for aspirants to your Senninship! Suppose you go round to another place, then perhaps . . .'

Here Gonsuké edged closer to him on his petulant blue-pantalooned knees, and began to argue in this way:

'Now, now, mister, that isn't quite honest, is it? What does your signboard say, anyhow? It says, "WE CAN GET YOU ANY JOB" in so many words. Since you promise us *any* job, you ought to find us *no matter what kind* of jobs we may ask for. But now, you may have lied about it all along, intentionally.'

---

*According to the ancient Chinese legend, a holy hermit who usually lives in the heart of a mountain, and has trained himself to various mystical powers, those of flying in the air at will and enjoying extreme longevity among them.

His argument being quite reasonable, the clerk could not very well blame him for his angry outburst.

'I can assure you, Mr Stranger, there's no trick there. It's all straight,' the clerk pleaded hastily, 'but if you insist on your strange request I must beg you to come round to us again tomorrow. We'll make inquiries today at all likely places we can think of.'

The clerk could see no other way out of it than to give him the promise and get him away, for the present anyhow. Needless to say, however, he had not the faintest idea, how could he indeed, of any household where they could teach their servant the secrets of Senninship. So on getting rid of the visitor, the clerk hastened to a physician living near his place.

To him he told the story of his strange client, and then asked in an anxious pleading tone, 'Now, please, Doctor, what sort of family do you think could train a fellow into a sennin, and that very quickly?'

The question apparently puzzled the doctor. He remained a while in pensive silence, arms folded across his chest, vaguely looking at a big pine-tree in the garden. It was the doctor's helpmate, a very shrewd woman, better known as Old Vixen, who answered for him, uninivited, on hearing the clerk's story:

'Why, nothing can be simpler. Send him on to us. We'll make him a sennin in a couple of years.'

'Will you, really, ma'am? That's great! Really I can't thank you enough for your kind offer. But frankly, I felt certain from the first that a doctor and a sennin were somehow closely related to each other.'

The clerk, who was blissfully ignorant of her design, bowed his thanks again and again, and left in great glee.

Our doctor followed him out with his eyes, looking as sour as anything, and then, turning round on his wife, brayed peevishly:

'You silly old woman, do you realize what a foolish thing you've gone and said, now? What the dickens would you do if the bumpkin should begin to complain some day that we hadn't taught him a scrap of your holy trick after so many years?'

But his wife, far from asking his pardon, turned up her nose at him, and quacked, 'Pugh! You dullard, you'd better mind your own business. A fellow who is as stupidly simple as you could hardly scrape enough in this eat-or-be-eaten world to keep body and soul together.' This counter-attack succeeded, and she pecked her husband into silence.

The next morning, as had been agreed upon, the clerk brought his boorish client to the doctor's. Country-bred as he was, Gonsuké came this particular day ceremoniously dressed in *haori* and *hakama*, perhaps in honour of this important occasion of his first day. Outwardly, however, he was in no way different from the ordinary peasant. His very commonness must have been a bit of a surprise to the doctor, who had been expecting to see something unusual in a would-be sennin. He eyed him curiously as one might a rare exotic animal such as a musk-deer brought over from far-off India, and then said, 'I am told that you wish to be a sennin, and I'm very curious to know whatever has put such a notion into your head.'

'Well, sir, I haven't much to tell there,' replied Gonsuké. 'Indeed it was quite simple. When I first came up to this town and looked at the great big castle, I just thought like this: that even our great ruler Taiko who lives up there must die some day; that you may live in the grandest way imaginable, but still you must come to dust like the rest of us. Well, in short, that all our life is a fleeting dream is just what I felt then.'

'Then,' Old Vixen promptly put in her word, 'you'd do anything if you could only be a sennin?'

'Yes, madam, if only I could be one.'

'Very good; then you'll live here and work for us for twenty years from today, and you shall be the happy possessor of the secrets at the end of your term.'

'Really, madam? I'm indeed very much obliged to you.'

'But,' she added, 'for twenty years to come you won't get a penny from us as wages. Is that understood?'

'Yes, ma'am, thanks, ma'am. I agree to all that.'

In this way started Gonsuké's twenty-year-service at the doctor's. He would draw water from the well, chop firewood, prepare every meal, and do all the scrubbing and sweeping for the family. But this was not all, for he would follow the doctor on his rounds, carrying a big medicine-chest on his back. Yet for all this labour Gonsuké never asked for a single penny. Indeed nowhere in Japan could you have found a better servant for less wages.

At last the twenty long years passed, and Gonsuké, again ceremoniously dressed in his family-crested *haori* as when he first came to them, presented himself before his master and mistress. To them he expressed his cordial thanks for all their kindness to him during the past twenty years. 'And now, sir,' he went on, 'would you kindly teach me today, as you promised twenty years ago today, how to become a sennin and attain eternal youth and immortality?'

'Here's a go,' sighed the doctor to himself at this request. After having worked him twenty long years for nothing, how in the name of humanity could he tell his servant now, that really he knew nothing of the way to Senninship? The doctor wriggled himself out of the dilemma, saying that it was not he but his wife who knew the secrets. 'So you must ask her to tell you,' he concluded, and turned woodenly away.

His wife, however, was sweetly unperturbed.

'Very well, then, I'll teach you,' she said, 'but, mind, you must do what I tell you, however difficult it may seem. Otherwise you could never be a sennin, and besides, you'll then have to work for us another twenty years without pay, or believe me, God Almighty will strike you dead on the spot.'

'Very good, madam, I'll do anything, however difficult it may be,' replied Gonsuké. He was now hugely delighted, and waited for her to give the word.

'Well then,' she said, 'climb that pine-tree in the garden.'

Utter stranger as she undoubtedly was to Senninship, her intentions may have been simply to impose any impossible task on him, and, in case of his failure, to secure his free services for another twenty years. At her order, however, Gonsuké started climbing the tree without a moment's hesitation.

'Go up higher,' she called after him, 'no, still higher, right up to the top.'

Standing near the edge of the verandah, she craned her neck to get a better view of her servant on the tree and now saw his *haori* fluttering high up among the topmost boughs of that very tall pine-tree.

'Now let go your right hand.'

Gonsuké gripped the bough with his left hand the tighter, and then let go his right in a gingerly sort of way.

'Next, let go your left hand as well!'

'Come, come, my good woman,' said her husband at last, now peering his anxious face upward from behind her. 'You know, with his left hand off the bough the bumpkin must fall to the ground. And right below there's the big stone, and he's a dead man as sure as I'm a doctor.'

'Right now I want none of your precious advice. Leave everything to me. — Hey, man, off with your left hand, do you hear?'

No sooner had she given the word than Gonsuké pushed away his hesitant left hand. Now with both hands off the bough, how could he stay on the tree? The next moment, as the doctor and his wife caught their breath, Gonsuké, yes, and his *haori*, too, were seen to come off the bough, and then . . . And then, why, w-w-what's this?—he stopped, he stopped! in mid-air, instead of dropping like a brick, and stayed on up in the bright noonday sky, posing like a marionette.

'I thank you both from the very bottom of my heart. You've made me a Sennin,' said Gonsuké from far above.

He was seen to make a very polite bow to them, and then he started climbing higher and higher, softly stepping on the blue sky, until he became a mere dot and disappeared in the fleecy clouds.

What became of the doctor and his wife no one knows. But the big pine-tree in their garden is known to have lived on for a long time, for it is told that a couple of centuries later a Yodoya Tatsugoro who wanted to see the tree clad in snow went to the trouble and expense of having the big tree, which was then more than twenty feet round, transplanted in his own garden.

A Woman Alone with Her Soul

Thomas Bailey Aldrich, *North American poet and novelist, was born in New Hampshire in 1835 and died in Boston in 1907. He was the author of* Cloth of Gold *(1874),* Wyndham Tower *(1879) and* An Old Town by the Sea *(1893).*

A woman is sitting alone in a house. She knows she is alone in the whole world: every other living thing is dead. The doorbell rings.

Ben-Tobith

Leonid Andreyev *(1871-1919) studied law at the universities of Moscow and St Petersburg but, after depressions which led to several suicide attempts, turned to writing, encouraged by Gorki. His sensational themes, treated in a highly realistic manner, made his reputation; amongst his works are* In the Fog *(1902) and* The Red Laugh *(1904), as well as numerous plays.*

On that dread day, when a universal wrong was wrought, and Jesus Christ was crucified between two thieves on Golgotha—on that day the teeth of Ben-Tobith, a trader of Jerusalem, had begun to ache unbearably from the earliest hours of the morning.

That toothache had begun even the day before, toward evening: at first his right jaw had begun to pain him slightly, while one tooth (the one just before the wisdom tooth) seemed to have become a little higher and, whenever the tongue touched it, felt a trifle painful. After supper, however, the ache had subsided entirely; Ben-Tobith forgot all about it and felt rather on good terms with the world—he had made a profitable deal that day, exchanging his old ass for a young and strong one, was in a very merry mood, and had not considered the ill-boding symptoms of any importance.

And he had slept very well and most soundly, but just before the dawn something had begun to trouble him, as though someone were rousing him to attend to some very important matter, and when Ben-Tobith angrily awoke, his teeth were aching, aching frankly and malevolently, in all the fullness of a sharp and piercing pain. And by now he could not tell whether it was only the tooth that had bothered him yesterday or whether other teeth had also made common cause with it: all his mouth and his head were filled with a dreadful sensation of pain, as though he were compelled to chew a thousand red-hot, sharp nails.

He took a mouthful of water from a clay jug: for a few moments the raging pain vanished; the teeth throbbed and undulated, and this sensation was actually pleasant in comparison with what he had felt before. Ben-Tobith lay down anew, bethought him of his newly acquired young ass, reflected how happy he would be if it were not for those teeth of his, and tried his best to fall asleep. But the water had been warm, and five minutes later the pain returned, raging worse than before, and Ben-Tobith sat up on his pallet and swayed to and fro like a pendulum. His whole face puckered up and was drawn toward his prominent nose, while on the nose itself, now all white from his torments, hung a bead of cold sweat.

And thus, swaying and groaning from his pain, did he greet the first rays of that sun which was fated to behold Golgotha with its three crosses and then grow dim from horror and grief.

Ben-Tobith was a good man and a kindly, with little liking for wronging anybody, yet when his wife awoke he told her many unpleasant things, even

17

though he was barely able to open his mouth, and complained that he had been left alone like a jackal, to howl and writhe in his pain. His wife accepted the unmerited reproaches with patience, since she realized that they were not uttered from an evil heart, and brought him many excellent remedies, such as purified rat droppings, to be applied to the cheek, a pungent infusion of scorpions, and a true shard of the tablets of the law, splintered off at the time Moses had shattered them.

The rat droppings eased the pain a little, but not for long; it was the same way with the infusion and the shard, for each time, after a short-lived relief, the pain returned with new vigor. And during the brief moments of respite Ben-Tobith consoled himself by thinking of the young ass and making plans concerning it, while at such times as his teeth worsened he moaned, became wroth with his wife, and threatened to dash his brains out against a stone if the pain would not abate. And all the while he kept pacing up and down the flat roof of his house, but avoided coming too near the edge thereof for very shame, since his whole head was swathed, like a woman's, in a shawl.

The children came running to him several times and, speaking very fast, told him something or other about Jesus of Nazareth. Ben-Tobith would stop his pacing and listen to them for a few moments with his face puckering but then stamp his foot in anger and drive them from him; he was a kindhearted man and loved children, but now he was wroth because they annoyed him with all sorts of trifles.

Nor was that the only unpleasant thing: the street, as well as all the roofs near by, were crowded with people who did not have a single thing to do, apparently, but stare at Ben-Tobith with his head swathed, like a woman's, in a shawl. And he was just about to come down from the roof when his wife told him:

'Look there—they're leading the robbers. Maybe that will make thee forget thy pain.'

'Leave me in peace, woman. Canst thou not see how I suffer?' Ben-Tobith answered her surlily.

But the words of his wife held out a vague hope that his toothache might let up, and he grudgingly approached the parapet of his roof. Putting his head to one side, shutting one eye and propping up his sore cheek with his hand, he made a wry, weepy face, and looked down.

An enormous mob, raising great dust and an incessant din, was going helter-skelter through the narrow street that ran uphill. In the midst of this mob walked the malefactors, bending under the weight of their crosses, while the lashes of the Roman legionaries writhed over their heads like black serpents. One of the condemned—that fellow with the long, light hair, his seamless chiton all torn and stained with blood—stumbled against a rock that had been thrown under his feet and fell. The shouts grew louder, and the motley crowd, like an iridescent sea, closed over the fallen man.

Ben-Tobith shuddered from pain—it was just as though someone had plunged a red-hot needle into his tooth and then given that needle a twist for good measure. He let out a long-drawn moan: 'Oo-oo-oo!' and left the parapet, wryly apathetic and in a vile temper.

'Hearken to them screaming!' he enviously mumbled, picturing to himself the widely open mouths, with strong teeth that did not ache, and imagined what a shout he himself would set up if only he were well.

And because of that mental picture his pain became ferocious, while his head bobbed fast, and he began to low like a calf: 'Moo-oo-oo!'

'They say He restored sight to the blind,' said Ben-Tobith's wife, who was glued to the parapet, and she skimmed a pebble toward the spot where Jesus, who had risen to his feet under the lashes, was now moving slowly.

'Yea, verily! If he would but rid me of my toothache it would suffice,' Ben-Tobith retorted sarcasticially, and added with a bitterness begotten of irritation: 'Look at the dust they are raising! For all the world like a drove of cattle. Somebody ought to take a stick to them and disperse them! Take me downstairs, Sarah.'

The good wife turned out to be right: the spectacle had diverted Ben-Tobith somewhat, although it may have been the rat droppings that had helped at last, and he succeeded in falling asleep. And when he awoke, the pain had practically vanished, and there was only a gumboil swelling on his right jaw, so small a gumboil that one could hardly notice it. His wife said that it was altogether unnoticeable, but Ben-Tobith smiled slyly at that: he knew what a kindhearted wife he had, and how she liked to say things that would please the hearer. Samuel the tanner, a neighbor, dropped in, and Ben-Tobith took him to see his young ass and listened with pride to the tanner's warm praises of the animal and its master.

Later on, heeding the plea of the inquisitive Sarah, the three of them set out for Golgotha, to have a look at the crucified. On the way Ben-Tobith told Samuel all about his misery from the very beginning, how last night he had felt a nagging ache in his right jaw, and how he had awakened in the night from the frightful pain. To make his recital graphic he assumed an expression of suffering, shut his eyes, tossed his head and moaned, while the grey-bearded Samuel shook his head commiseratingly and declared:

'Tsk-tsk-tsk! How that must have hurt!'

Ben-Tobith was so gratified by the sympathetic reception accorded to his story that he repeated it, and then went back to the remote time when his first tooth had begun to bother him—just one, a lower, on his left jaw. And thus, in animated talk, they reached Golgotha.

The sun, condemned to shed its light upon the world on that dread day, had already set beyond the distant knolls, and a ruddy scarlet streak was glowing like a bloodstain in the west. Against this background the crosses showed dark and indistinct, while some figures glimmered vague and white as they knelt at the foot of the central cross.

The people had long since dispersed; it was turning chill, and Ben-Tobith, after a casual glance at the crucified malefactors, took Samuel by the arm and discreetly headed him for home. He was in a particularly eloquent mood, and he wanted to round out the story of his toothache.

Thus did they wend their way homeward, and Ben-Tobith, to the accompaniment of Samuel's sympathetic nods and exclamations, assumed an expression of suffering, tossed his head, and moaned artfully, the while, from out the deep ravines, from the distant, sun-parched plains, the black night rose. As though it would screen from the sight of heaven the great malefaction the earth had wrought.

The Phantom Basket

John Aubrey, *British antiquary, born in Wiltshire in 1626, died in Oxford in 1697. His works include* Sacred Architecture *and* The Miscellanies *(1696), which deals with dreams and fantasies.*

Mr Trahern B.D. (Chaplain to Sir Orlando Bridgman Lord Keeper) a Learn'd and sober Person, was the Son of a Shoe-maker in Hereford: One Night as he lay in Bed, the Moon shining very bright, he saw the Phantome of one of the Apprentices sitting in a Chair in his red Wastcoat, and Headband about his Head, and Strap upon his Knee; which Apprentice was really abed and asleep with another Fellow-apprentice in the same Chamber, and saw him. The Fellow was Living 1671. Another time, as he was in Bed he saw a Basket come Sailing in the Air along by the Valence of his Bed; I think he said there was Fruit in the Basket: It was a Phantome. From himself.

The Drowned Giant

J. G. Ballard *(born 1930) is one of England's most successful writers of what has been called speculative fiction. He made his reputation in the late 1950s and 60s with a series of finely imagined fantasies and novels of catastrophes, turning to more personal and obsessive themes with* Crash *(1973) and* High-Rise *(1975). He achieved wider fame with* Empire of the Sun, *a semi-autobiographical novel set in Shanghai at the end of the war.*

On the morning after the storm the body of a drowned giant was washed ashore on the beach five miles to the north-west of the city. The first news of its arrival was brought by a nearby farmer and subsequently confirmed by the local newspaper reporters and the police. Despite this the majority of people, myself among them, remained sceptical, but the return of more and more eye-witnesses attesting to the vast size of the giant was finally too much for our curiosity. The library where my colleagues and I were carrying out our research was almost deserted when we set off for the coast shortly after two o'clock, and throughout the day people continued to leave their offices and shops as accounts of the giant circulated around the city.

By the time we reached the dunes above the beach a substantial crowd had gathered, and we could see the body lying in the shallow water two hundred yards away. At first the estimates of its size seemed greatly exaggerated. It was then at low tide, and almost all the giant's body was exposed, but he appeared to be a little larger than a basking shark. He lay on his back with his arms at his sides, in an attitude of repose, as if asleep on the mirror of wet sand, the reflection of his blanched skin fading as the water receded. In the clear sunlight his body glistened like the white plumage of a sea-bird.

Puzzled by this spectacle, and dissatisfied with the matter-of-fact explanations of the crowd, my friends and I stepped down from the dunes on to the shingle. Everyone seemed reluctant to approach the giant, but half an hour later two fishermen in wading boots walked out across the sand. As their diminutive figures neared the recumbent body a sudden hubbub of conversation broke out among the spectators. The two men were completely dwarfed by the giant. Although his heels were partly submerged in the sand, the feet rose to at least twice the fishermen's height, and we immediately realized that this drowned leviathan had the mass and dimensions of the largest sperm whale.

Three fishing smacks had arrived on the scene and with keels raised remained a quarter of a mile off-shore, the crews watching from the bows. Their discretion deterred the spectators on the shore from wading out across the sand. Impatiently everyone stepped down from the dunes and waited on the shingle slopes, eager for a closer view. Around the margins of the figure the sand had been washed away, forming a hollow, as if the giant had fallen out of the sky. The two fishermen were standing between the immense plinths of the feet, waving to us like tourists among the columns of some water-lapped temple on the Nile. For a moment I feared that the giant was merely asleep and might suddenly stir and clap his heels together, but his glazed eyes stared skywards, unaware of the minuscule replicas of himself between his feet.

The fishermen then began a circuit of the corpse, strolling past the long white flanks of the legs. After a pause to examine the fingers of the supine hand, they disappeared from sight between the arm and chest, then re-emerged to survey the head, shielding their eyes as they gazed up at its Grecian profile. The shallow forehead, straight high-bridged nose and curling lips reminded me of a Roman copy of Praxiteles, and the elegantly formed cartouches of the nostrils emphasized the resemblance to monumental sculpture.

Abruptly there was a shout from the crowd, and a hundred arms pointed towards the sea. With a start I saw that one of the fishermen had climbed on to the giant's chest and was now strolling about and signalling to the shore. There was a roar of surprise and triumph from the crowd, lost in a rushing avalanche of shingle as everyone surged forward across the sand.

As we approached the recumbent figure, which was lying in a pool of water the size of a field, our excited chatter fell away again, subdued by the huge physical dimensions of this moribund colossus. He was stretched out at a slight angle to the shore, his legs carried nearer the beach, and this foreshortening had disguised his true length. Despite the two fishermen standing on his abdomen, the crowd formed itself into a wide circle, groups of three or four people tentatively advancing towards the hands and feet.

My companions and I walked around the seaward side of the giant, whose hips and thorax towered above us like the hull of a stranded ship. His pearl-coloured skin, distended by immersion in salt water, masked the contours of the enormous muscles and tendons. We passed below the left knee, which was flexed slightly, threads of damp seaweed clinging to its sides. Draped loosely across the midriff, and preserving a tenuous propriety, was a shawl of heavy open-weaved material, bleached to a pale yellow by the water. A strong odour of brine came from the garment as it steamed in the sun, mingled with the sweet but potent scent of the giant's skin.

We stopped by his shoulder and gazed up at the motionless profile. The lips were parted slightly, the open eye cloudy and occluded, as if injected with some blue milky liquid, but the delicate arches of the nostrils and eyebrows invested the face with an ornate charm that belied the brutish power of the chest and shoulders.

The ear was suspended in mid-air over our heads like a sculptured doorway. As I raised my hand to touch the pendulous lobe someone appeared over the edge of the forehead and shouted down at me. Startled by this apparition, I stepped back, and then saw that a group of youths had climbed up on to the face and were jostling each other in and out of the orbits.

People were now clambering all over the giant, whose reclining arms provided a double stairway. From the palms they walked along the forearms to the elbow and then crawled over the distended belly of the biceps to the flat promenade of the pectoral muscles which covered the upper half of the smooth hairless chest. From here they climbed up on to the face, hand over hand along the lips and nose, or forayed down the abdomen to meet others who had straddled the ankles and were patrolling the twin columns of the thighs.

We continued our circuit through the crowd, and stopped to examine the outstretched right hand. A small pool of water lay in the palm, like the residue of another world, now being kicked away by the people ascending the arm. I tried to read the palm-lines that grooved the skin, searching for some clue to the giant's character, but the distension of the tissues had almost obliterated them, carrying away all trace of the giant's identity and his last tragic predicament. The huge muscles and wrist-bones of the hand seemed to deny any sensitivity to their owner, but the delicate flexion of the fingers and the well-tended nails, each cut symmetrically to within six inches of the quick, argued a certain refinement of temperament, illustrated in the Grecian features of the face, on which the townsfolk were now sitting like flies.

One youth was even standing, arms wavering at his sides, on the very tip of the nose, shouting down at his companions, but the face of the giant still retained its massive composure.

Returning to the shore, we sat down on the shingle, and watched the continuous stream of people arriving from the city. Some six or seven fishing boats had collected off-shore, and their crews waded in through the shallow water for a closer look at this enormous storm-catch. Later a party of police appeared and made a half-hearted attempt to cordon off the beach, but after walking up to the recumbent figure any such thoughts left their minds, and they went off together with bemused backward glances.

An hour later there were a thousand people present on the beach, at least two hundred of them standing or sitting on the giant, crowded along his arms and legs or circulating in a ceaseless mêlée across his chest and stomach. A large gang of youths occupied the head, toppling each other off the cheeks and sliding down the smooth planes of the jaw. Two or three straddled the nose, and another crawled into one of the nostrils, from which he emitted barking noises like a dog.

That afternoon the police returned, and cleared a way through the crowd for a party of scientific experts—authorities on gross anatomy and marine biology— from the university. The gang of youths and most of the people on the giant climbed down, leaving behind a few hardy spirits perched on the tips of the toes and on the forehead. The experts strode around the giant, heads nodding in vigorous consultation, preceded by the policemen who pushed back the press of spectators. When they reached the outstretched hand the senior officer offered to assist them up on to the palm, but the experts hastily demurred.

After they returned to the shore, the crowd once more climbed on to the giant, and was in full possession when we left at five o'clock, covering the arms and legs like a dense flock of gulls sitting on the corpse of a large fish.

I next visited the beach three days later. My friends at the library had returned to their work, and delegated to me the task of keeping the giant under observation and preparing a report. Perhaps they sensed my particular interest in the case, and it was certainly true that I was eager to return to the beach. There was nothing necrophilic about this, for to all intents the giant was still alive for me, indeed more alive than many of the people watching him. What I found so fascinating was partly his immense scale, the huge volumes of space occupied by his arms and legs, which seemed to confirm the identity of my own miniature limbs, but above all the mere categorical fact of his existence. Whatever else in our lives might be open to doubt, the giant, dead or alive, existed in an absolute sense, providing a glimpse into a world of similar absolutes of which we spectators on the beach were such imperfect and puny copies.

When I arrived at the beach the crowd was considerably smaller, and some two or three hundred people sat on the shingle, picnicking and watching the groups of visitors who walked out across the sand. The successive tides had carried the giant nearer the shore, swinging his head and shoulders towards the beach, so that he seemed doubly to gain in size, his huge body dwarfing the fishing boats beached beside his feet. The uneven contours of the beach had pushed his spine into a slight arch, expanding his chest and tilting back the head, forcing him into a more expressly heroic posture. The combined effects of seawater and the tumefaction of the tissues had given the face a sleeker and less youthful look. Although the vast proportions of the features made it impossible to assess the age and character of the giant, on my previous visit his classically modelled mouth and nose suggested that he had been a young man of discreet and modest temper. Now, however, he appeared to be at least in early middle age. The puffy cheeks, thicker nose and temples and narrowing eyes gave him a look of well-fed maturity that even now hinted at a growing corruption to come.

This accelerated post-mortem development of the giant's character, as if the latent elements of his personality had gained sufficient momentum during his life to discharge themselves in a brief final resumé, continued to fascinate me. It marked the beginning of the giant's surrender to that all-demanding system of time in which the rest of humanity finds itself, and of which, like the million twisted ripples of a fragmented whirlpool, our finite lives are the concluding products. I took up my position on the shingle directly opposite the giant's head, from where I could see the new arrivals and the children clambering over the legs and arms.

Among the morning's visitors were a number of men in leather jackets and cloth caps, who peered up critically at the giant with a professional eye, pacing out his dimensions and making rough calculations in the sand with spars of driftwood. I assumed them to be from the public works department and other municipal bodies, no doubt wondering how to dispose of this gargantuan piece of jetsam.

Several rather more smartly attired individuals, circus proprietors and the like, also appeared on the scene, and strolled slowly around the giant, hands in the pockets of their long overcoats, saying nothing to one another. Evidently its bulk was too great for their matchless enterprise. After they had gone the children continued to run up and down the arms and legs, and the youths wrestled with each other over the supine face, the damp sand from their feet covering the white skin.

The following day I deliberately postponed my visit until the late afternoon, and when I arrived there were fewer than fifty or sixty people sitting on the shingle. The giant had been carried still closer to the shore, and was now little more than seventy-five yards away, his feet crushing the palisade of a rotting breakwater. The slope of the firmer sand tilted his body towards the sea, and the bruised face was averted in an almost conscious gesture. I sat down on a large metal winch which had been shackled to a concrete caisson above the shingle, and looked down at the recumbent figure.

His blanched skin had now lost its pearly translucence and was spattered with dirty sand which replaced that washed away by the night tide. Clumps of seaweed filled the intervals between the fingers and a collection of litter and cuttle bones lay in the crevices below the hips and knees. But despite this, and the continuous thickening of his features, the giant still retained his magnificent Homeric stature. The enormous breadth of the shoulders, and the huge columns of the arms and legs, still carried the figure into another dimension, and the giant seemed a more authentic image of one of the drowned Argonauts or heroes of the Odyssey than the conventional human-sized portrait previously in my mind.

I stepped down on to the sand, and walked between the pools of water towards the giant. Two small boys were sitting in the well of the ear, and at the far end a solitary youth stood perched high on one of the toes, surveying me as I approached. As I had hoped when delaying my visit, no one else paid any attention to me, and the people on the shore remained huddled beneath their coats.

The giant's supine right hand was covered with broken shells and sand, in which a score of footprints were visible. The rounded bulk of the hip towered above me, cutting off all sight of the sea. The sweetly acrid odour I had noticed before was now more pungent, and through the opaque skin I could see the serpentine coils of congealed blood vessels. However repellent it seemed, this ceaseless metamorphosis, a visible life in death, alone permitted me to set foot on the corpse.

Using the jutting thumb as a stair-rail, I climbed up on to the palm and began my ascent. The skin was harder than I expected, barely yielding to my weight. Quickly I walked up the sloping forearm and the bulging balloon of the biceps. The face of the drowned giant loomed to my right, the cavernous nostrils and huge flanks of the cheeks like the cone of some freakish volcano.

Safely rounding the shoulder, I stepped out on to the broad promenade of the chest, across which the bony ridges of the rib-cage lay like huge rafters. The white skin was dappled by the darkening bruises of countless footprints, in which the patterns of individual heel-marks were clearly visible. Someone had built a small sandcastle on the centre of the sternum, and I climbed on to this partly demolished structure to give myself a better view of the face.

The two children had now scaled the ear and were pulling themselves into the right orbit, whose blue globe, completely occluded by some milk-coloured fluid, gazed sightlessly past their miniature forms. Seen obliquely from below, the face was devoid of all grace and repose, the drawn mouth and raised chin propped up by its gigantic slings of muscles resembling the torn prow of a colossal wreck. For the first time I became aware of the extremity of this last physical agony of the giant, no less painful for his awareness of the collapsing musculature and tissues. The absolute isolation of the ruined figure, cast like an abandoned ship upon the empty shore, almost out of sound of the waves, transformed his face into a mask of exhaustion and helplessness.

As I stepped forward, my foot sank into a trough of soft tissue, and a gust of fetid gas blew through an aperture between the ribs. Retreating from the fouled air, which hung like a cloud over my head, I turned towards the sea to clear my lungs. To my surprise I saw that the giant's left hand had been amputated.

I stared with bewilderment at the blackening stump, while the solitary youth reclining on his aerial perch a hundred feet away surveyed me with a sanguinary eye.

★

This was only the first of a sequence of depredations. I spent the following two days in the library, for some reason reluctant to visit the shore, aware that I had probably witnessed the approaching end of a magnificent illusion. When I next crossed the dunes and set foot on the shingle the giant was little more than twenty yards away, and with this close proximity to the rough pebbles all traces had vanished of the magic which once surrounded his distant wave-washed form. Despite his immense size, the bruises and dirt that covered his body made him appear merely human in scale, his vast dimensions only increasing his vulnerability.

His right hand and foot had been removed, dragged up the slope and trundled away by cart. After questioning the small group of people huddled by the breakwater, I gathered that a fertilizer company and a cattle food manufacturer were responsible.

The giant's remaining foot rose into the air, a steel hawser fixed to the large toe, evidently in preparation for the following day. The surrounding beach had been disturbed by a score of workmen, and deep ruts marked the ground where the hands and foot had been hauled away. A dark brackish fluid leaked from the stumps, and stained the sand and the white cones of the cuttlefish. As I walked down the shingle I noticed that a number of jocular slogans, swastikas and other signs had been cut into the grey skin, as if the mutilation of this motionless colossus had released a sudden flood of repressed spite. The lobe of one of the ears was pierced by a spear of timber, and a small fire had burnt out in the centre of the chest, blackening the surrounding skin. The fine wood ash was still being scattered by the wind.

A foul smell enveloped the cadaver, the undisguisable signature of putrefaction, which had at last driven away the usual gathering of youths. I returned to the shingle and climbed up on to the winch. The giant's swollen cheeks had now almost closed his eyes, drawing the lips back in a monumental gape. The once straight Grecian nose had been twisted and flattened, stamped into the ballooning face by countless heels.

When I visited the beach the following day I found, almost with relief, that the head had been removed.

★

Some weeks elapsed before I made my next journey to the beach, and by then the human likeness I had noticed earlier had vanished again. On close inspection the recumbent thorax and abdomen were unmistakably manlike, but as each of the limbs was chopped off, first at the knee and elbow, and then at shoulder and thigh, the carcass resembled that of any headless sea-animal—whale or whale-shark. With this loss of identity, and the few traces of personality that had clung tenuously to the figure, the interest of the spectators expired, and the foreshore was deserted except for an elderly beachcomber and the watchman sitting in the doorway of the contractor's hut.

A loose wooden scaffolding had been erected around the carcass, from which a dozen ladders swung in the wind, and the surrounding sand was littered with coils of rope, long metal-handled knives and grappling irons, the pebbles oily with blood and pieces of bone and skin.

I nodded to the watchman, who regarded me dourly over his brazier of burning coke. The whole area was pervaded by the pungent smell of huge squares of blubber being simmered in a vat behind the hut.

Both the thigh-bones had been removed, with the assistance of a small crane draped in the gauze-like fabric which had once covered the waist of the giant, and the open sockets gaped like barn doors. The upper arms, collar bones and pudenda had likewise been dispatched. What remained of the skin over the thorax and abdomen had been marked out in parallel strips with a tar brush, and the first five or six sections had been pared away from the midriff, revealing the great arch of the rib-cage.

As I left, a flock of gulls wheeled down from the sky and alighted on the beach, picking at the stained sand with ferocious cries.

Several months later, when the news of his arrival had been generally forgotten, various pieces of the body of the dismembered giant began to reappear all over the city. Most of these were bones, which the fertilizer manufacturers had found too difficult to crush, and their massive size, and the huge tendons and discs of cartilage attached to their joints, immediately identified them. For some reason, these disembodied fragments seemed better to convey the essence of the giant's original magnificence than the bloated appendages that had been subsequently amputated. As I looked across the road at the premises of the largest wholesale merchants in the meat market, I recognized the two enormous thigh-bones on either side of the doorway. They towered over the porters' heads like the threatening megaliths of some primitive druidical religion, and I had the sudden vision of the giant climbing to his knees upon these bare bones and striding away through the streets of the city, picking up the scattered fragments of himself on his return journey to the sea.

A few days later I saw the left humerus lying in the entrance to one of the shipyards (its twin for several years lay on the mud among the piles below the harbour's principal commercial wharf). In the same week the mummified right hand was exhibited on a carnival float during the annual pageant of the guilds.

The lower jaw, typically, found its way to the museum of natural history. The remainder of the skull has disappeared, but is probably still lurking in the waste grounds or private gardens of the city—quite recently, while sailing down the river, I noticed two ribs of the giant forming a decorative arch in a waterside garden, possible confused with the jaw-bones of a whale. A large square of tanned and tattoed skin, the size of an Indian blanket, forms a backcloth to the dolls and masks in a novelty shop near the amusement park, and I have no doubt that elsewhere in the city, in the hotels or golf clubs, the mummified nose and ears of the giant hang from the wall above a fireplace. As for the immense pizzle, this ends its days in the freak museum of a circus which travels up and down the north-west. This monumental apparatus, stunning in its proportions and sometime potency, occupies a complete booth to itself. The irony is that it is wrongly identified as that of a whale, and indeed most people, even those who first saw him cast up on the shore after the storm, now remember the giant, if at all, as a large beast.

The remainder of the skeleton, stripped of all flesh, still rests on the seashore, the clutter of bleached ribs like the timbers of a derelict ship. The contractor's hut, the crane and the scaffolding have been removed, and the sand being driven into the bay along the coast has buried the pelvis and backbone. In the winter the high curved bones are deserted, battered by the breaking waves, but in the summer they provide an excellent perch for the sea-wearying gulls.

Enoch Soames

Max Beerbohm *writer, humorist and caricaturist, born in London in 1872, died in Rapallo in 1956. Author of* A Defence of Cosmetics *(1896);* The Happy Hypocrite *(1897);* More *(1899);* Zuleika Dobson *(1911);* Seven Men *(1919);* And Even Now (1920).

When a book about the literature of the eighteen-nineties was given by Mr Holbrook Jackson to the world, I looked eagerly in the index for SOAMES, ENOCH. I had feared he would not be there. He was not there. But everybody else was. Many writers whom I had quite forgotten, or remembered but faintly, lived again for me, they and their work, in Mr Holbrook Jackson's pages. The book was as thorough as it was brilliantly written. And thus the omission found by me was an all the deadlier record of poor Soames' failure to impress himself on his decade.

I daresay I am the only person who noticed the omission. Soames had failed so piteously as all that! Nor is there a counterpoise in the thought that if he had had some measure of success he might have passed, like those others, out of my mind, to return only at the historian's beck. It is true that had his gifts, such as they were, been acknowledged in his lifetime, he would never have made the bargain I saw him make—that strange bargain whose results have kept him always in the foreground of my memory. But it is from those very results that the full piteousness of him glares out.

Not my compassion, however, impels me to write of him. For his sake, poor fellow, I should be inclined to keep my pen out of the ink. It is ill to deride the dead. And how can I write about Enoch Soames without making him ridiculous? Or rather, how am I to hush up the horrid fact that he *was* ridiculous? I shall not be able to do that. Yet, sooner or later, write about him I must. You will see, in due course, that I have no option. And I may as well get the thing done now.

In the Summer Term of '93 a bolt from the blue flashed down on Oxford. It drove deep, it hurtlingly embedded itself in the soil. Dons and undergraduates stood around, rather pale, discussing nothing but it. Whence came it, this meteorite? From Paris. Its name? Will Rothenstein. Its aim? To do a series of twenty-four portraits in lithograph. These were to be published from the Bodley Head, London. The matter was urgent. Already the Warden of A, and the Master of B, and the Regius Professor of C, had meekly 'sat'. Dignified and doddering old men, who had never consented to sit to any one, could not withstand this dynamic little stranger. He did not sue: he invited; he did not invite: he commanded. He was twenty-one years old. He wore spectacles that flashed more than any other pair ever seen. He was a wit. He was brimful of ideas. He knew Whistler. He knew Edmond de Goncourt. He knew every one in Paris. He knew them all by heart. He was Paris in Oxford. It was whispered that, so soon as he had polished off his selection of dons, he was going to include a few undergraduates. It was a proud day for me when I — I — was included. I liked Rothenstein not less than I feared him; and there arose between us a friendship that has grown ever warmer, and been more and more valued by me, with every passing year.

At the end of Term he settled in—or rather, meteoritically into—London. It was to him I owed my first knowledge of that forever enchanting little world-in-itself, Chelsea, and my first acquaintance with Walter Sickert and other august elders who dwelt there. It was Rothenstein that took me to see, in Cambridge Street, Pimlico, a young man whose drawings were already famous among the few—Aubrey Beardsley, by name. With Rothenstein I paid my first visit to the Bodley Head. By him I was inducted into another haunt of intellect and daring, the domino room of the Café Royal.

There, on that October evening—there, in that exuberant vista of gilding and crimson velvet set amidst all those opposing mirrors and upholding caryatids, with fumes of tobacco ever rising to the painted and pagan ceiling, and with the hum of presumably cynical conversation broken into so sharply now and again by the clatter of dominoes shuffled on marble tables, I drew a deep breath, and 'This indeed,' said I to myself, 'is life!'

It was the hour before dinner. We drank vermouth. Those who knew
Rothenstein were pointing him out to those who knew him only by name. Men
were constantly coming in through the swing-doors and wandering slowly up
and down in search of vacant tables, or of tables occupied by friends. One of
these rovers interested me because I was sure he wanted to catch Rothenstein's
eye. He had twice passed our table, with a hesitating look; but Rothenstein, in
the thick of a disquisition on Puvis de Chavannes, had not seen him. He was a
stooping, shambling person, rather tall, very pale, with longish and brownish
hair. He had a thin vague beard—or rather, he had a chin on which a large
number of hairs weakly curled and clustered to cover its retreat. He was an odd-
looking person; but in the 'nineties odd apparations were more frequent, I
think, than they are now. The young writers of that era—and I was sure this
man was a writer—strove earnestly to be distinct in aspect. This man had
striven unsuccessfully. He wore a soft black hat of clerical kind but of Bohemian
intention. and a grey waterproof cape which, perhaps because it was waterproof,
failed to be romantic. I decided that 'dim' was the *mot juste* for him. I had
already essayed to write, and was immensely keen on the *mot juste*, that Holy
Grail of the period.

The dim man was now again approaching our table, and this time he made up
his mind to pause in front of it. 'You don't remember me,' he said in a toneless
voice.

Rothenstein brightly focussed him. 'Yes, I do,' he replied after a moment,
with pride rather than effusion—pride in a retentive memory. 'Edwin Soames.'

'Enoch Soames,' said Enoch.

'Enoch Soames,' repeated Rothenstein in a tone implying that it was enough
to have hit on the surname. 'We met in Paris two or three times when you were
living there. We met at the Café Grouche.'

'And I came to your studio once.'

'Oh yes; I was sorry I was out.'

'But you were in. You showed me some of your paintings, you know . . . I
hear you're in Chelsea now.'

'Yes.'

I almost wondered that Mr Soames did not, after this monosyllable, pass
along. He stood patiently there, rather like a dumb animal, rather like a donkey
looking over a gate. A sad figure, his. It occurred to me that 'hungry' was
perhaps the *mot juste* for him; but—hungry for what? He looked as if he had
little appetite for anything. I was sorry for him; and Rothenstein, though he had
not invited him to Chelsea, did ask him to sit down and have something to
drink.

Seated, he was more self-assertive. He flung back the wings of his cape with a
gesture which—had not those wings been waterproof—might have seemed to
hurl defiance at things in general. And he ordered an absinthe. '*Je me tiens
toujours fidèle,*' he told Rothenstein, '*à la sorcière glauque.*'

'It is bad for you,' said Rothenstein drily.

'Nothing is bad for one,' answered Soames. '*Dans ce monde il n'y a ni de bien ni
de mal.*'

'Nothing good and nothing bad? How do you mean?'

'I explained it all in the preface to *Negations*.'

'*Negations*?'

'Yes; I gave you a copy of it.'

'Oh yes, of course. But did you explain—for instance—that there was no such thing as bad or good grammar?'

'N-no,' said Soames. 'Of course in Art there is the good and the evil. But in Life—no.' He was rolling a cigarette. He had weak white hands, not well washed, and with finger-tips much stained by nicotine. 'In Life there are illusions of good and evil, but'—his voice trailed away to a murmur in which the words '*vieux jeu*' and 'rococo' were faintly audible. I think he felt he was not doing himself justice, and feared that Rothenstein was going to point out fallacies. Anyway, he cleared his throat and said '*Parlons d'autre chose.*'

It occurs to you that he was a fool? It didn't to me. I was young, and had not the clarity of judgement that Rothenstein already had. Soames was quite five or six years older than either of us. Also, he had written a book.

It was wonderful to have written a book.

If Rothenstein had not been there, I should have revered Soames. Even as it was, I respected him. And I was very near indeed to reverence when he said he had another book coming out soon. I asked if I might ask what kind of book it was to be.

'My poems,' he answered. Rothenstein asked if this was to be the title of the book. The poet meditated on this suggestion, but said he rather thought of giving the book no title at all. 'If a book is good in itself—' he murmured, waving his cigarette.

Rothenstein objected that absence of title might be bad for the sale of a book. 'If,' he urged, 'I went into a bookseller's and said simply "Have you got?" or "Have you a copy of?" how would they know what I wanted?'

'Oh, of course I should have my name on the cover,' Soames answered earnestly. 'And I rather want,' he added, looking hard at Rothenstein, 'to have a drawing of myself as frontispiece.' Rothenstein admitted that this was a capital idea, and mentioned that he was going into the country and would be there for some time. He then looked at his watch, exclaimed at the hour, paid the waiter, and went away with me to dinner. Soames remained at his post of fidelity to the glaucous witch.

'Why were you so determined not to draw him?' I asked.

'Draw him? Him? How can one draw a man who doesn't exist?'

'He is dim,' I admitted. But my *mot juste* fell flat. Rothenstein repeated that Soames was non-existent.

Still, Soames had written a book. I asked if Rothenstein had read *Negations*. He said he had looked into it. 'But,' he added crisply, 'I don't profess to know anything about writing.' A reservation very characteristic of the period! Painters would not then allow that any one outside their own order had a right to any opinion about painting. This law (graven on the tablets brought down by Whistler from the summit of Fujiyama) imposed certain limitations. If other arts than painting were not utterly unintelligible to all but the men who practised them, the law tottered—the Monroe Doctrine, as it were, did not hold good. Therefore no painter would offer an opinion of a book without warning you at any rate that his opinion was worthless. No one is a better judge of literature than Rothenstein; but it wouldn't have done to tell him so in those days; and I knew that I must form an unaided judgement on *Negations*.

Not to buy a book of which I had met the author face to face would have been for me in those days an impossible act of self-denial. When I returned to Oxford for the Christmas Term I had duly secured *Negations*. I used to keep it lying carelessly on the table in my room, and whenever a friend took it up and asked what it was about I would say 'Oh, it's rather a remarkable book. It's by a man whom I know.' Just 'what it was about' I never was able to say. Head or tail was just what I hadn't made of that slim green volume. I found in the preface no clue to the exiguous labyrinth of contents, and in that labyrinth nothing to explain the preface.

Lean near to life, Lean very near—nearer.
  Life is web, and therein nor warp nor woof is, but web only.
  It is for this I am Catholick in church and in thought, yet do let swift Mood weave there what the shuttle of Mood wills.

These were the opening phrases of the preface, but those which followed were less easy to understand. Then came 'Stark: A *Conte*', about a midinette who, so far as I could gather, murdered, or was about to murder, a mannequin. It seemed to me like a story by Catulle Mendès in which the translator had either skipped or cut out every alternate sentence. Next, a dialogue between Pan and St Ursula—lacking, I rather felt, in 'snap'. Next, some aphorisms (entitled ἀφορίσματα). Throughout, in fact, there was a great variety of form; and the forms had evidently been wrought with much care. It was rather the substance that eluded me. Was there, I wondered, any substance at all? It did now occur to me: suppose Enoch Soames was a fool! Up cropped a rival hypothesis: suppose *I* was! I inclined to give Soames the benefit of the doubt. I had read *L'Après-midi d'un Faune* without extracting a glimmer of meaning. Yet Mallarmé—of course—was a Master. How was I to know that Soames wasn't another? There was a sort of music in his prose, not indeed arresting, but perhaps, I thought, haunting, and laden perhaps with meanings as deep as Mallarmé's own. I awaited his poems with an open mind.

And I looked forward to them with positive impatience after I had had a second meeting with him. This was on an evening in January. Going into the aforesaid domino room, I passed a table at which sat a pale man with an open book before him. He looked from his book to me, and I looked back over my shoulder with a vague sense that I ought to have recognized him. I returned to pay my respects. After exchanging a few words, I said with a glance to the open book, 'I see I am interrupting you,' and was about to pass on, but 'I prefer,' Soames replied in his toneless voice, 'to be interrupted,' and I obeyed his gesture that I should sit down.

I asked him if he often read here. 'Yes; things of this kind I read here,' he answered, indicating the title of his book—*The Poems of Shelley*.

'Anything that you really'—and I was going to say 'admire?' But 'I cautiously left my sentence unfinished, and was glad that I had done so, for he said, with unwonted emphasis, 'Anything second-rate.'

I had read little of Shelley, but 'Of course,' I murmured, 'he's very uneven.'

'I should have thought evenness was just what was wrong with him. A deadly evenness. That's why I read him here. The noise of this place breaks the rhythm. He's tolerable here.' Soames took up the book and glanced through the pages. He laughed. Soames' laugh was a short, single and mirthless sound from the throat, unaccompanied by any movement of the face or brightening of the eyes. 'What a period!' he uttered, laying the book down. And 'What a country!' he added.

I asked rather nervously if he didn't think Keats had more or less held his own against the drawbacks of time and place. He admitted that there were 'passages in Keats', but did not specify them. Of 'the older men', as he called them, he seemed to like only Milton. 'Milton,' he said, 'wasn't sentimental.' Also, 'Milton had a dark insight.' And again, 'I can always read Milton in the reading-room.'

'The reading-room?'

'Of the British Museum. I go there every day.'

'You do? I've only been there once. I'm afraid I found it rather a depressing place. It seemed to sap one's vitality.'

'It does. That's why I go there. The lower one's vitality, the more sensitive one is to great art. I live near the Museum. I have rooms in Dyott Street.'

'And you go round to the reading-room to read Milton?'

'Usually Milton.' He looked at me. 'It was Milton,' he certificatively added, 'who converted me to Diabolism.'

'Diabolism? Oh yes? Really?' said I, with that vague discomfort and that intense desire to be polite which one feels when a man speaks of his own religion. 'You—worship the Devil?'

Soames shook his head. 'It's not exactly worship,' he qualified, sipping his absinthe. 'It's more a matter of trusting and encouraging.'

'Ah, yes . . . But I had rather gathered from the preface to *Negations* that you were a—a Catholic.'

'*Je l'étais à cette époque.* Perhaps I still am. Yes, I'm a Catholic Diabolist.'

This profession he made in an almost cursory tone. I could see that what was upmost in his mind was the fact that I had read *Negations*. His pale eyes had for the first time gleamed. I felt as one who is about to be examined, *viva voce*, on the very subject in which he is shakiest. I hastily asked him how soon his poems were to be published. 'Next week,' he told me.

'And are they to be published without a title?'

'No. I found a title, at last. But I shan't tell you what it is,' as though I had been so impertinent as to inquire. 'I am not sure that it wholly satisfies me. But it is the best I can find. It does suggest something of the quality of the poems . . . Strange growths, natural and wild; yet exquisite,' he added, 'and many-hued, and full of poisons.'

I asked him what he thought of Baudelaire. He uttered the snort that was his laugh, and 'Baudelaire,' he said, 'was a *bourgeois malgré lui*.' France had had only one poet: Villon; 'and two-thirds of Villon were sheer journalism.' Verlaine was 'an *épicier malgré lui*.' Altogether, rather to my surprise, he rated French literature lower than English. There were 'passages' in Villiers de l'Isle-Adam. But 'I', he summed up, 'owe nothing to France.' He nodded at me. 'You'll see,' he predicted.

I did not, when the time came, quite see that. I thought the author of *Fungoids* did—unconsciously, no doubt—owe something to the young Parisian decadents, or to the young English ones who owed something to *them*. I still think so. The little book—bought by me in Oxford—lies before me as I write. Its pale-grey buckram cover and silver lettering have not worn well. Nor have its contents. Through these, with a melancholy interest, I have again been looking. They are not much. But at the time of their publication I had a vague suspicion that they *might* be. I suppose it is my capacity for faith, not poor Soames' work, that is weaker than it once was . . .

To a Young Woman

Thou art, who hast not been!
  Pale tunes irresolute
  And traceries of old sounds
  Blown from a rotted flute
Mingle with noise of cymbals rouged with rust,
Nor not strange forms and epicene
  Lie bleeding in the dust,
    Being wounded with wounds.
    For this it is
  That is thy counterpart
    Of age-long mockeries
Thou hast not been nor art!

There seemed to me a certain inconsistency as between the first and last lines of this. I tried, with bent brows, to resolve the discord. But I did not take my failure as wholly incompatible with a meaning in Soames' mind. Might it not rather indicate the depth of his meaning? As for the craftsmanship, 'rouged with rust' seemed to me a fine stroke, and 'nor not' instead of 'and' had a curious felicity. I wondered who the Young Woman was, and what she had made of it all. I sadly suspect that Soames could not have made more of it than she. Yet, even now, if one doesn't try to make sense at all of the poem, and reads it just for the sound, there is a certain grace of cadence. Soames was an artist— in so far as he was anything, poor fellow!

It seemed to me, when first I read *Fungoids*, that, oddly enough, the Diabolistic side of him was the best. Diabolism seemed to be a cheerful, even a wholesome, influence in his life.

NOCTURNE

Round and round the shutter'd Square
I stroll'd with the Devil's arm in mine.
No sound but the scrape of his hoofs was there
And the ring of his laughter and mine.
　　We had drunk black wine.

I scream'd 'I will race you, Master!'
'What matter,' he shriek'd, 'to-night
Which of us runs the faster?
There is nothing to fear to-night
　In the foul moon's light!'

Then I look'd at him in the eyes,
And I laugh'd full shrill at the lie he told
And the gnawing fear he would fain disguise.
It was true, what I'd time and again been told:
　He was old—old.

There was, I felt, quite a swing about that first stanza—a joyous and rollicking note of comradeship. The second was slightly hysterical perhaps. But I liked the third: it was so bracingly unorthodox, even according to the tenets of Soames' peculiar sect in the faith. Not much 'trusting and encouraging' here! Soames triumphantly exposing the Devil as a liar, and laughing 'full shrill,' cut a quite heartening figure, I thought—then! Now, in the light of what befell, none of his poems depresses me so much as 'Nocturne'.

I looked out for what the metropolitan reviewers would have to say. They seemed to fall into two classes: those who had little to say and those who had nothing. The second class was the larger, and the words of the first were cold; insomuch that

'Strikes a note of modernity throughout . . .These tripping numbers'—*Preston Telegraph*

was the sole lure offered in advertisements by Soames' publisher. I had hoped that when next I met the poet I could congratulate him on having made a stir; for I fancied he was not so sure of his intrinsic greatness as he seemed. I was but able to say, rather coarsely, when next I did see him, that I hoped *Fungoids* was 'selling splendidly'. He looked at me across his glass of absinthe and asked if I had bought a copy. His publisher had told him that three had been sold. I laughed, as at a jest.

'You don't suppose I *care*, do you?' he said, with something like a snarl. I disclaimed the notion. He added that he was not a tradesman. I said mildly that I wasn't, either, and murmured that an artist who gave truly new and great things to the world had always to wait long for recognition. He said he cared not a sou for recognition. I agreed that the act of creation was its own reward.

His moroseness might have alienated me if I had regarded myself as a nobody. But ah! hadn't both John Lane and Aubrey Beardsley suggested that I should write an essay for the great new venture that was afoot—*The Yellow Book*? And hadn't Henry Harland, as editor, accepted my essay? And wasn't it to be in the very first number? At Oxford I was still *in statu pupillari*. In London I regarded myself as very much indeed a graduate now—one whom no Soames could ruffle. Partly to show off, partly in sheer goodwill, I told Soames he ought to contribute to *The Yellow Book*. He uttered from the throat a sound of scorn for that publication.

Nevertheless, I did, a day or two later, tentatively ask Harland if he knew anything of the work of a man called Enoch Soames. Harland paused in the midst of his characteristic stride around the room, threw up his hands towards the ceiling, and groaned aloud: he had often met 'that absurd creature' in Paris and this very morning had received some poems in manuscript from him.

'Has he *no* talent?' he asked.

'He has an income. He's all right.' Harland was the most joyous of men and most generous of critics, and he hated to talk of anything about which he couldn't be enthusiastic. So I dropped the subject of Soames. The news that Soames had an income did not take the edge off solicitude. I learned afterwards that he was the son of an unsuccessful and deceased bookseller in Preston, but had inherited an annuity of £300 from a married aunt, and had no surviving relatives of any kind. Materially, then, he was 'all right'. But there was still a spiritual pathos about him, sharpened for me now by the possibility that even the praises of the *Preston Telegraph* might not have been forthcoming had he not been the son of a Preston man. He had a sort of weak doggedness which I could not but admire. Neither he nor his work received the slightest encouragement; but he persisted in behaving as a personage: always he kept his dingy little flag flying. Wherever congregated the *jeunes féroces* of the arts, in whatever Soho restaurant they had just discovered, in whatever music-hall they were most frequenting, there was Soames in the midst of them, or rather on the fringe of them, a dim but inevitable figure. He never sought to propitiate his fellow-writers, never bated a jot of his arrogance about his own work or of his contempt for theirs. To the painters he was respectful, even humble; but for the poets and prosaists of *The Yellow Book*, and later of *The Savoy*, he had never a word but of scorn. He wasn't resented. It didn't occur to anybody that he or his Catholic Diabolism mattered. When, in the autumn of '96, he brought out (at his own expense, this time) a third book, his last book, nobody said a word for or against it. I meant, but forgot, to buy it. I never saw it, and am ashamed to say I don't even remember what it was called. But I did, at the time of its publication, say to Rothenstein that I thought poor old Soames was really a rather tragic figure, and that I believed he would literally die for want of recognition. Rothenstein scoffed. He said I was trying to get credit for a kind heart which I didn't possess; and perhaps this was so. But at the private view of the New English Art Club, a few weeks later, I beheld a pastel portrait of 'Enoch Soames, Esq.' It was very like him, and very like Rothenstein to have done it. Soames was standing near it, in his soft hat and his waterproof cape, all through the afternoon. Anybody who knew him would have recognized the portrait at a glance, but nobody who didn't know him would have recognized the portrait from its bystander: it 'existed' so much more than he; it was bound to. Also, it had not that expression of faint happiness which on this day was discernible, yes, in Soames' countenance. Fame had breathed on him. Twice again in the course of the month I went to the New English, and on both occasions Soames himself was on view there. Looking back, I regard the close of that exhibition as having been virtually the close of his career. He had felt the breath of Fame against his cheek—so late, for such a little while; and at its withdrawal he gave in, gave up, gave out. He, who had never looked strong or well, looked ghastly now—a shadow of the shade he had once been. He still frequented the domino room, but, having lost all wish to excite curiosity, he no longer read books there. 'You read only at the Museum now?' asked I, with attempted cheerfulness, He said he never went there now. 'No absinthe there,' he muttered. It was the sort of thing that in the old days he would have said for effect; but it carried conviction now. Absinthe, erst but a point in the 'personality' he had striven so hard to build up, was solace and necessity now. He no longer called it *la sorcière glauque*. He had shed away all his French phrases. He had become a plain, unvarnished, Preston man.

Failure, if it be plain, unvarnished, complete failure, and even though it be a squalid failure, has always a certain dignity. I avoided Soames because he made me feel rather vulgar. John Lane had published, by this time, two little books of mine, and they had had a pleasant little success of esteem. I was a—slight but definite—'personality'. Frank Harris had engaged me to kick up my heels in the *Saturday Review*, Alfred Harmsworth was letting me do likewise in the *Daily Mail*. I was just what Soames wasn't. And he shamed my gloss. Had I known that he really and firmly believed in the greatness of what he as an artist had achieved, I might not have shunned him. No man who hasn't lost his vanity can be held to have altogether failed. Soames' dignity was an illusion of mine. One day in the first week of June, 1897, that illusion went. But on the evening of that day Soames went too.

I had been out most of the morning, and, as it was too late to reach home in time for luncheon, I sought 'the Vingtième'. This little place—Restaurant du Vingtième Siècle, to give it its full title—had been discovered in '96 by the poets and prosaists, but had now been more or less abandoned in favour of some later find. I don't think it lived long enough to justify its name; but at that time there it still was, in Greek Street, a few doors from Soho Square, and almost opposite to that house where, in the first years of the century, a little girl, and with her a boy named De Quincey, made nightly encampment in darkness and hunger among dust and rats and old legal parchments. The Vingtième was but a small whitewashed room, leading out into the street at one end and into a kitchen at the other. The proprietor and cook was a Frenchman, known to us at Monsieur Vingtième; the waiters were his two daughters, Rose and Berthe; and the food, according to faith, was good. The tables were so narrow, and were set so close together, that there was space for twelve of them, six jutting from either wall. Only the two nearest to the door, as I went in, were occupied. On one side sat a tall, flashy, rather Mephistophelian man whom I had seen from time to time in the domino room and elsewhere. On the other side sat Soames. They made a queer contrast in that sunlit room—Soames sitting haggard in that hat and cape which nowhere at any season had I seen him doff, and this other, this keenly vital man, at sight of whom I more than ever wondered whether he was a diamond merchant, a conjurer, or the head of a private detective agency. I was sure Soames didn't want my company; but I asked, as it would have seemed brutal not to, whether I might join him, and took the chair opposite to his. He was smoking a cigarette, with an untasted salmi of something on his plate and a half-empty bottle of Sauterne before him; and he was quite silent. I said that the preparations for the Jubilee made London impossible. (I rather liked them, really.) I professed a wish to go right away till the whole thing was over. In vain did I attune myself to his gloom. He seemed not to hear me nor even to see me. I felt that his behaviour made me ridiculous in the eyes of the other man. The gangway between the two rows of tables at the Vingtième was hardly more than two feet wide (Rose and Berthe, in their ministrations, had always to edge past each other, quarrelling in whispers as they did so), and any one at the table abreast of yours was practically at yours. I thought our neighbour was amused at my failure to interest Soames, and so, as I could not explain to him that my insistence was merely charitable, I became silent. Without turning my head, I had him well within my range of vision. I hoped I looked less vulgar than he in contrast with Soames. I was sure he was not an Englishman, but what *was* his nationality? Though his jet-black hair was *en brosse*, I did not think he was French. To Berthe, who waited on him, he spoke French fluently, but with a hardly native idiom and accent. I gathered that this was his first visit to the Vingtième; but Berthe was off-hand in her manner to him: he had not made a good impression. His eyes were handsome, but—like the Vingtième's tables— too narrow and set too close together. His nose was predatory, and the points of his moustache, waxed up beyond his nostrils, gave a fixity to his smile. Decidedly, he was sinister. And my sense of discomfort in his presence was intensified by the scarlet waistcoat which tightly, and so unseasonably in June, sheathed his ample chest. This waistcoat wasn't wrong merely because of the heat, either. It was somehow all wrong in itself. It wouldn't have done on Christmas morning. It would have struck a jarring note at the first night of 'Hernani'. I was trying to account for its wrongness when Soames suddenly and strangely broke silence. 'A hundred years hence!' he murmured, as in a trance.

'We shall not be here!' I briskly but fatuously added.

'We shall not be here. No,' he droned, 'but the Museum will still be just where it is. And the reading-room, just where it is. And people will be able to go and read there.' He inhaled sharply, and a spasm as of actual pain contorted his features.

I wondered what train of thought poor Soames had been following. He did not enlighten me when he said, after a long pause, 'You think I haven't minded.'

'Minded what, Soames?'

'Neglect. Failure.'

'*Failure?*' I said heartily. 'Failure?' I repeated vaguely. 'Neglect—yes, perhaps; but that's quite another matter. Of course you haven't been—appreciated. But what then? Any artist who—who gives—' What I wanted to say was, 'Any artist who gives truly new and great things to the world has always to wait long for recognition'; but the flattery would not out: in the face of his misery, a misery so genuine and so unmasked, my lips would not say the words.

And then—he said them for me. I flushed. 'That's what you were going to say, isn't it?' he asked.

'How did you know?'

'It's what you said to me three years ago, when *Fungoids* was published.' I flushed the more. I need not have done so at all, for 'It's the only important thing I ever heard you say,' he continued. 'And I've never forgotten it. It's a true thing. It's a horrible truth. But—d'you remember what I answered? I said "I don't care a sou for recognition." And you believed me. You've gone on believing I'm above that sort of thing. You're shallow. What should *you* know of the feelings of a man like me? You imagine that a great artist's faith in himself and in the verdict of posterity is enough to keep him happy . . . You've never guessed at the bitterness and loneliness, the'—his voice broke; but presently he resumed, speaking with a force that I had never known in him. 'Posterity! What use is it to *me*? A dead man doesn't know that people are visiting his grave—visiting his birthplace—putting up tablets to him—unveiling statues of him. A dead man can't read the books that are written about him. A hundred years hence! Think of it! If I could come back to life *then*—just for a few hours—and go to the reading-room, and *read*! Or better still: if I could be projected, now, at this moment, into that future, into that reading-room, just for this one afternoon! I'd sell myself body and soul to the devil, for that! Think of the pages and pages in the catalogue: "SOAMES, ENOCH" endlessly—endless editions, commentaries, prolegomena, biographies'—but here he was interrupted by a sudden loud creak of the chair at the next table. Our neighbour had half risen from his place. He was leaning towards us, apologetically intrusive.

'Excuse—permit me,' he said softly. 'I have been unable not to hear. Might I take a liberty? In this little restaurant-sans-façon'—he spread wide his hands—'might I, as the phrase is, "cut in"? '

I could but signify our acquiescence. Berthe had appeared at the kitchen door, thinking the stranger wanted his bill. He waved her away with his cigar, and in another moment had seated himself beside me, commanding a full view of Soames.

'Though not an Englishman,' he explained, 'I know my London well, Mr Soames. Your name and fame—Mr Beerbohm's too—very known to me. Your point is: who am *I*?' He glanced quickly over his shoulder, and in a lowered voice said 'I am the Devil.'

I couldn't help it: I laughed. I tried not to, I knew there was nothing to laugh at, my rudeness shamed me, but—I laughed with increasing volume. The Devil's quiet dignity, the surprise and disgust of his raised eyebrows, did but the more dissolve me. I rocked to and fro, I lay back aching. I behaved deplorably.

'I am a gentleman, and,' he said, with intense emphasis, 'I thought I was in the company of *gentlemen*.'

'Don't!' I gasped faintly. 'Oh, don't!'

'Curious, *nicht wahr*?' I heard him say to Soames. 'There is a type of person to whom the very mention of my name is—oh-so-awfully-funny! In your theatres the dullest *comédien* needs only to say "The Devil!" and right away they give him "the loud laugh that speaks the vacant mind". Is it not so?'

I had now just breath enough to offer my apologies. He accepted them, but coldly, and readdressed himself to Soames.

'I am a man of business,' he said, 'and always I would put things through "right now", as they say in the States. You are a poet. *Les affaires*—you detest them. So be it. But with me you will deal, eh? What you have said just now gives me furiously to hope.'

Soames had not moved, except to light a fresh cigarette. He sat crouched forward, with his elbows squared on the table, and his head just above the level of his hands, staring up at the Devil. 'Go on,' he nodded. I had no remnant of laughter in me now.

'It will be the more pleasant, our little deal,' the Devil went on, 'because you are—I mistake not?—a Diabolist.'

'A Catholic Diabolist,' said Soames.

The Devil accepted the reservation genially. 'You wish,' he resumed, 'to visit now—this afternoon as-ever-is—the reading-room of the British Museum, yes'? but of a hundred years hence, yes? *Parfaitement*. Time—an illusion. Past and future—they are as ever-present as the present, or at any rate only what you call "just-round-the-corner". I switch you on to any date. I project you—pouf! You wish to be in the reading-room just as it will be on the afternoon of June 3rd, 1997? You wish to find yourself standing in that room, just past the swing-doors, this very minute, yes? and to stay there till closing time? Am I right?'

Soames nodded.

The Devil looked at his watch. 'Ten past two,' he said. 'Closing time in summer same then as now: seven o'clock. That will give you almost five hours. At seven o'clock'—pouf!—you find yourself again here, sitting at this table. I am dining tonight *dans le monde—dans le higlif*. That concludes my present visit to your great city. I come and fetch you here, Mr Soames, on my way home.'

'Home?' I echoed.

'Be it never so humble!' said the Devil lightly.

'All right,' said Soames.

'Soames!' I entreated. But my friend moved not a muscle.

The Devil had made as though to stretch forth his hand across the table and touch Soames' forearm; but he paused in his gesture.

'A hundred years hence, as now,' he smiled, 'no smoking allowed in the reading-room. You would better therefore—'

Soames removed the cigarette from his mouth and dropped it into his glass of Sauterne.

'Soames!' again I cried. 'Can't you'—but the Devil had now stretched forth his hand across the table. He brought it slowly down on—the table-cloth.

Soames' chair was empty. His cigarette floated sodden in his wine-glass. There was no other trace of him.

For a few moments the Devil let his hand rest where it lay, gazing at me out of the corners of his eyes, vulgarly triumphant.

A shudder shook me. With an effort I controlled myself and rose from the chair. 'Very clever,' I said condescendingly. 'But—*The Time Machine* is a delightful book, don't you think? So entirely original!'

'You are pleased to sneer,' said the Devil, who had also risen, 'but it is one thing to write about a not possible machine; it is a quite other thing to be a Supernatural Power.' All the same, I had scored.

Berthe had come forth at the sound of our rising. I explained to her that Mr Soames had been called away, and that both he and I would be dining here. It was not until I was out in the open air that I began to feel giddy. I have but the haziest recollection of what I did, where I wandered, in the glaring sunshine of that endless afternoon. I remember the sound of carpenters' hammers all along Piccadilly, and the bare chaotic look of the half-erected 'stands'. Was it in the Green Park, or in Kensington Gardens, or *where* was it that I sat on a chair beneath a tree, trying to read an evening paper? There was a phrase in the leading article that went on repeating itself in my fagged mind—'Little is hidden from this august Lady full of the garnered wisdom of sixty years of Sovereignty.' I remember wildly conceiving a letter (to reach Windsor by express messenger told to await answer):

> MADAM—Well knowing that your Majesty is full of the garnered wisdom of sixty years of Sovereignty, I venture to ask your advice in the following delicate matter. Mr Enoch Soames, whose poems you may or may not know . . .

Was there *no* way of helping him—saving him? A bargain was a bargain, and I was the last man to aid or abet any one in wriggling out of a reasonable obligation. I wouldn't have lifted a little finger to save Faust. But poor Soames!—doomed to pay without respite an eternal price for nothing but a fruitless search and a bitter disillusioning . . .

Odd and uncanny it seemed to me that he, Soames, in the flesh, in the waterproof cape, was at this moment living in the last decade of the next century, poring over books not yet written, and seeing and seen by men not yet born. Uncannier and odder still, that tonight and evermore he would be in Hell. Assuredly, truth was stranger than fiction.

Endless that afternoon was. Almost I wished I had gone with Soames—not indeed to stay in the reading-room, but to sally forth for a brisk sight-seeing walk around a new London. I wandered restlessly out of the Park I had sat in. Vainly I tried to imagine myself an ardent tourist from the eighteenth century. Intolerable was the strain of the slow-passing and empty minutes. Long before seven o'clock I was back at the Vingtième.

I sat there just where I had sat for luncheon. Air came in listlessly through the open door behind me. Now and again Rose or Berthe appeared for a moment. I had told them I would not order any dinner till Mr Soames came. A hurdy-gurdy began to play, abruptly drowning the noise of a quarrel between some

Frenchmen further up the street. Whenever the tune was changed I heard the quarrel still raging. I had bought another evening paper on my way. I unfolded it. My eyes gazed ever away from it to the clock over the kitchen door . . .

Five minutes, now, to the hour! I remembered that clocks in restaurants are kept five minutes fast. I concentrated my eyes on the paper. I vowed I would not look away from it again. I held it upright, at its full width, close to my face, so that I had no view of anything but it . . . Rather a tremulous sheet? Only because of the draught, I told myself.

My arms gradually became stiff; they ached; but I could not drop them— now. I had a suspicion, I had a certainty. Well, what then? . . . What else had I come for? Yet I held tight that barrier of newspaper. Only the sound of Berthe's brisk footstep from the kitchen enabled me, forced me, to drop it, and to utter:

'What shall we have to eat, Soames?'

'*Il est souffrant, ce pauvre Monsieur Soames?*' asked Berthe.

'He's only—tired.' I asked her to get some wine—Burgundy—and whatever food might be ready. Soames sat crouched forward against the table, exactly as when last I had seen him. It was as though he had never moved—he who had moved so unimaginably far. Once or twice in the afternoon it had for an instant occurred to me that perhaps his journey was not to be fruitless—that perhaps we had all been wrong in our estimate of the works of Enoch Soames. That we had been horribly right was horribly clear from the look of him. But 'Don't be discouraged,' I falteringly said. 'Perhaps it's only that you—didn't leave enough time. Two, three centuries hence, perhaps—'

'Yes,' his voice came. 'I've thought of that.'

'And now—now for the more immediate future! Where are you going to hide? How would it be if you caught the Paris express from Charing Cross? Almost an hour to spare. Don't go on to Paris. Stop at Calais. Live in Calais. He'd never think of looking for you in Calais.'

'It's like my luck,' he said, 'to spend my last hours on earth with an ass.' But I was not offended. 'And a treacherous ass,' he strangely added, tossing across to me a crumpled bit of paper which he had been holding in his hand. I glanced at the writing on it—some sort of gibberish, apparently. I laid it impatiently aside.

'Come, Soames! pull yourself together! This isn't a mere matter of life and death. It's a question of eternal torment, mind you! You don't mean to say you're going to wait limply here till the Devil comes to fetch you?'

'I can't do anything else. I've no choice.'

'Come! This is "trusting and encouraging" with a vengeance! This is Diabolism run mad!' I filled his glass with wine. 'Surely, now that you've *seen* the brute—'

'It's no good abusing him.'

'You must admit there's nothing Miltonic about him, Soames.'

'I don't say he's not rather different from what I expected.'

'He's a vulgarian, he's a swell-mobsman, he's the sort of man who hangs about the corridors of trains going to the Riviera and steals ladies' jewel-cases. Imagine eternal torment presided over by *him*!'

'You don't suppose I look forward to it, do you?'

'Then why not slip quietly out of the way?'

Again and again I filled his glass, and always, mechanically, he emptied it; but the wine kindled no spark of enterprise in him. He did not eat, and I myself ate hardly at all. I did not in my heart believe that any dash for freedom could save him. The chase would be swift, the capture certain. But better anything than this passive, meek, miserable waiting. I told Soames that for the honour of the human race he ought to make some show of resistance. He asked what the human race had ever done for him. 'Besides,' he said, 'can't you understand that I'm in his power? You saw him touch me, didn't you? There's an end of it. I've no will, I'm sealed.'

I made a gesture of despair. He went on repeating the word 'sealed'. I began to realize that the wine had clouded his brain. No wonder! Foodless he had gone into futurity, foodless he still was. I urged him to eat at any rate some bread. It was maddening to think that he, who had so much to tell, might tell nothing. 'How was it all,' I asked, 'yonder? Come! Tell me your adventures.'

'They'd make first-rate "copy", wouldn't they?'

'I'm awfully sorry for you, Soames, and I make all possible allowances; but what earthly right have you to insinuate that I should make "copy", as you call it, out of you?'

The poor fellow pressed his hands to his forehead. 'I don't know,' he said. 'I had some reason, I'm sure . . . I'll try to remember.'

'That's right. Try to remember everything. Eat a little more bread. What did the reading-room look like?'

'Much as usual,' he at length muttered.

'Many people there?'

'Usual sort of number.'

'What did they look like?'

Soames tried to visualize them. 'They all,' he presently remembered, 'looked very like one another.'

My mind took a fearsome leap. 'All dressed in Jaeger?'

'Yes. I think so. Greyish-yellowish stuff.'

'A sort of uniform?' He nodded. 'With a number on it, perhaps?—a number on a large disc of metal sewn on to the left sleeve? DKF 78.910—that sort of thing?' It was even so. 'And all of them—men and women alike—looking very well-cared-for? very Utopian? and smelling rather strongly of carbolic? and all of them quite hairless?' I was right every time. Soames was only not sure whether the men and women were hairless or shorn. 'I hadn't time to look at them very closely,' he explained.

'No, of course not. But—'

'They stared at *me*, I can tell you. I attracted a great deal of attention.' At last he had done that! 'I think I rather scared them. They moved away whenever I came near. They followed me about at a distance, wherever I went. The men at the round desk in the middle seemed to have a sort of panic whenever I went to make inquiries.'

'What did you do when you arrived?'

Well, he had gone straight to the catalogue, of course—to the S volumes, and had stood long before SNN-SOF, unable to take this volume out of the shelf, because his heart was beating so . . . At first, he said, he wasn't disappointed— he only thought there was some new arrangement. He went to the middle desk and asked where the catalogue of *twentieth*-century books was kept. He gathered that there was still only one catalogue. Again he looked up his name, stared at the three little pasted slips he had known so well. Then he went and sat down for a long time . . .

'And then,' he droned, 'I looked up the *Dictionary of National Biography* and some encyclopædias . . . I went back to the middle desk and asked what was the best modern book on late nineteenth-century literature. They told me Mr T. K. Nupton's book was considered the best. I looked it up in the catalogue and filled in a form for it. It was brought to me. My name wasn't in the index, but—Yes!' he said with a sudden change of tone. 'That's what I'd forgotten. Where's that bit of paper? Give it me back.'

I, too, had forgotten that cryptic screed. I found it fallen on the floor, and handed it to him.

He smoothed it out, nodding and smiling at me disagreeably. 'I found myself glancing through Nupton's book,' he resumed. 'Not very easy reading. Some sort of phonetic spelling . . . All the modern books I saw were phonetic.'

'Then I don't want to hear any more, Soames, please.'

'The proper names seemed all to be spelt in the old way. But for that, I mightn't have noticed my own name.'

'Your own name? Really? Soames, I'm *very* glad.'

'And yours.'

'No!'

'I thought I should find you waiting here tonight. So I took the trouble to copy out the passage. Read it.'

I snatched the paper. Soames' handwriting was characteristically dim. It, and the noisome spelling, and my excitement, made me all the slower to grasp what T. K. Nupton was driving at.

The document lies before me at this moment. Strange that the words I here copy out for you were copied out for me by poor Soames just seventy-eight years hence . . .

From p. 234 of *Inglish Littracher 1890-1900*, bi T. K. Nupton, published by th Stait, 1992:

Fr. egzarmpl, a riter ov th time, naimd Max Beerbohm, hoo woz stil alive in th twentieth senchri, rote a stauri in wich e pautraid an immajnari karrakter kauld 'Enoch Soames'—a thurd-rait poit hoo beleevz imself a grate jeneus an maix a bargin with th Devvl in auder ter no wot posterriti thinx ov im! It iz a sumwot labud sattire but not without vallu az showing hou seriusli the yung men ov th aiteen-ninetiz took themselvz. Nou that the littreri profeshn haz bin auganized az a department of publik servis, our riters hav found their levvl an hav lernt ter doo their duti without thort ov th morro. 'Th laibrer iz werthi ov hiz hire,' an that iz aul. Thank hevvn we hav no Enoch Soameses amung us to-dai!

I found that by murmuring the words aloud (a device which I commend to my reader) I was able to master them, little by little. The clearer they became, the greater was my bewilderment, my distress and horror. The whole thing was a nightmare. Afar, the great grisly background of what was in store for the poor dear art of letters; here, at the table, fixing on me a gaze that made me hot all over, the poor fellow whom—whom evidently . . . but no: whatever down-grade my character might take in coming years, I should never be such a brute as to—

Again I examined the screed. 'Immajnari'—but here Soames was, no more imaginary, alas! than I. And 'labud'—what on earth was that? (To this day, I have never made out that word.) 'It's all very—baffling,' I at length stammered.

Soames said nothing, but cruelly did not cease to look at me.

'Are you sure,' I temporized, 'quite sure you copied the thing out correctly?'

'Quite'.

'Well, then it's this wretched Nupton who must have made—must be going to make—some idiotic mistake . . . Look here, Soames! you know me better than to suppose that I . . . After all, the name "Max Beerbohm" is not at all an uncommon one, and there must be several Enoch Soameses running around—or rather, "Enoch Soames" is a name that might occur to any one writing a story. And I don't write stories: I'm an essayist, an observer, a recorder . . . I admit that it's an extraordinary coincidence. But you must see—'

'I see the whole thing,' said Soames quietly. And he added, with a touch of his old manner, but with more dignity than I had ever known in him, *'Parlons d'autre chose.'*

I accepted that suggestion very promptly. I returned straight to the more immediate future. I spent most of the long evening in renewed appeals to Soames to slip away and seek refuge somewhere. I remember saying at last that if indeed I was destined to write about him, the supposed 'stauri' had better have at least a happy ending. Soames repeated those last three words in a tone of intense scorn. 'In Life and in Art,' he said, 'all that matters is an *inevitable* ending.'

'But,' I urged, more hopefully than I felt, 'an ending that can be avoided *isn't* inevitable.'

'You aren't an artist,' he rasped. 'And you're so hopelessly not an artist that, so far from being able to imagine a thing and make it seem true, you're going to make even a true thing seem as if you'd made it up. You're a miserable bungler. And it's like my luck.'

I protested that the miserable bungler was not I—was not going to be I—but T. K. Nupton; and we had a rather heated argument, in the thick of which it suddenly seemed to me that Soames saw he was in the wrong: he had quite physically cowered. But I wondered why—and now I guessed with a cold throb just why—he stared so, past me. The bringer of that 'inevitable ending' filled the doorway.

I managed to turn in my chair and to say, not without a semblance of lightness, 'Aha, come in!' Dread was indeed rather blunted in me by his looking so absurdly like a villain in a melodrama. The sheen of his tilted hat and of his shirtfront, the repeated twists he was giving to his moustache, and most of all the magnificence of his sneer, gave token that he was there only to be foiled.

He was at our table in a stride. 'I am sorry,' he sneered witheringly, 'to break up your pleasant party, but—'

'You don't: you complete it,' I assured him. 'Mr Soames and I want to have a little talk with you. Won't you sit? Mr Soames got nothing—frankly nothing—by his journey this afternoon. We don't wish to say that the whole thing was a swindle—a common swindle. On the contrary, we believe you meant well. But of course the bargain, such as it was, is off.'

The Devil gave no verbal answer. He merely looked at Soames and pointed with rigid forefinger to the door. Soames was wretchedly rising from his chair when, with a desperate quick gesture, I swept together two dinner-knives that were on the table, and laid their blades across each other. The Devil stepped sharp back against the table behind him, averting his face and shuddering.

'You are not superstitious!' he hissed.

'Not at all,' I smiled.

'Soames!' he said as to an underling, but without turning his face, 'put those knives straight!'

With an inhibitive gesture to my friend, 'Mr Soames,' I said emphatically to the Devil, 'is a *Catholic* Diabolist'; but my poor friend did the Devil's bidding, not mine; and now, with his master's eyes again fixed on him, he arose, he shuffled past me. I tried to speak. It was he that spoke. 'Try,' was the prayer he threw back at me as the Devil pushed him roughly out through the door, '*try* to make them know that I did exist!'

In another instant I too was through that door. I stood staring all ways—up the street, across it, down it. There was moonlight and lamplight, but there was not Soames nor that other.

Dazed, I stood there. Dazed, I turned back, at length, into the little room; and I suppose I paid Berthe or Rose for my dinner and luncheon, and for Soames': I hope so, for I never went to the Vingtième again. Ever since that night I have avoided Greek Street altogether. And for years I did not set foot even in Soho Square, because on that same night it was there that I paced and loitered, long and long, with some such dull sense of hope as a man has in not straying far from the place where he has lost something . . . 'Round and round the shutter'd Square'—that line came back to me on my lonely beat, and with it the whole stanza, ringing in my brain and bearing in on me how tragically different from the happy scene imagined by him was the poet's actual experience of that prince in whom of all princes we should put not our trust.

But—strange how the mind of an essayist, be it never so stricken, roves and ranges!—I remember pausing before a wide doorstep and wondering if perchance it was on this very one that the young De Quincey lay ill and faint while poor Ann flew as fast as her feet would carry her to Oxford Street, the 'stony-hearted stepmother' of them both, and came back bearing that 'glass of port wine and spices' but for which he might, so he thought, actually have died. Was this the very doorstep that the old De Quincey used to revisit in homage? I pondered Ann's fate, the cause of her sudden vanishing from the ken of her boyfriend; and presently I blamed myself for letting the past override the present. Poor vanished Soames!

And for myself, too, I began to be troubled. What had I better do? Would there be a hue and cry—Mysterious Disappearance of an Author, and all that? He had last been seen lunching and dining in my company. Hadn't I better get a hansom and drive straight to Scotland Yard? . . . They would think I was a lunatic. After all, I reassured myself, London was a very large place, and one very dim figure might easily drop out of it unobserved—now especially, in the blinding glare of the near Jubilee. Better say nothing at all, I thought.

And I was right. Soames' disappearance made no stir at all. He was utterly forgotten before any one, so far as I am aware, noticed that he was no longer hanging around. Now and again some poet or prosaist may have said to another, 'What has become of that man Soames?' but I never heard any such question asked. The solicitor through whom he was paid his annuity may be presumed to have made inquiries, but no echo of these resounded. There was something rather ghastly to me in the general unconsciousness that Soames had existed, and more than once I caught myself wondering whether Nupton, that babe unborn, were going to be right in thinking him a figment of my brain.

In that extract from Nupton's repulsive book there is one point which perhaps puzzles you. How is it that the author, though I have here mentioned him by name and have quoted the exact words he is going to write, is not going to grasp the obvious corollary that I have invented nothing? The answer can but be this: Nupton will not have read the later passages of this memoir. Such lack of thoroughness is a serious fault in any one who undertakes to do scholar's work. And I hope these words will meet the eye of some contemporary rival to Nupton and be the undoing of Nupton.

I like to think that some time between 1992 and 1997 somebody will have looked up this memoir, and will have forced on the world his inevitable and startling conclusions. And I have reasons for believing that this will be so. You realize that the reading-room into which Soames was projected by the Devil was in all respects precisely as it will be on the afternoon of June 3rd, 1997. You realize, therefore, that on that afternoon, when it comes round, there the self-same crowd will be, and there Soames too will be, punctually, he and they doing precisely what they did before. Recall now Soames' account of the sensation he made. You may say that the mere difference of his costume was enough to make him sensational in that uniformed crowd. You wouldn't say so if you had ever seen him. I assure you that in no period could Soames be anything but dim. The fact that people are going to stare at him, and follow him around, and seem afraid of him, can be explained only on the hypothesis that they will somehow have been prepared for his ghostly visitation. They will have been awfully waiting to see whether he really would come. And when he does come the effect will of course be—awful.

An authentic, guaranteed, proven ghost, but—only a ghost, alas! Only that. In his first visit, Soames was a creature of flesh and blood, whereas the creatures into whose midst he was projected were but ghosts, I take it—solid, palpable, vocal, but unconscious and automatic ghosts, in a building that was itself an illusion. Next time, that building and those creatures will be real. It is of Soames that there will be but the semblance. I wish I could think him destined to revisit the world actually, physically, consciously. I wish he had this one brief escape, this one small treat, to look forward to. I never forget him for long. He is where he is, and for ever. The more rigid moralists among you may say he has only himself to blame. For my part, I think he has been very hardly used. It is well that vanity should be chastened; and Enoch Soames' vanity was, I admit, above the average, and called for special treatment. But there was no need for vindictiveness. You say he contracted to pay the price he is paying; yes; but I maintain that he was induced to do so by fraud. Well-informed in all things, the Devil must have known that my friend would gain nothing by his visit to futurity. The whole thing was a very shabby trick. The more I think of it, the more detestable the Devil seems to me.

Of him I have caught sight several times, here and there, since that day at the Vingtième. Only once, however, have I seen him at close quarters. This was in Paris. I was walking, one afternoon, along the Rue d'Antin, when I saw him advancing from the opposite direction—over-dressed as ever, and swinging an ebony cane, and altogether behaving as though the whole pavement belonged to him. At thought of Enoch Soames and the myriads of other sufferers eternally in this brute's dominion, a great cold wrath filled me, and I drew myself up to my full height. But—well, one is so used to nodding and smiling in the street to anybody whom one knows, that the action becomes almost independent of oneself: to prevent it requires a very sharp effort and great presence of mind. I was miserably aware, as I passed the Devil, that I nodded and smiled to him. And my shame was the deeper and hotter because he, if you please, stared straight at me with the utmost haughtiness.

To be cut—deliberately cut—by *him!* I was, I still am, furious at having had that happen to me.

The Tail of the Sphinx

Ambrose Bierce (*born 1842), American journalist and short-story writer, is noted for his imagination and brilliant cynicism, as displayed in* Can Such Things Be? *(1893) and* The Devil's Dictionary *(1906). Tired of life, he disappeared in Mexico some time in 1913.*

A Dog of a taciturn disposition said to his Tail:

'Whenever I am angry you rise and bristle; when I am pleased you wag; when I am alarmed you tuck yourself in out of danger. You are too mercurial— you disclose all my emotions. My notion is that tails are given to conceal thought. It is my dearest ambition to be as impassive as the Sphinx.'

'My friend, you must recognize the laws and limitations of your being,' replied the Tail, with flexions appropriate to the sentiments uttered, 'and try to be great some other way. The Sphinx has one hundred and fifty qualifications for impassiveness which you lack.'

'What are they?' the Dog asked.

'One hundred and forty-nine tons of sand on its tail.'

'And—?'

'A stone tail.'

The Squid in Its Own Ink

Adolfo Bioy Casares, *Argentine writer born in Buenos Aires. Author of* La invención de Morel *(1940);* Plan de evasión *(1945);* La Trama celeste *(1948);* El sueño de los héroes *(1954);* Historia prodigiosa *(1955);* Guirnalda con amores *(1959);* El lado de la sombra *(1962).*

More has happened in this town during the last few days than in the whole of the rest of its history. In order fully to appreciate what I am saying, remember that I'm talking about one of the oldest towns in the province, one that has witnessed countless outstanding events: its foundation in the middle of the nineteenth century; cholera some time later—an outbreak which luckily did not reach major proportions; and the threat of a surprise attack by the Indians, which although it never actually happened, kept people in check for five years, when farms near the border were troubled by Indians. Leaving behind heroic times, I shall skip several visits by governors, members of parliament, candidates of every kind, as well as comics and one or two big names in sport, and, to come full circle, I shall end this short list with the Foundation Centenary party, a genuine pageant of homage and homilies.

As I am about to recount an event of great importance, let me first present my credentials to the reader. Of broad mind and advanced ideas, I devour any book I can get my hands on in my Spanish friend Villarroel's bookshop, from Doctor Jung to Hugo, Walter Scott and Goldoni, not forgetting the last little volume of *Scenes of Madrid.* My objective is culture, but I'm already approaching those 'damned thirty years' and I'm afraid I have more to learn than I already know. In short, I try to carry on and to illuminate my neighbours — all lovely, beautiful people, though overly fond of the siesta, a custom passed down from the Middle Ages and Obscurantism. I'm a teacher — primary school — and journalist. I practise my skill as a writer in modest local publications, now factotum for *The Sunflower* (a badly chosen title, giving rise to taunts and attracting an enormous amount of mistaken correspondence, since we are taken for a cereal publication), now for *Nueva Patria*.

The subject-matter of this chronicle has a special peculiarity I cannot omit: not only did the event in question take place in my home town, but it happened in the block where my whole life unfolded, where were my home, my school— my second home—and a hotel bar opposite the station, where we restless local youths would go night after night, very late. The epicentre of the phenomenon, or focus, if you like, was Juan Camargo's yard, the bottom of which adjoined the hotel on the east side and our yard on the north. And the phenomenon itself was heralded by a couple of circumstances which not everyone would have linked together: I mean the request for books and the withdrawal of the sprinkler.

Las Margaritas, don Juan's private *petit-hotel*, a real chalet with a flowery garden on to the street, takes up half the front and a small part of the bottom of the yard, where innumerable things were piled up, such as relics from ships at the bottom of the sea. As to the sprinkler, it always turned in the garden, so much so that it was one of the oldest traditions and one of the most interesting pecularities in our town.

One Sunday, early in the month, the sprinkler mysteriously went missing. Since it hadn't reappeared by the end of the week, the garden began to fade. Whilst many watched without seeing, there was one who was beset by curiosity from the first moment. This person infected the others, and at night, in the bar opposite the station, the lads would be bubbling with questions and comments. To the extent that, itching with natural, naïve curiosity, we uncovered something about which little was natural and which turned out to be quite a surprise.

We knew very well that don Juan was not a man who would carelessly cut off the water in the garden during a dry summer. We had so far considered him a pillar of the community. His portrait is a faithful representation of the character of our fifty-year-old: tall, of stout bearing, whitened hair combed in docile halves, whose waves form arches parallel to those of his moustache and to the lower ones of his watch chain. Other details reveal an old-fashioned gentleman: breeches, leather gaiters, spats. Throughout his life, governed by order and restraint, nobody, as far as I can remember, had ever spotted a weakness in him, be it drunkenness, loose women or a lapse into politics. In a past which we would willingly forget—which of us, if we're going to talk infamy, didn't let our hair down?— don Juan kept clean. Not for nothing did the very auditors of the Cooperative—hardly respectable people; layabouts, frankly—recognize his authority, etcetera. Not for nothing in those harsh years did that moustache constitute the handlebars the upright families of the village steered by.

It must be recognized that this exceptional man expounds old-fashioned ideas and that our ranks, themselves idealists, had so far not produced any great figures of comparable mettle. In a new country, new ideas are short on tradition. As everyone knows, without tradition there can be no stability.

Our hierarchy placed no one above this figure, except for doña Remedios, mother and only adviser to such an overwhelming son.

To complete the picture of those who live in the chalet, there is only one undoubtedly minor appendix to add, the godson, don Tadeíto, one of my students at evening classes. Since doña Remedios and don Juan rarely tolerate strangers in the house, neither as helpers nor as guests, the lad takes on the roles of labourer and assistant in the yard and as servant-boy in *Las Margaritas*. Add to this the fact that the poor devil regularly attends my classes and you will understand why I let rip at anyone who, jokingly or out of pure spite, calls him names, mocking him. That he was gloriously turned down for national service matters to me not at all, since envy is not one of my sins.

That particular Sunday, somewhere between two and four in the afternoon, there was a knock at my door, a deliberate effort, judging by the noise, to break it down. I staggered to my feet, murmured, 'It can be no other', uttered words inappropriate to a teacher and, as if this weren't a time for unpleasant visits, opened the door, sure that I would find don Tadeíto. I was right. There he was, smiling, his face so thin it didn't even block out the sun, which shone fully into my eyes. I understood he was asking straight out, and in that voice which suddenly drops, for first-, second- and third-year textbooks.

'Would you mind telling me what for?' I inquired irritably.

'Godfather asked for them,' he replied.

I handed over the books on the spot and forgot the episode as though it had all been part of a dream.

A few hours later, as I was on my way to the station, stretching out the walk to kill time, I noticed the sprinkler was missing in *Las Margaritas*. I mentioned this on the platform as we waited for the 19.30 Plaza express, which turned up at 20.54, and I mentioned it that night in the bar. I didn't refer to the request for the textbooks, and even less did I link one event with the other, because, as I said, I had barely registered the former in my memory.

I imagined that after such a restless day, we would get back into our usual stride. On Monday, at siesta-time, I joyfully said to myself, 'This time it's for real', but the fringe of my poncho was still tickling my nose when the rumpus started. Muttering, 'And what's up with him today? If I catch him kicking that door, I'll make him shed tears of blood,' I slipped on my espadrilles and went to the hall.

'Is interrupting your teacher to become a habit?' I growled on receiving back the pile of books.

The reply confused me totally, because all I got was, 'Godfather wants the third-, fourth- and fifth-year ones.'

'What for?' I managed to articulate.

'Godfather wants them,' explained don Tadeíto.

I handed over the books and went back to my bed, in search of sleep. I confess I did sleep, but I did so, believe me, in the air.

Later, on the way to the station, I saw that the sprinkler wasn't back in its place and that the yellowish tinge was spreading in the garden. I postulated all sorts of far-fetched ideas, and on the platform, as I showed off my body to frivolous groups of young ladies, my mind was still working on the interpretation of the mystery.

Watching the moon, enormous in the distant sky, one of us, I think it was Di Pinto, always given to the romantic notion of cutting the figure of a man of the country (for goodness' sake, in front of your lifelong friends!), commented, 'It's a dry moon. Let us not attribute, then, the removal of the device to a forecast of rain. Our don Juan must have had his reasons!'

Badaracco, a sharp lad, with a mole, because in previous times, apart from a bank salary, he earned a certain sum as an informant, asked me, 'Why don't you approach the idiot about it?'

'Who?'

'Your student,' he replied.

I approved the idea and applied it that night, after class. First I tried to dazzle don Tadeíto with the truism that rain is good for plants, then finally got straight to the point. The conversation went as follows:

'Is the sprinkler out of order?'

'No.'

'I don't see it in the garden.'

'Why would you see it?'

'Why wouldn't I?'

'Because it's watering the depot.'

I should explain that amongst ourselves we call the last shed in the yard, where don Juan piles up the materials which don't sell much, such as strange stoves and statues, monoliths and mizzenmasts, the depot.

Prompted by the desire to tell the lads the news about the sprinkler, I dismissed my student without questioning him on the other point. I both remembered and yelled after him at one and the same time. From the hallway, don Tadeíto looked at me with sheep's eyes.

'What does don Juan do with the books?'

'Well . . .' he shouted back, 'he puts them in the depot.'

Bewildered, I ran to the hotel. Just as I had predicted, the lads were perplexed by what I had to tell them. We all contributed an opinion, since it was a pity to say nothing at the time, and luckily nobody listened to anybody else. Or perhaps the landlord lent an ear, the enormous don Pomponio of the dropsical stomach, whom those in the group could barely tell apart from the pillars, tables and crockery, because we are blinded by pride of intellect. Don Pomponio's brassy voice, muffled by rivers of gin, called us to order. Seven faces looked up and fourteen eyes fixed on one shiny red face, split by his mouth, to inquire, 'Why don't you appoint a committee to go and ask don Juan himself for an explanation?'

His sarcasm awakened one of us, whose surname was Aldini, who takes correspondence courses and wears a white tie. Arching his eyebrows, he said to me, 'Why don't you tell your student to eavesdrop on conversations between doña Remedios and don Juan? Then use your cattle prod on him.'

'What prod?'

'Your schoolteacher's authority,' he clarified with hate.

'Does don Tadeíto have a good memory?' asked Badaracco.

'He does,' I asserted. 'Anything entering his skull is temporarily photographed.'

'Don Juan,' continued Aldini, 'asks doña Remedios' advice about everything.'

'Before a witness like his godson,' declared Di Pinto, 'they will talk in complete freedom.'

'If there is any mystery, it will be revealed,' Toledo prophesied.

Chazarreta, who works as an assistant at the market, grumbled, 'If there's no mystery, what is there?'

Since the conversation was getting sidetracked, Badaracco, famous for his equanimity, restrained the contenders. 'Lads,' he reprimanded them, 'you're old enought not to waste your energy.'

Just to have the last word, Toledo repeated, 'If there's any mystery, it will be revealed.'

It was revealed, but not before several days had passed.

Next siesta-time, just as I was falling into a deep sleep, naturally enough the knocks resounded. Judging by my palpitations, they were beating on the door and in my heart at the same time. Don Tadeíto was bringing back the books from the day before and asking for those of the first, second and third years of secondary school. As the more advanced book was outside my scope, we had to go to Villarroel's bookshop, wake up the Spaniard by banging loudly on the door and subsequently pacify him with the knowledge that it was don Juan who was asking for the books. As we had feared, the Spaniard asked, 'What's got into that man? Never in his life has he bought a book and all of a sudden . . . Needless to say, he only wants to borrow them.'

'Don't take it to heart, mate,' I reasoned, patting him on the back. 'You sound like an Argentine, you're so bitter.'

I told him about the previous requests for primary textbooks and maintained the strictest reserve as to the sprinkler, of whose disappearance, so he himself gave me to understand, he was perfectly aware. With the books under my arm I added, 'Tonight we're meeting in the bar of the hotel to debate all this. If you'd like to chip in, that's where you'll find us.'

We didn't see a soul on the way there and back, except for the butcher's rust-coloured dog, which must have been suffering from indigestion again, because even the humblest irrational being doesn't expose himself in his right mind to the heat of the two-o'clock sun.

I told my student to report to me verbatim the conversations between don Juan and doña Remedios. Not for nothing do they say that the punishment is in the crime. That night I was subjected to such torture as I had not foreseen in my rapacious curiosity: to listen to those interminably uninteresting dialogues recounted in every detail. I was occasionally about to make some cruel, ironic comment to the effect that I didn't care about doña Remedios' opinions on the last lot of yellow soap and the flannelette for don Juan's rheumatism but I restrained myself, for how could I leave what was to be considered important or not to the lad's discretion?

Needless to say, the next day he interrupted my siesta to bring the books back for Villarroel. That's when the first new development occurred: don Juan, said don Tadeíto, didn't want any more textbooks; he wanted old newspapers, which he was to buy by the kilo from the haberdashery, the butcher's and the baker's. In due course I discovered that the newspapers, like the books before them, were to end up in the depot.

Afterwards there came a period when nothing happened. The soul is never satisfied. I missed that same knocking at the door which before had wrenched me from my siesta. I wanted something to happen, good or bad. Accustomed to living intensely, I couldn't adjust to the lull. At last, one night the student, after an orderly inventory of the effects of salt and other nourishing substances on doña Remedios' system, without the slightest alteration in his tone to announce a change of subject, recited, 'Godfather said to doña Remedios that they have a guest living in the depot and he very nearly bumped into him the other day, because he was inspecting a sort of funfair swing which hadn't been entered in the books, and that he remained cool-headed although its state was pitiful and reminded him of a catfish gasping out of the lake. He said he hit on the idea of bringing a bucket of water, because without thinking he had understood that he was being asked for water and he wasn't going to let a fellow-creature die whilst he stood by and watched. He got no appreciable result and preferred to draw a drinking trough near rather than touch the visitor. He filled the trough with buckets of water but got no appreciable result. Suddenly he rememberd the sprinkler and, like a doctor who tries, he said, various remedies to save a dying man, he ran to fetch the sprinkler and connected it up. The result was visibly appreciable because the dying creature revived, as if breathing moist air suited him admirably. Godfather said he spent some time with the visitor, because he asked as best he could if he needed anything, and the visitor was, quite frankly, very sharp, and after a quarter of an hour was saying the odd word in Spanish and asking him for the basics so that he could teach himself. Godfather said he sent his godson to ask for the primary-school textbooks from the teacher. As the visitor was, quite frankly, very sharp, he learnt all the primary courses in two days, and in one what he felt like of secondary school. Next, said Godfather, he started to read the newspapers to find out what was going on in the world.'

'Did the conversation take place today?' I ventured to ask.

'Of course,' he answered. 'Whilst they were having coffee.'

'Did your godfather say anything else?'

'Of course, but I don't remember.'

'What do you mean, "I don't remember"?' I protested angrily.

'Well, you interrupted me,' the student explained.

'You're right. But you're not going to leave me like this,' I argued, 'dying of curiosity. Come on, make an effort.'

'Well, you interrupted me.'

'I know I interrupted you. It's all my fault.'

'All your fault,' he repeated.

'Don Tadeíto is a good man. He's not going to leave his teacher like this, half-way through a conversation, to carry on tomorrow or never.'

With deep sorrow he repeated, 'Or never.'

I was annoyed, as though something of great value were being stolen from me. I don't know why it was that I reflected that our dialogue consisted of repetitions, but I suddenly saw a glimmer of hope in that very thought. I repeated the last sentence in don Tadeíto's narrative. 'He read the papers to find out what was going on in the world.'

My student carried on indifferently, 'Godfather said that the visitor was stunned on discovering that the government of this world wasn't in the hands of worthy people, but rather in those of half-castes, if not complete ne'er-do-wells. That such a rabble should have the atom bomb in their care, said the visitor, was something which had to be seen to. If worthy people had it in their care, they would end up dropping it, because it is clear that when somebody has it, they drop it; but that it should be in the hands of that rabble just wasn't on. He said that they had discovered the bomb in other worlds before now, and such worlds inevitably blew up; that they didn't care if they blew up, since they were far away, but our world is nearby and they fear that they could be involved in a chain reaction.'

The incredible suspicion that don Tadeíto was making fun of me made me inquire of him gravely, 'Have you been reading *On Things You Can See in the Sky* by Doctor Jung?'

Fortunately he didn't hear the interruption and proceeded, 'Godfather said that he came from his planet in a vehicle made specially, with blood, sweat and tears, because over there there's a shortage of adequate materials and it's the result of years of investigation and work. That he came as a friend and liberator, and that he was asking for the full support of Godfather to execute his plan to save the world. Godfather said the interview with the visitor had taken place that afternoon and that he, at the gravity of the matter, hadn't hesitated to bother doña Remedios, to ask for her opinion, which he already took for granted was the same as his own.'

Since he did not resume after the pause which followed, I asked what the lady had answered.

'Ah, I don't know,' he replied.

'What do you mean, "Ah, I don't know"?' I repeated, angry once again.

'I left them talking together and came here, because it was time for my lessons. I thought to myself: when I'm not late, it makes my teacher happy.'

Shining with pride, his sheep's face awaited my congratulations. With admirable presence of mind I reflected that the lads wouldn't believe my story unless I took don Tadeíto along as a witness. I grabbed him violently by the arm and pushed him towards the bar. There were by friends, with the additoin of the Spaniard Villarroel.

As long as I am capable of remembering, I shall never forget that night. 'Gentlemen,' I shouted, as I pushed don Tadeíto against our table, 'I bring the explanation of the whole thing, important news and a witness who will not let me lie. In great detail, don Juan told his mother of the event and my faithful student didn't miss a word. In the depot in the yard, right here, the other side of this wall, is staying—guess who?—an inhabitant from another world. Don't be alarmed, gentlemen. Apparently the traveller is not of robust constitution, since

he cannot withstand the dry air of our city very well—we can still compete with
Córdoba—and to prevent him dying like a fish out of water, don Juan set up the
sprinkler for him, which constantly moistens the air in the depot. What's more,
apparently the motive for the arrival of the monster should not provoke anxiety.
He has come to save us, convinced that the world is going to be blown up by an
atom bomb, and he expressed his point of view to don Juan outright. Naturally
don Juan, whilst he drank his coffee, consulted doña Remedios. It is
unfortunate that this young man here'—I shook don Tadeíto, as though he were
a puppet—'left just in time not to hear doña Remedios' opinion, so we don't
know what they decided to do.'

'We do know,' said the bookseller, moving his thick wet lips like a snout.

I felt uncomfortable at having been corrected about news which I thought was
a scoop. I inquired, 'What do we know?'

'Don't get upset,' said Villarroel, who can see under water. 'If it's like you
say, all that about the traveller dying if they remove the sprinkler, don Juan has
condemned him to die. On my way here I passed *Las Margaritas* and by the light
of the moon I could distinguish perfectly the sprinkler watering the garden as
before.'

'I also saw it,' confirmed Chazarreta.

'With my hand on my heart,' murmured Aldini, 'I tell you the traveller
wasn't lying. Sooner or later we'll all be blown up by the atom bomb. I see no
escape.'

As though he were talking to himself, Badaracco said, 'Don't tell me that
those old people, between the two of them, have killed our last hope.'

'Don Juan doesn't like his position to be challenged,' said the Spaniard. 'He'd
rather the world blew up than have salvation come from someone else. It's a way
of loving humanity.'

'Reluctance at the unknown,' I commented. 'Obscurantism.'

They say that fear sharpens the mind. The truth is that something strange
hung over the bar that night, and we were all contributing ideas.

'Courage lads. Let's do something,' exhorted Badaracco. 'For the love of
humanity.'

'Why do you have, Mr Badaracco, so much love for humanity?' asked the
Spaniard.

Blushing, Badaracco stammered, 'I don't know. We all know.'

'What do we know, Mr Badaracco? If you think of men, do you find them
admirable? I find them the opposite: stupid, cruel, mean, envious,' declared
Villarroel.

'When there are elections,' agreed Chazarreta, 'your pretty humanity is
quickly exposed and shows itself just as it is. The worst always wins.'

'Is the love of humanity a hollow phrase?'

'No, Mr Teacher,' replied Villarroel. 'Let us call love of humanity
compassion for the pain of others and veneration for the works of our great
minds, for Cervantes' *Don Quixote*, for paintings by Velázquez and Murillo. In
neither form is that love worth anything as an argument to postpone the end of
the world. Only for men do these works exist, and after the end of the world—

the day will come, with the bomb or by natural causes—they will have no justification or excuse, believe me. As to compassion, it's a winner when the end is nigh . . . Since there is no way anyone will escape death, let it come soon for all of us, so that the sum of pain will be minimal!'

'We're wasting time with the preciousness of an academic discussion whilst right here, on the other side of this very wall, our last hope is dying,' I said with an eloquence which I was the first to admire.

'We have to act now,' observed Badaracco. 'Soon it will be too late.'

'If we invade his yard, don Juan might get angry,' suggested Di Pinto.

Don Pomponio, who had approached without our hearing him and gave us such a start that we jumped, proposed, 'Why don't you detail don Tadeíto as advance scout? That would be the prudent thing to do.'

'All right,' approved Toledo. 'Don Tadeíto is to connect the sprinkler in the depot and spy, to tell us what the traveller from another planet is like.'

We rushed out into the night, illuminated by the impassive moon. Practically in tears, Badaracco pleaded, 'Be generous, lads. No matter that we should put ourselves in danger. The fate of all the mothers and all the children in the world hangs on us.'

We scrambled in front of the yard; there were marches and countermarches, plottings and to-ings and fro-ings. Finally Badaracco gathered up courage and pushed don Tadeíto inside. My student came back after an endless wait to inform us: 'The catfish has died.'

We disbanded sadly. The bookseller came back with me. For some reason I don't fully understand, his company was a comfort to me.

Opposite *Las Margaritas*, whilst the sprinkler monotonously watered the garden, I exclaimed, 'I blame our lack of curiosity,' adding, looking absorbed at the constellations, 'How many Americas and infinite Terranovas have we lost tonight.'

'Don Juan,' said Villarroel, 'preferred to live within the constaints of a limited man. I admire his courage. We two, we don't even dare go in there.'

I said, 'It's late.'

'It's late', he repeated.

Guilty Eyes

Ah'med Ech Chiruani *is a name from a notebook, from a collection of folk tales. Nothing more is known of him.*

A man bought a girl for the sum of four thousand denarii. Looking at her one day, he burst into tears. The girl asked why he wept. He replied: 'Your eyes are so beautiful that they make me forget to worship God.' Later, when she was alone, the girl plucked out her eyes. 'Why do you so disfigure yourself? You have devalued your own worth.' She replied: 'I would not wish any part of me to stop you worshipping God.' That night, the man dreamed and heard a voice telling him: 'The girl devalued herself in your eyes, but she increased her value in ours and we have taken her from you.' When he awoke, he found four thousand denarii under his pillow. The girl was dead.

Anything You Want! . . .

Léon Bloy, *French writer, born in Perigueux (1846), died at Bourg la Reine (1917). Author of* Le Désespére *(1887);* Christophe Colomb devant les Taureaux *(1890);* Le Salut par les Juifs *(1892);* Sueur de Sang La Femme Pauvre *(1897);* Leon Bloy devant les Cochons *(1898);* Celle qui Pleure *(1906);* L'Ame de Napoléon *(1912).*

Maxence, weary after an evening of pleasure, arrived at the point where the main road crosses the Ruelle Dupleix, opposite the military academy. The place, merely unpleasant by daylight, had become, at one o'clock in the morning, a little sinister. The dark alley, especially, offered little reassurance: a muddy, neglected thoroughfare where artillerymen and cavalrymen lived and worked for pennies, in unspeakable quarters, which made the night reveller a trifle uneasy.

Nonetheless, he was contemplating it. A loud clamour could be heard coming from the Boulevard de Grenelle, a street that is was prudent to avoid, and a horror of being caught up in some drunken brawl made him feel inclined to turn into the dirty passage, at the other end of which he knew he would find a quieter street that would be more sympathetic to his amorous reverie.

He had just left his mistress's arms, and felt the need to dissipate his lust with a gentle and peaceful walk home, without interruption.

'Well, make your mind up—yes or no?' cried a horrible voice, trying to make itself sound agreeable.

Maxence saw, emerging from the shadows of a nearby wall, a gross woman who came towards him to offer the precious gift of her love.

'It won't cost much. Come with me and I'll do anything you want, sweetheart.'

She outlined a possible programme. The wayfarer listened, stock-still, as if hearing the pounding of his own heart. It was ridiculous, but he could not say why that voice moved him. The poor wretch could not have said why to save his life, but the feeling was real enough, and it turned into an unbearable anguish as he felt his mind drifting away on these shameful words, which somehow seemed to carry him back to his earliest days . . . sweet, wonderful memories which, recalled under such circumstances as these, were being horribly desecrated. His memories of childhood were sacred things, in contrast to his present existence which was—alas!—not at all glorious.

Whenever he needed to recover after a party or drinking-bout, he would call into his mind these memories, which always came rushing back to him, faithful and true, like shivering, abandoned lambs who only wanted to return to their shepherd . . .

But this time he had not called them. They had come unbidden—or, rather, it was *another voice* that had summoned them: a voice they clearly heeded as much as his own—and it was terrible not to understand how it could have happened.

Anything you want! I'll do anything you fancy, my dear . . . No, no — this was intolerable. His mother was dead, burned alive in a fire. He remembered a calcified hand, the only part of her that they had dared to show him.

His only sister, fifteen years his senior, who had raised him so tenderly, and from whom he had learned all that was good in him, had come to an equally tragic end. The ocean had swallowed her, together with fifty other passengers, in a notorious shipwreck off one of the most dangerous coastlines of the Gulf of Gascony. Her body had never been recovered.

These two tragic figures dominated his thoughts whenever he peered over the edge of his memory, as his own life took its course.

And now! It was horrible, monstrous, that this sow who clutched at him in the street, in this hellish place, had his sister's voice—the voice of his favourite creature in all the world, who had seemed to him an angel and whose feet, he believed, would have cleansed the filth of Sodom.

Admittedly, the voice had become immeasurably coarsened, had fallen from heaven and been dragged through slimy, murderous pits, but it was her voice all the same, and the sound of it made him want to run, screaming and sobbing, away.

In such ways can the dead mingle with the living—or those who pretend to be alive! Whilst the old whore offered him her vile flesh—and, Oh God!, in such language—he was hearing his sister, devoured by fish a quarter of a century before, enjoining him to worship God and love the poor.

'If you knew how lovely my thighs are!' said the crone.

'If you knew how lovely Jesus is!' said the saint.

'Come with me, you rascal; I have a good fire and a strong bed,' urged the hag.

'Never cause your guardian angel any pain,' murmured the other.

Without realizing it, he uttered the words that had filled his childhood *out loud*.

Hearing them, the whore was startled, and began to tremble. She raised her old, rheumy, bloodshot eyes—dull mirrors which seemed to reflect every scene of debauchery and every kind of torture—and looked sharply at him, like a drowning man looking for the last time at the sea-green sky through the window of water that is choking him.

There was a moment of silence.

'Sir,' she said at last, 'You must forgive me. I shouldn't have spoken to you. I'm just a wicked-minded old woman, a clown for the street-urchins to mock, and you should have kicked me into the gutter. Go home, and may God protect you.'

Maxence, astounded, watched as she disappeared into the shadows.

But she was right; he must go home. The midnight traveller turned towards the Boulevard de Grenelle, but very slowly. The encounter had completely overwhelmed him.

He had not gone ten paces when the old whore reappeared, running after him.

'Sir, I beg you, don't go that way!'

'And why should I not go that way?' he asked. 'It is on my way. I live in Vaugirard.'

'It doesn't matter if you return and take a different route altogether, even if it takes an hour longer. You'll be attacked if you go down that street. If you want to know, half the pimps in Paris are gathered there. They stretch from the abattoirs to the tobacco works. The police have given them the run of the place. There'll be no one there to look after you, and you'll walk straight into trouble.'

Maxence was tempted to reply that he had no need of protection but, fortunately, he realized that such bravado would be misplaced.

'Very well,' he said, 'I'll go back along by Les Invalides. It's a bit strong, though. I am very tired, and to have to make another detour is extremely annoying. They should send the cavalry in on these scoundrels.'

'There might be another way,' said the old woman, after a moment's hesitation.

'Really! And what might that be?'

Very humbly, she explained that as she was so well known in that delightful district, it would be easy for her to escort someone through . . .

'Only,' she added, with a surprising softness, 'people must think that you're a . . . friend, so you'll have to let me take your arm.'

Maxence hesitated too, fearing a trap. But some strange force was at work within him; his reluctance quickly vanished, and he was able to proceed unharmed through the dirty crowd on the arm of his creature, who greeted several villains as they passed, and who would have revolted Sin itself.

Not a word passed between them. He noticed, however, that she squeezed his arm and pressed against him much more than the situation warranted, and that her grasp seemed almost convulsive. The extraordinary anguish that he had felt lessened now that she was no longer speaking. He soon came to the conclusion that the whole thing had been some kind of hallucination, and everyone knows how useful this precious word can be in explaining any unusual sensation or foreboding.

When it was time for them to part, Maxence mumbled some banal word of thanks, and took out his purse with the intention of rewarding his strange, silent companion, who may have saved his life, but she stopped him with a gesture:

'No, sir, that's not what I want.'

Only then did he see that she was crying, as he had not dared to look at her during the half-hour that they had been walking together.

'What is the matter?' he asked, very moved. 'What *can* I do for you?'

'If you will let me embrace you,' she replied, 'that would be the greatest joy of my life—my disgusting life—and after that I think I should have the strength to die.'

Seeing that he assented, she threw herself upon him, groaning with love, and hugged him as if she wanted to devour him. A cry from the man she was smothering made her disentangle herself.

'Goodbye, Maxence, my little Maxence, my poor brother. Goodbye forever, and forgive me,' she cried. 'Now I can die.'

She fell before her brother could make any move to help her, and instantly her head was crushed under the wheel of a night wagon that was driving by at lightning speed.

Maxence no longer has a mistress. He is currently completing his novitiate as a lay brother at the monastery of Grande-Chartreuse.

Tlön, Uqbar, Orbis Tertius

Jorge Luis Borges *(1899-1986) born in Buenos Aires. Argentina's foremost modern writer and founder of several important periodicals in the 1920s. Author of* Fervor de Buenos Aires *(1923);* El Idioma de los Argentinos *(1928);* Cuaderno San Martin *(1929);* Evaristo Carriego *(1930);* Discussion *(1932);* Historia Universal de la Infamia *(1935), a collection of short stories;* Historia de la Eternidad *(1936);* El jardin de senderos que se bifurcan *(1941);* Ficciones *(1944; translated into English, 1962);* El Aleph *(1949);* Otras inquisiciones *(1952);* El hacedor *(1960; translated into English as* Dreamtigers, *1964).*

I owe the discovery of Uqbar to the conjunction of a mirror and an encyclopaedia. The unnerving mirror hung at the end of a corridor in a villa on Calle Goana, in Ramos Mejía; the misleading encyclopedia goes by the name of *The Anglo-American Cyclopaedia* (New York, 1917), and is a literal if inadequate reprint of the 1902 *Encyclopaedia Britannica*. The whole affair happened some five years ago. Bioy Casares had dined with me that night and talked to us at length about a great scheme for writing a novel in the first person, using a narrator who omitted or corrupted what happened and who ran into various contradictions, so that only a handful of readers, a very small handful, would be able to decipher the horrible or banal reality behind the novel. From the far end of the corridor, the mirror was watching us; and we discovered, with the inevitability of discoveries made late at night, that mirrors have something grotesque about them. Then Bioy Cesares recalled that one of the heresiarchs of Uqbar had stated that mirrors and copulation are abominable, since they both multiply the numbers of man. I asked him the source of that memorable sentence, and he replied that it was recorded in the *Anglo-American Cyclopaedia*, in its article on Uqbar. It so happened that the villa (which we had rented furnished) possessed a copy of that work. In the final pages of Volume XLVI, we ran across an article on Upsala; in the beginning of Volume XLVII, we found one on Ural-Altaic languages; but not one word on Uqbar. A little put out, Bioy consulted the index volumes. In vain he tried every possible spelling— Ukbar, Ucbar, Ooqbar, Ookbar, Oukbahr . . . Before leaving, he informed me it was a region in either Iraq or Asia Minor. I must say that I acknowledged this a little uneasily. I supposed that this undocumented country and its anonymous heresiarch had been deliberately invented by Bioy out of modesty, to substantiate a phrase. A futile examination of one of the atlases of Justus Perthes strengthened my doubt.

On the following day, Bioy telephoned me from Buenos Aires. He told me that he had in front of him the article on Uqbar, in Volume XLVI of the encyclopedia. It did not specify the name of the heresiarch, but it did note his doctrine, in words almost identical to the ones he had repeated to me, though, I would say, inferior from a literary point of view. He had remembered: 'Copulation and mirrors are abominable.' The text of the encyclopedia read: 'For one of those gnostics, the visible universe was an illusion or, more precisely, a sophism. Mirrors and fatherhood are abominable because they multiply it and extend it.' I said, in all sincerity, that I would like to see the article. A few days later, he brought it. This surprised me, because the scrupulous cartographic index of Ritter's *Erdkunde* completely failed to mention the name of Uqbar.

The volume which Bioy brought was indeed Volume XLVI of *The Anglo-American Cyclopaedia*. On the title page and spine, the alphabetical key was the same as in our copy, but instead of 917 pages, it had 921. These four additional pages consisted of the article on Uqbar—not accounted for by the alphabetical cipher, as the reader will have noticed. We ascertained afterwards that there was no other difference between the two volumes. Both, as I think I pointed out, are reprints of the tenth *Encyclopaedia Britannica*. Bioy had acquired his copy in one of a number of book sales.

We read the article with some care. The passage remembered by Bioy was perhaps the only startling one. The rest seemed probable enough, very much in keeping with the general tone of the work and, naturally, a little dull. Reading it over, we discovered, beneath the superficial authority of the prose, a fundamental vagueness. Of the fourteen names mentioned in the geographical section, we recognized only three—Khurasan, Armenia, and Erzurum—and they were dragged into the text in a strangely ambiguous way. Among the historical names, we recognized only one, that of the imposter, Smerdis the Magian, and it was invoked in a rather metaphorical sense. The notes appeared to fix precisely the frontiers of Uqbar, but the points of reference were all, vaguely enough, rivers and craters and mountain chains in that same region. We read, for instance, that the southern frontier is defined by the lowlands of Tsai Haldun and the Axa delta, and that wild horses flourish in the islands of that delta. This, at the top of page 918. In the historical sectoin (page 920), we gathered that, just after the religious persecutions of the thirteenth century, the orthodox sought refuge in the islands, where their obelisks have survived, and where it is a common enough occurrence to dig up one of their stone mirrors. The language and literature section was brief. There was one notable characteristic: it remarked that the literature of Uqbar was fantastic in character, and that its epics and legends never referred to reality, but to the two imaginary regions of Mlejnas and Tlön . . . The bibliography listed four volumes, which we have not yet come across, even although the third—Silas Haslam: *History of the Land Called Uqbar*, 1874—appears in the library catalogues of Bernard Quaritch.* The first, *Lesbare und lesenswerthe Bemerkungen über das Land Ukkbar in Klein-Asien*, is dated 1641, and is a work of Johann Valentin Andreä. The fact is signficant; a couple of years later I ran across that name accidentally in the thirteenth volume of De Quincey's *Writings*, and I knew that it was the name of a German theologian who, at the beginning of the seventeenth century, described the imaginary community of Rosae Crucis— the community which was later founded by others in imitation of the one he had preconceived.

That night, we visited the National Library. Fruitlessly we exhausted atlases, catalogues, yearbooks of geographical societies, memoirs of travellers and historians—nobody had ever been in Uqbar. Neither did the general index of Bioy's encyclopedia show the name. The following day, Carlos Mastronardi, to whom I had referred the whole business, caught sight, in a Corrientes and Talcahuano bookshop, of the black and gold bindings of *The Anglo-American Cyclopaedia* . . . He went in and looked up Volume XLVI. Naturally, there was not the slightest mention of Uqbar.

II

Some small fading memory of one Herbert Ashe, an engineer for the southern railroads, hangs on in the hotel in Androgué, between the luscious honeysuckle and the illusory depths of the mirrors. In life, he suffered from a sense of unreality, as do so many Englishmen; dead, he is not even the ghostly creature he was then. He was tall and languid; his limp squared beard had once been red. He was, I understand, a widower, and childless. Every so many years, he went to England to visit—judging by the photographs he showed us—a sundial and

---

*Haslam has also published *A General History of Labyrinths*.

some oak trees. My father and he had cemented (the verb is excessive) one of those English friendships which begin by avoiding intimacies and eventually eliminate speech altogether. They used to exchange books and periodicals; they would beat one another at chess, without saying a word . . . I remember him in the corridor of the hotel, a mathematics textbook in his hand, gazing now and again at the passing colours of the sky. One afternoon, we discussed the duodecimal numerical system (in which twelve is written 10). Ashe said that as a matter of fact, he was transcribing some duodecimal tables, I forget which, into sexagesimals (in which sixty is written 10), adding that this work had been commissioned by a Norwegian in Rio Grande do Sul. We had known him for eight years and he had never mentioned having stayed in that part of the country . . . We spoke of rural life, of *capangas*, of the Brazilian etymology of the word *gaucho* (which some old people in the east still pronounce *gaúcho*), and nothing more was said—God forgive me—of duodecimal functions. In September, 1937 (we ourselves were not at the hotel at the time), Herbert Ashe died of an aneurysmal rupture. Some days before, he had received from Brazil a stamped, registered package. It was a book, an octavo volume. Ashe left it in the bar where, months later, I found it. I began to leaf through it and felt a sudden curious lightheadedness, which I will not go into, since this is the story, not of my particular emotions, but of Uqbar and Tlön and Orbis Tertius. In the Islamic world, there is one night, called the Night of Nights, on which the secret gates of the sky open wide and the water in the water jugs tastes sweeter; if those gates were to open, I would not feel what I felt that afternoon. The book was written in English, and had 1001 pages. On the yellow leather spine, and again on the title page, I read these words: *A First Encyclopaedia of Tlön*. Volume XI. Hlaer to Jangr. There was nothing to indicate either date or place of origin. On the first page and on a sheet of silk paper covering one of the coloured engravings there was a blue oval stamp with the inscription: ORBIS TERTIUS. It was two years since I had discovered, in a volume of a pirated encyclopaedia, a brief description of a false country; now, chance was showing me something much more valuable, something to be reckoned with. Now, I had in my hands a substantial fragment of the complete history of an unknown planet, with its architecture and its playing cards, its mythological terrors and the sound of its dialects, its emperors and its oceans, its minerals, its birds, and its fishes, its algebra and its fire, its theological and metaphysical arguments, all clearly stated, coherent, without any apparent dogmatic intention or parodic undertone.

The eleventh volume of which I speak refers to both subsequent and preceding volumes. Néstor Ibarra, in an article (in the *N.R.F.*), now a classic, has denied the existence of those corollary volumes; Ezequiel Martínez Estrada and Drieu La Rochelle have, I think, succeeded in refuting this doubt. The fact is that, up to now, the most patient investigations have proved fruitless. We have turned the libraries of Europe, North and South America upside down—in vain. Alfonso Reyes, bored with the tedium of this minor detective work, proposes that we all take on the task of reconstructing the missing volumes, many and vast as they were: *ex ungue leonem*. He calculates, half seriously, that one generation of Tlönists would be enough. This bold estimate brings us back to the basic problem: who were the people who had invented Tlön? The plural is unavoidable, because we have unanimously rejected the idea of a single creator, some transcendental Leibnitz working in modest obscurity. We conjecture that this 'brave new world' was the work of a secret society of astronomers, biologists, engineers, metaphysicians, poets, chemists, mathematicians, moralists, painters, and geometricians, all under the supervision of an unknown genius. There are plenty of individuals who have mastered these various disciplines without having any facility for invention, far less for submitting that inventiveness to a strict, systematic plan. This plan is so vast that each individual contribution to it is infinitesimal. To begin with, Tlön was thought to be nothing more than a chaos, a free and irresponsible work of the imagination; now it was clear that it is a complete cosmos, and that the strict laws which govern it have been carefully formulated, albeit provisionally. It is enough to note that the apparent contradictions in the eleventh volume are the basis for proving the existence of the others, so lucid and clear is the scheme maintained in it. The popular magazines have publicized, with pardonable zeal, the zoology and topography of Tlön. I think, however, that its transparent tigers and its towers of blood scarcely deserve the unwavering attention of *all* men. I should like to take some little time to deal with its conception of the universe.

Hume remarked once and for all that the arguments of Berkeley were not only thoroughly unanswerable but thoroughly unconvincing. This dictum is emphatically true as it applies to our world; but it falls down completely in Tlön. The nations of that planet are congenitally idealist. Their language, with its derivatives—religion, literature, and metaphysics—presupposes idealism, For them, the world is not a concurrence of objects in space, but a heterogeneous series of independent acts. It is serial and temporal, but not spatial. There are no nouns in the hypothetical *Ursprache* of Tlön, which is the source of the living language and the dialects; there are impersonal verbs qualified by monosyllabic suffixes or prefixes which have the force of adverbs. For example, there is no word corresponding to the noun *moon*, but there is a verb *to moon* or *to moondle*. *The moon rose over the sea* would be written *hlör u fang axaxaxas mlö*, or, to put it in order: *upward beyond the constant flow there was moondling*. (Xul Solar translates it succinctly: *upward, behind the onstreaming it mooned.*)

The previous passage refers to the languages of the southern hemisphere. In those of the nothern hemisphere (the eleventh volume has little information on its *Ursprache*), the basic unit is not the verb, but the monosyllabic adjective. Nouns are formed by an accumulation of adjectives. One does not say moon; one says *airy-clear over dark-round* or *orange-faint-of-sky* or some other accumulation. In the chosen example, the mass of adjectives corresponds to a real object. The happening is completely fortuitous. In the literature of this hemisphere (as in the lesser world of Meinong), ideal objects abound, invoked and dissolved momentarily, according to poetic necessity. Sometimes, the faintest simultaneousness brings them about. There are objects made up of two sense elements, one visual, the other auditory—the colour of a sunrise and the distant call of a bird. Other objects are made up of many elements—the sun, the water against the swimmer's chest, the vague quivering pink which one sees when the eyes are closed, the feeling of being swept away by a river or by sleep. These second degree objects can be combined with others; using certain abbreviations, the process is practically an infinite one. There are famous poems made up of one enormous word, a word which in truth forms a poetic *object*, the creation of the writer. The fact that no one believes that nouns refer to an actual reality means, paradoxically enough, that there is no limit to the numbers of them. The languages of the northern hemisphere of Tlön include all the names in Indo-European languages—plus a great many others.

It is no exaggeration to state that in the classical culture of Tlön, there is only one discipline, that of psychology. All others are subordinated to it. I have remarked that the men of that planet conceive of the universe as a series of mental processes, whose unfolding is to be understood only as a time sequence. Spinoza attributes to the inexhaustibly divine in man the qualities of extension and of thinking. In Tlön, nobody would understand the juxtaposition of the first, which is only characteristic of certain states of being, with the second, which is a perfect synonym for the cosmos. To put it another way—they do not conceive of the spatial as everlasting in time. The perception of a cloud of smoke on the horizon and, later, of the countryside on fire and, later, of a half-extinguished cigar which caused the conflagration would be considered an example of the association of ideas.

This monism, or extreme idealism, completely invalidates science. To explain or to judge an event is to identify or unite it with another one. In Tlön, such connexion is a later stage in the mind of the observer, which can in no way affect or illuminate the earlier stage. Each state of mind is irreducible. The mere act of giving it a name, that is of classifying it, implies a falsification of it. From all this, it would be possible to deduce that there is no science in Tlön, let alone rational thought. The paradox, however, is that sciences exist, in countless number. In philosophy, the same thing happens as happens with the nouns in the northern hemisphere. The fact that any philosophical system is bound in advance to be a dialectical game, a *Philosophie des Als Ob,* means that systems abound, unbelievable systems, beautifully constructed or else sensational in effect. The metaphysicians of Tlön are not looking for truth, nor even for an approximation of it; they are after a kind of amazement. They consider metaphysics a branch of fantastic literature. They know that a system is nothing more than the subordination of all the aspects of the universe to some one of them. Even the phrase 'all the aspects' can be rejected, since it presupposes the impossible inclusion of the present moment, and of past moments. Even so, the plural, 'past moments' is inadmissible, since it supposes another impossible operation . . . One of the schools in Tlön has reached the point of denying time. It reasons that the present is undefined, that the future has no other reality than as present hope, that the past is no more than present memory.* Another school

---

*Russell (*The Analysis of Mind,* 1921, page 159) conjectures that our planet was created a few moments ago, and provided with a humanity which 'remembers' an illusory past.

declares that the *whole of time* has already happened and that our life is a vague memory or dim reflection, doubtless false and fragmented, of an irrevocable process. Another school has it that the history ot the universe, which contains the history of our lives and the most tenuous details of them, is the handwriting produced by a minor god in order to communicate with a demon. Another maintains that the universe is comparable to those code systems in which not all the symbols have meaning, and in which only that which happens every three hundredth night is true. Another believes that, while we are asleep here, we are awake somewhere else, and that thus every man is two men.

Among the doctrines of Tlön, none has occasioned greater scandal than the doctrine of materialism. Some thinkers have formulated it with less clarity than zeal, as one might put forward a paradox. To clarify the general understanding of this unlikely thesis, one eleventh century† heresiarch offered the parable of nine copper coins, which enjoyed in Tlön the same noisy reputation as did the Eleatic paradoxes of Zeno in their day. There are many versions of this 'feat of specious reasoning' which vary the number of coins and the number of discoveries. Here is the commonest:

On Tuesday, X ventures along a deserted road and loses nine copper coins. On Thursday, Y finds on the road four coins, somewhat rusted by Wednesday's rain. On Friday, Z comes across three coins in the road. On Friday morning, X finds two coins in the corridor of his house. [The heresiarch is trying to deduce from this story the reality, that is, the continuity, of the nine recovered coins.] It is absurd, he states, to suppose that four of the coins have not existed between Tuesday and Thursday, three between Tuesday and Friday afternoon, and two between Tuesday and Friday morning. It is logical to assume that they *have* existed, albeit in some secret way, in a manner whose understanding is concealed from men, in every moment, in all three places.

The language of Tlön is by its nature resistant to the formulation of this paradox; most people do not understand it. At first, the defenders of common sense confined themselves to denying the truth of the anecdote. They declared that it was a verbal fallacy, based on the reckless use of two neological expressions, not substantiated by common usage, and contrary to the laws of strict thought—the verbs *to find* and *to lose* entail a *petitio principii*, since they presuppose that the first nine coins and the second are identical. They recalled that any noun—*man, money, Thursday, Wednesday, rain*—has only metaphysical value. They denied the misleading detail 'somewhat rusted by Wednesday's rain', since it assumes what must be demonstrated—the continuing existence of the four coins between Thursday and Tuesday. They explained that equality is

---

† A century, in accordance with the duodecimal system, signifies a period of one hundred and forty-four years.

one thing and identity another, and formulated a kind of *reductio ad absurdum*, the hypothetical case of nine men who, on nine successive nights, suffer a violent pain. Would it not be ridiculous, they asked, to claim that this pain is the same one each time?* They said that the heresiarch was motivated mainly by the blasphemous intention of attributing the divine category of *being* to some ordinary coins: and that sometimes he was denying plurality, at other times not. They argued thus: that if equality entails identity, it would have to be admitted at the same time that the nine coins are only one coin.

Amazingly enough, these refutations were not conclusive. After the problem had been stated and restated for a hundred years, one thinker no less brilliant than the heresiarch himself, but in the orthodox tradition, advanced a most daring hypothesis. This felicitous supposition declared that there is only one Individual, and that this indivisible Individual is every one of the separate beings in the universe, and that those beings are the instruments and masks of divinity itself. X is Y and is Z. Z finds three coins because he remembers that X lost them. X finds only two in the corridor because he remembers that the others have been recovered. . . The eleventh volume gives us to understand that there were three principal reasons which led to the complete victory of this pantheistic idealism. First, it repudiated solipsism. Second, it made possible the retention of a psychological basis for the sciences. Third, it permitted the cult of the gods to be retained. Schopenhauer, the passionate and clear-headed Schopenhauer, advanced a very similar theory in the first volume of his *Parerga und Paralipomena*.

The geometry of Tlön has two somewhat distinct systems, a visual one and a tactile one. The latter system corresponds to our geometry; they consider it inferior to the former. The foundation of visual geometry is the surface, not the point. This system rejects the principle of parallelism, and states that, as man moves about, he alters the forms which surround him. The arithmetical system is based on the idea of indefinite numbers. It emphasizes the importance of the concepts *greater* and *lesser*, which our mathematicians symbolize as $>$ and $<$. It states that the operation of counting modifies quantities and changes them from indefinites into definites. The fact that several individuals counting the same quantity arrive at the same result is, say their psychologists, an example of the association of ideas or the good use of memory. We already know that in Tlön the source of all-knowing is single and eternal.

In literary matters too, the dominant notion is that everything is the work of one single author. Books are rarely signed. The concept of plagiarism does not exist; it has been established that all books are the work of one single writer, who is timeless and anonymous. Criticism is prone to invent authors. A critic will choose two dissimilar works—the *Tao Tê Ching* and *The Thousand and One Nights*, let us say—and attribute them to the same writer, and then with all probity explore the psychology of this interesting *homme de lettres*. . .

---

*Nowadays, one of the churches of Tlön maintains platonically that such and such a pain, such and such a greenish-yellow colour, such and such a temperature, such and such a sound etc., make up the only reality there is. All men, in the climatic instant of coitus, are the same man. All men who repeat one line of Shakespeare *are* William Shakespeare.

The books themselves are also odd. Works of fiction are based on a single plot, which runs through every imaginable permutation. Works of natural philosophy invariably include thesis and antithesis, the strict pro and con of a theory. A book which does not include its opposite, or 'counter-book', is considered incomplete.

Centuries and centuries of idealism have not failed to influence reality. In the very oldest regions of Tlön, it is not an uncommon occurrence for lost objects to be duplicated. Two people are looking for a pencil; the first one finds it and says nothing; the second finds a second pencil, no less real, but more in keeping with his expectation. These secondary objects are called *hrönir* and, even though awkward in form, are a little larger than the originals. Until recently, the *hrönir* were the accidental children of absent-mindedness and forgetfulness. It seems improbable that the methodical production of them has been going on for almost a hundred years, but so it is stated in the eleventh volume. The first attempts were fruitless. Nevertheless, the *modus operandi* is worthy of note. The director of one of the state prisons announced to the convicts that in an ancient river bed certain tombs were to be found, and promised freedom to any prisoner who made an important discovery. In the months preceding the excavation, printed photographs of what was to be found were shown the prisoners. The first attempt proved that hope and zeal could be inhibiting; a week of work with shovel and pick succeeded in unearthing no *hrön* other than a rusty wheel, postdating the experiment. This was kept a secret, and the experiment was later repeated in four colleges. In three of them the failure was almost complete; in the fourth (the director of which died by chance during the initial excavation), the students dug up—or produced—a gold mask, an archaic sword, two or three earthenware urns, and the moldered mutilated torso of a king with an inscription on his breast which has so far not been deciphered. Thus was discovered the unfitness of witnesses who were aware of the experimental nature of the search. . . Mass investigations produced objects which contradicted one another; now, individual projects, as far as possible spontaneous, are preferred. The methodical development of *hrönir*, states the eleventh volume, has been of enormous service to archaeologists. It has allowed them to question and even to modify the past, which nowadays is no less malleable or obedient than the future. One curious fact: the *hrönir* of the second and third degree—that is, the *hrönir* derived from another *hrön*, and the *hrönir* derived from the *hrön* of a *hrön*—exaggerate the flaws of the original; those of the fifth degree are almost uniform; those of the ninth can be confused with those of the second; and those of the eleventh degree have a purity of form which the originals do not possess. The process is a recurrent one; a *hrön* of the twelfth degree begins to deteriorate in quality. Stranger and more perfect than any *hrön* is sometimes the *ur*, which is a thing produced by suggestion, an object brought into being by hope. The great gold mask I mentioned previously is a distinguished example.

Things duplicate themselves in Tlön. They tend at the same time to efface themselves, to lose their detail when people forget them. The classic example is that of a stone threshold which lasted as long as it was visited by a beggar, and which faded from sight on his death. Occasionally, a few birds, a horse perhaps, have saved the ruins of an amphitheatre. (1940. *Salto Oriental*.)

Postscript. 1947. I reprint the foregoing article just as it appeared in *The Book of Fantasy*, 1940, omitting no more than some figures of speech, and a kind of burlesque summing up, which now strikes me as frivolous. So many things have happened since that date. . . . I will confine myself to putting them down.

In March, 1941, a manuscript letter by Gunnar Erfjord came to light in a volume of Hinton, which had belonged to Herbert Ashe. The envelope bore the postmark of Ouro Preto. The letter cleared up entirely the mystery of Tlön. The text of it confirmed Martínez Estrada's thesis. The elaborate story began one night in Lucerne or London, in the early seventeenth century. A benevolent secret society (which counted Dalgarno and, later, George Berkeley among its members) came together to invent a country. The first tentative plan gave prominence to 'hermetic studies', philanthropy, and the cabala. Andreä's curious book dates from that first period. At the end of some years of conventicles and premature syntheses, they realized that a single generation was not long enough in which to define a country. They made a resolution that each one of the master-scholars involved should elect a disciple to carry on the work. That hereditary arrangement prevailed; and after a hiatus of two centuries, the persecuted brotherhood reappeared in America. About 1824, in Memphis, Tennessee, one of the members had a conversation with the millionaire ascetic, Ezra Buckley. Buckley listened with some disdain as the other men talked, and then burst out laughing at the modesty of the project. He declared that in America it was absurd to invent a country, and proposed the invention of a whole planet. To this gigantic idea, he added another, born of his own nihilism*—that of keeping the enormous project a secret. The twenty volumes of the *Encyclopaedia Britannica* were then in circulation; Buckley suggested a systematic encyclopedia of the imaginary planet. He would leave the society his mountain ranges with their gold fields, his navigable rivers, his prairies where bull and bison roamed, his Negroes, his brothels, and his dollars, on one condition: 'The work will have no truck with the imposter Jesus Christ.' Buckley did not believe in God, but nevertheless wished to demonstrate to the nonexistent God that mortal men were capable of conceiving a world. Buckley was poisoned in Baton Rouge in 1828; in 1914, the society forwarded to its collaborators, three hundred in number, the final volume of the *First Encyclopaedia of Tlön*. The edition was secret; the forty volumes which comprised it (the work was vaster than any previously undertaken by men) were to be the basis for another work, more detailed, and this time written, not in English, but in some one of the languages of Tlön. This review of an illusory world was called, provisionally, *Orbis Tertius*, and one of its minor demiurges was Herbert Ashe, whether as an agent of Gunnar Erfjord, or as a full associate, I do not know. The fact that he received a copy of the eleventh volume would

---

*Buckley was a freethinker, a fatalist, and an apologist for slavery.

favour the second view. But what about the others? About 1942, events began to speed up. I recall with distinct clarity one of the first, and I seem to have felt something of its premonitory character. It occurred in an apartment on the Calle Laprida, facing a high open balcony which looked to the west. From Poitiers, the Princess of Faucigny Lucinge had received her silver table service. Out of the recesses of a crate, stamped all over with international markings, fine immobile pieces were emerging—silver plate from Utrecht and Paris, with hard heraldic fauna, a samovar. Amongst them, trembling faintly, just perceptibly, like a sleeping bird, was a magnetic compass. It shivered mysteriously. The princess did not recognize it. The blue needle longed for magnetic north. The metal case was concave. The letters on the dial corresponded to those of one of the alphabets of Tlön. Such was the first intrusion of the fantastic world into the real one. A disturbing accident brought it about that I was also witness to the second. It happened some months afterwards in a grocery store belonging to a Brazilian, in Cuchilla Negra. Amorim and I were on our way back from Sant'Anna. A sudden rising of the Tacuarembó river compelled us to test (and to suffer patiently) the rudimentary hospitality of the general store. The grocer set up some creaking cots for us in a large room, cluttered with barrels and wineskins. We went to bed, but were kept from sleeping until dawn by the drunkenness of an invisible neighbour, who alternated between shouting indecipherable abuse and singing snatches of *milongas*, or rather, snatches of the same *milonga*. As might be supposed, we attributed this insistent uproar to the fiery rum of the proprietor. . . At dawn, the man lay dead in the corridor. The coarseness of his voice had deceived us; he was a young boy. In his delirium, he had spilled a few coins and a shining metal cone, of the diameter of a die, from his heavy gaucho belt. A serving lad tried to pick up this cone—in vain. It was scarcely possible for a man to lift it. I held it in my hand for some minutes. I remember that it was intolerably heavy, and that after putting it down, its oppression remained. I also remember the precise circle it marked in my flesh. This manifestation of an object which was so tiny and at the same time so heavy left me with an unpleasant sense of abhorrence and fear. A countryman proposed that it be thrown into the rushing river. Amorim acquired if for a few pesos. No one knew anything of the dead man, only that 'he came from the frontier'. Those small and extremely heavy cones, made of a metal which does not exist in this world, are images of divinity in certain religions in Tlön.

Here I conclude the personal part of my narrative. The rest, when it is not in their hopes or their fears, is at least in the memories of all my readers. It is enough to recall or to mention subsequent events, in as few words as possible; that concave basin which is the collective memory will furnish the wherewithal to enrich or amplify them. About 1944, a reporter from the Nashville, Tennessee, *American* uncovered, in a Memphis library, the forty volumes of the *First Encyclopaedia of Tlön*. Even now it is uncertain whether this discovery was accidental, or whether the directors of the still nebulous *Orbis Tertius* condoned it. The second alternative is more likely. Some of the more improbable features of the eleventh volume (for example, the multiplying of the *hrönir*) had been either removed or modified in the Memphis copy. It is reasonable to suppose that these erasures were in keeping with the plan of projecting a world which would not be too incompatible with the real world. The dissemination of objects from Tlön throughout various countries would complement that plan. . .* The fact is that the international Press overwhelmingly hailed the 'find'. Manuals, anthologies, summaries, literal versions, authorized reprints, and pirated editions of the Master Work of Man poured and continue to pour out into the world. Almost immediately, reality gave ground on more than one point. The truth is that it hankered to give ground. Ten years ago, any symmetrical system whatsoever which gave the appearance of order—dialectical materialism, anti-Semitism, Nazism—was enough to fascinate men. Why not fall under the spell of Tlön and submit to the minute and vast evidence of an ordered planet? Useless to reply that reality, too, is ordered. It may be so, but in accordance with divine laws—I translate: inhuman laws—which we will never completely perceive. Tlön may be a labyrinth, but it is a labyrinth plotted by men, a labyrinth destined to be deciphered by men.

Contact with Tlön and the ways of Tlön have disintegrated this world. Captivated by its discipline, humanity forgets and goes on forgetting that it is the discipline of chess players, not of angels. Now, the conjectural 'primitive language' of Tlön has found its way into the schools. Now, the teaching of its harmonious history, full of stirring episodes, has obliterated the history which dominated my childhood. Now, in all memories, a fictitious past occupies the place of any other. We know nothing about it with any certainty, not even that it is false. Numismatics, pharmacology, and archaeology have been revised. I gather that biology and mathematics are awaiting their avatar. . . A scattered dynasty of solitaries has changed the face of the world. Its task continues. If our foresight is not mistaken, a hundred years from now someone will discover the hundred volumes of the *Second Encyclopaedia of Tlön*.

Then, English, French, and mere Spanish will disappear from this planet. The world will be Tlön. I take no notice. I go on revising, in the quiet of the days in the hotel at Androgué, a tentative translation into Spanish, in the style of Quevedo, which I do not intend to see published, of Sir Thomas Browne's *Urn Burial*.

---

*There remains, naturally, the problem of *matter* of which some of these objects consisted.

Odin

They say that an old man arrived one night, wrapped in a dark cloak, with the brim of his hat down over his eyes, at the court of Olaf Tryggvason, which had been converted to the new faith. The king asked him if he could do anything; the stranger replied that he could play the harp and tell stories. He played old tunes on the harp, he talked about Gudrun and Gunnar and, finally, he told of the birth of Odin. He said that the three Parcae came and that the first two promised much happiness, but the third said angrily, 'The child shall live no longer than the candle which burns at his side.' His parents then blew out the candle so that Odin shouldn't die. Olaf Tryggvason didn't believe the story; the stranger insisted that it was true, took out a candle and lit it. As they were watching it burn, the man said it was late and that he must go. When the candle had burned itself out, they went searching for him. A few steps from the king's house, Odin had died.

JORGE LUIS BORGES and DELIA INGENIEROS

The Golden Kite, The Silver Wind

Ray Bradbury (born 1920), American writer of fantasy and science fiction, began writing for cheap genre magazines in the 1940s, but developed a poetic, evocative style that is evident in collections such as Dark Carnival (1947), The October Country (1955) and The Martian Chronicles (1950), as well as in novels like Something Wicked This Way Comes (1962) and Fahrenheit 451 (1953).

'In the shape of a *pig*?' cried the Mandarin.

'In the shape of a pig,' said the messenger, and departed.

'Oh, what an evil day in an evil year,' cried the Mandarin. 'The town of Kwan-Si, beyond the hill, was very small in my childhood. Now it has grown so large that at last they are building a wall.'

'But why should a wall two miles away make my good father sad and angry all within the hour?' asked his daughter quietly.

' They build their wall,' said the Mandarin, 'in the shape of a pig! Do you see? Our own city wall is built in the shape of an orange. That pig will devour us, greedily!'

'Ah.'

They both sat thinking.

Life was full of symbols and omens. Demons lurked everywhere, Death swam in the wetness of an eye, the turn of a gull's wing meant rain, a fan held *so*, the tilt of a roof, and, yes, even a city wall was of immense importance. Travellers and tourists, caravans, musicians, artists, coming upon these two towns, equally judging the portents, would say, 'The city shaped like an orange? No! I will enter the city shaped like a pig and prosper, eating all, growing fat with good luck and prosperity!'

The Mandarin wept. 'All is lost! These symbols and signs terrify. Our city will come on evil days.'

'Then,' said the daughter, 'call in your stonemasons and temple builders. I will whisper from behind the silken screen and you will know the words.'

The old man clapped his hands despairingly. 'Ho, stonemasons! Ho, builders of towns and palaces!'

The men who knew marble and granite and onyx and quartz came quickly. The Mandarin faced them most uneasily, himself waiting for a whisper from the silken screen behind his throne. At last the whisper came.

'I have called you here,' said the whisper.

'I have called you here,' said the Mandarin aloud, 'because our city is shaped like an orange, and the vile city of Kwan-Si has this day shaped theirs like a ravenous pig——'

Here the stonemasons groaned and wept. Death rattled his cane in the outer courtyard. Poverty made a sound like a wet cough in the shadows of the room.

'And so,' said the whisper, said the Mandarin, 'you raisers of walls must go bearing trowels and rocks and change the shape of *our* city!'

The architects and masons gasped. The Mandarin himself gasped at what he had said. The whisper whispered. The Mandarin went on: 'And you will change our walls into a club which may beat the pig and drive it off!'

The stonemasons rose up, shouting. Even the Mandarin delighted at the words from his mouth, applauded, stood down from his throne. 'Quick!' he cried. 'To work!'

When his men had gone, smiling and bustling, the Mandarin turned with great love to the silken screen. 'Daughter,' he whispered, 'I will embrace you.' There was no reply. He stepped around the screen, and she was gone.

Such modesty, he thought. She had slipped away and left me with a triumph, as if it were mine.

The news spread through the city; the mandarin was acclaimed. Everyone carried stone to the walls. Fireworks were set off and the demons of death and poverty did not linger, as all worked together. At the end of the month the wall had been changed. It was now a mighty bludgeon with which to drive pigs, boars, even lions, far away. The Mandarin slept like a happy fox every night.

'I would like to see the Mandarin of Kwai-Si when the news is learned. Such pandemonium and hysteria; he will likely throw himself from a mountain! A little more of that wine, oh Daughter-who-thinks-like-a-son.'

But the pleasure was like a winter flower; it died swiftly. That very afternoon the messenger rushed into the courtroom. 'Oh, Mandarin, disease, early sorrow, avalanches, grasshopper plagues, and poisoned well water!'

The Mandarin trembled.

'The town of Kwan-Si,' said the messenger, 'which was built like a pig and which animal we drove away by changing our walls to a mighty stick, has now turned triumph to winter ashes. They have built their city's walls like a great bonfire to burn our stick!'

The Mandarin's heart sickened within him, like an autumn fruit upon an ancient tree.'Oh, gods! Travelers will spurn us. Tradesmen, reading the symbols, will turn from the stick, so easily destroyed, to the fire, which conquers all!'

'No,' said a whisper like a snowflake from behind the silken screen.

'No,' said the startled Mandarin.

'Tell my stonemasons,' said the whisper that was a falling drop of rain, 'to build our walls in the shape of a shining lake.'

The mandarin said this aloud, his heart warmed.

'And with this lake of water,' said the whisper and the old man, 'we will quench the fire and put it out forever!'

The city turned out in joy to learn that once again they had been saved by the magnificent Emperor of ideas. They ran to the walls and built them nearer to this new vision, singing, not as loudly as before, of course, for they were tired, and not as quickly, for since it had taken a month to build the wall the first time, they had had to neglect business and crops and therefore were somewhat weaker and poorer.

There then followed a succession of horrible and wonderful days, one in another like a nest of frightening boxes.

'Oh, Emperor,' cried the messenger, 'Kwan-Si has rebuilt their walls to resemble a mouth with which to drink all our lake!'

'Then,' said the Emperor, standing very close to his silken screen, 'build our walls like a needle to sew up that mouth!'

'Emperor!' screamed the messenger. 'They make their walls like a sword to break your needle!'

The Emperor held, trembling, to the silken screen. 'Then shift the stones to form a scabbard to sheathe that sword!'

'Mercy,' wept the messenger the following morn, 'they have worked all night and shaped their walls like lightning which will explode and destroy that sheath!'

Sickness spread in the city like a pack of evil dogs. Shops closed. The population, working now steadily for endless months upon the changing of the walls, resembled Death himself, clattering his white bones like musical instruments in the wind. Funerals began to appear in the streets, though it was the middle of summer, a time when all should be tending and harvesting. The Mandarin fell so ill that he had his bed drawn up by the silken screen and there he lay, miserably giving his architectural orders. The voice behind the screen was weak now, too, and faint, like the wind in the eaves.

'Kwan-Si is an eagle. Then our walls must be a net for that eagle. They are a sun to burn our net. Then we build a moon to eclipse their sun!'

Like a rusted machine, the city ground to a halt.

At last the whisper behind the screen cried out:

'In the name of the gods, send for Kwan-Si!'

Upon the last day of summer the Mandarin Kwan-Si, very ill and withered away, was carried into our Mandarin's courtroom by four starving footmen. The two mandarins were propped up, facing each other. Their breaths fluttered like winter winds in their mouths. A voice said:

'Let us put an end to this.'

The old men nodded.

'This cannot go on,' said the faint voice. 'Our people do nothing but rebuild our cities to a different shape every day, every hour. They have no time to hunt, to fish, to love, to be good to their ancestors and their ancestors' children.'

'This I admit,' said the mandarins of the towns of the Cage, the Moon, the Spear, the Fire, the Sword and this, that, and other things.

'Carry us into the sunlight,' said the voice.

The old men were borne out under the sun and up a little hill. In the late summer breeze a few very thin children were flying dragon kites in all the colors of the sun, and frogs and grass, the color of the sea and the color of coins and wheat.

The first Mandarin's daughter stood by his bed.

'See,' she said.

'Those are nothing but kites,' said the two old men.

'But what is a kite on the ground?' she said. 'It is nothing. What does it need to sustain it and make it beautiful and truly spiritual?'

'The wind, of course!' said the others.

'And what do the sky and the wind need to make *them* beautiful?'

'A kite, of course—many kites, to break the monotony, the sameness of the sky. Colored kites, flying!'

'So,' said the Mandarin's daughter. 'You, Kwan-Si, will make a last rebuilding of your town to resemble nothing more or less than the wind. And we shall build like a golden kite. The wind will beautify the kite and carry it to wondrous heights. And the kite will break the sameness of the wind's existence and give it purpose and meaning. One without the other is nothing. Together, all will be beauty and co-operation and a long and enduring life.'

Whereupon the two mandarins were so overjoyed that they took their first nourishment in days, momentarily were given strength, embraced, and lavished praise upon each other, called the Mandarin's daughter a boy, a man, a stone pillar, a warrior, and a true and unforgettable son. Almost immediately they parted and hurried to their towns, calling out and singing, weakly but happily.

And so, in time, the towns became the Town of the Golden Kite and the Town of the Silver Wind. And harvestings were harvested and business tended again, and the flesh returned, and disease ran off like a frightened jackal. And on every night of the year the inhabitants in the Town of the Kite could hear the good clear wind sustaining them. And those in the Town of the Wind could hear the kite singing, whispering, rising, and beautifying them.

'So be it,' said the Mandarin in front of his silken screen.

The Man Who Collected the First of September, 1973

Tor Åge Bringsvaerd *(born 1939), one of Norway's leading authors, has edited a number of science fiction anthologies, as well as writing plays, children's stories and novels. His best imaginative work is in* Karavane *(1974).*

I

Ptk discovered that he was about to lose his grip on reality. In fact it had been building up for years (he suddenly realized)—without his caring, without his giving it a thought. Perhaps he hadn't even been aware of it. Now the grey film had thickened to a crust, a stocking cap stretched over and encasing his arms, a sagging tent-like umbrella dimming out the outside world. The hands of his wristwatch flamed, and he no longer knew on which side his hair was parted: the mirror said the right, his hand the left. In the paper he read about a Frenchman who for various reasons had had himself imprisoned, naked, inside a small chamber 300 feet under the earth's surface. When he returned from isolation after three months, scientists were able to affirm that man has '*a natural rhythm—a built-in timekeeper*' and that this time-keeper '*is not adjusted to the sun, but counts 31 hours in the day-night cycle, instead of 24*'. But no one dared to make the inference, the only logic possibility . . . that man is a stranger, that Obstfelder was right, that our real home is another (and slower) globe—which, lighted by an unknown sun, takes seven hours more than the Earth to rotate about its own axis . . . that this is the genuine Eden—the garden we have been turned out from . . . Ptk pointed in amazement at his own mirror image, and neither aspirins nor valium was able to make him think otherwise.

II

Ptk decided to face his everyday, to try to orientate himself in the reality he was stranded in. He went out, bought all of that day's Oslo papers (Saturday the 18th of August 1973) and went home. He read them thoroughly—page by page, column by column. When at last he felt that he had got some sort of grip on Saturday the 18th of August, in the meantime Tuesday the 21st of August had arrived—and reality had changed its face three times. Ptk realized that the sum of information was too weighty for any single man to balance on his head. News fell in heaps around his feet, clung like ivy to his legs and tightened like a belt round his stomach. He fought in despair against Wednesday the 22nd and Thursday the 23rd. He dared not blink for fear that Friday the 24th might weigh down his eyelids. And even so . . . despite the best will in the world . . . Saturday the 25th went over his head completely.

III

Ptk realized that he'd acted in haste. He who consumes too much news has no time for boiling, frying or chewing it over, but is obliged to swallow everything raw and whole. Having considered political digestion and protective fatty layers of tissue, he decided to attack the problem from quite a different angle. Confronted with reality as a many-headed beast he resigned, but chose instead to cut off one of the heads, in order to get under the creature's skin by means of a detailed study of one single head. He selected the 1st of September 1973. In advance he had equipped a corner of his bedroom as a laboratory, and was all set with a typewriter, scissors, glue, paper and a 24-volume calf-bound encyclopaedia at hand.

IV

By the end of October Ptk had finished all the Norwegian papers from the 1st of September (including weekly papers). Without hesitation he delved into the study of papers from the rest of Scandinavia, primarily Denmark and Sweden. He had his fixed seat in the university library, and at night he stuck cuttings, notes and xerox copies on his bedroom walls. He developed an interest in curves and diagrams.

V

Soon his bedroom grew too small. In order to make his material for study as complete as possible, Ptk wrote to papers all over the world and asked for a copy from the 1st of September 1973—whether he had command of the language or not. He went to evening classes in Spanish and Russian.

VI

Four years later his flat had been exploited to the full. Apart from a cooker, a fridge, a bed, a coffee table and a wooden chair there was no furniture; no ornaments. the rooms were divided with hundreds of partitions, and the passages were so narrow that Ptk had to walk sidelong (very carefully) when he wanted to remind himself of an important cutting or add a new note. Working hours apart (Ptk was an accountant), he spent all his time in his historical archives. He neglected friends and relatives, and when he met one of them in the street (going to or from his office) he found it hard to carry on a sensible conversation. He grew more and more appalled at how little people knew of the 1st of September 1973. In the end he cut himself off completely, ignored invitations, had the telephone removed and made detours.

VII

Twice he had to find a bigger flat. By 1982 he knew—more or less—twenty different languages and dialects. But all the time there were more things to learn. The Subject turned out to be just about inexhaustible. Who would have guessed that so much had happened on exactly the 1st of September 1973? 'What a coincidence!' Ptk said to himself (he hadn't talked to anyone else for six years). 'What luck I had, choosing *that* particular day!' He still used the partition system, and busied himself organizing it all as systematically as possible. Not all subjects required the same amount of space. Some subjects, like Temperature and Wind, only needed half a wall, while others, as for instance Business and Finance, covered the whole dining room alone (all in all thirty walls, that is, about 4,050 sq. ft.).

VIII

On a grey and cloudy day in February 1983 a fire started in the Games and Sports department. Ptk was on his way home from a private lesson in Mongolian dialects. When he opened his front door the title fight world heavyweight was in flames, and as champion George Foreman struck a powerful right hook the Puerto Rican challenger photograph as well as the picture curled up. It was an absolute storm of fire. Nothing was saved. Before the fire brigade got there, the whole archive was in ashes. (Apart from the two basement store rooms, of course. But here he had mainly Deaths from the personal columns and un-sorted obituaries. All of peripheral interest.) Ptk was badly burnt, and spent the rest of his life (two years) in hospital.

IX

During these two years both doctors and patients tried in vain to get through to him. But whenever anyone spoke of the war in South America, Ptk talked of

South-East Asia. If anyone mentioned the EEC, Ptk replied that he thought there still was a Norweigian majority against it—certainly *he* was. If the other patients talked about games, Ptk always shook his head and mumbled something about an illegal punch and the first world championships in synchronized swimming starting in Belgrade. He now and then talked about two Englishmen rescued after being trapped in a mini-submarine on the floor of the Atlantic, he referred to the king as the crown prince and always spoke of the American president as 'Nixon'. If he was willing to reply at all. Most of the time he was not. 'A hopeless case,' the doctors said. 'There's nothing we can do.'

X

And when no one tried any more, Ptk was allowed the peace he so ardently yearned for. He spent his last three months lying happily on his back. One by one he brought forth the fragments, one by one he painstakingly put them together, starting at the back righthand corner of his brain and working leftwards. The picture of the 1st of September 1973 slowly grew in his mind, getting bigger and clearer day to day. Names and numbers melted into maps and diagrams. Border disputes and cinema advertisements merged. Ptk smiled. The picture filled his head. Some bits were still missing. He found them. His head became too small. The picture shattered his head and filled the whole hospital. Stil some bits were missing. A few. He found them. The picture shattered the hospital and filled all of the park outside, unfolded like a transparent film and became one with the trees, the birds and the sky. But then he'd already been dead . . . a quarter of an hour, one doctor said. Ten minutes, said the other. And neither noticed that it was autumn.

The Careless Rabbi

Martin Buber, *born in Austria, in 1878; died in Israel in 1965. Historian of the orthodox Hassidic sect and existential philosopher. His works include* Die Geschichten des Rabbi Nachman *(1906; translated into English as* The Tales of Rabbi Nachman, *1956),* Gog u. Magog *(1941; translated into English as* For the Sake of Heaven, *1945), and* Ich und Du *(1937; translated into English as* I and Thou, *1937).*

It is told:

Once Rabbi Elimelekh was eating the sabbath meal with his disciples. The servant set the soup bowl down before him. Rabbi Elimelekh raised it and upset it, so that the soup poured over the table. All at once young Mendel, later the rabbi of Rymanov, cried out: "Rabbi, what are you doing? They will put us all in jail!" The other disciples smiled at these foolish words. They would have laughed out loud, had not the presence of their teacher restrained them. He, however, did not smile. He nodded to young Mendel and said: "Do not be afraid, my son!"

Some time after this, it became known that on that day an edict directed against the Jews of the whole country had been presented to the emperor for his signature. Time after time he took up his pen, but something always happened to interrupt him. Finally he signed the paper. Then he reached for the sand-container but took the inkwell instead and upset it on the document. Hereupon he tore it up and forbade them to put the edict before him again.

The Tale and the Poet

Sir Richard Burton *(1821-90), the distinguished explorer, orientalist, polyglot and athropologist, translated* Las Lusiadas *by the Portuguese poet Luis de Camöes (c. 1524-80) as* The Lusiads *(1880), and the first unexpurgaged version of* A Thousand and One Nights.

Tulsi Das, the Hindu poet, created the tale of Hanuman and his army of monkeys. Years afterwards, a despot imprisoned him in a stone tower. Alone in his cell, he fell to meditating, and from his meditation came Hanuman and his monkey army, who laid low the city, broke open the tower, and freed Tulsi Das.

Fate is a Fool

Arturo Cancela, *Argentinian writer, born in Buenos Aires in 1882; died in the same city in 1957. Author of* Tres relatos Porteños *(1922);* El Burro de Maruf *(1925);* Palabras Socráticas *(1928)* Film Porteño *(1933).*

Pilar de Lusarreta, *Argentinian novelist and art critic. Author of a collection of tales of fantasy entitled* Job el Opulento *(1928)* Celimena sin Carazón *(1935); and of the play* El culto de los héroes *(in collaboration with Arturo Cancela, 1939): In 1964 she published* El manto de Noé .*

On how Juan Pedro Rearte made his entrance into the 20th century

The arguable popular principle that 'things come in threes' was never more objectionable than in the case of Juan Pedro Rearte. This old Argentine, who for fifteen years had been a coachman with the Buenos Aires Tram Company, broke his leg at the end of the last century. His was an allegorical turn-of-the-century accident: the tram he was driving ran into the last oxcart crossing the streets of the city centre. In the Láinez newspaper 'El Diario' this urban episode was highlighted as a final incident in the struggle between Civilization and Barbarism; and so, by virtue of the carelessness which prevented him from stopping the horses of his coach on the slope in Calle Comercio[1], Rearte was invested the character of symbol of Progress by the anonymous columnist.

The involuntary aggressor of the last cart from Tucumán was taken to the Charity Hospital, in one of whose wards he waited with the patience of the humble for time to weld together the two fragments of tibia which had been violently separated in the crash and no less violently put back in contact with each other by the hurried surgeon who had administered first aid. The good disciple of Pirovano, in order to save a few minutes—he had a commitment of a non-professional nature with one of the possible helpers at the Lezama Park charity fair, organized by the Ladies of the Trust—shortened the poor tram driver's right leg by four centimetres.

In his haste to attend the charity event, he had treated the fracture, which was direct and total, as though it were simple and incomplete, and given that the many miracles of Nature do not include that of correcting medical errors, Juan Pedro Rearte left the hospital limping, and limping he entered the twentieth century.

Short parenthesis on the Philosophy of History

He made his entrance, in his new capacity as an invalid, with some precipitation. (What person with a limp have you seen who doesn't walk in a hurry, nor what

[1] Humberto I was still triumphantly parading through the cities of Italy the crown and debonair moustache inherited from his father.

stammerer who doesn't talk in a rush? The majestic slowness is the most obvious sign of faith in the effort. People from our provinces are instinctively aware of this law and take advantage of it to the extent of combining, in some cases, solemnity with a stammer.)

We insist that the driver Rearte brought forward in unseemly fashion his entry into the present century, because the law of occupational accidents which should have protected him had not yet been decreed. It was not enacted until sixteen years later, but even had he had any inkling of it, he couldn't have waited in hospital all that time.

It's true that the most noticeable effect of that law has been the extension of periods of convalescence. Before it came into force, those injured in their daily work quickly either got better or died, which is the most complete cure for all ills, although the one offered the greatest resistance . . .

Juan Pedro Rearte chose to get back to work as soon as possible, without reflecting on the injustice of his fate or on the selfishness of the Company which, after fifteen years' service, left him to his misfortune.

Nothing could be further from his soul than such speculations. These belong in their entirety to the historian of this episode, who, like all historians, blends in his reflections the past and the present, the real and the possible, what was, what might have been and what should have been.

The Philosophy of History basically consists of that constant anachronism which twists with the imagination, in every sense, the inflexible determinism of facts.

The dandy and social order

Juan Pedro Rearte couldn't think, or even vaguely feel, any of the foregoing because like all those of his profession he was what was called in the colloquial language of the time a dandy. Now, the dandy was instinctively conservative, as are all men who are pleased with themselves[1], and there is nobody more vain about their person than those coachmen with their uniform peaked cap, carnation behind the ear, silk scarf around the neck, drainpipe trousers á la française and short boots with a high military heel. Their pride in their status was obvious at all times, in the arabesques they outlined in the air with their

---

[1] It is discontentment with oneself, whether due to obscurity of origin, a physical defect or the lack of brilliant spiritual conditions, that leads many men to revolutionary activity.

And, on the other hand, in every rebellious spirit there is a great underlying timidity. Revolutionary activity is the violent reaction of the timid who disturb society for encouragement. Which is the same as setting fire to somebody else's house in order to warm up.

Sometimes, in the course of revolutionary activity, when it is successful, the shy lose their timidity and become conservative. This is the secret psychological cause of the desertion of so many impetuous prophets who have left the emancipation of their people half way, merely because they achieved their own spiritual liberation first.

When I lose my literary shyness, I shall write a comedy full of sharp observations on the subject— amongst others, that austerity, revolutionary virtue par excellence, is a natural attitude in all those who are timid—a comedy I shall entitle *The Rodeos of the Timid Man* and which, I'm certain already, will not be a great success. It would be a different matter if it were premièred in Paris and were entitled *Le détour du timide*.

whips as they spurred on the horses; in the flourishes with which they embellished the most well-known phrases of popular tunes on their horns; in the dizzy dexterity with which they turned the brake handle; in the sly sweetness of their compliments to the maids, and in the mocking contempt of their insults to their rivals in the traffic.

Not until he left the high platform—mobile rostrum for compliments and insults—did the tram coachman return to his humble status as a proletarian. But that return to obscurity was too short to give him time to reflect on the insubstantiality of his pride.

Working ten hours a day, they had no leisure time, the source of all bad habits, particularly of the most terrible of all: the philosophical vice of pessimism and timidity . . .

The relics of a cohabitation

However, in the days following his discharge from hospital, Rearte had a few moments of leisure. As soon as he was out, he went to the Company's Administration where, as though he had willingly deserted his post, he shyly expressed his desire to return to work. They made him take a few steps 'to see how his leg was doing', and although his limp was very obvious, Mr McNab, the administrator, decided he could return to work in a fortnight's time. In addition he gave him fifty pesos, together with the advice that he should shorten the heel of his left boot by three centimetres in order to partly restore the balance of his bearing. Rearte spent the money, although he didn't follow the advice.

In the fortnight that passed until his return to work, he barely left his tidy celibate's bedroom, which he had occupied for the last ten years in a quiet house on calle Perú. He devoted all that time to caring for the two dozen pairs of canaries which were the luxury of his existence and the pride of his status as a breeder and tutor. The former, because all that multitude of songbirds had originated from a single couple legitimately inherited from a room-mate, who six years earlier had run off with all his savings and his only two suits; and the latter, because he had a special knack of teaching the chicks the tunes he played on his tramdriver's horn.

Of that ill-fated cohabitation, Rearte had left, in addition to the pair of canaries which, in compensation, had proved to be so fertile, two oil paintings and a few books. It is pointless to say that neither the paintings nor the books had reproduced like the birds. They were the same ones his disloyal room-mate had abandoned in his flight: 'The Meeting at the Cliff', in which the outline of an illustrious orator stood out like a rock on a sea of three thousand identical galleons; 'The July Revolution', where the bellicose decoration of the Park contrasted with the studied attitude of statesmanship of Alem; *The Unión Cívica: Its Origin and Trends, Official Publication*, an imposing volume which the tramdriver had never dared browse through; *White Magic and the Key to Dreams*, a work frequently borrowed by his neighbours; *The Lovers' Secretary*, to whose epistolary aid he would never dream of going and, finally, *The Businesses of Carlos Lanza,* by Eduardo Gutiérrez, a fictional story which had instilled in Rearte a bewildered mistrust of banks and bureaux de change.

On how a single cause can produce opposite effects

After that brief domestic respite which Rearte dedicated to teaching the first few bars of the waltz 'On the Waves' to his forty-eight canaries, our hero returned to the scene of his triumphs. He returned somewhat diminished in physical stature, but morally exalted by the glorious misfortune which earned him an allegorical item in 'El Diario'.

The obscure driver had for a time been the champion of progress, the destroyer of carts, the symbol of the great conquests of his century in the field of urban transport.

But, as the *Imitation of Christ* says, all human glory is ephemeral, and after a very few months of basking in it, that same progress of which he was made champion had left him behind.

Electric trams arrived on the scene, and although Rearte tried to become a motorman he couldn't because of his limp, which hindered him from ringing the warning bell. During training, each time he tried to kick with his heel in warning, he lost his balance . . . This episode, which provoked much merriment amongst the other learners, occasioned bitter reflections in the poor driver.

'So,' he said to himself, deeply melancholic, 'progress has left me with a limp and that same limp prevents me from following it, making me the champion of underdevelopment.'

And that, indeed, was how it was, for once the electrification of the tramlines was complete, Mr Bright, the new administrator, posted him to hitching carriages in Caridad station. With a team of increasingly scraggy horses, several times a day Rearte would take from inside the station to the middle of the street the old trams, which were becoming increasingly older, destined now to be a modest appendage to the motor coaches.

In this way he came to be, for several minutes, a parody of himself: of that witty and conquering Rearte who outlined arabesques in the air with his whip, wore a carnation behind his ear and played 'I like them all . . . I like them all' on his horn every time he saw a black woman.

A Road Accident

Fifteen years after resigning himself to being a ghost of his pristine glory on the street, Rearte arrived at the station earlier than usual. 'Bright's disease'—and not precisely the Bright of the Anglo Argentine Company—makes men become early risers. Complaining, with the palms of his hand on his waist and swearing through clenched teeth, the old driver sat on the windowsill of a low window, under the garage in which the trams were lined up with the wise air of beasts in the manger. Opposite him a half-closed tap dripped isochronously and melancholically, widening with imperceptible tenacity an eye in the water whose brightness livened up the hostile appearance of the depot.

'It must have been like that all night,' he thought. These nightwatchmen are becoming more and more careless. Good-for-nothings! I'd soon sort them out.'

He tried to adjust the tap, but after several fruitless attempts in which all he managed to do was splash his boots and hurt his finger, the rebellious tap continued to run, now with a sort of hoarse whistle like a teacher at the end of the year. In a few moments the water was overflowing from the stone basin which contained it and ran sinuously to the straight and predictable canal formed by the rails.

That feeble flow brought to his mind old times, when after four drops of rain the uneven roads of Buenos Aires would flood. Around the Cinco Esquinas . . . the mud! Even with extra draught it was impossible to get out of the mire, and you had to wait until the rain died down, sitting with the passengers on the backs of the seats to avoid the water which reached the step, sometimes flooding the inside of the coaches . . . But the people were different; they were all acquaintances, all friends, you knew who you were dealing with and who you were taking; you could have a chat and smoke a 'Sublime' or an 'Ideal' with anybody, and from the doorways, in summer, the famlies out for a breath of fresh air would send regards to your family . . .

The bell, announcing the scheduled time for the departure of the first coach, made him leave the tap, smilling at his memories and, still immersed in them, he bought and hitched the hairy team of nags to the carriage. That's what he, an Argentine of pure Spanish descent, who appreciated and was a friend of good beasts, had never been able to do with patience; to drive, along the worst roads in the city, those squalid horses, fed like pigs on a mess of bran and water.

'The truth is,' he thought, 'that they're not worth even that.'

He adjusted the chains, climbed into the driver's seat after wrapping his scarf around his neck, whistled a happy reveille between his teeth, spurred on the wretched horses with a click of the tongue and with an ironic 'Gee up, Bonito! Gee up, Pipón!' the tram set off amid the squeaking and creaking of all its hinges, couplings, windows and boards.

Outside, the electric tram must be waiting for him. Unusual that the bell wasn't jingling under the Spaniard Pedrosa's worn hell. But no: the road was clear and in the cold morning mist the city was fading, pale and melancholic like an old photograph. The chill air pecked at the driver's temples and hands. He would happily go for a ride, he thought; but he was distracted by the desperate gesturing from the street by a high mulatta, loaded with a basket covered by a white scarf.

'Stop, will you!' she shouted. 'Not paying attention, are you?'

Rearte suddenly drew to a halt and the black woman heaved aboard the trembling bulk of her flaccid flesh; the step creaked under the weight of her enormous espadrille and with a flash of white in between her fleshy lips, asked the tram conductor, 'Will you hand me by basket, now?.

He complied gallantly, and whilst the black woman searched her pocket full of crumbs and medals for the two pesos for the fare, they commented on the weather. 'It's a cool morning, isn't it?'

'Good for bathing in the river.'

'Enough to make you perish.'

Further on, from a low balcony, a chubby-cheeked maid signalled him to stop, shouting into the house, 'The tram, master, the tram's here!'

A solemn gentleman with frock coat and top hat rushed out, protesting vigourously, 'What a hopeless timetable! It's impossible to have breakfast, and even so one is late everywhere! Appalling service . . . taking advantage . . .'

'Good morning, Don Máximo,' the mulatta humbly cut in .

'Morning, Rosario,' and referring to something implicit, 'are they nice and tender?'

'Just out of the frying pan. Would you care for one?'

The solemn gentleman accepted a crispy pasty which scattered golden scales on the dull lapel of his frock coat.

Rearte was remembering those voices, the delicate aroma of cooking; he felt rejuvenated and involuntarily put his hand up to his ear to check whether the large carnation was in place, furtively picked from the plant which flowered in a large coffee tin in the yard. No, he wasn't wearing it—but of course! It was winter.

'Get away from there, boy, get away at once or I'll tell your father!' shouted Don Máximo to a boy running behind the coach with the obvious intention of jumping on.

'That's how accidents happen,' the black woman remarked.

Rearte lashed out right and left with his formidable whip, which the boy evaded by running away and mocking him from the road.

The bells were calling them to church in Balvanera; the black woman crossed herself devoutly, Don Máximo took off his hat. In the portico, two priests, one with a big belly and dirty-looking, the other scraggy and equally dirty, were talking excitedly, cassocks loose and holding their hats. Without any signal from them, the driver stopped the tram. After giving the service, Father Prudencio Heguera took the tram every day. He waited a couple of minutes, cap in hand, while the reverend said goodbye; Don Máximo coughed discreetly, the black woman cleared her throat and with a swirl of his skirts the priest sat down, greeting everyone like someone granting plenary indulgence.

Rosario was hiding her basket, pretending to look out of the window, twiddling her silver rings which shone on her dark bony hand.

'Up early, Don Máximo?'

'What does Your Reverence expect, Father Prudencio, with this Company's appalling service!'

'It's very chilly this morning, healthy breathing this air, gives you a good appetite . . . and after mass . . .'

'Did you attend last night's conference, in the National College, Father?'

'I couldn't make it, I had to prepare a sermon . . .'

'The events hall was too small to contain the public, with the 840 students, the teachers and guests . . .'

'What did you preach on?'

'On the Gospels . . .'

The priest turned round in his seat. 'And you, Rosario, always a good Christian?'

'As long as I'm not told to change . . .'

'And even if you were told to . . . They smell good today.'

Thin-voiced, the woman offered them. 'Would you care for one?'

Don Máximo threw some coins into her lap, saying, 'It's paid for.'

'Certainly not, certainly not,' protested the priest, affecting reluctance, and then, becoming distracted, 'Is there any news about our wages?'

'Not that I know of . . .'

'We haven't had anything since January . . .'

'Salaries for teachers and the priesthood should be sacred to the country; its present and its future are in our hands. It is scandalous to think that in yesterday's session, it was voted that two hundred thousand pesos on paper be spent on furnishing the Courts' archives . . .'

A maize-pudding cart crossed the mire of the corner of Piedad and Andes at a trot, drenching the conductor and passengers.

'You maniac!'

'Beast!'

'Peace, peace,' intervened the priest in conciliatory tone.

Taking advantage of the tram stopping, two elderly women walking along the street asked through the window, 'Will you be taking confession tomorrow, Father Prudencio?'

The reverend, concerned with the honesty of commerce, had a measure of maize pudding and milk filled to the brim, from *that maize pudding* which old people still recall and which disappeared along with cobblestones.

A pale sun filtered through the mist; the street began to fill with people and the familiar shouting of sellers joined the tooting of the tram; wood and newspaper sellers, pastry cooks, Basques with their churns at the side of their mounts and street vendors selling Paraguayan oranges and Brazilian bananas made a ready chorus for the dogcatcher's concert, to which the generation of '85 awoke every morning.

'Wouldn't you like a ride? I'll take you for free,' Rearte asked a dark plump girl scrubbing a doorstep.

The girl replied stonily, 'And you, do you want me to scrub your face for free?'

The tram became full opposite Piedad; Father Prudencio made room very deferentially to an elegant lady with a veil over her eyes and a rosary tangled around her extremely fine fingers. She barely responded condescendingly and made a friendly gesture to a man with a fair, salt-and-pepper beard.

'So early and on your own?'

'From church; you know I come every month specially to take communion. Any you, where are you off to at this hour by tram?'

'I'm on my way back, Teodorita, on my way back . . .'

'You're telling me! What a scandal!'

'The thing is, unfortunately I've come from the club; all night long discussing the propaganda programme.'

'Well, for Juárez to be chosen as candidate . . .'

'It's the only thing I'd dare deny to you, Teodorita; Don Bernardo has the support of reason.'

'And Juárez, that of the people. But tell me then, weren't you at the Colón last night?'

'I am not blessed with ubiquity. How was "Lucrezia"?'

" 'Lucrezia" was awful; but, on the other hand, if you'd seen Guillermina . . .'

'Don't be so critical. Let's talk about something else.'

'Are you scared? Oh well, since I've just come from confession and I've promised not to gossip . . .'

The gentleman tried to distract her. 'So, Borghi Mamo is not that great?'

'She wasn't very good, I assure you. When you think of Teodorini's "Lucrezia"! And the bass? In "Vieni, mia vendetta" I thought my eardrums would burst!'

A man with dandruff and thick elasticated boots with holes at the bunions sneezed; he was reading the news in 'La Nación'. 'Hey, this isn't bad.'

'What?' inquired a young man who was amusing himself by composing anagrams aloud out of the advertisements decorating the inside of the coach.

'They're asking for doormats in the tramways of San José de Flores, so that the passengers won't get cold feet; I suffer from that a great deal . . .'

A man with a handlebar moustache deferentially greeted another in a hazel-coloured overcoat and of foreign appearance. 'Congratulations, Icaza old chap; it seems to me that your proposal to the Council, which is so careless in these matters, couldn't be a better one . . .'

'It's the only way to put an end to the plagues of mosquitoes and the spreading of so many diseases . . .'

'What's it all about?' asked Dr Vélez from the other end.

'Something very simple. You just plough ten blocks of land around the depots and have canals take the sewage there so that they disappear by absorption . . .'

'Not to mention that with irrigation and fertilization, the soil will become very fertile indeed.'

The tram swerved so that passengers were thrown against each other, giving rise to terrible protestations.

'Have you hurt yourself, Teodorita?'

'Jesus, I'll never again take a tram even if I have to ask for transport at Cabral's at four in the morning!'

'These vehicles should be for men on their own . . .'

The 'La Nación' reader remarked on a terrible incident in the news. 'Listen to this, a poor old porter was having a quiet rest sitting on the kerb of the pavement, at the corner of Cangallo and La Florida, when a cart went by and ran over his foot . . .'

The clock at San Ignacio struck seven. The teacher bade farewell to the priest with his usual protestations, and the latter, half closing his eyelids, began to mutter a rosary. The elegant lady and the distinguished gentleman also got off. Two men travelling on the platform occupied the seats, forecasting the crisis in the British cabinet.

'Gladstone and his supporters will fall; the situation is imminent . . .'

'And what do yo think of the result of Dr Pellegrini's negotiations?'

'A skillful diplomat, superior intelligence, he'll secure the loan, I'm sure . . .'

The younger man inquired, 'Tell me, Mr Poblet, is it true that Rodriguez's land in San Juan is being auctinoed off?'

'Some hope, my friend! Don Ernesto is becoming richer all the time. A lucky Spaniard, if ever there was one!'

'I'm told that thirty leagues are on sale with no reserve price next to La Rosita and I imagined . . . If you could give me more precise details . . . I'm interested.'

'But of course! The land belongs to the Arcadinis, an old family who are travelling around Europe whilst a villain is managing it for them . . . Whoever buys it will become rich, land with a future, my dear Cambaceres . . .'

At that moment someone in a hurry consulted his watch. 'Good grief! Twenty past seven already!'

What! Rearte had let the scraggy beats go at their own pace, interested in the comments, and suddenly realized how behind schedule he was . . . He had to reach the Bajo del Retiro at seven thirty for the extra horses . . .

He whipped the horses enthusiastically and the galloped round the bend in Maipú at risk of derailing, and straightened up to head northwards.

Where Juan Pedro Rearte jumps 30 years

A formidable crash of glass and boards was drowning out the passengers' conversations. Spurred on by a nightmarish impatience, Rearte was desperately sounding his horn and crossing the intersections like a whirlwind. The gendarmes, in kepis and white shakos and spats, greeted him ironically as he went by, and from the high driver's seats of their coupés, the coachmen with long moustaches and pointed beards were encouraging him to go faster.

Proud of his horses, Rearte paid no attention to the passengers' desperate ringing of the bell . . .

Suddenly his vision blurred and, like a balloon bursting, the familiar landscape disappeared: the gendarmes in their kepis and white spats, the bearded coachdrivers, the maize-pudding carts, the Basque milkmen on horseback, the ladies in shawls and the gentlemen in top hats . . . Even the double row of low houses became lost on the horizon, merging like the last stretches of a railway line.

Rearte closed his eyes in resigned sadness so as not to see the last ghosts of his world annihilated: a lamplighter who disappeared elastically with his pole over his shoulder and a water cart dragged heavily by three small mules.

When he reopened them, he found himself lying by a doorway in the shadow of a seven-storey house. He was surrounded by a circle of people through whose legs he could see on the road the remains of the carriage and the inert bodies of the two nags lying in a pool of blood.

Next to him a fair-haired gendarme, notebook and pencil in hand like a diligent reporter, was questioning a pale and talkative motorman.

Rearte realized he had crashed into a electric tram, and by the already familiar symptoms he knew he had just broken his other leg.

On recovering consciousness, together with the pain, the only thing he was worried about was what day it was. 'What day is it?' he asked anxiously.

'July 26th,' the nurse who was feeling his ankle replied.

'What year?' insisted Rearte.

'1918,' answered the nurse, and added, as though to himself, 'The tibia appears to be broken in three places.'

'It's not much for a 30-year jump . . .' the old driver remarked philosophically.

Because thirty years earlier—on 26th July 1888—the horses had bolted on the same stretch and, according to the doctor, he had almost broken his shinbone.

After that stoical reflection, Juan Pedro Rearte closed his eyes, pretending to faint. He was ashamed at having become the object of public curiosity and having to answer policemen's urgent questions. He would have liked to have been questioned by one of those gendarmes with kepis and shakos, so arbitrary and so good-natured at the same time, the gendarmes of his youth. The present ones seemed foreign to him, and to make a statement to them seemed to him like abdicating his nationality.

And he was irritated above all by the amazement of the motorman, who didn't stop repeating, 'But how is it possible that this contraption could have crossed the whole of the city at this time and the wrong way? How is that possible?'

Rearte knew how it had been possible, because in the clashes between the deluded and reality, they have the ineffable key to the mystery. But how could he explain that to the common servant of a machine?

Fate is a fool . . .

Once in the ambulance, with the loquaciousness induced by the morphine, Rearte explained the mystery. 'The thing is, Fate is a rogue and a fool like the "gringos" . . . It was ordained by God, ever since I first got into a tram, that I had to break my left leg. I should have broken it thirty years ago, but I was saved by a miracle. In '90, at Lavalle and Paraná, the first day of the revolution, three bullets crossed the platform at knee height, without even brushing past my trousers. Later, when I crashed into the cart, Fate made a mistake and broke my right leg. And now, through fear that I would escape, it has set this trap to have it its own way. It's a real devil, isn't it!'

An Actual Authentic Ghost

Thomas Carlyle, *Scots historian and essayist. Born in Ecclefechan in 1795; died in London in 1881. Author of* The French Revolution *(1837),* Heroes and Hero-Worship *(1841);* Letters and Speeches of Oliver Cromwell *(1845);* Latter Day Pamphlets (1850); History of Frederick the Great *(1851), and many essays and lectures.*

'Again, could anything be more miraculous than an actual authentic Ghost? The English Johnson longed, all his life, to see one; but could not, though he went to Cock Lane, and thence to the church-vaults, and tapped on coffins. Foolish Doctor! Did he, never, with the mind's eye as well as with the body's, look round him into that full tide of human Life he so loved; did he never so much as look into Himself? The good Doctor was a Ghost, as actual and authentic as heart could wish; well-nigh a million of Ghosts were travelling the streets by his side. Once more I say, sweep away the illusion of Time; compress the threescore years into three minutes: what else was he, what else are we? Are we not Spirits, that are shaped into a body, into an Appearance; and that fade away again into air and invisibility?'

The Red King's Dream

Lewis Carroll *(pen-name of the Reverend Charles Lutwidge Dodgson) English writer and mathematician. Born at Daresbury in 1832, died at Guildford in 1898. Author of* Alice's Adventures in Wonderland *(1865),* Though the Looking-Glass *(1871),* Phantasmagoria *(1876),* The Hunting of the Snark *(1876) and* Sylvie and Bruno *(1889). He published his* Curiosa Mathematica *(1888-93) and* Symbolic Logic *(1896), both mathematical treatises, under his own name.*

'It's only the red King snoring,' said Tweedledee.

'Come and look at him!' the brothers cried, and they each took one of Alice's hands, and let her up to where the King was sleeping.

'Isn't he *lovely* sight?' said Tweedledum.

Alice couldn't say honestly that he was. He had a tall red night-cap on, with a tassel, and he was lying crumpled up into a sort of untidy heap, snoring loud— 'fit to snore his head off!' as Tweedledum remarked.

'I'm afraid he'll catch cold with lying on the damp grass,' said Tweedledee: 'and what do you think he's dreaming about?'

Alice said 'Nobody can guess that.'

'Why, about *you*!' Tweedledee exclaimed, capping his hand triumphantly. 'And if he left off dreaming about you, where do you suppose you'd be?'

'Where I am now, of course,' said Alice.

'Not you!' Tweedledee retorted contemptuously. 'You'd be nowhere. Why, you're only a sort of thing in his dream!'

'If that there King was to wake,' added Tweedledum, 'you'd go out—bang!—just like a candle!'

'I shouldn't!' Alice exclaimed indignanantly. 'Besides, if *I'm* only a sort of thing in his dream, what are *you*, I should like to know?'

'Ditto,' said Tweedledum.

'Ditto,' ditto!' cried Tweedledee.

He shouted this so loud that Alice couldn't help saying, 'Hush! You'll be waking him, I'm afraid, if you make so much noise.'

'Well, it's no use *your* talking about waking him,' said Tweedledum, 'when you're only one of the things in his dream. You know very well you're not real.'

'I *am* real!' said Alice, and began to cry.

'You won't make yourself a bit realler by crying,' Tweedledee remarked: 'there's nothing to cry about.'

'If I wasn't real,' Alice said—half-laughing though her tears, it all seemed so ridiculous— 'I shouldn't be able to cry.'

'I hope you don't suppose those are real tears?' Tweedledum interrupted in a tone of great contempt.

'I know they're talking nonsense,' Alice thought to herself: 'and it's foolish to cry about it.' So she brushed away her tears, and went on as cheerfully as she could, 'At any rate I'd better be getting out of the wood, for really it's coming on very dark. Do you think it's going to rain?'

Tweedledum spread a large umbrella over himself and his brother, and looked up into it. 'No, I don't think it is,' he said: 'at least—not under *here*. Nohow.'

The Tree of Pride

G. K. Chesterton, *English essayist, novelist and poet. Born in London in 1874; died in 1936. He published a vast amount of work, always lucid yet ardent. He wrote and revived various literary styles including novels, literary criticism, lyric poetry, biography, polemics, and detective stories. He is the author of essays on Robert Browning (1903) G. F. Watts (1904), and Charles Dickens (1906). His books include* Heretics *(1905);* The Man Who Was Thursday *(1908);* Orthodoxy *(1908);* Manalive *(1912);* Magic *(1913);* The Crimes of England *(1915);* A Short History of England *(1917);* The Uses of Diversity *(1920);* Father Brown Stories *(1927);* Collected Poems *(1927);* The Poet and the Lunatics *(1929);* Four Faultless Felons *(1930);* Autobiography *(1937); and* The Paradoxes of Mr Pond *(1936).*

If you go down to the Barbary Coast, where the last wedge of the forest narrows down between the desert and the great tideless sea, you will find the natives still telling a strange story about a saint of the Dark Ages. There, on the twilight border of the Dark Continent, you feel the Dark Ages. I have only visited the place once, though it lies so to speak, opposite to the Italian city where I lived for years, and yet you would hardly believe how the topsy-turveydom and transmigration of this myth somehow seemed less mad than they really are, with the wood loud with lions at night and that dark red solitude beyond. They say that the hermit St. Securis, living there among trees, grew to love them like companions; since, though great giants with many arms like Briareus, they were the mildest and most blameless of the creatures; they did not devour like the lions, but rather opened their arms to all the little birds. And he prayed that they might be loosened from time to time to walk like other things. And the trees were moved upon the prayers of Securis, as they were at the songs of Orpheus. The men of the desert were stricken from afar with fear, seeing the saint walking with a walking grove, like a schoolmaster with his boys. For the trees were thus freed under strict conditions of discipline. They were to return at the sound of the hermit's bell, and, above all, to copy the wild beasts in walking only—to destroy and devour nothing. Well, it is said that one of the trees heard a voice that was not the saint's; that, in the warm green twilight of one summer evening it became conscious of something sitting and speaking in its branches in the guise of a great bird, and it was that which once spoke from a tree in the guise of a great serpent. As the voice grew louder among its murmuring leaves the tree was torn with a great desire to stretch out and snatch at the birds that flew harmlessly about their nests, and pluck them to pieces. Finally, the tempter filled the tree-top with his own birds of pride, the starry pageant of the peacocks. And the spirit of the brute overcame the spirit of the tree, and it rent and consumed the blue-green birds till not a plume was left, and returned to the quiet tribe of trees. But they say that when spring came all the other trees put forth leaves, but this put forth feathers of a strange hue and pattern. And by that monstrous assimilation the saint knew of the sin and he rooted that one tree to the earth with a judgement so that evil should fall on any who removed it again.

The Tower of Babel

'. . . the story about that hole in the ground, that goes down nobody knows where, has always fascinated me rather. It's Mahomedan in form now; but I shouldn't wonder if the tale is a long way older than Mahomet. It's all about somebody they call the Sultan Aladin; not our friend of the lamp, of course, but rather like him in having to do with genii or giants or something of that sort. They say he commanded the giants to build him a sort of pagoda rising higher and higher above all the stars. The Utmost for the Highest, as the people said when they built the Tower of Babel. But the builders of the Tower of Babel were quite modest and domestic people, like mice, compared with old Aladin. They only wanted a tower that would reach heaven, a mere trifle. He wanted a tower that would *pass* heaven, and rise above it, and go on rising for ever and ever. And Allah cast him down to earth with a thunderbolt, which sank into the earth, boring a hole, deeper and deeper, till it made a well that was without a bottom as the tower was to have been without a top. And down that inverted tower of darkness the soul of the proud Sultan is falling for ever and ever.'

The Dream of the Butterfly

Chuang Tzu (c. 369-286 b.c.), *Chinese taoist philosopher. His work is full of allegorical tales, of which only thirty-three have survived. They were translated into English by Herbert A. Giles and published in 1926.*

The philosopher Chuang Tzu dreamed he was a butterfly, and when he woke up he said he did not know whether he was Chuang Tzu who had dreamed he was a butterfly, or a butterfly now dreaming that it was Chuang Tzu.

The Look of Death

Jean Cocteau *(1891-1963), Outstanding and amazingly prolific French writer. Of his books, the following is a selection. Poetry:* L'Opéra, L'Ange Heurtebise; *novels:* Le Grand Écart, Les Enfants Térribles; *criticism:* Le Rappel à l'ordre, Le Mystère Layc, Portraits-Souvenirs. *Plays include:* La Voix Humaine, Les Parents Térribles, Les Monstres Sacrés.

A young Persian gardener said to his Prince:
'Save me! I met Death in the garden this morning, and he gave me a threatening look. I wish that tonight, by some miracle, I might be far away, in Ispahan.'

The Prince lent him his swiftest horse.

That afternoon, as he was walking in the garden, the Prince came face to face with Death. 'Why,' he asked, 'did you give my gardener a threatening look this morning?'

'It was not a threatening look,' replied Death. 'It was an expression of surprise. For I saw him here this morning, and I knew that I would take him in Ispahan tonight.'

House Taken Over

Julio Cortazar *(1914- 84), Argentinian writer, who lived and worked in Europe. Author of* Los reyes *(1949);* Bestiario *(1951);* Final del juego *(1956);* La armas secretas *(1959);* Los premios *(translated into English as* The Winners, *1965;* Historias de cronopios y famas *(1962);* Rayuela *(1963; translated into English as* Hopscotch, *1966).*

We liked the house because, apart from its being old and spacious (in a day when old houses go down for a profitable auction of their construction materials), it kept the memories of great-grandparents, our paternal grandfather, our parents and the whole of childhood.

Irene and I got used to staying in the house by ourselves, which was crazy: eight people could have lived in that place and not have gotten in each other's way. We rose at seven in the morning and got the cleaning done, and about eleven I left Irene to finish off whatever rooms and went to the kitchen. We lunched at noon precisely; then there was nothing left to do but a few dirty plates. It was pleasant to take lunch and commune with the great hollow, silent house, and it was enough for us just to keep it clean. We ended up thinking, at times, that that was what had kept us from marrying. Irene turned down two suitors for no particular reason, and María Esther went and died on me before we could manage to get engaged. We were easing into our forties with the unvoiced concept that the quiet, simple marriage of sister and brother was the indispensible end to a line established in this house by our grandparents. We would die here someday, obscure and distant cousins would inherit the place, have it torn down, sell the bricks and get rich on the building plot; or more justly and better yet, we would topple it ourselves before it was too late.

Irene never bothered anyone. Once the morning housework was finished, she spent the rest of the day on the sofa in her bedroom, knitting. I couldn't tell you why she knitted so much; I think women knit when they discover that it's a fat excuse to do nothing at all. But Irene was not like that, she always knitted necessities, sweaters for winter, socks for me, handy morning robes and bedjackets for herself. Sometimes she would do a jacket, then unravel it the next moment because there was something that didn't please her; it was pleasant to see a pile of tangled wool in her knitting basket fighting a losing battle for a few hours to retain its shape. Saturdays I went downtown to buy wool; Irene had faith in my good taste, was pleased with the colours and never a skein got to be returned. I took advantage of these trips to make the rounds of the bookstores, uselessly asking if they had anything new in French literature. Nothing worthwhile had arrived in Argentina since 1939.

But it's the house I want to talk about, the house and Irene; I'm not very important. I wonder what Irene would have done without her knitting. One can reread a book, but once a pullover is finished you can't do it over again, it's some kind of disgrace. One day I found that the drawer at the bottom of the chiffonier, replete with moth-balls, was filled with shawls, white, green, lilac. Stacked amid a great smell of camphor—it was like a shop; I didn't have the nerve to ask her what she planned to do with them. We didn't have to earn our living—there was plenty coming in from the farms each month, even piling up. But Irene was only interested in the knitting and showed a wonderful dexterity, and for me the hours slipped away watching her, her hands like silver sea-urchins, needles flashing, and one or two knitting baskets on the floor, the balls of yarn jumping about. It was lovely.

How not to remember the layout of that house. The dining room, a living room with tapestries, the library and three large bedrooms in the section most recessed, the one that faced toward Rodríguez Peña. Only a corridor with its massive oak door separated that part from the front wing, where there was a bath, the kitchen, our bedrooms and the hall. One entered the house through a vestibule with enamelled tiles, and a wrought-iron grated door opened on to the living room. You had to come in through the vestibule and open the gate to go into the living room; the doors to our bedrooms were on either side of this, and opposite it was the corridor leading to the back section; going down the passage, one swung open the oak door beyond which was the other part of the house; or just before the door, one could turn to the left and go down a narrower passageway which led to the kitchen and the bath. When the door was open, you became aware of the size of the house; when it was closed, you had the impression of an apartment, like the ones they build today, with barely enough room to move around in. Irene and I always lived in this part of the house and hardly ever went beyond the oak door except to do the cleaning. Incredible how much dust collected on the furniture. It may be Buenos Aires is a clean city, but she owes it to her population and nothing else. There's too much dust in the air, the slightest breeze and it's back on the marble console tops and in the diamond patterns of the tooled-leather desk set. It's a lot of work to get it off with a feather duster; the motes rise and hang in the air, and settle again a minute later on the pianos and the furniture.

I'll always have a clear memory of it because it happened so simply and without fuss. Irene was knitting in her bedroom, it was eight at night, and I suddenly decided to put the water up for *mate*. I went down the corridor as far as the oak door, which was a ajar, then turned into the hall toward the kitchen, when I heard something in the library or the dining room. The sound came through muted and indistinct, a chair being knocked over on to the carpet or the muffled buzzing of a conversation. At the same time, or a second later, I heard it at the end of the passage which led from those two rooms toward the door. I hurled myself against the door before it was too late and shut it, leaned on it with the weight of my body; luckily, the key was on our side; moreover, I ran the great bolt into place, just to be safe.

I went down to the kitchen, heated the kettle, and when I got back with the tray of *mate*, I told Irene:

'I had to shut the door to the passage. They've taken over the back part.'

She let her knitting fall and looked at me with her tired, serious eyes.

'You're sure?'

I nodded.

'In that case,' she said, picking up her needles again, 'we'll have to live on this side.'

I sipped at the *mate* very carefully, but she took her time starting her work again. I remember it was a grey vest she was knitting. I liked that vest.

The first few days were painful, since we'd both left so many things in the part that had been taken over. My collection of French literature, for example, was still in the library. Irene had left several folios of stationery and a pair of slippers that she used a lot in the winter. I missed my briar pipe, and Irene, I think, regretted the loss of an ancient bottle of Hesperidin. It happened repeatedly (but only in the first few days) that we would close some drawer or cabinet and look at one another sadly.

'It's not here.'

One thing more among the many lost on the other side of the house.

But there were advantages, too. The cleaning was so much simplified that, even when we got up late, nine-thirty for instance, by eleven we were sitting around with our arms folded. Irene got into the habit of coming to the kitchen with me to help get lunch. We thought about it and decided on this: while I prepared the lunch, Irene would cook up dishes that could be eaten cold in the evening. We were happy with the arrangement because it was always such a bother to have to leave our bedrooms in the evening and start to cook. Now we made do with the table in Irene's room and platters of cold supper.

Since it left her more time for knitting, Irene was content. I was a little lost without my books, but so as not to inflict myself on my sister, I set about reordering papa's stamp collection; that killed some time. We amused ourselves sufficiently, each with his own thing, almost always getting together in Irene's bedroom, which was the more comfortable. Every once in a while, Irene might say:

'Look at this pattern I just figured out, doesn't it look like clover?'

After a bit it was I, pushing a small square of paper in front of her so that she could see the excellence of some stamp or another from Eupen-et-Malmédy. We were fine, and little by little we stopped thinking. You can live without thinking.

(Whenever Irene talked in her sleep, I woke up immediately and stayed awake. I never could get used to this voice from a statue or a parrot, a voice that came out of the dreams, not from a throat. Irene said that in my sleep I flailed about enormously and shook the blankets off. We had the living room between us, but at night you could hear everything in the house. We heard each other breathing, coughing, could even feel each other reaching for the light switch when, as happened frequently, neither of us could fall asleep.

Aside from our nocturnal rumblings, everything was quiet in the house. During the day there were the household sounds, the metallic click of knitting needles, the rustle of stamp-album pages turning. The oak door was massive, I think I said that. In the kitchen or the bath, which adjoined the part that was taken over, we managed to talk loudly, or Irene sang lullabies. In a kitchen there's always too much noise, the plates and glasses, for there to be interruptions from other sounds. We seldom allowed ourselves silence there, but when we went back to our rooms or to the living room, then the house grew quiet, half-lit, we ended by stepping around more slowly so as not to disturb one another. I think it was because of this that I woke up irremedially and at once when Irene began to talk in her sleep.)

Except for the consequences, it's nearly a matter of repeating the same scene over again. I was thirsty that night, and before we went to sleep, I told Irene that I was going to the kitchen for a glass of water. From the door of the bedroom (she was knitting) I heard the noise in the kitchen; if not the kitchen, then the bath, the passage off at that angle dulled the sound. Irene noticed how brusquely I had paused, and came up beside me without a word. We stood listening to the noises, growing more and more sure that they were on our side of the oak door, if not the kitchen then the bath, or in the hall itself at the turn, almost next to us.

We didn't wait to look at one another. I tok Irene's arm and forced her to run with me to the wrought-iron door, not waiting to look back. You could hear the noises, still muffled but louder, just behind us. I slammed the grating and we stopped in the vestibule. Now there was nothing to be heard.

'They've taken over our section,' Irene said. The knitting had reeled off from her hands and the yarn ran back toward the door and disappeared under it. When she saw that the balls of yarn were on the other side, she dropped the knitting without looking at it.

'Did you have time to bring anything?' I asked hopelessly.

'No, nothing.'

We had what we had on. I remembered fifteen thousand pesos in the wardrobe in my bedroom. Too late now.

I still had my wrist watch on and saw that it was 11 p.m. I took Irene around the waist (I think she was crying) and that was how we went into the street. Before we left, I felt terrible; I locked the front door up tight and tossed the key down the sewer. It wouldn't do to have some poor devil decide to go in and rob the house, at that hour and with the house taken over.

Being Dust

Santiago Dabove *Argentinian author, born in Moron in Argentina in 1889; died in 1951.* La muerta y su traje, *published posthumously, is a collection of his tales of fantasy.*

Mercilessly cruelty of circumstance! the doctors who were tending to me had to administer, at my insistent request, my desperate pleas, several injections of morphine and other substances that would file down the claws used to torture me by the unrelenting disease: a cruel trigeminal neuralgia.

I for my part took more poisons than Mithridates. The point was to dampen that species of voltaic battery or coil which tormented my trigeminal with its current of sharp, painful throbbing. But never let it be said that I have exhausted suffering, that nothing can exceed this pain; there will always be further suffering, further pain, further tears to endure. And don't take my complaints and expression of bitterness here as anything other than a variation on these singularly harsh words: 'There is no hope for the heart of man!' I said my goodbyes to the doctors, taking with me a syringe for hypodermic injections, opium pills and the whole arsenal of my pharmacopoeia.

I rode on horseback, as usual, across the forty kilometres I had often travelled between towns.

Just opposite that dusty abandoned cemetery which gave me the impression of a double death, the one it sheltered and its own—it was collapsing into ruins, brick by brick, piece by piece—disaster struck. Right opposite that ruin I met my bane, just like Jacob when the angel touched his thigh in the mist and exhausted him, as it couldn't actually defeat him. The hemiplegia, the paralysis which had been threatening me for a long time, knocked me off my horse. After I had fallen, the horse grazed for a while, and soon wandered away. I was left abandoned on that solitary route, where sometimes no human being passed by for several days. I did curse my fate; cursing had exhausted itself on my lips and no longer meant anything. Cursing for me had been the equivalent of the expressions of gratitude to fate made by someone whose life is rich in gifts.

As the ground on which I fell, on the side of the road, was hard, and as I might have to remain there for quite some time and I could hardly move, I devoted my energies to patiently digging the ground around my body with my pen-knife. The task turned out to be rather easy, because beneath the hard surface, the earth was spongy. I gradually buried myself in a sort of trench, which proved to be a tolerable bed, almost protected by the warm damp. The afternoon fled. My hope and my horse disappeared over the horizon. Night fell, dark and close. I had expected it like that, horrific and sticky with blackness, with the despair of worlds, with a moon and stars. Those first few black nights fear got the better of me. Leagues of fear, despair, memories! No, no, the memories come second! I'm not going to cry for myself, nor for . . . A fine persistent drizzle cried for me. At dawn the following day my body was stuck well into the earth. I devoted time to swallowing, enthusiastically and regularly, 'specimens'—pill after pill of opium, which must have determined the 'dream' preceding 'my death'.

It was a strange waking dream and a death-life. My body felt heavier than lead at times; at other times I didn't feel it at all, except for my head, which preserved its sensitivity.

Several days, I think, went by in that state and the black pills kept slipping into my mouth and, without being swallowed, slid down, settling below to turn everything into blackness and into earth.

My head felt and knew it belonged to an earthy body, inhabited by worms and beetles and criss-crossed with corridors freqented by ants. My body was feeling a certain warmth and a certain pleasure in being of mud and in becoming gradually hollower. That's the way it was, and the extraordinary thing was that my very arms, which initially maintained a certain independence of movement, also adopted a horizontal position. Only my head seemed to remain intact, nourished by the mud just like a plant. But since there is no respite in any condition, it had to gnash in self-defence at the birds of prey which wanted to eat its eyes and the flesh from its face. Judging by the tingling sensation I have inside me. I think I must have an ants' nest somewhere near my heart. I'm glad, but I feel impelled to walk, and you can't be made of mud and walk. Everything has to come to me; I shall not go in search of the dawn or the sunset, of any sensation.

A curious thing: the body is attacked by the gnawing forces of life and it is a hotchpotch in which no anatomist would distinguish anything other than mud, corridors and neat constructions of insects installing their home, and yet the brain preserves its intelligence.

I realized that my head was receiving the powerful nourishment of the earth, but directly, just like plants. The sap moved slowly up and down, instead of the blood, which nervously drives the heart. But what happens now? Things change. My head was almost happy to become like a bulb, a potato, a tuber, and now it's full of fear. The fear that one of those palaeontologists who spend their lives sniffing out death will discover it. Or that those political historians, the other funeral directors who turn up after unhumation, should notice the vegetalization of my head. But luckily they didn't see me.

. . . How sad! To be almost like the earth and still have hopes of moving, of loving.

If I want to move, I find I'm stuck, solidified with the earth. I'm diffusing, soon I'm going to be defunct. What a strange plant my head is! It's uniqueness cannot long remain unknown. Men discover everything, even a muddy two-cent coin.

My head bent mechanically towards the pocket watch I had placed at my side when I fell. The lid which closed over the clockwork was open and a small string of ants went in and out. I would have liked to clean it and put it away, but in which vestige of my suit, if everything of mine had practically turned into earth?

I felt that my transition to plant wasn't progressing much, because I was tormented by a strong desire to smoke. Absurd ideas crossed my mind: I wanted to be a tobacco plant so that I wouldn't need to smoke!

. . . The imperative need to move was giving way to the need to be firm and nourished by a rich, protective earth.

. . . At times I amuse myself watching the clouds float by with interest. How many shapes do they plan to assume before they no longer exist, mere masks of steam? Will they exhaust them all? Clouds amuse those who cannot do anything other than look at the sky, but, when they unsuccessfully repeat unto exhaustion their attempt to take on animal shapes, I feel so disappointed that I could watch impassively as a ploughshare came straight at my head.

. . . I'm going to be a plant but I don't feel it, because plants are aware of their ecstatic and selfish life. Their mode of amorous fulfilment and realization, through telegrams of pollen, cannot satisfy us like our close carnal love, but it is a matter of trying, and we'll see what their voluptiousness is like.

. . . But it is not easy to be content, and we would rub out what is written in the book of destiny if it hadn't already happened to us.

. . . How I've come to hate the term 'family tree': it reminds me too much of my tragic state of regression to a plant. I do not make an issue of dignity or privileges—the state of planthood is as honourable as animalhood— but, let's be logical; why don't they represent human ascendancies with a deer's antlers? It would be more in tune with the reality and animality of the matter.

. . . Alone in that desert, the days slowly passed over my sorrow and boredom. I estimated how long I'd been buried by the length of my beard. I noticed it was a bit swollen and, its horny nature just like nails and skin, it would fluff up like plant fibres. I consoled myself thinking that there are trees as expressive as an animal or human being. I remember seeing a poplar, a rope stretching from the sky to the earth. It was a leafy tree with short branches, very tall, prettier than a decorated mast. The wind, depending on its strength, drew from the foliage different expressions: a murmur, a rumour, almost a sound like a violin's bow, which makes the strings vibrate with graded speed and intensity.

. . . I heard a man's footsteps, the soles of a walker perhaps, or, because he couldn't afford the ticket to come this far, he has put something like a piston on his legs and steam pressure in his chest. He stopped as though he had suddenly braked in front of my bearded face. At first he was frightened and turned to flee; then, overcome by curiosity, he came back and, thinking perhaps of a crime, tried to dig me out with a pen-knife. I didn't know how to speak to him, because my voice was by then half-silent because of the almost complete absence of lungs. As though in secret, I said to him, 'Leave me alone, leave me alone! If you dig me out of the ground, as a man I will have nothing functional left and as a plant you will kill me. If you want to preserve my life and not merely be a policeman, don't kill this mode of existence in which there is actually something pleasant, innocent and desirable.'

The man didn't hear me, no doubt accustomed to the great voices of the country, and tried to go on digging. Then I spat in his face. He took offence and hit me with the back of his hand. His simplicity as a peasant, quick to react, no doubt asserted itself over any inclination towards investigation or inquiry. But it seemed to me that a wave of blood was rising to my head, and my choleric eyes were challenging, like those of a fencer buried with his swords and the skilful edge which aim to hurt.

The expression on the man's face of a distressed and helpful good person warned me that he wasn't of that chivalrous and duelling race. He seemed to want to move away without delving any deeper into the mystery . . . and indeed he went, twisting his neck back for a long time to keep on looking . . . But in all this there was something which made me shudder, something about myself.

A common occurrence with many a man when he becomes angry, my face became flushed. You will have noticed that without a mirror you cannot see much more of your face than the side of your nose and a very small part of your cheek and lip, all very blurred, and only by closing one eye. I, who had closed my left eye as though for a pistol duel, could glimpse on the right side in the images confused by being so close, in that cheek which had once been so fatigued by pain, I could glimpse, ah! the rising of a 'green flush'. Would it be sap or blood? If it was the latter, would the chlorophyll of peripheral cells give it an illusory green appearance? I don't know, but I think that each day I'm becoming less of a man.

. . . Opposite that old cemetery I was becoming a solitary cactus on which idle youths would test their pen-knives. With those huge fleshy gloved hands that cacti have, I would pat their sweaty backs and would inhale with pleasure 'their human smell'. Their smell? By that time, what with? All my senses were becoming duller in geometric progression.

Just as the varied and sharp sounds of door hinges will never become music, my animal frenzy, shrillness in creation, could not reconcile itself to the silent and serene activity of plants, with their subdued ease. And the only thing I understood was precisely what the latter don't know: that they are elements in the landscape.

Their innocence and tranquillity, their possible ecstasies, are perhaps equivalent to the intuition of beauty the 'scenery' they all go to make up offers to man.

. . . However highly human activity, change and movement are valued, in most cases man moves, walks, comes and goes in a long, filiform cage. He who has four very familiar walls as a horizon isn't so very different from he who travels along the same roads every day to fulfil tasks which are always the same, in much the same circumstances. All this tiring oneself is not worth the mutual, tacit kiss between a plant and the earth.

. . . But all this is nothing but a sophism. Each time 'I die more like a man and that death covers me in thorns and layers of chlorophyll.

. . . And now, opposite the dusty cemetery, opposite the anonymous ruin, the cactus 'to which I belong' disintegrates, its trunk cut by an axe. Ashes to ashes, dust to dust! Neutral? I don't know, but it will take quite some ferment to work again with matter like 'mine', so riddled with disappointments and defeat!

A Parable of Gluttony

Alexandra David-Neel, *French orientalist born in Paris. Lived in Tibet for many years, and was very familiar with Tibetan life, hagiography and customs.* Author of Initiations Lamaiques; Le Lama aux Cinq Sagesses; le Boudisme, ses Doctrines et ses Methodes; Les Theories Individualistes dans la Philosophie Chinoise.

A holy monk, so runs the story, met on his way a man who was boiling, near a river, a broth made with the fishes he had just caught. The monk, without uttering a word, took the pot and swallowed the boiling broth. The man was astonished to see how he could bear the touch of the boiling liquid, but yet scoffed at him reproaching him for his sinful gluttony. (Chinese and Korean Buddhist monks never eat animal food.) But the monk, still keeping silent, entered the river and micturated. And, then, with his water the fishes came out living and went away swimming in the river.

The Persecution of the Master

Then, in his eagerness to learn the doctrine that could save him from the purgatories, Naropa wanders from town to town, with the only result that each time he reaches a place where Tilopa is said to be staying, the latter had, invariably, just left it a little before his arrival.

Once, knocking at the door of a house, to beg food, a man comes out who offers him wine. Naropa feels deeply offended and indignantly refuses the impure beverge. The house and its master vanish immediately. The proud Brahmin is left alone on the solitary road, while a mocking voice laughs: 'That man was I: Tolopa.'

Another day, a villager askes Naropa to help him to skin a dead animal. Such work, in India, is done only by untouchable outcastes. The mere approach of such men makes a hindu, belonging to one of the pure castes, unclean. Naropa flees, utterly disgusted, and the invisible Tilopa scoffs at him: 'That man was myself.'

Again, the traveller sees a brutal husband who drags his wife by her hair, and when he interferes, the cruel fellow tells him: 'You had better help me, I want to kill her. At least, pass your way and let me do it.' Naropa can hear nothing more. He knocks the man down on the ground, sets free the woman . . . and lo! once more the phantasmagoria disappears while the same voice repeats scornfully: 'I was there, I: Tilopa.'

One evening, after a long tramp, he reaches a cemetery. A crumbled-down pyre is smouldering in a corner. At times, a dark reddish flame leaps from it, showing shrivelled-up carbonized remains. The glimmer alows Naropa to vaguely discern a man lying beside the pyre. He looks at him . . . a mocking laugh answers his inspection. He understood, he falls prostrate on the ground, holding Tilopa's feet and placing them on his head. This time the yogin does not disappear.

The Idle City

Lord Dunsany (*Edward John Moreton Drax Plunkett*), *Irish author, born in London in 1878; died in Ireland in 1957. Fought in the Boer War and in World War I. Author of* Time and the Gods (*1906*); The Sword of Welleran (*1908*); A Dreamer's Tales (*1910*); King Argimenes and the Unknown Warrior (*1911*); Unhappy Far-off Things (*1919*); The Curse of the Wise Woman (*1934*); *and an autobiography*, Patches of Sunlight (*1938*). *He also published his memoirs of World War II.*

There was once a city which was an idle city, wherein men told vain tales. And it was that city's custom to tax all men that would enter in, with the toll of some idle story in the gate.

So all men paid to the watchers in the gate the toll of an idle story, and passed into the city unhindered and unhurt. And in a certain hour of the night when the king of that city arose and went pacing swiftly up and down the chamber of his sleeping, and called upon the name of the dead queen, then would the watchers fasten up the gate and go into that chamber to the king, and, sitting on the floor, would tell him all the tales that they had gathered. And listening to them some calmer mood would come upon the king, and listening still he would lie down again and at last fall asleep, and all the watchers silently would arise and steal away from the chamber.

A while ago wandering, I came to the gate of that city. And even as I came a man stood up to pay his toll to the watchers. They were seated cross-legged on the ground between him and the gate, and each one held a spear. Near him two other travellers sat on the warm sand waiting. And the man said:

'Now the city of Nombros forsook the worship of the gods and turned towards God. So the gods threw their cloaks over their faces and strode away from the city, and going into the haze among the hills passed through the trunks of the olive groves into the sunset. But when they had already left the earth, they turned and looked through the gleaming folds of the twilight for the last time at their city; and they looked half in anger and half in regret, then turned and went away forever. But they sent back a Death, who bore a scythe, saying to it: 'Slay half in the city that forsook us, but half of them spare alive that they may yet remember their old forsaken gods..'

'But God sent a destroying angel to show that He was God, saying unto him: "Go down and show the strength of mine arm unto that city and slay half of the dwellers therein, yet spare a half of them that they may know that I am God." '

'And at once the destroying angel put his hand to his sword, and the sword came out of the scabbard with a deep breath, like to the breath that a broad woodman takes before his first blow at some giant oak. Thereat the angel pointed his arms downwards, and bending his head between them, fell forward from Heaven's edge, and the spring of his ankles shot him downwards with his wings furled behind him. So he went slanting earthward through the evening with his sword stretched out before him, and he was like a javelin that some hunter hath hurled that returneth again to the earth: but just before he touched it he lifted his head and spread his wings with the under feathers forward, and alighted by the bank of the broad Flavro that divides the city of Nombros. And down the bank of the Flavro he fluttered low, like to a hawk over a new-cut cornfield when the little creatures of the corn are shelterless, and at the same time down the other bank the Death from the gods went mowing.

'At once they saw each other, and the angel glared at the Death, and the Death leered back at him, and the flames in the eyes of the angel illumined with a red glare the mist that lay in the hollows of the sockets of the Death. Suddenly they fell on one another, sword to scythe. And the angel captured the temples of the gods, and set up over them the sign of God, and led into them the ceremonies and sacrifices of the gods; and all the while the centuries slipped quietly by going down the Flavro seawards.

'And now some worship God in the temple of the gods, and others worship the gods in the temple of God, and still the angel hath not returned again to the rejoicing choirs, and still the Death hath not gone back to die with the dead gods; but all through Nombros they fight up and down, and still on each side of the Flavro the city lives.'

And the watchers in the gate said, 'Enter in.'

Then another traveller rose up, and said:

'Solemnly between Huhenwazi and Nitcrana the huge grey clouds came floating. And those great mountains, heavenly Huhenwazi, and Nitcrana, the king of peaks, greeted them, calling them brothers. And the clouds were glad of their greeting for they meet with companions seldom in the lonely heights of the sky.

'But the vapours of evening said unto the earth-mist, 'What are those shapes that dare to move above us and to go where Nitcrana is and Huhenwazi?'

'And the earth-mist said in answer unto the vapours of evening, 'It is only an earth-mist that has become mad and has left the warm and comfortable earth, and has in his madness thought that his place is with Huhenwazi and Nitcrana.'

"Once," said the vapours of evening, "there were clouds, but this was many and many a day ago, as our forefathers have said. Perhaps the mad one thinks he is the clouds.'

'Then spake the earth-worms from the warm deeps of the mud, saying 'O, earth-mist, thou art inded the clouds, and there are no clouds but thou And as for Huhenwazi and Nitcrana, I cannot see them, and therefore they are not high, and there are no mountains in the world but those that I cast up every morning out of the deeps of the mud."

'And the earth-mist and the vapours of evening were glad at the voice of the earth-worms, and looking earthward believed what they had said.

'And indeed it is better to be as the earth-mist, and to keep close to the warm mud at night, and to hear the earth-worm's comfortable speech, and not to be a wanderer in the cheerless heights, but to leave the mountains alone with there vast aspect over all the cities of men, and from the whispers that they hear at evening of unknown distant Gods.'

And the watchers in the gate said, 'Enter in.'

Then a man stood up who came out of the west, and told a western tale. He said:

'There is a road in Rome that runs through an ancient temple that once the gods had loved; it runs along the top of a great wall, and the floor of the temple lies far down beneath it, of marble, pink and white.

'Upon the temple floor I counted to the number of thirteen hungry cats.

' "Sometimes," they said among themselves, "it was the gods that lived here, sometimes it was men, and now it's cats. So let us enjoy the sun on the hot marble before another people comes."

'For it was at that hour of a warm afternoon when my fancy is able to hear the silent voices.

'And the fearful leanness of all those thirteen cats moved me to go into a neighbouring fish shop, and there to buy a quantity of fishes. Then I returned and threw them all over the railing at the top of the great wall, and they fell for thirty feet, and hit the sacred marble with a smack.

'Now, in any other town but Rome, or in the minds of any other cats, the sight of fishes falling out of heaven had surely excited wonder. They rose slowly, and all stretched themselves, then they came leisurely towards the fishes. "It is only a miracle," they said in their hearts.'

And the watchers in the gate said, 'Enter in.'

Proudly and slowly, as they spoke, drew up to them a camel, whose rider sought for entrance to the city. His face shone with the sunset by which for long he had steered for the city's gate. Of him they demanded toll. Whereat he spoke to his camel, and the camel roared and kneeled, and the man descended from him. And the man unwrapped from many silks a box of divers metals wrought by the Japanese, and on the lid of it were figures of men who gazed from some shore at an isle of the Inland Sea. This he showed to the watchers, and when they had seen it, said, 'It has seemed to me that these speak to each other thus:

"Behold now Oojni, the dear one of the sea, the little mother sea that hath no storms. She goeth out from Oojni singing a song, and she returneth singing over her sands. Little is Oojni in the lap of the sea, and scarce to be perceived by wondering ships. White sails have never wafted her legends afar, they are told not by bearded wanderers of the sea. Her fireside tales are known not to the North, the dragons of China have not heard of them, nor those that ride on elephants through Ind.

"Men tell the tales and the smoke ariseth upwards; the smoke departeth and the tales are told.

"Oojni is not a name among the nations, she is not known of where the merchants meet, she is not spoken of by alien lips.

"Indeed, but Oojni is little among the isles, yet is she loved by those that know her coasts and her inland places hidden from the sea.

"Without glory, without fame, and without wealth, Oojni is greatly loved by a little people, and by a few; yet not by few, for all her dead still love her, and oft by night come whispering through her woods. Who could forget Oojni even among the dead?

"For here in Oojni, wot you, are homes of men, and gardens, and golden temples of the gods, and sacred places inshore from the sea, and many murmurous woods. And there is a path that winds over the hills to go into mysterious holy lands where dance by night the spirits of the woods, or sing unseen in the sunlight; and no one goes into these holy lands, for who that love Oojni would rob her of her mysteries, and the curious aliens come not. Indeed, but we love Oojni though she is so little; she is the little mother of our race, and the kindly nurse of all seafaring birds.

"And behold, even now caressing her, the gentle fingers of the mother sea, whose dreams are afar with that old wanderer Ocean.

"And yet let us forget not Fuzi-Yama, for he stands manifest over clouds and sea, misty below, and vague and indistinct, but clear above for all the isles to watch. The ships make all their journeys in his sight, the nights and the days go by him like a wind, the summers and winters under him flicker and fade, the lives of men pass quietly here and hence, and Fuzi-Yama watches there—and knows." '

And the watchers in the gate said 'Enter in.'

And I, too, would have told them a tale, very wonderful and very true; one that I had told in many cities, which as yet had no believers. But now the sun had set, and the brief twilight gone, and ghostly silences were rising from far and darkening hills. A stillness hung over that city's gate. And the great silence of the solemn night was more acceptable to the watchers in the gate than any sound of man. Therefore they beckoned to us, and motioned with their hands that we should pass untaxed into the city. And softly we went up over the sand, and between the high rock pillars of the gate, and a deep stillness settled among the watchers, and the stars over them twinkled undisturbed.

For how short a while man speaks, and withal how vainly. And for how long he is silent. Only the other day I met a king in Thebes, who had been silent already for four thousand years.

Tantalia

Macedonio Fernandez, *Argentinian metaphysicist and humorist, born in Buenos Aires in 1874, died in 1952. His extremely original work, which includes* No toda es Vigilia la de los Ojos Abiertos *(1928) and* Parpeles de Recienvenido *(1930), is distinguished for its intensity and continual inventiveness.*

The world is of tantalic inspiration.

First moment: The career of a little plant

He is finally convinced that his sentimentality, his capacity for affection, which has long been struggling to recover, is totally exhausted and, in the pain of this discovery, ponders and comes to the decision that perhaps caring for a fragile little plant, a minimal life, the most in need of affection, should be the first step in the re-education of his sentimentality.

A few days after this meditation and the projects pending, having no inkling of his thoughts but moved by a vague apprehension she had had of the emotional impoverishment taking place in him. She sent him a gift of a little clover plant.

He decided to adopt it to initiate the procedure he had been contemplating. He looked after it enthusiastically for some time, gradually becoming more aware of the infinite care and protection, susceptible to a fatal lapse, required to ensure the life of such a weak being, which a cat, a frost, a knock, heat or wind, could threaten. He felt intimidated by the possibility of seeing it die one day as a result of the slightest carelessness; but it was not only the fear of losing his beloved's gift. Talking with Her, worried just like all those who are passionate, the more so when that passion is flagging, it became an obsession that there was an intertwining of destinies of the life of the plant and their lives, or that of their love. It was She who one day came to tell him that the clover was the symbol of life of their love.

They began to fear that the little plant might die and that with it one of them might die, and, what's more, their love, the only death there is. They saw each other frequently, going over it in conversations, whilst the fear in which they found themselves trapped grew. They then decided to destroy the recognizable identity of the little plant so that, avoiding the bad omen which killing it would entail, there would be nothing identifiable in the world whose existence their life and love was subordinate; and in so doing, ensuring that they would never know whether that vegetable existence which had so uniquely become part of the vicissitudes of a human passion lived or died. Then they decided, at night, to lose it in a vast clover field somewhere unfamiliar to them.

Second moment: Identity of a clover

But the excitement which had been mounting in Him for some time, and the disappointment of both at having had to give up the attempt on which they had embarked to re-educate his sensitivity and the habit and affection emerging in him as he looked after the little plant, were translated into a covert deed on his return from the mission to forget in the shadows. On the way back, without Her noticing for certain, yet feeling a certain anxiety, He bent down and picked another clover.

'What are you doing?'

'Nothing.'

They parted at dawn, She somewhat frightened, both of them relieved at no longer seeing themselves dependent on the symbolic life of that little plant, and in both also was the fear that we feel at the point of no return, when we have just created an impossibility, as in this case the impossibility of ever knowing whether it was living and which one was the little plant which had initially been a gift of love.

Third moment: The torturer of a clover

'For sundry reasons and afflictions I find myself enjoying neither the pleasures of the intellect or art, nor sensual pleasures, which are there for the taking. I'm becoming deaf, music having been my greatest pleasure; the long walks amongst the hedgerows are becoming impossible because of a thousand details of physiological decadence. And similarly in other ways . . .

'This little clover plant has been chosen by me for Pain, out of a myriad others. Chosen! Poor thing! I'll see if I can create a world of Pain for it. I'll see if its Innocence and Torture become such that something explodes in Being, in Universality, so that Nothingness will claim and achieve total Cessation for itself and for the whole, for the world is such that there is not even individual death: a ceasing of the Whole or inexorable eternity for everyone. The only intelligible cessation is that of the Whole; the idea that he who had once 'felt' should cease to feel, the remaining reality still existing but he having ceased, is a contradiction in terms, an impossible concept.

'Chosen amongst millions, it befell you to be so, to be so for Pain! Not yet; from tomorrow I shall be an artist in Pain with you!

'For three days, sixty, seventy hours, the summer wind was constant, swinging within a small angle; it came and went from an accent and direction to a small variation of an accent and a direction, and my bedroom door, its swinging limited by its frame and a chair I placed in its path for this purpose, swung unceasingly, and the shutter of my window also banged unceasingly, at the mercy of the wind. Sixty, seventy hours of the door and shutter giving in minute by minute to their different pressures, and I likewise, sitting or swinging in the swingseat.

'It's as though I said to myself, this is Eternity. It's as though what I was feeling, that recipe of weariness, the senselessness of things, the aimlessness, the feeling of everything being the same—pain, pleasure, cruelty, kindness— spawned the thought of becoming the torturer of a little plant.

'I'll practise,' I repeated to myself, 'without trying any more to love again, torturing the weakest and most defenceless, the tamest and most vulnerable form of life; I'll be the torturer of this little plant. This is the poor little one chosen from thousands to put up with my creativeness and zeal as a torturer. Because, when I wanted to make a clover happy, I had had to give up the attempt and banish it from me under sentence of unrecognizability, the pendulum of my perverted and battered will swung to the other extreme, emerging all of a sudden in a contrary mutation, in dislike, and quickly gave rise to the idea of martyring innocence and isolation in order to obtain the suicide of the Cosmos by shame that so repulsive and cowardly a scene should thrive in its bosom. After all, the Cosmos has also created me!

'I deny Death. There could be no Death, not even as the occultation of one being for another, when for them all was love; and I don't deny it only as death for its own sake. If there is no death of he who once felt, why should the total cessation of being not exist, annihilation of the Whole? You are indeed possible, eternal Cessation. In you all those of us who do not believe in death but who are not satisfied with being, with life, would take refuge. And I believe that Desire can come to work directly on the cosmos, without mediation by our bodies, that Faith can move mountains; I believe, even though no other being might.

'I cannot rekindle the lascerating memory of the life of pain I planned, inventing new cruel methods each day to make it suffer without killing it.

'To skim over the matter, I would place it every day close to but untouched by the sun's rays and with the meticulousness of cruelty push it away as the patch of sunlight advanced. I watered it just enough to stop it from dying, whilst surrounding it with bowls of water, and I had invented realistic sounds of neighbouring rain and drizzle, which never refreshed it. To tempt and not give . . . The world is a table set with Temptation, with infinite obstacles interposed and no less a variety of impediments than of things offered. The world is of tantalic inspiration; a display of an immense making-itself-desired which is called Cosmos, or rather, Temptation. Everything a clover wants and everything a man wants is offered and denied. I also thought: tempt and deny. My internal orders, my tantalism, was to seek out the most exquisite states of torment without harming life, seeking on the contrary a fuller life, a more lively and excited sensitivity to suffering. And in this I succeeded, making it tremble from the pain of tantalic deprivation. But I could neither watch it nor touch it; my own actions filled me with disgust (when I pulled it up, that night so black in my spirit, I didn't look towards where it was and its contact was too odious to me). It would writhe at the sound of rain, the moist freshness always outside its reach.

'Chosen amongst millions for a martyr's destiny! Chosen! Poor thing! Oh, your Pain would leap over the world! When I pulled you up, you had already been chosen by my yearning to torment.'

Fourth moment: New smile

The radical, intimate formula of what He was doing so wretchedly was the ambition and anxiety of achieving the replacement of the Whole by Nothingness, of everything that there is, that there was, that is, of all the Reality of the material and spiritual. He thought that the Cosmos, the Real, couldn't survive long, being ashamed to harbour in its midst such a scene of torture inflicted on a member of one of the lower echelons of the weakest and most fragile of life-forms, because of the greater power and endowment of the living. Man tyrannizing a clover! So that's what the advent of man was about!

The irritation of denial of what has been offered can drive the most thoughtful of men to perversity. Thus the cowardly martyrdom, the disgusting satisfaction of the greater power in the treachery towards a minimal life.

He conceived of the equal possibility of Nothingness and Being, and thought a total substitution of the All-Being by the All-Nothingness plainly intelligible and possible. He, as the highest of Life Consciousness, as a man, and a man who is exceptionally endowed, was the one who could, in an ultimate refinement of thought, have found the mainspring, the talisman which could choose the option of Being for Nothingness, option or replacement or 'pushing out' of Being by Nothingness. Because truly, tell me if I'm mistaken, isn't it true that there is no mental element which can decide that Nothingness or Being differ in the *possibility* of being in some degree; is it not entirely possible that Nothingness should exist instead of Being. This is true, evident, because the world is or is not, but if it is, it is causalistic, and thus, its cessation, its not being, is causable; although the mainspring sought doesn't determine the cessation of Being, perhaps another might determine it . . . If the existence of the World or Nothingness are absolutely equally possible, in this equilibrium or balance of Being and Nothingness, a wisp, a dewdrop, a sigh, a desire, an idea, could be capable of pushing the alternative to a World of Non-Being from a World of Being.

One day the Saviour-of-Being would come . . .

(I comment and theorize on what He did, but I am not He.)

But She came one day: 'Tell me, what did you do that night, because I heard the dampened sound of a little plant being uprooted, the sound of the earth muffling the pulling up of a tender root? Is that what I heard?'

But He felt he was once more in his element after a long pilgrimage in search of the answer, and he burst into tears in Her arms and loved her once more, immensely, as before. They were tears which hadn't been shed for ten or twelve years which swelled his heart, which had made him want to blow up the world, and as he was reminded of the little scream, the humbling murmur of vegetable pain, of a torn rootlet, that was it! what his nature needed so that tears, overflowing, should rinse his entire being and return him to the days of his abundance of love . . . The suffocated scream of a suffering root in the earth, just as all Reality was able to decide towards Non-Being, was able to change His entire inner life.

I believe in it. And what the whole world believes is much more than I say I believe in—who is judged by their beliefs?—therefore don't accuse me of an absurd rashness in belief. Any woman believes that the life of her beloved can depend on the wilting of the carnation she gave him, if her beloved forgets to put water in the glass she once gave him. Every mother believes that her son who leaves with her 'blessing' departs protected from evil; every woman believes that what she prays for fervently can overcome fate. Everything-is-possible is my belief. Thus I believe it.

I am not deceived by the swollen verbiage of the placid ideology of many metaphysicians, with their opinions founded on opinions. An Event, an event which drives one mad with humiliation, with horror, the Secret, the Being-Mystery, the martyrdom of Vegetable Innocence for the maximum personalization of Consciousness: Man, for extreme non-mechanical power. I believe such an event, without need of proof, merely conceived by human consciousness, can edge towards Non-Being everything that is.

It is conceived; therefore Cessation is potentially caused. We can await it. But the miraculous re-creation of love conceived at the same time by the author will perhaps battle with Cessation or triumph later after the realization of Non-Being. In truth the psychological continuum of conscience is a series of cessations and re-creations rather than a continuum.

I have seen them love each other once again; but I cannot watch him or listen to him without experiencing sudden dread. I wish he had never made his terrible confession to me.

Eternal Life

James George Frazer *British social anthropologist, born in Glasgow in 1854, died in 1941. His major work is* The Golden Bough *(1890-1915). He also wrote* The Devil's Advocate: A Plea for Superstition *(1909) and* Totemism and Exogamy *(1910).*

A fourth story, taken down near Oldenburg in Holstein, tells of a jolly dame that ate and drank and lived right merrily and had all that heart could desire, and she wished to live always. For the first hundred years all went well, but after that she began to shrink and shrivel up, till at last she could neither walk nor stand nor eat nor drink. But die she could not. At first they fed her as if she were a little child, but when she grew smaller and smaller they put her in a glass bottle and hung her up in the church. And there she still hangs, in the church of St Mary, at Lübeck. She is as small as a mouse, but once a year she stirs.

A Secure Home

Elena Garro *Mexican writer, born in Puebla. Her books include the volume of comedies* Un hogar sólido *and the novel* Los recuerdos del porvenir *(1963).*

CLEMENTE (aged 60); DOÑA GERTRUDIS (aged 40); MAMÁ JESUSITA (aged 80); CATALINA (aged 5); VICENTE MEJÍA (aged 28); MUNI (aged 28); EVA, a foreigner (aged 20); LIDIA (aged 32).

(Interior of a small room with stone walls and ceiling. There are no windows or doors. To the left, built into the wall and also of stone, some bunks. In one of them, Mamá Jesusita, wearing a lace nightdress and lace sleeping-cap. The scene is very dark.)

VOICE OF DOÑA GERTRUDIS: Clemente, Clemente! I hear footsteps!

VOICE OF CLEMENTE: You're always hearing footsteps! Why are women so impatient? Always anticipating what's going to happen, prophesying disasters.

VOICE OF DOÑA GERTRUDIS: Well, I can hear them.

VOICE OF CLEMENTE: No, woman, you're always mistaken; you get carried away by your nostalgia for catastrophies . . .

VOICE OF DOÑA GERTRUDIS: That's true . . . but this time I'm not mistaken.

VOICE OF CATALINA: There are lots of feet, Gertrudis! (CATITA *emerges, in a white dress as worn around 1865, little black boots and a coral necklace around her neck. Her hair is pulled to the nape of her neck with a red bow.)* Goody, goody! Tralala, tralala! (CATITA *jumps and claps her hands.)*

DOÑA GERTRUDIS (appearing in a pink 1930s dress): Children don't make mistakes. Isn't it true, Aunt Catalina, that somebody's coming?

CATALINA: Yes, I know! I knew ever since they first came. I was so scared here, all alone!

CLEMENTE *(He appears in a black suit and white cuffs.):* I think they're right. Gertrudis! Gertrudis! Help me find my metacarpi! I'm always losing them and I can't shake hands without them.

VICENTE MEJÍA *(appearing dressed as a Juárez partisan):* You've read too much, Don Clemente; that's where the bad habit of forgetting things comes from. Look at me, complete in my uniform, always ready for any arrival!

MAMÁ JESUSITA *(straightening herself in her bunk and poking out her head, covered with the lace sleeping cap).* Catita is right! The footsteps are approaching. *(She puts one hand behind her ear, as though listening.)* The first ones have stopped . . . unless something awful has happened to the Ramírezes . . . this neighbourhood has already disappointed us several times.

CATALINA *(jumping):* You go to sleep, Jesusita! All you like doing is sleeping:

Sleep, sleep,
The cockerel's crowing
in San Agustin.
Is the bread done?

MAMÁ JESUSITA: And what do you expect me to do? They left me in my nightdress . . .

CLEMENTE: Don't complain, Doña Jesús. We think that out of respect . . .

MAMÁ JESUSITA: Out of respect! And out of respect, such lack of respect?

GERTRUDIS: Had I been there, mother . . . but what did you expect the girls and Clemente to do.

(*Above, we hear many footsteps. They stop. The sound of footsteps returns.*)

MAMÁ JESUSITA: Catita! Come here and polish my forehead; I want it to shine like the Pole Star. Blessed was the time when I ran around the house like lightning, sweeping, shaking the dust which fell on the piano in deceitful torrents of gold; later, when everything shone like a comet, to break the ice of my cubes left out in the open, and bathe with the water full of winter stars. Do you remember, Gertrudis? That was living; surrounded by my children, straight and clean as slate pencils.

GERTRUDIS: Yes, mother. And I also remember the little burnt cork you would use to paint rings under the eyes; and the lemons you used to eat so that your blood would become water; and those evenings when you would go with father to the Teatro de los Héroes. How pretty you looked with your fan and your earrings on!

MAMÁ JESUSITA: You see, child, life is so short! Every time I got to the box . . .

CLEMENTE: (*interrupting*): For pity's sake, now I can't find my femur!

MAMÁ JESUSITA: How inconsiderate! Interrupting a lady!

(CATITA, meanwhile, has been helping JESUSITA to fix her cap.)

VINCENTE: I saw Catita playing the trumpet with it.

GERTRUDIS: Aunt Catalina, where have you left Clemente's femur?

CATALINA: Jesusita! Jesusita! They want to take my trumpet away from me!

MAMÁ JESUSITA: Gertrudis, leave that child alone! And as to you, I say:
worse than my child being ill
is what it has done to her will . . .

GERTRUDIS: But mother, be fair, it's Clemente's femur!

CATALINA: You're horrid, mean! I'll hit you! It's not his femur, it's my sugar trumpet!

CLEMENTE (*to Gertrudis*): Perhaps she's eaten it? Your aunt is unbearable.

GERTRUDIS: I don't know, Clemente. She lost my broken collar-bone for me. She loved the whitewashed trails left by the scar. And it was my favourite bone! It reminded me of the doors of my house, surrounded by heliotrope. I told you I fell, didn't I? We'd been to the circus the night before. The whole of Chihuahua was there to see Ricardo Bell; suddenly a tightrope-walker came out, looking like a butterfly, and I never forgot her . . .

(*We hear a bang above and Gertrudis interrupts herself.*)

GERTRUDIS (*continuing*): . . . in the morning I went to the brambles, to dance on one foot, because all night long I dreamt I was her . . .

(*Above we hear a louder bang.*)

GERTRUDIS: . . . Of course, I didn't know I had bones. As a child, one doesn't know anything. Since I broke it, I always say it was the first bone I had. Life's full of surprises!

(*The bangs follow more rapidly,*)

VINCENTE (*smoothing his moustache*): No doubt. Somebody's coming, we have visitors. (*He sings.*)

> As night casts its shadow
> The moon glitters
> And in the lagoon
> The kingfisher sings . . .

MAMÁ JESUSITA: Be quiet, Vicente! It's not the time to sing. Look at those intrusive people! In my day, people said they would be coming before dropping in for a visit. There was more respect. Let's see who they bring us now. One of those strangers who married the girls! God strikes down the humble, as poor old Ramon used to say, God rest his soul.

VINCENTE: You haven't changed for the better, Jesusita! You find fault with everything. You used to be so cheerful; the only thing you enjoyed doing was dancing polkas. (*he hums 'Jesusita en Chihuahua' and dances a few steps.*) Do you remember how we used to dance at that Carnival? (*He carries on dancing.*) Your pink dress whirled around and around, and your neck was very close to my mouth . . .

MAMÁ JESUSITA: For goodness' sake, cousin Vicente! Don't remind me of those silly things.

VINCENTE (*laughing*): What would Ramon say now? He, so jealous . . . and you and me here together, whilst he rots alone, in Dolores' Pantheon.

GERTRUDIS: Uncle Vicente, be quiet! You'll be upsetting her.

CLEMENTE (*alarmed*): I've already explained to you, Doña Jesús, that at the time we had no money to move him.

MAMÁ JESUSITA: And the girls, what are they waiting for to bring him? Don't give me any explanations. You always were lacking in tact.

(*We hear a louder bang.*)

CATALINA: I saw light! (*A ray of light comes in.*) I saw a sabre! St Michael is coming to visit us again! Look at his spear!

VINCENTE: Are we all here? Well then, fall in and we will arise!

CLEMENTE: Muni and my sister-in-law are missing.

MAMÁ JESUSITA: You foreigners are always wandering off.

GERTRUDIS: Muni! Muni! Somebody's coming; perhaps it's one of your cousins. Don't you like it, son? You can play and laugh with them again. Let's see if it dispels your gloom.

(*EVA appears, foreign, fair-haired, tall, sad, very young, in a 1920s travelling dress.*)

EVA: Muni was around a moment ago. Muni, my son! Can you hear that beating? That's how the sea beats against the rocks of my house . . . none of you knew it . . . it was on a rock, tall as a wave. Beaten by the winds which rocked us at night. Swirls of salt covered its windows with sea stars. The whitewash in the kitchen became golden with my father's sunny hands . . . At night, the creatures of the wind, the sea, fire, salt, came in through the chimney, curled up in the flames, sang in the drips in the basins . . . Plink, plonk! Plink, plink, plink, plink, plonk! . . . And the iodine spread around the house like sleep . . . A shiny dolphin's tail heralded the day. Like that! With a cascade of scales and coral!

(EVA, *on saying the last phrase, raises her arm and points to the flood of light entering the crypt. Above, the first stone slab is removed. The room is bathed in sunlight. The luxurious dresses are dusty and the faces pale. The little girl* CATALINA *jumps with delight.*)

CATALINA: Look, Jesusita! Somebody's coming! Who's bringing him Jesusita: Doña Diphtheria or St Michael?

MAMÁ JESUSITA: Wait, child, we'll see!

CATALINA: Doña Diphtheria brought me. Do you remember her? She had fingers of cotton wool and didn't let me breathe. Did she frighten you, Jesusita?

MAMÁ JESUSITA: Yes, sister. I remember they took you away and the patio of the house was covered in purple petals. Mother cried a lot, and we girls too.

CATALINA: Silly! You didn't know you'd be coming to play with me? That day St Michael sat next to me and with his spear of fire he wrote it in the sky of my house. I couldn't read . . . and I read it. And was the Misses Simson's school pretty?

MAMÁ JESUSITA: Very pretty, Catita. Mother sent us with black bows . . . and you could no longer go.

CATALINA: And did you learn how to spell? That's what mother was going to send me there for. And since . . .

MUNI (*He enters in pyjamas, his face blue, with fair hair.*): Who could it be?

(*Above, through the piece of vault open to the sky, we can see the feet of a woman suspended in a circle of light.*)

GERTRUDIS: Clemente, Clemente, those are Lidia's feet! How lovely, my child, how lovely that you've died so soon!

(*Everyone is quiet. Lidia starts her descent, suspended by ropes. She comes upright, with a white dress, her arms crossed over her chest, her fingers making a cross, head bent and eyes closed.*)

CATALINA: Who's Lidia?

MUNI: Lidia? She's the daughter of Uncle Clemente and Aunt Gertrudis, Catita. (*He caresses the girl.*)

MAMÁ JESUSITA: That's all we needed! Now we have the whole set of grandchildren. What a lot of small fry! What's with the crematorium? Isn't that more modern? I thought it was at least more hygienic.

CATALINA: Isn't it true, Jesusita, that Lidia isn't real?

MAMÁ JESUSITA: If only it were, child! Here there is room for everyone, except poor old Ramon!

EVA: How she's grown! When I came she was as small as Muni.

(Lidia remains standing in their midst as they watch her. Then she opens her eyes.)

LIDIA: Father! *(She hugs him.)* Mother! Muni! *(She hugs them.)*

GERTRUDIS: You look very well, child.

LIDIA: And grandmother?

CLEMENTE: She couldn't get up. Do you remember we made the mistake of burying her in her nightdress?

MAMÁ JESUSITA: Yes, Lili, here I am lying down for ever and ever.

GERTRUDIS: My mother's ideas. You know, Lili, how composed she always was . . .

MAMÁ JESUSITA: The worst thing would be, child, to appear like this before Our Lord God. Don't you think it's wicked? Why didn't you think of bringing me a dress? That grey one, with the brocade ruffles and the little bunch of violets . . . but nobody remembers old people . . .

CATALINA: When St Michael comes to see us, she hides.

LIDIA: And who are you, darling?

CATALINA: Catita!

LIDIA: Ah, of course! We had her on the piano. Now she's in Evita's house. How sad when we saw her, so melancholic, painted in her white dress! I'd forgotten she was here.

VINCENTE: And aren't you pleased to meet me, niece?

LIDIA: Uncle Vicente! We also had you in the lounge, in uniform, and your medal was in a little red velvet box.

EVA: And don't you remember your Aunt Eva?

LIDIA: Aunt Eva! Yes, I can just remember you, with your fair hair in the sun . . . and I remember your purple parasol and your pale face under its lights, like that of a beautiful drowned woman . . . and your empty chair rocking to the rhythm of your song after you had gone.

(A voice erupts from the circle of light. A speech.)

VOICE: The generous earth of our beloved Mexico opens its arms to give you loving shelter. Virtuous lady, most exemplary mother, model wife, you leave an irremediable void . . .

MAMÁ JESUSITA: Who's talking to you with such familiarity?

LIDIA: It's Don Gregorio de la Huerta y Ramírez Puente, President of the Society for the Blind.

VINCENTE: What madness! And what are so many blind people doing together?

MAMÁ JESUSITA: But why does he treat you so familiarly?

GERTRUDIS: It's the fashion, mother, to talk familiarly to the dead.

VOICE: Most cruel loss, whose absence we shall grieve with growing sorrow with the passage of time, you deprive us of your overwhelming charm and you also leave a secure Christian home in the most pitiless orphanhood. Let homes tremble before the merciless Parcae . . .

CLEMENTE: Good God! Is that idiot still around?

MAMÁ JESUSITA: What's no good thrives!

LIDIA: Yes. And now she's Chair of the Bank, of the Knights of Colombus, of the flag and of Mother's Day . . .

VOICE: Only unshakable faith, Christian resignation and compassion . . .

CATALINA: Don Hilario always says the same thing.

MAMÁ JESUSITA: It's not Don Hilario, Catita. Don Hilario died a mere sixty-seven years ago . . .

CATALINA (*without hearing her*): When they brought me here, he said, 'A little angel has flown!' And it wasn't true. I was down here, alone, very frightened. Isn't that right, Vicente? Isn't it true that I don't tell lies?

VINCENTE: You're telling me! I arrived here, still dazed by the flashes, with open wounds and . . .what do I see? Catita crying: 'I want to see my mummy, I want to see my mummy!' What a battle this child gave me! I tell you, I even missed the French . . .

VOICE: *Requiescat in pace!* (*They begin to replace the stone slabs. The scene gradually darkens.*)

CATALINA: We were alone a long time, weren't we, Vicente? We didn't know what was happening, why nobody ever came back again.

MAMÁ JESUSITA: I've told you already, Catita, we went to Mexico. Then there was the Revolution . . .

CATALINA: Until one day Eva arrived. You said, Vicente, that she was a foreigner because we didn't know her.

VINCENTE: The situation was rather strained, and Eva didn't say a word to us.

EVA: I felt intimidated . . . and I was thinking of Muni . . . and my house . . . everything was so quiet here.

(*Silence. They replace the last slab.*)

LIDIA: And now what do we do?

CLEMENTE: Wait.

LIDIA: Still wait?

GERTRUDIS: Yes, child, you'll see.

EVA: You'll see everything you want to see, except your house with its white pine table and the waves in the windows and the boats' sails . . .

MUNI: Aren't you happy, Lilí?

LIDIA: Yes, Muni, especially seeing you. When I saw you lying that night in the yard of the police station with that smell of urine coming from broken slabs, and you sleeping on the bunk, amongst the policemen's feet, your pyjamas crumpled and your face blue, I asked myself, why, why?

CATALINA: So did I, Lilí. I had never seen a blue dead body. Jesusita told me later that cyanide has many brushes and only one tube of paint: blue.

MAMÁ JESUSITA: Leave the lad alone! Blue suits fair people very well.

MUNI: Why, cousin Lilí? Haven't you seen stray dogs wandering forever along the pavement, looking for bones in butchers' shops, full of flies, and the butcher, with his fingers soaked in blood from chopping so much meat? Well, I didn't want to walk along any more grim pavements looking for a bone amongst the blood. Nor to see the corners, props for drunks, places where dogs pee. I wanted a joyful city, full of suns and moons. A secure city, like the house we had as children: with a sun at each door, a moon for each window and planets in the rooms. Do you remember it, Lilí? It had a labyrinth of laughter. Its kitchen was a crossroads; its garden, the bed of all rivers; and the whole of it, the birth of nations . . .

LIDIA: A secure home, Muni! That's exactly what I wanted . . . And you know, they took me to a strange house and I found nothing there but clocks and some eyes without eyelids, which watched for years. I polished the floors, in order not to see the thousands of dead words the maids swept in the mornings. They polished the mirrors, to drive away our hostile looks. I was expecting that one morning the loving image would arise from its quicksilver. I would open books, in order to open up avenues in that circular inferno. I embroidered serviettes, with intertwined initials, to find the unbreakable magic thread which makes two names one . . .

MUNI: I know, Lilí.

LIDIA: But everything was in vain. The angry eyes never stopped looking at me. If I could find the spider which lived in my house, I would say to myself, with its invisible thread linking flower to light, apple to perfume, woman to man, I would sew beautiful eyelids on to these eyes which would look at me, and this house would enter the solar order. Each balcony would be a different country; its furniture would flower; sprinklers would sprout from its glasses; from the sheets, magic carpets to travel through a dream; from my children's hands, castles, flags and battles . . . but I couldn't find the thread, Muni . . .

MUNI: You told me at the polic station. In that strange yard, far away for ever from that other yard in whose sky a belltower told us the hours we had left to play.

LIDIA: Yes, Muni. And in you I kept the last day we were children. Afterwards there was only one: Lidia sitting facing the wall, waiting . . .

MUNI: I couldn't grow either, live on the the corners. I wanted my house . . .

EVA: So did I, Muni, my son, I wanted a secure home. So secure that the sea could beat against it every night, bang! bang!, and it would laugh with the laughter of my father, full of fishes and nets.

CLEMENTE: Lilí, aren't you happy? You'll find the thread and you'll find the spider. Now your house is the centre of the sun, the heart of every star, the root of every grass, the most secure point of every rock.

MUNI: Yes, Lilí, you don't know it yet, but suddenly you don't need a house, nor do you need a river. We shall not swim in Mescal; we shall be Mescal.

GERTRUDIS: Sometimes you'll feel very cold; and you'll be the snow falling in an unfamiliar city, on to grey roofs and red caps.

CATALINA: What I like most is to be a sweet in a little girl's mouth, or a gold thistle, to make those who read by a window cry!

MUNI: Don't worry when your eyes begin to disappear, because then you'll be all the eyes of the dogs looking at absurd feet.

MAMÁ JESUSITA: Oh, I hope you never have to be the blind eyes of a blind fish in the deepest sea. You don't know what a terrible feeling it gave me: it was like seeing and not seeing.

CATALINA (*laughing and clapping*): You also got very scared when you were the worm going in and out of your mouth!

VICENTE: For me, the worst thing was being the murderer's dagger.

MAMÁ JESUSITA: Now the rats will come back. Don't scream when you yourself scurry across your own face.

CLEMENTE: Don't tell her that, you'll scare her. It's frightening learning to be all those things.

GERTRUDIS: Especially since you barely learn to be a man in the world.

LIDIA: And could I be a pine tree with a spider's nest and build a secure home?

CLEMENTE: Of course. And you'll be the pine tree and the steps and the fire.

LIDIA: And then?

MAMÁ JESUSITA: Then God will call us to His bosom.

CLEMENTE: After you've learned to be everything, St Michael's spear will appear, centre of the Universe. And under its light will emerge the divine host of angels and we will enter the celestial order.

MUNI: I want to be the fold in an angel's tunic!

MAMÁ JESUSITA: Your colour would go very well; it'll give some beautiful reflections. And what will I do, encased in this nightdress?

CATALINA: I want to be God the Father's index finger!

EVERYONE IN CHORUS: Child!

EVA: And I a wave splattered with salt, transformed into a cloud!

LIDIA: And I the Virgin's seamstress's fingers, embroidering . . . embroidering . . .!

GERTRUDIS: And I the music from St Cecilia's harp.

VICENTE: And I the fury of St Gabriel's sword.

CLEMENTE: And I a particle of St Peter's stone.

CATALINA: And I the window which looks out on the world!

MAMÁ JESUSITA: There will be no more world, Catita, because we'll be all these things after the Last Judgement.

CATALINA (*crying*): There'll be no more world? And when am I going to see it? I haven't seen anything. I haven't even learned how to spell. I want there to be a world.

VICENTE: See it now, Catita!

(*In the distance we hear a trumpet.*)

MAMÁ JESUSITA: Jesus, Virgin most pure! The trumpet of the Last Judgement! And me in my nightdress! Forgive me, Lord, this immodesty . . .

LIDIA: No, Granny. It's the curfew. There's a barracks next to the pantheon.

MAMÁ JESUSITA: Ah! Yes, they've told me before, and I always forget. Whoever thought of putting a barracks so close to us? What a government! It's so confusing!

VICENTE: The curfew! I'm off. I'm the wind. The wind which opens all the doors I never opened, which climbs in a whirlwind the steps I never climbed, which runs through the streets new to my officer's uniform and lifts the skirts of beautiful unknown women . . . Ah, freshness! *(He disappears.)*

MAMÁ JESUSITA: Rascal!

CLEMENTE: Ah, rain on water! *(He disappears.)*

MUNI: Can you hear that? A dog is howling. Ah, melancholy! *(He disappears.)*

CATALINA: The table at which nine children are eating! I'm the game! *(She disappears.)*

MAMÁ JESUSITA: The fresh heart of a lettuce! *(She disappears.)*

EVA: Lightning sinking into the black sea! *(She disappears.)*

LIDIA: A secure home! That's what I am! The slabs of my tomb! *(She disappears.)*

The Man Who Did Not Believe in Miracles

Chu Fu Tze, who didn't believe in miracles, died; his son-in-law was watching over him. At dawn the coffin rose up of its own accord and hung noiselessly in the air, two feet from the ground. The pious son-in-law was terrified. 'Oh venerable father-in-law,' he begged. 'Don't destroy my faith that miracles are possible.' At that point the coffin descended slowly, and the son-in-law regained his faith.

—HERBERT A. GILES

Earth's Holocaust

Nathaniel Hawthorne *(1804-64) came from an old Puritan family and won acclaim for his sketches of New England life and his novel* The Scarlet Letter *(1850). He also wrote many imaginative stories such as 'Wakefield' and 'Mr Higginbotham's Catastrophe', which were enormously influential in the history of American writing.*

Once upon a time—but whether in the time past or time to come is a matter of little or no moment—this wide world had become so overburdened with an accumulation of wornout trumpery that the inhabitants determined to rid themselves of it by a general bonfire. The site fixed upon at the representation of the insurance companies, and as being as central a spot as any other on the globe, was one of the broadest prairies of the West, where no human habitation would be endangered by the flames, and where a vast assemblage of spectators might commodiously admire the show. Having a taste for sights of this kind, and imagining, likewise, that the illumination of the bonfire might reveal some profundity of moral truth heretofore hidden in mist or darnkess, I made it convenient to journey thither and be present. At my arrival, although the heap of condemned rubbish was as yet comparatively small, the torch had already been applied. Amid that boundless plain, in the dusk of the evening, like a far off star alone in the firmament, there was merely visible one tremulous gleam, whence none could have anticipated so fierce a blaze as was destined to ensue. With every moment, however, there came foot travellers, women holding up their aprons, men on horseback, wheelbarrows, lumbering baggage wagons, and other vehicles, great and small, and from far and near laden with articles that were judged fit for nothing but to be burned.

'What materials have been used to kindle the flame?' inquired I of a bystander; for I was desirous of knowing the whole process of the affair from beginning to end.

The person whom I addressed was a grave man, fifty years old or thereabout, who had evidently come thither as a looker on. He struck me immediately as having weighed for himself the true value of life and its circumstances, and therefore as feeling little personal interst in whatever judgment the world might form of them. Before answering my question, he looked me in the face by the kindling light of the fire.

'Oh, some very dry combustibles,' replied he, 'and extremely suitable to the purpose—no other, in fact, than yesterday's newspapers, last month's magazines, and last year's withered leaves. Here now comes some antiquated trash that will take fire like a handful of shavings.'

As he spoke some rough-looking men advanced to the verge of the bonfire, and threw in, as it appeared, all the rubbish of the herald's office—the blazonry of coat armor, the crests and devices of illustrious families, pedigrees that extended back, like lines of light, into the mist of the dark ages, together with stars, garters, and embroidered collars, each of which, as paltry a bawble as it might appear to be the uninstructed eye, had once possessed vast significance, and was still, in truth, reckoned among the most precious of moral or material facts by the worshippers of the gorgeous past. Mingled with this confused heap, which was tossed into the flames by armfuls at once, were innumerable badges of knighthood, comprising those of all the European soveriegnties, and Napoleon's decoration of the Legion of Honor, the ribbons of which were entangled with those of the ancient order of St Louis. There, too, were the medals of our own society of Cincinnati, by means of which, as history tells us, an order of hereditary knights came near being constituted out of the king quellers of the revolution. And besides, there were the patents of nobility of German counts and barons, Spanish grandees, and English peers, from the worm-eaten instruments signed by William the Conqueror down to the brand new parchment of the latest lord who has received his honors from the fair hand of Victoria.

At sight of the dense volumes of smoke, mingled with vivid jets of flame, that gushed and eddied forth from this immense pile of earthy distinctions, the multitude of plebeian spectators set up a joyous shout, and clapped their hands with an emphasis that made the welkin echo. That was their moment of triumph, achieved, after long ages, over creatures of the same clay and the same spiritual infirmities, who had dared to assume the privileges due only to Heaven's better workmanship. But now there rushed towards the blazing heap a grayhaired man, of stately presence, wearing a coat, from the breast of which a star, or other badge of rank, seemed to have been forcibly wrenched away. He had not the tokens of intellectual power in his face; but still there was the demeanor, the habitual and almost native dignity, of one who had been born to the idea of his own social superiority, and had never felt it questioned till that moment.

'People,' cried he, gazing at the ruin of what was dearest to his eyes with grief and wonder, but nevertheless with a degree of stateliness, — 'people, what have you done? This fire is consuming all that marked your advance from barbarism, or that could have prevented your relapse thither. We, the men of the privileged orders, were those who kept alive from age to age the old chivalrous spirit; the gentle and generous thought; the higher, the purer, the more refined and delicate life. With the nobles, too, you cast off the poet, the painter, the sculptor—all the beautiful arts; for we were their patrons, and created the atmosphere in which they flourish. In abolishing the majestic distinctions of rank, society loses not only its grace, but its steadfastness' —

More he would doubtless have spoken; but here there arose an outcry, sportive, contemptuous, and indignant, that altogether drowned the appeal of the fallen nobleman, insomuch that, casting one look of despair at his own half-burned pedigree, he shrunk back into the crowd, glad to shelter himself under his new-found insignificance.

'Let him thank his stars that we have not flung him into the same fire!' shouted a rude figure, spurning the embers with his foot. 'And henceforth let no man dare to show a piece of musty parchment as his warrant for lording it over his fellows. If he have strength of arm, well and good; it is one species of superiority. If he have wit, wisdom, courage, force of character, let these attributes do for him what they may; but from this day forward no mortal must hope for place and consideration by reckoning up the mouldy bones of his ancestors. That nonsense is done away.'

'And in good time,' remarked the grave observer by my side, in a low voice, however, 'if no worse nonsense comes in its place; but, at all events, this species of nonsense has fairly lived out its life.'

There was little space to muse or moralize over the embers of this time-honored rubbish; for, before it was half burned out, there came another multitude from beyond the sea, bearing the purple robes of royalty, and the crowns, globes, and sceptres of emperors and kings. All these had been condemned as useless bawbles, playthings at best, fit only for the infancy of the world or rods to govern and chastise it in its nonage, but with which universal manhood at its full-grown stature could no longer brook to be insulted. Into such contempt had these insignia now fallen that the gilded crown and tinselled robes of the player king from Drury Lane Theatre had been thrown in among the rest, doubtless as a mockery of his brother monarchs on the great stage of the world. It was a strange sight to discern the crown jewels of England glowing and flashing in the midst of the fire. Some of them had been delivered down from the time of the Saxon princes; others were purchased with vast revenues, or perchance ravished from the dead brows of the native potentates of Hindostan; and the whole now blazed with a dazzling lustre, as if a star had fallen in that spot and been shattered into fragments. The splendor of the ruined monarchy had no reflection save in those inestimable precious stones. But enough on this subject. It were but tedious to describe how the Emperor of Austria's mantle was converted to tinder, and how the posts and pillars of the French throne became a heap of coals, which it was impossible to distinguish from those of any other wood. Let me add, however, that I noticed one of the exiled Poles stirring up the bonfire with the Czar of Russia's sceptre, which he afterwards flung into the flames.

'The smell of singed garmets is quite intolerable here,' observed my new acquaintance, as the breeze enveloped us in the smoke of a royal wardrobe. 'Let us get to windward and see what they are doing on the other side of the bonfire.'

We accordingly passed around, and were just in time to witness the arrival of a vast procession of Washingtonians—as the votaries of temperance call themselves nowadays—accompanied by thousands of the Irish disciples of Father Mathew, with that great apostle at their head. They brought a rich contribution to the bonfire—being nothing less than all the hogsheads and barrels of liquor in the world, which they rolled before them across the prairie.

'Now, my children,' cried Father Mathew, when they reached the verge of the fire, 'one shove more, and the work is done. And now let us stand off and see Satan deal with his own liquor.'

Accordingly, having placed their wooden vessels within reach of the flames, the procession stood off at a safe distance, and soon beheld them burst into a blaze that reached the clouds and threatened to set the sky itself on fire. And well it might; for here was the whole world's stock of spirituous liqours, which, instead of kindling a frenzied light in the eyes of individual topers as of yore, soared upwards with a bewildering gleam that startled all mankind. It was the aggregate of that fierce fire which would otherwise have scorched the hearts of millions. Meantime numberless bottles of precious wine were flung into the blaze, which lapped up the contents as if it loved them, and grew, like other drunkards, the merrier and fiercer for what it quaffed. Never again will the insatiable thirst of the fire fiend be so pampered. Here were the treasures of famous bon vivants—liquors that had been tossed on ocean, and mellowed in the sun, and hoarded long in the recesses of the earth—the pale, the gold, the ruddy juice of whatever vineyards were most delicate—the entire vintage of Tokay—all mingling in one stream with the vile fluids of the common pothouse, and contributing to heighten the selfsame blaze. And while it rose in a gigantic spire that seemed to wave against the arch of the firmament and combine itself with the light of stars, the multitude gave a shout as if the broad earth were exulting in its deliverance from the curse of ages.

But the joy was not universal. Many deemed that human life would be gloomier than ever when that brief illumination should sink down. While the reformers were at work, I overheard muttered expostulations from several respectable gentlemen with red noses and wearing gouty shoes; and a ragged worthy, whose face looked like a hearth where the fire is burned out, now expressed his discontent more openly and boldly.

'What is this world good for,' said the last toper, 'now that we can never be jolly any more? What is to comfort the poor man in sorrow and perplexity? How is he to keep his heart warm against the cold winds of this cheerless earth? And what do you propose to give him in exchange for the solace that you take away? How are old friends to sit together by the fireside without a cheerful glass between them? A plague upon your reformation! It is a sad world, a cold world, a selfish world, a low world, not worth an honest fellow's living in, now that good fellowship is gone forever!'

This harangue excited great mirth among the bystanders; but, preposterous as was the sentiment, I could not help commiserating the forlorn condition of the last toper, whose boon companions had dwindled away from his side, leaving the poor fellow without a soul to countenance him in sipping his liquor, nor indeed any liquor to sip. Not that this was quite the true state of the case; for I had observed him at a critical moment filch a bottle of fourth-proof brandy that fell beside the bonfire and hide it in his pocket.

The spirituous and fermented liquors being thus disposed of, the zeal of the reformers next induced them to replenish the fire with all the boxes of tea and bags of coffee in the world. And now came the planters of Virginia, bringing their crops and tobacco. These, being cast upon the heap of inutility, aggregated it to the size of a mountain, and incensed the atmosphere with such potent fragrance that methought we should never draw pure breath again. The present sacrifice seemed to startle the lovers of the weed more than any that they had hitherto witnessed.

'Well, they've put my pipe out,' said an old gentleman flinging it into the flames in a pet. 'What is this world coming to? Everything rich and racy—all the

spice of life—is to be condemned as useless. Now that they have kindled the
bonfire, if these nonsensical reformers would fling themselves into it, all would
be well enough!'

'Be patient,' responded a staunch conservative; 'it will come to that in the
end. They will first fling us in, and finally themselves.'

From the general and systematic measures of reform I now turned to consider
the individual contributions to this memorable bonfire. In many instances these
were of a very amusing character. One poor fellow threw in his empty purse,
and another a bundle of counterfeit or insolvable bank notes. Fashionable ladies
threw in their last season's bonnets, together with heaps of ribbons, yellow lace,
and such other half-worn milliner's ware, all of which proved even more
evanescent in the fire than it had been in the fashion. A multitude of lovers of
both sexes—discarded maids or bachelors and couples mutually weary of one
another—tossed in bundles of perfumed letters and enamored sonnets. A hack
politician, being deprived of bread by the loss of office, threw in his teeth,
which happened to be false ones. The Rev. Sydney Smith—having voyaged
across the Atlantic for that sole purpose—came up to the bonfire with a bitter
grin and threw in certain repudiated bonds, fortified though they were with the
broad seal of a sovereign state. A little boy of five years old, in the premature
manliness of the present epoch, threw in his playthings; a college graduate his
diploma; an apothecary, ruined by the spread of homœopathy, his whole stock
of drugs and medicines; a physician his library; a parson his old sermons; and a
fine gentleman of the old school his code of manners, which he had formerly
written down for the benefit of the next generation. A widow, resolving on a
second marriage, slyly threw in her dead husband's miniature. A young man,
jilted by his mistress, would willingly have flung his own desperate heart into
the flames, but could find no means to wrench it out of his bosom. An American
author, whose works were neglected by the public, threw his pen and paper into
the bonfire, and betook himself to some less discouraging occupation. It
somewhat startled me to overhear a number of ladies, highly respectable in
appearance, proposing to fling their gowns and petticoats into the flames, and
assume the garb, together with the manners, duties, offices, and responsibili-
ties, of the opposite sex.

What favor was accorded to this scheme I am unable to say, my attention
being suddenly drawn to a poor, deceived, and half-delirious girl, who,
exclaiming that she was the most worthless thing alive or dead, attempted to cast
herself into the fire amid all that wrecked and broken trumpery of the world. A
good man, however, ran to her rescue.

'Patience, my poor girl!' said he, as he drew her back from the fierce embrace
of the destroying angel. 'Be patient, and abide Heaven's will. So long as you
possess a living soul, all may be restored to its first freshness. These things of
matter and creation of human fantasy are fit for nothing but to be burned when
once they have had their day; but your day is eternity!'

'Yes,' said the wretched girl, whose frenzy seemed now to have sunk down
into deep despondency—'yes and the sunshine is blotted out of it!'

It was now rumored among the spectators that all the weapons and munitions of war were to be thrown into the bonfire, with the exception of the world's stock of gunpowder, which, as the safest mode of disposing of it, had already been drowned in the sea. This intelligence seemed to awaken great diversity of opinion. The hopeful philanthropist esteemed it a token that the millennium was already come; while persons of another stamp, in whose view mankind was a breed of bulldogs, prophesied that all the old stoutness, fervor, nobleness, generosity, and magnanimity of the race would disappear—these qualities, as they affirmed, requiring blood for their nourishment. They comforted themselves, however, in the belief that the proposed abolition of war was impracticable for any length of time together.

Be that as it might, numberless great guns, whose thunder had long been the voice of battle—the artillery of the Armada, the battering trains of Marlborough, and the adverse cannon of Napoleon and Wellington—were trundled into the midst of the fire. By the continual addition of dry combustibles, it had now waxed so intense that neither brass nor iron could withstand it. It was wonderful to behold how these terrible instruments of slaughter melted away like playthings of wax. Then the armies of the earth wheeled around the mighty furnace, with their military music playing triumphant marches, and flung in their muskets and swords. The standard-bearers, likewise, cast one look upward at their banners, all tattered with shot holes and inscribed with the names of victorious fields; and, giving them a last flourish on the breeze, they lowered them into the flame, which snatched them upward in its rush towards the clouds. This ceremony being over, the world was left without a single weapon in its hands, except possibly a few old king's arms and rusty swords and other trophies of the Revolution in some of our state armories. And now the drums were beaten and the trumpets brayed all together, as a prelude to the proclamation of universal and eternal peace and the announcement that glory was no longer to be won by blood, but that it would henceforth be the contention of the human race to work out the greatest mutual good, and that beneficence, in the future annals of the earth, would claim the praise of valor. The blessed tidings were accordingly promulgated, and caused infinite rejoicings among those who had stood aghast at the horror and absurdity of war.

But I saw a grim smile pass over the seared visage of a stately old commander—by his warworn figure and rich military dress, he might have been one of Napoleon's famous marshals—who, with the rest of the world's soldiery, had just flung away the sword that had been familiar to his right hand for half a century.

'Ay! ay!' grumbled he. 'Let them proclaim what they please; but in the end, we shall find that all this foolery has only made more work for the armorors and cannon founders.'

'Why, sir,' exclaimed I, in astonishment, 'do you imagine that the human race will ever so far return on the steps of its past madness as to weld another sword or cast another cannon?'

'There will be no need,' observed, with a sneer, one who neither felt benevolence nor had faith in it. 'When Cain wished to slay his brother, he was at no loss for a weapon.'

'We shall see,' replied the veteran commander. 'If I am mistaken, so much the better; but in my opinion, without pretending to philosophize about the matter, the necessity of war lies far deeper than these honest gentlemen suppose. What! is there a field for all the petty disputes of individuals? and shall there be no great law court for the settlement of national difficulties? The battle field is the only court where such suits can be tried.'

'You forget, general,' rejoined I, 'that , in this advanced stage of civilization, Reason and Philanthropy combined will constitute just such a tribunal as is requisite.'

'Ah, I had forgotten that, indeed!' said the old warrior, as he limped away.

The fire was now to be replenished with materials that had hitherto been considered of even greater importance to the well being of society than the warlike munitions which we had already consumed. A body of reformers had travelled all over the earth in quest of the machinery by which the different nations were accustomed to inflict the punishment of death. A shudder passed through the multitude as these ghastly emblems were dragged forward. Even the flames seemed at first to shrink away, displaying the shape and murderous contrivance of each in a full blaze of light, which of itself was sufficient to convince mankind of the long and deadly error of human law. Those old implements of cruelty; those horrible monsters of mechanism; those inventions which seemed to demand something worse than man's natural heart to contrive, and which had lurked in the dusky nooks of ancient prisons, the subject of terror-stricken legend—were now brought forth to view. Headsmen's axes, with the rust of noble and royal blood upon them, and a vast collection of halters that had choked the breath of plebeian victims, were thrown in together. A shout greeted the arrival of the guillotine, which was thrust forward on the same wheels that had borne it from one to another of the blood-stained streets of paris. But the loudest roar of applause went up, telling the distant sky of the triumph of the earth's redemption, when the gallows made its appearance. An ill-looking fellow, however, rushed forward, and, putting himself in the path of the reformers, bellowed hoarsely, and fought with brute fury to stay their progress.

It was little matter of surprise, perhaps, that the executioner should thus do his best to vindicate and uphold the machinery by which he himself had his livelihood and worthier individuals their death; but it deserved special note that men of a far different sphere—even of that consecrated class in whose guardianship the world is apt to trust its benevolence—were found to take the hangman's view of the question.

'Stay, my brethren!' cried one of them. 'You are misled by a false philanthropy; you know not what to do. The gallows is a Heaven-ordained instrument. Bear it back, then, reverently, and set it up in its old place, else the world will fall to speedily ruin and desolation!'

'Onward! onward!' shouted a leader in the reform. 'Into the flames with the accursed instrument of man's blood policy! How can human law inculcate benevolence and love while it persists in setting up the gallows as its chief symbol? One heave more, good friends, and the world will be redeemed from its greatest error.'

A thousand hands, that nevertheless loathed the touch, now lent their assistance, and thrust the ominous burden far, far into the centre of the raging furnace. There its fatal and abhorred image was beheld, first black, then a red coal, then ashes.

'That was well done!' exclaimed I.

'Yes, it was well done,' replied, but with less enthusiasm than I expected, the thoughtful observer who was still at my side; 'well done, if the world be good enough for the measure. Death, however, is an idea that cannot easily be dispensed with in any condition between the primal innocence and that other p rity and perfection which perchance we are destined to attain after travelling round the full circle: but, at all events, it is well that the experiment should now be tried.'

'Too cold! too cold!' impatiently exclaimed the young and ardent leader in this triumph. 'Let the heart have its voice here as well as the intellect. And as for ripeness, and as for progress, let mankind always do the highest, kindest, noblest thing that, as any given period, it has attained the perception of; and surely that thing cannot be wrong nor wrongly timed.'

I know not whether it were the excitement of the scene, or whether the good people around the bonfire were really growing more enlightened every instant; but they now proceeded to measures in the full length of which I was hardly prepared to keep them company. For instance, some threw their marriage certificates into the flames, and declared themselves candidates for a higher, holier, and more comprehensive union than that which had subsisted from the birth of time under the form of the connubial tie. Others hastened to the vaults of banks and to the coffers of the rich—all of which were open to the first comer on this fated occasion—and brought entire bales of paper money to enliven the blaze, and tons of coin to be melted down by its intensity. Henceforth, they said, universal benevolence, uncoined and exhaustless, was to be the golden currency of the world. At this intelligence the bankers and speculators in the stocks grew pale, and a pickpocket, who had reaped a rich harvest among the crowd, fell down in a deadly fainting fit. A few men of business burned their daybooks and ledgers, the notes and obligations of their creditors, and all other evidences of debts due to themselves; while perhaps a somewhat larger number satisfied their zeal for reform with the sacrifice of any uncomfortable recollection of their own indebtment. There was then a cry that the period was arrived when the title deeds of landed property should be given to the flames, and the whole soil of the earth revert to the public, from whom it had been wrongfully abstracted and most unequally distributed among individuals. another party demanded that all written constitution, set forms of government, legislative acts, statute books, and everything else on which human invention had endeavoured to stamp its arbitrary laws, should at once be destroyed, leaving the consummated world as free as the man first created.

Whether any ultimate action was taken with regard to these propositions is beyond my knowledge; for, just then, some matters were in progress that concerned my sympathies more nearly.

'See! see! What heaps of books and pamphlets!' cried a fellow, who did not seem to be a lover of literature. 'Now we shall have a glorious blaze!'

'That's just the thing!' said a modern philosopher. 'Now we shall get rid of the weight of dead men's thought, which has hitherto pressed so heavily on the living intellect that it has been incompetent to any effectual self-exertion. Well done, my lads! Into the fire with them! Now you are enlightening the world indeed!'

'But what is to become of the trade?' cried a frantic bookseller.

'Oh, by all means, let them accompany their merchandise,' coolly observed an author. 'It will be a noble funeral pile!'

The truth was, that the human race had now reached a stage of progress so far beyond what the wisest and wittiest men of former ages had ever dreamed of that it would have been a manifest absurdity to allow the earth to be any longer encumbered with their poor achievements in the literary line. Accordingly a thorough and searching investigation had swept the booksellers' shops, hawkers' stands, public, and private libraries, and even the little book-shelf by the country fireside, and had brought the world's entire mass of printed paper, bound or in sheets, to swell the already mountain bulk of our illustrious bonfire. thick, heavy folios, containing the labours of lexicographers, commentators and encyclopaedists, were flung in, and falling among the embers with a leaden thump, smouldered away to ashes like rotten wood. The small, richly gilt French tomes of the last age, with the hundred volumes of Voltaire among them, went off in a brilliant shower of sparkles and little jets of flame; while the current literature of the same nation burned red and blue, and threw an infernal light over the visages of the spectators. converting them all to the aspect of party-coloured fiends. A collection of German stories emitted a scent of brimstone. The English standard authors made excellent fuel, generally exhibiting the properties of sound oak logs. Milton's works, in particular, sent up a powerful blaze, gradually reddening into a coal, which promised to endure longer than almost any other material of the pile. From Shakespeare there gushed a flame of such marvellous splendor that men shaded their eyes as against the sun's meridian glory; nor even when the works of his own elucidators were flung upon him did he cease to flash forth a dazzling radiance from beneath the ponderous heap. It is my belief that he is blazing as fervidly as ever.

'Could a poet but light a lamp at that glorious flame,' remarked I, 'he might then consume the midnight oil to some good purpose.'

'That is the very thing which modern poets have been too apt to do, or at least to attempt, answered a critic. 'The chief benefit to be expected from this conflagration of past literature undoubtedly is, that writers will henceforth be compelled to light their lamps at the sun or stars.'

'If they can reach so high,' said I, 'but that task requires a giant, who may afterwards distribute the light among inferior men. It is not every one that can seal the fire from heaven like Prometheus; but, when once he had done the deed, a thousand hearths were kindled by it.'

It amazed me much to observe how indefinite was the proportion between the physical mass of any given author and the property of brilliant and long-continued combustion. For instance, there was not a quarto volume of the last century—nor, indeed, of the present—that could compete in that particular with a child's little gilt-covered book, containing Mother Goose's melodies. *The Life and Death of Tom Thumb* outlasted the biography of Marlborough. An epic, indeed a dozen of them, was converted to white ashes before the single sheet of an old ballad was half consumed. In more than one case, too, when volumes of applauded verse proved incapable of anything better than a stifling smoke, an unregarded ditty of some nameless bard—perchance in the corner of a newspaper—soared up among the stars with a flame as brilliant as their own. Speaking of the properties of flame, methought Shelley's poetry emitted a purer light than almost any other productions of his day, contrasting beautifully with the fitful and lurid gleams and gushes of black vapor that flashed and eddied from the volumes of Lord Byron. As for Tom Moore, some of his songs diffused an odour like a burning pastil.

I felt particular interest in watching the combustion of American authors, and scrupulously noted by my watch the precise number of moments that changed most of them from shabbily-printed books to indistinguishable ashes. It would be invidious, however, if not perilous, to betray these awful secrets; so that I shall content myself with observing that it was not invariably the writer most frequent in the public mouth that made the most splendid appearance in the bonfire. I especially remember that a great deal of excellent inflammability was exhibited in a thin volume of poems by Ellery Channing; although, to speak the truth, there were certain portions that hissed and spluttered in a very disagreeable fashion. A curious phenomenon occurred in reference to several writers, native as well as foreign. Their books, though of highly respectable figure, instead of bursting into a blaze, or even smouldering out their substance in smoke, suddenly melted away in a manner that proved them to be ice.

If it be no lack of modesty to mention my own works, it must here be confessed that I looked for them with fatherly interest, but in vain. Too probably they were changed to vapor by the first action of the heat; at best, I can only hope that, in their quiet way, they contributed a glimmering spark or two to the splendor of the evening.

'Alas! and woe is me! thus bemoaned himself a heavy-looking gentleman in green spectacles. 'The world is utterly ruined, and there is nothing to live for any longer. The business of my life is snatched from me. Not a volume to be had for love or money!'

'This,' remarked the sedate observer beside me, 'is a bookworm—one of those men who are born to gnaw dead thoughts. His clothes, you see, are covered with the dust of libraries. He has no inward fountain of ideas; and, in good earnest, now that the old stock is abolished, I do not see what is to become of the poor fellow. Have you no word of comfort for him?'

'My dear sir,' said I to the desperate bookworm, 'is not Nature better than a book? Is not the human heart deeper than any system of philosophy? Is not life replete with more instruction than past observers have found it possible to write down in maxims? Be of good cheer. The great book of Time is still spread wide open before us; and, if we read it aright, it will be to us a volume of eternal truth.'

'Oh, my books, my books, my precious printed books!' reiterated the forlorn bookworm. 'My only reality was a bound volume; and now they will not leave me even a shadowy pamphlet!'

In fact, the last remnant of the literature of all the ages was now descending upon the blazing heap in the shape of a cloud of pamphlets from the press of the New World. These likewise were consumed in the twinkling of an eye, leaving the earth, for the first time since the days of Cadmus, free from the plague of letters—an enviable field for the authors of the next generation.

'Well, and does anything remain to be done?' inquired I somewhat anxiously. 'Unless we set fire to the earth itself, and then leap boldly off into infinite space, I know not that we can carry reform to any farther point.'

'You are vastly mistaken, my good friend,' said the observer. 'Believe me, the fire will not be allowed to settle down without the addition of fuel that will startle many persons who have lent a willing hand thus far.'

Nevertheless there appeared to be a relaxation of effort for a little time, during which, probably, the leaders of the movement were considering what should be done next. In the interval, a philosopher threw his theory into the flames—a sacrifice which, by those who knew how to estimate it, was pronounced the most remarkable that had yet been made. The combustion, however, was by no means brilliant. Some indefatigable people, scorning to take a moment's ease, now employed themselves in collecting all the withered leaves and fallen boughs of the forest, and thereby recruited the bonfire to a greater height than ever. But this was mere by-play.

'Here comes the fresh fuel that I spoke of,' said my companion.

'To my astonishment, the persons who now advanced into the vacant space around the mountain fire bore surplices and other priestly garments, mitres, crosiers, and a confusion of Popish and Protestant emblems, with which it seemed their purpose to consummate the great act of faith. Crosses from the spires of old cathedrals were cast upon the heap with as little remorse as if the reverence of centuries, passing in long array beneath the lofty towers, had not looked up to them as the holiest of symbols. The font in which infants were consecrated to God, the sacramental vessels whence piety received the hallowed draught, were given to the same destruction. Perhaps it most nearly touched my heart to see among these devoted relics fragments of the humble communion tables and undecorated pulpits which I recognized as having been torn from the meeting-houses of New England. Those simple edifices might have been permitted to retain all of sacred embellishment that their Puritan founders had bestowed, even though the mighty structure of St Peter's had sent it spoils to the fire of this terrible sacrifice. Yet I felt that these were but the externals of religion, and might most safely be relinquished by spirits that best knew their deep significance.

'All is well,' said I, cheerfully. 'The woodpaths shall be the aisles of our cathedral—the firmament itself shall be its ceiling. What needs an earthly roof between the Deity and his worshippers? Our faith can well afford to lose all the drapery that even the holiest men have thrown around it, and be only the more sublime in its simplicity.'

'True,' said my companion; 'but will they pause here?'

The doubt implied in his question was well founded. In the general destruction of books already described, a holy volume, that stood apart from the catalogue of human literature, and yet, in one sense, was at its head, had been spared. But the Titan of innovation—angel or fiend, double in his nature, and capable of deeds befitting both characters—at first shaking down only the old and rotten shapes of things, had now, as it appeared, laid his terrible hand upon the main pillars which supported the whole edifice of our moral and spiritual state. The inhabitants of the earth had grown too enlightened to define their faith within a form of words, or to limit the spiritual by any analogy to our material existence. Truths which the heavens trembled at were now but a fable of the world's infancy. Therefore, as the final sacrifice of human error, what else remained to be thrown upon the embers of that awful pile except the book which, though a celestial revelation to past ages, was but a voice from a lower sphere as regarded the present race of man? It was done! Upon the blazing heap of falsehood and wornout truth—things that the earth had never needed, or had ceased to need, or had grown childishly weary of—fell the ponderous church Bible, the great old volume that had lain so long on the cushion of the pulpit, and whence the pastor's solemn voice had given holy utterance on so many a Sabbath day. There, likewise, fell the family Bible, which the long-buried patriarch had read to his children—in prosperity or sorrow, by the fireside and in the summer shade of trees—and had bequeathed downward as the heirloom of generations. There fell the bosom Bible, the little volume that had been the soul's friend of some sorely-tried child of dust, who thence took courage, whether his trial were for life or death, steadfastly confronting both in the strong assurance of immortality.

All these were flung into the fierce and rioutous blaze; and then a mighty wind came roaring across the plain with a desolate howl, as if it were the angry lamentation of the earth for the loss of heaven's sunshine; and it shook the gigantic pyramid of flame and scattered the cinders of half-consumed abominations around the spectators.

'This is terrible!' said I, feeling that my cheek grew pale, and seeing a like change in the visages about me.

'Be of good courage yet,' answered the man with whom I had so often spoken. He continued to gaze steadily at the spectacle with a singular calmness, as if it concerned him merely as an observer. 'Be of good courage, nor yet exult too much; for there is far less both of good and evil in the effect of this bonfire than the world might be willing to believe.'

'How can that be?' exclaimed I, impatiently. 'Has it not consumed everything? Has it not swallowed up or melted down every human or divine appendage of our mortal state that had substance enough to be acted on by fire?

Will there be anything left us tomorrow morning better or worse than a heap of embers and ashes?'

'Assuredly there will,' said my grave friend. 'Come hither tomorrow morning, or whenever the combustible portion of the pile shall be quite burned out, and you will find among the ashes everything really valuable that you have seen cast into the flames. Trust me, the world of tomorrow will again enrich itself with the gold and diamonds which have been cast off by the world of today. Not a truth is destroyed nor buried so deep among the ashes but is will be raked up at last.'

This was a strange assurance. Yet I felt inclined to credit it, the more especially as I beheld among the wallowing flames a copy of the Holy Scriptures, the pages of which, instead of being blackened into tinder, only assumed a more dazzling whiteness as the finger marks of human imperfection were purified away. Certain marginal notes and commentaries, it is true, yielded to the intensity of the fiery test, but without detriment to the smallest syllable that had flamed from the pen of inspiration.

'Yes; there is the proof of what you say,' answered I, turning to the observer; but if only what is evil can feel the action of the fire, then, surely, the conflagration has been of inestimable utility. Yet, if I understand aright, you intimate a doubt whether the world's expectation of benefit would be realized by it.'

'Listen to the talk of these worthies,' said he, pointing to a group in front of the blazing pile; 'possibly they may teach you something useful without intending it.'

The persons whom he indicated consisted of that brutal and most earthly figure who had stood forth so furiously in defence of the gallows—the hangman, in short—together with the last thief and the last murderer all three of whom were clustered about the last toper. The latter was liberally passing the brandy bottle, which he had rescued from the general destruction of wines and spirits. This little convivial party seemed at the lowest pitch of despondency, as considering that the purified world must needs be utterly unlike the sphere that they had hitherto known, and therefore but a strange and desolate abode for gentlemen of their kidney.

'The best counsel for all of us is,' remarked the hangman, 'that, as soon as we have finished the last drop of liquor, I help you, my three friends, to a comfortable end upon the nearest tree, and then hang myself on the same bough. This is no world for us any longer.'

'Poh, poh, my good fellows!' said a dark-complexioned personage, who now joined the group—his complexion was indeed fearfully dark, and his eyes glowed with a redder light than that of the bonfire; 'be not so cast down, my dear friends; you shall see good days yet. There's one thing that these wiseacres have forgotten to throw into the fire, and without which all the rest of the conflagration is just nothing at all; yes, though they had burned the earth itself to a cinder.'

'And what may that be?' eagerly demanded the last murderer.

'What but the human heart itself?' said the dark-visaged stranger with a portentuous grin. 'And, unless they hit upon some method of purifying that foul cavern, forth from it will reissue all the shapes of wrong and misery—the same old shapes or worse ones—which they have taken such a vast deal of trouble to consume to ashes. I have stood by this livelong night and laughed in my sleeve at the whole business. Oh, take my word for it, it will be the old world yet!'

This brief conversation supplied me with a theme for lengthened thought. How sad a truth, if true it were, that man's agelong endeavour for perfection had served only to render him the mockery of the evil principle, from the fatal circumstance of an error at the very root of the matter! The heart, the heart— there was the little yet boundless sphere wherein existed the original wrong of which the crime and misery of this outward world were merely types. Purify that inward sphere, and the many shapes of evil that haunt the outward, and which now seem almost our only realities, will turn to shadowy phantoms and vanish of their own accord; but if we go no deeper than the intellect, and strive, with merely that feeble instrument, to discern and rectify what is wrong, our whole accomplishment will be a dream, so unsubstantial that it matters little whether the bonfire, which I have so faithfully described, were what we choose to call a real event and a flame that would scorch the finger, or only a phosphoric radiance and a parable of my own brain.

Ending for a Ghost Story

I. A. Ireland, *English savant born in Hanley in 1871. He claimed descent from the infamous impostor William H. Ireland, who had invented an ancestor, Wiliam Henrye Irlaunde, to whom Shakespeare had allegedly bequeathed his manuscripts. He published* A Brief History of Nightmares *(1899),* Spanish Literature *(1911),* The Tenth Book of Annals of Tacitus, newly done into English *(1911).*

'How eerie!' said the girl, advancing cautiously. And what a heavy door!' She touched it as she spoke and it suddenly swung to with a click.

'Good Lord!' said the man, 'I don't believe there's a handle inside. Why, you've locked us both in!'

'Not both of us. Only one of us,' said the girl, and before his eyes she passed straight through the door, and vanished.

The Monkey's Paw

W. W. Jacobs, *English humorist and prolific short-story writer, born in 1843, died in 1943. His works include* Many Cargoes *(1896),* The Skipper's Wooing *(1911)* and Sea Whispers *(1926).*

I

'Without, the night was cold and wet, but in the small parlour of Laburnum Villa the blinds were drawn and the fire burned brightly. Father and son were at chess; the former, who possessed ideas about the game involving radical changes, putting his king into such sharp and unnecessary perils that it even provoked comment from the white-haired old lady knitting placidly by the fire.

'Hark at the wind', said Mr White, who, having seen a fatal mistake after it was too late, was amiably desirous of preventing his son from seeing it.

'I'm listening,' said the latter, grimly surveying the board as he stretched out his hand. 'Check.'

'I should hardly think that he'd come tonight,' said his father, with his hand poised over the board.

'Mate,' replied the son.

'That's the worst of living so far out,' bawled Mr White, with sudden and unlooked-for violence; 'of all the beastly, slushy, out-of-the-way places to live in, this is the worst. Path's a bog, and the road's a torrent. I don't know what people are thinking about. I suppose because only two houses in the road are let, they think it doesn't matter.'

'Never mind, dear,' said his wife soothingly; 'perhaps you'll win the next one.'

Mr White looked up sharply, just in time to intercept a knowing glance between mother and son. The words died away on his lips, and he hid a guilty grin in his thin grey beard.

'There he is,' said Herbert White, as the gate banged to loudly and heavy footsteps came towards the door.

The old man rose with hospitable haste, and opening the door, was heard condoling with the new arrival. The new arrival also condoled with himself, so that Mrs White said, 'Tut, tut!' and coughed gently as her husband entered the room, followed by a tall, burly man, beady of eye and rubicund of visage.

'Sergeant-Major Morris,' he said, introducing him.

'The sergeant-major shook hands, and taking the proffered seat by the fire, watched contentedly while his host got out whisky and tumblers and stood a small copper kettle on the fire.

At the third glass his eyes got brighter, and he began to talk, the little family circle regarding with eager interest this visitor from distant parts, as he squared his broad shoulders in the chair and spoke of wild scenes and doughty deeds; of wars and plagues and strange peoples.

'Twenty-one years of it,' said Mr White, nodding at his wife and son. 'When he went away he was a slip of a youth in the warehouse. Now look at him.'

'He don't look to have taken much harm,' said Mrs White politely.

'I'd like to go to India myself,' said the old man, 'just to look round a bit, you know.'

'Better where you are,' said the sergeant-major, shaking his head. He put down the empty glass, and sighing softly, shook it again.

'I should like to see those old temples and fakirs and jugglers,' said the old man. 'What was that you started telling me the other day about a monkey's paw or something, Morris?'

'Nothing,' said the soldier hastily. 'Leastways nothing worth hearing.'

'Monkey's paw?' said Mrs White curiously.

'Well, it's just a bit of what you might call magic, perhaps,' said the sergeant-major offhandedly.

His three listeners leaned forward eagerly. The visitor absentmindedly put his empty glass to his lips and then set it down again. His host filled it for him.

'To look at,' said the sergeant-major, fumbling in his pocket, 'it's just an ordinary little paw, dried to a mummy.'

He took something out of his pocket and proffered it. Mrs White drew back with a grimace, but her son, taking it, examined it curiously.

'And what is there special about it?' inquired Mr White as he took it from his son, and having examined it, placed it upon the table.

'It had a spell put on it by an old fakir,' said the sergeant-major, 'a very holy man. He wanted to show that fate ruled people's lives, and that those who interfered with it did so to their sorrow. He put a spell on it so that three separate men could each have three wishes from it.'

His manner was so impressive that his hearers were conscious that their light laughter jarred somewhat.

'Well, why don't you have three, sir?' said Herbert White cleverly.

The soldier regarded him in the way that middle age is wont to regard presumptuous youth. 'I have,' he said quietly, and his blotchy face whitened.

'And did you really have the three wishes granted?' asked Mrs White.

'I did,' said the sergeant-major, and his glass tapped against his strong teeth.

'And has anybody else wished?' persisted the old lady.

'The first man had his three wishes. Yes,' was the reply; 'I don't know what the first two were, but the third was for death. That's how I got the paw.'

His tones were so grave that a hush fell upon the group.

'If you've had your three wishes, it's no good to you now, then, Morris,' said the old man at last. 'What do you keep it for?'

The soldier shook his head. 'Fancy, I suppose,' he said slowly. 'I did have some idea of selling it, but I don't think I will. It has caused enough mischief already. Besides, people won't buy. They think it's a fairy tale, some of them; and those who do think anything of it want to try it first and pay me afterward.'

'If you could have another three wishes,' said the old man, eyeing him keenly, 'would you have them?'

'I don't know,' said the other. 'I don't know.'

He took the paw, and dangling it between his forefinger and thumb, suddenly threw it upon the fire. White, with a slight cry, stooped down and snatched it off.

'Better let it burn,' said the soldier solemnly.

'If you don't want it, Morris,' said the other, 'give it to me.'

'I won't, said his friend doggedly. 'I threw it on the fire. If you keep it, don't blame me for what happens. Pitch it on the fire again like a sensible man.'

The other shook his head and examined his new possession closely. 'How do you do it?' he inquired.

'Hold it up in your right hand and wish aloud,' said the sergeant-major, 'but I warn you of the consequences.'

'Sounds like the *Arabian Nights*,' said Mrs White, as she rose and began to set the supper. 'Don't you think you might wish for four pairs of hands for me.'

Her husband drew the talisman from his pocket, and then all three burst into laughter as the sergeant-major, with a look of alarm on his face, caught him by the arm.

'If you must wish,' he said gruffly, 'wish for something sensible.'

Mr White dropped it back in his pocket, and placing chairs, motioned his friend to the table. In the business of supper the talisman was partly forgotten, and afterward the three sat listening in an enthralled fashion to a second instalment of the soldier's adventures in India.

'If the tale about the monkey's paw is not more truthful than those he has been telling us,' said Herbert, as the door closed behind their guest, just in time to catch the last train, 'we shan't make much out of it.'

'Did you give him anything for it, father?' inquired Mrs White, regarding her husband closely.

'A trifle,' said he, colouring slightly. 'He didn't want it, but I made him take it. And he pressed me again to throw it away.'

'Likely,' said Herbert, with pretended horror. 'Why, we're going to be rich, and famous, and happy. Wish to be an emperor, father, to begin with; then you can't be henpecked.'

He darted round the table, pursued by the maligned Mrs White armed with an antimacassar.

Mr White took the paw from his pocket and eyed it dubiously. 'I don't know what to wish for, and that's a fact,' he said slowly. 'It seems to me I've got all I want.'

'If you only cleared the house, you'd be quite happy, wouldn't you!' said Herbert, with his hand on his shoulder. 'Well, wish for two hundred pounds, then; that'll just do it.'

His father, smiling shamefacedly at his own credulity, held up the talisman, as his son, with a solemn face, somewhat marred by a wink at his mother, sat down at the piano and struck a few impressive chords.

'I wish for two hundred pounds,' said the old man distinctly.

A fine crash from the piano greeted the words, interrupted by a shuddering cry from the old man. His wife and son ran towards him.

'It moved,' he cried, with a glance of disgust at the object as it lay on the floor. 'As I wished, it twisted in my hand like a snake.'

'Well, I don't see the money,' said his son, as he picked it up and placed it on the table, 'and I bet I never shall.'

'It must have been your fancy, father,' said his wife, regarding him anxiously.

He shook his head. 'Never mind, though; there's no harm done, but it gave me a shock all the same.'

They sat down by the fire again while the two men finished their pipes. Outside, the wind was higher than ever, and the old man started nervously at the sound of a door banging upstairs. A silence unusual and depressing settled upon all three, which lasted until the old couple rose to retire for the night.

'I expect you'll find the cash tied up in a big bag in the middle of your bed,' said Herbert, as he bade them good night, 'and something horrible squatting up on top of the wardrobe watching you as you pocket you ill-gotten gains.'

He sat alone in the darkness, gazing at the dying fire, and seeing faces in it. The last face was so horrible and so simian that he gazed at it in amazement. It got so vivid that, with a little uneasy laugh, he felt on the table for a glass containing a little water to throw over it. His hand grasped the monkey's paw, and with a little shiver he wiped his hand on his coat and went up to bed.

II

In the brightness of the wintry sun next morning as it streamed over the breakfast table he laughed at his fears. There was an air of prosaic wholesomeness about the room which it had lacked on the previous night, and the dirty, shrivelled little paw was pitched on the side-board with a carelessness which betokened no great belief in its virtues.

'I suppose all old soldiers are the same,' said Mrs White. 'The idea of our listening to such nonsense! How could wishes be granted in these days? And if they could, how could two hundred pounds hurt you, father?'

'Might drop on his head from the sky,' said the frivolous Herbert.

'Morris said the things happened so naturally,' said his father, 'that you might if you so wished attribute it to coincidence.'

'Well, don't break into the money before I come back,' said Herbert as he rose from the table. 'I'm afraid it'll turn you into a mean, avaricious man, and we shall have to disown you.'

His mother laughed, and following him to the door, watched him down the road; and returning to the breakfast table, was very happy at the expense of her husband's credulity. All of which did not prevent her from scurrying to the door at the postman's knock, nor prevent her from referring somewhat shortly to retired sergeant-majors of bibulous habits when she found that the post brought a tailor's bill.

'Herbert will have some more of his funny remarks, I expect, when he comes home,' she said, as they sat at dinner.

'I dare say,' said Mr White, pouring himself out some beer; 'but for all that, the thing moved in my hand; that I'll swear to.'

'You thought it did,' said the old lady soothingly.

'I say it did,' replied the other. 'There was no thought about it; I had just—
What's the matter?'

His wife made no reply. She was watching the mysterious movements of a
man outside, who, peering in an undecided fashion at the house, appeared to be
trying to make up his mind to enter. In mental connexion with the two hundred
pound, she noticed that the stranger was well dressed, and wore a silk hat of
glossy newness. Three times he paused at the gate, and then walked on again.
The fourth time he stood with his hand upon it, and then with sudden
resolution flung it open and walked up the path. Mrs White at the same moment
placed her hands behind her, and hurriedly unfastening the strings of her apron,
put that useful article of apparel beneath the cushion of her chair.

She brought the stranger, who seemed ill at ease, into the room. He gazed at
her furtively, and listened in a preoccupied fashion as the old lady apologized for
the appearance of the room, and her husband's coat, a garment which he usually
reserved for the garden. She then waited as patiently as her sex would permit for
him to broach his business, but he was at first strangely silent.

'I—was asked to call,' he said at last, and stooped and picked a piece of cotton
from his trousers. 'I come from "Maw and Meggins".'

The old lady started. 'Is anything the matter?' she asked breathlessly. 'Has
anything happened to Herbert? What is it? What is it?'

Her husband interposed. 'There, there, mother,' he said hastily. 'Sit down,
and don't jump to conclusions. You've not brought bad news, I'm sure, sir,' and
he eyed the other wistfully.

'I'm sorry—' began the visitor.

'Is he hurt?' demanded the mother wildly.

The visitor bowed in assent. 'Badly hurt,' he said quietly, 'but he is not in any
pain.'

'Oh, thank God!' said the old woman, clasping her hands. 'Thank God for
that! Thank—'

She broke off suddenly as the sinister meaning of the assurance dawned upon
her and she saw the awful confirmation of her fears in the other's averted face.
She caught her breath, and turning to her slow-witted husband, laid her
trembling old hand upon his. There was a long silence.

'He was caught in the machinery,' said the visitor at length in a low voice.

'Caught in the machinery,' repeated Mr White, in a dazed fashion, 'yes.'

He sat staring blankly out of the window, and taking his wife's hand between
his own, pressed it as he had been wont to do in their old courting days nearly
forty years before.

'He was the only one left to us,' he said, turning gently to the visitor. 'It is
hard.'

The other coughed, and rising, walked slowly to the window. 'The firm
wished me to convey their sincere sympathy with you in your great loss,' he
said, without looking round. 'I beg that you will underatand I am only their
servant and merely obeying orders.'

There was no reply; the old woman's face was white, her eyes staring, and her breath inaudible; on the husband's face was a look such as his friend the sergeant might have carried into his first action.

'I was to say that Maw and Meggins disclaim all responsibility,' continued the other. 'They admit no liability at all, but in consideration of your son's services, they wish to present you with a certain sum as compensation.'

Mr White dropped his wife's hand, and rising to his feet, gazed with a look of horror at his visitor. His dry lips shaped the words, 'How much?'

'Two hundred pounds,' was the answer.

Unconscious of his wife's shriek, the old man smiled faintly, put out his hands like a sightless man, and dropped, a senseless heap to the floor.

III

In the huge new cemetery, some two miles distant, the old people buried their dead, and came back to the house steeped in shadow and silence. It was all over so quickly that at first they could hardly realize it, and remained in a state of expectation as though of something else to happen—something else which was to lighten this load, too heavy for old hearts to bear.

But the days passed, and expectation gave place to resignation—the hopeless resignation of the old, sometimes miscalled apathy. Sometimes they hardly exchanged a word, for now they had nothing to talk about, and their days were long to weariness.

It was about a week after that the old man, waking suddenly in the night, stretched out his hand and found himself alone. The room was in darkness, and the sound of subdued weeping came from the window. He raised himself in bed and listened.

'Come back,' he said tenderly. 'You will be cold.'

'It is colder for my son,' said the old woman, and wept afresh.

The sound of her sobs died away on he ears. The bed was warm, and his eyes heavy with sleep. He dozed fitfully, and then slept until a sudden wild cry from his wife awoke him with a start.

'The paw!' she cried wildly. 'The monkey's paw!'

He started up in alarm. 'Where? Where is it? What's the matter?'

She came stumbling across the room toward him. 'I want it,' she said quietly. 'You've not destroyed it?'

'It's in the parlour, on the bracket,' he replied, marvelling. 'Why?'

She cried and laughed together, and bending over, kissed his cheek.

'I only just thought of it,' she said hysterically. 'Why didn't I think of it before? Why didn't *you* think of it?'

'Think of what?' he questioned.

'The other two wishes,' she replied rapidly. 'We've only had one.'

'Was not that enough?' he demanded fiercely.

'No,' she cried triumphantly; 'We'll have one more. Go down and get it quickly, and wish our boy alive again.'

The man sat up in bed and flung the bedclothes from his quaking limbs. 'Good God, you are mad!' he cried, aghast.

'Get it,' she panted; 'get it quickly, and wish—Oh, my boy, my boy!'

Her husband struck a match and lit the candle. 'Get back to bed,' he said unsteadily. 'You don't know what you are saying.'

'We had the first wish granted,' said the old woman feverishly; 'why not the second?'

'A coincidence,' stammered the old man.

'Go and get it and wish,' cried his wife, quivering with excitement.

The old man turned and regarded her, and his voice shook. 'He has been dead ten days, and besides he—I would not tell you else, but—I could only recognize him by his clothing. If he was too terrible for you to see then, how now?'

'Bring him back,' cried the old woman, and dragged him towards the door. 'Do you think I fear the child I have nursed?'

He went down in the darkness, and felt his way to the parlour, and then to the mantelpiece. The talisman was in its place, and a horrible fear that the unspoken wish might bring his mutilated son before him ere he could escape from the room seized upon him, and he caught his breath as he found that he had lost the direction of the door. His brow cold with sweat, he felt his way round the table, and groped along the wall until he found himself in the small passage with the unwholesome thing in his hand.

Even his wife's face seemed changed as he entered the room. It was white and expectant, and to his fears seemed to have an unnatural look upon it. He was afraid of her.

'*Wish!*' she cried, in a strong voice.

'It is foolish and wicked,' he faltered.

'*Wish!*' repeated his wife.

He raised his hand. 'I wish my son alive again.'

The talisman fell to the floor, and he regarded it fearfully. Then he sank trembling into a chair as the old woman, with burning eyes, walked to the window and raised the blind.

He sat until he was chilled with the cold, glancing occasionally at the figure of the old woman peering through the window. The candle-end, which had burned below the rim of the china candle-stick, was throwing pulsating shadows on the ceiling and walls, until, with a flicker larger than the rest, it expired. The old man, with an unspeakable sense of relief at the failure of the talisman, crept back to his bed, and a minute or two afterward the old woman came silently and apathetically beside him.

Neither spoke, but lay silently listening to the ticking of the clock. A stair creaked, and a squeaky mouse scurried noisily through the wall. The darkness was oppressive, and after lying for some time screwing up his courage, he took the box of matches, and striking one, went downstairs for a candle.

At the foot of the stairs the match went out, and he paused to strike another; and at the same moment a knock, so quiet and stealthy as to be scarcely audible, sounded on the front door.

The matches fell from his hand and spilled in the passage. He stood motionless, his breath suspended until the knock was repeated. Then he turned and fled swiftly back to his room, and closed the door behind him. A third knock sounded through the house.

'*What's that?*' cried the old woman, starting up.

'A rat,' said the old man in shaking tones—'a rat. It passed me on the stairs.'

His wife sat up in bed listening. A loud knock resounded through the house.

'It's Herbert!' she screamed.'It's Herbert!'

She ran to the door, but her husband was before her, and catching her by the arm, held her tightly.

'What are you going to do?' he whispered hoarsely.

'It's my boy; it's Herbert!' she cried, struggling mechanically. 'I forgot it was two miles away. What are you holding me for? Let go. I must open the door.'

'For God's sake don't let it in,' cried the old man, trembling.

'You're afraid of your own son,' she cried, struggling. 'Let me go. I'm coming Herbert; I'm coming.'

There was another knock, and another. The old woman with a sudden wrench broke free and ran from the room. Her husband followed to the landing, and called after her appealingly as she hurried downstairs. He heard the chain rattle back and the bottom bolt drawn slowly and stiffly from the socket. Then the old woman's voice, strained and panting.

'The bolt,' she cried loudly. 'Come down. I can't reach it.'

But her husband was on his hands and knees groping wildly on the floor in search of the paw. If he could only find it before the thing outside got in. A perfect fusillade of knocks reverberated through the house, and he heard the scraping of a chair as his wife found the monkey's paw, and frantically breathed his third and last wish.

The knocking ceased suddenly, although the echoes of it were still in the house. He heard the chair drawn back, and the door opened. A cold wind rushed up the staircase, and a loud loud wail of disappointment and misery from his wife gave him courage to run down to her side, and then to the gate beyond. The street lamp flickering opposite shone on a quiet and deserted road.

What is a Ghost?

James Joyce, *Irish author, born in Dublin in 1882, died in Zurich in 1941. He was a brilliant technician, particularly with words. He published* Chamber Music *(1907),* Dubliners *(1914),* Portrait of the Artist as a Young Man *(1916),* Exiles *(1918),* Ulysses *(1921) and* Finnegans Wake *(1939).*

'What is a ghost? Stephen said with tingling energy. 'One who has faded into impalpabilty through death, through absence, through change of manners.'

May Goulding

SIMON

Think of your mother's people!

STEPHEN

Dance of death.

(Bang fresh barang bang of lacquey's bell, horse, nag, steer, piglings, Conmee on Christass, lame crutch and leg sailor in cockboat armfolded ropepulling hitching stamp hornpipe through and through. Baraabum! On nags hogs bellhorses Gadarene swine Corny in coffin steel shark stone onehandled Nelson two trickies Frauenzimmer plumstained from pram falling bawling. Gum he's a champion. Fuseblue peer from barrel rev. evensong Love on hackney jaunt Blazes blind coddoubled bicyclers Dilly with snowcake no fancy clothes. Then in last switchback lumbering up and down bump mashtub sort of viceroy and reine relish for tublumber bumpshire rose. Baraabum!

The couples fall aside. Stephen whirls giddily. Room whirls back. Eyes closed he totters. Red rails fly spacewards. Stars all around suns turn roundabout. Bright midges dance on walls. He stops dead.)

STEPHEN

Ho!

Stephen's mother, emaciated, rises stark through the floor, in leper grey with a wreath of faded orange blossoms and a torn bridal veil, her face worn and noseless, green with gravemould. Her hair is scant and lank. She fixes her bluecircled hollow eyesockets on Stephen and opens her toothless mouth uttering a silent word. A choir of virgins and confessors sing voicelessly.

THE CHOIR

Liliata rutilantium te confessorum . . .
Iubilantium te virginum . . .

(From the top of a tower Buck Mulligan, in particoloured jester's dress of puce and yellow and clown's cap with curling bell, stands gaping at her, a smoking buttered split scone in his hand.)

BUCK MULLIGAN

She's beastly dead. The pity of it! Mulligan meets the afflicted mother. *(he upturns his eyes)* Mercurial Malachi!

THE MOTHER

(with the subtle smile of death's madness) I was once the beautiful May Goulding. I am dead.

The Wizard Passed Over

Infante Don Juan Manuel, *Spanish prince, born in Escalona in 1282, died in Penafiel in 1349. He was the nephew of Alfonso X of Castile. A man of Latin culture and Islamic erudition, he is one of the fathers of Spanish prose. He wrote the* Libro de Patronio *(1128-35, translated into English by J. B. Trend in 1924).*

In the city of Santiago, there was a dean who had a burning desire to learn the art of magic. Hearing that don Illán of Toledo knew more about magic than anyone else, the dean went to Toledo in search of him.

The very morning he arrived, he went straight to don Illán's and found him reading in a room at the back of his house. Don Illán received the dean cordially and asked him to postpone telling him the object of his visit until after they had eaten. Showing his guest into pleasant quarters, don Illán said he felt very happy about the dean's visit. After their meal, the dean told don Illán why he had come, and he begged to be taught the craft of magic. Don Illán said that he already knew that his guest was a dean, a man of good standing and of good prospects, but that were he to teach him all his knowledge, the day might come when the dean would fail to repay his services—as men in high places are often wont to do. The dean swore that he would never forget Don Illán's bounty and that he would always be at his call. Once they came to an agreement, don Illán explained that the magic arts could not be learned save in a place of deep seclusion, and, taking the dean by the hand, he led him to the next room, in whose floor there was a large iron ring. Before this, however, he told the serving maid to prepare partridges for supper but not to put them on to roast until he so ordered.

Don Illán and his guest lifted the ring and went down a well-worn, winding stairway until it seemed to the dean they had gone down so far that the bed of the Tagus must now be above them. At the foot of the staircase was a cell, and in it were a library of books and a kind of cabinet with magic instruments. They were leafing through the books, when suddenly two men appeared bearing a letter for the dean, written by the bishop, his uncle, in which the bishop informed him that he was gravely ill, and that if the dean wanted to find him alive he should not tarry. The news was very upsetting to the dean—for one thing, because of his uncle's illness; for another, because he would be forced to interrupt his studies. In the end, choosing to stay, he wrote an apology and sent it to the bishop.

Three days passed, and there arrived several men in mourning bearing further letters for the dean, in which he read that the bishop had died, that a successor was being chosen, and that they hoped by the grace of God that the dean would be elected. The letters advised him to remain where he was, it seeming better that he be absent during his election.

Ten days elapsed, and two finely dressed squires came, throwing themselves down at the dean's feet and kissing his hands and greeting him as bishop. When don Illán saw these things, he turned to the new prelate with great joy and said that he thanked the Lord that such good news should have come to his house. He then asked for the now vacant deanery for his son. The bishop answered that he had already set aside the deanery for his own brother but that he would find the son some post in the Church, and he begged that they all three leave together for Santiago.

They made their way to the city of Santiago, where they were received with honours. Six months passed, and messengers from the pope came to the bishop, offering him the archbishopric of Toulouse and leaving in his hands the naming of a successor. When don Illán heard this, he reminded the archbishop of his old promise and asked for the vacated title for his son. The archbishop told him that he had already set aside the bishopric for his own uncle, his father's brother, but that as he had given his word to shed favour on don Illán, they should, together with the son, all leave for Toulouse. Don Illán had no recourse but to agree.

The three set out for Toulouse, where they were received with honours and Masses. Two years passed, and messengers from the pope came to the archbishop, elevating him to the cardinalate and leaving in his hands the naming of a successor. When don Illán learned this, he reminded the cardinal of his old promise and asked for the vacant title for his son. The cardinal told him that he had already set aside the archbishopric for his own uncle, his mother's brother—a good old man—but that if don Illán and his son were to accompany him to Rome, surely some favourable opportunity would present itself. Don Illán protested, but in the end he was forced to agree.

The three then set out for Rome, where they were received with honours, Masses, and processions. Four years elapsed, and the pope died, and our cardinal was elected to the papacy by all the other cardinals. Learning of this, don Illán kissed His Holiness's feet, reminded him of his old promise, and asked for the vacant cardinal's office for his son. The pope told don Illán that by now he was weary of his continued requests and that if he persisted in importuning him he would clap him in gaol, since he knew full well that don Illán was no more than a wizard and that in Toledo he had been a teacher of the arts of magic.

Poor don Illán could only answer that he was going back to Spain, and he asked the pope for something to eat during the long sea journey. Once more the pope refused him, whereupon don Illán (whose face had changed in a strange fashion) said in an unwavering voice, 'In that case, I shall have to eat the partridges that I ordered for tonight.'

The serving maid came forward, and don Illán ordered the partridges roasted. Immediately the pope found himself in the underground cell in Toledo, no more than dean of Santiago, and so taken aback with shame that he did not know what to say. Don Illán said that this test was sufficient, refused the dean his share of the partridges, and saw him to the door, where, taking leave of him with great courtesy, he wished him a safe journey home.

Josephine the Singer, or the Mouse Folk

Franz Kafka, *Austrian writer, born in Prague in 1883, died in Vienna in 1924. In all his books loneliness is a recurring theme; in almost all of them he dwells on the process of infinite and excruciating delay. His works include* Der Prozess *(1925; translated into English as* The Trial, *1933),* Der Schloss *(1926; translated into English as* The Castle, *1953),* Amerika *(1927) and many short stories, including the famous* Die Verwandlung *(1912; translated into English as* Metamorphosis *(1961).*

Our singer is called Josephine. Anyone who has not heard her does not know the power of song. There is no one but is carried away by her singing, a tribute all the greater as we are not in general a music-loving race. Tranquil peace is the music we love best; our life is hard, we are no longer able, even on occasions when we have tried to shake off the cares of daily life, to rise to anything so high and remote from our usual routine as music. But we do not much lament that; we do not get even so far; a certain practical cunning, which admittedly we stand greatly in need of, we hold to be our greatest distinction, and with a smile born of such cunning we are wont to console ourselves for all shortcomings, even supposing—only it does not happen—that we were to yearn once in a way for the kind of bliss which music may provide. Josephine is the sole exception; she has a love for music and knows too how to transmit it; she is the only one; when she dies, music—who knows for how long—will vanish from our lives.

I have often thought about what this music of hers really means. For we are quite unmusical; how is it that we understand Josephine's singing or, since Josephine denies that, at least think we can understand it. The simplest answer would be that the beauty of her singing is so great that even the most insensitive cannot be deaf to it, but this answer is not satisfactory. If it were really so, her singing would have to give one an immediate and lasting feeling of being something out of the ordinary, a feeling that from her throat something is sounding which we have never heard before and which we are not even capable of hearing, something that Josephine alone and no one else can enable us to hear. But in my opinion that is just what does not happen, I do not feel this and have never observed that others feel anything of the kind. Among intimates we admit freely to one another that Josephine's singing, as singing, is nothing out of the ordinary.

Is it in fact singing at all? Although we are unmusical we have a tradition of singing; in the old days our people did sing; this is mentioned in legends and some songs have actually survived, which, it is true, no one can now sing. Thus we have an inkling of what singing is, and Josephine's art does not really correspond to it. So is it singing at all? Is it not just a piping? And piping is something we all know about, it is the real artistic accomplishment of our people, or rather no mere accomplishment but a characteristic expression of our life. We all pipe, but of course no one dreams of making out that piping is an art, we pipe without thinking of it, indeed without noticing it, and there are even many among us who are quite unaware that piping is one of our characteristics. So if it were true that Josephine does not sing but only pipes and perhaps, as it seems to me at least, hardly rises above the level of our usual piping—yet, perhaps her strength is not even quite equal to our usual piping, whereas an ordinary farmhand can keep it up effortlessly all day long, besides doing his work—if that were all true, then indeed Josephine's alleged vocal skill might be disproved, but that would merely clear the ground for the real riddle which needs solving, the enormous influence she has.

After all, it is only a kind of piping that she produces. If you post yourself quite far away from her and listen, or, still better, put your judgment to the test, whenever she happens to be singing along with others, by trying to identify her voice, you will undoubtedly distinguish nothing but a quite ordinary piping tone, which at most differs a little from the others through being delicate or weak. Yet if you sit down before her, it is not merely a piping; to comprehend her art it is necessary not only to hear but to see her. Even if hers were only our usual workaday piping, there is first of all this peculiarity to consider, that here is someone making a ceremonial performance out of doing the usual thing. To crack a nut is truly no feat, so no one would ever dare to collect an audience in order to entertain it with nut-cracking. But if all the same one does do that and succeeds in entertaining the public, then it cannot be a matter of simple nut-cracking. Or it is a matter of nut-cracking, but it turns out that we have over-looked the art of cracking nuts because we were too skilled in it and that this newcomer to it first shows us its real nature, even finding it useful in making his effects to be rather less expert in nut-cracking than most of us.

Perhaps it is much the same with Josephine's singing; we admire in her what we do not at all admire in ourselves; in this respect, I may say, she is of one mind with us. I was once present when someone, as of course often happens, drew her attention to the folk piping everywhere going on, making only a modest reference to it, yet for Josephine that was more than enough. A smile so sarcastic and arrogant as she then assumed I have never seen; she, who in appearance is delicacy itself, conspicuously so even among our people who are prolific in such feminine types, seemed at that moment actually vulgar; she was at once aware of it herself, by the way, with her extreme sensibility, and controlled herself. At any rate she denies any connection between her art and ordinary piping. For those who are of the contrary opinion she has only contempt and probably unacknowledged hatred. This is not simple vanity, for the opposition, with which I too am half in sympathy, certainly admires her no less than the crowd does, but Josephine does not want mere admiration, she wants to be admired exactly in the way she prescribes, mere admiration leaves her cold. And when you take a seat before her, you understand her; opposition is possible only at a distance, when you sit before her, you know: this piping of hers is no piping.

Since piping is one of our thoughtless habits, one might think that people would pipe up in Josephine's audience too; her art makes us feel happy, and when we are happy we pipe; but her audience never pipes, it sits in mouselike stillness; as if we had become partakers in the peace we long for, from which our own piping at the very least holds us back, we make no sound. Is it her singing that enchants us or is it not rather the solemn stillness enclosing her frail little voice? Once it happened while Josephine was singing that some silly little thing in all innocence began to pipe up too. Now it was just the same as what we were hearing from Josephine; in front of us the piping sound that despite all rehearsal was still tentative and here in the audience the unselfconscious piping of a child; it would have been impossible to define the difference; but yet at once we hissed and whistled the interrupter down, although it would not really have been necessary, for in any case she would certainly have crawled away in fear and shame, whereas Josephine struck up her most triumphal notes and was quite beyond herself, spreading her arms wide and stretching her throat as high as it could reach.

That is what she is like always, every trifle, every casual incident, every nuisance, a creaking in the parquet, a grinding of teeth, a failure in the lighting incites her to heighten the effectiveness of her song; she believes anyhow that she is singing to deaf ears; there is no lack of enthusiasm and applause, but she has long learned not to expect real understanding, as she conceives it. So all disturbance is very welcome to her; whatever intervenes from outside to hinder the purity of her song, to be overcome with a slight effort, even with no effort at all, merely by confronting it, can help to awaken the masses, to teach them not perhaps understanding but awed respect.

And if small events do her such service, how much more do great ones. Our life is very uneasy, every day brings surprises, apprehensions, hopes, and terrors, so that it would be impossible for a single individual to bear it all did he not always have by day and night the support of his fellows; but even so it often becomes very difficult; frequently as many as a thousand shoulders are trembling under a burden that was really meant only for one pair. Then Josephine holds that her time has come. So there she stands, the delicate creature, shaken by vibrations especially below the breastbone, so that one feels anxious for her, it is as if she has concentrated all her strength on her song, as if from everything in her that does not directly subserve her singing all strength has been withdrawn, almost all power of life, as if she were laid bare, abandoned, committed merely to the care of good angels, as if while she is so wholly withdrawn and living only in her song a cold breath blowing upon her might kill her. But just when she makes such an appearance, we who are supposed to be her opponents are in the habit of saying: 'She can't even pipe; she has to put such a terrible strain on herself to force out not a song—we can't call it song—but some approximation to our usual customary piping.' So it seems to us, but this impression although, as I said, inevitable is yet fleeting and transient. We too are soon sunk in the feeling of the mass, which, warmly pressed body to body, listens with indrawn breath.

And to gather around her this mass of our people who are almost always on the run and scurrying hither and thither for reasons that are often not very clear, Josephine mostly needs to do nothing else than take up her stand, head thrown back, mouth half-open, eyes turned upwards, in the position that indicates her intention to sing. She can do this where she likes, it need not be a place visible a long way off, any secluded corner pitched on in a moment's caprice will serve as well. The news that she is going to sing flies around at once and soon whole processions are on the way there. Now, sometimes, all the same, obstacles intervene, Josephine likes best to sing just when things are most upset, many worries and dangers force us then to take devious ways, with the best will in the world we cannot assemble ourselves as quickly as Josephine wants, and on occasion she stands there in ceremonial state for quite a time without a sufficient audience—then indeed she turns furious, then she stamps her feet, swearing in most unmaidenly fashion; she actually bites. But even such behavour does no harm to her reputation; instead of curbing a little her excessive demands, people exert themselves to meet them; messengers are sent out to summon fresh hearers; she is kept in ignorance of the fact that this is being done; on the roads all around sentries can be seen posted who wave on newcomers and urge them to hurry; this goes on until at last a tolerably large audience is gathered.

What drives the people to make such exertions for Josephine's sake? This is no easier to answer than the first question about Josephine's singing, with which it is closely connected. One could eliminate that and combine them both in the second question, if it were possible to assert that because of her singing our people are unconditionally devoted to Josephine. But this is simply not the case; unconditional devotion is hardly known among us; ours are people who love slyness beyond everything, without any malice, to be sure, and childish whispering and chatter, innocent, superficial chatter, to be sure, but people of such a kind cannot go in for unconditional devotion, and that Josephine herself certainly feels, that is what she is fighting against with all the force of her feeble throat.

In making such generalized pronouncements, of course, one should not go too far, our people are all the same devoted to Josephine, only not unconditionally. For instance, they would not be capable of laughing at Josephine. It can be admitted: in Josephine there is much to make one laugh; and laughter for its own sake is never far away for us; in spite of all the misery of our lives quiet laughter is always, so to speak, at our elbows; but we do not laugh at Josephine. Many a time I have had the impression that our people interpret their relationship to Josephine in this way, that she, this frail creature, needing protection and in some way remarkable, in her own opinion remarkable for her gift of song, is entrusted to their care and they must look after her; the reason for this is not clear to anyone, only the fact seems to be established. But what is entrusted to one's care one does not laugh at; to laugh would be a breach of duty; the utmost malice which the most malicious of us wreak on Josephine is to say now and then: 'The sight of Josephine is enough to make one stop laughing.'

So the people look after Josephine much as a father takes into his care a child whose little hand—one cannot tell whether in appeal or command—is stretched out to him. One might think that our people are not fitted to exercise such paternal duties, but in reality they discharge them, at least in this case, admirably; no single individual could do what in this respect the people as a whole are capable of doing. To be sure, the difference in strength between the people and the individual is so enormous that it is enough for the nursling to be drawn into the warmth of their nearness and he is sufficiently protected. To Josephine, certainly, one does not dare mention such ideas. 'Your protection isn't worth an old song,' she says then. Sure, sure, old song, we think. And besides her protest is no real contradiction, it is rather a thoroughly childish way of doing, and childish gratitude, while a father's way of doing is to pay no attention to it.

Yet there is something else behind it which is not so easy to explain by this relationship between the people and Josephine. Josephine, that is to say, thinks just the opposite, she believes it is she who protects the people. When we are in a bad way politically or economically, her singing is supposed to save us, nothing less than that, and if it does not drive away the evil, at least gives us the strength to bear it. She does not put it in these words or in any other, she says very little anyhow, she is silent among the chatterers, but it flashes from her eyes, on her closed lips—few among us can keep their lips closed, but she can—it is plainly legible. Whenever we get bad news—and on many days bad news comes thick and fast at once, lies and half-truths included—she rises up at once, whereas usually she sits listlessly on the ground, she rises up and stretches her neck and tries to see over the heads of her flock like a shepherd before a thunderstorm. It is certainly a habit of children, in their wild, impulsive fashion, to make such claims, but Josephine's are not quite so unfounded as children's. True, she does not save us and she gives us no strength; it is easy to stage oneself as a savior of our people, inured as they are to suffering, not sparing themselves, swift in decision, well acquainted with death, timorous only to the eye in the atmosphere of reckless daring which they constantly breathe, and as prolific besides as they are bold—it is easy, I say, to stage oneself after the event as the savior of our people, who have always somehow managed to save themselves, although at the cost of sacrifices which make historians—generally speaking we ignore historical research entirely—quite horror-struck. And yet it is true that just in emergencies we hearken better than at other times to Josephine's voice. The menaces that loom over us make us quieter, more humble, more submissive to Josephine's domination; we like to come together, we like to huddle close to each other, especially on an occasion set apart from the troubles preoccupying us; it is as if we were drinking in all haste—yes, haste is necessary, Josephine too often forgets that—from a cup of peace in common before the battle. It is not so much a performance of songs as an assembly of the people, and an assembly where except for the small piping voice in front there is complete stillness; the hour is much too grave for us to waste it in chatter.

A relationship of this kind, of course, would never content Josephine. Despite all the nervous uneasiness that fills Josephine because her position has never been quite defined, there is still much that she does not see, blinded by her self-conceit, and she can be brought fairly easily to overlook much more, a swarm of flatterers is always busy about her to this end, thus really doing a public service—and yet to be only an incidental, unnoticed performer in a corner of an assembly of the people, for that, although in itself it would be no small thing, she would certainly not make us the sacrifice of her singing.

Nor does she need to, for her art does not go unnoticed. Although we are at bottom preoccupied with quite other things and it is by no means only for the sake of her singing that stillness prevails and many a listener does not even look up but buries his face in his neighbour's fur, so that Josephine up in front seems to be exerting herself to no purpose, there is yet something—it cannot be denied—that irresistably makes its way into us from Josephine's piping. This piping, which rises up where everyone else is pledged to silence, comes almost like a message from the whole people to each individual; Josephine's thin piping amidst the tumult of a hostile world. Josephine exerts herself, a mere nothing in voice, a mere nothing in execution, she asserts herself and gets across to us; it does us good to think of that. A really trained singer, if ever such a one should be found among us, we would certainly not endure at such a time and we should unanimously turn away from the senselessness of any such performance. May Josephine be spared from perceiving that the mere fact of our listening to her is proof that she is no singer. An intuition of it she must have, else why does she so passionately deny that we do listen, only she keeps on singing and piping her intuition away.

But there are other things she could take comfort from: we do really listen to her in a sense, probably much as one listens to a trained singer; she gets effects which a trained singer would try in vain to achieve among us and which are only produced precisely because her means are so inadequate. For this, doubtless, our way of life is mainly responsible.

Among our people there is no age of youth, scarcely the briefest childhood. Regularly, it is true, demands are put forward that the children should be granted a special freedom, a special protection, that their right to be a little carefree, to have a little senseless giddiness, a little play, that this right should be respected and the exercise of it encouraged; such demands are put forward and nearly everyone approves them, there is nothing one could approve of more, but there is also nothing, in the reality of our daily life, that is less likely to be granted, one approves these demands, one makes attempts to meet them, but soon all the old ways are back again. Our life happens to be such that a child, as soon as it can run about a little and a little distinguish one thing from another, must look after itself just like an adult; the areas on which, for economic reasons, we have to live in dispersion are too wide, our enemies too numerous, the dangers lying everywhere in wait for us too incalculable—we cannot shelter our children from the struggle for existence, if we did so, it would bring them to an early grave. These depressing considerations are reinforced by another, which is not depressing; the fertility of our race. One generation—and each is numerous—treads on the heels of another, the children have no time to be children. Other races may foster their children carefully, schools may be erected for their little ones, out of these schools the children may come pouring daily, the future of the race, yet among them it is always the same children that come out day after day for a long time. We have no schools, but from our race come pouring at the briefest intervals the innumerable swarms of our children, merrily lisping or chirping so long as they cannot yet pipe, rolling or tumbling along by sheer impetus so long as they cannot yet run, clumsily carrying everything before them by mass weight, so long as they cannot yet see, our children! And not the same children, as in those schools, no, always new children again and again, without end, without a break, hardly does a child appear than it is no more a child, while behind it new childish faces are already crowding so fast and so thick that they are indistinguishable, rosy with happiness. Truly, however delightful this may be and however much others may envy us for it, and rightly, we simply cannot give a real childhood to our children. And that has its consequences. A kind of unexpended ineradicable childishness pervades our people; in direct opposition to what is best in us, our infallible practical common sense, we often behave with the utmost foolishness, with exactly the same foolishness as children, senselessly, wastefully, grandiose-ly, irresponsibly, and all that often for the sake of some trivial amusement. And although our enjoyment of it cannot of course be so wholehearted as a child's enjoyment, something of this survives in it without a doubt. From this childishness of our people Josephine too has profited since the beginning.

Yet our people are not only childish, we are also in a sense prematurely old. Childhood and old age come upon us not as upon others. We have no youth, we are all at once grown-up, and then we stay grown-up too long, a certain weariness and hopelessness spreading from that leaves a broad trail through our people's nature, tough and strong in hope that it is in general. Our lack of musical gifts has surely some connection with this; we are too old for music, its excitement, its rapture do not suit our heaviness, wearily we wave it away; we content ourselves with piping; a little piping here and there, that is enough for us. Who knows, there may be talents for music among us; but if there were, the character of our people would suppress them before they could unfold. Josephine on the other hand can pipe as much as she will, or sing or whatever she likes to call it, that does not disturb us, that suits us, that we can well put up with; any music there may be in it is reduced to the least possible trace; a certain tradition of music is preserved, yet without making the slightest demand upon us.

But our people, being what they are, get still more than this from Josephine. At her concerts, especially in times of stress, it is only the very young who are interested in her singing as singing, they alone gaze in astonishment as she purses her lips, expels the air between her pretty front teeth, half dies in sheer wonderment at the sounds she herself is producing and after such a swooning swells her performance to new and more incredible heights, whereas the real mass of the people—this is plain to see—are quite withdrawn into themselves. Here in the brief intervals between their struggles our people dream, it is as if the limbs of each were loosened, as if the harried individual once in a while could relax and stretch himself at ease in the great, warm bed of the community. And into these dreams Josephine's piping drops note by note; she calls it pearl-like, we call it staccato; but at any rate here it is in its right place, as nowhere else, finding the moment wait for it as music scarcely ever does. Something of our poor brief childhood is in it, something of lost happiness that can never be found again, but also something of active daily life, of its small gaieties, unaccountable and yet springing up and not to be obliterated. And indeed this is all expressed not in full round tones but softly, in whispers, confidentially, sometimes a little hoarsely. Of course it is a kind of piping. Why not? Piping is our people's daily speech, only many a one pipes his whole life long and does not know it, where here piping is set free from the fetters of daily life and it sees too for a little while. We certainly should not want to do without these performances.

But from that point it is a long, long way to Josephine's claim that she gives us new strength and so on and so forth. For ordinary people, at least, not for her train of flatterers. 'What other explanation could there be?'—they say with quite shameless sauciness—'how else could you explain the great audiences, especially when danger is most imminent, which have even often enough hindered proper precautions being taken in time to avert danger.' Now, this last statement is unfortunately true, but can hardly be counted as one of Josephine's titles to fame, especially considering that when such large gatherings have been unexpectedly flushed by the enemy and many of our people left lying for dead, Josephine, who was responsible for it all, and indeed perhaps attracted the enemy by her piping, has always occupied the safest place and was always the first to whisk away quietly and speedily under cover of her escort. Still, everyone really knows that, and yet people keep running to whatever place Josephine decides on next, at whatever time she rises up to sing. One could argue from this that Josephine stands almost beyond the law, that she can do what she pleases, at the risk of actually endangering the community, and will be forgiven for everything. If this were so, even Josephine's claims would be entirely comprehensible, yes, in this freedom to be allowed her, this extraordinary gift granted to her and to no one else in direct contravention of the laws, one could see an admission of the fact that they marvel helplessly at her art, feel themselves unworthy of it, try to assuage the pity she rouses in them by making really desperate sacrifices for her and, to the same extent that her art is beyond their comprehension, consider her personality and her wishes to lie beyond their jurisdiction. Well, that is simply not true at all, perhaps as individuals the people may surrender too easily to Josephine, but as a whole they surrender unconditionally to no one, and not to her either.

For a long time back, perhaps since the very beginning of her artistic career, Josephine has been fighting for exemption from all daily work on account of her singing; she should be relieved of all responsibility for earning her daily bread and being involved in the general struggle for existence, which—apparently—should be transferred on her behalf to the people as a whole. A facile enthusiast—and there have been such—might argue from the mere unusualness of this demand, from the spiritual attitude needed to frame such a demand, that it has an inner justification. But our people draw other conclusions and quietly refuse it. Nor do they trouble much about disproving the assumptions on which it is based. Josephine argues, for instance, that the strain of working is bad for her voice, that the strain of working is of course nothing to the strain of singing, but it prevents her from being able to rest sufficiently after singing and to recuperate for more singing, she has to exhaust her strength completely and yet, in these circumstances, can never rise to the peak of her abilities. The people listen to her arguments and pay no attention. Our people, so easily moved, sometimes cannot be moved at all. Their refusal is sometimes so decided that even Josephine is taken aback, she appears to submit, does her proper share of work, sings as best she can, but all only for a time, then with renewed strength—for this purpose her strength seems inexhaustible—she takes up the fight again.

Now it is clear that what Josephine really wants is not what she puts into words. She is honourable, she is not work-shy, shirking in any case is quite unknown among us, if her petition were granted she would certainly live the same life as before, her work would not at all get in the way of her singing nor would her singing grow any better—what she wants is public, unambiguous, permanent recognition of her art, going far beyond any precedent so far known. But while almost everything else seems within her reach, this eludes her persistently. Perhaps she should have taken a different line of attack from the beginning, perhaps she herself sees that her approach was wrong, but now she cannot draw back, retreat would be self-betrayal, now she must stand or fall by her petition.

If she really had enemies, as she avers, they could get much amusement from watching this struggle, without having to lift a finger. But she has no enemies, and even though she is often criticized here and there, no one finds this struggle of hers amusing. Just because of the fact that the people show themselves here in their cold, judicial aspect, which is otherwise rarely seen among us. And however one may approve it in this case, the very idea that such an aspect might be turned upon oneself some day prevents amusement from breaking in. The important thing, both in the people's refusal and in Josephine's petition, is not the action itself, but the fact that the people are capable of presenting a stony, impenetrable front to one of their own, and that it is all the more impenetrable because in other respects they show an anxious paternal care, and more than paternal care, for this very member of the people.

Suppose that instead of the people one had an individual to deal with: one might imagine that this man had been giving in to Josephine all the time while nursing a wild desire to put an end to his submissiveness one fine day; that he had made superhuman sacrifices for Josephine in the firm belief that there was a natural limit to his capacity for sacrifice; yes, that he had sacrificed more than was needful merely to hasten the process, merely to spoil Josephine and encourage her to ask for more and more until she did indeed reach the limit with this last petition of hers; and that he then cut her off with a final refusal which was curt because long held in reserve. Now, this is certainly not how the matter stands, the people have no need of such guile, besides, their respect for Josephine is well tried and genuine, and Josephine's demands are after all so far-reaching that any simple child could have told her what the outcome would be; yet it may be that such considerations enter into Josephine's way of taking the matter and so add a certain bitterness to the pain of being refused.

But whatever her ideas on the subject, she does not let them deter her from pursuing the campaign. Recently she has even intensified her attack; hitherto she has used only words as her weapons but now she is beginning to have recourse to other means, which she thinks will prove more efficacious but which we think will run her into greater dangers.

Many believe that Josephine is becoming so insistent because she feels herself growing old and her voice falling off, and so she thinks it high time to wage the last battle for recognition. I do not believe it. Josephine would not be Josephine if that were true. For her there is no growing old and no falling off in her voice. If she makes demands it is not because of outward circumstances but because of an inner logic. She reaches for the highest garland not because it is momentarily hanging a little lower but because it is the highest; if she had any say in the matter she would have it still higher.

This contempt for external difficulties, to be sure, does not hinder her from using the most unworthy methods. Her rights seem beyond question to her; so what does it matter how she secures them; especially since in this world, as she sees it, honest methods are bound to fail. Perhaps that is why she has transferred the battle for her rights from the field of song to another which she cares little about. Her supporters have let it be known that, according to herself, she feels quite capable of singing in such a way that all levels of the populace, even to the remotest corners of the opposition, would find it a real delight, a real delight not by popular standards, for the people affirm that they have always delighted in her singing, but a delight by her own standards. However, she adds, since she cannot falsify the highest standards nor pander to the lowest, her singing will have to stay as it is. But when it comes to her campaign for exemption from work, we get a different story; it is of course also a campaign on behalf of her singing, yet she is not fighting directly with the priceless weapon of her song, so any instrument she uses is good enough. Thus, for instance, the rumor went around that Josephine meant to cut short her grace notes if her petition were not granted. I know nothing about grace notes, and have never noticed any in Josephine's singing. But Josephine is going to cut short her grace notes, not, for the present, to cut them out entirely, only to cut them short. Presumably she has carried out her threat, although I for one have observed no difference in her performance. The people as a whole listened in the usual way without making any pronouncement on the grace notes, nor did their response to her petition vary by a jot. It must be admitted that Josephine's way of thinking, like her figure, is often very charming. And so, for instance, after that performance, just as if her decision about the grace notes had been too severe or too sudden a move against the people, she announced that next time she would put in all the grace notes again. Yet after the next concert she changed her mind once more, there was to be definitely an end of these great arias with the grace notes; and until her petition was favorably regarded they would never recur. Well, the people let all these announcements, decisions and counterdecisions go in at one ear and out at the other, like a grown-up person deep in thought turning a deaf ear to a child's babble, fundamentally well disposed but not accessible.

Josephine, however, does not give in. The other day, for instance, she claimed that she had hurt her foot at work, so that it was difficult for her to stand up to sing; but since she could not sing except standing up, her songs would now have to be cut short. Although she limps and leans on her supporters, no one believes that she is really hurt. Granted that her frail body is extra sensitive, she is yet one of us and we are a race of workers; if we were to start limping every time we got a scratch, the whole people would never be done limping. Yet though she lets herself be led about like a cripple, though she shows herself in this pathetic conditoin oftener than usual, the people all the same listen to her singing thankfully and appreciatively as before, but do not bother much about the shortening of her songs.

Since she cannot very well go on limping forever, she thinks of something else, she pleads that she is tired, not in the mood for singing, feeling faint. And so we get a theatrical performance as well as a concert. We see Josephine's supporters in the background begging and imploring her to sing. She would be glad to oblige, but she cannot. They comfort and caress her with flatteries, they almost carry her to the selected spot where she is supposed to sing. At last, bursting inexplicably into tears, she gives way, but when she stands up to sing, obviously at the end of her resources, weary, her arms not widespread as usual but hanging lifelessly down, so that one gets the impression that they are perhaps a little too short—just as she is about to strike up, there, she cannot do it after all, an unwilling shake of the head tells us so and she breaks down before our eyes. To be sure, she pulls herself together again and sings, I fancy, much as usual; perhaps, if one has an ear for the finer shades of expression, one can even hear that she is singing with unusual feeling, which is, however, all to the good. And in the end she is actually less tired than before, with a firm tread, if one can use such a term for her tripping gait, she moves off, refusing all help from her supporters and measuring with cold eyes the crowd which respectfully makes way for her.

That happened a day or two ago; but the latest is that she has disappeared, just at a time when she was supposed to sing. It is not only her supporters who are looking for her, many are devoting themselves to the search, but all in vain; Josephine has vanished, she will not sing; she will not even be cajoled into singing, this time she has deserted us entirely.

Curiously, how mistaken she is in her calculations, the clever creature, so mistaken that one might fancy she has made no calculations at all but is only being driven on by her destiny, which in our world cannot be anything but a sad one. Of her own accord she abandons her singing, of her own accord she destroys the power she has gained over people's hearts. How could she ever have gained that power, since she knows so little about these hearts of ours? She hides herself and does not sing, but our people, quietly, without visible disappointment, a self-confident mass in perfect equilibrium, so constituted, even though appearances are misleading, that they can only bestow gifts and not receive them, even from Josephine, our people continue on their way.

Josephine's road, however, must go downhill. The time will soon come when her last notes sound and die into silence. She is a small episode in the eternal history of our people, and the people will get over the loss of her. Not that it will be easy for us; how can our gatherings take place in utter silence? Still, were they not silent even when Josephine was present? Was her actual piping notably louder and more alive than the memory of it will be? Was it even in her lifetime more than a simple memory? Was it not rather because Josephine's singing was already past losing in this way that our people in their wisdom prized it so highly?

So perhaps we shall not miss so very much after all, while Josephine, redeemed from the earthly sorrows which to her thinking lay in wait for all chosen spirits, will happily lose herself in the numberless throng of the heroes of our people, and soon, since we are no historians, will rise to the heights of redemption and be forgotten like all her brothers.

Before the Law

Before the Law stands a doorkeeper. To this doorkeeper there comes a man from the country and prays for admittance to the Law. But the doorkeeper says that he cannot grant admittance at the moment. The man thinks it over and then asks if he will be allowed in later. 'It is possible,' says the doorkeeper, 'but not at the moment.' Since the gate stands open, as usual, and the doorkeeper steps to one side, the man stoops to peer through the gateway into the interior. Observing that, the doorkeeper laughs and says: 'If you are so drawn to it, just try to go in despite my veto. But take note: I am powerful. And I am only the least of the doorkeepers. From hall to hall there is one doorkeeper after another, each more powerful than the last. The third doorkeeper is already so terrible that even I cannot bear to look at him.' These are difficulties the man from the country has not expected; the Law, he thinks, should surely be accessible at all times and to everyone, but as he now takes a closer look at the doorkeeper in his fur coat, with his big sharp nose and long, thin, black Tartar beard, he decides that it is better to wait until he gets permission to enter. The doorkeeper gives him a stool and lets him sit down at one side of the door. There he sits for days and years. He makes many attempts to be admitted, and wearies the doorkeeper by his importunity. The doorkeeper frequently has little interviews with him, asking him questions about his home and many other things, but the questions are put indifferently, as great lords put them, and always finish with the statement that he cannot be let in yet. The man, who has furnished himself with many things for his journey, sacrifices all he has, however valuable, to bribe the doorkeeper. The doorkeeper accepts everything, but always with the remark: 'I am only taking it to keep you from thinking you have omitted anything.' During these many years the man fixes his attention almost continuously on the doorkeeper. He forgets the other doorkeepers, and this first one seems to him the sole obstacle preventing access to the Law. He curses his bad luck, in his early years boldly and loudly; later, as he grows old, he only grumbles to himself. He becomes childish, and since in his yearlong contemplation of the doorkeeper he has come to know even the fleas on his fur collar, he begs the fleas as well to help him and to change the doorkeeper's mind. At length his eyesight begins to fail, and he does not know whether the world is really darker or whether his eyes are only deceiving him. Yet in his darkness he is now aware of a radiance that streams inextinguishably from the gateway of the Law. Now he has not very long to live. Before he dies, all his experiences in these long years gather themselves in his head to one point, a question he has not yet asked the doorkeeper. He waves him nearer, since he can no longer raise his stiffening body. The doorkeeper has to bend low towards him, much to the man's disadvantage. 'What do you want to know now?' asks the doorkeeper; 'you are insatiable.' 'Everyone strives to reach the Law,' says the man, 'so how does it happen that for all these many years no one but myself has ever begged for admittance?' The doorkeeper recognizes that the man has reached his end, and, to let his failing senses catch the words, roars in his ear: 'No one else could ever be admitted here, since this gate was made only for you. I am now going to shut it.'

The Return of Imray

Rudyard Kipling, *famous novelist, storyteller and epic poet, was born in Bombay in 1865, died in England in 1936. He won the Nobel Prize for Literature in 1907. Of his vast literary legacy, mention should be made of* Plain Tales from the Hills *(1887),* The Light That Failed *(1891),* The Seven Seas *(1896),* Stalky and Co. *(1899),* Kim *(1901),* The Five Nations *(1903),* Actions and Reactions *(1909),* A Diversity of Creatures *(1917),* The Years Between *(1918),* Debits and Credits *(1926),* Limits and Renewals *(1935), and* Something of Myself *(1937).*

> The doors were wide, the story saith,
> Out of the night came the patient wraith,
> He might not speak, and he could not stir
> A hair of the Baron's miniver—
> Speechless and strengthless, a shadow thin,
> He roved the castle to seek his kin.
> And oh, 'twas a piteous thing to see
> The dumb ghost follow his enemy!
>
> The Baron.

Imray achieved the impossible. Without warning, for no conceivable motive, in his youth, at the threshold of his career, he chose to disappear from the world—which is to say, the little Indian station where he lived.

Upon a day he was alive, well, happy, and in great evidence among the billiard tables at his Club. Upon a morning he was not, and no manner of search could make sure where he might be. He had stepped out of his place; he had not appeared at his office at the proper time, and his dog-cart was not upon the public roads. For these reasons, and because he was hampering, in a microscopical degree, the administration of the Indian Empire, that Empire paused for one microscopical moment to make inquiry into the fate of Imray. Ponds were dragged, wells were plumbed, telegrams were dispatched down the lines of railways and to the nearest seaport town—twelve hundred miles away; but Imray was not at the end of the drag-ropes nor the telegraph wires. He was gone, and his place knew him no more. Then the work of the great Indian Empire swept forward, because it could not be delayed, and Imray from being a man became a mystery—such a thing as men talk over at their tables in the Club for a month, and then forget utterly. His guns, horses, and carts were sold to the highest bidder. His superior officer wrote an altogether absurd letter to his mother, saying that Imray had unaccountably disappeared, and his bungalow stood empty.

After three or four months of the scorching hot weather had gone by, my friend Strickland, of the Police, saw fit to rent the bungalow from the native landlord. This was before he was engaged to Miss Youghal—an affair which has been described in another place—and while he was pursuing his investigations into native life. His own life was sufficiently peculiar, and men complained of his manners and customs. There was always food in his house, but there were no regular times for meals. He ate, standing up and walking about, whatever he might find at the sideboard, and this is not good for human beings. His domestic equipment was limited to six rifles, three shot-guns, five saddles, and a collection of stiff-jointed mahseer-rods, bigger and stronger than the largest salmon-rods. These occupied one half of his bungalow, and the other half was given up to Strickland and his dog Tietjens—an enormous Rampur slut who devoured daily the rations of two men. She spoke to Strickland in a language of her own; and whenever, walking abroad, she saw things calculated to destroy the peace of Her Majesty the Queen-Empress, she returned to her master and laid information. Strickland would take steps at once, and the end of his labours was trouble and fine and imprisonment for other people. The natives believed that Tietjens was a familiar spirit, and treated her with the great reverence that is born of hate and fear. One room in the bungalow was set apart for her special use. She owned a bedstead, a blanket, and a drinking-trough, and if anyone came into Strickland's room at night her custom was to knock down the invader and give tongue till someone came with a light. Strickland owed his life to her when he was on the Frontier in search of a local murderer, who came in the grey dawn to send Strickland much farther than the Andaman Islands. Tietjens caught the man as he was crawling into Strickland's tent with a dagger between his teeth; and after his record of iniquity was established in the eyes of the law he was hanged. From that date Tietjens wore a collar of rough silver, and employed a monogram on her night blanket; and the blanket was of double woven Kashmir cloth, for she was a delicate dog.

Under no circumstances would she be separated from Strickland; and once, when he was ill with fever, made great trouble for the doctors, because she did not know how to help her master and would not allow another creature to attempt aid. Macarnaght, of the Indian Medical Service, beat her over her head with a gun-butt before she could understand that she must give room for those who could give quinine.

A short time after Strickland had taken Imray's bungalow, my business took me through that Station, and naturally, the Club quarters being full, I quartered myself upon Strickland. It was a desirable bungalow, eight-roomed and heavily thatched against any chance of leakage from rain. Under the pitch of the roof ran a ceiling-cloth which looked just as neat as a white-washed ceiling. The landlord had repainted it when Strickland took the bungalow. Unless you knew how Indian bungalows were built you would never have suspected that above the cloth lay the dark three-cornered cavern of the roof, where the beams and the underside of the thatch harboured all manner of rats, bats, ants, and foul things.

Tietjens met me in the verandah with a bay like the boom of the bell of St Paul's, putting her paws on my shoulder to show she was glad to see me. Strickland had contrived to claw together a sort of meal which he called lunch, and immediately after it was finished went out about his business. I was left alone with Tietjens and my own affairs. The heat of the summer had broken up and turned to the warm damp of the rains. There was no motion in the heated air, but the rain fell like ramrods on the earth, and flung up a blue mist when it splashed back. The bamboo, and the custard apples, the poinsettias, and the mango trees in the garden stood still while the warm water lashed through them, and the frogs began to sing among the aloe hedges. A little before the light failed, and when the rain was at its worst, I sat in the back verandah and heard the water roar from the eaves, and scratched myself because I was covered with the thing called prickly heat. Tietjens came out with me and put her head in my lap and was very sorrowful; so I gave her biscuits when tea was ready, and I took tea in the back verandah on account of the little coolness found there. The rooms of the house were dark behind me. I could smell Strickland's saddlery and the oil on his guns, and I had no desire to sit among these things. My own servant came to me in the twilight, the muslin of his clothes clinging tightly to his drenched body, and told me that a gentleman had called and wished to see someone. Very much against my will, but only because of the darkness of the rooms, I went into the naked drawing-room, telling my man to bring the lights. There might or might not have been a caller waiting—it seemed to me that I saw a figure by one of the windows—but when the lights came there was nothing save the spikes of the rain without, and the smell of the drinking earth in my nostrils. I explained to my servant that he was no wiser than he ought to be, and went back to the verandah to talk to Tietjens. She had gone out into the wet, and I could hardly coax her back to me, even with biscuits with sugar tops. Strickland came home, dripping wet, just before dinner, and the first thing he said was:

'Has anyone called?'

I explained, with apologies, that my servant had summoned me into the drawing-room on a false alarm; or that some loafer had tried to call on Strickland, and thinking better of it, had fled after giving his name. Strickland ordered dinner, without comment, and since it was a real dinner with a white tablecloth attached, we sat down.

At nine o'clock Strickland wanted to go to bed, and I was tired too. Tietjens, who had been lying underneath the table, rose up, and sung into the least exposed verandah as soon as her master moved to his own room, which was next to the stately chamber set apart for Tietjens. If a mere wife had wished to sleep out of doors in that pelting rain it would not have mattered; but Tietjens was a dog, and therefore the better animal. I looked at Strickland, expecting to see him flay her with a whip. He smiled queerly, as a man would smile after telling some unpleasant domestic tragedy. 'She has done this ever since I moved in here,' said he. 'Let her go.'

The dog was Strickland's dog, so I said nothing, but I felt all that Strickland felt in being thus made light of. Tietjens encamped outside my bedroom window, and storm after storm came up, thundered on the thatch, and died away. The lightning spattered the sky as a thrown egg spatters a barn door, but the light was pale blue, not yellow; and, looking through my split bamboo blinds, I could see the great dog standing, not sleeping, in the verandah, the hackles alift on her back and her feet anchored as tensely as the drawn wire-rope of a suspension bridge. In the very short pauses of the thunder I tried to sleep, but it seemed that someone wanted me very urgently. He, whoever he was, was trying to call me by name, but his voice was no more than a husky whisper. The thunder ceased, and Tietjens went into the garden and howled at the low moon. Somebody tried to open my door, walked about and about through the house, and stood breathing heavily in the verandahs, and just when I was falling asleep I fancied that I heard a wild hammering and clamouring above my head or on the door.

I ran into Strickland's room and asked him whether he was ill, and had been calling me. He was lying on his bed half dressed, a pipe in his mouth. 'I thought you'd come,' he said. 'Have I been walking round the house recently?'

I explained that he had been tramping in the dining-room and the smoking-room and two or three other places, and he laughed and told me to go back to bed. I went back to bed and slept till the morning, but through all my mixed dreams I was sure I was doing someone an injustice in not attending to his wants. What those wants were I could not tell; but a fluttering, whispering, bolt-fumbling, lurking, loitering Someone was reproaching me for my slackness, and, half awake, I heard the howling of Tietjens in the garden and the threshing of the rain.

I lived in that house for two days. Strickland went to his office daily, leaving me alone for eight or ten hours with Tietjens for my only companion. As long as the full light lasted I was comfortable, and so was Tietjens; but in the twilight she and I moved into the back verandah and cuddled each other for company. We were alone in the house, but none the less it was much too fully occupied by a tenant with whom I did not wish to interfere. I never saw him, but I could see the curtains between the rooms quivering where he had just passed through; I could hear the chairs creaking as the bamboos sprung under a weight that had just quitted them; and I could feel when I went to get a book from the dining-room that somebody was waiting in the shadows of the front verandah till I should have gone away. Tietjens made the twilight more interesting by glaring into the darkened rooms with every hair erect, and following the motions of something that I could not see. She never entered the rooms, but her eyes moved interestedly: that was quite sufficient. Only when my servant came to trim the lamps and make all light and habitable she would come in with me and spend her time sitting on her haunches, watching an invisible extra man as he moved about behind my shoulder. Dogs are cheerful companions.

I explained to Strickland, gently as might be, that I would go over to the Club and find for myself quarters there. I admired his hospitality, was pleased with his guns and rods, but I did not much care for his house and its atmosphere. He heard me out to the end, and then smiled very wearily, but without contempt, for he is a man who understands things. 'Stay on,' he said, 'and see what this thing means. All you have talked about I have known since I took the bungalow. Stay on and wait. Tietjens has left me. Are you going too?'

I had seen him through one little affair, connected with a heathen idol, that had brought me to the doors of a lunatic asylum, and I had no desire to help him through further experiences. He was a man to whom unpleasantness arrived as do dinners to ordinary people.

Therefore I explained more clearly than ever that I liked him immensely, and would be happy to see him in the daytime; but that I did not care to sleep under his roof. This was after dinner, when Tietjens had gone out to lie in the verandah.

' 'Pon my soul, I don't wonder,' said Strickland, with his eyes on the ceiling-cloth. 'Look at that!'

The tails of two brown snakes were hanging between the cloth and the cornice of the wall. They threw long shadows in the lamplight.

'If you are afraid of snakes, of course—'said Strickland.

I hate and fear snakes, because if you look into the eyes of any snake you will see that it knows all and more of the mystery of man's fall, and that it feels all the contempt that the Devil felt when Adam was evicted from Eden. Besides which its bite is generally fatal, and it twists up trouser legs.

'You ought to get your thatch overhauled,' I said. 'Give me a mahseer-rod, and we'll poke 'em down.'

'They'll hide among the roof-beams,' said Strickland. 'I can't stand snakes overhead. I'm going up into the roof. If I shake 'em down, stand by with a cleaning-rod and break their backs.'

I was not anxious to assist Strickland in his work, but I took the cleaning-rod and waited in the dining-room, while Strickland brought a gardener's ladder from the verandah, and set it against the side of the room. The snake-tails drew themselves up and disappeared. We could hear the dry rushing scuttle of long bodies running over the baggy ceiling-cloth. Strickland took a lamp with him, while I tried to make clear to him the danger of hunting roof-snakes between a ceiling-cloth and a thatch, apart from the deterioration of property caused by ripping out ceiling-cloths.

'Nonsense!' said Strickland. 'They're sure to hide near the walls by the cloth. The bricks are too cold for 'em, and the heat of the room is just what they like.' He put his hand to the corner of the stuff and ripped it from the cornice. It gave with a great sound of tearing, and Strickland put his head through the opening into the dark of the angle of the roof-beams. I set my teeth and lifted the rod, for I had not the least knowledge of what might descend.

'H'm!' said Strickland, and his voice rolled and rumbled in the roof. 'There's room for another set of rooms up here, and, by Jove, someone is occupying 'em!'

'Snakes?' I said from below.

'No. It's a buffalo. Hand me up the two last joints of a mahseer-rod, and I'll prod it. It's lying on the main roof-beam.'

I handed up the rod.

'What a nest for owls and serpents! No wonder the snakes live here,' said Strickland, climbing farther into the roof. I could see his elbow thrusting with the rod. 'Come out of that, whoever you are! Heads below there! It's falling.'

I saw the ceiling-cloth nearly in the centre of the room sag with a shape that was pressing it downwards and downwards towards the lighted lamp on the table. I snatched the lamp out of danger and stood back. Then the cloth ripped out from the walls, tore, split, swayed, and shot down upon the table something that I dared not look at, till Strickland had slid down the ladder and was standing by my side.

He did not say much, being a man of few words; but he picked up the loose end of the tablecloth and threw it over the remnants on the table.

'It strikes me,' said he, putting down the lamp, 'our friend Imray has come back. Oh! you would, would you?'

There was a movement under the cloth, and a little snake wriggled out, to be back-broken by the butt of the mahseer-rod. I was sufficiently sick to make no remarks worth recording.

Strickland meditated, and helped himself to drinks. The arrangement under the cloth made no more signs of life.

'Is it Imray?' I said.

Strickland turned back the cloth for a moment, and looked.

'It is Imray,' he said; 'and his throat is cut from ear to ear.'

Then we spoke, both together and to ourselves: 'That's why he whispered about the house.'

Tietjens, in the garden, began to bay furiously. A little later her great nose heaved open the dining-room door.

She sniffed and was still. The tattered ceiling-cloth hung down almost to the level of the table, and there was hardly room to move away from the discovery.

Tietjens came in and sat down; her teeth bared under her lip and her forepaws planted. She looked at Strickland.

'It's a bad business, old lady,' said he. 'Men don't climb up into the roofs of their bungalows to die, and they don't fasten up the ceiling-cloth behind 'em. Let's think it out.'

'Let's think it out somewhere else,' I said.

'Excellent idea! Turn the lamps out. We'll get into my room.'

I did not turn the lamps out. I went into Strickland's room first, and allowed him to make the darkness. Then he followed me, and we lit tobacco and thought. Strickland thought. I smoked furiously, because I was afraid.

'Imray is back,' said Strickland. 'The question is—who killed Imray? Don't talk, I've a notion of my own. When I took this bungalow I took over most of Imray's servants. Imray was guileless and inoffensive, wasn't he?'

I agreed; though the heap under the cloth had looked neither one thing nor the other.

'If I call in all the servants they will stand fast in a crowd and lie like Aryans. What do you suggest?'

'Call 'em in one by one,' I said.

'They'll run away and give the news to all their fellows,' said Strickland. 'We must segregate 'em. Do you suppose your servant knows anything about it?'

'He may, for aught I know; but I don't think it's likely. He has only been here two or three days,' I answered. 'What's your notion?'

'I can't quite tell. How the dickens did the man get the wrong side of the ceiling-cloth?'

There was a heavy coughing outside Strickland's bedroom door. This showed that Bahadur Khan, his body servant, had waked from sleep and wished to put Strickland to bed.

'Come in,' said Strickland. 'It's a very warm night, isn't it?'

Bahadur Khan, a great, green-turbaned, six-foot Mohammedan, said that it was a very warm night; but that there was more rain pending, which, by his Honour's favour, would bring relief to the country.

'It will be so, if God pleases,' said Strickland, tugging off his boots. 'It is in my mind, Bahadur Khan, that I have worked thee remorselessly for many days—ever since that time when thou first camest into my service. What time was that?'

'Has the Heaven-born forgotten? It was when Imray Sahib went secretly to Europe without warning given; and I—even I—came into the honoured service of the protector of the poor.'

'And Imray Sahib went to Europe?'

'It is so said among those who were his servants.'

'And thou wilt take service with him when he returns?'

'Assuredly, Sahib. He was a good master, and cherished his dependants.'

'That is true. I am very tired, but I go buck-shooting tomorrow. Give me the little sharp rifle that I use for black-buck; it is in the case yonder.'

The man stooped over the case; handed barrels, stock, and fore-end to Strickland, who fitted all together, yawning dolefully. Then he reached down to the gun-case, took a solid-drawn cartridge, and slipped it into the breech of the 360 Express.

'And Imray Sahib has gone to Europe secretly! That is very strange, Bahadur Khan, is it not?'

'What do I know of the ways of the white man, Heaven-born?'

'Very little, truly. But thou shalt know more anon. It has reached me that Imray Sahib has returned from his so long journeyings, and that even now he lies in the next room, waiting his servant.'

'Sahib!'

The lamplight slid along the barrels of the rifle as they levelled themselves at Bahadur Khan's broad breast.

'Go and look!' said Strickland. 'Take a lamp. Thy master is tired, and he waits thee. Go!'

The man picked up a lamp, and went into the dining-room, Strickland following, and almost pushing him with the muzzle of the rifle. He looked for a moment at the black depths behind the ceiling-cloth; at the writhing snake under foot; and last, a grey glaze settling on his face, at the thing under the tablecloth.

'Hast thou seen?' said Strickland after a pause.

'I have seen. I am clay in the white man's hands. What does the Presence do?'

'Hang thee within the month. What else?'

'For killing him? Nay, Sahib, consider. Walking among us, his servants, he cast his eyes upon my child, who was four years old. Him he bewitched, and in ten days he died of the fever—my child!'

'What said Imray Sahib?'

'He said he was a handsome child, and patted him on the head; wherefore my child died. Wherefore I killed Imray Sahib in the twilight, when he had come back from office, and was sleeping. Wherefore I dragged him up into the roof-beams and made all fast behind him. The Heaven-born knows all things. I am the servant of the Heaven-born.'

Strickland looked at me above the rifle, and said, in the vernacular, 'Thou art witness to this saying? He has killed.'

Bahadur Khan stood ashen grey in the light of the one lamp. The need for justification came upon him very swiftly. 'I am trapped,' he said, 'but the offence was that man's. He cast an evil eye upon my child, and I killed and hid him. Only such as are served by devils,' he glared at Tietjens, couched stolidly before him, 'only such could know what I did.'

'It was clever. But thous shouldst have lashed him to the beam with a rope. Now, thou thyself wilt hang by a rope. Orderly!'

A drowsy policeman answered Strickland's call. He was followed by another, and Tietjens sat wondrous still.

'Take him to the police station,' said Strickland. 'There is a case toward.'

'Do I hang, then?' said Bahadur Khan, making no attempt to escape, and keeping his eyes on the ground.

'If the sun shines or the water runs—yes!' said Strickland.

Bahadur Khan stepped back one long pace, quivered, and stood still. The two policemen waited further orders.

'Go!' said Strickland.

'Nay; but I go very swiftly,' said Bahadur Khan. 'Look! I am even now a dead man.'

He lifted his foot, and to the little toe there clung the head of the half-killed snake, firm fixed in the agony of death.

'I come of land-holding stock,' said Bahadur Khan, rocking where he stood. 'It were a disgrace to me to go to the public scaffold: therefore I take this way. Be it remembered that the Sahib's shirts are correctly enumerated, and that there is an extra piece of soap in his wash-basin. My child was bewitched, and I slew the wizard. Why should you seek to slay me with the rope? My honour is saved, and—and—I die.'

At the end of an hour he died, as they die who are bitten by the little brown *karait,* and the policeman bore him and the thing under the tablecloth to their appointed places. All were needed to make clear the disappearance of Imray.

'This,' said Strickland, very calmly, as he climbed into bed, 'is called the nineteenth century. Did you hear what that man said?'

'I heard,' I answered. 'Imray made a mistake.'

'Simply and solely through not knowing the nature of the Oriental, and the coincidence of a little seasonal fever. Bahadur Khan had been with him for four years.'

I shuddered. My own servant had been with me for exactly that length of time. When I went over to my own room I found my man waiting, impassive as the copper head on a penny, to pull off my boots.

'What has befallen Bahadur Khan?' said I.

'He was bitten by a snake and died. The rest the Sahib knows,' was the answer.

'And how much of this matter hast thou known?'

'As much as might be gathered from One coming in in the twilight to seek satisfaction. Gently, Sahib. Let me pull off those boots.'

I had just settled to the sleep of exhaustion when I heard Strickland shouting from his side of the house—

'Tietjens has come back to her place!'

And so she had. The great deerhound was crouched statelily on her own bedstead on her own blanket, while, in the next room, the idle, empty ceiling-cloth waggled as it trailed on the table.

The Horses of Abdera

Leopoldo Lugones, *Argentinian writer, born in Rio Seco, in the province of Cordoba in 1874, died in el Tigre, Buenos Aires province, in 1938. He was at home in poetry, biography, history, homeric studies and fiction. His literary legacy includes the following titles:* Las Montañas del Oro *(1897),* Los Crepusculos del Jardin *(1905),* El Imperio Jesuistico *(1905),* Lunario Sentimental *(1909),* Odas Seculares *(1910),* Historia de Sarmiento *(1911),* El Payador *(1916),* El Libro de los Paisaies *(1917),* Mi Beligerancia *(1917),* La Torre de Casandra *(1919),* Nuevos Estudios Helenicas *(1928),* La Grande Argentina *(1930),* Roca *(1938).*

By the Aegean Sea lay the Thracian City of Abdera, which is now called Balastra and must not be confused with its Andalusian namesake, and which was famous for its horses. In Thrace, to win distinction for horses was no mean achievement, and Abdera's reputation in this regard was unsurpassed; each and every citizen took great pride in the care and rearing of these noble creatures, and their devotion to horses, carefully nurtured over many years until it had grown into a deeply-rooted tradition, had lead to wonderful results. The horses of Abdera commanded extraordinary prestige, and all the Thracian people from Cicilia to Bisalta paid a special tax to the Bithynians, the conquerors of Abdera. Moreover, the business of horse-rearing—a joy as well as a trade—occupied everyone, from the King down to the lowliest citizen.

This great tradition drew horse and master together much more closely than elsewhere in Thrace. The stable came to be regarded as a natural extension of the home, even (since enthusiasm leads to understandable excess) to the extent of allowing the horses to eat at table with their owners.

They were truly remarkable steeds, and the manner of their treatment might make one forget that they were beasts at all. Some slept under fine linen bedcovers and, since not a few vetinarians maintained that the equine race displayed artistic taste, others had the walls of their stalls decorated with simple frescoes, whilst in the horses' cemetery there were two or three real masterpieces among the conventionally over-elaborate gravestones. Abdera's most beautiful temple was dedicated to Orion, the horse that Neptune conjured from the ground with a single blow of his trident; and I believe that the current practice of carving a ship's prow in the shape of a horse's head derives from the temple decorations; in any event, the most common architectural decorations were the equestrian bas-reliefs. It was the King who showed the greatest devotion to horses, but his leniency towards his own steeds' mischief turned them into particularly ferocious creatures, so much so that Podargos and Flash of Light became names in dark and terrible legends; for it should be added that horses were given human names.

But on the whole the horses of Abdera were so well-trained that bridles were unnecessary and were used only for adornment—a practice greatly appreciated by the horses themselves. The usual method of communication with them was by the spoken word and, since it had been found that complete freedom from all constraint brought out their best qualities, they were left to roam freely to feed and frolic in the lush meadows reserved for them on the outskirts of the city, on the banks of the River Kossinites, except when they needed to be saddled or harnessed. A horn was then sounded to summon them in, and they were always extremely punctual, whether it was for work or for feeding. Their skill in all manner of circus tricks, even in parlour games, their bravery in combat, their self-possession during formal ceremonies—all defied credulity. The Hippodrome at Abdera thus became renowned not only for its troupes of acrobats but also for its bronze-armoured teams of horses and for its ceremonial funerals, so that people came from far and near to wonder at the excellence of the trainers and horses alike.

This practice of nurturing horses, cultivating and idealizing their qualities— in short, this humanizing of the equine race—gradually brought about something on which the Bithynians gloated as another glorious national achievement: the intelligence of the animals began to develop, as did their moral conscience. But this also lead to some instances of rather curious behaviour, which aroused much public debate.

A mare demanded mirrors in her stall. She tore them off the walls of her master's bedroom with her teeth, and when he protested she kicked them to pieces. When her whim was finally indulged, she became visibly coquettish. Another instance: Balios, the finest horse in the district, an elegant and highly-strung white colt who had survived two military campaigns and who thrilled at the sound of heroic hexameters, died of a broken heart. He had been striken with love for the wife of his master, the general, and the lady made no attempt to disguise what had happened. It was whispered that his bizarre *affaire* gratified her vanity. Things of this sort occurred frequently in the capital.

There were also cases of equine infanticide, which increased at such an alarming rate that they had to be forestalled by giving the foals to old, motherly mules. The horses developed tastes for fish and for hemp, and they raided the hemp plantations; they also began to rebel against their masters in a number of scattered outbreaks, and had to be quelled with burning irons, whips proving inadequate. This stern punishment was employed more and more as the horses became increasingly restless, despite all attempts to discipline them—but these were half-hearted at best, for the Bithynians were besotted with their horses and took no heed of the growing unrest.

Soon there were more significant occurrences. Two or three teams of horses banded together to attack a carter who had flogged an unruly mare. The horses began to resist being harnessed and yoked, and donkeys started to be used in their place. Some horses would not be saddled at all, but their wealthy owners still took no action, dismissing it with a laugh as a passing mood.

On a certain day, the horses ignored the sound of the horn and their owners had to go and round them up from the meadows, but the rebellion did not break out at once; it erupted later, when the tide had covered the beach with stranded fishes—as had often happened before. On this day, however, the horses gorged themselves on the fishes and then were seen ambling slowly and menacingly back towards the open meadows in the suburbs of the city. The conflict first broke out at midnight. Suddenly, the inhabitants of the outlying regions heard a muffled but persistent sound of thunder as the horses stampeded together in an attempt to storm the city. The cause was not discovered until later, however; at the time there was merely surprise at the unexpected sound coming out of the night's darkness, and no suspicion that an attack might be imminent.

Since the pasturelands were within the city walls nothing could contain the main assault, and since the horses also knew their master's houses inside out, the destruction was devastating. It was an appalling night, yet only in the day's light was the full extent of its horrors revealed.

Doors had been kicked down and they lay shattered on the ground, offering no obstacle to the hordes of frenzied horses pouring through in an unending stream. There was blood, for many citizens were crushed beneath the sharp hooves or torn apart by the great flashing teeth of the raging beasts, and men's own weapons were turned against them to wreak destruction. The city was paralysed by the surging mass, its skies darkened by the clouds of dust that it raised, and it was rent by a weird tumult in which cries of rage or of pain mingled with whinnyings as subtle as speech and the violent crashes of destruction: strange and horrifying sounds which added to the visible terror of the onslaught. The ground trembled with the ceaseless pounding of the rebellious hooves which, like a hurricane, grew and faded in intensity as frantic crowds of people rushed to and fro without purpose or clear direction. The horses plundered the fields of hemp and even the wine cellars—some of the beats, corrupted by luxurious living, had long coveted the latter—and their fury grew as they became intoxicated and maddened. Escape by sea was impossible, for the horses knew the purpose of the boats and barricaded the way to the harbour.

Only the fortress itself remained safe, and from within its walls men began to plan a defence. They fired arrows at any horse which approached, and if it fell within reach they dragged it inside for food.

Strange rumours spread amongst the cowering citizens: that the attack had been intended as nothing more than a pillaging expedition, and that the horses had battered down the doors and broken into the chambers merely to try and adorn themselves with the sumptuous draperies, the jewellery and the other finery that lay within. It was the resistance they met that had aroused their fury.

Others whispered of unthinkable acts of rapine, of women set upon and crushed with bestial violence on their own beds. They told of a virtuous young noblewoman who, racked with tears, had managed to stammer out the tale of her vile experience before she broke down utterly; how she was awakened in the dim lamp-light of her chamber by the foul, thick-lipped mouth of a black colt rubbing against hers, its lips curling with pleasure and revealing its loathsome teeth; how she cried out in sheer terror at the presence of an animal that had turned into a slavering beast, its eyes burning with an evil, human gleam full of lust, and how she was almost drowned in a sea of hot blood when the horse was run through by her servant's sword.

They told of cruel and deliberate murders, when mares gleefully bit their victims with the frenzy of she-devils as they crushed them with their hooves. They had slaughtered all the asses, but the mules had joined in the rebellion— mindlessly, revelling in destruction for its own sake and taking a particular pleasure in cruelly tormenting and then trampling dogs. All the while, the thunderous roar of the rampaging horses continued to shake the fortress, and the crashing sounds of the destruction grew louder. If the huddling citizens were to save their city from utter destruction they must escape somehow, though their assailants' sheer power in strength and number made it impossibly dangerous. The men gathered their arms; but, now that they had had a taste of what they had craved, the horses launched another attack.

A sudden silence preceded the assault. From the fortress the men could see the fearful army congregating, not without some confusion, in the hippodrome. This took the animals several hours and, when everything seemed ready, a sudden bout of prancing and a series of high-pitched neighings, the purpose of which was impossible to discern, threw the ranks into great disarray.

The sun was already setting when the first charge came. It was, if one may use the term, no more than a demonstration, for the animals confined themselves to running past the fortress and returned riddled with arrows.

They launched another attack from the furthest part of the city and its impact on the city's defences was enormous. The entire fortress reverberated beneath the storm of hooves, and its solid Doric ramparts were severely strained. This time the enemy was repulsed, but it very soon attacked again.

Most destructive were the shod horses and mules, which fell by the dozen; but, their numbers seemingly undiminished, they quickly closed their ranks in frantic rage.

The worst thing was that some had managed to put on fighting armour, and the steel mesh blunted the arrows. Others wore gaudy strips of cloth, others necklaces, and, childlike in their very fury, they would burst into unexpected frolics.

Some of them were recognized from the ramparts: Dione, Aedon, Amalthea, Xanthi! They greeted the men with joyous whinnies, arching their tails, then immediately charging at them with fiery jerks. One of them, obviously a leader, stood straight up on his hocks and walked some way like this, gracefully waving his forelegs in the air, as if he were dancing a military two-step, and writhing his neck with snake-like elegance, until an arrow pierced his chest.

Meanwhile, the attack was succeeding; the fortress walls were beginning to yield.

Suddenly, an alarm paralysed the beasts. Using each other's rumps and backs for support, they raised themselves one above the other and stretched out their necks to peer at the poplar grove that grew along the banks of the Kossinites; and when the defenders turned to look in the same direction, a fearful sight met their eyes.

Towering above the dark trees, horrifying against the early evening sky, the colossal head of a lion gazed towards the city. It was one of those wild pre-historic beasts which, although gradually dying out, still occasionally devastated the Rhodope Mountains. But never had anything so monstrous been seen before, for the head soared above the tallest trees, the matted hair of its mane merging with the twilight-tinged leaves.

They could see its enormous teeth gleaming brightly, its eyes half-closed against the light; its wild smell wafted towards them in the fitful breeze. Motionless against the trembling foliage, its gigantic mane glowing rusty-red, shining like gold in the setting sun, it rose on the horizon like one of those boulders upon which Pelasgian, as old as the mountains, carved his savage deities.

And suddenly it began to walk, as slowly as the ocean. You could hear the foliage being forced apart beneath its chest, and its bellow-like breathing, which, undoubtedly, would soon turn into a roar, making the whole city tremble with fear.

Despite their prodigious strength and numbers, the insurgent horses were unable to endure the presence of such a beast. In one thrust, they rushed to the beach, where they headed towards Macedonia, raising a storm of sand and foam, as many disappeared beneath the waves.

In the fortress, panic reigned. What could they do against such an enemy? What bronze door-hinge could resist its jaws? What wall could withstand its huge claws? They were already beginning to prefer past dangers (it had, after all, been a fight against civilized animals), too exhausted to even reload their bows, when the monster emerged from the trees.

Yet a roar did not break from its jaws: instead came a human war-cry, the aggressive 'hollo!' of battle, and in reply came the triumphant, joyous cries of 'hail!' and 'hip, hurrah!' from the fortress.

Oh, wondrous miracle!

Beneath the feline head the face of a deity, lit from above, appeared; and it blended magnificently with his honey-coloured skin, his marble chest, his arms of oak and his splendid muscles.

And a cry, a concerted cry of freedom, of gratitude, of pride, filled the evening air:

'It is Hercules, Hercules is coming!'

The Ceremony

Arthur Machen, *Welsh novelist, essayist, translator and journalist, born 1863. Fascinated by black magic and the supernatural, he wrote stories and novels on these themes, such as* The Great God Pan *(1894) and* The Hill of Dreams *(1907), dying in poverty in 1947.*

From her childhood, from those early and misty days which began to seem unreal, she recollected the grey stone in the wood.

It was something between the pillar and the pyramid in shape, and its grey solemnity amidst the leaves and the grass shone and shone from those early years, always with some hint of wonder. She remembered how, when she was quite a little girl, she had strayed one day, on a hot afternoon, from her nurse's side, and only a little way in the wood the grey stone rose from the grass, and she cried out and ran back in panic terror.

'What a silly little girl!' the nurse had said. 'It's only the — — stone.' She had quite forgotten the name that the servant had given, and she was always ashamed to ask as she grew older.

But always that hot day, that burning afternoon of her childhood when she had first looked consciously on the grey image in the wood, remained not a memory, but a sensation. The wide wood swelling like the sea, the tossing of the bright boughs in the sunshine, the sweet smell of the grass and flowers, the beating of the summer wind upon her cheek, the gloom of the underglade rich, indistinct, gorgeous, significant as old tapestry; she could feel it and see it all, and the scent of it was in her nostrils. And in the midst of the picture, where strange plants grew gross in shadow, was the old grey shape of the stone.

But there were in her mind broken remnants of another and far earlier impression. It was all uncertain, the shadow of a shadow, so vague that it might well have been a dream that had mingled with the confused waking thoughts of a little child. She did not know that she remembered, she rather remembered the memory. But again it was a summer day, and a woman, perhaps the same nurse, held her in her arms, and went through the wood. The woman carried bright flowers in one hand; the dream had in it a glow of bright red, and the perfume of cottage roses. Then she saw herself put down for a moment on the grass, and the red colour stained the grim stone, and there was nothing else— except that one night she woke up and heard the nurse sobbing.

She often used to think of the strangeness of very early life; one came, it seemed, from a dark cloud, there was a glow of light, but for a moment, and afterwards the night. It was as if one gazed at a velvet curtain, heavy, mysterious, impenetrable blackness, and then, for the twinkling of an eye, one spied through a pinhole a storied town that flamed, with fire about its walls and pinnacles. And then again the folding darkness, so that sight became illusion, almost in the seeing. So to her was that earliest, doubtful vision of the grey stone, of the red colour spilled upon it, with the incongruous episode of the nursemaid, who wept at night.

But the later memory was clear; she could feel, even now, the inconsequent terror that sent her away shrieking, running to the nurse's skirts. Afterwards, through the days of girlhood, the stone had taken its place amongst the vast array of unintelligible things which haunt every child's imagination. It was part of her life, to be accepted and not questioned; her elders spoke of many things which she could not understand, she opened books and was dimly amazed, and in the Bible there were many phrases which seemed strange. Indeed, she was often puzzled by her parents' conduct, by their looks at one another, by their half-words, and amongst all these problems which she hardly recognized as problems, was the grey ancient figure rising from dark grass.

Some semi-conscious impulse made her haunt the wood where shadow enshrined the stone. One thing was noticeable: that all through the summer months the passers-by dropped flowers there. Withered blossoms were always on the ground, amongst the grass, and on the stone fresh blooms constantly appeared. From the daffodil to the Michaelmas daisy there was marked the calendar of the cottage gardens, and in the winter she had seen sprays of juniper and box, mistletoe and holly. Once she had been drawn through the bushes by a red glow, as if there had been a fire in the wood, and when she came to the place, all the stone shone and all the ground about it was bright with roses.

In her eighteenth year she went one day into the wood, carrying with her a book that she was reading. She hid herself in a nook of hazel, and her soul was full of poetry, when there was a rustling, the rapping of parted boughs returning to their place. Her concealment was but a little way from the stone, and she peered through the net of boughs, and saw a girl timidly approaching. She knew her quite well: it was Annie Dolben, the daughter of a labourer, lately a promising pupil at Sunday school. Annie was a nice-mannered girl, never failing in her curtsey, wonderful for her knowledge of the Jewish Kings. Her face had taken an expression that whispered, that hinted strange things; there was a light and a glow behind the veil of flesh. And in her hand she bore lilies.

The lady hidden in hazels watched Annie come close to the grey image; for a moment her whole body palpitated with expectation, almost the sense of what was to happen dawned upon her. She watched Annie crown the stone with flowers, she watched the amazing ceremony that followed.

And yet, in spite of all her blushing shame, she herself bore blossoms to the wood a few months later. She laid white hot-house lilies upon the stone, and orchids of dying purple, and crimson exotic flowers. Having kissed the grey image with devout passion, she performed there all the antique immemorial rite.

The Riddle

Walter de la Mare *(1873-1956), English poet and novelist. His writing reveals his fascination with childhood, nature and dreams, notably in* Henry Brocken *(1904) and* The Listeners *(1912), and in his fine anthology* Come Hither *(1939).*

So these seven children, Ann and Matilda, James, William and Henry, Harriet and Dorothea, came to live with their grandmother. The house in which their grandmother had lived since her childhood was built in the time of the Georges. It was not a pretty house, but roomy, substantial, and square; and a great cedar tree outstretched its branches almost to the windows.

When the children were come out of the cab (five sitting inside and two beside the driver), they were shown into their grandmother's presence. They stood in a little black group before the old lady, seated in her bow-window. And she asked them each their names, and repeated each name in her kind, quavering voice. Then to one she gave a work-box, to William a jack-knife, to Dorothea a painted ball; to each a present according to age. And she kissed all her grand-children to the youngest.

'My dears,' she said, 'I wish to see all of you bright and gay in my house. I am an old woman, so that I cannot romp with you; but Ann must look to you, and Mrs Fenn, too. And every morning and every evening you must all come in to see your granny; and bring me smiling faces, that call back to my mind my own son Harry. But all the rest of the day, when school is done, you shall do just as you please, my dears. And there is only one thing, just one, I would have you remember. In the large spare bedroom that looks out on the slate roof there stands in the corner an old oak chest; aye, older than I, my dears, a great deal older; older than my grandmother. Play anywhere else in the house, but not there.' She spoke kindly to them all, smiling at them; but she was very old, and her eyes seemed to see nothing of this world.

And the seven children, though at first they were gloomy and strange, soon began to be happy and at home in the great house. There was much to interest and to amuse them there; all was new to them. Twice every day, morning and evening, they came in to see their grandmother, who every day seemed more feeble; and she spoke pleasantly to them of her mother, and her childhood, but never forgetting to visit her store of sugar-plums. And so the weeks passed by . . .

It was evening twilight when Henry went upstairs from the nursery by himself to look at the oak chest. He pressed his fingers into the carved fruit and flowers, and spoke to the dark-smiling heads at the corners; and then, with a glance over his shoulder, he opened the lid and looked in. But the chest concealed no treasure, neither gold nor baubles, nor was there anything to alarm the eye. The chest was empty, except that it was lined with silk of old-rose seeming darker in the dusk, and smelling sweet of pot-pourri. And while Henry was looking in, he heard the softened laughter and the clinking of the cups downstairs in the nursery; and out at the window he saw the day darkening. These things brought strangely to his memory his mother who in her glimmering white dress used to read to him in the dusk; and he climbed into the chest; and the lid closed gently down over him.

When the other six children were tired with their playing, they filed into their grandmother's room for her good-night and her sugar-plums. She looked out between the candles at them as if she were uncertain of something in her thoughts. The next day Ann told her grandmother that Henry was not anywhere to be found.

'Dearie me, child. Then he must be gone away for a time,' said the old lady. She paused. 'But remember, all of you, do not meddle with the oak chest.'

But Matilda could not forget her brother Henry, finding no pleasure in playing without him. So she would loiter in the house thinking where he might be. And she carried her wooden doll in her bare arms, singing under her breath all she could make up about it. And when one bright morning she peeped in on the chest, so sweet-scented and secret it seemed that she took her doll with her into it—just as Henry himself had done.

So Ann, and James, and William, Harriet and Dorothea were left at home to play together. 'Some day maybe they will come back to you, my dears,' said their grandmother, 'or maybe you will go to them. Heed my warning as best you may.'

Now Harriet and William were friends together, pretending to be sweethearts; while James and Dorothea liked wild games of hunting, and fishing and battles.

On a silent afternoon in October, Harriet and William were talking softly together, looking out over the slate roof at the green fields, and they heard the squeak and frisking of a mouse behind them in the room. They went together and searched for the small, dark hole from whence it had come out. But finding no hole, they began to finger the carving of the chest, and to give names to the dark-smiling heads, just as Henry had done. '*I* know! Let's pretend you are Sleeping Beauty, Harriet,' said William, 'and I'll be the Prince that squeezes through the thorns and comes in.' Harriet looked gently and strangely at her brother but she got into the box and lay down, pretending to be fast asleep, and on tiptoe William leaned over, and seeing how big was the chest, he stepped in to kiss the Sleeping Beauty and to wake her from her quiet sleep. Slowly the carved lid turned on its noiseless hinges. And only the clatter of James and Dorothea came in sometimes to recall Ann from her book.

But their old grandmother was very feeble, and her sight dim, and her hearing extremely difficult.

Snow was falling through the still air upon the roof; and Dorothea was a fish in the oak chest, and James stood over the hole in the ice, brandishing a walking-stick for a harpoon, pretending to be an Esquimau. Dorothea's face was red, and her wild eyes sparkled through her tousled hair. And James had a crooked scratch upon his cheek. 'You must struggle, Dorothea, and then I shall swim back and drag you out. Be quick now!' He shouted with laughter as he was drawn into the open chest. And the lid closed softly and gently down as before.

Ann, left to herself, was too old to care overmuch for sugar-plums, but she would go solitary to bid her grandmother good-night; and the old lady looked wistfully at her over her spectacles.

'Well, my dear,' she said with trembling head; and she squeezed Ann's fingers between her own knuckled finger and thumb. 'What lonely old people we two are, to be sure!' Ann kissed her grandmother's soft, loose cheek. She left the old lady sitting in her easy chair, her hands upon her knees, and her head turned sidelong towards her.

When Ann was gone to bed she used to sit reading her book by candlelight. She drew up her knees under the sheets, resting her book upon them. Her story was about fairies and gnomes, and the gently-flowing moonlight of the narrative seemed to illumine the white pages, and she could hear in fancy fairy voices, so silent was the great many-roomed house, and so mellifluent were the words of the story. Presently she put out her candle, and, with a confused babel of voices close to her ear, and faint swift pictures before her eyes, she fell asleep.

And in the dead of night she rose out of her bed in dream, and with eyes wide open yet seeing nothing of reality, moved silently through the vacant house. Past the room where her grandmother was snoring in brief, heavy slumber, she stepped lightly and surely, and down the wide staircase. And Vega the far-shining stood over against the window above the slate roof. Ann walked into the strange room beneath as if she were being guided by the hand towards the oak chest. There, just as if she were dreaming it was her bed, she laid herself down in the old-rose silk, in the fragrant place. But it was so dark in the room that the movement of the lid was indistinguishable.

Through the long day, the grandmother sat in her bow-window. Her lips were pursed, and she looked with dim, inquisitive scrutiny upon the street where people passed to and fro, and vehicles rolled by. At evening she climbed the stair and stood in the doorway of the large spare bedroom. The ascent had shortened her breath. Her magnifying spectacles rested upon her nose. Leaning her hand on the doorpost she peered in towards the glimmering square of window in the quiet gloom. But she could not see far, because her sight was dim and the light of day feeble. Nor could she detect the faint fragrance as of autumnal leaves. But in her mind was a tangled skein of memories—laughter and tears, and children long ago become old-fashioned, and the advent of friends, and last farewells. And gossiping fitfully, inarticulately, with herself, the old lady went down again to her window-seat.

Who Knows?

Guy de Maupassant, *French novelist and short-story writer, born in the Château de Miromesnil in 1850, died at Auteuil in 1893. He wrote various novels and two hundred and fifteen short stories. His works include* La Maison Tellier *(1881),* Les Soeurs Rondoli *(1884),* Bel Ami (1885), Contes du Jour et de la Nuit *(1885),* Le Horla *(1887),* Monsieur Parent *(1888),* La Main Gauche *(1889),* Notre Coeur *(1890), and* Le Lit *(1895), all of which have been translated.*

I

My God! My God! So at last I am going to put down in writing all that has happened to me! But how can I do it? How dare I do it? It's all so bizarre, so incomprehensible, so crazy!

If I were not certain about what I have seen, certain that there has been no weak link in my logic, no error in my investigations, no lapse in the relentless progression of my observations, I would consider myself simply the victim of some hallucination, deceived by some strange fantasy. After all, who knows?

I am writing this in a private mental hospital. But I have come in here of my own free will—as a precaution, and because I am afraid. Only one living soul knows my story: the doctor in charge here. And now I am going to write it down—I don't really know why. Perhaps it is so I can get it out of my system, for I can feel it rising within me, like an unbearable nightmare . . . Well, here it is.

I have always had a solitary disposition, always been a dreamer, a sort of lone philosopher, kind to others, content with little, bearing neither bitterness towards men, nor resentment towards heaven. I have always lived alone, as a result of a kind of uneasiness which comes over me when I am with other people. How can I explain this? I don't suppose I can explain it. It's not that I refuse to see people, or to chat to them, or to have dinner with friends, but when I've been with them for some time, even with the people I know best, I find that they weary me, tire me out, get on my nerves—and with a growing exasperation I long to see them go, or go away myself, so that I can be alone.

This feeling I have is more than a desire: it is a compelling necessity. And if I had to endure the continued presence of other people, if I had to go on listening to their conversation for any length of time, something would certainly happen to me. What exactly would it be? Ah, who knows? Perhaps I should faint—something like that.

I am so passionately fond of solitude that I can't even tolerate other people sleeping under the same roof. I can't bear to live in Paris because, for me, it seems like a lingering death. Not only do I suffer a spiritual death, but I also find that my body and nerves are tortured by the vast, swarming crowds of people who are living all around me, even when they are asleep. Oh, yes, I find the sleep of other human beings even harder to bear than their endless talking. And I can never get any rest myself when I know—or when I suspect—that on the other side of a wall there are lives being interrupted by those regular eclipses of consciousness which we call sleep.

Why do I feel like this? Who knows? Perhaps there is a very simple explanation: perhaps it's because I tire very quickly of anything which takes place outside of me, as it were. There are a lot of people in my situation . . .

One of the results of all this is that I become deeply attached to inanimate objects, which seem to me to take on the importance of living creatures. My house has become—or rather, *had* become—a whole world in which I lived a solitary yet active life, surrounded by physical things—familiar items of furniture and other odds and ends, which seemed to me to be as warm and friendly as human faces. I had gradually filled and adorned my home with these things, and when I was safe inside I felt as content and satisfied and genuinely happy as if I were in the arms of a loving woman whose familiar caress had become a gentle, tranquillizing necessity.

This house stood in a beautiful garden which isolated it from the roads; yet it was within reach of a town where, if I happened to feel like it, I could find all the social activities in which I took an occasional interest. All my servants slept in a building some distance away at the bottom of the kitchen-garden, which was surrounded by a high wall. The embrace of sombre nights in the silence of this house of mine, lost, hidden, submerged amongst the foliage of great trees, was so restful and so good for me that every evening I would delay going to bed for several hours, just so that I could enjoy it even longer.

On that particular day there had been a performance of Ernest Reyer's *Sigurd* at the theatre in town. It was the first time that I had heard this beautiful romantic opera, and it had given me the greatest of pleasure.

I was walking back home, at a brisk and cheerful pace, with my head full of rich melodies and pretty, fairy-tale scenes. It was very dark indeed—so dark, in fact, that I could hardly make out the edge of the main road, and several times I nearly fell into a ditch. The distance from the toll-gate to my house is about a mile, perhaps a little more—let us say twenty minutes at normal walking pace. It would be about one o'clock in the morning—possibly as late as half past one. As I walked, the sky ahead of me seemed to grow a little lighter, and a slender crescent-moon appeared, the melancholy crescent of the moon's last quarter. The crescent of the first quarter, the one you see rising at four or five o'clock in the evening, is bright, cheerful, glistening with silver, but the one you see rising after midnight is reddish, dismal, disturbing—the sinister moon of the Witches'

Sabbath. All those who are out late at night must have noticed this difference. The crescent of the first quarter, even if it is only as slender as a thread, sheds a cheerful radiance which gladdens the heart and lights up the earth sufficiently to leave clear-cut shadows. The crescent of the last quarter struggles to shed its dying light, which is so feeble that it hardly casts any shadows at all.

In the distance I noticed the gloomy mass of trees surrounding my garden, and for some reason or other I felt uneasy at the thought of entering it. I slackened my pace . . . The night was very mild. That great cluster of trees had the look of a tomb in which my house was buried.

I opened my gate and walked down the long avenue of sycamore trees which led up to the house. It was arched overhead, like a high tunnel, and ran past dense masses of shrubbery and round dark, moonlit lawns on which flower-beds superimposed their oval patches of wan colours.

When I got near the house I was overcome by a strange feeling of agitation. I stood still. There was not a sound to be heard. There was not a leaf stirring in the breeze. 'What on earth's the matter with me?' I thought. For ten years I had been coming home like this without feeling the slightest bit of anxiety. I was not afraid—and I never have been afraid—when coming home late at night. The mere sight of a strange man, some prowler or burglar, would have made me furious, and I would have leaped upon him without a moment's hesitation. Besides, I was armed: I had my revolver with me. But I did not touch it, because I was determined to master this nervousness stirring within me.

What was it? Some kind of premonition? Was it the mysterious foreboding which takes possession of a man's senses when he is about to see something inexplicable? Possibly. Who knows?

As I moved slowly forwards I felt my skin tingling all over, and when I got to the wall of my vast house with its closed shutters, I knew that I would have to wait a few minutes before I could open the door and go inside. So I sat down on a seat under the windows of my drawing-room. I stayed there for a while, trembling a little, with my head leaning back against the wall of the house, and my eyes wide open, staring at the gloomy foliage. For the first few moments I noticed nothing unusual. There was a sort of rushing sound in my ears—but I often get that. It sometimes seems as though I can hear trains going by, or bells ringing, or marching footsteps.

But soon these head-noises became louder, more distinct, more recognizable. I had been mistaken. It was not the usual surging in my arteries that was filling my ears with this murmuring sound, but a very peculiar, rather jumbled noise. And there was no doubt whatever that it was coming from inside my house.

Through the wall I could make out this continuous noise—more like a vibration than a noise, the sort of confused sound you would expect if a number of things were being moved about. It was as though all my articles of furniture were vibrating, being moved from their accustomed places, being gently dragged about the house.

Oh, I can assure you that for an appreciable time I doubted the evidence of my senses. But when I had pressed my ear against a shutter so I could get a getter idea of what was going on inside, I became absolutely convinced that something abnormal and incomprehensible was taking place in my home. I was not exactly afraid, but I was . . . how can I put it? . . . stunned with astonishment. I didn't even release the safety-catch on my revolver, because I felt sure there would be no need to use it . . . I simply waited.

I waited for a long time, unable to come to any decision, thinking very clearly, but beside myself with anxiety. I waited, standing there, listening all the time to the noise which was now growing louder, occasionally reaching a kind of violent intensity, which seemed like a growl of impatience or anger—a sort of mysterious rebellion.

Then, suddenly feeling ashamed of my cowardice, I took my bunch of keys, found the one I needed, pushed it into the keyhole, turned it fully in the lock and, pushing on the door with all my strength, I swung it open so violently that it banged against the inner wall.

The noise it made rang out like a gun-shot—and, instantly, as if in reply to this loud bang, from the whole of my house, from top to bottom, there came the most tremendous uproar. It was so unexpected, so horrible, so deafening, that I recoiled a few steps, and—though I still knew it was useless—I drew my revolver from its holster.

I waited—but not for long! Now I could hear an extraordinary stamping noise on the stairs, on the floors, on the carpets—not the stamping of shoes worn by human beings, but the stamping of crutches—wooden crutches, and iron crutches which made a noise like the clashing of cymbals . . . And then it was that I suddenly noticed an armchair on the threshold of my front door—the big armchair I always used when reading. It was going out of the house, swaying and waddling as it went . . . There it was, going off into the garden . . . Other chairs followed it, the ones out of my drawing-room. Then came the low couches, dragging themselves along like crocodiles on their short legs. Then out came all the rest of my chairs, leaping about like goats, and the little stools, bounding along like rabbits.

What a state I was in! I ran out and hid in the shrubbery, crouching down, unable to take my eyes off this march-past of my furniture—for every stick of it was going, one item after the other, some quickly, some slowly, depending on the size and weight. My piano, my huge grand piano, galloped past like a runaway horse, rattling and tinkling with music. The tiniest little objects were running over the gravel: the glasses, the goblets, in which the moonlight gleamed with the phosphorescence of glow-worms. The curtains and carpets were writhing and slithering along, like octopuses . . . Then I saw my writing-desk appear. It was a valuable antique from the eighteenth century and it contained all the letters I have ever received, the entire story of my personal life, a long story which has brought me much suffering! And there were photographs in there, too.

Suddenly, I was afraid no longer. I rushed forward and flung myself on this desk, grabbing hold of it as if I were tackling a burglar. But it continued irresistibly on its way, and in spite of all my struggles, in spite of all my anger, I couldn't even manage to slow it down. Struggling like a desperate man against this terrifying strength, I was flung to the ground still wrestling to hold it back.

Then it sent me rolling over, dragged me along the gravel—and the furniture that had been coming along behind it started to walk over me, trampling on my legs and bruising them badly. Then, as soon as I had let go of the desk, the rest of the furniture passed over my body, just like cavalry charging over a dismounted soldier.

By this time I was out of my mind with terror, but I managed to drag myself out of the drive and hide once again amongst the trees, from where I watched all my possessions disappearing into the night—every single one of them: the lowliest, the smallest, the most ordinary, even the ones I had never paid much attention to, but all of them belonging to me.

Then I heard, some distance away, the tremendous clatter of doors being shut. It came from my own house, which was now filled with the sonorous echoes of an empty house. The doors of the building slammed shut from top to bottom until finally the front-door, which in my folly I had opened to permit this mass escape, slammed shut last of all.

I took flight myself, running all the way to the town, and I only recovered my self-control when I got into the streets where there were a few people about, coming home late. I went and rang at the door of a hotel where I was well known. With my hands I had dashed the dirt off my clothes, and at the hotel I told the story that I had lost my bunch of keys, which also included the key to the kitchen-garden. I told them that this was where my servants were asleep in a detached building surrounded by the high wall which protected my fruit and vegetables from prowlers.

They gave me a bed, and though I buried myself under the sheets I couldn't sleep, but lay there waiting for daybreak, listening to the pounding of my heart. I had told somebody in the hotel to inform my servants of my whereabouts as soon as it was light, and at seven o'clock in the morning my valet banged on my door. From his face I could see that he was terribly upset.

'Something dreadful has happened during the night, monsieur,' he said. 'All your furniture has been stolen, monsieur—everything, absolutely everything, even down to the smallest articles.'

I felt pleased when I heard him say this. Why? Who knows? I was completely in control of myself, certain that I would be able to conceal my feelings and not tell anybody about what I had seen, certain that I could hide this thing, bury it deep in my mind like some frightful secret. I answered him by saying: 'It must be the same people as the ones who stole my keys. We must inform the police immediately. I'll get dressed and be with you in just a few moments.'

The investigations went on for five months. The police discovered nothing whatever. They could neither trace the smallest of my possesions nor uncover the slightest clue about the thieves. My God! If I had told them what I knew . . .If I had told them . . . they would have locked me up—me, not the thieves—me, the man who had been able to see what I had seen.

Oh, I knew how to keep my mouth shut. But I didn't start re-furnishing my house. It would have been quite pointless. The whole business would have started all over again. I didn't want to go back to my house. I never did go back. I never saw it again.

I came to Paris and stayed in a hotel. I consulted various doctors about the state of my nerves, something which has been worrying me a great deal ever since that appalling night.

They strongly advised me to travel. I took their advice . . .

II

I began with a trip to Italy. The sunshine there did me good. For six months I wandered from Genoa to Venice, from Venice to Florence, from Florence to Rome, from Rome to Naples. Then I travelled through Sicily, a place which has both wonderful scenery and wonderful historical sites, relics from the days of the Greeks and the Normans. I went over to Africa and made a safe journey across that great, calm yellow desert, peopled by camels, gazelles and nomadic Arabs, and where in the crystal-clear atmosphere there is no suggestoin of any haunting vision, either by night or day.

I returned to France by way of Marseilles, and, in spite of the Provençal gaiety, the fact that the skies were less bright than in Africa made me rather depressed. On returning to Europe I felt as a sick man must feel when he believes himself to be cured—and then a dull pain reminds him that the focus of infection has not been eliminated.

I came back to Paris, and after a month here I became bored. By now it was autumn, and before winter set in I wanted to take a trip through Normandy, where I had never been before.

I began by visiting Rouen, of course, and for a whole week I wandered in a state of ecstatic enthusiasm through this medieval city, this amazing museum of extraordinary Gothic buildings.

Now one afternoon, about four o'clock, I turned down a most peculiar street, along which flowed an inky-black stream called the Eau de Robec. I was gazing up at the queer, ancient façades of the houses when my attention was suddenly caught by the sight of a whole row of shops dealing in second-hand furniture.

How well they had chose their site, these sordid dealers in old junk. There they were in this weird alley, perched above this sinster-looking stream, and above them were the angular roofs of tiles and slates on which there still creaked the weather-cocks of a bygone age.

In the depths of these gloomy shops you could see a higgledy-piggledy assortment of carved chests, pottery from Rouen, Nevers and Moustiers, statues of various kinds, some painted, some in oak, images of saints, church ornaments, garments worn by priests; there were even holy chalices and an old wooden tabernacle painted gold, in which God no longer resided. Oh, what strange, mysterious grottoes there were in these tall houses crammed from cellar to attic with objects of every conceivable kind, objects whose life seemed to be over, and yet which had outlived their mortal owners—even outlived their century, their period and their fashion, so they could be bought as curios by new generations.

My passion for antiques was being aroused again in this stronghold of antique-dealers. I went from shop to shop, taking quick, light steps across the little bridges made from three or four rotten planks which lay across the evil-smelling water of the Eau de Robec.

Gracious God! What a shock! I found myself looking at one of my own wardrobes—one of the finest I had. It was standing at the side of a vaulted gallery which was cluttered up with antiques, a place which looked like the entrance to the catacombs of a cemetery for old furniture. I went up to the wardrobe, trembling all over, trembling so much that I hardly dared touch it. Hesitantly I reached out my hand. And yet it really was mine: a unique Louis XIII wardrobe, which would have been recognized straight away by anyone who had seen it even once. Suddenly looking a little further into the gloomy depths of this gallery, I noticed three of my armchairs, the ones upholstered in petit point tapestry, then, still deeper in the gallery, my two Henry II tables, so rare that people used to come all the way from Paris to see them.

Just imagine how I felt! Just think of my state of mind!

I moved further into the gallery. I was almost petrified with fear, but I am not a coward, and in spite of my agony of mind I moved forward, like a knight from the Dark Ages thrusting his way into a place that is haunted and bewitched. I went on, and at each step I took I found something that had belonged to me— my chandeliers, my books, my pictures, my curtains, my antique weapons— everything was there except the writing-desk containing my letters, and this was nowhere to be seen.

I went on, going down steps leading to lower floors, then climbing to ones higher up. I was all alone. I called out; but nobody answered. I was all alone— there was not another soul in this vast labyrinth of a building.

Night fell, and I had to sit there in the darkness on one of my own chairs, for I was determined not to leave the place. Every now and then I shouted out: 'Hello! Hello! Is anybody there?'

I must have been there for more than an hour when I heard the sound of footsteps—light, slow footsteps—coming from somewhere in the gallery. I nearly jumped up and ran out in the street but, bracing myself, I called out once again, and I saw a light appear in an adjoining room.

'Who's there?' asked a voice.

I replied: 'A customer.'

The answer came back: 'It's very late for you to be coming into a shop, isn't it?'

'I've been waiting for more than an hour,' I rejoined.

'You could come back tomorrow.'

'Tomorrow I shall have left Rouen.'

I simply dared not go towards him—and he was not coming out to me. The bright glow was still coming from his lamp and lighting up a tapestry which depicted two angels hovering over the corpses on a battle-field. This item, too, belonged to me.

I called out: 'Well, then? Are you coming?'

He replied: 'I'm waiting for you.'

I got up and went towards him.

In the middle of a large room there stood a little man, very short and very fat, phenomenally fat, like some hideous freak.

He had a thin, straggling beard, which was patchy and yellowish—and there was not a hair on his head! Not a hair! As he lifted up his candle at arm's length in order to see me better, his skull looked just like a little, round moon in this enormous room cluttered with old furniture. His face was wrinkled and bloated; his eyes were so sunken they could hardly be seen.

I bargained with him for three chairs which belonged to me, and paid him a large sum for them in cash, giving him only the number of my room and the name of the hotel. The chairs were to be delivered the following morning by nine o'clock.

Then I left. He saw me to the door, behaving very courteously.

I then went to the local superintendent of police and told him about how my furniture had been stolen and what I had just discovered.

He immediately sent a telegram to the department which had been investigating the burglary, and asked me to wait until he received the information he required. An hour later the reply came, confirming my story.

'I'm going to have this man arrested and questioned,' said the superintendent. 'And it must be done straight away because he might have got suspicious and had your belongings removed . . . If you can go and have a meal and come back in a couple of hours, I'll have him here by then, and I can question him again in your presence.'

'I can certainly do that, monsieur. I am extremely grateful to you.'

I went to my hotel and dined with a heartier appetite than I could have believed possible. I suppose I was feeling rather pleased about the way things had worked out. At last we had him.

Two hours later I went back to the police officer, who was waiting for me.

'Well, now, monsieur!' he said as soon as he saw me. 'We've not found this thief of yours. My men haven't been able to get their hands on him at all.'

'Ah!' I gasped, and suddenly felt as though I was going to faint.

'But,' I asked him, 'surely you've managed to find his house?'

'Yes, indeed. And I'm going to have it kept under surveillance until he gets back. But as for the man himself . . . disappeared!'

'Disappeared?'

'Yes, disappeared. He usually spends his evenings at the house of a neighbour, a woman who is a second-hand dealer, like himself—a queer old witch of a woman, a widow by the name of Bidoin. She hasn't seen him tonight, and she can't tell us where he is. We shall have to wait until tomorrow.'

I left the police station. Ah, those ancient streets of Rouen, how sinister, how disturbing, how haunted they now seemed to me!

I slept very badly that night, with a nightmare at the end of each brief interval of sleep.

The next day I waited until ten o'clock before going to the police. I didn't want to give them the impression that I was too anxious or in too much of a hurry.

The dealer had not turned up. His shop was still closed.

The superintendent said to me: 'I've taken all the necessary steps. I've been in touch with headquarters. I want you to come with us to this shop. I'll have it forced open, and then you can show me what belongs to you.'

We drove there in a carriage. Policemen were standing in front of the shop, and with them there was a locksmith—who soon opened it up for us.

When I went in I could see neither my cupboard, nor my armchairs, nor my tables, nor anything at all that had once furnished my house—nothing whatever, and yet the night before I could hardly move a step without coming across something of mine.

The superintendent was surprised, and at first he looked at me rather suspiciously.

I said: 'My word, monsieur, it's a remarkable coincidence that the furniture has disappeared at the same time as the dealer.'

'That's certainly true,' he said with a smile. 'You know, you were wrong to buy those things of yours yesterday—and pay for them as well. It'll have aroused his suspicions.'

'What I simply can't understand,' I said, 'is that every single space that was occupied by my furniture has now been filled by other articles.'

'Oh,' replied the superintendent, 'he's had all night—and probably been helped by accomplices as well. And I dare say this house communicates with the ones on each side . . . Don't worry, monsieur. I'm going to give this case my personal attention. Now we know his hide-out it won't be long before we get our hands on this villain.'

Ah, my heart, my heart, my poor heart, how madly it was beating!

I stayed in Rouen for a fortnight. The man never came back.

My God! My God! Who could ever have been any problem to a man like that, or caught him off his guard?

Now, when I had been in Rouen exactly a fortnight, on the morning of the fifteenth day, I received from the gardener who had been left in charge of my locked and empty house the following strange letter:

Dear Sir,

I beg to inform you that last night something happened which none of us can understand, not even the police. All the furniture has come back—all of it, with not a single thing missing. It's all here, down to the tiniest little things. The house is now exactly the same as it was on the night of the burglary. It's enough to drive you out of your mind. It happened in the middle of the night—between Friday and Saturday. The whole drive has got deep ruts in it, and it looks as though they'd dragged everything from the gate right up to the front-door. It was just like that the day everything disappeared.

We're waiting for you to come back, monsieur, and I remain,
                              Your obedient servant,
                                        Raudin, Philippe

Oh no! Oh no! No! No! No! I shall never go back!

I took this letter to the Rouen superintendent.

'It's a very clever piece of restitution,' he said. 'We'd better lie low for the time being. Don't worry; we'll nab this fellow one of these days.'

But they haven't nabbed him. Oh, no. They haven't nabbed him—and I'm as scared of him now as if he were a ferocious beast about to spring on me from behind my back.

Untraceable! That's what he is—untraceable. Nobody can possibly find him, this monster with the moon-like skull. They'll never catch him. He'll never go back to his shop. What does *he* care? I am the only person who could possibly confront him—and I don't want to!

No, I don't want to! I don't want to! I don't want to!

And, anyway, what if he does come back, what if he does return to his shop, who will be able to prove that my furniture was on his premises? Mine is the only evidence against him, and I'm well aware that the police are beginning to treat it with suspicion.

Oh, no! I couldn't go on living that kind of life. And yet I couldn't keep quiet about what I have seen. I couldn't go on living a normal life so long as I dreaded the possibility of this business starting all over again.

So I came to see the doctor who runs this private mental hospital, and I told him everything.

After he had spent a long time asking me questions, he said: 'Monsieur, would you be willing to stay here for a while?'

'Yes, monsieur. I'd be glad to.'

'Have you sufficient money?'

'Yes, monsieur.'

'Would you like any of your friends to come and visit you?'

'No, monsieur! No! I don't want anybody! The man from Rouen might try to get at me here—out of revenge.'

And I have been alone, all alone, for three months. My nerves are more or less calm now. I have only one fear . . . Suppose the antique-dealer went mad . . . and suppose they brought him into this place . . . Even the prisons are not safe . . .

The Shadow of the Players

I n one of the tales which make up the series of the *Mabinogion*, two enemy
kings play chess while in a nearby valley their respective armies battle and
destroy each other. Messengers arrive with reports of the battle; the kings do
not seem to hear them and, bent over the silver chessboard, they move the gold
pieces. Gradually it becomes apparent that the vicissitudes of the battle follow
the vicissitudes of the game. Toward dusk, one of the kings overturns the board
because he has been checkmated, and presently a blood-spattered horseman
comes to tell him: 'Your army is in flight. You have lost the kingdom.'

—EDWIN MORGAN

The Cat

H. A. **Murena** (*pseudonym of Hector Alberto Alvarez, 1923-*), *born in Buenos Aires. He has
published* Primer Testamento (*short stories, 1946*), La Vida Nueva (*poetry, 1951*), El juez
(*play, 1953*), El Pecado Original de America (*essays, 1954*), La Fatalidad de los Cuerpos
(*novel, 1955*), El Centro del Infierno (*short stories, 1956*), Las Leyes de la Noche (*short
story, 1958*), El Circulo de los Paraisos (*poetry, 1958*), El Escanalo y el Fuego (*poetry,
1959*), Homo Atomicus (*essays, 1961*), Relampago de la Duracion (*poetry, 1962*), Ensayos
Sobre Subversion (*essays, 1963*), El Demonio de la Armonia (*poetry, 1964*).

H ow long had he been shut away?
The May morning on which it took place, veiled by the mist, seemed as
unreal to him as the day he was born, an event perhaps truer than any other, but
which we only manage to think of as an incredible idea. When he suddenly
discovered the secret and impressive control the other one had over her, he
decided to do it. He told himself that perhaps he would operate for her sake, to
free her from a useless, degrading seduction. However, he was thinking of
himself, he was following a road first taken long ago. And that morning, leaving
the house, after it had all happened, he saw that the wind had driven away the
mist, and on raising his eyes before the blinding clarity, he saw in the sky a

black cloud which looked like a huge spider fleeing across a field of snow. But what he would never forget was that from that moment on, the other man's cat, the cat whose owner had boasted that he would never abandon him, began to follow him, with a certain indifference, almost with patience at his initial attempts to scare him off, until he became his shadow.

He found the boarding house, not too dirty or uncomfortable, for he still bothered about that. The cat was large and muscular, grey-haired, a dirty white in parts. He gave the impression of an old and degraded god who had not yet lost all his power to harm men. They didn't like him; they looked at him with fear and disgust; and with permission from his temporary owner, they threw him out. The next day, when he returned to his room, he found the cat installed there; sitting in the armchair, he barely raised his head, peered at him, and carried on dozing. They threw him out a second time, and he got back into the house, into the room, without anyone knowing how. So he won, because from then on the owner of the boarding house and her acolytes gave up the fight.

Can one conceive of a cat influencing the life of a man to the extent of altering its course?

At first he went out a lot; the habits of an easy life made that room, with its little lamp glowing a weak yellow, leaving many corners in shadow, with its surprisingly ugly and rickety furniture if you looked closely, purple forests, the sound of waves against the rocks. Without knowing why, he began to be able to contemplate pleasant images: the light of the lamp—for ever on—waned until it vanished, and, floating in the air, women covered in long clothes appeared, their faces the colour of blood or pale green, horses of an intense sky-blue . . .

The cat, meanwhile, remained undisturbed in his armchair.

One day he heard women's voices at his door. Although he tried, he couldn't make out what they were saying, but their tones were sufficient. It was as though he had an enormous flabby belly and they were driving a stake into it and he could feel the stimulus, but it was so distant, despite being extremely intense, that he realized it would be several hours before he could react. For one of the voices belonged to the owner of the boarding house, but the other one was *hers*: she must have finally discovered where he was.

He sat on the bed. He wanted to do something, and couldn't.

He watched the cat: he had also got up and was looking towards the shutters, but was very calm. That increased his feeling of impotence.

His whole body pulsated, and the voices didn't cease. He wanted to do something. Suddenly he felt such tension in his head that it seemed as though when it stopped he would disintegrate, dissolve.

Then he opened his mouth, not knowing for a moment why he did so, and finally he miaowed; shrilly, with infinite despair, he miaowed.

The Story of the Foxes

Niu Chiao, *ninth-century Chinese poet and savant. He wrote more than thirty books.*

Wang saw two Foxes standing on their hind legs and leaning against a tree. One of them held a sheet of paper in its hand, and they laughed together as though they were sharing a joke. Wang tried to frighten them off but they stood their ground, and finally he shot at the one holding the page. The Fox was hit in the eye and Wang took away the piece of paper. At the inn Wang told the story to the other guests. While he spoke a gentleman having a bandaged eye came in. He listened to Wang's story with interest and asked if he might not be shown the paper. Wang was just about to produce it when the innkeeper noticed that the the newcomer had a tail. 'He's a Fox!' he shouted, and on the spot the gentleman turned into a Fox and fled. The Foxes tried time after time to recover the paper, which was filled with indecipherable writing, but were repeatedly set back. Wang decided at last to return home. On the road he met his whole family, who were on their way to the capital. They said that he had ordered them to undertake the journey, and his mother showed him the letter in which he asked them to sell off all their property and join him in the city. Wang, studying the letter, saw that the page was blank. Although they no longer had a roof over their heads, he ordered, 'Let's go back.'

One day a younger brother appeared whom everyone had given up for dead. He asked about the family's misfortunes and Wang told him the whole story. 'Ah,' said the brother when Wang came to the part about the Foxes, 'there lies the root of all the evil.' Wang showed him the page in question. Tearing it from Wang's hand, the brother stuffed the sheet into his pocket and said, 'At last I have back what I wanted.' Then, changing himself into a Fox, he made his escape.

The Atonement

Silvina Ocampo, *Argentinian writer born in Buenos Aires. Author of:* The Forgotten Journey *(1937);* Inventory of the Motherland *(1942);* Metric Spaces *(1945);* Garden Sonnets *(1948);* The Autobiography of Irene *(1948);* The Poems of Love in Despair *(1949);* The Names *(1953);* The Fury *(1960);* The Guests *(1961);* The Bitter for the Sweet *(1962).*

Antonio summoned Ruperto and I to the room at the back of the house. Imperiously, he told us to sit down. The bed was made. He went out to the patio and opened the door of the birdcage, then came back and lay down on the bed.

'I'm going to show you a trick', he said.

'Are you going to be hired by the circus?' I asked.

He whistled two or three times and Favorita, Maria Callas and Mandarin, who was red, all flew into the room. Staring at the ceiling, he again gave a whistle, more high pitched and tremulous this time. Was this the trick? Why had he summoned us, Ruperto and I? Why had he not waited for Cleobula to arrive? I thought that the whole purpose of this show was to demonstrate that Ruperto was not blind, but mad, and that he would prove it in a moment of emotion, in the face of Antonio's distress. The canaries flying around made me feel tired. My memories flew around my mind with the same insistence. They say that at the moment of death one reviews one's whole life—I relived mine that afternoon with a remote feeling of sadness.

I could see, as clearly as if the image were painted on the wall, my wedding to Antonio at five in the afternoon, in the month of December.

It was already hot and when we arrived at our house, to my surprise, from the window in the bedroom where I took off my wedding dress and veil, I saw a canary.

Now I realize that it was, in fact, Mandarin pecking at the only remaining orange on the tree in the patio.

Antonio didn't stop kissing me when he saw me so engrossed in the spectacle. The bird's merciless pecking of the orange fascinated me. I contemplated the scene until Antonio dragged me trembling to the bed, which, surrounded with wedding presents, had been a source of pleasure to him and of terror to me on the eve of our wedding. The dark-red velvet bedspread had a stagecoach journey embroidered on it. I shut my eyes and hardly knew what happened afterwards. Love is also a journey; for many days after that, I learnt its lessons, without seeing or understanding the pleasure and the pain that it causes. At the beginning, I think that Antonio and I loved each other equally, with no difficulty other than that which my conscience and his timidity created.

The tiny house with its equally tiny garden is situated at the entrance to the village. The fresh mountain air surrounds us and we can see the nearby countryside when we open the windows.

We already had a radio and a fridge. Numerous friends would come to our house on days when there was a holiday or to celebrate some event in the family. What more could we ask for? Cleobula and Ruperto would visit us more often because they had been friends of ours since childhood. Antonio had fallen in love with me, they had known this. He hadn't looked for me, he hadn't chose me, rather I had chosen him. His only ambition was to be loved by his wife and that she should remain faithful to him. He attached little importance to money.

Ruperto would sit in a corner of the patio and, while he was tuning his guitar, would ask, without any preamble, for a mate tea, or an orange juice if it was hot. I thought of him as one of the many friends or relatives who were like part of the furniture in the house, that one only notices when they are broken or put in a different place.

'These canaries sing well', Cleobula would invariably remark, but, had she been able to kill them with a broom, she would have done so because she hated them. What would she have said if she had seen them perform so many ridiculous tricks without Antonio having to give them a single little lettuce leaf or a single sweet!

Automatically, I would hand the mate or the glass of orange juice to Ruperto, sitting in the shade of the vine where he always sat, in a Vienna chair, like a dog in its corner. I didn't think of him as a woman thinks of a man, there was not the slightest hint of flirtatiousness in the way I treated him. Often, after having washed my hair, with my wet hair held back by clips, looking an absolute fright, or maybe with my toothbrush in my mouth and with toothpaste on my lips, or my hands covered in soap when I was about to wash some clothes, an apron tied at my waist, with a large stomach like a pregnant woman, I would open the door and ask him to come in without even looking at him. Often in my carelessness, I think he saw me come out of the bathroom wrapped in a towel, shuffling along in my slippers like an old woman.

Chusco, Albahaca and Serranito flew to the container which held little thorny arrows. Carrying the arrows, they would enthusiastically fly to other containers which held a dark liquid in which they dipped the minute tips of the arrows. They looked like toy birds, cheap penholders or the decorations on a grandmother's hat.

Cleobula, who is not a malicious person, had noticed and told me that Ruperto stared at me far too intently. 'What eyes!' he'd repeat incessantly. 'What wonderful eyes!'

'I've managed to keep my eyes open when I sleep', murmured Antonio. 'It's one of the cleverest tricks I've ever managed to do.'

I jumped when I heard his voice. Was that the trick? After all, what was so extraordinary about it?

'Like Ruperto', I said with a strange voice.

'Like Ruperto', repeated Antonio. 'The canaries obey my orders more easily than my eyelids.'

The three of us were in that darkened room as if in penance. But what possible link could there be between his eyes being open during sleep and the orders he gave to the canaries? No wonder Antonio left me somehow perplexed—he was so different from other men!

Cleobula had also assured me that while Ruperto tuned his guitar he would look me over from the tip of my hair to the tips of my feet. One night, falling asleep, half drunk in the patio, his eyes had stayed fixed on me. The result of this was that I became self-conscious and maybe even flirtatious. Ruperto looked at me through a kind of mask into which his animal-like eyes were set, eyes that he didn't close, even to sleep. With a mysterious intensity, he would fix his eyes on me when he was thirsty, God knows with what intention, just as he fixed them on the glass of orange juice or mate tea that I served him. No one in the whole province, in the whole world had eyes that stared so—a deep shining blue, like fragments of sky, set them apart from the others, whose eyes seemed dull or dead. Ruperto was not a man, he was a pair of eyes, without face, without voice, without a body, or so it seemed to me but Antonio didn't share my feeling. During the months when my lack of awareness came to exasperate him, at the slightest excuse he would talk to me abruptly or make me do arduous tasks, as if I had been his slave instead of his wife. It grieved me to see how Antonio had changed.

Men are so strange! What was the trick that he wanted to show us? The business about the circus hadn't been a joke.

Soon after we were married, he began to frequently miss work, with the excuse that he had a headache or an inexplicable queasiness in his stomach. Were all husbands like this?

At the back of the house, the huge birdcage full of canaries that Antonio had always looked after so conscientiously lay forgotten. In the morning, if I had the time, I'd clean the birdcage, put canary grass, water and lettuce in the white containers and when the females were going to lay eggs, I'd prepare the little nests. Antonio had always looked after these things, but he no longer showed the slightest interest in doing it or even in my doing it.

We had been married for two years and not one child! Instead, how many young had the canaries given birth to!

The smell of musk and cedar filled the room. The canaries smelt like hens, Antonio of tobacco and sweat, but Ruperto smelt only of alcohol. People told me he often got drunk. The room was so dirty! Canary grass, breadcrumbs, lettuce leaves, cigarette ends and ash were scattered over the floor.

Since childhood, Antonio had spent his free time training animals. He first put his art into practice, for he was a true artist, with a dog, a horse, then with a skunk that had had an operation and that he carried around for a time in his pocket. Later, when he met me, he thought of training canaries because I liked them. During the months of our courtship, so as to win my heart, he had sent the canaries to me carrying little pieces of paper with romantic messages written on them or flowers tied with a little ribbon. From the house where he lived to mine there were fifteen large blocks; the winged messengers went from his house to mine without faltering. Incredible as it may seem, they managed to put the flowers in my hair and a little message in the pocket of my blouse.

Canaries putting flowers in my hair and little papers in my pocket, was that not more difficult than the ridiculous things they were doing with those wretched little arrows?

Antonio came to enjoy great prestige in the village. 'If you hypnotized women like you do birds nobody would resist your charms', his aunts would tell him in the hope that their nephew would marry some millionairess. As I have already mentioned, Antonio was not interested in money. Since the age of fifteen he had worked as a mechanic and he had all he wanted, which is what he offered me when he proposed. We needed nothing else to make us happy. I couldn't understand why Antonio didn't find an excuse to keep Ruperto away. Any reason would have been good enough for the purpose, even if no more than a quarrel over work or politics, which, without escalating into a fullblown fight using fists or weapons, would have meant that Ruperto was barred from entering our house. Antonio didn't let any of his feelings show, except for in that change of character which only I knew how to interpret. Going against my natural modesty, I realized that because of me my husband, whom I had always considered the most reasonable of men, was being driven out of his mind with jealousy.

Antonio whistled and took off his vest. His naked torso seemed made of bronze. I trembled to look at him. I remembered that before marrying him I blushed when I saw a statue which looked very much like him. Had I not seen him naked before? Why was I so surprised?

But Antonio's character underwent another change which calmed me somewhat: he went from being apathetic to being extremely active, from being melancholy he appeared to become cheerful. His life became full of mysterious occupations, of a coming and going which seemed to denote great interest in life. After dinner, we didn't even have a moment's peace to listen to the radio or to read the daily papers, or just to do nothing, or to talk for a while about the events of the day. Neither were Sundays or holidays an excuse to allow ourselves a rest. I, who am like Antonio's mirror image, became possessed by his restlessness and, overpowered by the necessity to keep up with my husband's enigmatic occupations, paced around the house, tidying wardrobes that had already being tidied or washing spotless cushion covers. His love and assiduous care for the birds redoubled and took up a large part of the day. He added new sections to the birdcage and the little dead tree which stood at its centre was replaced by another larger and more graceful one which made the cage more attractive.

Dropping their arrows, two of the canaries started to fight: the little feathers flew around the room, Antonio's face grew dark with anger. Would he be capable of killing them? Cleobula had told me that he was cruel. 'He looks as if he carries a knife at his belt', she had added.

Antonio now no longer allowed me to clean out the birdcage. At that time he left the marital bed to sleep in the room which was used as a storeroom at the back of the house. Antonio slept on an ottoman where my brother used to take a nap when he came to visit us but he would spend what I suspect were sleepless nights, as I could hear him pacing up and down until dawn. Sometimes he would shut himself for hours at a time in that wreched room.

One by one the canaries let the little arrows drop from their beaks. They landed on the back of a chair and started singing softly. Antonio sat up and looking at Maria Callas, whom he had always called 'the Queen of Disobedience', he uttered a word that I could not understand. The canaries started to fly around again.

I tried to follow his movements through the painted windowpanes. I cut my hand on purpose with a knife so that I dared knock at his door. When he opened, a whole flock of canaries flew out in the direction of the birdcage. Antonio dressed my wound but, as if he suspected that it was just an excuse to attract his attention, his manner was abrupt and suspicious. At that time he made a journey by bus which lasted two weeks—I don't know where he went and he returned with a bag full of plants.

I gave a sideways glance to my sttained skirt. Birds are so small and so dirty. When had they stained my skirt? I looked at them with hatred—I like to be clean even in a darkened room.

Ruperto, unaware of the bad feeling that his visits caused, came as often as usual and had the same habits. Sometimes, when I left the patio to avoid his glances, my husband would find an excuse to make me return. It seemed as if he somehow enjoyed that which he found so unpleasant. Ruperto's stares now seemed obscene: they undressed me in the shade of the vine and made me do shameful things when, at dusk, a fresh breeze stroked my cheeks. Antonio, on the other hand, never looked at me or, so Cleobula told me, pretended not to. For a time, one of my most ardent desires was to have never known him, never married him or felt his careess so as to have been able to meet him, discover him, give myself to him. But who regains that which he has already lost?

I sat up—my legs hurt. I don't like to be still for so long. How I envy birds flying! But I pity canaries. They seem to suffer when they obey commands.

Antonio didn't try to stop Ruperto's visits, on the contrary, he encouraged them. During the carnival, one night that he stayed until very late, he went to the extreme of inviting him to stay at our house. We had to put him in the room that Antonio provisionally slept in. That night, as if it were the most natural thing in the world, we slept together again, my husband and I, in the marital bed. From that moment my life returned to normal, or so I thought.

In a corner, under the table with the light on it, I could just make out the famous doll. I thought of picking it up. As if I had actually gone to do so, Antonio said to me:

'Don't move'.

I remembered that day during carnival week when I was tidying the rooms, I had discovered as a punishment for my sins, the rag doll, lying on Antonio's wardrobe, with large blue eyes made of cloth with two dark circles in the centre made to look like pupils. Had it been dressed as a gaucho it could have decorated our bedroom. Laughing, I showed it to Antonio, who took it from me with annoyance. 'It's a souvenir from my childhood', he told me. 'I don't like you touching my things'.

'What harm is there in touching a doll that you played with in your childhood? I know boys who played with dolls, are you ashamed of it? Aren't you a grown man now?' I asked him.

'I don't have to give you any explanation. The best thing is for you to shut up.'

In a temper, Antonio again placed the doll on top of the wardrobe and didn't say a word to me for several days. But we slept together again as in happier times.

I passed my hand over my damp forehead. Had my curlers come undone? Luckily, there was no mirror in the room as I would not have resisted the temptation of looking at myself instead of looking at the canaries that I found so silly.

Antonio often shut himself in the back room and I noticed that he left the door of the birdcage open so that one of the little birds could fly in through the window. One afternoon, driven by my curiosity, I spied on him. I had to stand on a chair, as the window was very high up (this naturally did not allow me to look inside the room when I was passing through the patio).

I could see Antonio's naked torso. Was it my husband or a statue? He accused Ruperto of being mad, but maybe he was even more mad. How much money had he spent on buying canaries, instead of buying me a washing machine!

One day I caught sight of the doll lying on the bed. A whole group of little birds fluttered around it. The room had been transformed into a kind of laboratory. In a earthenware container, there was a pile of leaves, stems and dark pieces of bark. In another container there was some little arrows made with thorns. In another one there was a shining brown liquid. It seemed as if I had already seen those objects in dreams and, so as to put an end to my perplexity, I recounted the scene to Cleobula who told me:

'That is what the Indians do: they use arrows dipped in Curare.'

I didn't ask her what 'Curare' meant. Nor did I know if she was telling me this with scorn or with admiration.

'They are given to witchcraft. Your husband is an Indian.' And on seeing my surprise, she asked, 'Didn't you know?'

Annoyed, I shook my head. My husband was my husband. I had never thought of him belonging to another race or to a world other than my own.

'How do you know?' I asked vehemently.

'Haven't you looked at his eyes, his high cheek bones? Haven't you noticed how Indian he is? Mandarin, even Maria Callas are more frank than he is. His reserve, his way of not answering a question, his way of treating women, isn't that enough to prove that he is an Indian? My mother knows all about it. They took him away from a settlement when he was five years old. Maybe that is what you like about him, his mysteriousness which sets him apart from other men.'

Antonio was sweating and the sweat made his torso shine. Such a solid young man and wasting his time! If I had married Juan Leston, the lawyer, or Roberto Cuentas, the bookkeeper, I would probably not have suffered so much. But what sensitive woman marries for money? They say there are men who train fleas and what is the point of that?

I lost faith in Cleobula. Undoubtedly, she told me that my husband was

Indian so as to hurt me or to make me lose my faith in him. But on leafing through a history book which showed illustrations of Indian settlements and Indians on horseback carrying bolas*, I saw the similarity between Antonio and those naked men adorned with feathers. I also noticed that what had maybe attracted me to Antonio was the difference between him and my brothers and their friends, the dark colour of his skin, his slanting eyes and that Indian look about him which Cleobula mentioned with perverse enjoyment.

'What about the trick?' I asked.

Antonio didn't answer me. He was staring at the canaries which began flying around the room again. Mandarin separated himself from his companions and from the darkness he could be heard singing like a lark.

My solitude increased. I told no one of my worries.

During Easter week, Antonio insisted that Ruperto stayed as a guest in our house for the second time. It was raining, as it tends to do during Easter week. We went to church with Cleobula to do the Stations of the Cross.

'How is the Indian?' asked Cleobula insolently.

'Who?'

'The Indian, your husband', she answered. 'That's what everyone in the village calls him'.

'I like Indians. Even if my husband were not one I would still like them', I answered, trying to continue my prayers.

Antonio was in an attitude of prayer. Had he ever prayed before? On our wedding day, my mother had asked him to receive communion but Antonio did not comply.

Meanwhile Antonio and Ruperto's friendship grew stronger. A kind of camaraderie, from which I was somehow excluded, united them in a way which seemed genuine. At that time, Antonio showed off his powers. So as to occupy himself, he would send the canaries with messages to Ruperto. People said that they were using them to play some kind of cardgame, as they did once exchange some Spanish cards. Were they making fun of me? The game that the two men were playing annoyed me and I decided not to take them seriously. Did I have to concede that friendship was more important than love? Nothing had separated Antonio and Ruperto. Instead, Antonio, unjustly in some way, had moved away from me. My pride as woman suffered. Ruperto continued to stare at me. That whole drama, had it been nothing but a farce? Did I miss the conjugal drama, the torment that had resulted from the jealousy of a husband driven mad for so many days?

We still loved each other in spite of everything.

In a circus Antonio could earn money with his tricks, why not? Maria Callas nodded her little head to one side, then to the other and landed on the back of a chair.

One morning, Antonio came into my room and, as if announcing that the house was on fire, said to me:

---

*Weapon used by Argentine gauchos which consists of several ropes tied together with metal balls at the ends.

'Ruperto is dying. They came to fetch me. I am going to see him.'

Busying myself with chores in the house, I waited for Antonio until midday. He returned when I was washing my hair.

'Come on', he said to me. 'Ruperto is in the patio. I saved him.'

'How? Was it a joke?'

'Not at all. I saved him with artificial respiration.'

Not understanding anything, I quickly tied back my hair, dressed and went out to the patio. Ruperto stood immobile by the door and was staring unseeingly at the tiles on the patio floor. Antonio brought a chair to him so that he could sit down.

Antonio didn't look at me, he looked at the ceiling as if he were holding his breath. Mandarin unexpectedly flew by Antonio and stuck one of the little arrows in his arm. I clapped as I thought this would please Antonio. Nevertheless it seemed a ridiculous trick. Why did he not use his ingenuity to cure Ruperto! On that fatal day, Ruperto, sitting down, covered his face with his hands. How he had changed! I looked at his cold inanimate face, his dark hands.

When would they leave me alone! I had to put my wet hair into curlers. I asked Ruperto, trying to hid my annoyance:

'What's happened?'

A long silence which made the birds' singing clearly audible quivered in the sun. Ruperto answered at last:

'I dreamt that the canaries were pecking my arms, my neck, my chest, that I couldn't shut my eyelids to protect my eyes. I dreamt that my arms and my legs were heavy like sacks of sand. I couldn't scare away with my hands the horrible beaks that were pecking at my eyes. I was sleeping without being asleep as if I had taken some kind of drug. When I awoke from that dream which was not a dream, I saw darkness. But I could hear the birds singing and the normal morning noises. Making a huge effort, I called my sister, who came to me. With a voice that was not my own I said:

' "You have to call Antonio so that he can save me." "What from?" asked my sister. I couldn't say another single word. My sister ran out and came back half an hour later with Antonio. Half an hour which had seemed like a whole century to me! Slowly as Antonio moved my arms, I regained my strength but not my sight.'

'I am going to make a confession to you', murmured Antonio and he added slowly, 'but without words.'

Favorita followed Mandarin and stuck a little arrow in Antonio's neck. Maria Callas hovered over him for an instant before sticking another little arrow in his chest. Antonio's eyes, staring fixedly at the ceiling, seemed to change colour. Was Antonio an Indian? Could an Indian have blue eyes? His eyes somehow looked like Ruperto's.

'What does all this mean?' I mused.

'What is he doing?' said Ruperto, who did not understand anything.

Antonio didn't answer. He remained immobile like a statue while the canaries pierced him with the inoffensive-looking arrows. I went up to the bed and shook him.

'What does all this mean?', I said. 'Answer me. Answer me.'

He did not reply. In tears, I embraced him and threw myself over his body. Losing any self-restraint, I kissed him on the mouth as only a film star could have done. A flock of canaries fluttered around my head.

That morning Antonio looked at Ruperto with horror. I now understood that Antonio was doubly guilty. So that nobody would find out about his crime, he had said to me and had said afterwards to everybody:

'Ruperto has gone mad. He thinks he is blind but he can see as well as any of us.'

Just as the light had left Ruperto's eyes, love left our house. It was almost as if his glances were necessary to our love. The gatherings in the patio had become quiet and dull. Antonio fell into a deep gloom. He would explain to me:

'A friend's madness is worse than death. Ruperto can see but he thinks he is blind'.

I thought despairingly, maybe with jealousy, that friendship was more important than love in the life of a man.

When I stopped kissing Antonio and took my face away from his, I saw that the canaries were about to peck at his eyes. I covered his face with my face and hair, which is as thick as a shawl. I ordered Ruperto to shut the door and windows so that the room should be in complete darkness, waiting for the canaries to go to sleep. My legs ached. How long did I remain like that? I don't know. Slowly I understood Antonio's confession. It was a confession that united us in a frenzied misfortune. I understood the pain that he had endured when sacrificing in such an ingenious way, with a minute dose of Curare and the winged monsters which obeyed his whimsical commands, the eyes of Ruperto, his friend, and his own, so that they would not be able to look at me, poor things, ever again.

The Man Who Belonged to Me

Giovanni Papini, *Italian short-story writer and essayist. Born in Florence in 1871; died in Florence in 1956. Translator of Berkeley, Bergson, Boutroux, James and Schopenhauer. Author of* Il tragico quotidiano *(1906),* Vita de Nessuno *(1912),* Un Uomo Finito *(1912),* L'uomo Carducci *(1918),* L'Europa Occidentale contro la Mitteleuropa *(1918),* Sant' Agostino *(1931).*

I

I can't say exactly how long Amico Dite's body and soul had been following mine, because I left off keeping a diary years ago. I am rather absent-minded, so probably I did not notice what day my second shadow (a solid and more or less living shadow) happened to make its entrance on the dim stage of my life.

One morning, as I was leaving home, I noticed I was being followed by a man of about forty, who wore a long blue overcoat; he seemed gay and lively (but not too much so) and followed me at a respectful distance so that I could not very well turn round and ask him what he was doing. I had nothing in particular to do, and I had only come out to get away from the sound of a wood fire crackling in the grate; so I amused myself watching this man although there was nothing remarkable about his appearance. I was sure he wasn't a detective, because I'm so lacking in physical courage, and I so much dislike being talked about that I have always kept out of active politics, and laziness and clumsiness in any sort of manual work have saved me from earning my living through crime. I didn't think this man in blue could be a thief after my purse. Everyone in the neighbourhood knew I was rather poor; and you could tell I wasn't rich by looking at my clothes, which were untidy, not studiedly careless.

Although there was no reason why I should have been followed, I began going round and round the complicated streets in the middle of the town, to make sure I hadn't made a mistake about it. The man still followed me, looking more and more pleased as he went on. I turned off into one of the principal streets, and began to walk more quickly; but there was still the same distance between me and the man in blue. I went into a post office to buy a three-halfpenny stamp; the unknown man came into the same shop and also bought a three-halfpenny stamp. Then I got into a tram; my smiling follower got in too, and when I got out, he got out just behind me. I bought a paper and he bought exactly the same paper. I sat down on a bench, and he sat down on another bench quite close to me; I took out a cigarette, and he took one out too and waited to light his until I had lit mine.

All this amused me and irritated me at the same time. 'He may be a humorist with nothing to do,' I thought, 'so he wants to amuse himself at my expense.' At last I made up my mind to solve the problem in the quickest way possible, so I went and stood in front of the man as if I were going to ask him who he was and what he wanted. But there was no need for me to ask him. The man in blue got up, took off his hat, smiled and said very quickly: 'Excuse me—I'll explain everything—but first let me introduce myself: I am Amico Dite. I haven't any definite occupation but that doesn't really matter. I've got lots of things to tell you but . . . well, up till now . . . I wanted to write to you—I actually *did* write to you two or three times but I don't always send the letters I write. Otherwise I'm quite an ordinary kind of person, although you might sometimes think . . .'

Here Amico Dite stopped and hesitated a little; then he went on quickly, as if he had suddenly remembered something extremely important:

'Wouldn't you like to drink something? A drop of Marsala perhaps—or some coffee?'

We both went off together quickly as if we both had the same instinct to get the matter cleared up then and there. As soon as we saw a café we both dashed in, like people who want a drink at once in a great hurry. However, we sat down in a corner by the fire, without ordering anything. The café was little, and all full of smoke and cabbies and the waiter looked a fearful scoundrel; but we hadn't time to choose anywhere else.

'I should like to know . . .' I began.

'I'll tell you all about everything,' said the man. 'I don't want to keep anything from you. I'm in rather a difficult and unfortunate situation—but I'll tell you at once, I have the greatest trust in you. Here I am, then; I put myself in your hands. I'm yours to do what you like with . . .'

'But I don't see . . .'

'I assure you, you'll see everything in a moment. Let me explain. Didn't I tell you who I was. I know, my name doesn't tell you anything about me. Well, I'll tell you what sort of person I am—I'm an ordinary man—appallingly ordinary; but I want to live in an extraordinary way, to have a really thrilling and amazing life.'

'Forgive me . . .'

'Yes, yes. I'll forgive everything. Only as I told you, I simply must say what I have to say . . . I trust you implicitly. You shall be my saviour, my spiritual adviser, and master of my body and my soul. I'm too cautious, too respectable; I'm too much of a gentleman—too much just like myself. You've written so many fantastic stories, so may extraordinary novels—and I've lived so much among all your characters that I dream about them in the night and think about them in the daytime. I sometimes think I see them in the street and then, I get absolutely wild and despairing, I want to suppress them and forget them for ever and ever . . .'

'Thank you . . . but . . .'

'Wait one moment, please. I'll explain now why I thought about you and why I followed you. A few days ago I said to myself: "You are a fool, the kind of person you can meet anywhere any day; and you've got this craze of wanting to live a glorious life, all risks and adventures, like the people in six-penny stories and cheap novels. But you've no imagination so you can't expect to have that sort of life. The only thing to do is to look round till you find an author who makes up extra-ordinary characters, and make him a present of your life so that he can do whatever he likes with it and turn it into something really exciting and beautiful and unexpected . . ." '

'So you'd like me to . . .?'

'Just a moment, please. In a few minutes I shall do exactly what you want and then you can stop my talking when you like, only now I would like to finish what I've got to say. I still belong to myself for the moment! I've only one thing to tell you and that is—I've chosen you to be my director and so I make you a present of my life and whatever money you want to help you make it interesting. You have plenty of imagination and you'll easily be able to break the ghastly monotony of my life. Up till now you have only been able to control imaginary people; but to day you've got a real man, who moves and who suffers and you can do whatever you like with him. I put myself in your hands—not like a corpse though. You wouldn't know what to do with me if I died—but like a mechanical toy, an amazing marionette that can talk and laugh and do whatever you order it to. From now on, I give you my life and a thousand pounds a year, to pay for all the things you'll need to make my life picturesque and adventurous. I've got the proper document here in my pocket . . . waiter, a pen and ink! There's only the date and you signature missing. Say yes or no, just as you feel, but say it quickly!'

I pretended to think it over for a few seconds, but I had really made up my mind already. Amico Dite was fulfilling one of my oldest desires. I had always been a little grieved that I could make up the lives only of imaginary people. In my spare moments I often thought of what I would do if I had a real flesh-and-blood creature to do what I liked with. Now the very man was offering himself up to me, with a good income thrown in as well.

'I never waste time in bargaining,' I said after my pretended consideration, 'so I'll accept your offer although you must realize what a great responsibility it is for me, taking charge of a soul and a body as well. Let's see the conditions . . .'

Amico Dite handed me an official-looking document in a thick gray paper cover and I read it in a few moments. Everything was in order. By signing this paper I became the rightful owner of the wealth and life of Amico Dite, the only condition being that I should constantly be directing him so that he should lead an illustrious and adventurous life. The contract lasted a year, but it could be renewed if Amico Dite was satisfied with the way I managed him.

I signed without hestitation and left Amico Dite immediately; after having promised to write to him next day and ordering him not to follow me but to have some strong drink. And as I was going out I saw him ordering, with his usual charming smile, one of the most celebrated bitters in the world.

II

That evening I did not go to bed as terribly bored as I usually did. I had something new and important to think about, that was quite worth spending a sleepless night for. A man had become my property, and really belonged to me. I could lead him, drive him, send him anywhere I wanted; I could experiment with him and give him strange emotions and unheard of adventures.

Now what could I make him do next day? Ought I to order him to do some fixed thing, or should I leave him in the dark and then spring something on him suddenly? Finally I chose something that combined the two methods. Next day I wrote and told him that until he heard to the contrary, he was to sleep all day and spend the night out of doors wandering about in all sorts of lonely places. Next day I went to an estate agent's and took a lonely house outside the town for six months. Then I hired two of the unemployed who were looking for work for the winter. In four days everything was ready. On the appointed evening I had Amico Dite followed, and when he had got out into a lonely place, my accomplices attacked him and took him, gagged and bound, to the house I had ready. Unfortunately no one noticed what we were doing, and no one reported the mysterious disappearance of Amico Dite; so I had to provide for two strong men, who wanted paying as well as feeding, for several months.

The worst of it was that I had not the slightest idea what to do with this man who belonged to me. On the evening of his gift, I had thought that kidnapping him would be an excellent beginning for an exciting life but I had not bothered to think about what could happen afterwards. Yet even Amico Dite's life wanted its next instalment at once, like a newspaper serial.

As I could think of nothing better I resorted to the old trick of sending to live with him, in the little house where I had installed him, a woman who was always masked and never spoke to him. It was very difficult finding a woman who would agree to do this; and even more difficult to train her, and even then she wouldn't engage herself for more than a month. Luckily Amico Dite was something of a misogynist and was over forty, so none of the things you might have expected actually did happen. After a fortnight I realized that I should have to change my tactics; so I had my two unemployed set my man free, and I sent him back to his home.

I began to realize that Amico Dite hadn't behaved in the least like the ordinary man he said he was when he made me take charge of him like this. Who else but a really queer person would have imagined such a subtle kind of slavery?

A man I knew who was an excellent swordsman agreed to help me at this juncture. One day, when Amico Dite was sitting quietly drinking a glass of milk in a very smart café, this man came up and glared at him; then he jostled him and as soon as Dite said something, he slapped him two or three times quite calmly as if he did not want to hurt him too much. Amico Dite asked my permission to send his seconds to challenge the man who had insulted him; I produced two of my friends who obliged him to fight although he did not want to in the least. Amico Dite knew nothing whatever about duelling and it was just because of this that he struck out violently at the very beginning and wounded his adversary seriously. I took this opportunity of explaining to him that he must leave the town at once, but he would not hear of going away without me;

he preferred being tried before the Court, and so he got himself sentenced to three months' imprisonment.

I really thought I should be free from him for that time, but after a day or two I began thinking it was my duty to set Amico Dite free. It seemed almost impossible; but, by means of bribes, I managed to convince two people that what I was doing was an excellent thing; and so, perfectly disguised, Amico Dite succeeded in getting out of the prison one day just before dawn. This time he really had to go into exile, so I had to leave my house, my work and my country all in order to arrange his escape.

When we reached London I was in a greater muddle than ever. I couldn't speak a word of English, and in the midst of that huge unknown city I was less than ever in a position to find any exciting adventures for my man's benefits. Finally I had to ask the advice of a private detective, who gave me some vague instructions in abominable French. After consulting a good map of London, I took Amico Dite into the most disreputable parts, but, to my great annoyance, nothing whatever happened to him there. We came across the usual drunken sailors, the usual painted brazen-faced women, and numbers of noisy thrifty 'viveurs,' but no one paid any attention to us; perhaps they thought we were something to do with the police, we looked so sure of ourselves wandering round the mazes of little streets that are all exactly alike.

Then I had the idea of sending Amico Dite all by himself into the North of England, and giving him only twenty or thirty shillings beyond his railway fare. As he knew no English either I hoped something very disagreeable might happen to him or, better still, that he might never come back at all. I was really getting tired of this man who belonged to me, and for whom I worked so hard and gave up so much; I was simply longing for the day when I could get back to my own dear old town full of cafés and loiterers. But after a fortnight had gone by Amico Dite came back to London in perfect health and spirits. He had come across an Italian friend of his in Edinburgh—a 'cellist who had gone to Scotland years ago, and who had asked him to stay and amused him during the time he was there.

But I wouldn't give up yet. In some newspaper I had seen the address of a little club for psychical research, that was looking for new members; it promised them they would see real spirits, ghosts who could talk and so on. I ordered Amico Dite to apply for membership immediately and to go there regularly every evening. He kept on going for a week and saw nothing at all; then one morning he came to me and told me that he had actually met a ghost, but that it wasn't much better than ordinary men. Indeed it seemd to have been rather more foolish than most people because it stole his handkerchief, took away his chair from under him, pulled his hair and hit him in the back.

'Well, really,' he said, 'I don't think there's been anything really extraordinary in what you've made me do. Excuse me if I speak to you openly—but I think you must agree with me that in your novels you've got much more originality and more amusing imagination than in real life. Just think—kidnapping, then a masked woman and a duel, then escape and now ghosts! You don't seem to have been able to think of anything better than these old-fashioned tricks—the sort of thing you get in French novels. There are much more thrilling things in Hoffmann and Poe, and much more thrilling things in Hofmann and Poe, and much more ingenious ideas in Gaboriau and Ponson du Terrail. I really can't understand this sudden collapse of your imagination. At the very beginning I used to do everything you did, really expecting to have an exciting life; but I soon came to the conclusion that your life was just like anyone else's, and I supposed you must keep all your invention for your novels: but now I'm beginning to doubt this as well, and much as I dislike doing it I am obliged to tell you that unless you find something better to make me do I shall have to look for another master, even before our contract has run out.'

Pride prevented my answering this extraordinary ingratitude. I thought to myself how for months—ever since I had taken over control of that man—I had not been master of my own life; I had been obliged to leave all my work in the middle, to leave my country, to worry myself inventing romantic adventures and reliable people to carry them out. Since I had taken possession of Amico Dite's life, I had had to sacrifice the whole of my own life to him. I, nominally his master, had really degenerated into his slave; or at best, merely the manager of his personal existence. As he said, he must find something 'more impressive' than what I had done for him, and moreover, something that had no need of accomplices. After having thought the matter over quietly for a day or two, I wrote to him as follows:

'My dear Dite,—Since you belong to me according to a formal contract, I can arrange for your life or your death as I see fit. I therefore order you to shut yourself up in your room on Saturday night at eight o'clock; then lie down on your bed and take one of the pills here enclosed. At half past eight take another one and at *nine exactly* take the third. Should you disobey my orders I give up any responsibility I may ever have had for your life, from this day onwards.'

I knew that Amico Dite would not flinch at the fear of death. In spite of being so particular, he was a gentleman and had a great respect for his word and signature. I bought a strong emetic and arranged to be at his house just before nine—that is, just before he took the last pill, which would inevitably kill him if he took it.

On Saturday evening I ordered a cab for eight o'clock, because I lived in a boarding house a long way from where Amico Dite was staying. The cab did not turn up until a quarter past eight, so I impressed on the driver the fact that I was in a great hurry. The horse started off, indeed, with a sort of pseudo-gallop, but after about ten minutes he stumbled and fell down in the street. It seemed hopeless to try to pick him up so I quickly paid the cabby and looked round for another cab. Luckily I found one at once and I calculated that at nine o'clock exactly I ought to be at Amico Dite's house. I began to worry a little nevertheless because there was a thick fog and even if we were only five minutes late, it meant that the poor man would certainly be dead.

Then suddenly the cab pulled up. We were at the end of an important street full of cars and 'buses, and a policeman held up his hand to stop our going by. I leapt out of the cab like a madman and rushed up to the huge policeman, trying to make him understand that I was in a great hurry and that a man's life was at stake.

But he either did not understand or would not understand. I had to go the rest of the way on foot, but partly because of the fog and partly because I did not know London very well, I took a wrong turning and I only noticed I was going in the wrong direction when I'd been rushing along for about ten minutes. So, still running, I turned back and went in the other direction. It was only a few minutes before nine, and I was making prodigious efforts so as to get there in time. But I only reached the boarding house at seven minutes past nine, and rang the bell frantically. The moment someone opened it, I rushed into Amico Dite's room. He was lying in his shirt-sleeves on the bed, pale and stiff as a corpse. I shook him and called him by name; I felt whether his heart was beating and whether he was breathing still. No: he was indeed a corpse; the little box I had sent him was empty. Amico Dite had kept his word to the last. I had intended to give him the terror of certain death and then the shock of resurrection; but instead I had given him death, real and irrevocable death.

I stayed all night in his room, numb with grief. In the morning I was found with the dead man, as pale and as silent as he. My papers were all confiscated, and my last letter to Dite was found as well. The trial was extremely short because I did not even put up a defence or show the contract I still had put away somewhere. It is several years now since I have been in prison; but I am not sorry for what I have done. Amico Dite has made my life much more worth telling than it would have been without him, and I don't think I have managed so badly even though in the year in which he belonged to me I spent a good deal more than the thousand pounds he gave me.

RANI

Carlos Peralta, *Argentine writer. Author of a satirical book* Manual del gorila; *and a book of essays. He has been editor or director of various magazines, writing for them and other publications. He signs his satirical and humorous work with the pseudonym Carlos del Peral. He has several translations to his name and has also worked on filmscripts.*

Between Don Pedro the butcher and I there existed only a rather restricted relationship so far. Our lives were very different. For him, to exist was to cut up animals tirelessly in the foetid coolness of the butcher's shop; for me, to tear numerous pages from a cheap pad and slip them into the typewriter. Almost all our daily deeds were subject to differing rituals. I would visit him to pay my bill, but I wouldn't go to his daughter's engagment party, for example. Not that I would have had any objection to doing so, had the case arisen. However, what interested me most was not the private attitudes I might have but the general search for closer relationships between men, for a greater exchange between those rituals.

I was ruminating on these ideas when I noticed the butcher leaving, barely managing to carry a basket with a quarter of beef.

'Would that be for the restaurant around the corner?' I asked.

'No. It's for across the road, flat 4B.'

'They must have a "frigidaire",' said a female verbal ghost which took power over me.

'They have the same thing every day,' answered Don Pedro.

'You don't say. They eat all that?'

'Well, if they don't eat it, tough on them, wouldn't you say?' said the butcher.

I very soon found out that 4B was occupied by a childless couple. The man was short and wore brown. The woman must be very lazy, because she was always dishevelled when she received the butcher. Apart from that and the quarter of beef, which as far as I could see was their only bad habit, they were orderly people. They never returned home after sunset, at about eight o'clock in summer and five in winter. Once, the concierge had told Don Pedro, they must have thrown a very noisy party, because two neighbours complained. Apparently some comedian had been imitating animal noises.

'Shh!' said Don Pedro, lifting a tragic bloodstained finger to his lips. A man dressed in brown came in, undoubtedly the same one who ate two cows a week, or at least one, if he was assisted by his noble consort. Being in a hurry, he didn't see me. He got his wallet and begun counting out large, crisp bills.

'Four thousand,' he said. 'Six hundred . . . and two. Here you are.'

'Hello, Carracido,' I said to him. 'Do you remember me?' I'd met him years ago. He was a lawer. 'We seem to be neighbours.'

'How are you, Peralta? How are things? Do you live nearby?' he asked with his old administrative warmth.

'Next door to you. Things seem to be going well for you, apparently. Eating well, aren't you?'

'No,' he said. 'I make do with anything. And anyway, you understand, my liver.'

'But then, how come . . . ?'

'Ah, you mean the meat? No, that's something else.' He seemed to become gloomy and then gave a sort of false laugh, like a cough. 'I've got a lot to do. Goodbye, friend. Come around to my house early one afternoon, on Saturday or Sunday. I live at number 860, flat 4B.' He hesitated. 'You know, I'd like to have a chat with you.' I could have sworn there was a pleading note in his voice, which intrigued me.

'I will,' I replied. 'See you Saturday.'

Don Pedro followed him with his gaze. 'Goodness knows what's up with him,' he said. 'Each family is a world unto itself.'

Years go by and you never see an old school friend, a fellow-student from university days, a colleague from work; that day I met two. First Carracido, then Gómez Campbell, with whom I went for a coffee at the Boston, and told him I'd seen Carracido. He remembered him and didn't like the memory, that was obvious.

'I don't like that chap,' he said later. 'He's a nasty character, full of troubles and goings-on.'

'He seems pretty harmless to me,' I remarked.

He kept quiet whilst the waiter served coffee. 'I met him many years ago,' he said. 'Before joining the Ministry he worked at the Credit Bank. He was already married. Just think, I had to report him because he had taken a stack of money to the races. They nearly sacked him, but he was a friend of the manager's and was able to replace the missing money, and got away with it. Afterwards he was appointed consultant at the Ministry. The man began to prosper. I think he came into an inheritance, too.'

This Gómez Campbell, I haven't mentioned it to you yet, was a bit of a bad sort.

'I was pleased, honestly,' continued Gómez, 'and I went to congratulate him. Do you know what he said to me? "Shut up, you hypocrite", that's what he called me. I, who was the first to go and congratulate him, with open arms, with the greatest respect. That is just not on. Men should know how to forget quarrels and trifles. And if they don't know, like this Carracido, sooner or later they'll be punished.' He paused to highlight the severity of his admonition. 'It was through him I got the job, after a lot of trying. And now, you know, I think he's not getting on with his wife. She goes her own way and he goes his. You can see she's too pretty and too big for him, and since the inheritance was from his father-in-law, a number of houses, he has to put up with her.'

The band was happily murdering a waltz.

'He can go to blazes as far as I'm concerned,' Gómez Campbell finished. 'Just see how things are: he's been having affairs with all the employees at the Ministry. His wife ignores him, of course.'

We soon said goodbye. That casual encounter, sustained by vilification and curiosity, exhausted itself pretty quickly. Gómez Campbell shook my hand coldly and disappeared into calle Florida. Carracido seemed more and more exciting to me, a great meat-eater, Don Juan, married to a beautiful and presumably unfaithful woman, quite a gambler and something of a thief. The truth is we never really know anyone.

I meant to go early on Saturday, but couldn't. I had intended finishing a short story I was to hand in on Monday (perhaps this same one) but I didn't manage it. I had a bath, put on clean clothes, felt rather frustrated and went to number 860, flat 4B. It was half-past seven. Carracido received me very politely, but somewhat uneasily, opening the door very slowly.

'Hello,' he said. 'I wasn't expecting you. You're a bit late.'

'Listen, if you have something to do, we'll leave it until tomorrow or the day after.'

'No,' he said with genuine warmth. 'No, come in. Just a moment, I'll call my wife.'

The furniture was in various styles, but the combination was not unpleasant. The only thing which clashed was the vicuña skin covering the couch, torn lengthwise as though with a knife and almost split in two. Moreover, the legs of the couch opened too far outwards. I stroked the skin and left it as I heard Carracido's voice.

'This is Rani,' he said.

I looked at her, fascinated. Everything I can say would not be enough. I don't know—I don't think I've ever seen a more beautiful woman, more intense green eyes, a more perfect and delicate movement. I got up and shook her hand, never taking my eyes off hers. She barely lowered her eyelids and sat beside me on the couch, silent, smiling, with an easy feline grace. Making an effort I looked away from her towards the window, but without ceasing to keep in my mind those legs which moved with the gentleness and energy of the waves. Outside, nothing stained the soft blue of the Buenos Aires sunset save for a cloud which was just then changing colour from copper to purple. An incongruous noise distracted me: Carracido was drumming his fingers on the table at the speed of an express train. I looked at him and he stopped.

'Rani, your bath must be ready by now,' he said.

'Yes, dear,' she replied sweetly, stretching her hand, closed and tight, over the vicuña skin.

'Rani,' insisted Carracido.

Tacit command, I thought to myself. He's jealous; he wants her to go.

The woman got up and disappeared through a door. First she turned around and looked at me.

'We could go for a drink in the bar,' suggested Carracido. This annoyed me and I said to him, 'Shame. It's nice here. I'd rather stay, if you don't mind.'

He hestitated, but his warmth returned, as well as that pleading quality I had noticed before, that dog-like air.

'All right,' he said. 'Perhaps that would be best after all. God knows what's best.' He went to the sideboard and brought a bottle and two glasses. Before sitting down, he looked at his watch.

Gómez Campbell is right, I said to myself. This man must bear his wife's whims with more naturalness than a bull.

And at that moment the purring began. First slow, deep and low; then more violent. It was a purr, but what a purr! I felt as though my head were in a beehive. And I couldn't have drunk one glassful.

'It's nothing,' said Carracido solicitously. 'It'll pass.'

The purring came from the inner bedrooms. It was followed by a loud outburst which made me leap to my feet.

'What was that?' I yelled, going towards the door.

'Nothing, nothing,' he replied firmly, blocking my way.

I didn't answer him; I pushed him away so violently that he fell to one side, on the armchair.

'Don't shout!' he said stupidly. And then, 'Don't be scared!' I had already opened the door. At first I didn't see a thing; then, a sinuous shape approached me in the darkness.

It was a tiger. A huge tiger, totally out of place, striped, fearful and advancing. I pulled back; as though in a dream, I felt Carracido take me by the arm. I pushed him again, this time forwards, reached the front door, opened it and got into the lift. The tiger stopped in front of me. It had Rani's amethyst necklace around its shiny neck. I covered my eyes so as not to see its green eyes and pressed the button.

The tiger followed as I descended, bounding down the stairs. I went up again and the tiger went up. I went down, and this time it got tired of the game; it snorted triumphantly and went out into the street. I went back the flat.

'Why didn't you do as I said?' said Carracido. 'Now she's gone, you idiot!' He poured himself a glass of whisky and drank it in one go. I did likewise. Carracido leant his head on his arms and sobbed. 'I'm a peaceful man,' he hiccupped. 'I married Rani never dreaming that at night she turned into a tiger.'

He was apologizing. It was incredible, but he was apologizing.

'You've no idea what it was like at first, when we lived in the suburbs . . .' he began, like anyone who shares a secret.

'What do I care where you lived!' I shouted in exasperation. 'We have to call the police, the zoo, the circus. You can't let a tiger loose in the street!'

'No, have no fear. My wife won't harm anyone. She sometimes frightens people at little. Don't complain,' he added, now a little drunk. 'I told you to come early. The worst thing is I don't know what to do; last week I had to sell off some land very cheaply in order to pay the butcher . . .'

He drank down two or three glasses like an animal.

'They say there is an Indian here in Buenos Aires . . . a magician . . . One of these days I'll go and see him; perhaps he can do something.'

He stopped talking and continued sobbing quietly.

I smoked for a long while. I imagined—what a nightmare—some of the habitual scenes of his life. Rani ruining the couch, because she wasn't allowed to frolic. Rani devouring the raw meat at some time during the night, or weaving her long body in and out of the furniture. And Carracido there, watching her . . . when would she sleep?

'Bumburumbum,' said Carracido, definitely drunk. He let his head fall to one side, inert, like an object. Gradually his sobs were replaced by the sound of peaceful snoring. He had finally returned to the simple world of work, documents, files. There was a little bone under the armchair.

I stayed until daylight. I must have slept too. At about seven o'clock the bell rang. I opened the door. It was Rani. Her hair was uncombed, her clothes in a mess, her nails dirty. She seemed confused and ashamed. I turned my head away so as not to hurt her; I let her come in, went out and left. Don Pedro was right: each family is a world unto itself.

Afterwards I moved to another neighbourhood. Several months later—it's strange how things unfold and we think of them as coincidences, in order not to despair—I met Gómez Campbell again, one night, in a bar on Rivadavia at about number 5,000, opposite the square. I told him the story. Perhaps he thought I was mad; he changed the subject. We left, walking in silence through the square, and saw Carracido with a huge dog. A large dog, true, but tame and calm, with an amethyst collar. I could swear it looked at me with its wide green eyes. Its owner hadn't seen us.

'The Indian!' I exclaimed. 'Poor Carracido, it looks like his problem has been partly alleviated. Shall we go and see the couple?'

'Don't,' said Gómez Campbell, frightened and upset. 'Don't greet him. I don't like these things. I'm a straight chap. The best thing with these people is not to become involved.'

In vain I told him that I considered as harmful the distance which is maintained between one man and another in Buenos Aires and the displeasure at the peculiarities of others, in vain I advised him to be tolerant and understanding. I don't think he even heard me.

The Blind Spot

Barry Perowne, *British crime fiction writer. He took the Raffles character, created at the turn of the century by W. W. Hornung, and wrote new short stories featuring this aristocratic crook. Other works include* Arrest This Man *(1932),* Enemy of Women *(1934),* Ladies in Retreat *(1935),* Girl at Zero *(1939),* Blonde with Escort *(1940), and* The Tilted Moon *(1949).*

Annixter loved the little man like a brother. He put an arm around the little man's shoulders, partly from affection and partly to prevent himself from falling.

He had been drinking earnestly since seven o'clock the previous evening. It was now nudging midnight, and things were a bit hazy. The lobby was full of the thump of hot music; down two steps, there were a lot of tables, a lot of people, a lot of noise. Annixter had no idea what this place was called, or how he had got here, or when. He had been in so many places since seven o'clock the previous evening.

'In a nutshell,' confided Annixter, leaning heavily on the little man, 'a woman fetches you a kick in the face, or fate fetches you a kick in the face. Same thing, really—a woman and fate. So what? So you think it's the finish, an' you go out and get plastered. You get good an' plastered,' said Annixter, 'an' you brood.

'You sit there an' you drink as' you brood—an' in the end you find you've brooded up just about the best idea you ever had in your life! 'At's the way it goes,' said Annixter, 'an' 'at's my philosophy—the harder you kick a playwright, the better he works!'

He gestured with such vehemence that he would have collapsed if the little man hadn't steadied him. The little man was poker-backed, his grip was firm. His mouth was firm, too—a straight line, almost colourless. He wore hexagonal rimless spectacles, a black hard-felt hat, a neat pepper-and-salt suit. He looked pale and prim beside the flushed, rumpled Annixter.

From her counter, the hat-check girl watched them indifferently.

'Don't you think,' the little man said to Annixter, 'you ought to go home now? I've been honoured you should tell me the scenario of your play, but—'

'I had to tell someone,' said Annixter, 'or blow my top! Oh, boy, what a play, what a play! What a murder, eh? That climax—'

The full, dazzling perfection of it struck him again. He stood frowning, considering, swaying a little—then nodded abruptly, groped for the little man's hand, warmly pumphandled it.

'Sorry I can't stick around,' said Annixter. 'I got work to do.'

He crammed his hat on shapelessly, headed on a slightly elliptical course across the lobby, thrust the double doors open with both hands, lurched out into the night.

It was, to his inflamed imagination, full of lights, winking and tilting across the dark. *Sealed Room* by James Annixter. No. *Room Reserved* by James—No, no. *Blue room. Room Blue. Room Blue* by James Annixter—

He stepped, oblivious, off the kerb, and a taxi, swinging in towards the place he had just left, skidded with suddenly locked, squealing wheels on the wet road.

Something hit Annixter violently in the chest, and all the lights he had been seeing exploded in his face.

Then there weren't any lights.

Mr James Annixter, the playwright, was knocked down by a taxi late last night when leaving the Casa Havana. After hospital treatment for shock and superficial injuries, he returned to his home.

The lobby of the Casa Havana was full of the thump of music; down two steps there were a lot of tables, a lot of people, a lot of noise. The hat-check girl looked wonderingly at Annixter—at the plaster on his forehead, the black sling which supported his left arm.

'My,' said the hat-check girl, 'I certainly didn't expect to see *you* again so soon!'

'You remember me, then?' said Annixter, smiling.

'I ought to,' said the hat-check girl. 'You cost me a night's sleep! I heard those brakes squeal right after you went out the door that night—and there was a sort of a thud!' She shuddered. 'I kept hearing it all night long. I can still hear it now—a week after! Horrible!'

'You're sensitive,' said Annixter.

'I got too much imagination,' the hat-check girl admitted. 'F'rinstance, I just *knew* it was you even before I run to the door and see you lying there. That man you was with was standing just outside. "My heavens," I says to him, "it's your friend!" '

'What did he say?' Annixter asked.

'He says, "He's not my friend. He's just someone I met." Funny, eh?'

Annixter moistened his lips.

'How d'you mean,' he said carefully, 'funny? I *was* just someone he'd met.'

'Yes, but—man you been drinking with,' said the hat-check girl, 'killed before your eyes. Because he must have seen it; he went out right after you. You'd think he'd 'a' been interested, at least. But when the taxi driver starts shouting for witnesses it wasn't his fault, I looks around for that man—an' he's gone!'

Annixter exchanged a glance with Ransome, his producer, who was with him. It was a slightly puzzled, slightly anxious glance. But he smiled, then, at the hat-check girl.

'Not quite "killed before his eyes," ' said Annixter. 'Just shaken up a bit, that's all.'

There was no need to explain to her how curious, how eccentric, had been the effect of that 'shaking up' upon his mind.

'If you could 'a' seen yourself lying there with the taxi's lights shining on you—'

'Ah, there's that imagination of yours!' said Annixter.

He hesitated for just an instant, then asked the question he had come to ask—the question which had assumed so profound an importance for him.

He asked, 'That man I was with—who was he?'

The hat-check girl looked from one to the other. She shook her head.

'I never saw him before,' she said, 'and I haven't seen him since.'

Annixter felt as though she had struck him in the face. He had hoped, hoped desperately, for a different answer; he had counted on it.

Ransome put a hand on his arm, restrainingly.

'Anyway,' said Ransom, 'as we're here, let's have a drink.'

They went down the two steps into the room where the band thumped. A waiter led them to a table, and Ransome gave him an order.

'There was no point in pressing that girl,' Ransome said to Annixter. 'She doesn't know the man, and that's that. My advice to you, James, is: Don't worry. Get your mind on to something else. Give yourself a chance. After all, it's barely a week since—'

'A week!' Annixter said. 'Hell, look what I've done in that week! The whole of the first two acts, and the third act right up to that crucial point—the climax of the whole thing: the solution: the scene that the play stands or falls on! It would have been done, Bill—the whole play, the best thing I ever did in my life—it would have been finished two days ago if it hadn't been for this—' he knuckled his forehead—'this extraordinary blind spot, this damnable little trick of memory!'

'You had a very rough shaking-up—'

'That?' Annixter said contemptuously. He glanced down at the sling on his arm. 'I never even felt it; it didn't bother me. I woke up in the ambulance with my play as vivid in my mind as the moment the taxi hit me—more so, maybe, because I was stone cold sober then, and knew what I had. A winner—a thing that just couldn't miss!'

'If you'd rested,' Ransome said, 'as the doc told you, instead of sitting up in bed there scribbling night and day—'

'I had to get it on paper. Rest?' said Annixter, and laughed harshly. 'You don't rest when you've got a thing like that. That's what you live for—if you're a playwright. That *is* living! I've lived eight whole lifetimes, in those eight characters, during the past five days. I've lived so utterly in them, Bill, that it wasn't till I actually came to write that last scene that I realized what I'd lost! Only my whole play, that's all! How was Cynthia stabbed in that windowless room into which she had locked and bolted herself? How did the killer get to her? *How was it done?*

'Hell,' Annixter said, 'scores of writers, better men than I am, have tried to put that sealed room murder over—and never quite done it convincingly: never quite got away with it: been over-elaborate, phony! I had it—heaven help me, *I* had it! Simple, perfect, glaringly obvious when you've seen it! And it's my whole play—the curtain rises on that sealed room and falls on it! That was my revelation—*how it was done!* That was what I got, by way of playwright's compensation, because a woman I thought I loved kicked me in the face—I brooded up the answer to the sealed room! And a taxi knocked it out of my head!'

He drew a long breath.

'I've spent two days and two nights, Bill, trying to get that idea back—*how it was done!* It won't come. I'm a competent playwright; I know my job; I could finish my play, but it'd be like all those others—not quite right, phony! It wouldn't be *my play!* But there's a little man walking around this city somewhere—a little man with hexagonal glasses—who's got my idea in his head! He's got it because I told it to him. I'm going to find that little man, and get back what belongs to me! I've got to! Don't you see that, Bill? I've *got* to!'

If the gentleman who, at the Casa Havana on the night of January 27th, so patiently listened to a playwright's outlining of an idea for a drama will communicate with the Box No. below, he will hear of something to his advantage.

A little man who had said, 'he's not my friend. He's just someone I met—'
A little man who'd seen an accident but hadn't waited to give evidence—
The hat-check girl had been right. There *was* something a little queer about that.
A little queer?
During the next few days, when the advertisements he'd inserted failed to bring any reply, it began to seem to Annixter very queer indeed.
His arm was out of its sling now, but he couldn't work. Time and again he sat down before his almost completed manuscript, read it through with close, grim attention, thinking, 'It's *bound* to come back this time!'—only to find himself up

against that blind spot again, that blank wall, that maddening hiatus in his memory.

He left his work and prowled the streets; he haunted bars and saloons; he rode for miles on buses and subway, especially at the rush hours. He saw a million faces, but the face of the little man with hexagonal glasses he did not see.

The thought of him obsessed Annixter. It was unjust, it was torture to think that a little, ordinary, chance-met citizen was walking blandly around somewhere with the last link of his, the celebrated James Annixter's play—the best thing he'd ever done—locked away in his head. And with no idea of what he had: without the imagination, probably, to appreciate what he had! And certainly with no idea of what it meant to Annixter!

Or *had* he some idea? Was he, perhaps, not quite so ordinary as he'd seemed? Had he seen those advertisements, drawn from them tortuous inferences of his own? Was he holding back with some scheme for shaking Annixter down for a packet?

The more Annixter thought about it, the more he felt that the hat-check girl had been right, that there was something very queer indeed about the way the little man had behaved after the accident.

Annixter's imagination played around the man he was seeking, tried to probe into his mind, conceived reasons for his fading away after the accident, for his failure to reply to the advertisements.

Annixter's was an active and dramatic imagination. The little man who had seemed so ordinary began to take on a sinister shape in Annixter's mind—

Both the moment he actually saw the little man again, he realized how absurd that was. It was so absurd that it was laughable. The little man was so respectable; his shoulders were so straight; his pepper-and-salt suit was so neat; his black hard-felt hat was set so squarely on his head—

The doors of the subway train were just closing when Annixter saw him, standing on the platform with a brief case in one hand, a folded evening paper under his other arm. Light from the train shone on his prim, pale face; his hexagonal spectacles flashed. He turned towards the exit as Annixter lunged for the closing doors of the train, squeezed between them on to the platform.

Craning his head to see above the crowd, Annixter elbowed his way through, ran up the stairs two at a time, put a hand on the little man's shoulder.

'Just a minute,' Annixter said. 'I've been looking for you.'

The little man checked instantly., at the touch of Annixter's hand. Then he turned his head and looked at Annixter. His eyes were pale behind the hexagonal, rimless glasses—a pale grey. His mouth was a stright line, almost colourless.

Annixter loved the little man like a brother. Merely finding the little man was a relief so great that it was like the lifting of a black cloud from his spirits. He patted the little man's shoulder affectionately.

'I've got to talk to you,' said Annixter. 'It won't take a minute. Let's go somewhere.'

The little man said, 'I can't imagine what you want to talk to me about.'

He moved slightly to one side, to let a woman pass. The crowd from the train

had thinned, but there were still people going up and down the stairs. The little
man looked, politely inquiring, at Annixter.

Annixter said, 'Of course you can't, it's so damned silly! But it's about that
play—'

'Play?'

Annixter felt a faint anxiety.

'Look,' he said, 'I was drunk that night—I was very, very drunk! But looking
back, my impression is that you were dead sober. You were, weren't you?'

'I've never been drunk in my life.'

'Thank heaven for that!' said Annixter. 'Then you won't have any difficulty
in remembering the little point I want you to remember.' He grinned, shook his
head. 'You had me going there, for a minute. I thought—'

'I don't know what you thought,' the little man said. 'But I'm quite sure
you're mistaking me for somebody else. I haven't any idea what you're talking
about. I never saw you before in my life. I'm sorry. Good night.'

He turned and stared up the stairs. Annixter stared after him. He couldn't
believe his ears. He stared blankly after the little man for an instant, then a rush
of anger and suspicion swept away his bewilderment. He raced up the stairs,
caught the little man by the arm.

'Just a minute,' said Annixter. 'I may have been drunk, but—'

'That,' the little man said, 'seems evident. Do you mind taking your hand off
me?'

Annixter controlled himself. 'I'm sorry,' he said. 'Let me get this right,
though. You say you've never seen me before. Then you weren't at the Casa
Havana on the 27th—somewhere between ten o'clock and midnight? You didn't
have a drink or two with me, and listen to an idea for a play that had just come
into my mind?'

The little man looked steadily at Annixter.

'I've told you,' the little man said. 'I've never set eyes on you before.'

'You didn't see me get hit by a taxi?' Annixter pursued, tensely. 'You didn't
say to the hat-check girl, "He's not my friend. He's just someone I met"?'

'I don't know what you're talking about,' the little man said sharply.

He made to turn away, but Annixter gripped his arm again.

'I don't know,' Annixter said, between his teeth, 'anything about your private
affairs, and I don't want to. You may have had some good reason for wanting to
duck giving evidence as a witness of that taxi accident. You may have some good
reason for this act you're pulling on me, now. I don't know and I don't care. But
it is an act! You *are* the man I told my play to!

'I want you to tell that story back to me as I told it to you; I have my reasons—
personal reasons, of concern to me and me only. I want you to tell the story back
to me—that's all I want! I don't want to know who you are, or anything about
you. *I just want you to tell me that story!*'

'You ask,' the little man said, 'an impossibility, since I never heard it.'

Annixter kept an iron hold on himself.

He said, 'Is it money? Is this some sort of a hold-up? Tell me what you want;
I'll give it to you. Lord help me, I'd go so far as to give you a share in the play!

That'll mean real money. I know, because I know my business. And maybe—
maybe,' said Annixter, struck by a sudden thought, '*you* know it, too! Eh?'

'You're insane or drunk!' the little man said.

With a sudden movement, he jerked his arm free, raced up the stairs. A train
was rumbling in, below. People were hurrying down. He weaved and dodged
among them with extraordinary celerity.

He was a small man, light, and Annixter was heavy. But the time he reached
the street, there was no sign of the little man. He was gone.

Was the idea, Annixter wondered, to steal his play? By some wild chance did the
little man nurture a fantastic ambition to be a dramatist? Had he, perhaps,
peddled his precious manuscripts in vain, for years, around the managements?
Had Annixter's play appeared to him as a blinding flash of hope in the gathering
darkness of frustration and failure: something he had imagined he could safely
steal because it had seemed to him the random inspiration of a drunkard who by
morning would have forgotten he had ever given birth to anything but a
hangover?

That, Annixter thought, would be a laugh! That would be irony—

He took another drink. It was his fifteenth since the little man with the
hexagonal glasses had given him the slip, and Annixter was beginning to reach
the stage where he lost count of how many places he had had drinks in tonight.
It was also the stage, though, where he was beginning to feel better, where his
mind was beginning to work.

He could imagine just how the little man must have felt as the quality of the
play he was being told, with hiccups, gradually had dawned upon him.

'This is mine!' the little man would have thought. 'I've got to have this. He's
drunk, he's soused, he's bottled—he'll have forgotten every word of it by the
morning! Go on! Go on, mister! Keep talking!'

That was a laugh, too—the idea that Annixter would have forgotten his play
by the morning. Other things Annixter forgot, unimportant things; but never in
his life had he forgotten the minutest detail that was to his purpose as a
playwright. Never!

Except once, because a taxi had knocked him down.

Annixter took another drink. He needed it. He was on his own now. There
wasn't any little man with hexagonal glasses to fill in that blind spot for him.
The little man was gone. He was gone as though he'd never been. To hell with
him! Annixter had to fill in that blind spot himself. He *had* to do it—somehow!

He had another drink. He had quite a lot more drinks. The bar was crowded
and noisy, but he didn't notice the noise—till someone came up and slapped
him on the shoulder. It was Ransome.

Annixter stood up, leaning with his knuckles on the table.

'Look, Bill,' Annixter said, 'how about this? Man forgets an idea, see? He
wants to get it back—gotta get it back! Idea comes from inside, works
outwards—right? So he starts on the outside, works back inward. How's that?'

He swayed, peering at Ransome.

'Better have a little drink,' said Ransome. 'I'd need to think that out.'

'I,' said Annixter, '*have* thought it out!' He crammed his hat shapelessly on to his head. 'Be seeing you, Bill. I got work to do!'

He started, on a slightly tacking course, for the door—and his apartment.

It was Joseph, his 'man,' who opened the door of his apartment to him, some twenty minutes later. Joseph opened the door while Annixter's latchkey was still describing vexed circles around the lock.

'Good evening, sir,' said Joseph.

Annixter stared at him. 'I didn't tell you to stay in tonight.'

'I hadn't any real reason for going out, sir,' Joseph explained. He helped Annixter off with his coat. 'I rather enjoy a quiet evening in, once in a while.'

'You got to get out of here,' said Annixter.

'Thank you, sir,' said Joseph. 'I'll go and throw a few things into a bag.'

Annixter went into his big living-room-study, poured himself a drink.

The manuscript of his play lay on the desk. Annixter, swaying a little, glass in hand, stood frowning down at the untidy stack of yellow paper, but he didn't begin to read. He waited until he heard the outer door click shut behind Joseph, then he gathered up his manuscript, the decanter and a glass, and the cigarette box. Thus laden, he went into the hall, walked across it to the door of Joseph's room.

There was a bolt on the inside of this door, and the room was the only one in the apartment which had no window—both facts which made the room the only one suitable to Annixter's purpose.

With his free hand, he switched on the light.

It was a plain little room, but Annixter noticed, with a faint grin, that the bedspread and the cushion in the worn basket chair were both blue. Appropriate, he thought—a good omen. *Room Blue* by James Annixter—

Joseph had evidently been lying on the bed, reading the evening paper; the paper lay on the rumpled quilt, and the pillow was dented. Beside the head of the bed, opposite the door, was a small table littered with shoebrushes and dusters.

Annixter swept this paraphernalia onto the floor. He put his stack of manuscript, the decanter and glass and cigarette box on the table, and went across and bolted the door. He pulled the basket chair up to the table, sat down, lighted a cigarette.

He leaned back in the chair, smoking, letting his mind ease into the atmosphere he wanted—the mental atmosphere of Cynthia, the woman in his play, the woman who was afraid, so afraid that she had locked and bolted herself into a windowless room, a sealed room.

'This is how she sat,' Annixter told himself, 'just as I'm sitting now: in a room with no windows, the door locked and bolted. Yet he got at her. He got at her with a knife—in a room with no windows, the door remaining locked and bolted on the inside. *How was it done?*'

There was a way in which it could be done. He, Annixter, had thought of that way; he had conceived it, invented it—and forgotten it. His idea had produced the circumstances. Now, deliberately, he had reproduced the circumstances, that he might think back to the idea. He had put his person in the position of the victim, that his mind might grapple with the problem of the murderer.

It was very quiet: not a sound in the room, the whole apartment. For a long time, Annixter sat unmoving. He sat unmoving until the intensity of his concentration began to waver. Then he relaxed. He pressed the palms of his hands to his forehead for a moment, then reached for the decanter. He splashed himself a strong drink. He had almost recovered what he sought; he had felt it close, had been on the very verge of it.

'Easy,' he warned himself, 'take it easy. Rest. Relax. Try again in a minute.'

He looked around for something to divert his mind, picked up the paper from Joseph's bed.

At the first words that caught his eye, his heart stopped.

The woman, in whose body were found three knife wounds, any of which might have been fatal, was in a windowless room the only door to which was locked and bolted on the inside. These elaborate precautions appear to have been habitual with her, and no doubt she went in continual fear of her life, as the police know her to have been a persistent and pitiless blackmailer.

Apart from the unique problem set by the circumstance of the sealed room is the problem of how the crime could have gone undiscovered for so long a period, the doctor's estimate from the condition of the body as some twelve to fourteen days.

Twelve to fourteen days—

Annixter read back over the remainder of the story; then let the paper fall to the floor. The pulse was heavy in his head. His face was grey. Twelve to fourteen days? He could put it closer than that. *It was exactly thirteen nights ago that he had sat in the Casa Havana and told a little man with hexagonal glasses how to kill a woman in a sealed room!*

Annixter sat very still for a minute. Then he poured himself a drink. It was a big one, and he needed it. He felt a strange sense of wonder, of awe.

They had been in the same boat, he and the little man—thirteen nights ago. They had both been kicked in the face by a woman. One, as a result, had conceived a murder play. The other had made the play reality!

'And I actually, tonight, offered him a share!' Annixter thought. 'I talked about "real" money!'

That was a laugh. All the money in the universe wouldn't have made that little man admit that he had seen Annixter before—that Annixter had told him the plot of a play about how to kill a woman in a sealed room! Why, he, Annixter, was the one person in the world who could denounce that little man! Even if he couldn't tell them, because he had forgotten, just *how* he had told the little man the murder was to be committed, he could still put the police on the little man's track. He could describe him, so that they could trace him. And once on his track, the police would ferret out links, almost inevitably, with the dead woman.

A queer thought—that he, Annixter, was probably the only menace, the only danger, to the little prim, pale man with the hexagonal spectacles. The only menace—as, of course, the little man must know very well.

He must have been very frightened when he had read that the playwright who had been knocked down outside the Casa Havana had only received 'superficial injuries.' He must have been still more frightened when Annixter's advertisements had begun to appear. *What must he have felt tonight, when Annixter's hand had fallen on his shoulder?*

A curious idea occured, now, to Annixter. It was from tonight, precisely from tonight, that he was a danger to that little man. He was, because of the inferences the little man must infallibly draw, a deadly danger as from the moment the discovery of the murder in the sealed room was published. That discovery had been published tonight and the little man had had a paper under his arm—

Annixter's was a lively and resourceful imagination.

It was, of course, just in the cards that, when he'd lost the little man's trail at the subway station, the little man might have turned back, picked up *his*, Annixter's trail.

And Annixter had sent Joseph out. He was, it dawned slowly upon Annixter, alone in the apartment—alone in a windowless room, with the door locked and bolted on the inside, at his back.

Annixter felt a sudden, icy and wild panic.

He half rose, but it was too late.

It was too late, because at that moment the knife slid, thin and keen and delicate, into his back, fatally, between the ribs.

Annixter's head bowed slowly forward until his cheek rested on the manuscript of his play. He made only one sound—a queer sound, indistinct, yet identifiable as a kind of laughter.

The fact was, Annixter had just remembered.

The Wolf

Caius Petronius Arbitrus, *probable author of* The Satyricon, *who lived and died in the Roman Empire in the first century. The only information about this author has come down via the writings of Tacitus* (Annals, *Book XVI, chapters XVII, XVIII, XIX). He is the putative author of a major work of fiction,* The Satyricon, *of which only a few prose and verse fragments have survived.*

'When I was still in service, we were living down a narrow street—Gavilla owns the house now—and there as heaven would have it, I fell in love with the wife of Terentius the innkeeper.

'You all used to know Melissa from Tarentium, an absolute peach to look at. Honest to god, it wasn't her figure or just sex that made me care for her, it was more because she had such a nice nature. If I asked her for anything, it was never refused. She made a penny, I got half of it. I gave her what I had to look after and she never let me down.

'One day her husband died out on the estate. So I did my best to get her by hook or by crook. After all, you know, a friend in need is a friend indeed.

'Luckily the master had gone off to Capua to fix up some odds and ends. I seized my chance and I talked a guest of ours into walking with me as far as the fifth milestone. He was a soldier as it happened, and as brave as hell. About cock-crow we shag off, and the moon was shining like one o'clock. We get to where the tombs are and my chap starts making for the grave-stones, while I, singing away, sits down and starts counting them. Then just as I looked in my mate's direction, he stripped off and laid all his clothes by the side of the road. My heart was in my mouth, I stood there like a corpse. Anyway, he pissed a ring round his clothes and suddenly turned into a wolf. Don't think I'm joking, I wouldn't tell a lie about this for a fortune. However, as I began to say, after he turned into a wolf, he started howling and rushed off into the woods.

'At first I didn't know where I was, then I went up to collect his clothes—but they'd turned to stone. If ever a man was dead with fright, it was me. But I pulled out my sword, and I fairly slaughtered the early morning shadows till I arrived at my girl's house.

'I was just like a ghost when I got in, I practically gasped my last, the sweat was pouring down my crotch, my eyes were blank and staring—I could hardly get over it. It came as a surprise to my poor Melissa to find I'd walked over so late.

' "If you'd come a bit earlier," she said, "at least you could've helped us. A wolf got into the grounds and went for all the livestock—it was a shambles. But he didn't have the last laugh, even though he got away. One of the slaves put a spear right through his neck."

'I couldn't close my eyes again after I heard this. But when it was broad daylight I rushed off home like the innkeeper after the robbery. And when I came to the spot where his clothes had turned to stone, I found nothing but bloodstains. However, when I got home, my soldier friend was lying in bed like a great ox with the doctor seeing to his neck. I realized he was a werewolf and afterwards I couldn't have taken a bite of bread in his company, not if you killed me for it. If other people think differently about this, that's up to them. But me—if I'm telling a lie may all your guardian spirits strike me down!'

The Bust

Manuel Peyrou, *Argentine writer born in San Nicolás de los Arroyos (province of Buenos Aires). Author of* La espada dormida *(1944);* El estruendo de las rosas *(1948);* La noche repetida *(1953);* Las leyes del juego *(1959);* El árbol de Judas *(1961);* Acto y Ceniza *(1963).*

He tied the knot in his tie and, as he tugged downwards to tighten it, pressed the material with his fingers, so that there was a fold from the knot, a pleat in the middle, avoiding any small creases. He put on his blue coat and checked the overall effect. For him, being impeccable was a form of comfort. Satisfied—well satisfied—he left, carefully closing the front door behind him. He had been unable to be at the church, but hoped to arrive at his sister's house before ten. It was the wedding day of his eldest nephew, who, more than a relative, was his friend. He went past the concièrges of the neighbouring houses and casually wished them good night. His was an elegant silhouette, despite his age: tall, dark, his hair lightly streaked with silver.

The display cabinets in the room with the gifts exhibited expensive jewellery. A necklace of various different gemstones diffused a tiny rainbow on its red case in the background; a topaz ring, a pair of bright earrings and a few other artificial miniature meteors glittered under the lights. He checked whether the brooch he had chosen for his brand-new niece and the diamond cufflinks for the groom had pride of place. Satisfied, he went forth in search of the new couple.

'Don't tell me it isn't odd!' his nephew suddenly said, taking him by surprise. He had been in the same room and not noticed his presence.

'I don't know what you're talking about . . .' he replied, stopping in his tracks.

'The bust . . . or whatever it is . . .'

He followed the youth's gaze and then approached, frowning. His instinct had taught him to disdain the habit displayed by those who live in the capital of laughing at what they don't understand.

'Yes . . . it's peculiar . . . but it's not bad. It's got something of Blumpel about it . . .'

His nephew didn't answer. He took a few steps towards it, walked around the pedestal which supported the bust and said, 'I think it looks worst seen from the front.'

'From the front? Which is the front?' He stopped and frowned. 'I don't think it has a front. In any case, I don't think it's right that you should attribute to the author an intention he was probably far from having.'

'I don't know, Uncle; but I think it's an intrusion, a dark presence in a place which is full of light things . . .'

'Fantasies, son, fantasies. You've always been very imaginative. And you always forget the most important thing. For instance, who gave it to you?'

'Here's the card. I've not heard the name before.'

His uncle took the card and studied it carefully; he turned it over and then looked at the front again, with his usual frown, as though he could make out fingerprints or any other trace simply by looking at it.

'Perhaps it's an old classmate you've forgotten about?' he suggested, handing back the tiny rectangular card.

'No. I've checked the list I made before sending the invitations. The name isn't on it.'

His uncle went up to the bust and looked at it close to. 'Haven't you seen this little bronze plaque?' he asked. 'Perhaps you didn't see it because it was covered in dust. Look, it says: "The man of this century".'

'So it does,' the young man replied. 'I hadn't noticed it. But which century does it refer to? And whichever it is, I don't like it. I can't explain, but I don't like it. I'd like to chuck it out.'

Eduardo Adhemar looked at him calmly. He felt his abundant, unvarying tenderness rising; he had always liked to be the arbiter of his relatives' decisions. 'I don't think you should do that,' he said. 'In any case,' he added, suddenly inspired, 'you could take advantage of the opportunity to do something original. And while you're at it, take advantage of the gift too . . .'

His excitement encouraged his nephew. 'Yes, but I don't know how . . . It's a perfectly useless article . . .'

'That's just it,' replied Eduardo Adhemar. 'Because it's useless, it's good for a present.'

His nephew was shocked by the bust. He didn't think it would go down very well if he gave it to anybody. 'It's a form of provocation,' he said. 'And people have already seen it here . . .'

Adhemar was a pleasant and educated dilettante; he would discourse superficially on anything and took pleasure in it. He looked at his nephew with an ironic frown. 'Why do you insist on seeing this bust from an aesthetic point of view?' he asked. 'I suggest you view it as something peculiar, mysterious.' His nephew blinked at him. 'For example, imagine a being who lacked the possibility of becoming real. Nature, say, had five projects for the horse and chose the one we know. The other four have remained a mystery, but they do not lack interest for that reason. Perhaps there was one with extremely long legs, like stilts, and another with long hair, like a sheep, and another with a prehensile tail—most useful in the forest. Perhaps this is the man which might have been. Not that I see it like that. I only like it as a theory. I prefer to imagine it in a dark street, emerging from a carriage entrance; a shapeless being to our present concept, with two pairs of arms and the nose to one side, talking in barks and saying; "Excuse me, I'm the rejected project for Man".'

'You would reply, "I see your kind at the club every night".'

'Don't talk nonsense,' replied Adhemar, who was very sensible when other people became imaginative.

'I prefer the idea of the gift,' said his nephew. 'But for whom? Most of my friends are here and even if they haven't seen it, they soon will . . .'

Eduardo Adhemar remembered. 'I know! Send it to Olegario! He isn't here.

He went to his farm yesterday and is getting married in a fortnight.'

When Eduardo Adhemar arrived a fortnight later at Olegario M. Banfield's house, he had already forgotten the matter. Perhaps that's why—probably for no other reason—he got a fright when he came face to face with the bust when going from one room to another, having checked to his satisfaction that the presents received by the couple were not as expensive as those received by his niece and nephew. The bust was in a corner of the room and yet seemed to be the centre of the lighting and décor. Adhemar greeted two or three people and left.

A month later, when it was already summer, he went to another reception; the company chairman's son was getting married. He felt a bit uncomfortable in the Banking and Stock Exchange environment. He knew that the chairman— a very deserving man, hardworking, but with no background—boasted about being his friend, and that the owner of the house was going to introduce him enthusiastically to a number of rich bourgeois women. But the tyranny of business conventions didn't allow him to think up any excuses. He turned up with his usual propriety, which sometimes sparkled in a light youthful display— a flower, a novel tie—and his undoubtedly distinguished air. He greeted the hosts and the bride and groom, and then, allowing no time for the introductions which were already pouring forth from the chairman's wife, expressed with almost childish impatience his desire to see the presents. They climbed up a stairway bordered with baskets of flowers to the first floor. The bust was in the centre of the large room, under the crystal chandelier.

During the summer and later, in the autumn, Eduardo Adhemar attended two or three more weddings. At all of them he came across the bust. He spaced out his social commitments and restricted himself to going to the club in the afternoon and sometimes at night.

One unsettled night at the beginning of winter he was comfortably installed drinking his whisky and reading the paper when a conversation behind him made him sit up and listen. Two members were talking excitedly. Judging by the few words he was able to make out, he realized they were talking about the bust. 'Luckily they had time to . . .' The sentence was unfinished because a waiter went by rattling a tray of glasses. What had to be done in time? wondered Adhemar. A trace of humour, an incident arising in a moment of joviality on his nephew's wedding day, seemed to have had unforeseeable consequences. He had set something in motion, a habit, a fashion, a force. He didn't know what, but decided to find out. Unfortunately he wasn't on speaking terms with either of the gentlemen. They had fallen out on the day of the renewal of the board. He decided to be alert during the next few days in case he heard other allusions to the bust. One afternoon he got to the lounge just at the end of a conversation amongst several friends. He thought he understood that someone had held that there existed several busts. But that idea was triumphantly refuted by Pedrito Defferrari Marenco, the young lawyer and politician, who was fast becoming one of the new names in the Traditional Party. It was a single bust, which everyone nervously got rid of as soon as they received it. Adhemar, in a sort of dizzy state, kept quiet.

From then on he started feeling deeply worried. The reasons for his disquiet did not respond to an egotistic feeling; he understood—sitting in his usual armchair in the club, he analysed his situation in detail—that a generous impulse, although still hidden, was increasingly and silently taking over. He started to think constantly about his nephew, his happiness, his profession, aspects of his married life. The couple had not yet returned from a long trip to Europe and Adhemar suffered real anxiety during the weeks prior to their return. When they finally arrived, he had to restrain himself for a few days. One afternoon he invited the young man to have a whisky at the club. After talking about trivia related to the trip, he carefully explored the topics which interested him. Everything was fine; his nephew and his wife were happy, they had plenty of money and his profession as an engineer was the young man's fulfilled vocation. Adhemar smiled imperceptibly, satisfied, like a conspirator.

But two or three days later he noted with alarm that he began to be interested in the fate of Olegario Banfield, the friend to whom his nephew had given the bust. The problem was rather more difficult, because his friendship with Banfield was limited and there weren't many excuses to see him. He started, nonetheless, to visit friends they had in common in order to obtain details; he invented innumerable subterfuges and excuses to find out everything about the life of young Olegario and his wife. He achieved his aim, of course, and was satisfied once again. The next few investigations turned out to be more complicated, because as he went on he came across people virtually unknown to him. He therefore resorted to a private investigation agency. At first he found it difficult to overcome Inspector Molina's professional distrust. The latter, an experienced man, naturally thought of affairs of the heart. It is normal for a gentleman of means to have an expensive liaison and to yearn for relative faithfulness; it is also normal for him to try to obtain proof of that faithfulness. But when the investigation had to extend to ten or fifteen newly created households, the inspector finally accepted the reasons put forward by Adhemar. All the work, the gentlemen explained, was to be done with a view to creating a file; a large credit company, whose identity had to be kept secret for the time being, was preparing an enormous moral and financial register of the country. Adhemar noticed a hint of irony in the inspector on two or three occasions, but since the man carried out his work conscientiously he immediately forgot about that. The inspector for his part received a considerable monthly instalment for his activities, so he soon abandoned all considerations irrelevant to his routine work and cooperated most efficiently.

After some time Adhemar realized it was impossible to get a picture of somebody's life, starting from possession of the bust, without knowing about their previous life. Only by comparison could he get a precise picture. This spread infinitely complicated the investigations. In order to assist the inspector, Adhemar himself decided to take action. For days and nights he held interviews, requested reports, followed unknown people along the street for long periods. After a few months, one misty night when he was wandering around the Recoleta district, he got a fright. A slight form, almost a shadow, half-seen as he turned his face, made him suspect that he also was being followed. The blood throbbed at his temples; a feeling of horror was about to paralyse him. He managed to quicken his step, turned two or three corners unexpectedly—or what he thought was unexpectedly—and finally reached his house. A few hours later, he had calmed down. He had pried into the lives of others; did he have the right to prevent somebody spying on him? But he didn't think any more about it because he was very tired; his physical state and his energy had flagged over the past few weeks.

For a month he continued his work, always with the feeling of being closely observed, until an upset stomach and a slight stitch in his left side forced him to go and visit the doctor. It was nothing to worry about, the latter explained. A diet, reduced alcohol intake, a series of injections and he would be as good as new. He returned to his flat in Calle Arenales and got into bed. The following day was his birthday and he wanted to be well enough to receive his friends. But when he woke up, he realized that his gathering was doomed. A sharp pain, rheumatism or whatever it was, made all movement impossible. His slight discomfort had turned into lumbago.

He spent the day in bed. His manservant let in two or three friends who came to wish him well; a few presents also arrived. At nine o'clock that night he left, having asked permission to go to the cinema. Adhemar suggested that he leave the door ajar in case any more friends turned up. Half an hour later he heard a knock and a messenger came in without waiting for a reply. He was struggling under a very heavy parcel, which he left on the hall table. Then he approached the bed, handed him a letter and left. In the next room, the parcel was a dark shadow. Bent double by the pain, unable to sit up, Adhemar opened the letter and took out a card. He had never seen the name before. Yes, he had seen it before: the night of his nephew's wedding, on the card accompanying the bust! Anxiously, he stretched out his arm and picked up the telephone. He put the earpiece to his ear; it was dead. He made another painful, fruitless effort to sit up. A growing oppression, like a tide, filled his chest and rose and rose.

Under the archway of the hall, darkness spread like spilt coffee and advanced into the bedroom.

The Cask of Amontillado

Edgar Allan Poe, *American writer. Born in Boston in 1809, died in hospital in New York in 1849. The inventor of the crime fiction genre, who revived the gothic fantasy genre. He influenced writers as diverse as Baudelaire and Chesterton, Conan Doyle and Paul Valéry. His* works include The narrative of Arthur Gordon Pym *(1838),* Tales of the Grotesque and the Arabesque *(1839),* Tales *(1845),* The Raven and Other Poems *(1845),* Eureka *(1848). His works have been reproduced in almost all the other media.*

(ROME)

The thousand injuries of Fortunato I had borne as I best could; but when he ventured upon insult, I vowed revenge. You, who so well know the nature of my soul, will not suppose, however, that I gave utterance to a threat. *At length* I would be avenged; this was a point definitively settled—but the very definitiveness with which it was resolved precluded the idea of risk. I must not only punish, but punish with impunity. A wrong is unredressed when retribution overtakes its redresser. It is equally unredressed when the avenger fails to make himself felt as such to him who has done the wrong.

It must be understood that neither by word nor deed had I given Fortunato cause to doubt my good-will. I continued, as was my wont, to smile in his face, and he did not perceive that my smile *now* was at the thought of his immolation.

He had a weak point—this Fortunato—although in other regards he was a man to be respected and even feared. He prided himself on his connoisseurship in wine. Few Italians have the true virtuoso spirit. For the most part their enthusiasm is adopted to suit the time and opportunity—to practise imposture upon the British and Austrian millionaires. In painting and gemmary, Fortunato, like his countrymen, was a quack—but in the matter of old wines he was sincere. In this respect I did not differ from him materially: I was skilful in the Italian vintages myself, and bought largely whenever I could.

It was about dusk, one evening during the supreme madness of the carnival season, that I encountered my friend. He accosted me with excessive warmth, for he had been drinking much. The man wore motley. He had on a tight-fitting parti-striped dress, and his head was surmounted by the conical cap and bells. I was so pleased to see him that I thought I should never have done wringing his hand.

I said to him, 'My dear Fortunato, you are luckily met. How remarkably well you are looking today! But I have received a pipe of what passes for Amontillado, and I have my doubts.'

'How?' said he. 'Amontillado? A pipe? Impossible! And in the middle of the carnival!'

'I have my doubts,' I replied; 'and I was silly enough to pay the full Amontillado price without consulting you in the matter. You were not to be found, and I was fearful of losing a bargain.'

'Amontillado!'

'I have my doubts.'

'Amontillado!'

'And I must satisfy them.'

'Amontillado!'

'As you are engaged, I am on my way to Luchesi. If anyone has a critical turn, it is he. He will tell me — —'

'Luchesi cannot tell Amontillado from Sherry.'

'And yet some fools will have it that his taste is a match for your own.'

'Come, let us go.'

'Whither?'

'To your vaults.'

'My friend, no; I will not impose upon your good-nature. I perceive you have an engagement. Luchesi—'

'I have no engagement; come.'

'My friend, no. It is not the engagement, but the severe cold with which I perceive you are afflicted. The vaults are insufferably damp. They are encrusted with nitre.'

'Let us go, nevertheless. The cold is merely nothing. Amontillado! You have been imposed upon. And as for Luchesi, he cannot distinguish Sherry from Amontillado.'

Thus speaking, Fortunato possessed himself of my arm. Putting on a mask of black silk, and drawing a roquelaire closely about my person, I suffered him to hurry me to my palazzo.

There were no attendants at home; they had absconded to make merry in honor of the time. I had told them that I should not return until the morning, and had given them explicit orders not to stir from the house. These orders were sufficient, I well knew, to insure their immediate disappearance, one and all, as soon as my back was turned.

I took from their sources two flambeaus, and giving one to Fortunato, bowed him through several suites of rooms to the archway that led into the vaults. I passed down a long and winding staircase, requesting him to be cautious as he followed. We came at length to the foot of the descent, and stood together on the damp ground of the catacombs of the Montresors.

The gait of my friend was unsteady, and the bells upon his cap jingled as he strode.

'The pipe,' said he.

'It is farther on,' said I; 'but observe the white web-work which gleams from these cavern walls.'

He turned towards me, and looked into my eyes with two filmy orbs that distilled the rheum of intoxication.

'Nitre?' he asked, at length.

'Nitre,' I replied. 'How long have you had that cough?'

'Ugh! ugh! ugh!—ugh! ugh! ugh!—ugh! ugh! ugh!—ugh! ugh! ugh!—ugh! ugh! ugh!'

My poor friend found it impossible to reply for many minutes.

'It is nothing,' he said, at last.

'Come,' I said, with decision, 'we will go back; your health is precious. You are rich, respected, admired, beloved; you are happy, as once I was. You are a man to be missed. For me it is no matter. We will go back; you will be ill, and I cannot be responsible. Besides, there is Luchesi—'

'Enough,' he said; 'the cough is a mere nothing; it will not kill me. I shall not die of a cough.'

'True—true,' I replied; 'and, indeed, I had no intention of alarming you unnecessarily—but you should use all proper caution. A draught of this Medoc will defend us from the damps.'

Here I knocked off the neck of a bottle which I drew from a long row of its fellows that lay upon the mould.

'Drink,' I said, presenting him the wine.

He raised it to his lips with a leer. He paused and nodded to me familiarly, while his bells jingled.

'I drink,' he said, 'to the buried that repose around us.'

'And I to your long life.'

He again took my arm, and we proceeded.

'These vaults,' he said, 'are extensive.'

'The Montresors,' I replied, 'were a great and numerous family.'

'I forget your arms.'

'A huge human foot d'or, in a field azure; the foot crushes a serpent rampant whose fangs are imbedded in the heel.'

'And the motto?'

'*Nemo me impune laccessit.*'

'Good!' he said.

The wine sparkled in his eyes and the bells jingled. My own fancy grew warm with the Medoc. We had passed through walls of piled bones, with casks and puncheons intermingling, into the inmost recesses of the catacombs. I passed again, and this time I made bold to seize Fortunato by an arm above the elbow.

'The nitre!' I said; 'see, it increases. It hangs like moss upon the vaults. We are below the river's bed. The drops of moisture trickle among the bones. Come, we will go back ere it is too late. Your cough—'

'It is nothing,' he said; 'let us go on. But first, another draught of the Medoc.'

I broke and reached him a flagon of De Grâve. He emptied it at a breath. His eyes flashed with a fierce light. He laughed and threw the bottle upwards with a gesticulation I did not understand.

I looked at him in surprise. He repeated the movement—a grotesque one.

'You do not comprehend?' he said.

'Not I,' I replied.

'Then you are not of the brotherhood.'

'How?'

'You are not of the masons.'

'Yes, yes,' I said, 'yes, yes.'

'You? Impossible! A mason?'

'A mason,' I replied.

'A sign,' he said.

'It is this,' I answered, producing a trowel from beneath the folds of my roquelaire.

'You jest,' he exclaimed, recoiling, a few paces. 'But let us proceed to the Amontillado.'

'Be it so,' I said, replacing the tool beneath the cloak, and again offering him my arm. He leaned upon it heavily. We continued our route in search of the Amontillado. We passed through a range of low arches, descended, passed on, and, descending again, arrived at a deep crypt, in which the foulness of the air caused our flambeaus rather to glow than flame.

At the most remote end of the crypt there appeared another less spacious. Its walls had been lined with human remains, piled to the vault overhead, in the fashion of the great catacombs of Paris. Three sides of this interior crypt were still ornamented in this manner. From the fourth the bones had been thrown down, and lay promiscuously upon the earth, forming at one point a mound of some size. Within the wall thus exposed by the displacing of the bones, we perceived a still interior recess, in depth about four feet, in width three, in height six or seven. It seemed to have been constructed for no especial use within itself, but formed merely the interval between two of the colossal supports of the roof of the catacombs, and was backed by one of their circumscribing walls of solid granite.

It was in vain that Fortunato, uplifting his dull torch, endeavored to pry into the depth of the recess. Its termination the feeble light did not enable us to see.

'Proceed,' I said; 'herein is the Amontillado. As for Luchesi—'

'He is an ignoramus,' interrupted my friend, as he stepped unsteadily forward, while I followed immediately at his heels. In an instant he had reached the extremity of the niche, and finding his progress arrested by the rock, stood stupidly bewildered. A moment more and I had fettered him to the granite. In its sufrace were two iron staples, distant from each other about two feet, horizontally. From one of these depended a short chain, from the other a padlock. Throwing the links about his waist, it was but the work of a few seconds to secure it. He was too much astounded to resist. Withdrawing the key, I stepped back from the recess.

'Pass your hand,' I said, 'over the wall; you cannot help feeling the nitre. Indeed it is *very* damp. Once more let me *implore* you to return. No? Then I must positively leave you. But I must first render you all the little attentions in my power.'

'The Amontillado!' ejaculated my friend, not yet recovered from his astonishment.

'True,' I replied; 'the Amontillado.'

As I said these words I busied myself among the pile of bones of which I have before spoken. Throwing them aside, I soon uncovered a quantity of building stone and mortar. With these materials and with the aid of my trowel, I began vigourously to wall up the entrance of the niche.

I had scarcely laid the first tier of the masonry when I discovered that the intoxication of Fortunato had in a great measure worn off. The earliest indication I had of this was a low moaning cry from the depth of the recess. It was *not* the cry of a drunken man. There was then a long and obstinate silence. I laid the second tier, and the third, and the fourth; and then I heard the furious vibrations of the chain. The noise lasted for several minutes, during which, that I might hearken to it with the more satisfaction, I ceased my labors and sat down upon the bones. When at last the clanking subsided, I resumed the trowel, and finished without interruption the fifth, the sixth, and the seventh tier. The wall was now nearly upon a level with my breast. I again paused, and holding the flambeaus over the mason-work, threw a few feeble rays upon the figure within.

A succession of loud and shrill screams, bursting suddenly from the throat of the chained form, seemed to thrust me violently back. For a brief moment I hestitated—I trembled. Unsheathing my rapier, I began to grope with it about the recess; but the thought of an instant reasured me. I placed my hand upon the solid fabric of the catacombs, and felt satisfied. I reapproached the wall. I replied to the yells of him who clamored. I re-echoed—I aided—I surpassed them in volume and in strength. I did this, and the clamorer grew still.

It was now midnight, and my task was drawing to a close. I had completed the eighth, the ninth, and the tenth tier. I had finished a portion of the last and the eleventh; there remained but a single stone to be fitted and plastered in. I struggled with its weight; I placed it partially in its destined position. But now there came from out the niche a low laugh that erected the hairs upon my head. It was succeeded by a sad voice, which I had difficulty in recognizing as that of the noble Fortunato. The voice said—

'Ha! ha! ha!—he! he! he!—a very good joke indeed—an excellent jest. We will have many a rich laugh about it at the palazzo—he! he! he!—over our wine—he! he! he!'

'The Amontillado!' I said.

'He! he! he!—he! he! he!—yes, the Amontillado. But is it not getting late? Will not they be awaiting us at the palazzo,—the Lady Fortunato and the rest? Let us be gone.'

'Yes,' I said, 'let us be gone.'

'*For the love of God, Montresor!*'

'Yes,' I said, 'for the love of God!'

But to these words I hearkened in vain for a reply. I grew impatient. I called aloud—

'Fortunato!'

No answer. I called again—

'Fortunato!'

No answer still. I thrust a torch through the remaining aperture and let it fall within. There came forth in return only a jingling of the bells. My heart grew sick—on account of the dampness of the catacombs. I hastened to make an end of my labor. I forced the last stone into its position; I plastered it up. Against the new masonry I re-erected the old rampart of bones. For the half of a century no mortal has disturbed them. *In pace requiescat.*

The Tiger of Chao-ch'êng

P'U Sung Ling *was the author of a huge collection of tales and legends, as familiar in China as the* Arabian Nights. *Biographical details are scanty, but we know that in 1651 he was a graduate of ten years' standing. His great work has been translated as* Strange Stories from a Chinese Studio, *or* Lao Tse.

At Chao-ch'êng there lived an old woman more than seventy years of age, who had an only son. One day he went up to the hills and was eaten by a tiger, at which his mother was so overwhelmed with grief that she hardly wished to live. With tears and lamentations she ran and told her story to the magistrate of the place, who laughed and asked her how she thought the law could be brought to bear on a tiger. But the old woman would not be comforted, and at length the magistrate lost his temper and bade her begone. Of this, however, she took no notice; and then the magistrate, in compassion for her great age and unwilling to resort to extremities, promised her that he would have the tiger arrested. Even then she would not go until the warrant had been actually issued; so the magistrate, at a loss what to do, asked his attendants which of them would undertake the job. Upon this one of them, Li Nêng, who happened to be gloriously drunk, stepped forward and said that he would; whereupon the warrant was immediately issued and the old woman went away. When our friend, Li Nêng, got sober, he was sorry for what he had done; but reflecting that the whole thing was a mere trick of his master's to get rid of the old woman's importunities, did not trouble himself much about it, handing in the warrant as if the arrest had been made. 'Not so,' cried the magistrate, 'you said you could do this, and now I shall not let you off.' Li Nêng was at his wits' end, and begged that he might be allowed to impress the hunters of the district. This was conceded; so collecting together these men, he proceeded to spend day and night among the hills in the hope of catching a tiger, and thus making a show of having fulfilled his duty.

A month passed away, during which he received several hundred blows with the bamboo, and at length, in despair, he betook himself to the Ch'êng-huang temple in the eastern suburb, where, falling on his knees, he prayed and wept by turns. By-and-by a tiger walked in, and Li Nêng, in a great fright, thought he was going to be eaten alive. But the tiger took no notice of anything, remaining seated in the doorway. Li Nêng then addressed the animal as follows:— 'O tiger, if thou didst slay that old woman's son, suffer me to bind thee with this cord;' and, drawing a rope from his pocket, threw it over the animal's neck. The tiger drooped its ears, and allowing itself to be bound, followed Li Nêng to the magistrate's office. The latter then asked it, saying, 'Did you eat the old woman's son?' to which the tiger replied by nodding its head; whereupon the magistrate rejoined, 'That murderers should suffer death has ever been the law. Besides, this old woman had but one son, and by killing him you took from her the sole support of her declining years. But if now you will be as a son to her, your crime shall be pardoned.' The tiger again nodded assent, and accordingly the magistrate gave orders that he should be released, at which the old woman was highly incensed, thinking that the tiger ought to have paid with its life for the destruction of her son.

Next morning, however, when she opened the door of her cottage, there lay a dead deer before it; and the old woman, by selling the flesh and skin, was able to purchase food. From that day this became a common event, and sometimes the tiger would even bring her money and valuables, so that she became quite rich, and was much better cared for than she had been even by her own son. Consequently, she became very well-disposed to the tiger, which often came and slept in the verandah, remaining for a whole day at a time, and giving no cause of fear either to man or beast. In a few years the old woman died, upon which the tiger walked in and roared its lamentations in the hall. However, with all the money she had saved, she was able to have a splendid funeral; and while her relatives were standing round the grave, out rushed a tiger and sent them all running away in fear. But the tiger merely went up to the mound, and after roaring like a thunder-peal, disappeared again. Then the people of that place built a shrine in honour of the Faithful Tiger, and it remains there to this day.

How We Arrived at the Island of Tools

François Rabelais, *French satrical writer. Born in Chinon about 1494, died in Paris in 1553. He was a cleric who practised medicine in various cities in southern France. He travelled extensively throughout France and Italy. Most famous for* Pantagruel and Gargantua *(1532-1564). He also published* Topographiae Antiquae Romae Epistola *(1534),* Supplicatio pro Apostasia *(1535) and* La Sciomachie *(1549).*

We ballasted our stomachs well, and sailed on, the wind at our stern; with our main mizzen aloft, we reached Tool Island in less than two days. It was deserted land with a vast number of trees bearing hoes, mattocks, pickaxes, scythes, sickles, spades, trowels, hatchets, pruning bills, saws, shears, adzes, scissors, pincers, shovels, augers and wimbles. Others bore daggers, poniards, dirks, knives, scimitars, broadblades, cutlasses, rippers, knives and arrows.

Did you wish a tool or weapon, you had but to shake the tree: it fell at your feet like a plum. What is more, it fell snugly to earth to meet a hollow stalk of scabbard-grass which enclosed it like a sheath. You had to take care it did not land on your head, on your foot or on any other part of your body, since, to be sheathed properly, it fell point downward. It might thus seriously wound any one who was not spry.

Below another kind of tree—I don't know its name—I saw various species of tall grasses that looked like pikestaves, lancehilts, spear-shafts, halberdshafts, partisan hafts, handles and stakes. These grew all the way up to the trees, where heads, steels, points, helves, blades and hafts met; the trees furnishing the appropriate blade for each wooden utensil, as carefully as fond mothers provide coats for infants ere they grow out of swaddling clothes.

In order to convince you that Plato, Anaxagoras and Democritus (no mean philosophers!) were right when they assigned intellect and feeling to plants, I must add that these trees were in reality animals, if you will. How did they differ from beasts? They had skin, flesh, tissues, veins, arteries, ligaments, nerves, cartilages, glands, bones, marrow, humors, matrices, brains and articulation. These were not immediately apparent, as in the case of animals, but existed and functioned none the less, as Theophrastus proved in his *Treatise on Plants*. These trees differed from animals merely in that their heads (*i.e.* trunks) grew downwards, their hair (*i.e.* roots) was invisible, their feet (*i.e.* branches) kicked out into the air. These trees, in other words, looked like a man or beast standing on his head.

From leagues hence, and weeks aforetime, you, O my beloved venereals, feel, in your sciatic legs and rheumatic shoulders, the coming of rain, wind and calm. Your very bones presage a change of weather. So these trees, through root, stock, sap and gum, sensed the kind of staff growing beneath them, and prepared a blade to suit it.

To be sure, all things, God excepted, are subject to error: even Nature is not exempt, since Nature, too, produces deformities and monstrosities. Occasionally, these trees wrought amiss. A pikestaff, growing high aloft the earth, rose to meet a tool-bearing tree, and found itself accidentally fastened, not to a metal head, but to a broom. (What matter? That grotesque implement would serve the better to scour the chimney.) A spearshaft, pushing up from the ground, might meet a pair of garden shears? (Very good: it would serve to trim trees and rid the garden of caterpillars!) The haft of a halberd found itself joined to the blade of a scythe, with results I can describe only as hermaphroditic in appearance. (Why worry? It would do yeoman service in the mowing season.)

Verily, to put one's trust in the Lord is a noble thing!

We returned to the ships. On our way, I glimpsed, behind God knows what bushes, God knows what people, doing God knows what, and God knows how. They were sharpening God knows what blades, which they held in God knows what place, and wielded to God knows what advantages . . .

The Music On The Hill

Saki *(pseudonym of H. H. Munro), English writer born at Akyab, Burma, died in 1916 in World War I in the assault on Beaumont Hamel. His work includes* The Rise of the Russian Empire *(1900),* Not So Stories *(1902),* When William Came *(1913),* Beasts and Super-Beasts *(1914),* The Stories of Saki *(1930).*

Sylvia Seltoun ate her breakfast in the morning-room at Yessney with a pleasant sense of ultimate victory, such as a fervent Ironside might have permitted himself on the morrow of Worcester fight. She was scarcely pugnacious by temperament, but belonged to that more successful class of fighters who are pugnacious by circumstance. Fate had willed that her life should be occupied with a series of small struggles, usually with the odds slightly against her, and usually she had just managed to come through winning. And now she felt that she had brought her hardest and certainly her most important struggle to a successful issue. To have married Mortimer Seltoun, 'Dead Mortimer' as his more intimate enemies called him, in the teeth of the cold hostility of his family, and in spite of his unaffected indifference to women, was indeed an achievement that had needed some determination and adroitness to carry through; yesterday she had brought her victory to its concluding stage by wrenching her husband away from Town and its group of satellite watering-places and 'settling him down,' in the vocabulary of her kind, in this remote wood-girt manor farm which was his country house.

'You will never get Mortimer to go,' his mother said carpingly, 'but if he once goes he'll stay; Yessney throws almost as much a spell over him as Town does. One can understand what holds him to Town, but Yessney—' and the dowager had shrugged her shoulders.

There was a sombre almost savage wildness about Yessney that was certainly not likely to appeal to town-bred tastes, and Sylvia, notwithstanding her name, was accustomed to nothing much more sylvan than 'leafy Kensington.' She looked on the country as something excellent and wholesome in its way, which was apt to become troublesome if you encouraged it overmuch. Distrust of town-life had been a new thing with her, born of her marriage with Mortimer, and she had watched with satisfaction the gradual fading of what she called 'the Jermyn-Street-look' in his eyes as the woods and heather of Yessney had closed in on them yesternight. Her will-power and strategy had prevailed; Mortimer would stay.

Outside the morning-room windows was a triangular slope of turf, which the indulgent might call a lawn, and beyond its low hedge of neglected fuschia bushes a steeper slope of heather and bracken dropped down into cavernous combes overgrown with oak and yew. In its wild open savagery there seemed a stealthy linking of the joy of life with the terror of unseen things. Sylvia smiled complacently as she gazed with a School-of-Art appreciation at the landscape, and then of a sudden she almost shuddered.

'It is very wild,' she said to Mortimer, who had joined her; 'one could almost think that in such a place the worship of Pan had never quite died out.'

'The worship of Pan never has died out,' said Mortimer. 'Other newer gods have drawn aside his votaries from time to time, but he is the Nature-God to whom all must come back at last. He has been called the Father of all the Gods, but most of his children have been stillborn.'

Sylvia was religious in an honest, vaguely devotional kind of way, and did not like to hear her beliefs spoken of as mere aftergrowths, but it was at least something new and hopeful to hear Dead Mortimer speak with such energy and conviction on any subject.

'You don't really believe in Pan?' she asked incredulously.

'I've been a fool in most things,' said Mortimer quietly, 'but I'm not such a fool as not to believe in Pan when I'm down here. And if you're wise you won't disbelieve in him too boastfully while you're in his country.'

It was not till a week later, when Sylvia had exhausted the attractions of the woodland walks round Yessney, that she ventured on a tour of inspection of the farm buildings. A farmyard suggested in her mind a scene of cheerful bustle, with churns and flails and smiling dairymaids, and teams of horses drinking knee-deep in duck-crowded ponds. As she wandered among the gaunt grey buildings of Yessney manor farm her first impression was one of crushing stillness and desolation, as though she had happened on some lone deserted homestead long given over to owls and cobwebs; then came a sense of furtive watchful hostility, the same shadow of unseen things that seemed to lurk in the wooded combes and coppices. From behind heavy doors and shuttered windows came the restless stamp of hoof or rasp of chain halter, and at times a muffled bellow from some stalled beast. From a distant corner a shaggy dog watched her with intent unfriendly eyes; as she drew near it slipped quietly into its kennel, and slipped out again as noiselessly when she had passed by. A few hens, questing for food under a rick, stole away under a gate at her approach. Sylvia felt that if she had come across any human beings in this wilderness of barn and byre they would have fled wraith-like from her gaze. At last, turning a corner quickly, she came upon a living thing that did not fly from her. Astretch in a pool of mud was an enormous sow, gigantic beyond the town-woman's wildest computation of swine-flesh, and speedily alert to resent and if necessary repel the unwonted intrusion. It was Sylvia's turn to make an unobtrusive retreat. As she threaded her way past rickyards and cowsheds and long blank walls, she started suddenly at a strange sound—the echo of a boy's laughter, golden and equivocal. Jan, the only boy employed on the farm, a tow-headed, wizen-faced yokel, was visibly at work on a potato clearing half-way up the nearest hill-side, and Mortimer, when questioned, knew of no other probable or possible begetter of the hidden mockery that had ambushed Sylvia's retreat. The memory of that untraceable echo was added to her other impressions of a furtive sinister 'something' that hung around Yessney.

Of Mortimer she saw very little; farm and woods and trout-streams seemed to swallow him up from dawn till dusk. Once, following the direction she had seen him take in the morning, she came to an open space in a nut copse, further shut in by huge yew trees, in the centre of which stood a stone pedestal surmounted by a small bronze figure of a youthful Pan. It was a beautiful piece of workmanship, but her attention was chiefly held by the fact that a newly cut bunch of grapes had been placed as an offering at its feet. Grapes were none too plentiful at the manor house, and Sylvia snatched the bunch angrily from the pedestal. Contemptuous annoyance dominated her thoughts as she strolled slowly homeward, and then gave way to a sharp feeling of something that was very near fright; across a thick tangle of undergrowth a boy's face was scowling at her, brown and beautiful, with unutterably evil eyes. It was a lonely pathway, all pathways round Yessney were lonely for the matter of that, and she sped forward without waiting to give a closer scrutiny to this sudden apparition. It was not till she had reached the house that she discovered that she had dropped the bunch of grapes in her flight.

'I saw a youth in the wood today,' she told Mortimer that evening, 'brown-faced and rather handsome, but a scoundrel to look at. A gipsy lad, I suppose.'

'A reasonable theory,' said Mortimer, 'only there aren't any gipsies in these parts at present.'

'Then who was he?' asked Sylvia, and as Mortimer appeared to have no theory of his own, she passed on to recount her finding of the votive offering.

'I suppose it was your doing,' she observed; 'it's a harmless piece of lunacy, but people would think you dreadfully silly if they knew of it.'

'Did you meddle with it in any way?' asked Mortimer.

'I—I threw the grapes away. It seemed so silly,' said Sylvia, watching Mortimer's impassive face for a sign of annoyance.

'I don't think you were wise to do that,' he said reflectively. 'I've heard it said that the Wood Gods are rather horrible to those who molest them.'

'Horrible perhaps to those that believe in them, but you see I don't,' retorted Sylvia.

'All the same,' said Mortimer in his even, dispassionate tone, 'I should avoid the woods and orchards if I were you, and give a wide berth to the horned beasts on the farm.'

It was all nonsense, of course, but in that lonely wood-girt spot nonsense seemed able to rear a bastard brood of uneasiness.

'Mortimer,' said Sylvia suddenly, 'I think we will go back to Town some time soon.'

Her victory had not been so complete as she had supposed; it had carried her on to ground that she was already anxious to quit.

'I don't think you will ever go back to Town,' said Mortimer. He seemed to be paraphrasing his mother's prediction as to himself.

Sylvia noted with dissatisfaction and some self-contempt that the course of her next afternoon's ramble took her instinctively clear of the network of woods. As to the horned cattle, Mortimer's warning was scarcely needed, for she had always regarded them as of doubtful neutrality at the best: her imagination unsexed the most matronly dairy cows and turned them into bulls liable to 'see red' at any moment. The ram who fed in the narrow paddock below the orchards she had adjudged, after ample and cautious probation, to be of docile temper; today, however, she decided to leave his docility untested, for the usually tranquil beast was roaming with every sign of restlessness from corner to corner of his meadow. A low, fitful piping, as of some reedy flute, was coming from the depth of a neighbouring copse, and there seemed to be some subtle connection between the animal's restless pacing and the wild music from the wood. Sylvia turned her steps in an upward direction and climbed the heather-clad slopes that stretched in rolling shoulders high above Yessney. She had left the piping notes behind her, but across the wooded combes at her feet the wind brought her another kind of music, the straining bay of hounds in full chase. Yessney was just on the outskirts of the Devon-and-Somerset country, and the hunted deer sometimes came that way. Sylvia could presently see a dark body, breasting hill after hill, and sinking again and again out of sight as he crossed the combes, while behind him steadily swelled that relentless chorus, and she grew tense with the excited sympathy that one feels for any hunted thing in whose capture one is not directly interested. And at last he broke through the outermost line of oak scrub and fern and stood panting in the open, a fat September stag carrying a well-furnished head. His obvious course was to drop down to the brown pools of Undercombe, and thence make his way towards the red deer's favoured sanctuary, the sea. To Sylvia's surprise, however, he turned his head to the upland slope and came lumbering resolutely onward over the heather. 'It will be dreadful,' she thought, 'the hounds will pull him down under my very eyes.' But the music of the pack seemed to have died away for a moment, and in its place she heard again that wild piping, which rose now on this side, now on that, as though urging the failing stag to a final effort. Sylvia stood well aside from his path, half hidden in a thick growth of whortle bushes, and watched him swing stiffly upward, his flanks dark with sweat, the coarse hair on his neck showing light by contrast. The pipe music shrilled suddenly around her, seeming to come from the bushes at her very feet, and at the same moment the great beast slewed round and bore directly down upon her. In an instant her pity for the hunted animal was changed to wild terror at her own danger; the thick heather roots mocked her scrambling efforts at flight, and she looked frantically downward for a glimpse of oncoming hounds. The huge antler spikes were within a few yards of her, and in a flash of numbing fear she remembered Mortimer's warning, to beware of horned beasts on the farm. And then with a quick throb of joy she saw that she was not alone; a human figure stood a few paces aside, knee-deep in the whortle bushes.

'Drive it off!' she shrieked. But the figure made no answering movement.

The antlers drove straight at her breast, the acrid smell of the hunted animal was in her nostrils, but her eyes were filled with the horror of something she saw other than her oncoming death. And in her ears rang the echo of a boy's laughter, golden and equivocal.

Where Their Fire Is Not Quenched

May Sinclair, *English writer, born in Cheshire in 1865, died at Aylesbury in 1946. Author of* The Divine Fire *(1904),* The Three Sisters *(1914), and* Mary Oliver *(1919).*

There was nobody in the orchard. Harriott Leigh went out, carefully, through the iron gate into the field. She had made the latch slip into its notch without a sound.

The path slanted widely up the field from the orchard gate to the site under the elder tree. George Waring waited for her there.

Years afterwards, when she thought of George Waring she smelt the sweet, hot, wine-scent of the elder flowers. Years afterwards, when she smelt elder flowers she saw George Waring, with his beautiful, gentle face, like a poet's or a musician's, his black-blue eyes, and sleek, olive-brown hair. He was a naval lieutenant.

Yesterday he had asked her to marry him and she had consented. But her father hadn't, and she had come to tell him that and say good-bye before he left her. His ship was to sail the next day.

He was eager and excited. He couldn't believe that anything could stop their happiness, that anything he didn't want to happen could happen.

'Well?' he said.

'He's a perfect beast, George. He won't let us. He says we're too young.'

'I was twenty last August,' he said, aggrieved.

'And I shall be seventeen in September.'

'And this is June. We're quite old, really. How long does he mean us to wait?'

'Three years.'

'Three years before we can be engaged even—Why, we might be dead.'

She put her arms round him to make him feel safe. They kissed; and the sweet, hot, wine-scent of the elder flowers mixed with their kisses. They stood, pressed close together, under the elder tree.

Across the yellow fields of charlock they heard the village clock strike seven. Up in the house a gong clanged.

'Darling, I must go,' she said.

'Oh stay—Stay *five* minutes.'

He pressed her close. It lasted five minutes, and five more. Then he was running fast down the road to the station, while Harriott went along the field-path, slowly, struggling with her tears.

'He'll be back in three months,' she said. 'I can live through three month.'

But he never came back. There was something wrong with the engines of his ship, the *Alexandra*. Three weeks later she went down in the Mediterranean, and George with her.

Harriott said she didn't care how soon she died now. She was quite sure it would be soon, because she couldn't live without him.

Five years passed.

The two lines of beech trees stretched on and on, the whole length of the Park, a broad green drive between. When you came to the middle they branched off right and left in the form of a cross, and at the end of the right arm there was a white stucco pavilion with pillars and a three-cornered pediment like a Greek temple. At the end of the left arm, the west entrance to the Park, double gates and a side door.

Harriott, on her stone seat at the back of the pavilion, could see Stephen Philpotts the very minute he came through the side door.

He had asked her to wait for him there. It was the place he always chose to read his poems aloud in. The poems were a pretext. She knew what he was going to say. And she knew what she would answer.

There were elder bushes in flower at the back of the pavilion, and Harriott throught of George Waring. She told herself that George was nearer to her now than he could ever have been, living. If she married Stephen she would not be unfaithful, because she loved him with another part of herself. It was not as though Stephen were taking George's place. She loved Stephen with her soul, in an unearthly way.

But her body quivered like a stretched wire when the door opened and the young man came towards her down the drive under the beech trees.

She loved him; she loved his slenderness, his darkness and sallow whiteness, his black eyes lighting up with the intellectual flame, the way his black hair swept back from his forehead, the way he walked, tiptoe, as if his feet were lifted with wings.

He sat down beside her. She could see his hands tremble. She felt that her moment was coming; it had come.

'I wanted to see you alone because there's something I must say to you. I don't quite know how to begin. . . .'

Her lips parted. She panted lightly.

'You've heard me speak of Sybill Foster?'

Her voice came stammering, 'N-no, Stephen. Did you?'

'Well, I didn't mean to, till I knew it was all right. I only heard yesterday.'

'Heard what?'

'Why, that she'll have me. Oh, Harriott—do you know what it's like to be terribly happy?'

She knew. She had known just now, the moment before he told her. She sat there, stone-cold and stiff, listening to his raptures, listening to her own voice saying she was glad.

Ten years passed.

Harriott Leigh sat waiting in the drawing-room of a small house in Maida Vale. She lived there ever since her father's death two years before.

She was restless. She kept on looking at the clock to see if it was four, the hour that Oscar Wade had appointed. She was not sure that he would some, after she had sent him away yesterday.

She now asked herself, why, when she had sent him away yesterday, she had let him come to-day. Her motives were not altogether clear. If she really meant what she had said then, she oughtn't to let him come to her again. Never again.

She had shown him plainly what she meant. She could see herself, sitting very straight in her chair, uplifted by a passionate integrity, while he stood before her, hanging his head, ashamed and beaten; she could feel again the throb in her voice as she kept on saying that she couldn't, she couldn't; he must see that she couldn't; that no, nothing would make her change her mind; she couldn't forget he had a wife; that he must think of Muriel.

To which he had answered savagely: 'I needn't. That's all over. We only live together for the look of the thing.'

And she, serenely, withgreat dignity: 'And for the look of the thing, Oscar, we must leave off seeing each other. Please go.'

'Do you mean it?'

'Yes. We must never see each other again.'

And he had gone then, ashamed and beaten.

She could see him, squaring his broad shoulders to meet the blow. And she was sorry for him. She told herself she had been unnecessarily hard. Why shouldn't they see each other again, now he understood where they must draw the line? Until yesterday the line had never been very clearly drawn. Today she meant to ask him to forget what he had said to her. Once it was forgotten, they could go ono being friends as if nothing had happened.

It was four o'clock. Half-past. Five. She had finished tea and given him up when, between the half-hour and six o'clock, he came.

He came as he had come a dozen times, with his measured, deliberate, thoughtful tread, carrying himself well braced, with a sort of held-in arrogance, his great shoulders heaving. He was a man of about forty, broad and tall, lean-flanked and short-necked, his straight, handsome features showing small and even in the big square face and in the flush that swamped it. The close-clipped, reddish-brown moustache bristled forwards from the push-out upper lip. His small, flat eyes shone, reddish-brown, eager and animal.

She liked to think of him when he was not there, but always at the first sight of him she felt a slight shock. Physically, he was very far from her admired ideal. So different from George Waring and Stephen Philpotts.

He sat down, facing her.

There was an embarrassed silence, broken by Oscar Wade.

'Well, Harriott, you said I could come.' He seemed to be throwing the responsibility on her.

'So I suppose you've forgiven me,' he said.

'Oh, yes, Oscar, I've forgiven you.'

He said she'd better show it by coming to dine with him somewhere that evening.

She could give no reason to herself for going. She simply went.

He took her to a restaurant in Soho. Oscar Wade dined well, even extravagantly, giving each dish its importance. She liked his extravagance. He had none of the mean virtues.

It was over. His flushed, embarrassed silence told her what he was thinking. But when he had seen her home, he left her at her garden gate. He had thought better of it.

She was not sure whether she were glad or sorry. She had had her moment of righteous exaltation and she had enjoyed it. But there was no joy in the weeks that followed it. She had given up Oscar Wade because she didn't want him very much; and now she wanted him furiously, perversely, because she had given him up. Though he had no resemblance to her ideal, she couldn't live without him.

She dined with him again and again, till she knew Schnebler's Restaurant by heart, the white panelled walls picked out with gold; the white pillars, and the curling gold fronds of their capitals; the thick crimson velvet cushions, that clung to her skirts; the glitter of silver and glass on the innumerable white circles of the tables. And the faces of the diners, red, white, pink, brown, grey and sallow, distorted and excited; the curled mouths that twisted as they ate; the convoluted electric bulbs pointing, pointing down at them, under the red, crinkled shades. All shimmering in a thick air that the red light stained as wine stains water.

And Oscar's face, flushed with his dinner. Always, when he leaned back from the table and brooded in silence she knew what he was thinking. His heavy eyelids would lift; she would find his eyes fixed on hers, wondering, considering.

She knew now what the end would be. She thought of George Waring, and Stephen Philpotts, and of her life, cheated. She hadn't chosen Oscar, she hadn't really wanted him; but now he had forced himself on her she couldn't afford to let him go. Since George died no man had loved her, no other man ever would. And she was sorry for him when she thought of him going from her, beaten and ashamed.

She was certain, before he was, of the end. Only she didn't know when and where and how it would come. That was what Oscar knew.

It came at the close of one of their evenings when they had dined in a private sitting-room. He said he couldn't stand the heat and noise of the public restaurant.

She went before him, up a steep, red-carpeted stair to a white door on the second landing.

From time to time they repeated the furtive, hidden adventure. Sometimes she met him in the room above Schnebler's. Sometimes, when her maid was out, she received him at her house in Maida Vale. But that was dangerous, not to be risked too often.

Oscar declared himself unspeakably happy. Harriott was not quite sure. This was love, the thing she had never had, that she had dreamed of, hungered and thirsted for; but now she had it she was not satisfied. Always she looked for something just beyond it, some mystic, heavenly rapture, always beginning to come, that never came. There was something about Oscar that repelled her. But because she had taken him for her lover, she couldn't bring herself to admit that it was a certain coarseness. She looked another way and pretended it wasn't there. To justify herself, she fixed her mind on his good qualities, his generosity, his strength, the way he had built up his engineering business. She made him take her over his works, and show her his great dynamos. She made him lend her the books he read. But always, when she tried to talk to him, he let her see that *that* wasn't what she was there for.

'My dear girl, we haven't time,' he said. 'It's waste of our priceless moments.'

She persisted. 'There's something wrong about it all if we can't talk to each other.'

He was irritated. 'Woman never seem to consider that a man can get all the talk he wants from other men. What's wrong is our meeting in this unsatisfactory way. We ought to live together. It's the only sane thing. I would, only I don't want to break up Muriel's home and make her miserable.'

'I thought you said she wouldn't care.'

'My dear, she cares for her home and her position and the children. You forget the children.'

Yes. She had forgotten the children. She had forgotten Muriel. She had left off thinking of Oscar as a man with a wife and children and a home.

He had a plan. His mother-in-law was coming to stay with Muriel in October and he would get away. He would go to Paris, and Harriott should come to him there. He could say he went on business. No need to lie about it; he *had* business in Paris.

He engaged rooms in an hotel in the rue de Rivoli. They spent two weeks there.

For three days Oscar was madly in love with Harriott and Harriott with him. As she lay awake she would turn on the light and look at him as he slept at he side. Sleep made him beautiful and innocent; it laid a fine, smooth tissue over his coarseness; it made his mouth gentle; it entirely hid his eyes.

In six days reaction had set in. At the end of the tenth day, Harriott, returning with Oscar from Montmartre, burst into a fit of crying. When questioned, she answered wildly that the Hotel Saint Pierre was too hideously ugly; it was getting on her nerves. Mercifully Oscar explained her state as fatigue following excitement. She tried hard to believe that she was miserable because her love was purer and more spiritual than Oscar's; but all the time she knew perfectly well she had cried from pure boredom. She was in love with Oscar, and Oscar bored her. Oscar was in love with her, and she bored him. At close quarters, day in and day out, each was revealed to the other as an incredible bore.

At the end of the second week she began to doubt whether she had ever been really in love with him.

Her passion returned for a little while after they got back to London. Freed from the unnatural strain which Paris had put on them, they persuaded themselves that their romantic temperaments were better fitted to the old life of casual adventure.

Then, gradually, the sense of danger began to wake in them. They lived in perpetual fear, face to face with all the chances of discovery. They tormented themselves and each other by imagining possibilities that they would never have considered in their first fine moments. It was as though they were beginning to ask themselves if it were, after all, worth while running such awful risks, for all they go out of it. Oscar still swore that if he had been free he would have married her. He pointed out that his intentions at any rate were regular. But she asked herself: Would I marry *him*? Marriage would be the Hotel Saint Pierre all over again, without any possibility of escape. But, if she wouldn't marry him, was she in love with him? That was the test. Perhaps it was a good thing he wasn't free. Then she told herself that these doubts were morbid, and that the question wouldn't arise.

One evening Oscar called to see her. He had come to tell her that Muriel was ill.

'Seriously ill?'

'I'm afraid so. It's pleurisy. May turn to pneumonia. We shall know one way or another in the next few days.'

A terrible fear seized upon Harriott. Muriel might die of her pleurisy; and if Muriel died, she would have to marry Oscar. He was looking at her queerly, as if he knew what she was thinking, and she could see that the same thought had occurred to him and that he was frightened too.

Muriel got well again; but their danger had enlightened them. Muriel's life was now inconceivably precious to them both; she stood between them and that permanent union, which they dreaded and yet would not have the courage to refuse.

After enlightenment the rupture.

It came from Oscar, one evening when he sat with her in her drawing-room.

'Harriott,' he said, 'do you know I'm thinking seriously of settling down?'

'How do you mean, settling down?'

'Patching it up with Muriel, poor girl . . . Has it never occured to you that this little affair of ours can't go on forever?'

'You don't want it to go on?'

'I don't want to have any humbug about it. For God's sake, let's be straight. If it's done, it's done. Let's end it decently.'

'I see. You want to get rid of me.'

'That's a beastly way of putting it.'

'Is there any way that isn't beastly? The whole thing's beastly. I should have thought you'd have stuck to it now you've made it what you wanted. When I haven't an ideal, I haven't a single illusion, when you've destroyed everything you didn't want.'

'What didn't I want?'

'The clean, beautiful part of it. The part *I* wanted.'

'My part at least was real. It was cleaner and more beautiful than all that putrid stuff you wrapped it up in. You were a hypocrite, Harriott, and I wasn't. You're a hypocrite now if you say you weren't happy with me.'

'I was never really happy. Never for one moment. There was always something I missed. Something you didn't give me. Perhaps you couldn't.'

'No. I wasn't spiritual enough,' he sneered.

'You were not. And you made me what you were.'

'Oh, I noticed that you were always very spiritual *after* you'd got what you wanted.'

'What I wanted?' she cried. 'Oh, my God—'

'If you ever knew what you wanted.'

'What—I—wanted,' she repeated, drawing out her bitterness.

'Come,' he said, 'why not be honest? Face facts. I was awfully gone on you. You were awfully gone on me—once. We got tired of each other and it's over. But at least you might own we had a good time while it lasted.'

'A good time?'

'Good enough for me.'

'For you, because for you love only means one thing. Everything that's high and noble in it you dragged down to that, till there's nothing left for us but that. *That's* what you made of love.'

Twenty years passed.

It was Oscar who died first, three years after the rupture. He did it suddenly one evening, falling down in a fit of apoplexy.

His death was an immense relief to Harriott. Perfect security had been impossible as long as he was alive. But now there wasn't a living soul who knew her secret.

Still, in the first moment of shock Harriott told herself that Oscar dead would be nearer to her than ever. She forgot how little she had wanted him to be near her, alive. And long before the twenty years had passed she had contrived to persuade herself that he had never been near to her at all. It was incredible that she had ever known such a person as Oscar Wade. As for their affair, she couldn't think of Harriott Leigh as the sort of woman to whom such a thing could happen. Schnebler's and the Hotel Saint Pierre ceased to figure among prominent images of her past. Her memories, if she had allowed herself to remember, would have clashed disagreeably with the reputation for sanctity which she had now acquired.

For Harriott at fifty-two was the friend and helper of the Reverend Clement Farmer, Vicar of St. Mary the Virgin's, Maida Vale. She worked as a deaconess in his parish, wearing the uniform of a deaconess, the semi-religious gown, the cloak, the bonnet and veil, the cross and rosary, the holy smile. She was also secretary to the Maida Vale and Kilburn Home for Fallen Girls.

Her moments of excitement came when Clement Farmer, the lean, austere likeness of Stephen Philpotts, in his cassock and lace-bordered surplice, issued from the vestry, when he mounted the pulpit, when he stood before the altar rails and lifted up his arms in the Benediction; her moments of ecstasy when she received the Sacrament from his hands. And she had moments of calm happiness when his study door closed on their communion. All these moments were saturated with a solemn holiness.

And they were insignificant compared with the moment of her dying.

She lay dozing in her white bed under the black crucifix with the ivory Christ. The basins and medicine bottles had been cleared from the table by her pillow; it was spread for the last rites. The priest moved quietly about the room, arranging the candles, the Prayer Book and the Holy Sacrament. Then he drew a chair to her bedside and watched with her, waiting for her to come up out of her doze.

She woke suddenly. Her eyes were fixed upon him. She had a flash of lucidity. She was dying, and her dying made her supremely important to Clement Farmer.

'Are you ready?' he asked.

'Not yet. I think I'm afraid. Make me not afraid.'

He rose and lit the two candles on the altar. He took down the crucifix from the wall and stood it against the foot-rail of the bed.

She sighed. That was not what she had wanted.

'You will not be afraid now,' he said.

'I'm not afraid of the hereafter. I suppose you get used to it. Only it may be terrible just at first.'

'Our first state will depend very much on what we are thinking of at our last hour.'

'There'll be my—confession,' she said.

'And after it you will receive the Sacrament. Then you will have your mind fixed firmly upon God and your Redeemer . . . Do you feel able to make your confession now, Sister? Everything is ready.'

Her mind went back over her past and found Oscar Wade there. She wondered: Should she confess to him about Oscar Wade? One moment she thought it was possible; the next she knew that she couldn't. She could not. It wasn't necessary. For twenty years he had not been part of her life. No. She wouldn't confess about Oscar Wade. She had been guilty of other sins.

She made a careful selection.

'I have cared too much for the beauty of this world . . . I have failed in charity to my poor girls. Because of my intense repugnance to their sin . . . I have thought, often, about—people I love, when I should have been thinking about God.'

After that she received the Sacrament.

'Now,' he said, 'there is nothing to be afraid of.'

'I won't be afraid if—if you would hold my hand.'

He held it. And she lay still a long time, with her eyes shut. Then he heard her murmuring something. He stopped close.

'This—is—dying. I thought it would be horrible. And it's bliss . . . Bliss.'

The priest's hand slackened, as if at the bidding of some wonder. She gave a weak cry.

'Oh—don't let me go.'

His grasp tightened.

'Try,' he said, 'to think about God. Keep on looking at the crucifix.'

'If I look,' she whispered, 'you won't let go my hand?'

'I will not let you go.'

He held it till it was wrenched from him in the last agony.

She lingered for some hours in the room where these things had happened.

Its aspects was familiar and yet unfamiliar, and slightly repugnant to her. The altar, the crucifix, the lighted candles, suggested some tremendous and awful experience the details of which she was not able to recall. She seemed to remember that they had been connected in some way with the sheeted body on the bed; but the nature of the connection was not clear; and she did not associate the dead body with herself. When the nurse came in and laid it out, she saw that it was the body of a middle-aged woman. Her own living body was that of a young woman of about thirty-two.

Her mind had no past and no future, no sharp-edged, coherent memories, and no idea of anything to be done next.

Then, suddenly, the room began to come apart before her eyes, to split into shafts of floor and furniture and ceiling that shifted and were thrown by their commotion into different planes. They leaned slanting at every possible angle; they crossed and overlaid each other with a transparent mingling of dislocated perspectives, like reflections fallen on an interior seen behind glass.

The bed and the sheeted body slid away somewhere out of sight. She was standing by the door that still remained in position.

She opened it and found herself in the street, outside a building of yellowish-grey brick and freestone, with a tall slated spire. Her mind came together with a palpable click of recognition. This object was the Church of St. Mary the

Virgin, Maida Vale. She could hear the droning of the organ. She opened the door and slipped in.

She had gone back into a definite space and time, and recovered a certain limited section of coherent memory. She remembered the rows of pitch-pine benches, with their Gothic peaks and mouldings; the stone-coloured walls and pillars with their chocolate stencilling; the hanging rings of lights along the aisles of the nave; the high altar with its lighted candles, and the polished brass cross, twinkling. These things were somehow permanent and real, adjusted to the image that now took possession of her.

She knew what she had come there for. The service was over. The choir had gone from the chancel; the sacristan moved before the altar, putting out the candles. She walked up the middle aisle to a seat that she knew under the pulpit. She knelt down and covered her face with her hands. Peeping sideways through her fingers, she could see the door of the vestry on her left at the end of the north aisle. She watched it steadily.

Up in the organ loft the organist drew out the Recessional, slowly and softly, to its end in the two solemn, vibrating chords.

The vestry door opened and Clement Farmer came out, dressed in his black cassock. He passed before her, close, close outside the bench where she knelt. He paused at the opening. He was waiting for her. There was something he had to say.

She stood up and went towards him. He still waited. He didn't move to make way for her. She came close, closer than she had ever come to him, so close that his features grew indistinct. She bent her head back, peering short-sightedly, and found herself looking into Oscar Wade's face.

He stood still, horribly still, and close, barring her passage.

She drew back; his heaving shoulders followed her. He leaned forward, covering her with his eyes. She opened her mouth to scream and no sound came.

She was afraid to move lest he should move with her. The heaving of his shoulders terrified her.

One by one the lights in the side aisles were going out. The lights in the middle aisle would go next. They had gone. If she didn't get away she would be shut up with him there, in the appalling darkness.

She turned and moved towards the north aisle, groping, steadying herself by the book ledge.

When she looked back, Oscar Wade was not there.

Then she remembered that Oscar Wade was dead. Therefore, what she had seen was not Oscar; it was his ghost. He was dead; dead seventeen years ago. She was safe from him for ever.

When she came out on the steps of the church she saw that the road it stood in had changed. It was not the road she remembered. The pavement on this side was raised slightly and covered in. It ran under a succession of arches. It was a long gallery walled with glittering shop windows on one side; on the other a line of tall grey columns divided it from the street.

She was going along the arcades of the rue de Rivoli. Ahead of her she could see the edge of an immense grey pillar jutting out. That was the porch of the Hotel Saint Pierre. The revolving glass doors swung forward to receive her; she crossed the grey, sultry vestibule under the pillared arches. She knew it. She knew the porter's shining, wine-coloured, mahogany pen on her left, and the shining, wine-coloured, mahogany barrier of the clerk's bureau on her night; she made straight for the great grey carpeted staircase; she climbed the endless flights that turned round and round the caged-in shaft of the well, past the latticed doors of the lift, and came up on to a landing that she knew, and into the long, ash-grey, foreign corridor lit by a dull window at one end.

It was there that the horror of the place came on her. She had no longer any memory of St. Mary's Church, so that she was unaware of her backward course through time. All space and time were here.

She remembered she had to go to the left, the left.

But there was something there; where the corridor turned by the window; at the end of all the corridors. If she went the other way she would escape it.

The corridor stopped there. A blank wall. She was driven back past the stairhead to the left.

At the corner, by the window, she turned down another long ash-grey corridor on her right, and to the right again where the night-light spluttered on the table-flap at the turn.

This third corridor was dark and secret and depraved. She knew the soiled walls, and the warped door at the end. There was a sharp-pointed streak of light at the top. She could see the number on it now, 107.

Something had happened there. If she went in it would happen again.

Oscar Wade was in the room waiting for her behind the closed door. She felt him moving about in there. She leaned forward, her ear to the key-hole, and listened. She could hear the measured, deliberate, thoughtful footsteps. They were coming from the bed to the door.

She turned and ran; her knees gave way under her; she sank and ran on, down the long grey corridors and the stairs, quick and blind, a hunted beast seeking for cover, hearing his feet coming after her.

The revolving doors caught her and pushed her out into the street.

The strange quality of her state was this, that it had no time. She remembered dimly that there had once been a thing called time; but she had forgotten altogether what it was like. She was aware of things happening and about to happen; she fixed them by the place they occupied, and measured their duration by the space she went through.

So now she thought: If I could only go back and get to the place where it hadn't happened.

To get back farther—

She was walking now on a white road that went between broad grass borders. To the right and left were the long raking lines of the hills, curve after curve, shimmering in a thin mist.

The road dropped to the green valley. It mounted the humped bridge over the river. Beyond it she saw the twin gables of the grey house pricked up over the high, grey garden wall. The tall iron gate stood in front of it between the ball-topped stone pillars.

And now she was in a large, low-ceilinged room with drawn blinds. She was standing before the wide double bed. It was her father's bed. The dead body, stretched out in the middle under the drawn white sheet, was her father's body.

The outline of the sheet sank from the peak of the upturned toes to the shin bone, and from the high bridge of the nose to the chin.

She lifted the sheet and folded it back across the breast of the dead man. The face she saw then was Oscar Wade's face, stilled and smoothed in the innocence of sleep, the supreme innocence of death. She stared at it, fascinated, in a cold, pitiless joy.

Oscar was dead.

She remembered how he used to lie like that beside her in the room in the Hotel Saint Pierre, on his back with his hands folded on his waist, his mouth half open, his big chest rising and falling. If he was dead, it would never happen again. She would be safe.

The dead face frightened her, and she was about to cover it up again when she was aware of a light heaving, a rhythmical rise and fall. As she drew the sheet up tighter, the hands under it began to struggle convulsively, the broad ends of the fingers appeared above the edge, clutching it to keep it down. The mouth opened; the eyes opened; the whole face stared back at her in a look of agony and horror.

Then the body drew itself forwards from the hips and sat up, its eyes peering into her eyes; he and she remained for an instant motionless, each held there by the other's fear.

Suddenly she broke away, turned and ran, out of the room, out of the house.

She stood at the gate, looking up and down the road, not knowing by which way she must go to escape Oscar. To the right, over the bridge and up the hill and across the downs she would come to the arcades of the rue de Rivoli and the dreadful grey corridors of the hotel. To the left the road went through the village.

If she could get further back she would be safe, out of Oscar's reach. Standing by her father's death-bed she had been young, but not young enough. She must get back to the place where she was younger still, to the Park and the green drive under the beech trees and the white pavilion at the cross. She knew how to find it. At the end of the village the high road ran right and left, east and west, under the Park walls; the south gate stood there at the top looking down the narrow street.

She ran towards it through the village, past the long grey barns of Goodyer's farm, pat the grocer's shop, past the yellow front and blue sign of the 'Queen's Head,' past the post office, with its one black window blinking under its vine, past the church and the yew-trees in the churchyard, to where the south gate made a delicate black pattern on the green grass.

These things appeared insubstantial, drawn back behind a sheet of air that shimmered over them like thin glass. They opened out, floated pat and away from her; and instead of the high road and park walls she saw a London street of dingy white façades and instead of the south gate the swinging glass doors of Schnebler's Restaurant.

The glass doors swung open and she passed into the restaurant. The scene beat on her with the hard impact of reality: the white and gold panels, the white pillars and their curling gold capitals, the white circles of the tables, glittering, the flushed faces of the diners, moving mechanically.

She was driven forward by some irresistible compulsion to a table in the corner, where a man sat alone. The table napkin he was using hid his mouth, and jaw, and chest; and she was not sure of the upper part of the face above the straight, drawn edge. It dropped; and she saw Oscar Wade's face. She came to him, dragged, without power to resist; she sat down beside him, and he leaned to her over the table; she could feel the warmth of his red, congested face; the smell of wine floated towards her on his thick whisper.

'I knew you would come.'

She ate and drank with him in silence, nibbling and sipping slowly, staving off the abominable moment it would end in.

At last they got up and faced each other. His long bulk stood before her, above her; she could almost feel the vibration of its power.

'Come,' he said. 'Come.'

And she went before him, slowly, slipping out through the maze of the tables, hearing behind her Oscar's measured, deliberate, thoughtful tread. The steep, red-carpeted staircase rose up before her.

She swerved from it, but he turned her back.

'You know the way,' he said.

At the top of the flight she found the white door of the room she knew. She knew the long windows guarded by drawn muslin blinds; the gilt looking-glass over the chimney-piece that reflected Oscar's head and shoulders grotesquely between two white porcelain babies and bulbous limbs and garlanded loins, she knew the sprawling stain on the drab carpet by the table, the shabby, infamous couch behind the screen.

They moved about the room, turning and turning in it like beasts in a cage, uneasy, inimical, avoiding each other.

At last they stood still, he at the window, she at the door, the length of the room between.

'It's no good your getting away like that,' he said. 'There couldn't be any other end to it—to what we did.'

'But that *was* ended.'

'Ended there, but not here.'

'Ended for ever. We've done with it for ever.'

'We haven't. We've got to begin again. And go on. And go on.'

'Oh, no. No. Anything but that.'

'There isn't anything else.'

'We can't. We can't. Don't you remember how it bored us?'

'Remember? Do you suppose I'd touch you if I could help it . . . That's what we're here for. We must. We must.'

'No. No. I shall get away—now.'

She turned to the door to open it.

'You can't,' he said. 'The door's locked.'

'Oscar—what did you do that for?'

'We always did it. Don't you remember?'

She turned to the door again and shook it; she beat on it with her hands.

'It's no use, Harriott. If you got out now you'd only have to come back again. You might stave it off for an hour or so, but what's that in an immortality?'

'Immortality?'

'That's what we're in for.'

'Time enough to talk about immortality when we're dead . . . Ah—'

They were being drawn towards each other across the room, moving slowly, like figures in some monstrous and appalling dance, their heads thrown back over their shoulders, their faces turned from the horrible approach. Their arms rose slowly, heavy with intolerable reluctance; they stretched them out towards each other, aching, as if they held up an overpowering weight. Their feet dragged and were drawn.

Suddenly her knees sank under her; she shut her eyes; all her being went down before him in darkness and terror.

It was over. She had got away, she was going back, back, to the green drive of the Park, between the beech trees, where Oscar had never been, where he would never find her. When she passed through she south gate her memory became suddenly young and clean. She forgot the rue de Rivoli and the Hotel Saint Pierre; she forgot Schnebler's Restaurant and the room at the top of the stairs. She was back in her youth. She was Harriott Leigh going to wait for Stephen Philpotts in the pavilion opposite the west gate. She could feel herself, a slender figure moving fast over the grass between the lines of the great beech trees. The freshness of her youth was upon her.

She came to the heart of the drive where it branched right and left in the form of a cross. At the end of the right arm the white Greek temple, with its pediment and pillars, gleamed against the wood.

She was sitting on their seat at the back of the pavilion, watching the side door that Stephen would come in by.

The door was pushed open; he came towards her, light and young, skimming between the beech trees with his eager, tiptoeing stride. She rose up to meet him. She gave a cry.

'Stephen!'

It had been Stephen. She had seen him coming. But the man who stood before her between the pillars of the pavilion was Oscar Wade.

And now she was walking along the field-path that slanted from the orchard door to the stile; further and further back, to where young George Waring waited for her under the elder tree. The smell of the elder flowers came to her over the field. She could feel on her lips and in all her body the sweet, innocent excitement of her youth.

'George, oh, George?'

As she went along the field-path she had seen him. But the man who stood waiting for her under the elder tree was Oscar Wade.

'I told you it's no use getting away, Harriott. Every path brings you back to me. You'll find me at every turn.'

'But how did you get *here*?'

'As I got into the pavilion. As I got into your father's room, on to his death bed. Because I *was* there. I am in all your memories.'

'My memories are innocent. How could you take my father's place, and Stephen's, and George Waring's? You?'

'Because I did take them.'

'Never. My love for *them* was innocent.'

'Your love for me was part of it. You think the past affects the future. Has it never struck you that the future may affect the past? In your innocence there was the beginning of your sin. You *were* what you *were to be*.'

'I shall get away,' she said.

'And, this time, I shall go with you.'

The stile, the elder tree, and the field floated away from her. She was going under the beech trees down the Park drive towards the south gate and the village, slinking close to the right-hand row of trees. She was aware that Oscar Wade was going with her under the left-hand row, keeping even with her, step by step, and tree by tree. And presently there was grey pavement under her feet and a row of grey pillars on her right hand. They were walking side by side down the rue de Rivoli towards the hotel.

They were sitting together now on the edge of the dingy white bed. Their arms hung by their sides, heavy and limp, their heads drooped, averted. Their passion weighed on them with the unbearable, unescapable boredom of immortality.

'Oscar—how long will it last?'

'I can't tell you. I don't know whether *this* is one moment of eternity, or the eternity of one moment.'

'It must end some time,' she said. 'Life doesn't go on for ever. We shall die.'

'Die? We *have* died. Don't you know what this is? Don't you know where you are? This is death. We're dead, Harriott. We're in hell.'

'Yes. There can't be anything worse than this.'

'This isn't the worst. We're not quite dead yet, as long as we've life in us to turn and run and get away from each other; as long as we can escape into our memories. But when you've got back to the farthest memory of all and there's nothing beyond it—When there's no memory but this—

'In the last hell we shall not run away any longer; we shall find no more roads, no more passages, no more open doors. We shall have no need to look for each other.

'In the last death we shall be shut up in this room, behind that locked door, together. We shall lie here together, for ever and ever, joined so fast that even God can't put us asunder. We shall be one flesh and one spirit, one sin repeated for ever, and ever; spirit loathing flesh, flesh loathing spirit; you and I loathing each other.'

'Why? Why?' she cried.
'Because that's all that's left us. That's what you made of love.'

The darkness came down swamping, it blotted out the room. She was walking along a garden path between high borders of phlox and larkspur and lupin. They were taller than she was, their flowers swayed and nodded above her head. She tugged at the tall stems and had no strength to break them. She was a little thing.

She said to herself then that she was safe. She had gone back so far that she was a child again; she had the blank innocence of childhood. To be a child, to go small under the heads of the lupins, to be blank and innocent, without memory, was to be safe.

The walk led her out through a yew hedge on to a bright green lawn. In the middle of the lawn there was a shallow round pond in a ring of rockery cushioned with small flowers, yellow and white and purple. Gold-fish swam in the olive brown water. She would be safe when she saw the gold-fish swimming towards her. The old one with the white scales would come up first, pushing up his nose, making bubbles in the water.

At the bottom of the lawn there was a privet hedge cut by a broad path that went through the orchard. She knew what she would find there; her mother was in the orchard. She would lift her up in her arms to play with the hard red balls of the apples that hung from the tree. She had got back to the farthest memory of all; there was nothing beyond it.

There would be an iron gate in the wall of the orchard. It would lead into a field.

Something was different here, something that frightened her. An ash-grey door instead of an iron gate.

She pushed it open and came into the last corridor of the Hotel Saint Pierre.

The Cloth which Weaves Itself

Among the sacred objects belonging to a sultan of Menangcabow named Gaggar Allum was the cloth *sansistah kallah*, which weaves itself, and adds one thread yearly of fine pearls, and when that cloth shall be finished the world will be no more.

—W.W. SKEAT

Universal History

William Olaf Stapledon, *English utopian and early science fiction writer. Born in 1887, died in 1950. Author of* A Modern Theory of Ethics *(1915),* Last and First Men *(1930),* Last Men in London *(1932),* Star Maker *(1937),* Philosophy and Living *(1939).*

In one inconceivably complex cosmos, whenever a creature was faced with several possible courses of action, it took them all, thereby creating many distinct temporal dimensions and distinct histories of the cosmos. Since in every evolutionary sequence of the cosmos there were very many creatures, and each was constantly faced with many possible courses, and the combinations of all their courses were innumerable, an infinity of distinct universes exfoliated from every moment of every temporal sequence in this cosmos.

A Theologian In Death

Emmanuel Swedenborg *(1688-1772), Swedish theologian, scientist and mystic. Author of* Daedalus Hyperboreus *(1716),* Economia Regni Animalis *(1704),* De Coelo et Inferno *(1758),* Apocalysis Revelata *(1766),* Thesaurus Bibliorum Embelaticus et Allegoricus *(1859-68). Swedenborg has been translated into eighty eastern and western languages.*

The angels told me that when Melancthon died he was provided with a house deceptively like the one in which he lived in this world. (This happens to most newcomers in eternity upon their first arrival—it is why they are ignorant of their death, and think they are still in the natural world.) All the things in his room were similar to those he had had before—the table, the desk with its drawers, the shelves of books. As soon as Melancthon awoke in this new abode, he sat at his table, took up his literary work, and spent several days writing—as usual—on justification by faith alone, without so much as a single word on charity. This omission being remarked by the angels, they sent messengers to question him. 'I have proved beyond refutation,' Melancthon replied to them, 'that there is nothing in charity essential to the soul, and that to gain salvation faith is enough.' He spoke with great assurance, unsuspecting that he was dead and that his lot lay outside Heaven. When the angels heard him say these things, they departed.

After a few weeks, the furnishings in his room began to fade away and disappear, until at last there was nothing left but the armchair, the table, the paper, and his inkstand. What is more, the walls of the room became encrusted with lime, and the floor with a yellow glaze. Melancthon's own clothes were now much coarser. He wondered at these changes, but he went on writing about faith while denying charity, and was so persistent in this exclusion that he was suddenly transported underground to a kind of workhouse, where there were other theologians like him. Locked up for a few days, Melancthon fell to doubting his doctrine, and was allowed to return to his former room. He was now clad in a hairy skin, but he tried hard to convince himself that what had just happened to him was no more than a hallucination, and he went back to extolling faith and belittling charity.

One evening, Melancthon felt cold. He began examining the house, and soon discovered that the other rooms no longer matched those of his old house in the natural world. One was cluttered with instruments whose use he did not understand; another had shrunk so small that entrance was impossible; a third had not changed, but its doors and windows opened onto vast sandbanks. One of the rooms at the back of the house was full of people who worshipped him and who kept telling him that no theologian was ever as wise as he. These praises pleased him, but since some of the visitors were faceless and others seemed dead he ended up hating and distrusting them. It was at this point that he decided to write something concerning charity. The only difficulty was that what he wrote one day he could not see the next. This was because the pages had been written without conviction.

Melancthon received many visits from persons newly dead, but he felt shame at being found in so run-down a lodging. In order to have them believe he was in Heaven, he hired a neighboring magician, who tricked the company with appearances of peace and splendor. The moment his visitors had gone—and sometimes a little before—these adornments vanished, leaving the former plaster and draftiness.

The last I heard of Melancthon was that the magician and one of the faceless men had taken him away into the sand hills, where he is now a kind of servant of demons.

The Encounter

A tale from the T'ang Dynasty (618-906 a.d.)

Ch'ienniang was the daughter of Chang Yi, a public official in Hunan province. She had a cousin named Wang Chu, an intelligent and handsome youth. The two cousins had grown up together and, since Chang Yi both loved and approved of the boy, he said he would accept Wang Chu as his son-in-law. Both the young people heard and marked the promise; she was an only child and spent all her time with her cousin; their love grew day by day. And the day came when they were no longer children and their relations grew intimate. Unfortunately, her father, Chang Yi, was the only person around who did not notice. One day a young public official asked Chang Yi for his daughter's hand. The father, heedless or forgetful of his earlier promise, consented. Ch'ienniang, torn between love and filial piety, nearly died of grief; the young man fell into such despair that he resolved to leave the district rather than watch his mistress married to another man. He invented some pretext or other and told his uncle that he must go to the capital. When the uncle was unable to dissuade him, he supplied the youth with funds along with some presents and offered him a farewell banquet. In a desperate state, Wang Chu did not leave off moaning throughout the feast and was more than ever determined to go away rather than persist in a hopeless love affair.

The youth embarked one afternoon; he had sailed only a few miles when night fell. He ordered his sailor to tie up so that they might rest. But Wang Chu could not fall asleep; some time around midnight he heard footsteps approaching. He got up and called out: 'Who is it, walking about at this hour of the night?' 'I, Ch'ienniang,' came the reply. Surprised and overjoyed he brought her aboard. She told him that she had hoped and expected to be his wife, that her father had been unjust, and that she could not resign herself to their separation. She had also feared that, finding himself alone in a strange land, he might have been driven to suicide. And so she had defied general disapproval and parental wrath and had now come to follow him wherever he might go. The happily re-united pair thereupon continued the journey on to Szechwan.

Five years of happiness passed, and she bore Wang Chu two children. But there was no news of Ch'ienniang's family and every day she thought of her father. It was the only cloud in their happy sky. She did not know whether or not her parents were still alive; and one night she confessed her anxiety to Wang Chu. Because she was an only daughter she felt guilty of a grave filial impiety. 'You have the heart of a good daughter and I will stand by you,' Wang Chu told her. 'Five years have passed and they will no longer be angry with us. Let us go home.' Ch'ienniang rejoiced and they made ready to go back with their children.

259

When the ship reached their native city, Wang Chu told Ch'ienniang: 'We cannot tell in what state of mind we will find your parents. Let me go on alone to find out.' At sight of the house, he could feel his heart pounding. Wang Chu saw his father-in-law, knelt down, made his obeisance, and begged his pardon. Chang Yi gazed upon him with amazement and said: 'What are you talking about? For the past five years, Ch'ienniang has been lying in bed, in a coma. She has not gotten up once.'

'But I have told you the truth,' said Wang Chu. 'She is well, and awaits us on board the ship.'

Chang Yi did not know what to think and sent two maids-in-waiting to see Ch'ienniang. They found her seated aboard ship, beautifully gowned and radiant; she asked them to convey her fondest greetings to her parents. Struck with wonder, the maids-in-waiting returned to the parental house, where Chang Yi's bewilderment increased. Meanwhile, the sick girl had heard the news, and now seemed freed of her ill. There was a new light in her eyes. She rose from her bed and dressed in front of her mirror. Smiling and without a word, she made her way towards the ship. At the same time, the girl on the ship began walking toward the house. The two met on the river-bank. There they embraced and the two bodies merged, so that only one Ch'ienniang remained, as youthful and lovely as ever. Her parents were overjoyed, but they ordered the servants to keep quiet, to avoid commentaries.

For more than forty years Wang Chu and Ch'ienniang lived together in happiness.

The Three Hermits

Count Leo Tolstoy (1828-1910), one of Russia's greatest writers and philosophers, is the celebrated author of War and Peace and Ann Karenina as well as many collections of stories and folk tales.

A Bishop was sailing from Archangel to the Solovétsk Monastery, and on the same vessel were a number of pilgrims on their way to visit the shrines at that place. The voyage was a smoooth one. The wind favourable and the weather fair. The pilgrims lay on deck, eating, or sat in groups talking to one another. The Bishop, too, came on deck, and as he was pacing up and down he noticed a group of men standing near the prow and listening to a fisherman, who was pointing to the sea and telling them something. The Bishop stopped, and looked in the direction in which the man was pointing. He could see nothing, however, but the sea glistening in the sunshine. He drew nearer to listen, but when the man saw him, he took off his cap and was silent. The rest of the people also took off their caps and bowed.

'Do not let me disturb you, friends,' said the Bishop. 'I came to hear what this good man was saying.'

'The fisherman was telling us about the hermits,' replied one, a tradesman, rather bolder than the rest.

'What hermits?' asked the Bishop, going to the side of the vessel and seating himself on a box. 'Tell me about them. I should like to hear. What were you pointing at?'

'Why, that little island you can just see over there,' answered the man, pointing to a spot ahead and a little to the right. 'That is the island where the hermits live for the salvation of their souls.'

'Where is the island ?' asked the Bishop. 'I see nothing.'

'There, in the distance, if you will please look along my hand. Do you see that little cloud? Below it, and a bit to the left, there is just a faint streak. That is the island.'

The Bishop looked carefully, but his unaccustomed eyes could make out nothing but the water shimmering in the sun.

'I cannot see it,' he said. 'But who are the hermits that live there?'

'They are holy men,' answered the fisherman. 'I had long heard tell of them, but never chanced to see them myself till the year before last.'

And the fisherman related how once, when he was out fishing, he had been stranded at night upon that island, not knowing where he was. In the morning, as he wandered abut the island, he came across an earth hut, and met an old man standing near it. Presently two others came out, and after having fed him and dried his things, they helped him mend his boat.

'And what are they like?' asked the bishop.

'On is a small man and his back is bent. He wears a priest's cassock and is very old; he must be more than a hundred, I should say. He is so old that the white of his beard is taking a greenish tinge, but he is always smiling, and his face is as bright as an angel's from heaven. The second is taller but he also is very old. He wears a tattered, peasant coat. His beard is broad, and of a yellowish grey colour. He is a strong man. Before I had time to help him, he turned my boat over as if it were only a pail. He too is kindly and cheerful. The third is tall, and has a beard as white as snow and reaching to his knees. He is stern, with over-hanging eyebrows; and he wears nothing but a piece of matting tied round his waist.'

'And did they speak to you?' asked the Bishop.

'For the most part they did everything in silence, and spoke but little even to one another. One of them would just give a glance, and the others would understand him. I asked the tallest whether they had lived there long. He frowned, and muttered something as if he were angry; but the oldest one took his hand and smiled, and then the tall one was quiet. The oldest one only said: "Have mercy upon us," and smiled.'

While the fisherman was talking, the ship had drawn nearer to the island.

'There, now you can see it plainly, if your Lordship will please to look,' said the tradesman, pointing with his hand.

The Bishop looked, and now he really saw a dark streak—which was the island. Having looked at it a while, he left the prow of the vessel, and going to the stern, asked the helmsman:

'What island is that?'

'That one,' replied the man, 'has no name. There are many such in this sea.'

'Is it true that there are hermits who live there for the salvation of their souls?'

'So it is said, your Lordship, but I don't know if it's true. Fishermen say they have seen them; but of course they may only be spinning yarns.'

'I should like to land on the island and see these men,' said the Bishop. 'How could I manage it?'

'The ship cannot get close to the island,' replied the helmsman, 'but you might be rowed there in a boat. You had better speak to the captain.'

The captain was sent for and came.

'I should like to see these hermits,' said the Bishop. 'Could I not be rowed ashore?'

The captain tried to dissuade him.

'Of course it could be done,' said he, 'but we should lose much time. And if I might venture to say so to your Lordship, the old men are not worth your pains. I have heard say that they are foolish old fellows, who understand nothing and never speak a word, any more than the fish in the sea.'

'I wish to see them,' said the Bishop, 'and I will pay you for your trouble and loss of time. Please let me have a boat.'

There was no help for it; so the order was given. The sailors trimmed the sails, the steersman put up the helm, and the ship's course was set for the island. A chair was placed at the prow for the Bishop, and he sat there, looking ahead. The passengers all collected at the prow, and gazed at the island. Those who had the sharpest eyes could presently make out the rocks on it, and then a mud hut was seen. At last one man saw the hermits themselves. The captain brought a telescope and, after looking through it, handed it to the Bishop.

'It's right enough. There are three men standing on the shore. There, a little to the right of that big rock.'

The Bishop took the telescope, got it into position, and he saw the three men: a tall one, a shorter one, and one very small and bent, standing on the shore and holding each other by the hand.

The captain turned to the Bishop.

'The vessel can get no nearer in that this, your Lordship. If you wish to go ashore, we must ask you to go in the boat, while we anchor here.'

The cable was quickly let out; the anchor cast, and the sails furled. There was a jerk, and the vessel shook. Then, a boat having been lowered, the oarsmen jumped in, and the Bishop descended the ladder and took his seat. The men pulled at their oars and the boat moved rapidly towards the island. When they came within a stone's throw, they saw three old men: a tall one with only a piece of matting tied round his waist: a shorter one in a tattered peasant coat, and a very old one bent with age and wearing an old cassock—all three standing hand in hand.

The oarsmen pulled in to the shore, and held on with the boathook while the Bishop got out.

The old men bowed to him, and he gave them his blessing, at which they bowed still lower. Then the Bishop began to speak to them.

'I have heard,' he said, 'that you, godly men, live here saving your own souls and praying to our Lord Christ for your fellow men. I, an unworthy servant of Christ, am called, by God's mercy, to keep and teach His flock. I wished to see you, servants of God, and to do what I can to teach you, also.'

The old men looked at each other smiling, but remained silent.

'Tell me,' said the Bishop, 'what you are doing to save your souls, and how you serve God on this island.'

The second hermit sighed, and looked at the oldest, the very ancient one. The latter smiled, and said:

'We do not know how to serve God. We only serve and support ourselves, servant of God.'

'But how do you pray to God?' asked the Bishop.

'We pray in this way,' replied the hermit. 'Three are ye, three are we, have mercy upon us.'

And when the old man said this, all three raised their eyes to heaven, and repeated:

'Three are ye, three are we, have mercy upon us!'

The Bishop smiled.

'You have evidently heard something about the Holy Trinity,' said he. 'But you do not pray aright. You have won my affection, godly men. I see you wish to please the Lord, but you do not know how to serve Him. That is not the way to pray; but listen to me, and I will teach you. I will teach you, not a way of my own, but the way in which God in the Holy Scriptures has commanded all men to pray to Him.'

And the Bishop began explaining to the hermits how God had revealed Himself to men; telling them of God the Father, and God the Son, and God the Holy Ghost.

'God the Son came down on earth,' said he, 'to save men, and this is how He taught us all to pray. Listen, and repeat after me: "Our Father." '

And the first old man repeated after him, 'Our Father,' and the second said, 'Our Father,' and the third said, 'Our Father.'

'Which art in heaven,' continued the Bishop.

The first hermit repeated, 'Which art in heaven,' but the second blundered over the words, and the tall hermit could not say them properly. His hair had grown over his mouth so that he could not speak plainly. The very old hermit, having no teeth, also mumbled indistinctly.

The Bishop repeated the words again, and the old men repeated them after him. The Bishop sat down on a stone, and the old men stood before him, watching his mouth, and repeating the words as he uttered them. And all day long the Bishop laboured, saying a word twenty, thirty, a hundred times over, and the old men repeated it after him. They blundered, and he corrected them, and made them begin again.

The Bishop did not leave off till he had taught them the whole of the Lord's Prayer so that they could not only repeat it after him, but could say it by themselves. The middle one was the first to know it, and to repeat the whole of it alone. The Bishop made him say it again and again, and at last the others could say it too.

It was getting dark and the moon was appearing over the water, before the Bishop rose to return to the vessel. When he took leave of the old men they all bowed down to the ground before him. He raised them, and kissed each of them, telling them to pray as he had taught them. Then he got into the boat and returned to the ship.

And as he sat in the boat and was rowed to the ship he could hear the three voices of the hermits loudly repeating the Lord's Prayer. As the boat drew near the vessel their voices could no longer be heard, but they could still be seen in the moonlight, standing as he had left them on the shore, the shortest in the middle, the tallest on the right, the middle one on the left. As soon as the Bishop had reached the vessel and got on board, the anchor was weighed and the sails unfurled. The wind filled them and the ship sailed away, and the Bishop took a seat in the stern and watched the island they had left. For a time he could still see the hermits, but presently they disappeared from sight, though the island was still visible. At last it too vanished, and only the sea was to be seen, rippling in the moonlight.

The pilgrims lay down to sleep, and all was quiet on deck. The Bishop did not wish to sleep, but sat alone at the stern, gazing at the sea where the island was no longer visible, and thinking of the good old men. He thought how pleased they had been to learn the Lord's Prayer; and he thanked God for having sent him to teach and help such godly men.

So the Bishop sat, thinking, and gazing at the sea where the island had disappeared. And the moonlight flickered before his eyes, sparkling, now here, now there, upon the waves. Suddenly he saw something white and shining, on the bright path which the moon cast across the sea. Was it a seagull, or the little gleaming sail of some small boat? The Bishop fixed his eyes on it, wondering.

'It must be a boat sailing after us,' thought he, 'but it is overtaking us very rapidly. It was far, far away a minute ago, but now it is much nearer. It cannot be a boat, for I can see no sail; but whatever it may be, it is following us and catching us up.'

And he could not make out what it was. Not a boat, nor a bird, nor a fish! It was too large for a man, and besides a man could not be out there in the midst of the sea. The Bishop rose, and said to the helmsman:

'Look there, what is that, my friend? What is it?' the Bishop repeated, though he could now see plainly what it was—the three hermits running upon the water, all gleaming white, their grey beards shining, and approaching the ship as quickly as though it were not moving.

The steersman looked, and let go the helm in terror.

'Oh Lord! The hermits are running after us on the water as though it were dry land!'

The passengers, hearing him, jumped up and crowded to the stern. They saw the hermits coming along hand in hand, and the two outer ones beckoning the ship to stop. All three were gliding along upon the water without moving their feet. Before the ship could be stopped, the hermits had reached it, and raising their heads, all three as with one voice, began to say:

'We have forgotten your teaching, servant of God. As long as we kept repeating it we remembered, but when we stopped saying it for a time, a word dropped out, and now it has all gone to pieces. We can remember nothing of it. Teach us again.'

The Bishop crossed himself, and leaning over the ship's side, said:

'Your own prayer will reach the Lord, men of God. It is not for me to teach you. Pray for us sinners.'

And the Bishop bowed low before the old men; and they turned and went back across the sea. And a light shone until daybreak on the spot where they were lost to sight.

Macario

B. Traven *is one of the most mysterious figures in all literature, the author of* The Death Ship *(1926),* The Treasure of the Sierra Madre *(1927) and* The Rebellion of the Hanged *(1936), and proletarian stories and novels set in South America and Mexico. He has been identified with the German revolutionary Ret Marut, with his own agent, the American Hal Croves, and most recently as a Pole named Otto Feige.*

Macario, the village woodchopper, had one overwhelming desire which he had nourished for fifteen years.

It was not riches he wanted, nor a well-built house instead of that ramshackle old hut in which he lived with his wife and his eleven children who wore rags and were always hungry. What he craved more than anything in this world— what he might have traded his very soul for—was to have a roast turkey all for himself combined with the opportunity to eat it in peace, deep in the woods unseen by his ever-hungry children, and entirely alone.

His stomach never fully satisfied, he would leave home before sunrise every morning in the year, weekday and Sunday alike, rain or shine. He would disappear into the woods and by nightfall bring back a load of chopped wood carried on his back.

That load, meaning a full day's job, would sell for one bit, sometimes even less than that. During the rainy season, though, when competition was slow, he would get as much as two bits now and then for his load of fuel.

Two bits meant a fortune to his wife, who looked even more starved than her husband, and who was known in the village as the Woman with the Sad Eyes.

Arriving home after sunset, Macario would throw off his pack with a heavy groan, stagger into his hut and drop with an audible bump upon a low crudely made chair brought to the equally crude table by one of the children.

There he would spread both his arms upon the table and say with a tired voice: 'Oh, Mother, I am tired and hungry, what have we for supper?'

'Black beans, green chilli, tortillas, salt and lemon tea,' his wife would answer.

It was always the same menu with no variation whatever. Knowing the answer long before he was home, he merely asked so as to say something and, by so doing, prevent his children from believing him merely a dumb animal.

When supper was set before him in earthen vessels, he would be profoundly asleep. His wife would shake him: 'Father, supper's on the table.'

'We thank our good Lord for what he allows us poor sinners,' he would pray, and immediately start eating.

Yet hardly would he swallow a few mouthfuls of beans when he would note the eyes of his children resting on his face and hands, watching him that he might not eat too much so that they might get a little second helping since the first had been so very small. He would cease eating and drink only the tea, brewed of *zacate de limon*, sweetened with a little chunk of *piloncillo*.

Having emptied the earthen pot he would, with the back of his hand, wipe his mouth, moan pitifully, and in a prayerful voice say: 'Oh, dear Lord in heaven, if only once in all my dreary life I could have a roast turkey all for myself, I would then die happily and rest in peace until called for the final reckoning. Amen.'

Frequently he would not say that much, yet he would never fail to say at least: 'Oh, good Lord, if only once I could have a roast turkey all for myself.'

His children had heard that lamentation so often that none of them paid attention to it any longer, considering it their father's particular way of saying grace after supper.

He might just as well have prayed that he would like to be given one thousand doubloons, for there was not the faintest likelihood that he would ever come into the possession of roast chicken, let alone a heavy roast turkey whose meat no child of his had ever tasted.

His wife, the most faithful and the most abnegating companion a man would wish for, had every reason to consider him a very good man. He never beat her; he worked as hard as any man could. On Saturday nights only he would take a three-centavo's worth nip of mezcal, and no matter how little money she had, she would never fail to buy him that squeeze of a drink. She would buy it at the general store because he would get less than half the size for the same money if he bought the drink in the village tavern.

Realizing how good a husband he was, how hard he worked to keep the family going, how much he, in his own way, loved her and the children, the wife began saving up any penny she could spare of the little money she earned doing odd jobs for other villagers who were slightly better off than she was.

Having thus saved penny by penny for three long years, which had seemed to her an eternity, she at last could lay her hands on the heaviest turkey brought to the market.

Almost exploding with joy and happiness, she took it home while the children were not in. She hid the fowl so that none would see it. Not a word she said when her husband came home that night, tired, worn out and hungry as always, and as usual praying to heaven for his roast turkey.

The children were sent to bed early. She feared not that her husband might see what she was about, for he had already fallen asleep at the table and, as always, half an hour later he would drowsily rise and drag himself to his cot upon which he would drop as if clubbed down.

If there ever was prepared a carefully selected turkey with a true feeling of happiness and profound joy guiding the hands and the taste of a cook, this one certainly was. The wife worked all through the night to get the turkey ready before sunrise.

Macario got up for his day's work and sat down at the table for his lean breakfast. He never bothered saying good morning and was not used to hearing it said by his wife or anybody in the house.

If something was amiss on the table or if he could not find his machete or the ropes which he needed for tying up the chopped wood, he would just mumble something, hardly opening his lips. As his utterings were few and these few always limited to what was absolutely necessary, his wife would understand him without ever making a mistake.

Now he rose, ready to leave.

He came out, and while standing for a few seconds by the door of his shack looking at the misty gray of the coming day, his wife placed herself before him as though in his way. For a brief moment he gazed at her, slightly bewildered because of that strange attitude of hers. And there she handed him an old basket in which was the roast turkey, trimmed, stuffed and garnished, all prettily wrapped up in fresh green banana leaves.

'There now, there, dear husband, there's the roast turkey you've been praying for during so many long years. Take it along with you to the deepest and densest part of the woods where nobody will disturb you and where you can eat it all alone. Hurry now before the children smell it and get aware of that precious meal, for then you could not resist giving it to them. Hurry along.'

He looked at her with his tired eyes and nodded. *Please* and *thanks* were words he never used. It did not even occur to him to let his wife have just one little bite of that turkey because his mind, not fit to handle more than one thought at a time, was at this instant exclusively occupied with his wife's urging to hurry and run away with his turkey lest the children get up before he could leave.

He took his time finding himself a well-hidden place deep in the woods and as

he, because of so much wandering about, had become sufficiently hungry by
now, he was ready to eat his turkey with genuine gusto. He made his seat on the
ground very comfortable, washed his hands in a brook near-by, and everything
was as perfect as it should be at such a solemn occasion—that is, the fulfillment
of a man's prayer said daily for an almost uncountable number of years.

With a sigh of utter happiness, he leaned his back against the hollow trunk of
a heavy tree, took the turkey out of the basket, spread the huge banana leaves
before him on the ground and laid the bird upon them with a gesture as if he
were offering it to the gods. He had in mind to lie down after the meal and sleep
the whole day through and so turn this day, his saint's day, into a real holiday—
the first in his life since he could think for himself.

On looking at the turkey so well prepared and taking in that sweet aroma of a
carefully and skilfully roasted turkey, he muttered in sheer admiration: 'I must
say this much of her, she's a great and wonderful cook. It is sad that she never
has the chance to show her skill.'

That was the most profound praise and the highest expression of thanks he
could think of. His wife would have burst with pride and she would have been
happy beyond words had he only once in his life said that in her presence. This,
though, he would never have been able to do, for in her presence such words
would simply refuse to pass his lips.

Holding the bird's breast down with his left hand, he firmly grabbed with his
right one of the turkey's thick legs to tear it off.

And while he was trying to do so, he suddenly noted two feet standing right
before him, hardly two yards away.

He raised his eyes up along the black, tightly fitting pants which covered low
riding boots as far down as the ankles and found, to his surprise, a Charro in full
dress, watching him tear off the turkey's leg.

The Charro wore a sombrero of immense size, richly trimmed with gold laces.
His short leather coat was adorned with the richest gold, silver and multicolored
silk embroidery one could imagine. To the outside seams of the Charro's black
trousers, and reaching from the belt down to where they came to rest upon the
heavy spurs of pure silver, a row of gold coins was sewn. A slight move the
Charro would make now and then while he was speaking to Macario caused
these gold coins to send forth a low, sweet-sounding tinkle. He had a black
moustachio, the Charro had, and a beard like a goat's. His eyes were pitch
black, very narrow and piercing, so that one might virtually believe them
needles.

When Macario's eyes reached his face, the stranger smiled, thin-lipped and
somewhat malicious. He evidently thought his smile a most charming one, by
which any human, man or woman, would be enticed beyond help.

'What do you say, friend, about a fair bite of your tasty turkey for a hungry
horseman,' he said in a metallic voice. 'See, friend, I've had a long ride all
through the night and now I'm nearly starved and so, please, for hell's sake,
invite me to partake of your lunch.'

'It's not lunch in the first place,' Macario corrected, holding onto his turkey as if he thought that bird might fly away at any moment. 'And in the second place, it's my holiday dinner and I won't part with it for anybody, whoever he may be. Do you understand?'

'No, I don't. Look here, friend, I'll give you my heavy silver spurs just for that thick leg you've grabbed,' the Charro bargained, moistening his lips with a thin dark red tongue which, had it been forked, might have been that of a snake.

'I have no use for spurs whether they are of iron, brass, silver or gold trimmed with diamonds all over, because I have no horse to ride on.' Macario judged the value of his roast turkey as only a man would who had waited for that meal for many years.

'Well then, friend, if it is worth that much to you, I'll cut off all these gold coins which you see dangling from my trousers and I'll give them to you for a half breast of that turkey of yours. What about that?'

'That money would do me no good. If I spent only one single coin they'd clap me in jail right away and there torture me until I'd tell them where I stole it, and after that they'd chop off one hand of mine for being a thief. What could I, a woodchopper, do with one hand less when, in fact, I could use four if only the Lord had been kind enough to let me have that many.'

Macario, utterly unconcerned over the Charro's insistence, once more tried to tear off the leg and start eating when the visitor interrupted him again: 'See here, friend, I own these woods, the whole woods, and all the woods around here, and I'll give you these woods in exchange for just one wing of your turkey and a fistful of the fillings. All these woods, think of it.'

'Now you're lying, stranger. These woods are not yours, they're the Lord's, or I couldn't chop in here and provide the villagers with fuel. And if they were your woods and you'd give them to me for a gift or in payment for a part of my turkey, I wouldn't be any richer anyhow because I'd have to chop them just as I do now.'

Said the Charro: 'Now listen, my good friend—'

'Now you listen,' Macario broke in impatiently. 'You aren't my good friend and I'm not your good friend and I hope I never will be your good friend as long as God saves my soul. Understand that. And now go back to hell where you came from and let me eat my holiday dinner in peace.'

The Charro made a horribly obscene grimace, swore at Macario and limped off, cursing the world and all mankind.

Macario looked after him, shook his head and said to himself: 'Who'd expect to meet such funny jesters in these woods? Well, I suppose it takes all kinds of people and creatures to make it truly our Lord's world.'

He sighed and laid his left hand on the turkey's breast as he had done before and with his right grasped one of the fowl's legs.

And again he noted two feet standing right before him at the same spot where, only a half minute earlier, the Charro had been standing.

Ordinary huaraches, well-worn as though by a man who has wandered a long and difficult road, covered these two feet. Their owner was quite obviously very tired and weary, for his feet seemed to sag at the arches.

Macario looked up and met a very kind face, thinly bearded. The wanderer was dressed in very old, but well-washed, white cotton pants and a shirt of the same stuff, and he looked not very different from the ordinary Indian peasant of the country.

The wanderer's eyes held Macario's as though by a charm and Macario became aware that in this pilgrim's heart were combined all the goodness and kindnesses of earth and heaven, and in each of the wanderer's eyes he saw a little golden sun, and each little golden sun seemed to be but a little golden hole through which one might crawl right into heaven and see Godfather Himself in all His glory.

With a voice that sounded like a huge organ playing from a distance far away, the wandereer said: 'Give unto me, my good neighbor, as I shall give unto you. I am hungry, very hungry indeed. For see, my beloved brother, I have come a long way. Pray, let me have that leg which you are holding and I shall truly and verily bless you for it. Just that leg, nothing else. It will satisfy my hunger and it will give me new strength, for very long still is my way before reaching my father's house.'

'You're a very kind man, wanderer, the kindest of men that ever were, that are today, and that are to come,' Macario said, as though he was praying before the image of the Holy Virgin.

'So I beg of you, my good neighbor, give me just one half of the bird's breast, you certainly will not miss it much.'

'Oh, my beloved pilgrim,' Macario explained as if he were speaking to the archbishop whom he had never seen and did not know but whom he believed the highest of the highest on earth. 'If you, my Lord, really mean to say that I won't miss it much, I shall answer that I feel terribly hurt in my soul because I can't say anything better to you, kind man, but that you are very much mistaken. I know I should never say such a thing to you for it comes close to blasphemy, yet I can't help it, I must say it even should that cost me my right to enter heaven, because your eyes and your voice make me tell the truth.

'For you see, your Lordship, I must not miss even the tiniest little morsel of this turkey. This turkey, please, oh please, do understand, my Lord, was given me as a whole and was meant to be eaten as a whole. It would no longer be a whole turkey were I to give away just a little bit not even the size of a fingernail. A whole turkey—it was what I have yearned for all my life, and not to have it now after a lifetime of praying for it would destroy all the happiness of my good and faithful wife who has sacrificed herself beyond words to make me that great gift. So, please, my Lord and Master, understand a poor sinner's mind. Please, I pray you, understand.'

And the wanderer looked at Macario and said unto him: 'I do understand you, Macario, my noble brother and good neighbor, I verily do understand you. Be blessed for ever and ever and eat your turkey in peace. I shall go now, and passing through your village I shall go near your hut where I shall bless your good wife and all your children. Be with the Lord. Good-bye.'

Not once while he had made these speeches to the Charro and to the wanderer had it occurred to Macario, who rarely spoke more than fifty words a day, to stop to think what had made him so eloquent—why it is was that he, in the depths of the woods, could speak as freely and easily as the minister in church and use words and expressions which he had never known before. It all came to him without his realizing what was happening.

He followed the pilgrim with his eyes until he could see him no longer.

He shook his head sadly.

'I most surely feel sorry about him. He was so very tired and hungry. But I simply could do nothing else. I would have insulted my dear wife. Besides, I cannot spare a leg or part of the breast, come what may, for it would no longer be a whole turkey then.'

And again he seized the turkey's leg to tear it off and start his dinner when, again he noted two feet standing before him and at the same spot the others had stood a while ago.

These two feet were standing in old-fashioned sandals, and Macario thought that the man must be a foreigner from far-off lands, for he had never seen sandals like these before.

He looked up and stared at the hungriest face he had ever believed possible. That face had no flesh. It was all bone. And all bone were the hands and the legs of the visitor. His eyes seemed to be but two very black holes hidden deep in the fleshless face. The mouth consisted of two rows of strong teeth, bared of lips.

He was dressed in a faded bluish-white flowing mantle which, as Macario noted, was neither cotton nor silk nor wool nor any fabric he know. He held a long staff in one hand for support.

From the stranger's belt, which was rather carelessly wound around his waist, a mahogany box, scratched all over, with a clock ticking audibly inside, was dangling on a bit of a string.

It was that box hanging there instead of the hourglass which Macario had expected that confused him at first as to what the new visitor's social standing in the world might be.

The newcomer now spoke. He spoke with a voice that sounded like two sticks clattering one against the other.

'I am very hungry, compadre, very, very hungry.'

'You don't need to tell me. I can see that, compadre,' Macario asserted, not in the least afraid of the stranger's horrible appearance.

'Since you can see that and since you have no doubt that I need something substantial in my stomach, would you mind giving me that leg of the turkey you are holding?'

Macario gave forth a desperate groan, shrugged and lifted up his arms in utter helplessness.

'Well,' he said, with mourning in his voice, 'what can a poor mortal do against fate? I've been caught at last. There's no way out any more. It would have been a great adventure, the good God in heaven knows it, but fate doesn't want it that way. I shall never have a whole turkey for myself, never, never and never, so what can I do? I must give in. All right compadre, get your belly's fill; I know what hunger is like. Sit down, hungry man, sit down. Half the turkey's yours and be welcome to it.'

'Oh, compadre, that is fine, very fine,' said the hungry man, sitting down on the ground opposite Macario and widening his row of teeth as if he were trying to grin.

Macario could not make out for sure what the stranger meant by that grin, whether it was an expression of thanks or a gesture of joy at having been saved from a sure death by starvation.

'I'll cut the bird in two,' Macario said, in a great hurry now lest another visitor might come up and make his own part a third only. 'Once I've cut the bird in two, you just look the other way and I'll lay my machete flat between the two halves and you tell which half you want, that next to the edge or that next to the back. Fair enough, Bone Man?'

'Fair enough, compadre.'

So they had dinner together. And a mighty jolly dinner it was, with much clever talking on the part of the guest and much laughter on the side of the host.

'You know, compadre,' Macario presently said, 'at first I was slightly upset because you didn't fit into the picture of you I had in my mind. That box of mahogany with the clock in it which you carry hanging from your belt confused me quite a bit and made it hard for me to recognize you promptly. What has become of your hourglass, if it isn't a secret to know?'

'No secret at all, no secret at all. You may tell the world if it itches you to do so. You see, it was like this. There was a big battle in full swing somewhere around Europe, which is the fattest spot on earth for me next to China. And I tell you, compadre, that battle kept me on the run as if I were still a youngster. Hither and thither I had to dart until I went nearly mad and was exhausted entirely. So, naturally, I could not take proper care of myself as I usually do to keep me fit. Well, it seems a British cannon ball fired in the wrong direction by a half-drunken limey smashed my cherished hourglass so completely that it could not be mended again by old smith Pluto who likes doing such odd jobs. I looked around and around everywhere, but I could not buy a satisfactory new one since they are made no longer, save for decorations on mantel pieces which, like all such silly knickknacks, are useless. I tried to swipe one in museums, but to my horror I discovered that they were all fakes, not a genuine instrument among them.'

A chunk of tender white meat which he chewed at this instant let him forget his story for a while. Remembering that he had started to tell something without finishing it, he now asked: 'Oh, well, where was I with my tale, compadre?'

'The hourglass in all the museums were all fakes wherever you went to try one out.'

'Right. Yes, now isn't it a pity that they build such wonderful great museums around things which are only fakes? Coming back to the point: there I was without a correctly adjusted hourglass, and many mistakes were bound to happen. Then it came to pass not long afterwards that I visited a captain sitting in his cabin of a ship that was rapidly sinking away under him and with the crew all off in boats. He, the captain I mean, having refused to leave his ship, had hoisted the Union Jack and was stubbornly sticking by his ship whatever might happen to her, as would become a loyal British captain. There he now sat in his cabin, writing up his log-book.

'When he saw me right before him, he smiled at me and said: "Well, Mr Bone Man—Sir, I mean, seems my time is up." "It is, skipper," I confirmed, also smiling to make it easier for him and make him forget the dear ones he would leave behind. He looked at his chronometer and said: "Please, sir, just allow me fifteen seconds more to jot down the actual time in my log-book." "Granted," I answered. And he was all happiness that he could write in the correct time. Seeing him so very happy, I said: "What about it, Cap'n, would you mind giving me your chronometer? I reckon you can spare it now since you won't have any use for it any longer, because aboard the ship you will sail from now on you won't have to worry about time at all. You see, Cap'n, as a matter of fact my hourglass was smashed by a British cannon ball fired by a drunken British gunner in the wrong direction, and so I think it only fair and just that I should have in exchange for my hourglass a British-made chronometer." '

'Oh, so that's what you call that funny-looking little clock—a chronometer. I didn't know that,' Macario broke in.

'Yes, that's what it is called,' the hungry man admitted with a grin of his bared teeth. 'The only difference is that a chronometer is a hundred times more exact in telling the correct time than an ordinary watch or a clock. Well, compadre, where was I?'

'You asked the ship's master for the chro . . .'

'. . . nometer. Exactly. So when I asked him to let me have that pretty timepiece he said: "Now, you are asking for just the very thing, for it happens that this chronometer is my personal property and I can dispose of it any way it damn pleases me. If it were the company's I would have to deny you that beautiful companion of mine. It was perfectly adjusted a few days before we went on this rather eventful voyage and I can assure you, Mr Bone Man, that you can rely on this instrument a hundred times better than on any of your old-fashioned glasses." So I took it with me on leaving the rapidly sinking ship. And that's how I came to carry this chronometer instead of that shabby outdated hourglass I used to have in bygone days.

'And I can tell you one thing, compadre, this British-made gadget works so perfectly that, since I got hold of it, I have never yet missed a single date, whereas before that many a man for whom the coffin or the basket or an old sack had already been brought into the house escaped me. And I tell you, compadre, escaping me is bad business for everybody concerned, and I lose a good lot of my reputation whenever something of this sort happens. But it won't happen anymore now.'

So they talked, told one another jokes, dry ones and juicy ones, laughed a great deal together, and felt as jolly as old friends meeting each other after a long separation.

The Bone Man certainly liked the turkey, and he said a huge amount of good words in praise of the wife who had cooked the bird so tastily.

Entirely taken in by that excellent meal he, now and then, would become absent-minded and forget himself, and try to lick his lips which were not there with a tongue which he did not have.

But Macario understood that gesture and regarded it as a sure and unmistakable sign that his guest was satisfied and happy in his own unearthly way.

'You have had two visitors before today, or have you?' the Bone Man asked in the course of their conversation.

'True. How did you know, compadre?'

'How did I know? I have to know what is going on around the world. You see, I am the chief of the secret police of—of—well, you know the Big Boss. I am not allowed to mention His name. Did you know them—those two visitors, I mean?'

'Sure I did. What do you think I am, a heathen?'

'The first one was what we call our main trouble.'

'The Devil, I knew him all right,' Macario said confidently. 'That fellow can come to me in any disguise and I'd know him anywhere. This time he tried looking like a Charro, but smart as he thinks he is, he had made a few mistakes in dressing up, as foreigners are apt to do. So it wasn't hard for me to see that he was a counterfeit Charro.'

'Why didn't you give him a small piece of your turkey then, since you knew who he was? That hop-about-the-world can do you a great deal of harm, you know.'

'Not to me, compadre. I know all his tricks and he won't get me. Why should I give him part of my turkey? He had so much money that he had not pockets enough to put it in and so had to sew it outside on his pants. At the next inn he passes he can buy if he wishes a half dozen roast turkeys and a couple of young roast pigs besides. He didn't need a leg or a wing of my turkey.'

'But the second visitor was—well, you know Whom I refer to. Did you recognize Him?'

'Who wouldn't? I am a Christian. I would know Him anywhere. I felt awfully sorry that I had to deny Him a little bite, for I could see that He was very hungry and terribly in need of some food. But who am I, poor sinner, to give Our Lord a little part of my turkey. His father owns the whole world and all the birds because He made everything. He may give His Son as many roast turkeys as the Son wants to eat. What is more, Our Lord, Who can feed five thousand hungry people with two fishes and five ordinary loaves of bread all during the same afternoon, and satisfy their hunger and have still a few dozens of sacks full of crumbs left over—well, compadre, I thought that He Himself can feed well on just one little leaf of grass if He is really hungry. I would have considered it a really grave sin giving Him a leg of my turkey. And another thing, He Who can turn water into wine just by saying so can just as well cause that little ant walking here on the ground and picking up a tiny morsel to turn into a roast turkey with all the fillings and trimmings and sauces known in heaven.

'Who am I, a poor woodchopper with eleven brats to feed, to humiliate Our Lord by making Him accept a leg of my roast turkey touched with my unclean hands? I am a faithful son of the Church, and as such I must respect the power and might and dignity of Our Lord.'

'That's an interesting philosophy, compadre,' the Bone Man said. 'I can see that your mind is strong, and that your brain functions perfectly in the direction of that human virtue which is strongly concerned with safeguarding one's property.'

'I've never heard of that, compadre.' Macario's face was a blank.

'The only thing that baffles me now is your attitude toward me, compadre.' The Bone Man was cleaning up a wing bone with his strong teeth as he spoke. 'What I would like to hear is why did you give me half of your turkey when just a few minutes before you had denied as little as a leg or a wing to the Devil and also to Our Lord?'

'Ah,' Macario exclaimed, throwing up both his hands to emphasize the exclamation. And 'Ah,' he said once more, 'that's different; with you that's very different. For one thing, I'm a human being and I know what hunger is and how it feels to be starved. Besides, I've never heard as yet that you have any power to create or to perform miracles. You're just an obedient servant of the Supreme Judge. Nor have you any money to buy food with, for you have no pockets in your clothes. It's true I had the heart to deny my wife a bite of that turkey which she prepared for me with all her love put in for extra spices. I had the heart because, lean as she is, she doesn't look one-tenth as hungry as you do. I was able to put up enough will power to deny my poor children, always crying for food, a few morsels of my roast turkey. Yet, no matter how hungry my children are, none of them looks one-hundredth as hungry as you do.'

'Now, compadre, come, come. Don't try to sell me that,' the dinner guest clattered, making visible efforts to smile. 'Out with the truth. I can bear it. You said "For one thing" when you started explaining. Now tell me the other thing as well. I can stand the truth.'

'All right then,' Macario said quietly. 'You see, compadre, I realized the very moment I saw you standing before me that I would not have any time left to eat as little as one leg, let alone the whole turkey. So I said to myself, as long as he eats too, I will be able to eat, and so I made it fifty-fifty.'

The visitor turned his deep eyeholes in great surprise upon his host. Then he started grinning and soon he broke into a thundering laughter which sounded like heavy clubs drumming a huge empty barrel. 'By the great Jupiter, compadre, you are a shrewd one, indeed you are. I cannot remember having met such a clever and quick-witted man for a long time. You deserve, you truly and verily deserve to be selected by me for a little service, a little service which will make my lonely existence now and then less boresome to me. You see, compadre, I like playing jokes on men now and then as my mood will have it. Jokes that don't hurt anybody, and they amuse me and help me to feel my job is, somehow, less unproductive, if you know what I mean.'

'I guess I know how you mean it.'

'Do you know what I am going to do so as to pay honestly for the dinner you offered me?'

'What, compadre? Oh, please, sir, your lordship, don't make me your assistant. Not that, please, anything else you wish, but not your helper.'

'I don't need an assistant and I have never had one. No, I have another idea. I shall make you a doctor, a great doctor who will outwit all those haughty learned physicians and superspecialists who are always playing their nasty little tricks with the idea that they can put one over on me. That's what I am going to do: make you a doctor. And I promise you that your roast turkey shall be paid for a millionfold.'

Speaking thus he rose, walked some twenty feet away, looked searchingly at the ground, at that time of the year dry and sandy, and called back: 'Compadre, bring your *guaje* bottle over here. Yes, I mean that bottle of yours which looks as though it were of some strange variety of pumpkin. But first pour out all the water which is still in it.'

Macario obeyed and came close to where his guest waited for him. The visitor spat seven times upon the dry ground, remained quiet for a few minutes and then, all of a sudden, crystal-clear water sputtered out of that sandy soil.

'Hand me your bottle,' the Bone Man said.

He knelt down by the little pool just forming and with one hand spooned up the water and poured it into Macario's *guaje* bottle. This procedure took quite some time, for the mouth of the bottle was extremely small.

When the bottle, which held about a quart, was full, the Bone Man, still kneeling by the pool, tapped the soil with one hand and the water immediately disappeared from view.

'Let's go back to our eating place, compadre,' the visitor suggested.

Once more they sat down together. The Bone Man handed Macario the bottle. 'This liquid in your bottle will make you the greatest doctor known in the present century. One drop of this fluid will cure any sickness, and I include any sickness known as a fatal and as an incurable one. But mind, and mind well, compadre, once the last drop is gone, there will be no more of that medicine and your curing power will exist no longer.'

Macario was not at all excited over that great gift. 'I don't know if I should take that present from you. You see, compadre, I've been happy in my own way. True it is that I've been hungry always all through my life; always I've been tired, always been struggling with no end in view. Yet that's the way with people in my position. We accept that life because it was given us. It's for that reason we feel happy in our way—because we always try making the best of something very bad and apparently hopeless. This turkey we ate together today has been the very peak of my life's ambition. I never wanted to go up higher in all my desires than to have one roast turkey with all the trimmings and fillings all for myself, and be allowed to eat it in peace and all alone with no hungry children's eyes counting every little bite going into my hungry stomach.'

'That's just why. You didn't have your roast turkey all by yourself. You gave me half of it, and so your life's ambition is still not accomplished.'

'You know, compadre, that I had no choice in the matter.'

'I suppose you are right. Anyway, whatever the reason, your one and only desire in this world has not yet been satisfied. You must admit that. So, if you wish to buy another turkey without waiting for it another fifteen or twenty years, you will have to cure somebody to get the money with which to buy that turkey.'

'I never thought of that,' Macario muttered, as if speaking to himself. 'I surely must have a whole roast turkey all for myself, come what may, or I'll die a most unhappy man.'

'Of course, compadre, there are a few more things which you ought to know before we part for a while.'

'Yes, what is it, tell me.'

'Wherever you are called to a patient you will see me there also.'

On hearing that, unprepared as he was for the catch, Macario got the shivers.

'Don't get frightened, compadre, no one else will see me; and mind you well what I am going to tell you now. If you see me standing at your patient's feet, just put one drop of your medicine into a cup or glass of fresh water, make him drink it, and before two days are gone he will be all right again, sane and sound for a good long time to come.'

'I understand,' Macario nodded pensively.

'But if,' the Bone Man continued, 'you see me standing at your patient's head, do not use the medicine; for if you see me standing thus, he will die no matter what you do and regardless of how many brilliant doctors attempt to snatch him away from me. In that case do not use the medicine I gave you because it will be wasted and be only a loss to you. You must realize, compadre, that this divine power to select the one that has to leave the world—while some other, be he old or a scoundrel, shall continue on earth—this power of selection I cannot transfer to a human being who may err or become corrupt. That's why the final decision in each particular case must remain with me, and you must obey and respect my selection.'

'I won't forget that, sir,' Macario answered.

'You had better not. Well, now, compadre, let us say goodbye. The dinner was excellent, exquisite I should call it, if you understand that word. I must admit, and I admit it with great pleasure, that I have had an enjoyable time in your company. By all means, that dinner you gave me will restore my strength for another hundred years. Would that when my need for another meal is as urgent as it was today, I may find as generous a host as you have been. Much obliged, compadre. A thousand thanks. Good-bye.'

'Good-bye, compadre.'

Macario spoke as though he were walking from a heavy dream, yet immediately he realized that he had not been dreaming.

Before him on the ground were the well-picked bones of that half turkey which his guest had eaten with so much delight.

Mechanically he cleaned up all the morsels which had dropped and stuffed them into his mouth, so that nothing should be wasted, all the while trying to find the meaning of the several adventures that were crammed into the limited space of his mind.

The thing most difficult for him to understand was how it had been possible for him to talk so much and talk what he believed was very clever as, in his opinion, only a learned man could do. But then he knew that when in the woods he always had very clever thoughts; only at home in the presence of his wife and children he had no thoughts whatever and his mouth was as if glued and it cost him much labor to get out of it one full sentence.

Soon he got tired and presently lay down under a tree to sleep the rest of the day, as he had promised himself that he would after his holiday dinner.

No fuel did he bring back that night.

His wife had not a red cent in the house with which to buy food the next day.

Yet she did not reproach him for having been lazy, as in fact she never criticized anything he did or did not. The truth was that she felt immensely happy to be alive. For, during the day, at about noon, when she was busy in the yard washing the children's rags, a strange golden ray which, so it appeared, came not from the sun, but from an unknown source, had touched her whole body, while at the same time she had heard inside her heart a sweet music as if played by a huge organ from far, far above the earth.

From that moment on and all the whole day she had felt as though lifted from the ground, and her mind had been at peace as she could not remember having ever felt before. Nothing of this phenomenon did she tell her husband. She kept it to herself like a very sacred property all her own.

When she served supper there was still some reflection of that golden ray visible on her face.

Even her husband noted it on giving her a casual glance. But he said nothing, for he was still heavily occupied with his own fortunes of the day.

Before he went to sleep that night, later than usual, for he had slept well during the day out in the woods, his wife asked him timidly: 'How was the turkey, dear husband?'

'What do you think was the matter with it since you ask me how it was? What do you mean? Was there something wrong with it? It was quite all right as far as I could judge, with the little experience I've had eating roast turkey.'

With not a single word did he mention his visitors.

When he had turned about to go to his cot, she looked at him, watching his face sidewise and thoughtfully. Something was new in him, something had come over him. Never before had he talked that much to her at one breath.

Next day was a hungry one for the whole family. Their breakfast, including that of Macario's, was always lean. Yet this morning his wife had to make it smaller still, for it had to be stretched into two more meals.

Soon Macario was through with the few mouthfuls of black beans seasoned with green chilli and a pot of *atole* for a drink. Complain he did not because he realized that the blame was on him.

He took up his machete, his axe and his ropes and stepped out into the misty morning.

Considering the way he went about his usual hard task of chopping wood, he might was well have forgotten about the precious medicine and all that went with it.

Only a few paces had he gone when his wife called after him: 'Husband, your water bottle.'

This reminded him like a flash that the whole adventure of the day before might after all not have been a dream but reality. Last night, on thinking of the happenings, he had reached the conclusion that it might have been but sort of an imagination caused by a stomach not used to being filled up with roast turkey.

'It's still full of water,' the wife said, bringing the *guaje* bottle out and shaking it. 'Shall I pour the old water out and put in fresh water?' she asked, while playing with the cork cut from a corn cob.

'Yes, I know, woman, it's still full,' Macario answered, not a bit afraid that his wife might be too hasty and spill the miraculous liquid away. 'Yesterday I drank from the little brook. Just give me the bottle full as it is. The water is good; I got it out there in the woods.'

On his way to work and some fair distance away from his hut which was the last at his side of the village, he hid the bottle in dense bushes, partly covering it with soil.

That night he brought home one of the biggest loads of heavy fine dry fuel such as he had not delivered for many months. It was sold at three bits, a price unheard of, and was sold that same night on the first call the older boy made. So the family felt like having come into a million.

Next day Macario went about his job as usual.

On the night before he had told his wife casually that he had broken his *guaje* bottle because a heavy trunk had dropped upon it, and she had to give him another one of the several they kept in the house. These bottles cost them nothing, for the older boys discovered them growing wild in the bush somewhere.

Again he brought home that night a good load of chopped wood, yet this time he found his family in a pitiful distress.

His wife, her face swollen her eyes red from long crying, rushed at him the moment he came in. 'Reginito is dying, my poor little baby, Regino, will be gone in a halfhour,' and she broke into heartbreaking lamentation, tears streaming down her face.

Helplessly and stupidly he looked at her the way he always looked if something in the house happened which was out of the gloomy routine by which this home of his was run. When his wife stepped aside, he noted that there were present several neighbors, all women, partly standing, partly squatting close to the cot on which the child had been bedded.

His was the poorest family in the village, yet they were among the best liked for their questions, their honesty, their modesty, and because of that unearned virtue that the poor are always liked better than the rich anywhere and by everybody.

Those women, in their neighborly zeal to help the so very poor Macario, and on hearing of the child's being sick, had brought with them all sorts of herbs, roots, bits of bark as used by the villagers in cases of sickness. The village had no doctor and no drug store and for that reason, perhaps, it also had no undertaker.

Every woman had brought a different kind of medicinal herb or remedy. And every one of the women made a different suggestion as to what should be done to save the child. For hours that little creature had been tortured with scores of different treatments and had been given teas brewed from roots, herbs and ground snake bones mixed with a powder obtained from charred toads.

'He ate too much,' one woman said, seeing his father coming to the child's bed.

'His bowels are all twisted up, there's no help,' another one corrected the first one.

'Wrong, compadre, it's an infection of the stomach, he is done for.'

The one next to her observed: 'We've done everything possible, he can't live another hour. One of our kids died the same way. I know it. I can see by his little shrunken face that he is winged already for his flight to heaven, little angel, poor little angel.' She broke into a loud sob.

Not in the least minding the women's chatter, Macario looked at his little son whom he seemed to love best of all as he was the youngest of the bunch. He liked his innocent smile and felt happy in his way when the little tyke would now and then sit on his lap for a few minutes and play with his tiny fingers upon the man's face. Often it occurred to Macario that the only reason for being alive rested with the fact that there always would be a little baby around the house smiling at him innocently and beating his nose and cheeks with his little fists.

The child was dying; no doubt of that. The mirror held by a woman before the baby's mouth showed no mark of breath. His heartbeat could practically no longer be noted by one or the other woman who would press her ear upon the child's chest.

The father stood there and gazed at his baby without knowing whether he ought to step closer still and touch the little face or remain where he was, or say something to his wife or to one of the other women, or talk to the children who were timidly crowded into one corner of the room where they all sat as if they were guilty of the baby's misfortune. They had had no dinner and they felt sure there would be no supper tonight as thier mother was in a horrible state of mind.

Macario turned slowly about, walked to the door and went out into the darkness of the night.

Not knowing what to do or where to go since his home was all in a turmoil, tired as he was from his very hard day's labor, and feeling as though he were to sink down on his knees, he took, as if automatically, the path which led to the woods—his realm where he was sure to find the quiet of which he was so badly in need.

Arriving at the spot where, in the early morning, he had buried the *guaje* bottle, he stopped, searched for the exact place, took out the bottle, and quicker than he had moved in many years ran back to his hut.

'Give me a cup filled with fresh clean water,' he ordered in a loud and determined voice on opening the door.

His wife hurried as if given new hope, and in a few seconds she brought an earthen cup of water.

'Now, folks, you leave the room. Get out of here, all of you, and leave me alone with that sone of mine. I'll see what I can do about it.'

'No use, Macario, can't you see he has only a few minutes left? You'd better kneel down and say the prayers with us while he is breathing his last, so that his soul may be saved,' one of the women told him.

'You heard what I said and you do as you've been advised,' he said, sharply cutting off any further protest.

Never before had his wife heard him speak in such a harsh, commanding manner. Almost afraid of him, she urged the women out of the hut.

They were all gone.

Macario closed the door behind them, turned to the cot, and when he looked up he saw his bony dinner guest standing opposite him, the cot with the child in it between the two.

The visitor stared at him out of his deep dark holes he had for eyes, hesitated, shrugged, and slowly, as though still weighing his decision, moved toward the baby's feet, remaining there for the next few seconds while the father poured a generous dose of the medicine into the cup filled with water.

Seeing his partner shaking his head in disapproval, Macario remembered that only one drop would have sufficed for the cure. Yet, it was too late now, and the liquid could not be returned to the bottle, for it was already mixed with fresh water.

Macario lifted the baby's head, forced the little mouth open and let the drink trickle into it, taking care that nothing was spilled. To his great joy he noted that the baby, once his mouth had been moistened, started to swallow voluntarily. Soon he had taken the whole to its last drop.

Hardly could the medicine have reached his stomach when the child began to breathe freely. Color returned slowly but visibly to his pale face, and he moved his head in search of better comfort.

The father waited a few minutes longer, and seeing that the baby was recovering miraculously fast, he called in his wife.

Only one look did the mother give her baby when she fell to her knees by the cot and cried out loud: 'Glory be to God and the Holy Virgin. I thank you, Lord in Heaven; my little baby will live.'

Hearing the mother's excited outburst, all the women who had been waiting outdoors rushed in, and seeing what had happened while the father had been alone with his son they crossed themselves, gasped and stared at Macario as if noting his existence for the first time and as though he were a stranger in the house.

One hour later the whole village was assembled at Macario's to see with their own eyes whether it was true what the women, running about the village, were telling the people.

The baby, his cheeks rosy, his little fists pressed close to his chin, was profoundly asleep, and anybody could see that all danger was past.

Next morning Macario got up at his usual time, sat down at the table for his breakfast, looked for his machete, ax and ropes and, taciturn as always, left home to go out to the woods and there chop fuel for the villagers. The bottle with the medicine he took along with him and buried at the same spot from which he had taken it the night before.

So he went about his job for the next six weeks when one night, on returning home, he found Ramiro waiting for him. Ramiro asked him, please, to come around to his place and see what he might do about his wife who had been sick for several days and was now sinking fast.

Ramiro, the principal storekeeper and merchant of the whole community and the richest man in the municipality, explained that he had heard of Macario's curing powers and that he would like him to try his talents on his young wife.

'Fetch me a little bottle, a very little glass bottle from your store. I'll wait for you here and think over what I perhaps could do for your wife.'

Ramiro brought the bottle, an empty medicine flask.

'What are you going to do with the bottle, Macario?'

'Leave that to me, Ramiro. You just go home and wait for me. I have to see your wife first before I can say whether or not I can save her. She'll hold on all right until I come, don't worry over that. In the meantime, I will go out in the fields and look for some herbs which I know to be good medicine.'

He went into the night, searched for his bottle, filled the little crystal flask half full with the precious liquid, buried the bottle again and walked to Ramiro's who lived in one of the three one-story brick houses the village boasted.

He found the woman rapidly nearing her end, and she was as close to it as had been his little son.

Ramiro looked at Macario's eyes. Macario shrugged for an answer. After a while he said: 'You'd better go out now and leave me alone with your wife.'

Ramiro obeyed. Yet, extremely jealous of his young and very pretty wife, pretty even now when near her death, he peeped through a hole in the door to watch Macario's doings.

Macario, already close to the door, turned abruptly with the intention to ask for a glass of fresh water.

Ramiro, his eyes still pressed to the door, was not quick enough in getting away and so, when Macario, by a resolute pull, opened the door, Ramior fell full length into the room.

'Not very decent of you, Ramiro,' Macario said, comprehending what the jealous man had been about. 'Just for that I should decline giving your young wife back to you. You don't deserve her, you know that, don't you?'

He stopped in great surprise.

He could not understand himself what had come over him this very minute. Why he, the poorest and humblest man in the village, a common woodchopper, had dared to speak to the haughtiest and richest man, the millionaire of the village, in a manner which the judge at the county court would hardly have risked. But seeing Ramiro, that mighty and powerful man, standing before him humiliated and with the gesture of a beggar trembling with fear that Macario might refuse to heal his wife, Macario had suddenly become aware that he had become a great power himself, a great doctor of whom that arrogant Ramiro expected miracles.

Very humble now, Ramiro begged Macario's forgiveness for having spied upon him, and in the most pitiful way he pleaded with him to save his wife, who was about to give him, in less than four months, his first child.

'How much would you ask for giving her back to me sane and healthy like she was before?'

'I do not sell my medicine for prices, I do not set prices. It's you, Ramiro, who have to make the price. Only you can know what your wife is worth to you. So name the price yourself.'

'Would ten doubloons do, my dear good Macario?'

'That's what your wife is worth to you? Only ten doubloons?'

'Don't take it that way, dear Macario. Of course she means far more to me than all my money. Money I can make again any day that God will allow me to live. But once my wife is gone, where would I find another one like her? Not in this world. I'll make it one hundred doubloons then, only, please, save her.'

Macario knew Ramiro well, only too well did he know him. Both had been born and raised in that village. Ramiro was the son of the richest merchant of the village as he himself was the richest man today—whereas Macario was the son of the poorest day laborer in the community as he himself was now the poorest woodchopper with the biggest family of the whole village to support. And as he knew Ramiro so very well, nobody would have to tell him that, once the merchant's wife was cured, her husband would try to chisel down on the one hundred doubloons as much as he possibly could, and if Macario did not yield there would be a long and nasty fight between the two men for many years to come.

Realizing all that, Macario now said: 'I'll take the ten doubloons which you offered me first.'

'Oh, thank you, Macario, I thank you, indeed I do, and not for cutting down on the price but that you're willing to cure her. I shall never forget what you have done for us, I'm sure, I shall never forget it. I only hope that the unborn will be safe also.'

'It surely will,' Macario said, assured of his success since he had seen his bony dinner companion standing where he liked best to see him.

'Now, bring me a glass of fresh water,' he told Ramiro.

The water was brought and Macario counselled the merchant: 'Don't you dare peep in again for, mind you, if you do I might fail and it will be all your fault. So remember, no spying, no peeping. Now, leave me alone with the patient.'

This time Macario was extremely careful in not spending more than exactly one drop of the valuable liquid. As hard as he could he even tried to cut that one drop into two halves. By his talk with Ramiro he had suddenly understood how much his medicine was really worth if such a proud and rich man as Ramiro would humble himself before the woodchopper for no other reason than that his wife might be cured by the poor woodman's medicine.

In realizing that, he visioned what his future might be like if he would forget about his woodchopping and stick by his medicine exclusively. Naturally enough, the quintessence of that future was an unlimited supply of roast turkeys any time he wanted them.

His one-time dinner guest, seeing him cutting the one drop in half, nodded approvingly when Macario looked at him for advice.

Two days after Ramiro's wife had recovered fully, she told her husband that she was positively sure that the baby had not been hurt in the least by her sickness, as she could feel him all right.

Ramiro in his great joy handed Macario the ten gold pieces, not only without prattling over that high price but with a hundred thanks thrown in. He invited the whole Macario family to his store where everyone, husband, wife, and all the children, was allowed to take as much home as everybody could carry in his arms. Then he threw a splendid dinner to which the Macarios were invited as his guests of honor.

Macario built a real house now for his family, bought some pieces of good land and began cultivating them, because Ramiro had loaned him one hundred doubloons at very low interest.

Ramiro had done so not solely out of gratitude. He was too shrewd a businessman to loan out money without thinking of fat gains. He realized that Macario had a great future ahead of him, and that it would be a very sound investment to keep Macario in the village and make people come here to see him, rather than have him take up his residence in a city. The more visitors the village would have on account of Macario's fame, the more important would grow Ramiro's business. In expectation of this development in the village's future, Ramiro added to his various lines in business that of banking.

He gambled fast on Macario and he won. He won far beyond his most fantastic dreams.

It was he who did all the advertising and all the propaganda to draw attention to Macario's great gift. Hardly had he sent out a few letters to business friends in the city, than sick people flocked to the village in the hope of being cured of their maladies, many having been declared uncurable by learned physicians.

Soon Macario could build himself a mansion. He bought up all the land around and converted it into gardens and parks. His children were sent to schools and universities as far as Paris and Salamanca.

As his one-time dinner guest had promised him, so it came to pass, Macario's half turkey was paid for a millionfold.

Regardless of his riches and his fame, Macario remained honest and uncorrupted. Anyone who wanted to be cured was asked how much his health was worth to him. And as Macario had done in his first case, so he did ever after in all other cases—that is, the patients or their relatives would decide the price.

A poor man or woman who had no more to offer than one silver peso or a pig or a rooster, he would heal just as well as the rich who, in many instances, had made prices as high as twenty thousand doubloons. He cured men and women of the highest nobility, many of whom had crossed the ocean and had come from Spain, Italy, Portugal, France and other countries and who had come for no other reason than to see him and consult him.

Whoever came to consult him would be told frankly that he could do nothing to save him, if Macario saw the Bone Man stand at the patient's head. Nothing did he charge for that consultation.

People, whoever they were, accepted his final verdict without discussion. No longer would they try arguing with him, once he had told them that they were beyond help.

More or less half the people consulting him were saved; the other half were claimed by his partner. It happened often for weeks at a time that he would not meet one patient whom he could cure, because his dinner guest would decide differently. Such weeks the people in the land called 'his low-power periods.'

While at the beginning of his practice he was able to cut a drop of his precious medicine into two, he soon learned to cut each drop into eight. He acquired all devices known then by which a drop might be divided up into practically an infinite number of mites. Yet, no matter how much he cut and divided, regardless of how cleverly he administered each dose to make it as small as possible and yet retain its effectiveness, the medicine had frightfully fast become scarcer and scarcer.

He had drained the *guaje* bottle during the first month of his practice, once he had observed the true value of the liquid. He knew that a *guaje* bottle will not only soak into its walls a certain amount of any fluid it may hold, but worse, the liquid will evaporate, and rather fast, through the bottle's walls. It is for that reason that water kept in a *guaje* bottle of the kind natives use will stay always cool even should the day be very hot.

So he had taken out the medicine and poured it into bottles of dark glass, tightly sealed.

The last little bottle had been opened months ago, and one day Macario noted to his horror that there were only about two drops left. Consequently, he decided to make it known that he would retire from practice and cure nobody any longer.

By now he had become really old and felt that he had a right to spend the last few years of his life in peace.

These last two drops he meant to keep for members of his family exclusively, and especially for his beloved wife, whom he had had to cure two times during the last ten years and whom he was afraid he might lose—a loss which would be very difficult for him to bear.

Just about that same time it so happened that the eight-year-old son of the viceroy, don Juan Marquez de Casafuerte, the highest personage of New Spain, fell sick.

The best doctors were called for help. None could do anything for the boy. The doctors admitted frankly that this boy had been stricken by a sickness not known to medical science.

The viceroy had heard of Macario. Who hadn't? But he owed it to his dignity, education and high social and political position to consider Macario a quack, the more so since he was called thus by every doctor who had a title from an accredited university.

The child's mother, however, less given to dignity when the life of her son was at stake, made life for the viceroy so miserable that finally he saw no other way out of his dilemma than to send for Macario.

Macario disliked travelling and rarely left his village, and then only for short trips. Yet, an order given by the viceroy himself had to be obeyed under penalty of death.

So he had to go.

Brought before the viceroy he was told what was expected of him.

The viceroy, still not believing in the so-called miracles which Macario was said to have performed, spoke to him in the same way as he would have spoken to any native wood-chopper.

'It was not I who called you, understand that, my good man. Her Highness, la Marquesa, insisted on bringing you here to save our son whom, so it appears, no learned medico can cure. I make it quite clear to you that in case you actually save our child, one-fourth of the fortune which I hold here in New Spain shall be yours. Besides, you may ask anything you see here in my palace, whatever it is that catches your fancy and whatever its value. That shall be yours also. Apart from all that, I personally shall hand you a license which will entitle you to practise medicine anywhere in New Spain with the same rights and privileges as any learned medico, and you shall be given a special letter with my seal on it which will give you immunity for life against any arrest by police or soldiers, and which will safeguard you against any unjustified court action. I believe, my good man, that this is a royal payment for your service.'

Macario nodded, yet said nothing.

The viceroy went on: 'What I promised you in the case that you save our son follows exactly the suggestion made by Her Highness, La Marquesa, my wife, and what I promise I always keep.'

The Marquez stopped for a few seconds, as if waiting for Macario to say something.

Macario, however, said nothing and made no gesture.

'But now, listen to my own suggestions,' the viceroy continued. 'If you should fail to save our son, I shall hand you over to the High Court of the Inquisition, charging you with the practice of witchcraft under pact with the Devil, and you shall be burned alive at the stake on the Alameda and in public.'

Again the viceroy stopped to see what expression his threat had made upon Macario.

Macario paled, but still said nothing.

'Have you understood in full what I have said?'

'I have, Your Highness,' Macario said briefly, trembling slightly as he attempted to make an awkward bow.

'Now, I personally shall show you to our sick child. Follow me.'

They entered the boy's room where two nurses were in attendance, merely watching the child's slow decline, unable to do anything save keep him comfortable. His mother was not present. She had, by the doctor's order, been confined to her room as she was close to a complete breakdown.

The boy was resting on a bed becoming his age, a light bed made of fine wood, though not rich looking.

Macario went close and looked around for a sign of his dinner guest.

Slightly, so as not to make his gesture seem suspicious, he touched a special little pocket in his trousers to be sure he had the crystal flask with the last two drops of medicine about him.

Now he said: 'Will you, Your Highness, I pray, leave this room for one hour, and will Your Highness, please, give orders that everybody else will leave, too, so that I may remain alone with the young patient?'

The Marquez hesitated, evidently being afraid that this ignorant peasant might do his son some harm if left alone with him.

Macario, noting that expression of uneasiness shown by the viceroy, recalled, at this very instant, his first cure of a patient not of his own family, that is, Ramiro's young wife in his native village. Ramiro had hesitated in a similar way when told to leave the room and let Macario alone with the young woman in bed.

These two cases of hesitation had been the only ones he had ever experienced during his long practice. And Macario wondered whether that might carry some significance in his destiny, that perhaps today, with only two little drops of his medicine left, he beheld the same expression of hesitancy in a person who wanted a great service done but did not trust the man who was the only one who could render that service.

He was now alone with the boy.

And suddenly there appeared his partner, taking his stand at the boy's head.

The two, Macario and the Bone Man, had never again spoken one to the other since they had had a turkey dinner together. Whenever they would meet in a sickroom, they would only look at each other, yet not speak.

Macario had never asked of his partner any special favour. Never had he claimed from him any individual whom the Bone Man had decided to take. He even had to let go two grandchildren of his without arguing his dinner guest's first claim.

This time everything was different. He would be burned alive at the stake as a witch doctor convicted of having signed a pact with the Devil. His children, now all of them in highly honoured positions, would fall into disgrace, because their father had been condemned by the Holy Inquisition to suffer the most infamous death a Christian could die. All his fortune and all his landed property, which he had meant to leave to his children and grandchildren, would be confiscated and given to the Church. He did not mind losing his fortune. It had never meant much to him personally anyhow.

What he did mind above all was the happiness of his children. But more still than his children he was, in this most terrible moment of his whole life, thinking of his beloved wife.

She would go crazy with grief on learning what had happened to him in that strange, vast city so far away from home, and she would be unable to come to his aid or even comfort him during his last hours on earth. It was for her sake, not for his own, that this time he decided to fight it out with the Bone Man.

'Give me that child,' he pleaded, 'give him to me for old friendship's sake. I've never asked any favor of you, not one little favor for the half turkey you ate with so much gusto when you needed a good dinner more than anything else. You gave me voluntarily what I had not asked you for. Give me that boy, and I'll pour out the last drop of your medicine and break the bottle, so that not even one little wet spot be left inside to be used for another cure. Please, oh please, give me that boy. It isn't for my sake that I ask you this. It is for my dear, faithful, loyal and beloved wife's. You know, or at least you can imagine, what it means for a Christian family if one of its members is burned at the stake alive and in public. Please, let me have the boy. I shall not take or touch the riches offered me for curing him. You found me a poor man and I was happy then in my own way. I don't mind being poor again, as I used to be. I'm willing to chop wood again for the villagers as I did when we met for the first time.'

The Bone Man looked at him with his deep black holes for a long time. If he had a heart he was questioning it at this moment. Now he looked down before him as though he were deliberating this case from every angle to find the most perfect solution. Obviously, his orders were to take the child away. He could not express his thoughts by his eyes or his face, yet his gestures clearly showed his willingness to help a friend in dire need, for by his attitude he tried to explain that, in this particular case, he was powerless to discover a way out which would meet halfway the problems of both.

Again, for a very long while, his look rested upon the boy as though judging more carefully still Macario's plea against the child's fate, destined before he was born.

And again he looked at Macario as if pitying him and as though he felt deeply distressed.

Presently he shook his head slowly as might someone in great sadness who finds himself utterly helpless in a desperate situation.

He opened his fleshless jaws, and with a voice that sounded like heavy wooden sticks clubbed on a board he said: 'I am sorry, compadre, very sorry, but in this case I can do nothing to help you out of that uncomfortable pool you have been put into. All I can say is that in few of my cases I have felt sadder than in this, believe me, compadre. I can't help it, I must take that boy.'

'No, you mustn't. You mustn't. Do you hear me, you must not take that child,' Macario yelled in great despair. 'You must not, you cannot take him. I won't let you.'

The Bone Man shook his head again, but said nothing.

And now, with a resolute jerk, Macario grabbed the boy's bed and quickly turned it round so that his partner found himself standing at the boy's feet.

Immediately the Bone Man vanished from sight for two or three seconds and, like a flash, appeared at the boy's head once more.

Quickly Macario again turned the bed so that the Bone Man would stand at the feet, and again the Bone Man disappeared from the child's feet and stood at the boy's head.

Macario, wild with madness, turned the bed round and round as if it were a wheel. Yet, whenever he stopped, for taking a breath, he would see his dinner guest standing at the boy's head, and Macario would start his crazy game again by which he thought that he might cheat the claimant out of his chosen subject.

It was too much for the old man, turning that bed round and round without gaining more than two seconds from eternity.

If, so he thought, he could stretch these two seconds into twenty hours only and leave the city under the viceroy's impression that the boy was cured, he might escape that horrible punishment which he had been condemned to suffer.

He was so tired now that he could not turn the bed once more. Touching, as if by a certain impulse, the little pocket in his trousers, he discovered that the crystal flask with the last two drops of the precious medicine in it had been smashed during his wild play with the bed.

Fully realizing that loss and its significance, he felt as if he had been drained of the last spark of his life's energy and that his whole life had become empty.

Vaguely, he gazed about the room as though coming out of a trance in which he had been held for an uncountable number of years, centuries perhaps. He recognized that his fate was upon him and that it would be useless to fight against it any longer.

So, letting his eyes wander around the whole room, he came to look at the boy's face and he found the boy gone.

As if felled he dropped to the floor, entirely exhausted.

Lying there motionless, he heard his one-time dinner guest speaking to him, softly this time.

He heard him say: "Once more, compadre, I thank you for the half turkey which you so generously gave me and which restored my strength, then waning, for another hundred years of tedious labor. It certainly was exquisite, if you understand that word. But now, coming to where we are at thi shour, see, compadre, I have no power to save you from being burned at the stake on the Alameda and in public, because that is beyond my jurisdiction. Yet, I can save you from being burned alive and from being publicly defamed. And this, compadre, I shall do for old friendship's sake, and because you have always played fair and never tried to cheat me. A royal payment you received and you honored it like a royal payment. You have lived a very great man. Good-bye, compadre."

Macario opened his eyes and, on looking backwards, he saw his one-time dinner guest standing at his head.

Macario's wife, greatly worried over her husband's not coming home, called all the men of the village morning to help her find Macario, who might be hurt somewhere deep in the woods and unable to return without help.

After several hours of searching, he was discovered at the densest part of the woods in a section far away from the village, so far that nobody would ever dare go there alone.

He was sitting on the ground, his body comfortably snuggled in the hollow of a huge tree trunk, dead, a big beautiful smile all over his face.

Before him on the ground banana leaves were spread out, serving as a tablecloth, and on them were lying the carefully cleaned bones of a half turkey.

Directly opposite, separated by a space of about three feet, there also were, in a like manner, banana leaves spread, on which was the other half of the turkey, but untouched.

"How strange!" said his wife, thick tears welling out of her sad eyes. "I wonder why he cut the turkey in two? It was his dream all during his life to eat it all himself! I just wonder who he had invited to eat the other half of his turkey. Whoever he was, he must have been a fine and noble and very gentle person, or Macario wouldn't have died so very, very happy."

The Infinite Dream of Pao-Yu

Ts'ao Chan (Hsueh Ch'in), *Chinese novelist, born in the Province of Kiangsu in c.1716, died in 1764. Ten years before his death he began work on the long novel for which he is famous,* The Dream of the Red Chamber. *Like* Kin Ping Mei *and other novels of the realistic school, it is full of surreal and fantastic episodes.*

So before he knew what had happened Pau-Yu's head nodded, and he fell asleep. It seemed to him presently that he was in a great flower-garden which was extraordinarily like his own garden at home. 'Is it possible,' he said to himself in his dream, 'that there is really another garden so exactly like mine?' While he was thus wondering to himself, there suddenly appeared in front of him a number of girls who seemed all to be waiting-maids in some great house. And Pao-Yu, more than ever surprised, said to himself again—'Can it really be that someone else has waiting-maids so exactly like Hsi-Jen, Ping-erh, and all my own maids at home?' Presently one of the girls called out: 'Look, there's Pao-Yu! How ever did he get out here?' Pao-Yu naturally supposed that she knew it was he, and coming forward, he said: 'I was just going for a walk, and got here quite by accident. I suppose this garden belongs to some family that my people visit. But in any case, dear Sisters, let me join you in your walk.' No sooner had he finished speaking than the girls burst into peals of laughter. 'What a silly mistake!' they said: 'We thought you were our younger master Pao-Yu. But of course you are not half so good-looking and do not talk nearly so nicely.' So they were servants of another Pao-Yu! 'Dear Sisters,' he said to them, 'tell me who then *is* your master?' 'He is Pao-Yu,' they said. 'It was his grandmother and mother who wished him to use these two characters Pao (precious) and Yu (jade), hoping that such a name would make him have a long and happy life; and though we are only servants, it pleases him very much that we too should call him by this name. But where do you come from, we should like to know, and whose seedy little drudge are you, that you should use the same characters in your name? You dare try that on again, and we'll beat your nasty little body into jelly!' Another of them said, laughing: 'Come on! Let's get away as quick as we can. What would our Pao-Yu think if he saw us talking to such a ragamuffin?' Another said: 'If we stay near him much longer we shall all smell nasty!' And at one streak they were gone.

Pao-Yu was very much downcast. 'No one,' he thought, 'has ever before treated me so rudely. Why should these particular girls have taken such a dislike to me? And is there really another Pao-Yu? I must somehow discover.' While these thoughts were passing through his mind he had been walking on without noticing where he was going, and he now found himself in a courtyard that seemed strangely familiar. 'Can there then,' he asked himself, 'be another courtyard exactly like ours at home?' He went up some steps and walked straight into a room. Here the first thing he saw was a young man lying on a bed, round which sat a number of girls laughing and playing while they did their needlework. The boy on the bed kept on sighing heavily, till at last one of the girls said to him—'Pao-Yu, why do you keep on sighing? Can't you get to sleep? No doubt you are worried over your cousin's illness. But it is silly to make such a fuss.' When the real Pao-Yu heard this he was more than ever astonished. . . . 'I have been having such an odd dream,' said the young man on the bed. 'I thought I was in a great flower-garden, where I met some girls who called me nasty names and would not play with me. But I followed them back to the house, and there what should I find but another Pao-Yu, lying senseless on his bed, for all the world like an empty bag. His thoughts and feelings seemed all to have flown somewhere far, far away.' When the real Pao-Yu heard this dream, he could not contain himself and cried out to the boy on the bed: 'I came to look for a Pao-Yu; and now it seems that you are the one!' The boy on the bed rose and coming quickly toward him, embraced him, saying: 'So you are Pao-Yu, and it was not a dream!' 'A dream!' cried Pao-Yu. 'No, indeed. It was more true than truth itself.' But hardly had he finished speaking when someone came to the door, crying: 'Mr. Pao-Yu is to go to his father's room at once.' At the sound of these words both Pao-Yus trembled from head to foot. The dream Pao-Yu rushed away, and as he left the room the real Pao-Yu called after him: 'Come back soon, Pao-Yu! Come back.' His maid Hsi-Jen was by the bed, and hearing him calling out his own name in his dreams she woke him, and said, laughing: 'Where is this Pao-Yu that you are calling to?' Though he was no longer asleep, his mind was dazed and confused. 'There he is,' he said, pointing sleepily at the door. 'He has just gone out.' 'Why, you are still dreaming!' said Hsi-Jen, much amused. 'Do you know what it is you are staring at, screwing up your eyes and making such a funny face? It is your own reflection in the mirror!'

The Mirror of Wind-to-Moon

Chia Jui hated Phœnix whenever he thought of her treachery, but then he would see Phœnix's image before him, lovely as ever and now all the more to be desired because he knew that she had never cared for him, and he would tell himself that he would gladly die if he could have her in his arms for but one brief moment. He knew better, though, than to let himself be seen again at the Yungkuofu.

This proved only the beginning of his real troubles. Chia Yung and Chia Chiang pressed him for the notes and his grandfather imposed on him more severe tasks as a punishment for his recent escapades. His desire being stimulated by the constant image of Phœnix, he gave way to evil habits and slept but poorly. The two nights of exposure soon produced their effects and Chia Jui was laid up in bed. In a year's time he became a victim to a host of aches and oppressions. His sleep was infested with nightmares from which he would awake in deliriums. Of such tonic simples as cinnamon, *futze*, *peh-chia*, *meitung*, *yuchu*, he took pounds upon pounds during his illness. The doctors later prescribed the sole use of the best grade of ginseng, something that Tai-Ju could not afford. Madame Wang was appealed to, but as Phœnix was acting for Madame Wang, the supply of ginseng thus secured did not last very long.

One day a lame Taoist mendicant was asking for alms in the street and proclaimed that he could cure ailments of the soul. His cries reached Chia Jui, who begged his family to send for the Taoist. The latter looked at him and said: 'Your affliction is not something to be remedied with medicine. I have a treasure that will heal you if you will follow my directions.' He took from his sleeves a mirror that was polished on both sides. It bore the inscription 'The Precious Mirror to Wind-and-Moon.' He said to Chia Jui: 'This mirror is made by the Goddess of Disillusionment of the Ethereal and Spiritual Palace in the Sphere of the Primordial Void and has curative qualities for diseases resulting from impure thoughts and self-destructive habits. It can save the world and restore life. It is intended for youths such as you are. But do not look into the right side. Only use the reverse. In three days I shall be back to get the mirror and to congratulate you on your recovery.' He went away without taking any reward.

Chia Jui took the mirror and looked into the reverse side as the Taoist had directed. He threw it down with an oath, for he saw a gruesome skeleton staring at him with hollow eyes. He cursed the Taoist for playing such a crude joke upon him. Then he thought he would see what was on the right side. He took up the mirror and looked. Phœnix, in her best clothes, stood beckoning to him. Chia Jui felt himself wafted into a mirror world, wherein he fulfilled his desire for Phœnix. He woke up from his trance and found the mirror lying wrong side up, revealing the repulsive skeleton. He felt exhausted from the voluptuous experience that the more deceptive side of the mirror gave him, but it was so delicious that he could not resist the temptation of looking into the right side again. Again he saw Phœnix beckoning to him and again he yielded to the temptation. This happened three or four times. When he was about to leave the illusive world of the mirror on his last visit, he was seized by two men and put in chains.

'Just a moment, officers,' Chia Jui pleaded. 'Let me take my mirror with me.' These were his last words.

The Desire to be a Man

Comte P.H. Villiers de L'isle Adam, *French writer, born at Saint Brieux in 1840, died in Paris in 1889. He contributed novels, short stories and plays to the literature of fantasy. He is the author of* Isis *(1862),* Claire Lenoir *(1866),* La Revolte *(1870),* Contes Cruels *(1883),* Axel *(1885; translated into English, 1925),* L'Amour Suprême *(1886),* L'Eve Future *(1886),* Le Secret de l'echafaud *(1888) and* Histoires Insolites *(1888).*

For Monsieur Catulle Mendés

> . . . Nature might stand up and say
> to all the world: 'This was a man!'
> SHAKESPEARE: *Julius Caesar*

The Stock Exchange clock struck midnight, under a starry sky. At that time the citizens were still subject to military law, and, in accordance with the curfew regulations, the waiters of those establishments which were still lit up were hurriedly closing their doors.

Inside the boulevard cafés the gas butterflies of the chandeliers fluttered quickly away, one by one, into the darkness. Outside could be heard the noise of the chairs being arranged in quartets on the marble-topped tables; it was the psychological moment when every café proprietor thinks fit to show the last customers, with an arm ending in a napkin, the Caudine Forks of the back door.

That Sunday the sad October wind was whistling through the streets. A few yellow leaves, dusty and rustling, were blown along by the squalls, touching the stones and skimming the asphalt, and then, like bats, disappeared into the shadows, arousing the idea of commonplace days lived through once for all. The theatres of the Boulevard du Crime where, during the evening, all the Medicis, Salviatis, and Montefeltres had been stabbing one another with the utmost fervour, stood silent, their mute portals guarded by their caryatids. Carriages and pedestrians became fewer from one moment to the next; here and there, the sceptical lanterns of rag-pickers gleamed already, phosphorescent glows given off by the rubbish-heaps over which they were wandering.

Under a street lamp level with the Rue Hauteville, at the corner of a fairly luxurious-looking café, a tall passer-by had come to a stop, as if automatically hesitating to cross the roadway separating him from the Boulevard Bonne-Nouvelle. He had a saturnine face, a smooth chin, a somnambulist's walk, long greying hair under a Louis Treize hat, black gloves holding an ivory-headed stick, and an old greatcoat in royal blue, trimmed with dubious astrakhan.

Was this tardy stroller on his way home? Had the mere chance of a walk late at night brought him to that street-corner? It would have been difficult to decide from his appearance. However, the fact remains that, suddenly noticing on his

294

right one of those mirrors—as tall and narrow as himself—which sometimes stand like public looking-glasses outside leading cafés, he halted abruptly, planted himself opposite his reflection, and deliberately looked himself up and down, from his boots to his hat. Then, all of a sudden, raising his hat with an old-world gesture, he greeted himself with a certain courtesy.

His head, thus unexpectedly bared, then revealed him as none other than the famous tragedian Esprit Chaudval, born Lepeinteur and known as Monanteuil, the scion of a worthy family of Saint-Malo pilots, and whom the mysteries of Providence had induced to become a leading man in the provinces, a star abroad, and the often fortunate rival of Frédérick Lemaître.

While he was considering himself with this sort of stupor, the waiters in the nearby café were helping their last customers into their overcoats and fetching their hats, others were noisily emptying the contents of the nickel money boxes and piling the day's takings on a tray. This haste and bustle was due to the ominous presence of two policemen who had suddenly appeared at the door and were standing there with folded arms, harrying the laggardly landlord with their cold gaze.

Soon the shutters were bolted into their iron frames, apart from the one over the mirror, which by a strange oversight was forgotten in the general hurry.

Then silence descended on the boulevard. Only Chaudval, heedless of everybody's departure, had remained in his ecstatic posture on the corner of the Rue Hauteville, on the pavement in front of the forgotten mirror.

This pale, moonlit looking-glass seemed to give the actor the feeling he would have had bathing in a pond. Chaudval shivered.

Alas, the fact is that in that cruel, dark crystal, the actor had just seen himself growing old.

He noticed that his hair, which only yesterday had still been grizzly, was turning silver; he was finished! It was goodbye to curtains and crowns, goodbye to the roses of Thalia and the laurels of Melpomene. It was time to take leave for ever, with handshakes and tears, of the Ellevious and the Laruettes, of the grand liveries and the soft curves of the Dugazons and the *ingénues*!

It was time to get down in a hurry from the chariot of Thespis and watch it drive away with his colleagues; to see the baubles and streamers which, that morning, had fluttered from the wind of Hope, disappear in the twilight round a distant bend in the road.

Chaudval, suddenly conscious of his fifty years (he was a good fellow), heaved a sigh. A mist passed in front of his eyes; a sort of wintry fever took hold of him and a hallucination dilated his pupils.

The haggard fixity with which he was gazing into the providential mirror ended up by giving his eyes that ability to enlarge objects and endow them with importance which physiologists have observed in individuals under the stress of intense emotion.

The long mirror was accordingly deformed under the gaze of his eyes, which were filled with dim, murky ideas. Childhood memories of beaches and silvery waves danced about in his brain. And the mirror, doubtless because of the stars deepening its surface, reminded him at first of the sleeping waters of a gulf.

Then, billowing out even more, thanks to the old man's sighs, the mirror took on the appearance of the sea and the night, those two old friends of lonely hearts.

He revelled for some time in his vision, but then the street lamp which was reddening the cold drizzle behind him, above his head, struck him, reflected as it was in the depths of the dreadful mirror, as like the glow of a blood-red lighthouse, luring the doomed vessel of his future to shipwreck.

He shook off his hallucination and drew himself up to his full height, with a nervous burst of bitter, cynical laughter which startled the two policeman under the trees. Luckily for the actor, the latter, taking him for some drunkard or jilted lover, continued their official stroll without paying any attention to the wretched Chaudval.

'Very well, let us give up!' he said simply in an undertone, like the condemned man who, suddenly roused from sleep, says to the executioner: 'I am at your service.'

The old actor then launched into a dazed monologue.

'I acted prudently the other evening,' he went on, 'when I asked my good comrade Mademoiselle Pinson (who shares the Minister's confindence and even his bed) to obtain for me, between two ardent confessions, that post as lighthouse-keeper which my ancestors occupied on the Atlantic coast. Ah! Now I understand the weird effect the reflection of this street lamp in this mirror had on me! It was that idea at the back of my mind. Pinson will send me my letter of appointment, that's certain. And then I shall retire into my lighthouse like a rat into a cheese. I shall guide the ships in the distance, across the sea. A lighthouse always gives the impression of a stage-set. I am alone in the world: without a doubt it is the perfect refuge for my old age.'

All of a sudden Chaudval interrupted his reverie.

'Good Lord!' he said, feeling inside his greatcoat. 'But . . . that letter the postman delivered just as I was coming out must be the reply . . . I was going into this café to read it, and I forgot all about it! I'm losing my grip, and no mistake! . . . Good, here it is!'

Chaudval had just taken out of his pocket a large envelope from which, as soon as he broke the seal, a ministerial letter fell to the ground. He feverishly picked it up and read it at a single glance, in the red glow of the street lamp.

'My lighthouse! My letter of appointment!' he exclaimed. 'Saved, thank God!' he added, as if out of force of habit and in a falsetto voice so sudden and so different from his own that he looked around, thinking that somebody else had spoken.

'Come, now,' he said, 'calm down . . . and *be a man!*'

But at these words Esprit Chaudval, born Lepeinteur and known as Monanteuil, stopped as if changed into a statue of salt; this remark seemed to have petrified him.

'Eh?' he went on after a pause. 'What did I tell myself just then? To be a Man? . . . After all, why not?'

He folded his arms reflectively.

'For nearly half a century now I have been *acting* and *playing* other men's passions without ever feeling them—for at bottom I have never felt anything. So I am like those other men just for fun! So I am nothing but a shadow! Passions, feelings, *real* actions—that is what makes a genuine Man. Consequently, since my age forces me to rejoin Mankind, I must find myself some passions or *real* feelings—seeing that that is the *sine qua non* without which nobody can call himself a Man.

'There's a piece of good reasoning for you; it's positively bursting with common sense. So now to choose the passion most in keeping with my resuscitated nature.'

He meditated, then went on sadly:

'Love? . . . too late . . . Glory? . . . I have tasted it . . . Ambition? . . . let us leave that nonsense to the politicians!'

All of a sudden he gave a cry.

'I have it!' he said. 'Remorse! *There's* a passion that suits my dramatic temperament.'

He looked at himself in the mirror, assuming an expression which was drawn and convulsed as if by some supernatural horror.

'That's it!' he concluded. 'Nero! Macbeth! Orestes! Hamlet! Erostratus! The ghosts! Oh, yes, I want to see some real ghosts too! Like all those lucky fellows who could not take a single step without meeting a ghost.'

He struck his forehead.

'But how? . . . I'm as innocent as a lamb unwilling to be born.'

And after another pause he went on:

'But that doesn't matter! Where there's a will there's a way! I'm entitled to become what I ought to be, whatever the cost. I'm entitled to be a man. Do I have to commit crimes in order to feel remorse? All right, so be it: what does it matter, provided it is in a good cause? Yes indeed, so be it!'

At this point he began to improvise a dialogue.

'I shall perpetrate some dreadful crimes . . . When? . . . Straight away. I cannot wait until tomorrow . . . What crimes? . . . A single one! But a grandiose crime, of extraordinary cruelty, calculated to rouse all the Furies from the Underworld! . . . And what crime is that? . . . Why, the most impressive of all! I have it! A fire! I just have time to start a fire, pack my bags, come back, duly hidden behind the window of a cab, to enjoy my victory in the midst of the horrified crowd, collect the curses of the dying—and catch the train for the north-west with enough remorse put by to last me the rest of my days. Then I shall go and hide in my brightly-lit eyrie on the shores of the Ocean—where the police will never find me, for the simple reason that my crime is *disinterested*. And there I shall die alone.'

Here Chaudval drew himself up and improvised this positively classical line:

'Saved from suspicion by the grandeur of the crime.'

The great artist looked around to make sure he was alone, picked up a stone, and concluded:

'Well, that's settled. And from now on *you* won't reflect anybody else.'

And he threw the stone at the mirror which shattered into a thousand shining pieces.

Having performed this duty, Chaudval made off in a hurry—as if satisfied
with this first energetic feat—and rushed towards the boulevards, where, a few
minutes later, he hailed a cab, jumped into it, and disappeared.

Two hours later, the flames of a huge fire, coming from some big warehouses
stocked with petroleum, oil, and matches, were reflected in every window-pane
in the Faubourg du Temple. Soon squads of firemen, rolling and pushing their
pumps, came running up from all sides, the mournful wail of their horns
rousing the inhabitants of that populous district from their sleep. Countless
hurried steps rang out on the pavement: the Place du Château-d'Eau and the
adjoining streets were crowded with people. Already human chains were being
hurriedly organized. Within less than a quarter of an hour a cordon of troops
had been formed round the fire. In the blood-red light of the torches, policemen
were holding the people back.

The carriages, trapped in the crowds, had come to a standstill. Everybody
was shouting. Distant screams could be made out amidst the dreadful crackling
of the flames. The victims of the fire, caught in the inferno, were howling, and
the roofs of the houses falling in on them. About a hundred families, those of the
workers employed in the burning buildings, were left penniless and homeless.

In the distance, a solitary cab, loaded with two bulky trunks, was standing
behind the crowd at the Château-d'Eau. And in that cab sat Esprit Chaudval,
born Lepeinteur and known as Monanteuil, drawing aside the blind from time
to time and contemplating his handiwork.

'Oh!' he whispered to himself. 'How loathsome I feel in the eyes of God and
men! Yes, that's the work of a criminal, sure enough!'

The kindly old actor's face lit up.

'O wretched man!' he muttered. 'What sleepless nights I'm going to enjoy
among the ghosts of my victims! I can feel burgeoning within me the soul of
Nero, burning Rome out of artistic fervour, of Erostratus, burning the temple
of Ephesus out of a desire for glory, of Rostopchin, burning Moscow out of
patriotism, of Alexander, burning Persepolis out of love for his immortal
Thaïs! . . . I for my part burn out of duty, having no other means of *existence*. I
burn because I owe it to myself. I burn to fulfil an obligation. What a man I'm
going to be! How I'm going to live! Yes, at last I'm going to find out what it's
like to be tortured by remorse. What wonderful nights of delicious horror I'm
going to spend! Ah, I breathe again! I'm born again! I exist! When I think that I
was an actor! Now, as I'm nothing in the coarse eyes of mankind but a gallows-
bird, let us fly like the wind! Let us hide in our lighthouse, to enjoy our remorse
there in peace.'

In the evening, two days later, Chaudval, reaching his destination safely, took
possession of his lonely old lighthouse on the north coast: a ruined building with
an antiquated beacon which ministerial compassion had rekindled for his sake.

The light was of scarcely any use: it was just an excrescence, a sinecure, a
dwelling with a lamp on top, which nobody needed except Chaudval.

So the worthy tragedian, having moved his bed into the lighthouse, together
with stocks of food and a tall mirror in which to study his facial expressions,
promptly shut himself up there, secure from all human suspicion.

Around him moaned the sea, in which the ancient abyss of the heavens bathed the light of its stars. He watched the waves attacking his tower under the shifts of the winds, much as the Stylite must have gazed at the sands being hurled against his column by the shimiel.

In the distance he followed with unthinking eyes the smoke of steamships or the sails of fishing boats.

As he went up and down the stone staircase, the dreamer kept forgetting his fire.

On the evening of the third day, sitting in his room, sixty feet above the waves, he was re-reading a Paris newspaper which told the story of the catastrophe which had taken place two days before.

An unknown malefactor had thrown some matches into the petroleum cellars. A colossal fire, which had kept the firemen and the people out in the Faubourg du Temple.

Nearly a hundred victims had died; unfortunate families had been plunged into the direst poverty.

The whole place was in mourning and still smoking.

The name of the person who had committed this heinous crime was unknown, and so above all was the criminal's motive.

When he read this, Chaudval jumped for joy and, feverishly rubbing his hands, exclaimed:

'What a triumph! What a wonderful scoundrel I am! How I'm going to be haunted! How many ghosts I'm going to see! I knew that I should become a Man! Oh, I admit that the means I used was drastic, but it had to be, it had to be!'

Reading the Paris newspaper again, Chaudval noticed that a special performance was being given in aid of those who had suffered from the fire, and murmured:

'Well, well! I ought to have put my talent at the service of my victims. It would have been my farewell performance. I would have declaimed Orestes, I would have been marvellously true to life . . .'

Thereupon Chaudval began living in his lighthouse.

And the evenings and the nights fell, and followed one after another.

Something happened which astounded the actor. Something horrifying!

Contrary to his hopes and expectations, his conscience failed to torment him. Not a single ghost appeared. He felt nothing, *absolutely nothing*!

He could not believe the Silence. He could not get over it.

Sometimes, looking at himself in the mirror, he noticed that his debonair expression had not changed. Then he would hurl himself in a fury on his signals, altering them in the radiant hope of sinking some far-off ship, so as to rouse, quicken, stimulate his rebellious remorse, and awaken the longed-for ghosts.

It was all to no purpose.

His attempted crimes came to nothing. His efforts were in vain. He felt nothing. His efforts were in vain. He felt nothing. He did not see a single threatening phantom. He found it impossible to sleep any more, he was so stifled by shame and despair. The result was that when, one night, he suffered a

stroke in his luminous eyrie, he had a death-agony in which—amid the noise of
the ocean, with the sea-winds buffeting his tower lost in infinity—he cried out:

'Ghosts! . . . For the love of God! . . . Let me see one ghost at least! . . . *I've
earned it!'*

But the God he was invoking did not grant him this favour—and the old actor
died, still expressing, in his vain rhetoric, his ardent longing to see some
ghosts . . . *without realizing that he himself was what he was looking for.*

Memnon, or Human Wisdom

Voltaire *was the pen-name of François Marie Arouet (1694-1778), French philosopher,
playright and satirist whose most famous work is* Candide *(1764).*

Memnon one day took it into his head to become a great philosopher. There
are few men who have not, at some time or other, conceived the same wild
project. Says Memnon to himself: To be a perfect philosopher, and of course to
be perfectly happy, I have nothing to do but to divest myself entirely of
passions; and nothing is more easy, as everybody knows. In the first place, I will
never be in love; for, when I see a beautiful woman, I will say to myself, These
cheeks will one day grow wrinkled, these eyes be encircled with vermilion, that
bosom become flabby and pendant, that head bald and palsied. Now I have only
to consider her at present in imagination, as she will afterwards appear; and
certainly a fair face will never turn my head.

In the second place, I will be always temperate. It will be in vain to tempt me
with good cheer, with delicious wines, or the charms of society. I will have only
to figure to myself the consequences of excess, an aching head, a loathing
stomach, the loss of reason, of health, and of time. I will then only eat to supply
the waste of nature; my health will be always equal, my ideas pure and
luminous. All this is so easy that there is no merit in accomplishing it.

But, says Memnon, I must think a little of how I am to regulate my fortune:
why, my desires are moderate, my wealth is securely placed with the Receiver
General of the finances of Nineveh: I have wherewithal to live independent; and
that is the greatest of blessing. I shall never be under the cruel necessity of
dancing attendance at court: I will never envy anyone, and nobody will envy
me; still, all this is easy. I have friends, continued he, and I will preserve them,
for we shall never have any difference; I will never take amiss anything they may
say or do; and they will behave in the same way to me. There is no difficulty in
all this.

Having thus laid his little plan of philosophy in his closet, Memnon put his head out of the window. He saw two women walking under the plane trees near his house. The one was old, and appeared quite at her ease. The other was young, handsome, and seemingly much agitated: she sighed, she wept, and seemed on that account still more beautiful. Our philosopher was touched, not to be sure, with the beauty of the lady (he was too much determined not to feel any uneasiness of that kind) but with the distress which he saw her in. He came downstairs and accosted the young Ninevite in the design of consoling her with philosophy. That lovely person related to him, with an air of great simplicity, and in the most affecting manner, the injuries she sustained from an imaginary uncle; with what art he had deprived her of some imaginary property, and of the violence which she pretended to dread from him. 'You appear to me,' said she, 'a man of such wisdom that if you will condescend to come to my house and examine into my affairs, I and persuaded you will be able to draw me from the cruel embarrassment I am at present involved in.' Memnon did not hesitate to follow her, to examine her affairs philosophically and to give her sound counsel.

The afficted lady led him into a perfumed chamber, and politely made him sit down with her on a large sofa, where they both placed themselves opposite to each other in the attitude of conversation, their legs crossed; the one eager in telling her story, the other listening with devout attention. The lady spoke with downcast eyes, whence there sometimes fell a tear, and which, as she now and then ventured to raise them, always met those of the sage Memnon. Their discourse was full of tenderness, which redoubled as often as their eyes met. Memnon took her affairs exceedingly to heart, and felt himself every instant more and more inclined to oblige a person so virtuous and so happy. By degrees, in the warmth of conversation, they ceased to sit opposite; they drew nearer; their legs were no longer crossed. Memnon counseled her so closely and gave her such tender advices that neither of them could talk any longer of business nor well knew what they were about.

At his interesting moment, as may easily be imagined, who should come in but the uncle; he was armed from head to foot, and the first thing he said was, that he would immediately sacrifice, as was just, the sage Memnon and his niece; the latter, who made her escape, knew that he was well enough disposed to pardon, provided a good round sum were offered to him. Memnon was obliged to purchase his safety with all he had about him. In those days people were happy in getting so easily quit. America was not then discovered, and distressed ladies were not nearly as dangerous as they are now.

Memnon, covered with shame and confusion, got home to his own house; there he found a card inviting him to dinner with some of his intimate friends. If I remain at home alone, said he, I shall have my mind so occupied with this vexatious adventure that I shall not be able to eat a bit, and I shall bring upon myself some disease. It will therefore be prudent in me to go to my intimate friends, and partake with them of a frugal repast. I shall forget in the sweets of their society that folly I have this morning been guilty of. Accordingly, he attends the meeting; he is discovered to be uneasy at something, and he is urged to drink and banish care. A little wine, drunk in moderation, comforts the heart of god and man: so reasons Memnon the philosopher, and becomes intoxicated. After the repast, play is proposed. A little play with one's intimate friends is a harmless pastime. He plays and loses all that is in his purse, and four times as much on his word. A dispute arises on some circumstances in the game, and the disputants grow warm: one of his intimate friends throws a dice box at his head, and strikes out one of his eyes. The philosopher Memnon is carried home to his house, drunk and penniless, with the loss of an eye.

He sleeps out his debauch, and when his head has got a little clear, he sends his servant to the Receiver General of the finances of Nineveh to draw a little money to pay his debts of honor to his intimate friends. The servant returns and informs him that the Receiver General had that morning been declared a fraudulent bankrupt and that by this means an hundred families are reduced to poverty and despair. Memnon, almost beside himself, puts a plaster on his eye and a petition in his pocket, and goes to court to solicit justice from the king against the bankrupt. In the saloon he meets a number of ladies all in the highest spirits, and sailing along with hoops four-and-twenty feet in circumference. One of them, who knew him a little, eyed him askance, and cried aloud, 'Ah! What a horrid monster!' Another, who was better acquainted with him thus accosts him, 'Good-morrow, Mr. Memnon. I hope you are very well, Mr. Memnon. La, Mr. Memnon, how did you lose your eye?' And, turning upon her heel, she tripped away without waiting an answer. Memnon hid himself in a corner and waited for the moment when he could throw himself at the feet of the monarch. That moment at last arrived. Three times he kissed the earth, and presented his petition. His gracious majesty received him very favorably, and referred the paper to one of his satraps, that he might give him an account of it. The satrap takes Memnon aside and says to him with a haughty air and satirical grin, 'Hark ye, you fellow with the one eye, you must be a comical dog indeed, to address yourself to the king rather than to me; and still more so, to dare to demand justice against an honest bankrupt, whom I honor with my protection, and who is nephew to the waiting-maid of my mistress. Proceed no further in this business, my good friend, if you wish to preserve the eye you have left.'

Memnon, having thus in his closet resolved to renounce women, the excesses of the table, play and quarreling, but especially having determined never to go to court, had been in the short space of four-and-twenty hours, duped and robbed by a gentle dame, had got drunk, had gamed, had been engaged in a quarrel, had got his eye knocked out, and had been at court where he was sneered at and insulted.

Petrified with astonishment, and his heart broken with grief, Memnon returns homeward in despair. As he was about to enter his house, he is repulsed by a number of officers who are carrying off his furniture for the benefit of his creditors: he falls down almost lifeless under a plane tree. There he finds the fair dame, of the morning, who was walking with her dear uncle; and both set up a loud laugh on seeing Memnon with his plaster. The night approached, and Memnon made his bed on some straw near the walls of his house. Here the ague seized him, and he fell asleep in one of the fits, when a celestial spirit appeared to him in a dream.

It was all resplendent with light: it had six beautiful wings, but neither feet nor head nor tail, and could be likened to nothing. 'What art thou?' said Memnon. 'Thy good genius,' replied the spirit. 'Restore to me then my eye, my health, my fortune, my reason,' said Memnon; and he related how he had lost them all in one day. 'These are adventures which never happen to us in the world we inhabit,' said the spirit. 'And what world do you inhabit?' said the man of affliction. 'My native country,' replied the other, 'is five hundred millions of leagues distant from the sun, in a little star near Sirius, which you see from hence.' 'Charming country!' said Memnon. 'And are there indeed no jades to dupe a poor devil, no intimate friends that win his money, and knock out an eye for him, no fraudulent bankrupts, no satraps that make a jest of you while they refuse you justice?' 'No,' said the inhabitant of the star, 'we have nothing of what you talk of; we are never duped by women, because we have none among us; we never commit excesses at table, because we neither eat nor drink; we have no bankrupts, because with us there is neither silver nor gold; our eyes cannot be knocked out because we have not bodies in the form of yours; and satraps never do us injustice because in our world we are all equal.' 'Pray, my lord,' then said Memnon, 'without women and without eating how do you spend your time?' 'In watching,' said the genius, 'over the other worlds that are entrusted to us; and I am now come to give you consolation.' 'Alas!' replied Memnon, 'why did you not come yesterday to hinder me from committing so many indiscretions?' 'I was with your elder brother Hassan,' said the celestial being. 'He is still more to be pitied than you are. His Most Gracious Majesty the Sultan of the Indies, in whose court he has the honor to serve, has caused both his eyes to be put out for some small indiscretion; and he is now in a dungeon, his hands and feet loaded with chains.' ' 'Tis a happy thing truly,' said Memnon, 'to have a good genius in one's family, when out of two brothers one is blind of an eye, the other blind of both: one stretched upon straw, the other in a dungeon.' 'Your fate will soon change,' said the animal of the star. 'It is a true, you will never recover your eye, but, except that, you may be sufficiently happy if you never again take it into your head to be a perfect philosopher.' 'It is then impossible?' said Memnon. 'As impossible as to be perfectly wise, perfectly strong, perfectly powerful, perfectly happy. We ourselves are very far from it. There is a world indeed where all this is possible; but, in the hundred thousand millions of worlds dispersed over the regions of space, everything goes on by degrees. There is less philosophy, and less enjoyment on the second than in the first, less in the third than in the second, and so forth till the last in the scale, where all are completely fools.' 'I am afraid,' said Memnon, 'that our little terraqueous globe here is the madhouse of those hundred thousand millions of worlds of which Your Lordship does me the honor to speak.' 'Not quite,' said the spirit, 'but very nearly: everything must be in its proper place.' 'But are those poets and philosophers wrong, then, who tell us that everything is for the best?' 'No, they are right, when we consider things in relation to the gradation to the whole universe.' 'Oh! I shall never believe it till I recover my eye again,' said poor Memnon.

The Man Who Liked Dickens

Evelyn Waugh *(1903-66), was born in London and educated at Oxford. His first book was a biography of Dante Gabriel Rossetti, but his reputation was made by a series of satirical novels in the 1920s and 30s:* Decline and Fall, Vile Bodies, Black Mischief *and so on. Later novels include* Brideshead Revisited *(1945) and the 'Sword of Honour' trilogy. 'The Man Who Liked Dickens' was later modified and incorporated into one of his best novels,* A Handful of Dust.

Although Mr. McMaster had lived in Amazonas for nearly sixty years, no one except a few families of Shiriana Indians was aware of his existence. His house stood in a small savannah, one of those little patches of sand and grass that crop up occasionally in that neighbourhood, three miles or so across, bounded on all sides by forest.

The stream which watered it was not marked on any map; it ran through rapids, always dangerous and at most seasons of the year impassable, to join the upper waters of the River Uraricuera, whose course, though boldly delineated in every school atlas, is still largely conjectural. None of the inhabitants of the district, except Mr. McMaster, had ever heard of the republic of Colombia, Venezuela, Brazil or Bolivia, each of whom had at one time or another claimed its possession.

Mr. McMaster's house was larger than those of his neighbours, but similar in character—a palm-thatch roof, breast-high walls of mud and wattle, and a mud floor. He owned a dozen or so head of puny cattle which grazed in the savannah, a plantation of cassava, some banana and mango trees, a dog, and, unique in the neighbourhood, a single-barrelled, breech-loading shotgun. The few commodities which he employed from the outside world came to him through a long succession of traders, passed from hand to hand, bartered for in a dozen languages at the extreme end of one of the longest threads in the web of commerce that spreads from Manaos into the remote fastness of the forest.

One day, while Mr. McMaster was engaged in filling some cartridges, a Shiriana came to him with the news that a white man was approaching through the forest, alone and very sick. He closed the cartridge and loaded his gun with it, put those that were finished into his pocket and set out in the direction indicated.

The man was already clear of the bush when Mr. McMaster reached him, sitting on the ground, clearly in a bad way. He was without hat or boots, and his clothes were so torn that it was only by the dampness of his body that they adhered to it; his feet were cut and grossly swollen, every exposed surface of skin was scarred by insect and bat bites; his eyes were wild with fever. He was talking to himself in delirium, but stopped when Mr. McMaster approached and addressed him in English.

'I'm tired,' the man said; then: 'Can't go on any farther. My name is Henty

304

and I'm tired. Anderson died. That was a long time ago. I expect you think I'm
very odd.'

'I think you are ill, my friend.'

'Just tired. It must be several months since I had anything to eat.'

Mr. McMaster hoisted him to his feet and, supporting him by the arm, led
him across the hummocks of grass towards the farm.

'It is a very short way. When we get there I will give you something to make
you better.'

'Jolly kind of you.' Presently he said: 'I say, you speak English. I'm English,
too. My name is Henty.'

'Well, Mr. Henty, you aren't to bother about anything more. You're ill and
you've had a rough journey. I'll take care of you.'

They went very slowly, but at length reached the house.

'Lie there in the hammock. I will fetch something for you.'

Mr. McMaster went into the back room of the house and dragged a tin
canister from under a heap of skins. It was full of a mixture of dried leaf and
bark. He took a handful and went outside to the fire. When he returned he put
one hand behind Henty's head and held up the concoction of herbs in a calabash
for him to drink. He sipped, shuddering slightly at the bitterness. At last he
finished it. Mr. McMaster threw out the dregs on the floor. Henty lay back in
the hammock sobbing quietly. Soon he fell into a deep sleep.

'Ill-fated' was the epithet applied by the Press to the Anderson expedition to the
Parima and upper Uraricuera region of Brazil. Every stage of the enterprise
from the preliminary arrangements in London to its tragic dissolution in
Amazonas was attacked by misfortune. It was due to one of the early set-backs
that Paul Henty became connected with it.

He was not by nature an explorer; an even-tempered, good-looking young
man of fastidious tastes and enviable possessions, unintellectual, but apprecia-
tive of fine architecture and the ballet, well travelled in the more accessible parts
of the world, a collector though not a connoisseur, popular among hostesses,
revered by his aunts. He was married to a lady of exceptional charm and beauty,
and it was she who upset the good order of his life by confessing her affection for
another man for the second time in the eight years of their marriage. The first
occasion had been a short-lived infatuation with a tennis professional, the
second was a captain in the Coldstream Guards, and more serious.

Henty's first thought under the shock of this revelation was to go out and dine
alone. He was a member of four clubs, but at three of them he was liable to meet
his wife's lover. Accordingly he chose one which he rarely frequented, a semi-
intellectual company composed of publishers, barristers, and men of scholar-
ship awaiting election to the Athenæum.

Here, after dinner, he fell into conversation with Professor Anderson and first
heard of the proposed expedition to Brazil. The particular misfortune that was
retarding arrangements at the moment was defalcation of the secretary with two-
thirds of the expedition's capital. The principals were ready—Professor
Anderson, Dr. Simmons the anthropologist, Mr. Necher the biologist, Mr.

Brough the surveyor, wireless operator and mechanic—the scientific and
sporting apparatus was packed up in crates ready to be embarked, the necessary
facilities had been stamped and signed by the proper authorities but unless
twelve hundred pounds was forthcoming the whole thing would have to be
abandoned.

Henty, as had been suggested, was a man of comfortable means; the
expedition would last from nine months to a year; he could shut his country
house—his wife, he reflected, would want to remain in London near her young
man—and cover more than the sum required. There was a glamour about the
whole journey which might, he felt, move even his wife's sympathies. There and
then, over the club fire, he dicided to accompany Professor Anderson.

When he went home that evening he announced to his wife: 'I have decided
what I shall do'.

'Yes, darling?'

'You are certain that you no longer love me?'

'*Darling*, you *know*, I *adore* you.'

'But you are certain you love this guardsman, Tony what-ever-his-name-is,
more?'

'Oh, yes, *ever* so much more. Quite a different thing altogether.'

'Very well, then. I do not propose to do anything about a divorce for a year.
You shall have time to think it over. I am leaving next week for the Uraricuera.'

'Golly, where's that?'

'I am not perfectly sure. Somewhere in Brazil, I think. It is unexplored. I
shall be away a year.'

'But darling, how ordinary! Like people in books—big game, I mean, and all
that.'

'You have obviously already discovered that I am a very ordinary person.'

'Now, Paul, don't be disagreeable—oh, there's the telephone. It's probably
Tony. If it is, d'you mind terribly it I talk to him alone for a bit?'

But in the ten days of preparation that followed she showed greater
tenderness, putting off her soldier twice in order to accompany Henty to the
shops where he was choosing his equipment and insisting on his purchasing a
worsted cummerbund. On his last evening she gave a supper-party for him at
the Embassy to which she allowed him to ask any of his friends he liked; he
could think of no one except Professor Anderson, who looked oddly dressed,
danced tirelessly and was something of a failure with everyone. Next day Mrs.
Henty came with her husband to the boat train and presented him with a pale
blue, extravagantly soft blanket, in a suede case of the same colour furnished
with a zip fastener and monogram. She kissed him good-bye and said, 'Take
care of yourself in wherever it is.'

Had she gone as far as Southampton she might have witnessed two dramatic
passages. Mr. Brough got no farther than the gangway before he was arrested
for debt—a matter of £32; the publicity given to the dangers of the expedition
was responsible for the action. Henty settled the account.

The second difficulty was not to be overcome so easily. Mr. Necher's mother
was on the ship before them; she carried a missionary journal in which she had

just read an account of the Brazilian forests. Nothing would induce her to permit her son's departure; she would remain on board until he came ashore with her. If necessary, she would sail with him, but go into those forests alone he should not. All argument was unavailing with the resolute old lady who eventually, five minutes before the time of embarkation, bore her son off in triumph, leaving the company without a biologist.

Nor was Mr. Brough's adherence long maintained. The ship in which they were travelling was a cruising liner taking passengers on a round voyage. Mr. Brough had not been on board a week and had scarcely accustomed himself to the motion of the ship before he was engaged to be married; he was still engaged, although to a different lady, when they reached Manaos and refused all inducements to proceed farther, borrowing his return fare from Henty and arriving back in Southampton engaged to the lady of his first choice, whom he immediately married.

In Brazil the officials to whom their credentials were addressed were all out of power. While Henty and Professor Anderson negotiated with the new administrators, Dr. Simmons proceeded up river to Boa Vista where he established a base camp with the greater part of the stores. These were instantly commandeered by the revolutionary garrison, and he himself imprisoned for some days and subjected to various humiliations which so enraged him that, when released, he made promptly for the coast, stopping at Manaos only long enough to inform his colleagues that he insisted on leaving his case personally before the central authorities at Rio.

Thus while they were still a month's journey from the start of their labours, Henty and Professor Anderson found themselves alone and deprived of the greater part of their supplies. The ignominy of immediate return was not to be borne. For a short time they considered the advisability of going into hiding for six months in Madeira or Teneriffe, but even there detection seemed probable; there had been too many photographs in the illustrated papers before they left London. Accordingly, in low spirits, the two explorers at last set out alone for the Uraricuera with little hope of accomplishing anything of any value to anyone.

For seven weeks they paddled through green, humid tunnels of forest. They took a few snapshots of naked, misanthropic Indians, bottled some snakes and later lost them when their canoe capsized in the rapids; they overtaxed their digestions, imbibing nauseous intoxicants at native galas, they were robbed of the last of their sugar by a Guianese prospector. Finally, Professor Anderson fell ill with malignant malaria, chattered feebly for some days in his hammock, lapsed into coma and died, leaving Henty alone with a dozen Maku oarsmen, none of whom spoke a word of any language known to him. They reversed their course and drifted down stream with a minimum of provisions and no mutual confidence.

One day, a week or so after Professor Anderson's death, Henty awoke to find that his boys and his canoe had disappeared during the night, leaving him with only his hammock and pyjamas some two or three hundred miles from the nearest Brazilian habitation. Nature forbade him to remain where he was although there seemed little purpose in moving. He set himself to follow the course of the stream, at first in the hope of meeting a canoe. But presently the whole forest became peopled for him with frantic apparitions, for no conscious reason at all. He plodded on, now wading in the water, now scrambling through the bush.

Vaguely at the back of his mind he had always believed that the jungle was a place full of food, that there was danger of snakes and savages and wild beasts, but not of starvation. But now he observed that this was far from being the case. The jungle consisted solely of immense tree trunks, embedded in a tangle of thorn and vine rope, all far from nutritious. On the first day he suffered hideously. Later he seemed anaesthetized and was chiefly embarrassed by the behaviour of the inhabitants who came out to meet him in footman's livery, carrying his dinner, and then irresponsibly disappeared or raised the covers of their dishes and revealed live tortoises. Many people who knew him in London appeared and ran round him with derisive cries, asking him questions to which he could not possibly know the answers. His wife came, too, and he was pleased to see her, assuming that she had got tired of her guardsman and was there to fetch him back, but she soon disappeared, like all the others.

It was then that he remembered that it was imperative for him to reach Manaos; he redoubled his energy, stumbling against boulders in the stream and getting caught up among the vines. 'But I mustn't waste my breath,' he reflected. They he forgot that, too, and was conscious of nothing more until he found himself lying in a hammock in Mr. McMaster's house.

His recovery was slow. At first, days of lucidity alternated with delirium, then his temperature dropped and he was conscious even when most ill. The days of fever grew less frequent, finally occurring in the normal system of the tropics between long periods of comparative health. Mr. McMaster dosed him regularly with herbal remedies.

'It's very nasty,' said Henty, 'but it does do good.'

'There is medicine for everything in the forest,' said Mr. McMaster; 'to make you well and to make you ill. My mother was an Indian and she taught me many of them. I have learned others from time to time from my wives. There are plants to cure you and give you fever, to kill you and send you mad, to keep away snakes, to intoxicate fish so that you can pick them out of the water with your hands like fruit from a tree. There are medicines even I do not know. They said that it is possible to bring dead people back to life after they have begun to stink, but I have not seen it done.'

'But surely you are English?'

'My father was—at least a Barbadian. He came to British Guiana as a missionary. He was married to a white woman but he left her in Guiana to look for gold. Then he took my mother. The Shiriana women are ugly but very devoted. I have had many. Most of the men and women living in this savannah are my children. That is why they obey—for that reason and because I have the gun. My father lived to a great age. It is not twenty years since he died. He was a man of education. Can you read?'

'Yes, of course.'

'It is not everyone who is so fortunate. I cannot.'

Henty laughed apologetically. 'But I suppose you haven't much opportunity here.'

'Oh, yes, that is just it. I have a great many books. I will show you when you are better. Until five years ago there was an Englishman—at least a black man, but he was well educated in Georgetown. He died. He used to read to me every day until he died. You shall read to me when you are better.'

'I shall be delighted to.'

'Yes, you shall read to me,' Mr. McMaster repeated, nodding over the calabash.

During the early days of his convalescence Henty had little conversation with his host; he lay in the hammock staring up at the thatched roof and thinking about his wife, rehearsing over and over again different incidents in their life together, including her affairs with the tennis professional and the soldier. The days, exactly twelve hours each, passed without distinction. Mr. McMaster retired to sleep at sundown, leaving a little lamp burning—a hand-woven wick drooping from a pot of beef fat—to keep away vampire bats.

The first time that Henty left the house Mr. McMaster took him for a stroll around the farm.

'I will show you the black man's grave,' he said, leading him to a mound between the mango trees. 'He was very kind to me. Every afternoon until he died, for two hours, he used to read to me. I think I will put up a cross—to commemorate his death and your arrival—a pretty idea. Do you believe in God?'

'I've never really thought about it much.'

'You are perfectly right. I have thought about it a *great* deal and I still do not know . . . Dickens did.'

'I suppose so.'

'Oh yes, it is apparent in all his books. You will see.'

That afternoon Mr. McMaster began the construction of a headpiece for the negro's grave. He worked with a large spokeshave in a wood so hard that it grated and rang like metal.

At last when Henty had passed six or seven consecutive days without fever, Mr. McMaster said, 'Now I think you are well enough to see the books.'

At one end of the hut there was a kind of loft formed by a rough platform erected up in the eaves of the roof. Mr. McMaster propped a ladder against it and mounted. Henty followed, still unsteady after his illness. Mr. McMaster sat on the platform and Henty stood at the top of the ladder looking over. There was a heap of small bundles there, tied up with rag, palm leaf and raw hide.

'It has been hard to keep out the worms and ants. Two are practically destroyed. But there is an oil the Indians know how to make that is useful.'

He unwrapped the nearest parcel and handed down a calf-bound book. It was an early American edition of *Bleak House*.

'It does not matter which we take first.'

'You are fond of Dickens?'

'Why, yes, of course. More than fond, far more. You see, they are the only books I have ever heard. My father used to read them and then later the black man . . . and now you. I have heard them all several times by now but I never get tired; there is always more to be learned and noticed, so many characters, so many changes of scene, so many words. . . . I have all Dickens's books except those that the ants devoured. It takes a long time to read them all—more than two years.'

'Well,' said Henty lightly, 'they will well last out my visit.'

'Oh, I hope not. It is delightful to start again. Each time I think I find more to enjoy and admire.'

They took down the first volume of *Bleak House* and that afternoon Henty had his first reading.

He had always rather enjoyed reading aloud and in the first year of marriage had shared several books in this way with his wife, until one day, in one of her rare moments of confidence, she remarked that it was torture to her. Sometimes after that he had thought it might be agreeable to have children to read to. But Mr. McMaster was a unique audience.

The old man sat astride his hammock opposite Henty, fixing him throughout with his eyes, and following the words, soundlessly, with his lips. Often when a new character was introduced he would say, 'Repeat the name, I have forgotten him,' or, 'Yes, yes, I remember her well. She dies, poor woman.' He would frequently interrupt with questions; not as Henty would have imagined about the circumstances of the story—such things as the procedure of the Lord Chancellor's Court or the social conventions of the time, though they must have been unintelligible, did not concern him—but always about the characters. 'Now, why does she say that? Does she really mean it? Did she feel faint because of the heat of the fire or of something in that paper?' He laughed loudly at all the jokes and at some passages which did not seem humorous to Henty, asking him to repeat them two or three times; and later at the description of the sufferings of the outcasts in 'Tom-all-alone' tears ran down his cheeks into his beard. His comments on the story were usually simple. 'I think that Dedlock is a very proud man,' or, 'Mrs Jellyby does not take enough care of her children.' Henty enjoyed the readings almost as much as he did.

At the end of the first day the old man said, 'You read beautifully, with a far better accent than the black man. And you explain better. It is almost as though my father were here again.' And always at the end of a session he thanked his guest courteously. 'I enjoyed that very much. It was an extremely distressing chapter. But, if I remember rightly, it will all turn out well.'

By the time that they were well into the second volume, however, the novelty of the old man's delight had begun to wane, and Henty was feeling strong enough to be restless. He touched more than once on the subject of his departure, asking about canoes and rains and the possibility of finding guides. But Mr. McMaster seemed obtuse and paid no attention to these hints.

One day, running his thumb through the pages of *Bleak House* that remained to be read, Henty said, 'We still have a lot to get through. I hope I shall be able to finish it before I go.'

'Oh, yes,' said Mr. McMaster. 'Do not disturb yourself about that. You will have time to finish it, My friend.'

For the first time Henty noticed something slightly menacing in his host's manner. That evening at supper, a brief meal of farine and dried beef eaten just before sundown, Henty renewed the subject.

'You know, Mr. McMaster, the time has come when I must be thinking about getting back to civilization. I have already imposed myself on your hospitality for too long.'

Mr. McMaster bent over his plate, crunching mouthfuls of farine, but made no reply.

'How soon do you think I shall be able to get a boat? . . . I said how soon do you think I shall be able to get a boat? I appreciate all your kindness to me more than I can say, but . . .'

'My friend, any kindness I may have shown is amply repaid by your reading of Dickens. Do not let us mention the subject again.'

'Well, I'm very glad you have enjoyed it. I have, too. But I really must be thinking of getting back . . .'

'Yes,' said Mr. McMaster. 'The black man was like that. He thought of it all the time. But he died here . . .'

Twice during the next day Henty opened the subject but his host was evasive. Finally he said, 'Forgive me, Mr. McMaster, but I really must press the point. When can I get a boat?'

'There is no boat.'

'Well, the Indians can build one.'

'You must wait for the rains. There is not enough water in the river now.'

'How long will that be?'

'A month . . .two months . . .'

They had finished *Bleak House* and were nearing the end of *Dombey and Son* when the rain came.

'Now it is time to make preparations to go.'

'Oh, that is impossible. The Indians will not make a boat during the rainy season—it is one of their superstitions.'

'You might have told me.'

'Did I not mention it? I forgot.'

Next morning Henty went out alone while his host was busy, and, looking as aimless as he could, strolled across the savannah to the group of Indian houses. There were four or five Shirianas sitting in one of the doorways. They did not look up as he approached them. He addressed them in the few words of Maku he had acquired during the journey but they made no sign whether they understood him or not. Then he drew a sketch of a canoe in the sand, he went through some vague motions of carpentry, pointed from them to him, then made motions of giving something to them and scratched out the outlines of a gun and hat and a few other recognizable articles of trade. One of the women giggled, but no one gave any sign of comprehension, and he went away unsatisfied.

At their midday meal Mr. McMaster said: 'Mr Henty, the Indians tell me you have been trying to speak with them. It is easier that you say anything you wish through me. You realize, do you not, that they would do nothing without my authority. They regard themselves, quite rightly in most cases, as my children.'

'Well, as a matter of fact, I was asking them about a canoe.'

'So they gave me to understand . . . and now if you have finished your meal perhaps we might have another chapter. I am quite absorbed in the book.'

They finished *Dombey and Son*; nearly a year had passed since Henty had left England, and his gloomy foreboding of permanent exile became suddenly acute when, between the pages of *Martin Chuzzlewit*, he found a document written in pencil in irregular characters.

Year 1919.

I James McMaster of Brazil do swear to Barnabas Washington of Georgetown that if he finish this book in fact Martin Chuzzlewit I will let him go away back as soon as finished.

There followed a heavy pencil *X*, and after it: *Mr. McMaster made this mark signed Barnabas Washington.*

'Mr. McMaster,' said Henty, 'I must speak frankly. You saved my life, and when I get back to civilization I will reward you to the best of my ability. I will give you anything within reason. But at present you are keeping me here against my will. I demand to be released.'

'But, my friend, what is keeping you? You are under no restraint. Go when you like.'

'You know very well that I can't get away without your help.'

'In that case you must humour an old man. Read me another chapter.'

'Mr. McMaster, I swear by anything you like that when I get to Manaos I will find someone to take my place. I will pay a man to read to you all day.'

'But I have no need of another man. You read so well.'

'I have read for the last time.'

'I hope not,' said Mr. McMaster politely.

That evening at supper only one plate of dried meat and farine was brought in and Mr. McMaster ate alone. Henty lay without speaking, staring at the thatch.

Next day at noon a single plate was put before Mr. McMaster, but with it lay his gun, cocked, on his knee, as he ate. Henty resumed the reading of *Martin Chuzzlewit* where it had been interrupted.

Weeks passed hopelessly. They read *Nicholas Nickleby* and *Little Dorrit* and *Oliver Twist*. Then a stranger arrived in the savannah, a half-caste prospector, one of that lonely order of men who wander for a lifetime through the forests, tracing the little streams, sifting the gravel and, ounce by ounce, filling the little leather sack of gold dust, more often than not dying of exposure and starvation with five hundred dollars' worth of gold hung round their necks. Mr. McMaster was vexed at his arrival, gave him farine and *passo* and sent him on his journey within an hour of his arrival, but in that hour Henty had time to scribble his name on a slip of paper and put it into the man's hand.

From now on there was hope. The days followed their unvarying routine; coffee at sunrise, a morning of inaction while Mr. Mcmaster pottered about on the business of the farm, farine and *passo* at noon, Dickens in the afternoon, farine and *passo* and sometimes some fruit for supper, silence from sunset to dawn with the small wick glowing in the beef fat and the palm thatch overhead dimly discernible: but Henty lived in quiet confidence and expectation.

Some time, this year or the next, the prospector would arrive at a Brazilian village with news of his discovery. The disasters to the Anderson expedition would not have passed unnoticed. Henty could imagine the headlines that must have appeared in the popular Press; even now probably there were search parties working over the country he had crossed; any day English voices might sound over the savannah and a dozen friendly adventurers come crashing through the bush. Even as he was reading, while his lips mechanically followed the printed pages, his mind wandered away from his eager, crazy host opposite, and he began to narrate to himself incidents of his home-coming—the gradual re-encounters with civilization; he shaved and bought new clothes at Manaos, telegraphed for money, received wires of congratulation; he enjoyed the leisurely river journey to Belem, the big liner to Europe; savoured good claret and fresh meat and spring vegetables; he was shy at meeting his wife and uncertain how to address her . . . '*Darling*, you've been much longer than you said. I quite thought you were lost . . .'

And then Mr. McMaster interrupted. 'May I trouble you to read that passage again? It is one I particularly enjoy.'

The weeks passed; there was no sign of rescue, but Henty endured the day for hope of what might happen on the morrow; he even felt a slight stirring of cordiality towards his gaoler and was therefore quite willing to join him when, one evening after a long conference with an Indian neighbour, he proposed a celebration.

'It is one of the local feast days,' he explained, 'and they have been making *piwari*. You may not like it, but you should try some. We will go across to this man's home tonight.'

Accordingly after supper they joined a party of Indians that were assembled round the fire in one of the huts at the other side of the savannah. they were singing in an apathetic, monotonous manner and passing a large calabash of liquid from mouth to mouth, Separate bowls were brought for Henty and Mr. McMaster, and they were given hammocks to sit in.

'You must drink it all without lowering the cup. That is the etiquette.'

Henty gulped the dark liquid, trying not to taste it. But it was not unpleasant, hard and muddy on the palate like most of the beverages he had been offered in Brazil, but with a flavour of honey and brown bread. He leant back in the hammock feeling unusually contented. Perhaps at that very moment the search party was in camp a few hours' journey from them. Meanwhile he was warm and drowsy. The cadence of song rose and fell interminably, liturgically. Another calabash of *piwari* was offered him and he handed it back empty. He lay full length watching the play of shadows on the thatch as the Shirianas began to dance. Then he shut his eyes and thought of England and his wife and fell asleep.

He awoke, still in the Indian hut, with the impression that he had outslept his usual hour. By the position of the sun he knew it was late afternoon. No one else was about. He looked for his watch and found to his surprise that it was not on his wrist. He had left it in the house, he supposed, before coming to the party.

'I must have been tight last night,' he reflected. 'Treacherous drink, that.' He had a headache and feared a recurrence of fever. He found when he set his feet to the ground that he stood with difficulty; his walk was unsteady and his mind confused as it had been during the first weeks of his convalescence. On the way across the savannah he was obliged to stop more than once, shutting his eyes and breathing deeply. When he reached the house he found Mr. McMaster sitting there.

'Ah, my friend, you are late for the reading this afternoon. There is scarcely another half-hour of light. How do you feel?'

'Rotten. That drink doesn't seem to agree with me.'

'I will give you something to make you better. The forest has remedies for everything; to make you awake and to make you sleep.'

'You haven't seen my watch anywhere?'

'You have missed it?'

'Yes. I thought I was wearing it. I say, I've never slept so long.'

'Not since you were a baby. Do you know how long? Two days.'

'Nonsense. I can't have.'

'Yes, indeed. It is a long time. It is a pity because you missed our guests.'

'Guests?'

'Why, yes. I have been quite gay while you were asleep. Three men from outside. Englishmen. It is a pity you missed them. A pity for them, too, as they particularly wished to see you. But what could I do? You were so sound asleep. They had come all the way to find you, so—I thought you would not mind—as you could not greet them yourself I gave them a little souvenir, your watch. They wanted something to take home to your wife who is offering a great reward for news of you. They were very pleased with it. And they took some photographs of the little cross I put up to commemorate your coming. They were pleased with that, too. They were very easily pleased. But I do not suppose they will visit us again, our life here is so retired . . . no pleasures except reading . . . I do not suppose we shall ever have visitors again . . . well, well, I will get you some medicine to make you feel better. Your head aches, does it not . . . We will not have any Dickens to-day . . . but to-morrow, and the day after that, and the day after that. Let us read *Little Dorrit* again. There are passages in that book I can never hear without the temptation to weep.'

Pomegranate Seed

Edith Wharton *(1862-1937) was born in New York City, marrying Edward Wharton in 1885. Under Henry James's influence she wrote novels analysing modern life, such as* The House of Mirth *(1905) and the New England tragedy* Ethan Frome *(1911). She also wrote many short stories, collected in* Tales of Men and Ghosts *(1910) and* Xingu *(1916).*

Charlotte Ashby paused on her doorstep. Dark had descended on the brilliancy of the March afternoon, and the grinding rasping street life of the city was at its highest. She turned her back on it, standing for a moment in the old-fashioned, marble-flagged vestibule before she inserted her key in the lock. The sash curtains drawn across the panes of the inner door softened the light within to a warm blur through which no details showed. It was the hour when, in the first months of her marriage to Kenneth Ashby, she had most liked to return to that quiet house in a street long since deserted by business and fashion. The contrast between the soulless roar of New York, its devouring blaze of lights, the oppression of its congested traffic, congested houses, lives, minds and this veiled sanctuary she called home, always stirred her profoundly. In the very heart of the hurricane she had found her tiny islet—or thought she had. And now, in the last months, everything was changed, and she always wavered on the doorstep and had to force herself to enter.

While she stood there she called up the scene within: the hall hung with old prints, the ladder-like stairs, and on her left her husband's long shabby library, full of books and pipes and worn armchairs inviting to meditation. How she had loved that room! Then, upstairs, her own drawing room, in which, since the death of Kenneth's first wife, neither furniture nor hangings had been changed, because there had never been money enough, but which Charlotte had made her own by moving furniture about and adding more books, another lamp, a table for the new reviews. Even on the occasion of her only visit to the first Mrs. Ashby—a distant, self-centered woman, whom she had known very slightly— she had looked about her with an innocent envy, feeling it to be exactly the drawing room she would have liked for herself; and now for more than a year it had been hers to deal with as she chose—the room to which she hastened back at dusk on winter days, where she sat reading by the fire, or answering notes at the pleasant roomy desk, or going over her step-children's copybooks, till she heard her husband's step.

Sometimes friends dropped in; sometimes—oftener—she was alone; and she liked that best, since it was another way of being with Kenneth, thinking over what he had said when they parted in the morning, imagining what he would say when he sprang up the stairs, found her by herself and caught her to him.

Now, instead of this, she thought of one thing only—the letter she might or might not find on the hall table. Until she had made sure whether or not it was there, her mind had no room for anything else. The letter was always the same—a square grayish envelope with 'Kenneth Ashby, Esquire,' written on it in bold but faint characters. From the first it had struck Charlotte as peculiar that anyone who wrote such a firm hand should trace the letters so lightly; the address was always written as thought there were not enough ink in the pen, or the writer's wrist were too weak to bear upon it. Another curious thing was that, in spite of its masculine curves, the writing was so visibly feminine. Some hands are sexless, some masculine, at first glance; the writing on the gray envelope, for all its strength and assurance, was without doubt a woman's. The envelope never bore anything but the recipient's name; no stamp, no address. The letter was presumably delivered by hand—but by whose? No doubt it was slipped into the letter box, whence the parlormaid, when she closed the shutters and lit the lights, probably extracted it. At any rate, it was always in the evening, after dark, that Charlotte saw it lying there. She thought of the letter in the singular, as 'it,' because, though there had been several since her marriage—seven, to be exact—they were so alike in appearance that they had become merged in one another in her mind, become one letter, become 'it.'

The first had come the day after their return from their honeymoon—a journey prolonged to the West Indies, from which they had returned to New York after an absence of more than two months. Re-entering the house with her husband, late on the first evening—they had dined at his mother's—she had seen, alone on the hall table, the grey envelope. Her eye fell on it before Kenneth's, and her first thought was: 'Why, I've seen that writing before'; but where she could not recall. The memory was just definite enough for her to identify the script whenever it looked up at her faintly from the same pale envelope; but on that first day she would have thought no more of the letter if, when her husband's glance lit on it, she had not chanced to be looking at him. It all happened in a flash—his seeing the letter, putting out his hand for it, raising it to his shortsighted eyes to decipher the faint writing, and then abruptly withdrawing the arm he had slipped through Charlotte's, and moving away to the hanging light, his back turned to her. She had waited—waited for a sound, an exclamation; waited for him to open the letter; but he had slipped it into his pocket without a word and followed her into the library. And there they had sat down by the fire and lit their cigarettes, and he had remained silent, his head thrown back broodingly against the armchair, his eyes fixed on the hearth, and presently had passed his hand over his forehead and said: 'Wasn't it unusually hot at my mother's tonight? I've got a splitting head. Mind if I take myself off to bed?'

That was the first time. Since then Charlotte had never been present when he had received the letter. It usually came before he got home from his office, and she had to go upstairs and leave it lying there. But even if she had not seen it, she would have known it had come by the change in his face when he joined her—which, on those evenings, he seldom did before they met for dinner. Evidently, whatever the letter contained, he wanted to be by himself to deal with it; and when he reappeared he looked years older, looked emptied of life and courage, and hardly conscious of her presence. Sometimes he was silent for the rest of the evening; and if he spoke, it was usually to hint some criticism of her household arrangements, suggest some change in the domestic administration, to ask, a little nervously, if she didn't think Joyce's nursery governess was rather young and flighty, or if she herself always saw to it that Peter—whose throat was delicate—was properly wrapped up when he went to school. At such times Charlotte would remember the friendly warnings she had received when she became engaged to Kenneth Ashby: 'Marrying a heartbroken widower! Isn't that rather risky? You know Elsie Ashby absolutely dominated him'; and how she had jokingly replied: 'He may be glad of a little liberty for a change.' And in this respect she had been right. She had needed no one to tell her, during the first months, that her husband was perfectly happy with her. When they came back from their protracted honeymoon the same friends said: 'What have you done to Kenneth? He looks twenty years younger'; and this time she answered with careless joy: 'I suppose I've got him out of his groove.'

But what she noticed after the grey letters began to come was not so much his nervous tentative faultfinding—which always seemed to be uttered against his will—as the look in his eyes when he joined her after receiving one of the letters. The look was not unloving, not even indifferent; it was the look of a man who had been so far away from ordinary events that when he returns to familiar things they seem strange. She minded that more than the faultfinding.

Though she had been sure from the first that the handwriting on the grey envelope was a woman's, it was long before she associated the mysterious letters with any sentimental secret. She was too sure of her husband's love, too confident of filling his life, for such an idea to occur to her. It seemed far more likely that the letters—which certainly did not appear to cause him any sentimental pleasure—were addressed to the busy lawyer than to the private person. Probably they were from some tiresome client—women, he had often told her, were nearly always tiresome as clients—who did not want her letters opened by his secretary and therefore had them carried to his house. Yes; but in that case the unknown female must be unusually troublesome, judging from the effect her letters produced. Then again, though his professional discretion was exemplary, it was odd that he had never uttered an impatient comment, never remarked to Charlotte, in a moment of expansion, that there was a nuisance of a woman who kept badgering him about a case that had gone against her. He had made more than one semiconfidence of the kind—of course without giving names or details; but concerning this mysterious correspondent his lips were sealed.

There was another possibility: what is euphemistically called an 'old entanglement.' Charlotte Ashby was a sophisticated woman. She had few illusions about the intricacies of the human heart; she knew that there were often old entanglements. But when she had married Kenneth Ashby, her friends, instead of hinting at such a possibility, had said: 'You've got your work cut out for you. Marrying a Don Juan is a sinecure to it. Kenneth's never looked at another woman since he first saw Elsie Corder. During all the years of their marriage he was more like an unhappy lover than a comfortably contented husband. He'll never let you move an armchair or change the place of a lamp;

and whatever you venture to do, he'll mentally compare with what Elsie would have done in your place.'

Except for an occasional nervous mistrust as to her ability to manage the children—a mistrust gradually dispelled by her good humour and the children's obvious fondness for her—none of these forebodings had come true. The desolate widower, of whom his nearest friends said that only his absorbing professional interests had kept him from suicide after his first wife's death, had fallen in love, two years later, with Charlotte Gorse, and after an impetuous wooing had married her and carried her off on a tropical honeymoon. And ever since he had been as tender and lover-like as during those first radiant weeks. Before asking her to marry him he had spoken to her frankly of his great love for his first wife and his despair after her sudden death; but even then he had assumed no stricken attitude, or implied that life offered no possibility of renewal. He had been perfectly simple and natural, and had confessed to Charlotte that from the beginning he had hoped the future held new gifts for him. And when, after their marriage, they returned to the house where his twelve years with his first wife had been spent, he had told Charlotte at once that he was sorry he couldn't afford to do the place over for her, but that he knew every woman had her own views about furniture and all sorts of household arrangements a man would never notice, and had begged her to make any changes she saw fit without bothering to consult him. As a result, she made as few as possible; but his way of beginning their new life in the old setting was so frank and unembarrassed that it put her immediately at her ease, and she was almost sorry to find that the portrait of Elsie Ashby, which used to hang over the desk in his library, had been transferred in their absence to the children's nursery. Knowing herself to be the indirect cause of this banishment, she spoke of it to her husband; but he answered: 'Oh, I thought they ought to grow up with her looking down on them.' The answer moved Charlotte, and satisfied her; and as the time went by she had to confess that she felt more at home in her house, more at ease and in confidence with her husband, since that long coldly beautiful face on the library wall no longer followed her with guarded eyes. It was as if Kenneth's love had penetrated to the secret she hardly acknowledged to her own heart—her passionate need to feel herself the sovereign even of his past.

With all this stored-up happiness to sustain her, it was curious that she had lately found herself yielding to a nervous apprehension. But there the apprehension was; and on this particular afternoon—perhaps because she was more tired than usual, or because of the trouble of finding a new cook or, for some other ridiculously trivial reason, moral or physical—she found herself unable to react against the feeling. Latchkey in hand, she looked back down the silent street to the whirl and illumination of the great thoroughfare beyond, and up at the sky already aflare with the city's nocturnal life. 'Outside there,' she thought, 'skyscrapers, advertisements, telephones, wireless, airplanes, movies, motors, and all the rest of the twentieth century; and on the other side of the door something I can't explain, can't relate to them. Something as old as the world, as mysterious as life. . . . Nonsense! What am I worrying about? There hasn't been a letter for three months now—not since the day we came back from the country after Christmas. . . . Queer that they always seem to come after our holidays! . . . Why should I imagine there's going to be one tonight!'

No reason why, but that was the worst of it—one of the worst!—that there were days when she would stand there cold and shivering with the premonition of something inexplicable, intolerable, to be faced on the other side of the curtained panes; and when she opened the door and went in, there would be nothing; and on other days when she felt the same premonitory chill, it was justified by the sight of the grey envelope. so that ever since the last had come she had taken to feeling cold and premonitory every evening, because she never opened the door without thinking the letter might be there.

Well, she'd had enough of it: that was certain. She couldn't go on like that. If her husband turned white and had a headache on the days when the letter came, he seemed to recover afterward; but she couldn't. With her the strain had become chronic, and the reason was not far to seek. Her husband knew from whom the letter came and what was in it; he was prepared beforehand for whatever he had to deal with, and master of the situation, however bad; whereas she was shut out in the dark with her conjectures.

'I can't stand it! I can't stand it another day!' she exclaimed aloud, as she put her key in the lock. She turned the key and went in; and there on the table, lay the letter.

II

She was almost glad of the sight. It seemed to justify everything, to put a seal of definiteness on the whole blurred business. A letter for her husband: a letter from a woman—no doubt another vulgar case of 'old entanglement.' What a fool she had been ever to doubt it, to rack her brains for less obvious explanations! She took up the envelope with a steady contemptuous hand, looked closely at the faint letters, held it against the light and just discerned the outline of the folded sheet within. She knew that now she would have no peace till she found out what was written on that sheet.

Her husband had not come in; he seldom got back from his office before half-past six or seven, and it was not yet six. She would have time to take the letter up to the drawing room, hold it over the kettle which at that hour always simmered by the fire in expectation of her return, solve the mystery and replace the letter where she had found it. No one would be the wiser, and her gnawing uncertainty would be over. The alternative, of course, was to question her husband; but to do that seemed even more difficult. She weighed the letter between thumb and finger, looked at it again under the light, started up the stairs with the envelope—and came down again and laid it on the table.

'No, I evidently can't,' she said, disappointed.

What should she do, then? She couldn't go up alone to that warm welcoming room, pour out her tea, look over her correspondence, glance at a book or review—not with that letter lying below and the knowledge that in a little while her husband would come in, open it and turn into the library alone, as he always did on the days when the grey envelope came.

Suddenly she decided. she would wait in the library and see for herself; see what happened between him and the letter when they thought themselves unobserved. She wondered the idea had never occurred to her before. By leaving the door ajar, and sitting in the corner behind it, she could watch him unseen. . . Well, then, she would watch him! She drew a chair into the corner, sat down, her eyes on the crack, and waited.

As far as she could remember, it was the first time she had ever tried to surprise another person's secret, but she was conscious of no compunction. She simply felt as if she were fighting her way through a stifling fog that she must at all costs get out of.

At length she heard Kenneth's latchkey and jumped up. The impulse to rush out and meet him had nearly made her forget why she was there; but she remembered in time and sat down again. From her post she covered the whole range of his movements—saw him enter the hall, draw the key from the door and take off his hat and overcoat. Then he turned to throw his gloves on the hall table, and at that moment he saw the envelope. The light was full on his face, and what Charlotte first noted there was a look of surprise. Evidently he had not expected the letter—had not thought of the possibility of its being there that day. But though he had not expected it, now that he saw it he knew well enough what it contained. He did not open it immediately, but stood motionless, the color slowly ebbing from his face. Apparently he could not make up his mind to touch it; but at length he put out his hand, opened the envelope, and moved with it to the light. In doing so he turned his back on Charlotte, and she saw only his bent head and slightly stooping shoulders. Apparently all the writing was on one page, for he did not turn the sheet but continued to stare at it for so long that he must have reread it a dozen times—or so it seemed to the woman breathlessly watching him. At length she saw him move; he raised the letter still closer to his eyes, as though he had not fully deciphered it. Then he lowered his head, and she saw his lips touch the sheet.

'Kenneth!' she exclaimed, and went on out into the hall.

The letter clutched in his hand, her husband turned and looked at her. 'Where were you?' he said, in a low bewildered voice, like a man waked out of his sleep.

'In the library, waiting for you.' She tried to steady her voice: 'What's the matter! What's in that letter? You look ghastly.'

Her agitation seemed to calm him, and he instantly put the envelope into his pocket with a slight laugh. 'Ghastly? I'm sorry. I've had a hard day in the office—one or two complicated cases. I look dog-tired, I suppose.'

'You didn't look tired when you came in. It was only when you opened that letter—'

He had followed her into the library, and they stood gazing at each other. Charlotte noticed how quickly he had regained his self-control; his profession had trained him to rapid mastery of face and voice. She saw at once that she would be at a disadvantage in any attempt to surprise his secret, but at the same moment she lost all desire to maneuver, to trick him into betraying anything he wanted to conceal. Her wish was still to penetrate the mystery, but only that she might help him to bear the burden it implied. 'Even if it *is* another woman,' she thought.

'Kenneth,' she said, her heart beating excitedly, 'I waited here on purpose to see you come in. I wanted to watch you while you opened that letter.'

His face, which had paled, turned to dark red; then it paled again. 'That letter? Why especially that letter?'

'Because I've noticed that whenever one of those letters comes it seems to have such a strange effect on you.'

A line of anger she had never seen before came out between his eyes, and she said to herself: 'The upper part of his face is too narrow; this is the first time I ever noticed it.'

She heard him continue, in the cool and faintly ironic tone of the prosecuting lawyer making a point: 'Ah, so you're in the habit of watching people open their letters when they don't know you're there?'

'Not in the habit. I never did such a thing before. But I had to find out what she writes to you, at regular intervals, in those grey envelopes.'

He weighed this for a moment; then: 'The intervals have not been regular,' he said.

'Oh, I dare say you've kept a better account of the dates than I have,' she retorted, her magnanimity vanishing at his tone. 'All I know is that every time that woman writes to you—'

'Why do you assume it's a woman?'

'It's a woman's writing. Do you deny it?'

He smiled. 'No, I don't deny it. I asked only because the writing is generally supposed to look more like a man's.'

Charlotte passed this over impatiently. 'And this woman—what does she write to you about?'

Again he seemed to consider a moment. 'About business.'

'Legal business?'

'In a way, yes. Business in general.'

'You look after her affairs for her?'

'Yes.'

'You've looked after them for a long time?'

'Yes. A very long time.'

'Kenneth, dearest, won't you tell me who she is?'

'No. I can't.' He paused, and brought out, as if with a certain hesitation: 'Professional secrecy.'

The blood rushed from Charlotte's heart to her temples. 'Don't say that— don't!'

'Why not?'

'Because I saw you kiss the letter.'

The effect of the words was so disconcerting that she instantly repented having spoken them. Her husband, who had submitted to her cross-questioning with a sort of contemptuous composure, as though he were humoring an unreasonable child, turned on her a face of terror and distress. For a minute he seemed unable to speak; then, collecting himself, with an effort, he stammered out: 'The writing is very faint; you must have seen me holding the letter close to my eyes to try to decipher it.'

'No; I saw you kissing it.' He was silent. 'Didn't I see you kissing it?'

He sank back into indifference. 'Perhaps.'

'What possible difference can it make to you? The letter is on business, as I told you. Do you suppose I'd lie about it? The writer is a very old friend whom I haven't seen for a long time.'

'Men don't kiss business letters, even from women who are very old friends, unless they have been their lovers, and still regret them.'

He shrugged his shoulders slightly and turned away, as if he considered the discussion at an end and were faintly disgusted at the turn it had taken.

'Kenneth!' Charlotte moved toward him and caught hold of his arm.

He paused with a look of weariness and laid his hand over hers. 'Won't you believe me?' he asked gently.

'How can I? I've watched these letters come to you—for months now they've been coming. Ever since we came back from the West Indies—one of them greeted me the very day we arrived. And after each one of them I see their mysterious effect on you, I see you disturbed, unhappy, as if someone were trying to estrange you from me.'

'No, dear; not that. Never!'

She drew back and looked at him with passionate entreaty. 'Well, then, prove it to me, darling. It's so easy!'

He forced a smile. 'It's not easy to prove anything to a woman who's once taken an idea into her head.'

'You've only got to show me the letter.'

His hand slipped from hers and he drew back and shook his head.

'You won't?'

'I can't.'

'Then the woman who wrote it is your mistress.'

'No, dear. No.'

'Not now, perhaps. I suppose she's trying to get you back, and you're struggling, out of pity for me. My poor Kenneth!'

'I swear to you she never was my mistress.'

Charlotte felt the tears rushing to her eyes. 'Ah, that's worse, then—that's hopeless! The prudent ones are the kind that keep their hold on a man. We all know that.' She lifted her hands and hid her face in them.

Her husband remained silent; he offered neither consolation nor denial, and at length, wiping away her tears, she raised her eyes almost timidly to his.

'Kenneth, think! We've been married such a short time. Imagine what you're making me suffer. You say you can't show me this letter. You refuse even to explain it.'

'I've told you the letter is on business. I will swear to that too.'

'A man will swear to anything to screen a woman. If you want me to believe you, at least tell me her name. If you'll do that, I promise you I won't ask to see the letter.'

There was a long interval of suspense, during which she felt her heart beating against her ribs in quick admonitory knocks, as if warning her of the danger she was incurring.

'I can't,' he said at length.

'Not even her name?'

'No.'

'You can't tell me anything more?'

'No.'

Again a pause; this time they seemed both to have reached the end of their arguments and to be helplessly facing each other across a baffling waste of incomprehension.

Charlotte stood breathing rapidly, her hands against her breast. She felt as if she had run a hard race and missed the goal. She had meant to move her husband and had succeeded only in irritating him; and this error of reckoning seemed to change him into a stranger, a mysterious incomprehensible being whom no argument or entreaty of hers could reach. The curious thing was that she was aware in him of no hostility or even impatience, but only of a remoteness, an inaccessibility, far more difficult to overcome. She felt herself excluded, ignored, blotted out of his life. But after a moment or two, looking at him more calmly, she saw that he was suffering as much as she was. His distant guarded face was drawn with pain; the coming of the grey envelope, though it always cast a shadow, had never marked him as deeply as this discussion with his wife.

Charlotte took heart; perhaps, after all, she had not spent her last shaft. She drew nearer and once more laid her hand on his arm. 'Poor Kenneth! If you knew how sorry I am for you—'

She thought he winced slightly at this expression of sympathy, but he took her hand and pressed it.

'I can think of nothing worse than to be incapable of loving long,' she continued, 'to feel the beauty of a great love and to be too unstable to bear its burden.'

He turned on her a look of wistful reproach. 'Oh, don't say that of me. Unstable!'

She felt herself at last on the right tack, and her voice trembled with excitement as she went on: 'Then what about me and this other woman? Haven't you already forgotten Elsie twice within a year?'

She seldom pronounced his first wife's name; it did not come naturally to her tongue. She flung it out now as if she were flinging some dangerous explosive into the open space between them, and drew back a step, waiting to hear the mine go off.

Her husband did not move; his expression grew sadder, but showed no resentment. 'I have never forgotten Elsie,' he said.

Charlotte could not repress a faint laugh. 'Then, you poor dear, between the three of us—'

'There are not—' he began; and then broke off and put his hand to his forehead.

'Not what?'

'I'm sorry; I don't believe I know what I'm saying. I've got a blinding headache.' He looked wan and furrowed enough for the statement to be true, but she was exasperated by his evasion.

'Ah, yes; the grey envelope headache!'

She saw the surprise in his eyes. 'I'd forgotten how closely I've been watched,' he said coldly. 'If you'll excuse me, I think I'll go up and try an hour in the dark, to see if I can get rid of this neuralgia.'

She wavered; then she said, with desperate resolution: I'm sorry your head aches. But before you go I want to say that sooner or later this question must be settled between us. Someone is trying to separate us, and I don't care what it costs me to find out who it is.' She looked him steadily in the eyes. 'If it costs me your love, I don't care! If I can't have your confidence I don't want anything from you.'

He still looked at her wistfully. 'Give me time.'

'Time for what? It's only a word to say.'

'Time to show you that you haven't lost my love or my confidence.'

'Well, I'm waiting.'

He turned toward the door, and then glanced back hesitatingly. 'Oh, do wait, my love.' he said, and went out of the room.

She heard his tired step on the stairs and the closing of his bedroom door above. Then she dropped into a chair and buried her face in her folded arms. Her first movement was one of compunction; she seemed to herself to have been hard, unhuman, unimaginative. 'Think of telling him that I didn't care if my insistence cost me his love! The lying rubbish!' She started up to follow him and unsay the meaningless words. But she was checked by a reflection. He had had his way, after all; he had eluded all attacks on his secret, and now he was shut up alone in his room, reading that other woman's letter.

III

She was still reflecting on this when the surprised parlormaid came in and found her. No, Charlotte said, she wasn't going to dress for dinner; Mr. Ashby didn't want to dine. He was very tired and had gone up to his room to rest; later she would have something brought on a tray to the drawing room. She mounted the stairs to her bedroom. Her dinner dress was lying on the bed, and at the sight the quiet routine of her daily life took hold of her and she began to feel as if the strange talk she had just had with her husband must have taken place in another world, between two beings who were not Charlotte Gorse and Kenneth Ashby, but phantoms projected by her fevered imagination. She recalled the year since her marriage—her husband's constant devotion: his persistent, almost too insistent tenderness: the feeling he had given her at times of being too eagerly dependent on her, too searchingly close to her, as if there were not air enough between her soul and his. It seemed preposterous, as she recalled all this, that a few moments ago she should have been accusing him of an intrigue with another woman! But then, what—

Again she was moved by the impulse to go up to him, beg his pardon and try to laugh away the misunderstanding. But she was restrained by the fear of forcing herself upon his privacy. He was troubled and unhappy, oppressed by some grief or fear; and he had shown her that he wanted to fight out his battle alone. It would be wiser, as well as more generous, to respect his wish. Only, how strange, how unbearable, to be there, in the next room to his, and feel herself at the other end of the world! In her nervous agitation she almost regretted not having had the courage to open the letter and put it back on the hall table before he came in. At least she would have known what his secret was, and the bogy might have been laid. For she was beginning now to think of the mystery as something conscious, malevolent: a secret persecution before which he quailed, yet from which he could not free himself. Once or twice in his evasive eyes she thought she had detected a desire for help, an impulse of confession, instantly restrained and suppressed. It was as if he felt she could have helped him if she had known, and yet had been unable to tell her!

There flashed through her mind the idea of going to his mother. She was very fond of old Mrs. Ashby, a firm-fleshed clear-eyed old lady, with an astringent bluntness of speech which responded to the forthright and simple in Charlotte's own nature. There had been a tacit bond between them ever since the day when Mrs. Ashby Senior, coming to lunch for the first time with her new daughter-in-law, had been received by Charlotte downstairs in the library, and glancing up at the empty wall above her son's desk, had remarked laconically: 'Elsie gone, eh?' adding, at Charlotte's murmured explanation: 'Nonsense. Don't have her back. Two's company.' Charlotte, at this reading of her thoughts, could hardly refrain from exchanging a smile of complicity with her mother-in-law; and it seemed to her now that Mrs. Ashby's almost uncanny directness might pierce to the core of this new mystery. But here again she hesitated, for the idea almost suggested a betrayal. What right had she to call in anyone, even so close a relation, to surprise a secret which her husband was trying to keep from her? 'Perhaps, by and by, he'll talk to his mother of his own accord,' she thought, and then ended: 'But what does it matter? He and I must settle it between us.'

She was still brooding over the problem when there was a knock on the door and her husband came in. He was dressed for dinner and seemed surprised to see her sitting there, with her evening dress lying unheeded on the bed.

'Aren't you coming down?'

'I thought you were not well and had gone to bed,' she faltered.

He forced a smile. 'I'm not particularly well, but we'd better go down.' His face, though still drawn, looked calmer than when he had fled upstairs an hour earlier.

'There it is; he knows what's in the letter and has fought his battle out again, whatever it is,' she reflected, 'while I'm still in darkness.' She rang and gave a hurried order that dinner should be served as soon as possible—just a short meal, whatever could be got ready quickly, as both she and Mr. Ashby were rather tired and not very hungry.

Dinner was announced, and they sat down to it. At first neither seemed able to find a word to say; then Ashby began to make conversation with an assumption of ease that was more oppressive than his silence. 'How tired he is! How terribly overtired!' Charlotte said to herself, pursuing her own thoughts while he rambled on about municipal politics, aviation, and an exhibition of modern French painting, the health of an old aunt and the installing of the automatic telephone. 'Good heavens, how tired he is!'

When they dined alone they usually went into the library after dinner, and Charlotte curled herself up on the divan with her knitting while he lit a pipe. But this evening, by tacit agreement, they avoided the room in which their strange talk had taken place, and went up to Charlotte's room.

They sat down near the fire, and Charlotte said: 'Your pipe?' after he had put down his hardly tasted coffee.

He shook his head. 'No, not tonight.'

'You must go to bed early; you look terribly tired. I'm sure they overwork you at the office.'

'I suppose we all overwork at times.'

She rose and stood before him with sudden resolution. 'Well, I'm not going to have you use up your strength slaving in that way. It's absurd. I can see you're ill.' She bent over him and laid her hand on his forehead. 'My poor old Kenneth. Prepare to be taken away soon on a long holiday.'

He looked up at her startled. 'A holiday?'

'Certainly. Didn't you know I was going to carry you off at Easter? We're going to start in a fortnight on a month's voyage to somewhere or other. On any one of the big cruising steamers.' She paused and bent closer, touching his forehead with her lips. 'I'm tired, too, Kenneth.'

He seemed to pay no heed to her last words, but sat, his hands on his knees, his head drawn back a little from her caress, and looked up at her with a stare of apprehension. 'Again? My dear, we can't; I can't possibly go away.'

'I don't know why you say "again," Kenneth; we haven't taken a real holiday this year.'

'At Christmas we spend a week with the children in the country.'

'Yes, but this time I mean away from the children, from servants, from the house. From everything that's familiar and fatiguing. Your mother will love to have Joyce and Peter with her.'

He frowned and slowly shook his head. 'No, dear; I can't leave them with my mother.'

'Why, Kenneth, how absurd! She adores them. You didn't hesitate to leave them with her for over two months when we went to the West Indies.'

He drew a deep breath and stood up uneasily. 'That was different.'

'Different? Why?'

'I mean, at that time I didn't realize—' He broke off as if to choose his words and then went on: 'My mother adores the children, as you say. But she isn't always very judicious. Grandmothers always spoil children. And sometimes she talks before them without thinking.' He turned to his wife with an almost pitiful gesture of entreaty. 'Don't ask me to, dear.'

Charlotte mused. It was true that the elder Mrs. Ashby had a fearless tongue, but she was the last woman in the world to say or hint anything before her grandchildren at which the most scrupulous parent could take offence. Charlotte looked at her husband in perplexity.

'I don't understand.'

'Not now—not yet.' He put up his hands and pressed them against his temples. 'Can't you see that there's no use in insisting? I can't go away, no matter how much I might want to.'

Charlotte still scrutinized him gravely. 'The question is, *do* you want to?'

He returned her gaze for a moment; then his lips began to tremble, and he said, hardly above his breath: 'I want—anything you want.'

'And yet—'

'Don't ask me. I can't leave—I can't.'

'You mean that you can't go away out of reach of those letters!'

Her husband had been standing before her in an uneasy half-hesitating attitude; now he turned abruptly away and walked once or twice up and down the length of the room, his head bent, his eyes fixed on the carpet.

Charlotte felt her resentfulness rising with her fears. 'It's that,' she persisted. 'Why not admit it? You can't live without them.'

He continued his troubled pacing of the room; then he stopped short, dropped into a chair and covered his face with his hands. From the shaking of his shoulders, Charlotte saw that he was weeping. She had never seen a man cry, except her father after her mother's death, when she was a little girl; and she remembered still how the sight had frightened her. she was frightened now; she felt that her husband was being dragged away from her into some mysterious bondage, and that she must use up her last atom of strength in the struggle for his freedom, and for hers.

'Kenneth—Kenneth!' she pleaded, kneeling down beside him. 'Won't you listen to me? Won't you try to see what I'm suffering? I'm not unreasonable, darling, really not. I don't suppose I should ever have noticed the letters if it hadn't been for their effect on you. It's not my way to pry into other people's affairs; and even if the effect had been different—yes, yes, listen to me—if I'd seen that the letters made you happy, that you were watching eagerly for them, counting the days between their coming, that you wanted them, that they gave you something I haven't known how to give—why, Kenneth, I don't say I shouldn't have suffered from that, too: but it would have been in a different way, and I should have had the courage to hide what I felt, and the hope that someday you'd come to feel about me as you did about the writer of the letters. But what I can't bear is to see how you dread them, how they make you suffer, and yet how you can't live without them and won't go away lest you should miss one during your absence. Or perhaps,' she added, her voice breaking into a cry of accusation—'perhaps it's because she's actually forbidden you to leave. Kenneth, you must answer me! Is that the reason? Is it because she's forbidden you that you won't go away with me?'

She continued to kneel at his side, and raising her hands, she drew his gently down. She was ashamed of her persistence, ashamed of uncovering that baffled disordered face, yet resolved that no such scruples should arrest her. His eyes were lowered, the muscles of his face quivered; she was making him suffer even more than she suffered herself. Yet this no longer restrained her.

'Kenneth, is it that? She won't let us go away together?'

Still he did not speak or turn his eyes to her, and a sense of defeat swept over her. After all, she thought, the struggle was a losing one. 'You needn't answer. I see I'm right,' she said.

Suddenly, as she rose, he turned and drew her down again. His hands caught hers and pressed them so tightly that she felt her rings cutting into her flesh. There was something frightening, convulsive in his hold; it was the clutch of a man who felt himself slipping over a precipice. He was staring up at her now as if salvation lay in the face she bent over him. 'Of course we'll go away together. We'll go wherever you want,' he said in a low confused voice; and putting his arm about her, he drew her close and pressed his lips on hers.

IV

Charlotte had said to herself: 'I shall sleep tonight,' but instead she sat before her fire into the small hours, listening for any sound that came from her husband's room. But he, at any rate, seemed to be resting after the tumult of the evening. Once or twice she stole to the door and in the faint light that came in from the street through his open window she saw him stretched out in heavy sleep—the sleep of weakness and exhaustion. 'He's ill,' she thought—'he's undoubtedly ill. And it's not overwork; it's this mysterious persecution.'

She drew a breath of relief. She had fought through the weary fight and the victory was hers—at least for the moment. If only they could have started at once—started for anywhere! She knew it would be useless to ask him to leave before the holidays; and meanwhile the secret influence—as to which she was still so completely in the dark—would continue to work against her, and she would have to renew the struggle day after day till they started on their journey. But after that everything would be different. If once she could get her husband away under other skies, and all to herself, she never doubted her power to release him from the evil spell he was under. Lulled to quiet by the thought, she too slept at last.

When she woke, it was long past her usual hour, and she sat up in bed surprised and vexed at having overslept herself. She always liked to be down to share her husband's breakfast by the library fire; but a glance at the clock made it clear that he must have started long since for his office. To make sure, she jumped out of bed and went into his room, but it was empty. No doubt he had looked in on her before leaving, seen that she still slept, and gone downstairs without disturbing her; and their relations were sufficiently lover-like for her to regret having missed their morning hour.

She rang and asked if Mr. Ashby had already gone. Yes, nearly an hour ago, the maid said. He had given orders that Mrs. Ashby should not be waked and that the children should not come to her till she sent for them. . . . Yes, he had gone up to the nursery himself to give the order. All this sounded usual enough, and Charlotte hardly knew why she asked: 'And did Mr. Ashby leave no other message?'

Yes, the maid said, he did; she was so sorry she'd forgotten. He'd told her, just as he was leaving, to say to Mrs. Ashby that he was going to see about their passages, and would she please be ready to sail tomorrow?

Charlotte echoed the woman's 'Tomorrow,' and sat staring at her incredulously. 'Tomorrow—you're sure he said to sail tomorrow?'

'Oh, ever so sure, ma'am. I don't know how I could have forgotten to mention it.'

'Well, it doesn't matter, Draw my bath, please.' Charlotte sprang up, dashed through her dressing, and caught herself singing at her image in the glass as she sat brushing her hair. It made her feel young again to have scored such a victory. The other woman vanished to a speck on the horizon, as this one, who ruled the foreground, smiled back at the reflection of her lips and eyes. He loved her, then—he loved her as passionately as ever. He had divined what she had suffered, had understood that their happiness depended on their getting away at once, and finding each other again after yesterday's desperate groping in the fog. The nature of the influence that had come between them did not much matter to Charlotte now; she had faced the phantom and dispelled it. 'Courage—that's the secret! If only people who are in love weren't always so afraid of risking their happiness by looking it in the eyes.' As she brushed back her light abundant hair it waved electrically above her head, like the palms of victory. Ah, well, some women knew how to manage men, and some didn't— and only the fair—she gaily paraphrased—deserve the brave! Certainly she was looking very pretty.

The morning danced along like a cockleshell on a bright sea—such a sea as they would soon be speeding over. She ordered a particularly good dinner, saw the children off to their classes, had her trunks brought down, consulted with the maid about getting out summer clothes—for of course they would be heading for heat and sunshine—and wondered if she oughtn't to take Kenneth's flannel suits out of camphor. 'But how absurd,' she reflected, 'that I don't yet know where we're going!' She looked at the clock, saw that it was close to noon and decided to call him up at his office. There was a slight delay; then she heard his secretary's voice saying that Mr. Ashby had looked in for a moment early, and left again almost immediately. . . . Oh, very well; Charlotte would ring up later. How soon was he likely to be back? The secretary answered that she couldn't tell; all they knew in the office was that when he left he had said he was in a hurry because he had to go out of town.

Out of town! Charlotte hung up the receiver and sat blankly gazing into new darkness. Why had he gone out of town? And where had he gone? And of all days, why should he have chosen the eve of their suddenly planned departure? She felt a faint shiver of apprehension. Of course he had gone to see that woman—no doubt to get her permission to leave. He was as completely in bondage as that; and Charlotte had been fatuous enough to see the palms of victory on her forehead. She burst into a laugh and, walking across the room, sat down again before her mirror. What a different face she saw! The smile on her pale lips seemed to mock the rosy vision of the other Charlotte. But gradually her colour crept back. After all, she had a right to claim the victory, since her

THE BOOK OF FANTASY

husband was doing what she wanted, not what the other woman exacted of him. It was natural enough, in view of his abrupt decision to leave the next day, that he should have arrangements to make, business matters to wind up; it was not even necessary to suppose that his mysterious trip was a visit to the writer of the letters. He might simply have gone to see a client who lived out of town. Of course they would not tell Charlotte at the office; the secretary had hesitated before imparting even such meagre imformation as the fact of Mr. Ashby's absence. Meanwhile she would go on with her joyful preparations, content to learn later in the day to what particular island of the blest she was to be carried.

The hours wore on, or rather were swept forward on a rush of eager preparations. At last the entrance of the maid who came to draw the curtain roused Charlotte from her labours, and she saw to her surprise that the clock marked five. And she did not yet know where they were going the next day! She rang up her husband's office and was told that Mr. Ashby had not been there since the early morning. She asked for his partner, but the partner could add nothing to her information, for he himself, his suburban train having been behind time, had reached the office after Ashby had come and gone. Charlotte stood perplexed; then she decided to telephone to her mother-in-law. Of course Kenneth, on the eve of a month's absence, must have gone to see his mother. The mere fact that the children—in spite of his vague objections—would certainly have to be left with old Mrs. Ashby, made it obvious that he would have all sorts of matters to decide with her. At another time Charlotte might have felt a little hurt at being excluded from their conference, but nothing mattered now but that she had won the day, that her husband was still hers and not another woman's. Gaily she called up Mrs. Ashby, heard her friendly voice, and began: 'Well, did Kenneth's news surprise you? What do you think of our elopement?'

Almost instantly, before Mrs. Ashby could answer, Charlotte knew what her reply would be. Mrs. Ashby had not seen her son, she had had no word from him and did not know what her daughter-in-law meant. Charlotte stood silent in the intensity of her surprise. 'But then, where *has* he been?' she thought. Then, recovering herself, she explained their sudden decision to Mrs. Ashby, and in doing so, gradually regained her own self-confidence, her conviction that nothing could ever again come between Kenneth and herself. Mrs. Ashby took the news calmly and approvingly. She, too, had thought that Kenneth looked worried and overtired, and she agreed with her daughter-in-law that in such cases change was the surest remedy. 'I'm always so glad when he gets away. Elsie hated travelling; she was always finding pretexts to prevent his going anywhere. With you, thank goodness, it's different.' Nor was Mrs. Ashby surprised at his not having had time to let her know of his departure. He must have been in a rush from the moment the decision was taken; but no doubt he'd drop in before dinner. Five minutes' talk was really all they needed. 'I hope you'll gradually cure Kenneth of his mania for going over and over a question that could be settled in a dozen words. He never used to be like that, and if he carried the habit into his professional work he'd soon lose all his clients. . . . Yes, do come in for a minute, dear, if you have time; no doubt he'll turn up while you're here.' The tonic ring of Mrs. Ashby's voice echoed on reassuringly in the silent room while Charlotte continued her preparations.

Toward seven the telephone rang, and she darted to it. Now she would know! But it was only from the conscientious secretary, to say that Mr. Ashby hadn't been back, or sent any word, and before the office closed she thought she ought to let Mrs. Ashby know. 'Oh, that's all right. Thanks a lot! Charlotte called out cheerfully, and hung up the receiver with a trembling hand. But perhaps by this time, she reflected, he was at his mother's. She shut her drawers and cupboards, put on her hat and coat and called up to the nursery that she was going out for a minute to see the children's grandmother.

Mrs. Ashby lived nearby, and during her brief walk through the cold spring dusk Charlotte imagined that every advancing figure was her husband's. But she did not meet him on the way, and when she entered the house she found her mother-in-law alone. Kenneth had neither telephoned nor come. Old Mrs. Ashby sat by her bright fire, her knitting needles flashing steadily through her active old hands, and her mere bodily presence gave reassurance to Charlotte. Yes, it was certainly odd that Kenneth had gone off for the whole day without letting any of them know; but, after all, it was to be expected. A busy lawyer held so many threads in his hands that any sudden change of plan would oblige him to make all sorts of unforeseen arrangements and adjustments. He might have gone to see some client in the suburbs and been detained there: his mother remembered his telling her that he had charge of the legal business of a queer old recluse somewhere in New Jersey, who was immensely rich but too mean to have a telephone. Very likely Kenneth had been stranded there.

But Charlotte felt her nervousness gaining on her. When Mrs. Ashby asked her at what hour they were sailing the next day and she had to say she didn't know—that Kenneth had simply sent her word he was going to take their passages—the uttering of the words again brought home to her the strangeness of the situation. Even Mrs. Ashby conceded that it was odd; but she immediately added that it only showed what a rush he was in.

'But, mother, it's nearly eight o'clock! He must realize that I've got to know when we're starting tomorrow.'

'Oh, the boat probably doesn't sail till evening. Sometimes they have to wait till midnight for the tide. Kenneth's probably counting on that. After all, he has a level head.'

Charlotte stood up. 'It's not that. Something has happened to him.'

Mrs. Ashby took off her spectacles and rolled up her knitting. 'If you begin to let yourself imagine things—'

'Aren't you in the least anxious?'

'I never am till I have to be. I wish you'd ring for dinner, my dear. You'll stay and dine? He's sure to drop in here on his way home.'

Charlotte called up her own house. No, the maid said, Mr. Ashby hadn't come in and hadn't telephoned. She would tell him as soon as he came that Mrs. Ashby was dining at his mother's. Charlotte followed her mother-in-law into the dining room and sat with parched throat before her empty plate, while Mrs, Ashby dealt calmly and efficiently with a short but carefully prepared repast.

'You'd better eat something, child, or you'll be as bad as Kenneth. . . . Yes, a little more asparagus, please, Jane.'

She insisted on Charlotte's drinking a glass of sherry and nibbling a bit of toast; then they returned to the drawing room, where the fire had been made up, and cushions in Mrs. Ashby's armchair shaken out and smoothed. How safe and familiar it all looked; and out there, somewhere in the uncertainty and mystery of the night, lurked the answer to the two women's conjectures, like an indistinguishable figure prowling on the threshold. At last Charlotte got up and said: 'I'd better go back. At this hour Kenneth will certainly go straight home.'

Mrs. Ashby smiled indulgently. 'It's not very late, my dear. It doesn't take two sparrows long to dine.'

'It's after nine.' Charlotte bent down to kiss her. 'The fact is, I can't keep still.'

Mrs. Ashby pushed aside her work and rested her two hands on the arms of her chair. 'I'm going with you,' she said, helping herself up.

Charlotte protested that it was too late, that it was not necessary, that she would call up as soon as Kenneth came in, but Mrs. Ashby had already rung for her maid. She was slightly lame, and stood resting on her stick while her wraps were brought. 'If Mr. Kenneth turns up, tell him he'll find me at his own house,' she instructed the maid as the two women got into the taxi which had been summoned. During the short drive Charlotte gave thanks that she was not returning home alone. There was something warm and substantial in the mere fact of Mrs. Ashby's nearness, something that corresponded with the clearness of her eyes and the texture of her fresh firm complexion. As the taxi drew up she laid her hand encouragingly on Charlotte's. 'You'll see; there'll be a message.'

The door opened at Charlotte's ring and the two entered. Charlotte's heart beat excitedly; the stimulus of her mother-in-law's confidence was beginning to flow through her veins.

'You'll see—you'll see,' Mrs. Ashby repeated.

The maid who opened the door said no, Mr. Ashby had not come in, and there had been no message from him.

'You're sure the telephone's not out of order?' his mother suggested; and the maid said, well, it certainly wasn't half an hour ago; but she'd just go and ring up to make sure. She disappeared, and Charlotte turned to take off her hat and cloak. As she did so her eyes lit on the hall table, and there lay a grey envelope, her husband's name faintly traced on it. 'Oh!' she cried out, suddenly aware that for the first time in months she had entered her house without wondering if one of the grey letters would be there.

'What is it, my dear?' Mrs. Ashby asked with a glance of surprise.

Charlotte did not answer. She took up the envelope and stood staring at it as if she could force her gaze to penetrate to what was within. Then an idea occurred to her. She turned and held out the envelope to her mother-in-law.

'Do you know that writing?' she asked.

Mrs. Ashby took the letter. She had to feel with her other hand for her eyeglasses, and when she had adjusted them she lifted the envelope to the light. 'Why!' she exclaimed; and then stopped. Charlotte noticed that the letter shook in her usually firm hand. 'But this is addressed to Kenneth,' Mrs. Ashby said at length, in a low voice. Her tone seemed to imply that she felt her daughter-in-law's question to be slightly indiscreet.

'Yes, but no matter,' Charlotte spoke with sudden decision. 'I want to know—do you know the writing?'

Mrs. Ashby handed back the letter. 'No,' she said distinctly.

The two women had turned into the library. Charlotte switched on the electric light and shut the door. She still held the envelope in her hand.

'I'm going to open it,' she announced.

She caught her mother-in-law's startled glance. 'But, dearest—a letter not addressed to you? My dear, you can't!'

'As if I cared about that—now!' She continued to look intently at Mrs. Ashby. 'This letter may tell me where Kenneth is.'

Mrs. Ashby's glossy bloom was effaced by a quick pallor; her firm cheeks seemed to shrink and wither. 'Why should it? What makes you believe—It can't possibly—'

Charlotte held her eyes steadily on that altered face. 'Ah, then you *do* know the writing?' she flashed back.

'Know the writing? How should I? With all my son's correspondents. . . . What I do know is—' Mrs. Ashby broke off and looked at her daughter-in-law entreatingly, almost timidly.

Charlotte caught her by the wrist. 'Mother! What do you know? Tell me! You must!'

'That I don't believe any good ever came of a woman's opening her husband's letters behind his back.'

The words sounded to Charlotte's irritated ears as flat as a phrase culled from a book of moral axioms. She laughed impatiently and dropped her mother-in-law's wrist. 'Is that all? No good can come of this letter, opened or unopened. I know that well enough. But whatever ill comes, I mean to find out what's in it.' Her hands had been trembling as they held the envelope, but now they grew firm, and her voice also. She still gazed intently at Mrs. Ashby. 'This is the ninth letter addressed in the same hand that has come to Kenneth since we've been married. Always these same grey envelopes. I've kept count of them because after each one he has been like a man who has had some dreadful shock. It takes him hours to shake off their effect. I've told him so. I've told him I must know from whom they come, because I can see they're killing him. He won't answer my questions; he promised to go away with me—to get away from them.'

Mrs. Ashby, with shaking steps, had gone to one of the armchairs and sat down in it, her head drooping forward on her breast. 'Ah,' she murmured.

'So now you understand—'

'Did he tell you it was to get away from them?'

'He said, to get away—to get away. He was sobbing so that he could hardly speak. But I told him I knew that was why.'

'And what did he say?'

'He took me in his arms and said he'd go wherever I wanted.'

'Ah, thank God!' said Mrs. Ashby. There was a silence, during which she continued to sit with head bowed, and eyes averted from her daughter-in-law. At last she looked up and spoke. 'Are you sure there have been as many as nine?'

'Perfectly. This is the ninth. I've kept count.'

'And he has absolutely refused to explain?'

'Absolutely.'

Mrs. Ashby spoke through pale contracted lips. 'When did they begin to come? Do you remember?'

Charlotte laughed again. 'Remember? The first one came the night we got back from our honeymoon.'

'All that time?' Mrs. Ashby lifted her head and spoke with sudden energy. 'Then—yes, open it.'

The words were so unexpected that Charlotte felt the blood in her temples, and her hands began to tremble again. She tried to slip her finger under the flap of the envelope, but it was so tightly stuck that she had to hunt on her husband's writing table for his ivory letter opener. As she pushed about the familiar objects his own hands had so lately touched, they sent through her the icy chill emanating from the little personal effects of someone newly dead. In the deep silence of the room the tearing of the paper as she slit the envelope sounded like a human cry. She drew out the sheet and carried it to the lamp.

'Well?' Mrs. Ashby asked below her breath.

Charlotte did not move or answer. She was bending over the page with wrinkled brows, holding it nearer and nearer to the light. Her sight must be blurred, or else dazzled by the reflection of the lamplight on the smooth surface of the paper, for, strain her eyes as she would, she could discern only a few faint strokes, so faint and faltering as to be nearly undecipherable.

'I can't make it out,' she said.

'What do you mean, dear?'

'The writing's too indistinct. . . . Wait.'

She went back to the table and, sitting down close to Kenneth's reading lamp, slipped the letter under a magnifying glass. All this time she was aware that her mother-in-law was watching her intently.

'Well, it's no clearer. I can't read it.'

'You mean the paper is an absolute blank?'

'No, not quite. There is writing on it. I can make out something like "mine"—oh, and "come." It might be "come".'

Mrs. Ashby stood up abruptly. Her face was even paler than before. She advanced to the table and, resting her two hands on it, drew a deep breath. 'Let me see,' she said, as if forcing herself to a hateful effort.

Charlotte felt the contagion of her whiteness. 'She knows', she thought. She pushed the letter across the table. Her mother-in-law lowered her head over it in silence, but without touching it with her pale wrinkled hands.

Charlotte stood watching her as she herself, when she had tried to read the letter, had been watched by Mrs. Ashby. The latter fumbled for her eyeglasses, held them to her eyes, and bent still closer to the outspread page, in order, as it seemed, to avoid touching it. The light of the lamp fell directly on her old face, and Charlotte reflected what depths of the unknown may lurk under the clearest and most candid lineaments. She had never seen her mother-in-law's features express any but simple and sound emotions—cordiality, amusement, a kindly sympathy; now and again a flash of wholesome anger. Now they seemed to wear a look of fear and hatred, of incredulous dismay and almost cringing defiance. It was as if the spirits warring within her had distorted her face to their own likeness. At length she raised her head. 'I can't—I can't,' she said in a voice of childish distress.

'You can't make it out either?'

She shook her head, and Charlotte saw two tears roll down her cheeks.

'Familiar as the writing is to you?' Charlotte insisted with twitching lips.

Mrs. Ashby did not take up the challenge. 'I can make out nothing—nothing.'

'But you do know the writing?'

Mrs. Ashby lifted her head timidly; her anxious eyes stole with a glance of apprehension around the quite familiar room. 'How can I tell? I was startled at first. . . .'

'Startled by the resemblance?'

'Well, I thought—'

'You'd better say it out, mother! You knew at once it was *her* writing?'

'Oh, wait, my dear,—wait.'

'Wait for what?'

Mrs. Ashby looked up; her eyes, travelling slowly past Charlotte, were lifted to the blank wall behind her son's writing table.

Charlotte, following the glance, burst into a shrill laugh of accusation. 'I needn't wait any longer! You've answered me now! You're looking straight at the wall where her picture used to hang!'

Mrs. Ashby lifted her hand with a murmur of warning. 'Sh-h.'

'Oh, you needn't imagine that anything can ever frighten me again!' Charlotte cried.

Her mother-in-law still leaned against the table. Her lips moved plaintively. 'But we're going mad—we're both going mad. We both know such things are impossible.'

Her daughter-in-law looked at her with a pitying stare. 'I've known for a long time now that everything was possible.'

'Even this?'

'Yes, exactly this.'

'But this letter—after all, there's nothing in this letter—'

'Perhaps there would be to him. How can I tell? I remember his saying to me once that if you were used to a handwriting the faintest stroke of it became legible. Now I see what he meant. He *was* used to it.'

'But the few strokes that I can make out are so pale. No one could possibly read that letter.'

Charlotte laughed again. 'I suppose everything's pale about a ghost,' she said stridently.

'Oh, my child—my child—don't say it!'

'Why shouldn't I say it, when even the bare walls cry it out? What difference does it make if her letters are illegible to you and me? If even you can see her face on that blank wall, why shouldn't he read her writing on this blank paper? Don't you see that she's everywhere in this house, and the closer to him because to everyone else she's become invisible?' Charlotte dropped into a chair and covered her face with her hands. A turmoil of sobbing shook her head to foot. At length a touch on her shoulder made her look up, and she saw her mother-in-law bending over her. Mrs. Ashby's face seemed to have grown still smaller and more wasted, but it had resumed its usual quiet look. Through all her tossing anguish, Charlotte felt the impact of that resolute spirit.

'Tomorrow—tomorrow. You'll see. There'll be some explanation tomorrow.'

Charlotte cut her short. 'An explanation? Who's going to give it, I wonder?'

Mrs. Ashby drew back and straightened herself heroically. 'Kenneth himself will,' she cried out in a strong voice. Charlotte said nothing, and the old woman went on: 'But meanwhile we must act; we must notify the police. Now, without a moment's delay. We must do everything—everything.'

Charlotte stood up slowly and stiffly; her joints felt as cramped as an old woman's. 'Exactly as if we thought it could do any good to do anything?'

Resolutely Mrs. Ashby cried: 'Yes!' and Charlotte went up to the telephone and unhooked the receiver.

Lukundoo

Edward Lucas White *(1866-1934) was born in Bergen, New Jersey, but spent most of his life in Baltimore, attending Johns Hopkins University. He wrote poems and historical novels such as* El Supremo *and* Andivius Hedulio, *as well as fantasy and horror stories, which he said came to him in dreams.*

'It stands to reason,' said Twombly, 'that a man must accept the evidence of his own eyes, and when eyes and ears agree, there can be no doubt. He has to believe what he has both seen and heard.'

'Not always,' put in Singleton, softly.

Every man turned towards Singleton. Twombly was standing on the hearthrug, his back to the grate, his legs spread out, with his habitual air of dominating the room. Singleton, as usual, was as much as possible effaced in a corner. But when Singleton spoke he said something. We faced him in that flattering spontaneity of expectant silence which invites utterance.

'I was thinking,' he said, after an interval, 'of something I both saw and heard in Africa.'

Now, if there was one thing we had found impossible, it had been to elicit from Singleton anything definite about his African experiences. As with the Alpinist in the story, who could tell only that he went up and came down, the sum of Singleton's revelations had been that he went there and came away. His words now riveted our attention at once. Twombly faded from the hearthrug, but not one of us could ever recall having seen him go. The room readjusted itself, focused on Singleton, and there was some hasty and furtive lighting of fresh cigars. Singleton lit one also, but it went out immediately, and he never relit it.

I

We were in the Great Forest, exploring for pigmies. Van Rieten had a theory that the dwarfs found by Stanley and others were a mere cross-breed between ordinary negroes and the real pigmies. He hoped to discover a race of men three feet tall at most, or shorter. We had found no trace of any such beings.

Natives were few, game scarce; food, except game, there was none; and the deepest, dankest, drippingest forest all about. We were the only novelty in the country, no native we met had even seen a white man before, most had never heard of white men. All of a sudden, late one afternoon, there came into our camp an Englishman, and pretty well used up he was, too. We had heard no rumour of him; he had not only heard of us but had made an amazing five-day march to reach us. His guide and two bearers were nearly as done up as he. Even though he was in tatters and had five days' beard on, you could see he was naturally dapper and neat and the sort of man to shave daily. He was small, but wiry. His face was the sort of British face from which emotion has been so carefully banished that a foreigner is apt to think the wearer of the face incapable of any sort of feeling; the kind of face which, if it has any expression at all, expresses principally the resolution to go through the world decorously, without intruding upon or annoying anyone.

His name was Etcham. He introduced himself modestly, and ate with us so deliberately that we should never have suspected, if our bearers had not had it from his bearers, that he had had but three meals in the five days, and those small. After we had lit up he told us why he had come.

'My chief is ve'y seedy,' he said between puffs. 'He is bound to go out if he keeps this way. I thought perhaps . . .'

He spoke quietly in a soft, even tone, but I could see little beads of sweat oozing out on his upper lip under his stubby moustache, and there was a tingle of repressed emotion in his tone, a veiled eagerness in his eye, a palpitating inward solicitude in his demeanour that moved me at once. Van Rieten had no sentiment in him; if he was moved he did not show it. But he listened. I was surprised at that. He was just the man to refuse at once. But he listened to Etcham's halting, difficult hints. He even asked questions.

'Who is your chief?'

'Stone,' Etcham lisped.

That electrified both of us.

'Ralph Stone?' we ejaculated together.

Etcham nodded.

For some minutes Van Rieten and I were silent. Van Rieten had never seen him, but I had been a classmate of Stone's, and Van Rieten and I had discussed him over many a camp fire. We had heard of him two years before, south of Luebo in the Balunda country, which had been ringing with his theatrical strife against a Balunda witch-doctor, ending in the sorcerer's complete discomfiture and the abasement of his tribe before Stone. They had even broken the fetish-man's whistle and given Stone the pieces. It had been like the triumph of Elijah over the prophets of Baal, only more real to the Balunda.

We had thought of Stone as far off, if still in Africa at all, and here he turned up ahead of us and probably forestalling our quest.

II

Etcham's naming of Stone brought back to us all his tantalizing story, his fascinating parents, their tragic death; the brilliance of his college days; the dazzle of his millions; the promise of his young manhood; his wide notoriety, so nearly real fame; his romantic elopement with the meteoric authoress whose sudden cascade of fiction had made her so great a name so young, whose beauty and charm were so much heralded; the frightful scandal of the breach-of-promise suit that followed; his bride's devotion through it all; their sudden quarrel after it was all over; their divorce; the too much advertised announcement of his approaching marriage to the plaintiff in the breach-of-promise suit; his precipitate remarriage to his divorced bride; their second quarrel and second divorce; his departure from his native land; his advent in the dark continent. The sense of all this rushed over me and I believe Van Rieten felt it, too, as he sat silent.

Then he asked:

'Where is Werner?'

'Dead,' said Etcham. 'He died before I joined Stone.'

'You were not with Stone above Luebo?'

'No,' said Etcham, 'I joined him at Stanley Falls.'

'Who is with him?' Van Rieten asked.

'Only his Zanzibar servants and the bearers,' Etcham replied.

'What sort of bearers?' Van Rieten demanded.

'Mang-Battu men,' Etcham responded simply.

Now that impressed both Van Rieten and myself greatly. It bore out Stone's reputation as a notable leader of men. For up to that time no one had been able to use Mang-Battu as bearers outside of their own country, or to hold them for long or difficult expeditions.

'Were you long among the Mang-Battu?' was Van Rieten's next question.

'Some weeks,' said Etcham. 'Stone was interested in them and made up a fair-sized vocabulary of their words and phrases. He had a theory that they are an offshoot of the Balunda and he found much confirmation in their customs.'

'What do you live on?' Van Rieten inquired.

'Game, mostly,' Etcham lisped.

'How long has Stone been laid up?' Van Rieten next asked.

'More than a month,' Etcham answered.

'And you have been hunting for the camp?' Van Rieten exclaimed.

Etcham's face, burnt and flayed as it was, showed a flush.

'I missed some easy shots,' he admitted ruefully. 'I've not felt ve'y fit myself.'

'What's the matter with your chief?' Van Rieten inquired.

'Something like carbuncles,' Etcham replied.

'He ought to get over a carbuncle or two,' Van Rieten declared.

'They are not carbuncles,' Etcham explained. 'Nor one or two. He has had dozens, sometimes five at once. If they had been carbuncles he would have been dead long ago. But in some ways they are not so bad, though in others they are worse.'

'How do you mean?' Van Rieten queried.

'Well,' Etcham hesitated, 'they do not seem to inflame so deep nor so wide as carbuncles, nor to be so painful, nor to cause so much fever. But then they seem to be part of a disease that affects his mind. He let me help him dress the first, but the others he has hidden most carefully, from me and from the men. He keeps his tent when they puff up, and will not let me change the dressings or be with him at all.'

'Have you plenty of dressings?' Van Rieten asked.

'We have some,' said Etcham doubtfully. 'But he won't use them; he washes out the dressings and uses them over and over.'

'How is he treating the swellings?' Van Rieten inquired.

'He slices them off clear down to flesh level, with his razor.'

'What?' Van Rieten shouted.

Etcham made no answer but looked him steadily in the eyes.

'I beg your pardon,' Van Rieten hastened to say. 'You startled me. They can't be carbuncles. He'd have been dead long ago.'

'I thought I had said they are not carbuncles,' Etcham lisped.

'But the man must be crazy!' Van Rieten exclaimed.

'Just so,' said Etcham. 'He is beyond my advice or control.'

'How many has he treated that way?' Van Rieten demanded.

'Two, to my knowledge,' Etcham said.

'Two?' Van Rieten queried.

Etcham flushed again.

'I saw him,' he confessed, 'through a crack in the hut. I felt impelled to keep him a watch on him, as if he was not responsible.'

'I should think not,' Van Rieten agreed. 'And you saw him do that twice?'

'I conjecture,' said Etcham, 'that he did the like with all the rest.'

'How many has he had?' Van Rieten asked.

'Dozens,' Etcham lisped.

'Does he eat?' Van Rieten inquired.

'Like a wolf,' said Etcham. 'More than any two bearers.'

'Can he walk?' Van Rieten asked.

'He crawls a bit, groaning,' said Etcham simply.

'Little fever, you say,' Van Rieten ruminated.

'Enough and too much,' Etcham declared.

'Has he been delirious?' Van Rieten asked.

'Only twice,' Etcham replied; 'once when the first swelling broke, and once later. He would not let anyone come near him then. But we could hear him talking, talking steadily, and it scared the natives.'

'Was he talking their patter in delirium?' Van Rieten demanded.

'No,' said Etcham, 'but he was talking some similiar lingo. Hamed Burghash said he was talking Balunda. I know too little Balunda. I do not learn languages readily. Stone learned more Mang-Battu in a week than I could have learned in a year. But I seemed to hear words like Mang-Battu words. Anyhow, the Mang-Battu bearers were scared.'

'Scared?' Van Rieten repeated, questioningly.

'So were the Zanzibar men, even Hamed Burghash, and so was I,' said Etcham, 'only for a different reason. He talked in two voices.'

'In two voices,' Van Rieten reflected.

'Yes,' said Etcham, more excitedly than he had yet spoken. 'In two voices, like a conversation. One was his own, one a small, thin, bleaty voice like nothing I ever heard. I seemed to make out, among the sounds the deep voice made, something like Mang-battu words I knew, as *nedru*, *metababa*, and *nedo*, their terms for "head," "shoulder," "thigh," and perhaps *kudra* and *nekere* ("speak" and "whistle"); and among the noises of the shrill voice *matomipa*, *angunzi*, and *kamomami* ("kill," "death," and "hate"). Hamed Burghash said he also heard those words. He knew Mang-Battu far better than I.'

'What did the bearers say?' Van Rieten asked.

'They said, "*Lukundoo, Lukundoo!*" ' Etcham replied. 'I did not know that word; Hamed Burghash said it was Mang-Battu for "leopard." '

'It's Mang-Battu for "witchcraft," ' said Van Rieten.

'I don't wonder they thought so,' said Etcham. 'It was enough to make one believe in sorcery to listen to those two voices.'

'One voice answering the other?' Van Rieten asked perfunctorily.

Etcham's face went grey under his tan.

'Sometimes both at once,' he answered huskily.

'Both at once!' Van Rieten ejaculated.

'It sounded that way to the men, too,' said Etcham. 'And that was not all.'

He stopped and looked helplessly at us for a moment.

'Could a man talk and whistle at the same time?' he asked.

'How do you mean?' Van Rieten queried.

'We could hear Stone talking away, his big, deep-chested baritone rumbling along, and through it all we could hear a high, shrill whistle, the oddest, wheezy sound. You know, no matter how shrilly a grown man may whistle, the note has a different quality from the whistle of a boy or a woman or a little girl. They sound more treble, somehow. Well, if you can imagine the smallest girl who could whistle keeping it up tunelessly right along, that whistle was like that, only even more piercing, and it sounded right through Stone's bass tones.'

'And you didn't go to him?' Van Rieten cried.

'He is not given to threats,' Etcham disclaimed. 'But he had threatened, not volubly, nor like a sick man, but quietly and firmly, that if any man of us (he lumped me in with the men) came near him while he was in his trouble, that man should die. And it was not so much his words as his manner. It was like a monarch commanding respected privacy for a deathbed. One simply could not transgress.'

'I see,' said Van Rieten shortly.

'He's ve'y seedy,' Etcham repeated helplessly. 'I thought perhaps . . .'

His absorbing affection for Stone, his real love for him, shone out through his envelope of conventional training. Worship of Stone was plainly his master passion.

Like many competent men, Van Rieten had a streak of hard selfishness in him. It came to the surface then. He said we carried our lives in our hands from day to day just as genuinely as Stone; that he did not forget the ties of blood in imperilling one party for a very problematical benefit to a man probably beyond any help; that it was enough of a task to hunt for one party; that if two were united, providing food would be more than doubly difficult; that the risk of starvation was too great. Deflecting our march seven full days' journey (he complimented Etcham on his marching powers) might ruin our expedition entirely.

III

Van Rieten had logic on his side and he had a way with him. Etcham sat there apologetic and deferential, like a fourth-form schoolboy before a headmaster. Van Rieten wound up.

'I am after pigmies, at the risk of my life. After pigmies I go.'

'Perhaps, then, these will interest you,' said Etcham, very quietly.

He took two objects out of the side-pocket of his blouse, and handed them to Van Rieten. They were round, bigger than big plums, and smaller than small peaches, about the right size to enclose in an average hand. They were black, and at first I did not see what they were.

'Pigmies!' Van Rieten exclaimed. 'Pigmies, indeed! Why, they wouldn't be two feet high! Do you mean to claim that these are adult heads?'

'I claim nothing,' Etcham answered evenly. 'You can see for yourself.'

Van Rieten passed one to me. The sun was just setting and I examined it closely. A dried head it was, perfectly preserved, and the flesh as hard as Argentine jerked beef. A bit of a vertebra stuck out where the muscles of the vanished neck had shrivelled into folds. The puny chin was sharp on a projecting jaw, the minute teeth white and even between the retracted lips, the tiny nose was flat, the little forehead retreating, there were inconsiderable clumps of stunted wool on the Lilliputian cranium. There was nothing babyish, childish or youthful about the head; rather it was mature to senility.

'Where did these come from?' Van Rieten inquired.

'I do not know,' Etcham replied precisely. 'I found them among Stone's effects while rummaging for medicines or drugs or anything that could help me to help him. I do not know where he got them. But I'll swear he did not have them when we entered this district.'

'Are you sure?' Van Rieten queried, his eyes big and fixed on Etcham's.

'Ve'y sure,' lisped Etcham.

'But how could he have come by them without your knowledge?' Van Rieten demurred.

'Sometimes we were apart ten days at a time hunting,' said Etcham. 'Stone is not a talking man. He gave me no account of his doings, and Hamed Burghash keeps a still tongue and a tight hold on the men.'

'You have examined these heads?' Van Rieten asked.

'Minutely,' said Etcham.

Van Rieten took out his notebook. He was a methodical chap. He tore out a leaf, folded it and divided it equally into three pieces. He gave one to me and one to Etcham.

'Just for a test of my impressions,' he said, 'I want each of us to write separately just what he is most reminded of by these heads. Then I want to compare the writings.'

I handed Etcham a pencil and he wrote. Then he handed the pencil back to me and I wrote.

'Read the three,' said Van Rieten, handing me his piece.

Van Rieten had written:

'An old Balunda witch-doctor.'

Etcham had written:

'An old Mang-Battu fetish-man.'

I had written:

'An old Katongo magician.'

'There!' Van Rieten exclaimed. 'Look at that! There is nothing Wagabi or Batwa or Wambuttu or Wabotu about these heads. Nor anything pigmy either.'

'I thought as much,' said Etcham.

'And you say he did not have them before?'

'To a certainty he did not,' Etcham asserted.

'It is worth following up, said Van Rieten. 'I'll go with you. And first of all, I'll do my best to save Stone.'

He put out his hand and Etcham clasped it silently. He was grateful all over.

IV

Nothing but Etcham's fever of solicitude could have taken him in five days over the track. It took him eight days to retrace with full knowledge of it and our party to help. We could not have done it in seven, and Etcham urged us on, in a repressed fury of anxiety, no mere fever of duty to his chief, but a real ardour of devotion, a glow of personal adoration for Stone which blazed under his dry conventional exterior and showed in spite of him.

We found Stone well cared for. Etcham had seen to a good high thorn *zareeba* round the camp, the huts were well built and thatched, and Stone's was as good as their resources would permit. Hamed Burghash was not named after two Seyyids for nothing. He had in him the making of a sultan. He had kept the

Mang-Battu together, not a man had slipped off, and he had kept them in order. Also he was a deft nurse and a faithful servant.

The two other Zanzibaris had done some creditable hunting. Though all were hungry, the camp was far from starvation.

Stone was on a canvas cot and there was a sort of collapsible camp-stool-table, like a Turkish tabouret, by the cot. It had a water-bottle and some vials on it and Stone's watch, also his razor in its case.

Stone was clean and not emanciated, but he was far gone; not unconscious, but in a daze; past commanding or resisting anyone. He did not seem to see us enter or to know we were there. I should have recognized him anywhere. His boyish dash and grace had vanished utterly, of course. But his head was even more leonine; his hair was still abundant, yellow and wavy; the close, crisped blond beard he had grown during his illness did not alter him. He was big and big-chested yet. His eyes were dull and he mumbled and babbled mere meaningless syllables, not words.

Etcham helped Van Rieten to uncover him and look him over. He was in good muscle for a man so long bedridden. There were no scars on him except about his knees, shoulders and chest. On each knee and above it he had a full score of roundish cicatrices, and a dozen or more on each shoulder, all in front. Two or three were open wounds and four or five barely healed. He had no fresh swellings, except two, one to each side, on his pectoral muscles, the one on the left being higher up and farther out than the other. They did not look like boils or carbuncles, but as if something blunt and hard were being pushed up through the healthy flesh and skin, not much inflamed.

'I should not lance those,' said Van Rieten, and Etcham assented.

They made Stone as comfortable as they could, and just before sunset we looked in at him again. He was lying on his back, and his chest showed big and massive yet, but he lay as if in a stupor. We left Etcham with him and went into the next hut, which Etcham had resigned to us. The jungle noises were no different there than anywhere else for months past, and I was soon fast asleep.

V

Some time in the pitch dark I found myself awake and listening. I could hear two voices, one Stone's, the other sibilant and wheezy. I knew Stone's voice after all the years that had passed since I heard it last. The other was nothing like I remembered. It had less volume than the wail of a new-born baby, yet there was an insistent carrying power to it, like the shrilling of an insect. As I listened I heard Van Rieten breathing near me in the dark; then he heard me and realized that I was listening too. Like Etcham I knew little Balunda, but I could make out a word or two. The voices alternated, with intervals of silence between.

Then suddenly both sounded at once and fast. Stone's baritone basso, full as if he were in perfect health, and that incredibly stridulous falsetto, both jabbering at once like the voices of two people quarrelling and trying to talk each other down.

'I can't stand this,' said Van Rieten. 'Let's have a look at him.'

He had one of those cylindrical electric night-candles. He fumbled about for it, touched the button and beckoned me to come with him. Outside the hut he motioned me to stand still, and instinctively turned off the light, as if seeing made listening difficult.

Except for a faint glow from the embers of the bearers' fire we were in complete darkness, little starlight struggled through the trees, the river made but a faint murmur. We could hear the two voices together and then suddenly the creaking voice changed into a razor-edged, slicing whistle, indescribably cutting, continuing right through Stone's grumbling torrent of croaking words.

'Good God!' exclaimed Van Rieten.

Abruptly he turned on the light.

We found Etcham utterly asleep, exhausted by his long anxiety and the exertions of his phenomenal march, and relaxed completely now that the load was in a sense shifted from his shoulders to Van Rieten's. Even the light on his face did not wake him.

The whistle had ceased and the two voices now sounded together. Both came from Stone's cot, where the concentrated white ray showed him lying just as we had left him, except that he had tossed his arms above his head and had torn the coverings and bandages from his chest.

The swelling on the right breast had broken. Van Rieten aimed the centre line of the light at it and we saw it plainly. From his flesh, grown out if it, there protruded a head, such a head as the dried specimens Etcham had shown us, as if it were a miniature of the head of a Balunda fetish-man. It was black, shining black as the blackest African skin; it rolled the whites of its wicked, wee eyes and showed its microscopic teeth between lips repulsive in their red fullness, even in so diminutive a face. It had crisp, fuzzy wool on its minikin skull, it turned malignantly from side to side and chittered incessantly in that inconceivable falsetto. Stone babbled brokenly against its patter.

Van Rieten turned from Stone and waked Etcham, with some difficulty. When he was awake and saw it all, Etcham stared and said not one word.

'You saw him slice off two swellings?' Van Rieten asked.

Etcham nodded, chokingly.

'Did he bleed much?' Van Rieten demanded.

've'y little,' Etcham replied.

'You hold his arms,' said Van Rieten to Etcham.

He took up Stone's razor and handed me the light. Stone showed no sign of seeing the light or of knowing we were there. But the little head mewled and screeched at us.

Van Rieten's hand was steady, and the sweep of the razor even and true. Stone bled amazingly little and Van Rieten dressed the wound as if it had been a bruise or scrape.

Stone had stopped talking the instant the excrescent head was severed. Van Rieten did all that could be done for Stone and then fairly grabbed the light from me. Snatching up a gun he scanned the ground by the cot and brought the butt down once and twice, viciously.

We went back to our hut, but I doubt if I slept.

VI

Next day, near noon, in broad daylight, we heard the two voices from Stone's hut. We found Etcham dropped asleep by his charge. The swelling on the left had broken, and just such another head was there miauling and spluttering. Etcham woke up and the three of us stood there and glared. Stone interjected hoarse vocables into the tinkling gurgle of the portent's utterance.

Van Rieten stepped forward, took up Stone's razor and knelt down by the cot. The atomy of a head squealed a wheezy snarl at him.

Then suddenly Stone spoke English.

'Who are you with my razor?'

Van Rieten started back and stood up.

Stone's eyes were clear now and bright, they roved about the hut.

'The end,' he said; 'I recognize the end. I seem to see Etcham, as if in life. But Singleton! Ah, Singleton! Ghosts of my boyhood come to watch me pass! And you, strange spectre with the black beard and my razor! Aroint ye all!'

'I'm no ghost, Stone,' I managed to say. 'I'm alive. So are Etcham and Van Rieten. We are here to help you.'

'Van Rieten!' he exclaimed. 'My work passes on to a better man. Luck go with you, Van Rieten.'

Van Rieten went nearer to him.

'Just hold still a moment, old man,' he said soothingly. 'It will be only one twinge.'

'I've held still for many such twinges,' Stone answered quite distinctly. 'Let me be. Let me die in my own way. The hydra was nothing to this. You can cut off ten, a hundred, a thousand heads, but the curse you can not cut off, or take off. What's soaked into the bone won't come out of the flesh, any more than what's bred there. Don't hack me any more. Promise!'

His voice had all the old commanding tone of his boyhood and it swayed Van Rieten as it always had swayed everybody.

'I promise,' said Van Rieten.

Almost as he said the word Stone's eyes filmed again.

Then we three sat about Stone and watched that hideous, gibbering prodigy grow up out of Stone's flesh, till two horrid, spindling little black arms disengaged themselves. The infinitesimal nails were perfect to the barely perceptible moon at the quick, the pink spot on the palm was horridly natural. These arms gesticulated and the right plucked towards Stone's blond beard.

'I can't stand this,' Van Rieten exclaimed and took up the razor again.

Instantly Stone's eyes opened, hard and glittering.

'Van Rieten break his word?' he enunciated slowly. 'Never!'

'But we must help you,' Van Rieten gasped.

'I am past all help and all hurting,' said Stone. 'This is my hour. This curse is not put on me; it grew out of me, like this horror here. Even now I go.'

His eyes closed and we stood helpless, the adherent figure spouting shrill sentences.

In a moment Stone spoke again.

'You speak all tongues?' he asked quickly.

And the mergent minikin replied in sudden English:

'Yea, verily, all that you speak,' putting out its microscopic tongue, writhing its lips and wagging its head from side to side. We could see the thready ribs on its exiguous flanks heave as if the thing breathed.

'Has she forgiven me?' Stone asked in a muffled strangle.

'Not while the moss hangs from the cypresses,' the head squeaked. 'Not while the stars shine on Lake Pontchartrain will she forgive.'

And then Stone, all with one motion, wrenched himself over on his side. The next instant he was dead.

When Singleton's voice ceased the room was hushed for a space. We could hear each other breathing. Twombly, the tactless, broke the silence.

'I presume,' he said, 'you cut off the little minikin and brought it home in alcohol.'

Singleton turned on him a stern countenance.

'We buried Stone,' he said, 'unmutilated as he died.'

'But,' said the unconscionable Twombly, 'the whole thing is incredible.'

Singleton stiffened.

'I did not expect you to believe it,' he said; 'I began by saying that although I heard and saw it, when I look back on it I cannot credit it myself.'

The Donguys

Juan Rodolfo Wilcock, *born in Buenos Aires. He has published poetry and prose books in Spanish and Italian, including:* Libro de poemas y canciones *(1940);* Ensayos de Poesía Lírica *(1945);* Persecución de las Musas Menores *(1945);* Paseo Sentimental *(1946);* Sexto *(1953);* Il Caos *(1960);* Fatti Inquietanti *(1961);* Luoghi Comuni *(1961);* Teatro in prosa e versi *(1962).*

I

Suspended vertically from the greyness like those curtains of little chains which keep out the flies in dairies whilst shutting out neither the air which sustains them nor people, the rain was falling between the Andes and me when I reached Mendoza, making it impossible to see the mountains although I could sense their presence in the gullies, which all seemed to be descending from the same pyramid.

The following morning I went up to the terrace of the hotel and saw that in fact the tops were white under the gaps in the sky amongst nomadic clouds. I wasn't surprised, partly because of a postcard with a banal view of the Inca's Bridge bought by chance in a gift shop which turned out to be different from reality; as for many travellers, from a distance they looked to me like the mountains of Switzerland.

The day I was transferred I rose before dawn and got ready in the damp and the faint light. We left by car at seven o'clock; with me were two engineers, Balsa and Balsocci, both quite incapable of knowing an anagram from a greeting. In the outskirts, the light of dawn was beginning to fall on deformed cacti on shapeless hillocks: we crossed the river Mendoza, which at this time of year stands out more than anything else for its thundering noise under the blue beam of bright summer lights shining towards the bottom of the valley, without looking at it, and then we entered the mountains.

Balsocci talked with Balso in a duet and at one point said, 'Barnaza eats more than a donguy.'

Balsa glanced at me sideways and after another discussion of news from abroad, tried to sound me out, 'Have they explained to you, Engineer, the reason we're building the monumental Punta de Vacas hotel?'

I knew, but nobody had actually explained it to me: I replied, 'No.' And I followed that with the pathetic offering, 'I imagine it is being built to encourage tourism.'

'Yes, to encourage tourism, ha, ha. To salve their conscience, you should say (Balsocci).

I didn't say, but I did say to them, 'I don't understand,' although I did.

'We'll tell you certain secret details later,' Balsa explained to me, 'which concern the construction and which you will therefore be informed of when we hand over the plans, specifications and other construction details to you. For the time being, allow us to impose on your patience a little.'

I suppose that between the two of them they couldn't create a mystery in fourteen years. Their only honesty—involuntary—consisted in making everything they were thinking obvious; for instance, instead of hiding something they would just *look* as though they were hiding something, and so on.

I observed my brave new world. Certain moments superimposed themselves onto the next few hours and days, as when you return for example for the second time to the open square in Sienna and enter from the other side, you think that the entrance you first used is by now famous. Changeable between two rocks as tall as the obelisk, one black, one red, I caught a memorable vision and devoted myself to taking in another great landscape: close to the thundering crash of the river I reflected that the moment was a tunnel and I would emerge a changed man.

We continued like a buzzing insect between green, yellow and purple sheets of basalt and granite along a dangerous road. Balsa asked me, 'Is your family in Buenos Aires?'

'I don't have a family.'

'Ah, I understand,' he replied, because for them there was always the possibility of not understanding, not even that.

'And do you intend staying here long?' (Balsocci).

'I don't know; the contract mentioned the construction of unspecified monumental hotels, which naturally could go on for an indefinite period.'

'As long as the height doesn't bother you . . .' (Balsocci, hopeful).

'You don't even notice 2,400 metres, specially not if you're young.' (Balsa, equally hopeful).

The luxurious skies were changing into blankets of clouds squashed in between the hills: soon it was raining amongst rainbows, then the rain turned into snow. We stopped for a white coffee at the house of a 50-year-old Slav friend of theirs, married to a 20-year-old Argentine woman, in charge of the maintenance of the railway and swapping the rails around, those futile jobs of the poor. This painfully thin woman seemed to suffer merely from living, but filled me with such desire that I had to step outside in order not to stare at her like a monkey. I sank my feet into the fresh snow; I took off my gloves and squeezed a ball, tested it with my lips, bit it with my teeth, tore pieces of bark off the branches, urinated, slipped and fell on a frozen ditch.

When we left, the snow was feathering the car windows and the damp penetrated my boots. At times we went alongside the river and at others we would catch sight of it at the bottom of a precipice.

'Those who fall into the water are dragged far away, to be found naked and skinned' (Balsa).

'Why? (Me).

'Because the water beats them against the rocks' (Balsa).

'The water rushes by at seven metres per second. A few days ago a foreman, Antonio, fell from the footbridge; his wife is in Mendoza waiting for his body and we can't find him' (Balsocci).

'True, we should have a look now and then and see if we can see him' (Balsa).

At the bottom of the valley a simple picture unveiled itself in the sunshine On one side, Uspallata with poplars and leafless willows, on the other the road which continued upwards along a red gorge between solitary rivers.

Those rivers of the Andes, rapid, clearer than air, with their round pebbles, green, purple, yellow and marbled, always washed clean, with neither bugs nor nymphs amongst ageless blocks which some strange thing brought and left behind—modern rivers, because they have no history. Sometimes I listen to them standing on a rock, under the invisible sky, cloudless and birdless; amongst springs, hearing torrents, thinking of nothing.

They have the names of colours, Blanco, Colorado and Negro; some appear in front of you, some jump out at you (they say there are guanacos, but so far I haven't seen any); they all come to the valley and in the summer they swell, changing places and colours, carrying incredible quantities of mud.

We pass a geologically interesting yellow alluvial elevation called Paramillo de Juan Pobre and reach the site at lunch-time. It's not exactly in Punta de Vacas but some two kilometres before; this annoyed me because I thought that in winter the snow might leave me stranded without a woman, assuming I fancied any of them. Later I calmed down as I understood that in any case I could always walk there, even though the moraines fell—these are cones of mineral detritus which periodically slide down, covering roads and railways.

The building occupies a sort of platform a good way away from the landslides. The ground is sloping, bordered on one side by a stream which after forming a respectable seven-metre waterfall, falls pathetically into the valley like a trickle from a tap. In this place anything that didn't get here on wheels is basalt, slate or arum and similar weeds. A hill like a red saw or the roof of a church, or rather that of St Pancras Station in London, closes the other side of the gorge; the sky is so narrow here that the sun appears at nine thirty and sets at four thirty, quickly, as though embarrassed by the cold and wind which will follow.

The wind! How will the rich women of Buenos Aires manage to live here, always so careful with their hairdos, with these winds which make rocks roll as though they were nothing? I can just hear them saying what a headache it gives them, and that in some way encourages me to finish the first hotel soon and develop a kind of simple window which once opened cannot be closed. In a few days' time we shall be opening the temporary section, if that pain Enrique doesn't turn up.

After lunch the two engineers showed me the plans and the site. They were very pleased that no architect had been involved, and had commissioned the decoration of the building from a marble-cutter in Mendoza with whom there is a disagreement over a batch of a hundred and twenty-eight crosses destined for the bedrooms, whose size is not stipulated in any of the specifications. The crosses sent are in black granitite and one metre high; I, who had thought of them, insist on putting them there, but Balsocci fears them. The truth is I went over the top, but so far, poor things, they have let themselves be horribly manipulated and, not counting the underaged girl at the post-office and this chronicle, I was finding it difficult to keep myself amused: I managed to insert the inner tube of a football into one of the main concrete columns in the staff annexe when they were filling it, but when the shuttering was removed, you could see where the inner tube had rested against the wood; they had to inject cement into the gap, and the incident has become a confused legend which periodically occasions the dismissal of someone on the staff. The ball belonged to Balsocci.

We went back to the office and my colleagues tackled the secret part of my initiation. I had no need to pretend any curiosity since I was interested in hearing them talk about it.

II

BALSOCCI. Haven't you noticed anything strange lately in Buenos Aires?
ME. No, nothing.
BALSA. Let's not beat about the bush (*as though he suddenly decided to delve amongst the branches of a leafy skull*). Have you never heard of the donguys?
ME. No. What are they?

BALSA. You must have seen in the underground from Constitución to Boedo that the train doesn't reach Boedo station because it's unfinished, it stops at a temporary station with wooden flooring. The tunnel continues and where the digging was interrupted, the hole has been boarded up.

BALSOCCI. The donguys appeared through that hole.

ME. What are they?

BALSA. I'll tell you . . .

BALSOCCI. They say it is the animal destined to replace man on Earth.

BALSA. Let me explain. There are certain leaflets, whose circulation has been banned, which analyse the opinion of foreign and Argentine experts. I've read them. They say that during different eras, different animals predominated in the world, for whatever reason. Now man predominates because he has a highly developed nervous system which allows him to impose himself over the rest. But this new animal called donguy . . .

BALSOCCI. They call it donguy because it was first studied by a French biologist, Donneguy (*he writes it down and shows it to me*) and in England they called it the Donneguy Pig, but everyone calls it donguy.

ME. Is it a pig?

BALSA. It looks like a semi-transparent hog.

ME. And what does the donguy do?

BALSA. Its digestive system is so advanced that these animals can eat anything, even earth, iron, cement, jellyfish, whatever, they swallow everything in sight. What a nasty creature!

BALSOCCI. They're blind, deaf, live in the dark, a sort of worm like a transparent hog.

ME. Do they repoduce?

BALSA. Like flies. Through shoots, just think.

ME. And they're from Boedo?

BALSOCCI. That's where they started, but then they also started in other stations, especially those with dead-end tunnels or underground depots; Constitución is riddled with them, in Palermo there are loads of them in the tunnel which was begun for the extension to Belgrano. But afterwards they started in the other lines, they must have dug a tunnel, the Chacarita, Primera Junta lines. You should see the Plaza Once tunnel.

BALSA. And abroad! Wherever there was a tunnel, it became riddled with donguys. In London they were even laughing, apparently, because they have so many miles of tunnels; in Paris, in New York, in Madrid. As though they spread seeds.

BALSOCCI. They weren't allowing ships arriving from an infected port to dock there, they were afraid they'd be bringing donguys in the hold. But that didn't save them, they're even better off than we are.

BALSA. In our country they try not to scare people, that's why they never say anything, it's a secret told only to the professionals, and also to a few non-professionals.

BALSOCCI. They must be killed, but who can kill them? If they're given poison they may eat it or not, either way, but it does nothing to them, they eat it quite happily just like any other mineral. If they're gassed, the bastards block the tunnels and escape by another route. They dig tunnels everywhere, you cannot attack them directly. You can't flood them or demolish the tunnels because the city's foundations might subside. Needless to say, they wander about the basement and sewers as though they owned them . . .

BALSA. You must have heard of those buildings collapsing these last few months. The Lanús depots, for instance—that was their work. They want to dominate man.

BALSOCCI. Oh! man isn't dominated that easily, nobody can dominate him, but if they eat him . . .

ME. They eat him?

BALSOCCI. And how! Five donguys can eat a person in a minute, everything, bones, clothes, shoes, teeth, even his identity card, if you'll forgive the exaggeration.

BALSA. They like them. It's they're favourite food, most unfortunate.

ME. Are there any proven cases?

BALSOCCI. Cases? Ha, ha. In a Welsh coal-mine they ate 550 miners in one night; they blocked their exit.

BALSA. In the capital, they ate a team of eight workmen who were repairing the railway between Loria and Medrano. They closed in on them.

BALSOCCI. My suggestion is that we infect them with some disease.

BALSA. So far, there's no solution. I don't see how they can innoculate a disease into a jellyfish.

BALSOCCI. Those wise men! I suppose the inventor of the hydrogen bomb against us could also invent something, a few wretched little blind pigs. The Russians, for instance, who are so intelligent.

BALSA. Yes, do you know what the Russians are doing? Trying to create a light-resistant strain of donguy.

BALSOCCI. Their problem.

BALSA. Yes, theirs. But they don't matter. We would disappear. It can't be true. It must be a rumour like so many others. I don't believe a word of what I've just told you.

BALSOCCI. First we thought of solving the problem by constructing buildings on piles, but on one hand there's the cost, and on the other they can always demolish them from below.

BALSA. That's why we build our monumental hotels here. I bet they can't dig under the Andes! And those who are in the know are dying to come here. We'll see how long they last.

BALSOCCI. They could also dig under the rocks, but they'd take ages; and meanwhile I suppose somebody will do something.

BALSA. Don't breathe a word of this. Anyway, you've no family in Buenos Aires. That's why we limit excavations for the foundations to a minumum and none of the planned hotels have basements or a top floor.

III

The air in Buenos Aires has a special colloidal quality for transmitting false rumours intact. In other places, the atmosphere deforms what it hears, but by the river lies are cleanly transmitted. In his days of extroversion, every human being can make up specific rumours without the need to proclaim them on a corner in order for them to come back unchanged a week later.

That's why when I heard about the donguys two and a half years ago I consigned them to the level of flying saucers, but a friend with varied interests who had just come from Europe and had it on good authority confirmed the news. Right from the first I found them charming and looked forward to a profitable association.

At the time my interest in Virginia, a sales assistant in a silk shop, was in parabolic decline, and my next interest in a black woman called Colette was growing. My detachment from Virginia took the form of nights in Lezama Park, although her stupidity was provoking an unseemly prolongation of the procedure.

One of those nights when I was suffering most at witnessing suffering, we were caressing on the twin steps over some store in the park where the gardeners keep their tools. The door to one of these storerooms was open; in the dark void I suddenly saw eight or ten nervous donguys which didn't dare come out because of a hint of lousy light. They were the first I'd seen; I approached with Virginia and showed them to her. Virginia was wearing a light-coloured skirt with a pattern of large pots of chrysanthemums: I remember it because she fainted in my arms with fright and luckily stopped crying that night for the first time. I took her unconscious to the open door and threw her in.

The donguy's mouth is a cylinder lined with horn-like teeth, and shredding in a helical motion. I watched with natural curiosity; in the dark I could make out the chrysanthemum skirt and on it the epileptic movement of the huge masticating slugs. I went home disgusted but happy; I was singing as I left the park.

That deserted, damp park with broken statues and a thousand modern vulgarities for the ignorami, with flowers like stars and only one good fountain, almost a South American park: how many liaisons of people who call plumbago jasmine has it seen die away under its dusty palm trees.

There I got rid of Colette, of a Polish woman who lent me the money for my motorbike, an untrustworthy minor, and finally Rosa, putting them to sleep with a special sweet. But Rosa at one point excited me so much that I was reckless enough to give her my telephone number, and although she promised to destroy the scrap of paper and learn it by heart, her brother once saw her call me and saw the number she was dialling, such that soon after her disappearance Enrique turned up and started pestering me. That's why I accepted this job, temporarily giving up all enjoyment like the prehistoric kings who had to fast for forty days in the mountains.

I find distraction from this vow of chastity in my own way, solving hieroglyphs and preparing things for Enrique. For instance, when I arrived, the footbridge over the river Mendoza was nothing but one of those scattered by the deluge in the thirties, which twisted the bridges, and a cable along the side to hold on to. A certain Antonio fell from there, and on that pretext I had the cable removed and replaced by a long pipe hooked onto a pole at each end. Now it's easier to hold on to when you cross and, to unhook the pipe when somebody else is crossing.

Other distractions might be setting fire with a match to the bushes surrounding the workmen's tents when it's cold, because they are so resinous that they burn on their own. Once I organized a one-person picnic which consisted of always going up and up with several ham, egg and lettuce sandwiches, but I got so fed up with climbing that I turned back at midday. That morning I saw inexplicably dirty glaciers and on the boulders above found black flowers, the first I've seen. As there was no earth, only sharp, loose stones, I was interested in seeing the roots; the flower measured some five centimetres, but clearing the stones I uncovered some two metres of soft stem which disappeared into the rubble like a smooth black string; I thought it would continue for another hundred metres and I found it rather disgusting.

Another time I saw a black sky over fluorescent snow which absorbed all the light of the moon; it looked like a negative of the world and was worth seeing.

Lord Arthur Savile's Crime
A Study of Duty

Oscar Wilde *(1854-1900), Irish-born poet, dramatist and writer of stories and fables, who enjoyed brilliant success with plays like* Lady Windermere's Fan *and* The Importance of Being Earnest. *A homosexual scandal wrecked his life, but produced masterpieces in* The Ballad of Reading Gaol *and* De Profundis.

It was Lady Windermere's last reception before Easter, and Bentinck House was even more crowded than usual. Six Cabinet Ministers had come on from the Speaker's Levée in their stars and ribands, all the pretty women wore their smartest dresses, and at the end of the picture-gallery stood the Princess Sophia of Carlsrühe, a heavy Tartar-looking lady, with tiny black eyes and wonderful emeralds, talking bad French at the top of her voice, and laughing immoderately at everything that was said to her. It was certainly a wonderful medley of people. Gorgeous peeresses chatted affably to violent Radicals, popular preachers brushed coat-tails with eminent sceptics, a perfect bevy of bishops kept following a stout prima-donna from room to room, on the staircase stood several Royal Academicians, disguised as artists, and it was said that at one time the supper-room was absolutely crammed with geniuses. In fact, it was one of Lady Windermere's best nights, and the Princess stayed till nearly half-past eleven.

As soon as she had gone, Lady Windermere returned to the picture-gallery, where a celebrated political economist was solemnly explaining the scientific theory of music to an indignant virtuoso from Hungary, and began to talk to the Duchess of Paisley. She looked wonderfully beautiful with her grand ivory throat, her large blue forget-me-not eyes, and her heavy coils of golden hair. *Or pur* they were—not that pale straw colour that nowadays usurps the gracious name of gold, but such gold as is woven into sunbeams or hidden in strange amber; and they gave to her face something of the frame of a saint, with not a little of the fascination of a sinner. She was a curious psychological study. Early in life she had discovered the important truth that nothing looks so like innocence as an indiscretion; and by a series of reckless escapades, half of them quite harmless, she had acquired all the privileges of a personality. She had more than once changed her husband; indeed, Debrett credits her with three marriages; but as she had never changed her lover, the world had long ago ceased to talk scandal about her. She was now forty years of age, childless, and with that inordinate passion for pleasure which is the secret of remaining young.

Suddenly she looked eagerly round the room, and said, in her clear contralto voice, 'Where is my chiromantist?'

'Your what, Gladys?' exclaimed the Duchess, giving an involuntary start.

'My chiromantist, Duchess; I can't live without him at present.'

'Dear Gladys! you are always so original,' murmured the Duchess, trying to remember what a chiromantist really was, and hoping it was not the same as a chiropodist.

'He comes to see my hand twice a week regularly,' continued Lady Windermere, 'and is most interesting about it.'

'Good heavens!' said the Duchess to herself, 'he is a sort of chiropodist after all. How very dreadful. I hope he is a foreigner at any rate. It wouldn't be quite so bad then.'

'I must introduce him to you.'

'Introduce him!' cried the Duchess; 'you don't mean to say he is here?' and she began looking about for a small tortoise-shell fan and a very tattered lace shawl, so as to be ready at a moment's notice.

'Of course he is here; I would not dream of giving a party without him. He tells me I have a pure psychic hand, and that if my thumb had been the least little bit shorter, I should have been a confirmed pessimist, and gone into a convent.'

'Oh, I see!' said the Duchess, feeling very much relieved; 'he tells fortunes, I suppose?'

'And misfortunes, too,' answered Lady Windermere, 'any amount of them. Next year, for instance, I am in great danger, both by land and sea, so I am going to live in a balloon, and draw up my dinner in a basket every evening. It is all written down on my little finger, or on the palm of my hand, I forget which.'

'But surely that is tempting Providence, Gladys.'

'My dear Duchess, surely Providence can resist temptation by this time. I think every one should have their hands told once a month so as to know what not to do. Of course, one does it all the same, but it is so pleasant to be warned.

Now if some one doesn't go and fetch Mr. Podgers at once, I shall have to go myself.'

'Let me go, Lady Windermere,' said a tall handsome young man, who was standing by, listening to the conversation with an amused smile.

'Thanks so much, Lord Arthur; but I am afraid you wouldn't recognize him.'

'If he is as wonderful as you say, Lady Windermere, I couldn't well miss him. Tell me what he is like, and I'll bring him to you at once.'

'Well, he is not a bit like a chiromantist. I mean he is not mysterious, or esoteric, or romantic-looking. He is a little, stout man, with a funny, bald head, and great gold-rimmed spectacles; something between a family doctor and a country attorney. I'm really very sorry, but it is not my fault. People are so annoying. All my pianists look exactly like poets; and all my poets look exactly like pianists; and I remember last season asking a most dreadful conspirator to dinner, a man who had blown up ever so many people, and always wore a coat of mail, and carried a dagger up his shirt-sleeve; and do you know that when he came he looked just like a nice old clergyman, and cracked jokes all the evening? Of course, he was very amusing, and all that, but I was awfully disappointed; and when I asked him about the coat of mail, he only laughed, and said it was far too cold to wear in England. Ah, here is Mr. Podgers! Now, Mr. Podgers, I want you to tell the Duchess of Paisley's hand. Duchess, you must take your glove off. No, not the left hand, the other.'

'Dear Gladys, I really don't think it is quite right,' said the Duchess, feebly unbuttoning a rather soiled kid glove.

'Nothing interesting ever is,' said Lady Windermere: '*on a fait le monde ainsi.* But I must introduce you. Duchess, this is Mr. Podgers, my pet chiromantist. Mr. Podgers, this is the Duchess of Paisley, and if you say that she has a larger mountain of the moon than I have, I will never believe in you again.'

'I am sure, Gladys, there is nothing of the kind in my hand,' said the Duchess gravely.

'Your Grace is quite right,' said Mr. Podgers, glancing at the little fat hand with its short square fingers, 'the mountain of the moon is not developed. The line of life, however, is excellent. Kindly bend the wrist. Thank you. Three distinct lines of the *rascette*! You will live to a great age, Duchess, and be extremely happy. Ambition—very moderate, line of intellect not exaggerated, line of heart—'

'Now, do be discreet, Mr. Podgers,' cried Lady Windermere.

'Nothing would give me greater pleasure,' said Mr. Podgers, bowing, 'if the Duchess ever had been, but I am sorry to say that I see great permanence of affection, combined with a strong sense of duty.'

'Pray go on, Mr. Podgers,' said the Duchess, looking quite pleased.

'Economy is not the least of your Grace's virtues,' continued Mr. Podgers, and Lady Windermere went off into fits of laughter.

'Economy is a very good thing,' remarked the Duchess complacently; 'when I married Paisley he had eleven castles, and not a single house fit to live in.'

'And now he has twelve houses, and not a single castle,' cried Lady Windermere.

'Well, my dear,' said the Duchess, 'I like—'

'Comfort,' said Mr. Podgers, 'and modern improvements, and hot water laid on in every bedroom. Your Grace is quite right. Comfort is the only thing our civilization can give us.'

'You have told the Duchess's character admirably, Mr. Podgers, and now you must tell Lady Flora's'; and in answer to a nod from the smiling hostess, a tall girl with sandy Scotch hair, and high shoulder-blades, stepped awkwardly from behind the sofa, and held out a long, bony hand with spatulate fingers.

'Ah, a pianist! I see,' said Mr. Podgers, 'an excellent pianist, but perhaps hardly a musician. Very reserved, very honest, and with a great love of animals.'

'Quite true!' exclaimed the Duchess, turning to Lady Windermere, 'absolutely true! Flora keeps two dozen collie dogs at Macloskie, and would turn our town house into a menagerie if her father would let her.'

'Well, that is just what I do with my house every Thursday evening,' cried Lady Windermere, laughing, 'only I like lions better than collie dogs.'

'Your one mistake, Lady Windermere,' said Mr. Podgers, with a pompous bow.

'If a woman can't make her mistakes charming, she is only a female,' was the answer. 'But you must read some more hands for us. Come, Sir Thomas, show Mr. Podgers yours'; and a genial-looking old gentleman, in a white waistcoat, came forward, and held out a thick rugged hand, with a very long third finger.

'An adventurous nature; four long voyages in the past, and one to come. Been shipwrecked three times. No, only twice, but in danger of a shipwreck your next journey. A strong Conservative, very punctual and with a passion for collecting curiosities. Had a severe illness between the ages of sixteen and eighteen. Was left a fortune when about thirty. Great aversion to cats and Radicals.'

'Extraordinary!' exclaimed Sir Thomas: 'you must really tell my wife's hand, too.'

'Your second wife's,' said Mr. Podgers quietly, still keeping Sir Thomas's hand in his. 'Your second wife's. I shall be charmed'; but Lady Marvel, a melancholy-looking woman, with brown hair and sentimental eyelashes, entirely declined to have her past or her future exposed; and nothing that Lady Windermere could do would induce Monsieur de Koloff, the Russian Ambassador, even to take his gloves off. In fact, many people seemed afraid to face the odd little man with his stereotyped smile, his gold spectacles, and his bright, beady eyes, and when he told poor Lady Fermor right out before every one, that she did not care a bit for music, but was extremely fond of musicians, it was generally felt that chiromancy was a most dangerous science, and one that ought not to be encouraged, except in a tête-à-tête.

Lord Arthur Savile, however, who did not know anything about Lady Fermor's unfortunate story, and who had been watching Mr. Podgers with a great deal of interest, was filled with an immense curiosity to have his own hand read, and feeling somewhat shy about putting himself forward, crossed over to the room to where Lady Windermere was sitting, and, with a charming blush, asked her if she thought Mr. Podgers would mind.

LORD ARTHUR SAVILE'S CRIME

'Of course he won't mind,' said Lady Windermere, 'that is what he is here for. All my lions, Lord Arthur, are performing lions, and jump through hoops whenever I ask them. But I must warn you beforehand that I shall tell Sybil everything. She is coming to lunch with me to-morrow, to talk about bonnets, and if Mr. Podgers finds out that you have a bad temper, or a tendency to gout, or a wife living in Bayswater, I shall certainly let her know all about it.'

Lord Arthur smiled, and shook his head. 'I am not afraid,' he answered. 'Sybil knows me as well as I know her.'

'Ah! I am a little sorry to hear you say that. The proper basis for marriage is a mutual misunderstanding. No, I am not at all cynical, I have merely got experience, which, however, is very much the same thing. Mr. Podgers, Lord Arthur Savile is dying to have his hand read. Don't tell him that he is engaged to one of the most beautiful girls in London, because that appeared in the *Morning Post* a month ago.'

'Dear Lady Windermere,' cried the Marchioness of Jedburgh, 'do let Mr. Podgers stay here a little longer. He has just told me I should go on the stage, and I am so interested.'

'If he has told you that, Lady Jedburgh, I shall certainly take him away. Come over at once, Mr. Podgers, and read Lord Arthur's hand.'

'Well,' said Lady Jedburgh, making a little *moue* as she rose from the sofa, 'if I am not to be allowed to go on the stage, I must be allowed to be part of the audience at any rate.'

'Of course; we are all going to be part of the audience,' said Lady Windermere; 'and now, Mr. Podgers, be sure and tell us something nice. Lord Arthur is one of my special favourites.'

But when Mr. Podgers saw Lord Arthur's hand he grew curiously pale, and said nothing. A shudder seemed to pass through him, and his great bushy eyebrows twitched convulsively, in an odd, irritating way they had when he was puzzled. Then some huge beads of perspiration broke out on his yellow forehead, like a poisonous dew, and his fat fingers grew cold and clammy.

Lord Arthur did not fail to notice these strange signs of agitation, and, for the first time in his life, he himself felt fear. His impulse was to rush from the room, but he restrained himself. It was better to know the worst, whatever it was, than to be left in this hideous uncertainty.

'I am waiting, Mr. Podgers,' he said.

'We are all waiting,' cried Lady Windermere, in her quick, impatient manner, but the chiromantist made no reply.

'I believe Arthur is going on the stage,' said Lady Jedburgh, 'and that, after your scolding, Mr. Podgers is afraid to tell him so.'

Suddenly Mr. Podgers dropped Lord Arthur's right hand, and seized hold of his left, bending down so low to examine it that the gold rims of his spectacles seemed almost to touch the palm. For a moment his face became a white mask of horror, but he soon recovered his *sang-froid*, and looking up at Lady Windermere, said with a forced smile, 'It is the hand of a charming young man.'

'Of course it is!' answered Lady Windermere, 'but will he be a charming husband? That is what I want to know.'

'All charming young men are,' said Mr. Podgers.

'I don't think a husband should be too fascinating,' murmured Lady Jedburgh pensively, 'it is so dangerous.'

'My dear child, they never are too fascinating,' cried Lady Windermere. 'But what I want are details. Details are the only things that interest. What is going to happen to Lord Arthur?'

'Well, within the next few months Lord Arthur will go on a voyage—'

'Oh yes, his honeymoon, of course!'

'And lose a relative.'

'Not his sister, I hope?' said Lady Jedburgh, in a piteous tone of voice.

'Certainly not his sister,' answered Mr. Podgers, with a deprecating wave of the hand, 'a distant relative merely.'

'Well, I am dreadfully disappointed,' said Lady Windermere. 'I have absolutely nothing to tell Sybil to-morrow. No one cares about distant relatives nowadays. They went out of fashion years ago. However, I suppose she had better have a black silk by her; it always does for church, you know. And now let us go to supper. They are sure to have eaten everything up, but we may find some hot soup. François used to make excellent soup once, but he is so agitated about politics at present, that I never feel quite certain about him. I do wish General Boulanger would keep quiet. Duchess, I am sure you are tired?'

'Not at all, dear Gladys,' answered the Duchess, waddling towards the door. 'I have enjoyed myself immensely, and the chiropodist, I mean the chiromantist, is most interesting. Flora, where can my tortoise-shell fan be? Oh, thank you, Sir Thomas, so much. And my lace shawl, Flora? Oh, thank you, Sir Thomas, very kind, I'm sure'; and the worthy creature finally managed to get downstairs without dropping her scent-bottle more than twice.

All this time Lord Arthur Savile had remained standing by the fireplace, with the same feeling of dread over him, the same sickening sense of coming evil. He smiled sadly at his sister, as she swept past him on Lord Plymdale's arm, looking lovely in her pink brocade and pearls, and he hardly heard Lady Windermere when she called to him to follow her. He thought of Sybil Merton, and the idea that anything could come between them made his eyes dim with tears.

Looking at him, one would have said that Nemesis had stolen the shield of Pallas, and shown him the Gorgon's head. He seemed turned to stone, and his face was like marble in its melancholy. He had lived the delicate and luxurious life of a young man of birth and fortune, a life exquisite in its freedom from sordid care, its beautiful boyish insouciance; and now for the first time he had become conscious of the terrible mystery of Destiny, of the awful meaning of Doom.

How mad and monstrous it all seemed! Could it be that written on his hand, in characters that he could not read himself, but that another could decipher, was some fearful secret of sin, some blood-red sign of crime? Was there no escape possible? Were we no better than chessmen, moved by an unseen power, vessels the potter fashions at his fancy, for honour or for shame? His reason revolted against it, and yet he felt that some tragedy was hanging over him, and that he had been suddenly called upon to bear an intolerable burden. Actors are so fortunate. They can choose whether they will appear in tragedy or in comedy, whether they will suffer or make merry, laugh or shed tears. But in real life it is different. Most men and women are forced to perform parts for which they have no qualifications. Our Guildensterns play Hamlet for us, and our Hamlets have to jest like Prince Hal. The world is a stage, but the play is badly cast.

Suddenly Mr. Podgers entered the room. When he saw Lord Arthur he started, and his coarse, fat face became a sort of greenish-yellow colour. The two men's eyes met, and for a moment there was silence.

'The Duchess has left one of her gloves here, Lord Arthur, and has asked me to bring it to her,' said Mr. Podgers finally. 'Ah, I see it on the sofa! Good evening.'

'Mr Podgers, I must insist on your giving me a straightforward answer to a question I am going to put to you.'

'Another time, Lord Arthur, but the Duchess is anxious. I am afraid I must go.'

'You shall not go. The duchess is in no hurry.'

'Ladies should not be kept waiting, Lord Arthur,' said Mr. Podger, with his sickly smile. 'The fair sex is apt to be impatient.'

Lord Arthur's finely-chiselled lips curled in petulant disdain. The poor Duchess seemed to him of very little importance at that moment. He walked across the room to where Mr. Podgers was standing, and held his hand out.

'Tell me what you saw there,' he said. 'Tell me the truth. I must know it. I am not a child.'

Mr Podger's eyes blinked behind his gold-rimmed spectacles, and he moved uneasily from one foot to the another, while his fingers played nervously with a flash watch-chain.

'What makes you think that I saw anything in your hand, Lord Arthur, more than I told you?'

'I know you did, and I insist on your telling me what it was. I will pay you. I will give you a cheque for a hundred pounds.'

The green eyes flashed for a moment, and then became dull again.

'Guineas?' said Mr. Podgers at last, in a low voice.

'Certainly. I will send you a cheque to-morrow. What is your club?'

'I have no club. That is to say, not just at present. My address is . . . , but allow me to give you my card'; and producing a bit of gilt-eged pasteboard from his waistcoat pocket, Mr. Podgers handed it, with a low bow, to Lord Arthur, who read on it, '*Mr. Septimus R. Podgers, Professional Chiromantist, 1030 West Moon Street.*'

'My hours are from ten to four,' murmured Mr. Podgers mechanically, 'and I make a reduction for families.'

'Be quick,' cried Lord Arthur, looking very pale, and holding his hand out.

Mr Podgers glanced nervously round, and drew the heavey *portiére* across the door.

'It will take a little time, Lord Arthur, you had better sit down.'

'Be quick, sir,' cried Lord Arthur again, stamping his foot angrily on the polished floor.

Mr. Podgers smiled, drew from his breast-pocket a small magnifying glass, and wiped it carefully with his handkerchief.

'I am quite ready,' he said.

II

Ten minutes later, with face blanched by terror, and eyes wild with grief, Lord Arthur Savile rushed from Bentinck House, crushing his way through the crowd of fur-coated footmen that stood round the large striped awning, and seeming not to see or hear anything. The night was bitter cold, and the gas-lamps round the square flared and flickered in the keen wind; but his hands were hot with fever, and his forehead burned like fire. On and on he went, almost with the gait of a drunken man. A policeman looked curiously at him as he passed, and a beggar, who slouched from an archway to ask for alms, grew frightened, seeing misery greater than his own. Once he stopped under a lamp, and looked at his hands. He thought he could detect the stain of blood already upon them, and a faint cry broke from his trembling lips.

Murder! that is what the chiromantist had seen there. Murder! The very night seemed to know it, and the desolate wind to howl it in his ear. The dark corners of the streets were full of it. It grinned at him from the roofs of the houses.

First he came to the Park, whose sombre woodland seemed to fascinate him. He leaned wearily against the railings, cooling his brow against the wet metal, and listening to the tremulous silence of the trees. 'Murder! murder!' he kept repeating, as though iteration could dim the horror of the word. The sound of his own voice made him shudder, yet he almost hoped that Echo might hear him, and wake the slumbering city from its dreams. He felt a mad desire to stop the casual passer-by, and tell him everything.

Then he wandered across Oxford Street into narrow, shameful alleys. Two women with painted faces mocked at him as he went by. From a dark courtyard came a sound of oaths and blows, followed by shrill screams, and, huddled upon a damp door-step, he saw the crooked-back forms of poverty and eld. A strange pity came over him. Were these children of sin and misery predestined to their end, as he to his? Were they like him, merely the puppets of a monstrous show?

And yet it was not the mystery, but the comedy of suffering that struck him; its absolute uselessness, its grotesque want of meaning. How incoherent everything seemed! How lacking in all harmony! He was amazed at the discord between the shallow optimism of the day, and the real facts of existence. He was still very young.

After a time he found himself in front of Marylebone Church. The silent roadway looked like a long riband of polished silver, flecked here and there by the dark arabesques of waving shadows. Far into the distance curved the line of flickering gas-lamps, and outside a little walled-in house stood a solitary hansom, the driver asleep inside. He walked hastily in the direction of Portland

Place, now and then looking round, as though he feared that he was being followed. At the corner of Rich Street stood two men, reading a small bill upon a hoarding. An odd feeling of curiosity stirred him, and he crossed over. As he came near, the word 'Murder', printed in black letters, met his eye. He started, and a deep flush came into his cheek. It was an advertisement offering a reward for any information leading to the arrest of a man of medium height, between thirty and forty years of age, wearing a billycock hat, a black coat, and check trousers, and with a scar upon his right cheek. He read it over and over again, and wondered if the wretched man would be caught, and how he had been scarred. Perhaps, some day, his own name might be placarded on the walls of London. Some day, perhaps, a price would be set on his head also.

The thought made him sick with horror. He turned on his heel, and hurried into the night.

Where he went he hardly knew. He had a dim memory of wandering through a labyrinth of sordid houses, and it was bright dawn when he found himself at last in Piccadilly Circus. As he strolled home towards Belgrave Square, he met the great waggons on their way to Covent Garden. The white-smocked carters, with their pleasant sunburnt faces and coarse curly hair, strode sturdily on, cracking their whips, and calling out now and then to each other; on the back of a huge grey horse, the leader of a jangling team, sat a chubby boy, with a bunch of primroses in his battered hat, keeping tight hold of the mane with his little hands, and laughing; and the great piles of vegetables looked like masses of jade against the morning sky, like masses of green jade against the pink petals of some marvellous rose. Lord Arthur felt curiously affected, he could not tell why. There was something in the dawn's delicate loveliness that seemed to him inexpressibly pathetic, and he thought of all the days that break in beauty, and that set in storm. These rustics, too, with their rough, good-humoured voices, and their nonchalant ways, what a strange London they saw! A London free from the sin of night and the smoke of day, a pallid, ghost-like city, a desolate town of tombs! He wondered what they thought of it, and whether they knew anything of its splendour and its shame, of its fierce, fiery-coloured joys, and its horrible hunger, of all it makes and mars from morn to eve. Probably it was to them merely a mart where they brought their fruit to sell, and where they tarried for a few hours at most, leaving the streets still silent, the houses still asleep. It gave him pleasure to watch them as they went by. Rude as they were, with their heavy, hob-nailed shoes, and their awkward gait, they brought a little of Arcady with them. He felt that they had lived with Nature, and that she had taught them peace. He envied them all that they did not know.

By the time hea had reached Belgrave Square the sky was a faint blue, and the birds were beginning to twitter in the gardens.

III

When Lord Arthur woke it was twelve o'clock, and the midday sun was streaming through the ivory-silk curtains of his room. He got up and looked out of the window. A dim haze of heat was hanging over the great city, and the roofs of the houses were like dull silver. In the flickering green of the square below some children were flitting about like white butterflies, and the pavement was crowded with people on their way to the Park. Never had life seemed lovelier to him, never had the things of evil seemed more remote.

Then his valet brought him a cup of chocolate on a tray. After he had drunk it, he drew aside a heavy *portiére* of peach-coloured plush, and passed into the bathroom. The light stole softly from above, through thin slabs of transparent onyx, and the water in the marble tank glimmered like a moonstone. He plunged hastily in, till the cool ripples touched throat and hair, and then dipped his head right under, as though he would have wiped away the stain of some shameful memory. When he stepped out he felt almost at peace. The exquisite physical conditions of the moment had dominated him, as indeed often happens in the case of very finely-wrought natures, for the senses, like fire, can purify as well as destroy.

After breakfast, he flung himself down on a divan and lit a cigarette. On the mantel-shelf, framed in dainty old brocade, stood a large photograph of Sybil Merton, as he had seen her first at Lady Noel's ball. The small, exquisitely-shaped head drooped slightly to one side, as though the thin, reed-like throat could hardly bear the burden of so much beauty; the lips were slightly parted, and seemed made for sweet music; and all the tender purity of girlhood looked out in wonder from the dreaming eyes. With her soft, clinging dress of *crêpe de chine*, and her large leaf-shaped fan, she looked like one of those delicate little figures men find in the olive-woods near Tanagra; and there was a touch of Greek grace in her pose and attitude. Yet she was not *petite*. She was simply perfectly proportioned—a rare thing in an age when so many women are either over life-size or insignificant.

Now as Lord Arthur looked at her, he was filled with the terrible pity that is born of love. He felt that to marry her, with the doom of murder hanging over his head, would be a betrayal like that of Judas, a sin worse than any the Borgias had ever dreamed of. What happiness could there be for them when at any moment he might be called upon to carry out the awful prophecy written in his hand? What manner of life would be theirs while Fate still held this fearful fortune in the scales? The marriage must be postponed, at all costs. Of this he was quite resolved. Ardently though he loved the girl, and the mere touch of her fingers, when they sat together, made each nerve of his body thrill with exquisite joy, he recognised none the less clearly where his duty lay, and was fully conscious of the fact that he had no right to marry until he had committed the murder. This done, he could stand before the altar with Sybil Merton, and give his life into her hands without terror of wrong-doing. This done, he could take her to his arms, knowing that she would never have to blush for him, never have to hang her head in shame. But done it must be first; and the sooner the better for both.

Many men in his position would have preferred the primrose path of dalliance to the steep heights of duty; but Lord Arthur was too conscientious to set pleasure above principle. There was more than mere passion in his love; and Sybil was to him a symbol of all that is good and noble. For a moment he had a natural repugnance against what he was asked to do, but it soon passed away. His heart told him that it was not a sin, but a sacrifice; his reason reminded him that there was no other course open. He had to choose between living for himself and living for others, and terrible though the task laid upon him undoubtedly was, yet he knew that he must not suffer selfishness to triumph over love. Sooner or later we are all called upon to decide on the same issue—of us all the same question is asked. To Lord Arthur it came early in life—before his nature had been spoiled by the calculating cynicism of middle age, or his heart corroded by the shallow, fashionable egotism of our day, and he felt no hesitation about doing his duty. Fortunately also, for him, he was no mere dreamer, or idle dilettante. Had he been so, he would have hesitated, like Hamlet, and let irresolution mar his purpose. But he was essentially practical. Life to him meant action, rather than thought. He had that rarest of all things, common sense.

The wild, turbid feelings of the previous night had by this time completely passed away, and it was almost with a sense of shame that he looked back upon his mad wanderings from street to street, his fierce emotional agony. The very sincerity of his sufferings made them seem unreal to him now. He wondered how he could have been so foolish as to rant and rave about the inevitable. The only question that seemed to trouble him was, whom to make away with; for he was not blind to the fact that murder, like the religions of the Pagan world, requires a victim as well as a priest. Not being a genius, he had no enemies, and indeed he felt that this was not the time for the gratification of any personal pique or dislike, the mission in which he was engaged being one of great and grave solemnity. He accordingly made out a list of his friends and relatives on a sheet of notepaper, and after careful consideration, decided in favour of Lady Clementina Beauchamp, a dear old lady who lived in Curzon Street, and was his own second cousin by his mother's side. He had always been very fond of Lady Clem, as everyone called her, and as he was very wealthy himself, having come into all Lord Rugby's property when he came of age, there was no possibility of his deriving any vulgar monetary advantage by her death. In fact, the more he thought over the matter, the more she seemed to him to be just the right person, and, feeling that any delay would be unfair to Sybil, he determined to make his arrangements at once.

The first thing to be done was, of course, to settle with the chiromantist; so he sat down at a small Sheraton writing-table that stood near the window, drew a cheque for £105, payable to the order of Mr. Septimus Podgers, and enclosing it in an envelope, told his valet to take it to West Moon Street. He then telephoned to the stables for his hansom, and dressed to go out. As he was leaving the room he looked back at Sybil Merton's photograph, and swore that, come what may, he would never let her know what he was doing for her sake, but would keep the secret of his self-sacrifice hidden always in his heart.

On his way to the Buckingham, he stopped at a florist's, and sent Sybil a beautiful basket of narcissi, with lovely white petals and staring pheasants' eyes, and on arriving at the club went straight to the library, rang the bell, and ordered the waiter to bring him a lemon-and-soda, and a book on Toxicology.

He had fully decided that poison was the best means to adopt in this troublesome business. Anything like personal violence was extremely distasteful to him, and besides, he was very anxious not to murder Lady Clementina in any way that might attract public attention, as he hated the idea of being lionized at Lady Windermere's, or seeing his name figuring in the paragraphs of vulgar society-newspapers. He had also to think of Sybil's father and mother, who were rather old-fashioned people, and might possibly object to the marriage if there was anything like a scandal, though he felt certain that if he told them the whole facts of the case they would be the very first to appreciate the motives that had actuated him. He had every reason, then, to decide in favour of poison. It was safe, sure, and quiet, and did away with any necessity for painful scenes, to which, like most Englishmen, he had a rooted objection.

Of course the science of poisons, however, he knew absolutely nothing, and as the waiter seemed quite unable to find anything in the library but *Ruff's Guide* and *Bailey's Magazine* he examined the book-shelves himself, and finally came across a handsomely-bound edition of the *Pharmacopæia*, and a copy of Erskine's *Toxicology*, edited by Sir Mathew Reid, the President of the Royal College of Physicians, and one of the oldest members of the Buckingham, having been elected in mistake for somebody else; a *contretemps* that so enraged the Committee, that when the real man came up they black-balled him unanimously. Lord Arthur was a good deal puzzled at the technical terms used in both books, and had begun to regret that he had not paid more attention to his classics at Oxford, when in the second volume of Erskine, he found a very interesting and complete account of the properties of aconitine, written in fairly clear English. It seemed to him to be exactly the poison he wanted. It was swift—indeed, almost immediate, in its effect—perfectly painless, and when taken in the form of a gelatine capsule, the mode recommended by Sir Mathew, not by any means unpalatable. He accordingly made a note, upon his shirt-cuff, of the amount necessary for a fatal dose, put the books back in their places, and strolled up St. James's Street, to Pestle and Humbey's, the great chemists. Mr. Pestle, who always attended personally on the aristocracy, was a good deal surprised at the order, and in a very deferential manner murmured something about a medical certificate being necessary. However, as soon as Lord Arthur explained to him that it was for a large Norwegian mastiff that he was obliged to get rid of, as it showed signs of incipient rabies, and had already bitten the coachman twice in the calf of the leg, he expressed himself as being perfectly satisfied, complimented Lord Arthur on his wonderful knowledge of Toxicology, and had the prescription made up immediately.

Lord Arthur put the capsule into a pretty little silver *bonbonnière* that he saw in a shop window in Bond Street, threw away Pestle and Humbey's ugly pill-box, and drove off at once to Lady Clementina's.

'Well, *monsieur le mauvais sujet*,' cried the old lady, as he entered the room, 'why haven't you been to see me all this time?'

'My dear Lady Clem, I never have a moment to myself,' said Lord Arthur, smiling.

'I suppose you mean that you go about all day along with Miss Sybil Merton, buying *chiffons* and talking nonsense? I cannot understand why people make such a fuss about being married. In my day we never dreamed of billing and cooing in public, or in private for that matter.'

'I assure you I have not seen Sybil for twenty-four hours, Lady Clem. As far as I can make out, she belongs entirely to her milliners.'

'Of course; that is the only reason you come to see an ugly old woman like myself. I wonder you men don't take warning. *On a fait des folies pour moi*, and here I am, a poor rheumatic creature, with a false front and a bad temper. Why, if it were not for dear Lady Jansen, who sends me all the worst French novels she can find, I don't think I could get through the day. Doctors are no use at all, except to get fees out of one. They can't even cure my heartburn.'

'I have brought you a cure for that, Lady Clem,' said Lord Arthur gravely. 'It is a wonderful thing, invented by an American.'

'I don't think I like American inventions, Arthur. I am quite sure I don't. I read some American novels lately, and they were quite nonsensical.'

'Oh, but there is no nonsense at all about this, Lady Clem! I assure you it is a perfect cure. You must promise to try it'; and Lord Arthur brought the little box out of his pocket, and handed it to her.

'Well, the box is charming, Arthur. Is it really a present? That is very sweet of you. And is this the wonderful medicine? It looks like a *bonbon*. I'll take it at once.'

'Good heavens! Lady Clem,' cried Lord Arthur, catching hold of her hand, 'you mustn't do anything of the kind. It is a homœopathic medicine, and if you take it without having heartburn, it might do you no end of harm. Wait till you have an attack, and take it then. You will be astonished at the result'.

'I should like to take it now,' said Lady Clementine, holding up to the light the little transparent capsule, with its floating bubble of liquid aconitine. 'I am sure it is delicious. The fact is that, though I hate doctors, I love medicines. However, I'll keep it till my next attack.'

'And when will that be?' asked Lord Arthur eagerly. 'Will it be soon?'

'I hope not for a week. I had a very bad time yesterday morning with it. But one never knows'

'You are sure to have one before the end of the month then, Lady Clem?'

'I am afraid so. But how sympathetic you are to-day, Arthur! Really, Sybil has done you a great deal of good. And now you must run away, for I am dining with some very dull people, who won't talk scandal, and I know that if I don't get my sleep now I shall never be able to keep awake during dinner. Good-bye, Arthur, give my love to Sybil, and thank you so much for the American medicine.'

'You won't forget to take it, Lady Clem, will you?' said Lord Arthur, rising from his seat.

'Of course I won't, you silly boy. I think it is most kind of you to think of me, and I shall write and tell you if I want any more.'

Lord Arthur left the house in high spirits, and with a feeling of immense relief.

That night he had an inverview with Sybil Merton. He told her how he had been suddenly placed in a position of terrible difficulty, from which neither honour nor duty would allow him to recede. He told her that the marriage must be put off for the present, as until he had got rid of his fearful entanglements, he was not a free man. He implored her to trust him, and not to have any doubts about the future. Everything should come right, but patience was necessary.

The scene took place in the conservatory of Mr. Merton's house, in Park Lane, where Lord Arthur had dined as usual. Sybil had never seemed more happy, and for a moment Lord Arthur had been tempted to play the coward's part, to write to Lady Clementina for the pill, and to let the marriage go on as if there was no such person as Mr. Podgers in the world. His better nature, however, soon asserted itself, and even when Sybil flung herself weeping into his arms, he did not falter. The beauty that stirred his senses had touched his conscience also. He felt that to wreck so fair a life for the sake of a few months' pleasure would be a wrong thing to do.

He stayed with Sybil till nearly midnight, comforting her and being comforted in turn, and early the next morning he left for Venice, after writing a manly, firm letter to Mr. Merton about the necessary postponement of the marriage.

IV

In Venice he met his brother, Lord Surbiton, who happened to have come over from Corfu in his yacht. The two young men spent a delightful fortnight together. In the morning they rode on the Lido, or glided up and down the green canal in their long black gondola; in the afternoon they usually entertained visitors on the yacht; and in the evening they dined at Florian's, and smoked innumerable cigarettes on the Piazza. Yet somehow Lord Arthur was not happy. Every day he studied the obituary column in the *Times*, expecting to see a notice of Lady Clementina's death, but every day he was disappointed. He began to be afraid that some accident had happened to her, and often regretted that he had prevented her taking the aconitine when she had been so anxious to try its effect. Sybil's letters, too, though full of love, and trust, and tenderness, were often very sad in their tone, and sometimes he used to think that he was parted from her for ever.

After a fortnight Lord Surbiton got bored with Venice, and determined to run down the coast to Ravenna, as he heard that there was some capital cock-shooting in the Pinetum. Lord Arthur at first refused absolutely to come, but Surbiton, of whom he was extremely fond, finally persuaded him that if he stayed at Danielli's by himself he would be moped to death, and on the morning of the 15th they started, with a strong nor'east wind blowing, and a rather choppy sea. The sport was excellent, and the free, open-air life brought the colour back to Lord Arthur's cheek, but about the 22nd be became anxious about Lady Clementina, and, in spite of Surbiton's remonstrances, came back to Venice by train.

As he stepped out of his gondola on to the hotel steps, the proprietor came forward to meet him with a sheaf of telegrams. Lord Arthur snatched them out of his hand, and tore them open. Everything had been quite successful. Lady Clementina had died quite suddenly on the night of the 17th!

His first thought was for Sybil, and he sent her off a telegram announcing his immediate return to London. He then ordered his valet to pack his things for the night mail, sent his gondoliers about five times their proper fare, and ran up to his sitting-room with a light step and a buoyant heart. There he found three letters waiting for him. One was from Sybil herself, full of sympathy and condolence. The others were from his mother, and from Lady Clementina's solicitor. It seemed that the old lady had dined with the Duchess that very night, had delighted every one by her wit and *esprit*, but had gone home somewhat early, complaining of heartburn. In the morning she was found dead in her bed, having apparently suffered no pain. Sir Mathew Reid had been sent for at once, but, of course, there was nothing to be done, and she was to be buried on the 22nd at Beauchamp Chalcote. A few days before she died she had made her will, and left Lord Arthur her little house in Curzon Street, and all her furniture, personal effects, and pictures, with the exception of her collection of miniatures, which was to go to her sister, Lady Margaret Rufford, and her amethyst necklace, which Sybil Merton was to have. The property was not of much value; but Mr. Mansfield, the solicitor, was extremely anxious for Lord Arthur to return at once, if possible, as there were a great many bills to be paid, and Lady Clementina had never kept any regular accounts.

Lord Arthur was very much touched by Lady Clementina's kind remembrance of him, and felt that Mr. Podgers had a great deal to answer for. His love of Sybil, however, dominated every other emotion, and the consciousness that he had done his duty gave him peace and comfort. When he arrived at Charing Cross, he felt perfectly happy.

The Mertons received him very kindly. Sybil made him promise that he would never again allow anything to come between them, and the marriage was fixed for the 7th June. Life seemed to him once more bright and beautiful, and all his old gladness came back to him again.

One day, however, as he was going over the house in Curzon Street, in company with Lady Clementina's solicitor and Sybil herself, burning packages of faded letters and turning out drawers of odd rubbish, the young girl suddenly gave a cry of delight.

'What have you found, Sybil?' said Lord Arthur, looking up from his work, and smiling.

'This lovely little silver *bonbonnière*, Arthur. Isn't it quaint and Dutch? Do give it to me! I know amethysts won't become me till I am over eighty.'

It was the box that had held the aconitine.

Lord Arthur started, and a faint blush came into his cheek. He had almost entirely forgotten what he had done, and it seemed to him a curious coincidence that Sybil, for whose sake he had gone through all that terrible anxiety, should have been the first to remind him of it.

'Of course you can have it, Sybil, I gave it to poor Lady Clem myself.'

'Oh! thank you, Arthur; and may I have the *bonbon* too? I had no notion that Lady Clementina liked sweets. I thought she was far too intellectual.'

Lord Arthur grew deadly pale, and a horrible idea crossed his mind.

'*Bonbon*, Sybil? What do you mean?' he said in a slow, hoarse voice.

'There is one in it, that is all. It looks quite old and dusty, and I have not the slightest intention of eating it. What is the matter, Arthur? How white you look!

Lord Arthur rushed across the room, and seized the box. Inside it was the amber-coloured capsule, with its poison-bubble. Lady Clementina had died a natural death after all!

The shock of the discovery was almost too much for him. He flung the capsule into the fire, and sank on the sofa with a cry of despair.

V

Mr. Merton was a good deal distressed at the second postponement of the marriage, and Lady Julia, who had already ordered her dress for the wedding, did all in her power to make Sybil break off the match. Dearly, however, as Sybil loved her mother, she had given her whole life into Lord Arthur's hands, and nothing that Lady Julia could say could make her waver in her faith. As for Lord Arthur himself, it took him days to get over his terrible disappointment, and for a time his nerves were completely unstrung. His excellent common sense, however, soon asserted itself, and his sound, practical mind did not leave him long in doubt about what to do. Poison having proved a complete failure, dynamite, or some other form of explosive, was obviously the proper thing to try.

He accordingly looked again over the list of his friends and relatives, and, after careful consideration, determined to blow up his uncle, the Dean of Chichester. The Dean, who was a man of great culture and learning, was extremely fond of clocks, and had a wonderful collection of timepieces, ranging from the fifteenth century to the present day, and it seemed to Lord Arthur that this hobby of the good Dean's offered him an excellent opportunity for carrying out his scheme. Where to procure an explosive machine was, of course, quite another matter. The London Directory gave him no information on the point, and he felt that there was very little use in going to Scotland Yard about it, as they never seemed to know anything about the movements of the dynamite faction till after an explosion had taken place, and not much even then.

Suddenly he thought of his friend Rouvaloff, a young Russian of very revolutionary tendencies, whom he had met at Lady Windermere's in the winter. Count Rouvaloff was supposed to be writing a life of Peter the Great, and to have come over to England for the purpose of studying the documents relating to that Tsar's residence in this country as a ship carpenter; but it was generally suspected that he was a Nihilist agent, and there was no doubt that the Russian Embassy did not look with any favour upon his presence in London. Lord Arthur felt that he was just the man for his purpose, and drove down one morning to his lodgings in Bloomsbury, to ask his advice and assistance.

'So you are taking up politics seriously?' said Count Rouvaloff, when Lord Arthur had told him the object of his mission; but Lord Arthur, who hated swagger of any kind, felt bound to admit to him that he had not the slightest interest in social questions, and simply wanted the explosive machine for a purely family matter, in which no one was concerned but himself.

Count Rouvaloff looked at him for some moments in amazement, and then seeing that he was quite serious, wrote an address on a piece of paper, initialled it, and handed it to him across the table.

'Scotland Yard would give a good deal to know this address, my dear fellow.'

'They shan't have it,' cried Lord Arthur, laughing; and after shaking the young Russian warmly by the hand he ran downstairs, examined the paper, and told the coachman to drive to Soho Square.

There he dismissed him, and strolled down Greek Street, till he came to a place called Bayle's Court. He passed under the archway, and found himself in a curious *cul-de-sac*, that was apparently occupied by a French laundry, as a perfect network of clothes-lines was stretched across from house to house, and there was a flutter of white linen in the morning air. He walked right to the end, and knocked at a little green house. After some delay, during which every window became a blurred mass of peering faces, the door was opened by a rather rough-looking foreigner, who asked him in very bad English what his business was. Lord Arthur handed him the paper Count Rouvaloff had given him. When the man saw it he bowed, and invited Lord Arthur into a very shabby front parlour on the ground floor, and in a few moments Herr Winckelkopf, as he was called in England, bustled into the room, with a very wine-stained napkin round his neck, and a fork in his left hand.

'Count Rouvaloff has given me an introduction to you,' said Lord Arthur, bowing, 'and I am anxious to have a short interview with you on a matter of business. My name is Smith, Mr. Robert Smith, and I want you to supply me with an explosive clock.'

'Charmed to meet you, Lord Arthur,' said the genial little German, laughing. 'Don't look so alarmed, it is my duty to know everybody, and I remember seeing you one evening at Lady Windermere's. I hope her ladyship is quite well. Do you mind sitting with me while I finish my breakfast? There is an excellent *paté*, and my friends are kind enough to say that my Rhine wine is better than any they get at the German Embassy,' and before Lord Arthur had got over his surprise at being recognized, he found himself seated in the back-room, sipping the most delicious Marcobrünner out of a pale yellow hock-glass marked with the Imperial monogram, and chatting in the friendliest manner possible to the famous conspirator.

'Explosive clocks,' said Herr Winckelkopf, 'are not very good things for foreign exportation, as, even if they succeed in passing the Custom House, the train service is so irregular, that they usually go off before they have reached their proper destination. If, however, you want one for home use, I can supply you with an excellent article, and guarantee that you will be satisfied with the result. May I ask for whom it is intended? If it is for the police, or for any one connected with Scotland Yard, I am afraid I cannot do anything for you. The English detectives are really our best friends, and I have always found that by relying on their stupidity, we can do exactly what we like. I could not spare one of them.'

'I assure you,' said Lord Arthur, 'that it has nothing to do with the police at all. In fact, the clock is intended for the Dean of Chichester.'

'Dear me! I had no idea that you felt so strongly about religion, Lord Arthur. Few young men do nowadays.'

'I am afraid you overrate me, Herr Winckelkopf,' said Lord Arthur, blushing. 'The fact is, I really know nothing about theology.'

'It is a purely private matter then?'

'Purely private.'

Herr Winckelkopf shrugged his shoulders, and left the room, returning in a few minutes with a round cake of dynamite about the size of a penny, and a pretty little French clock, surmounted by an ormolu figure of Liberty trampling on the hydra of Despotism.

Lord Arthur's face brightened up when he saw it. 'That is just what I want,' he cried, 'and now tell me how it goes off.'

'Ah! there is my secret,' answered Herr Winckelkopf, contemplating his invention with a justifiable look of pride; 'let me know when you wish it to explode, and I will set the machine to the moment.'

'Well, today is Tuesday, and if you could sent it off at once—'

'That is impossible; I have a great deal of important work on hand for some friends of mine in Moscow. Still, I might send it off tomorrow.'

'Oh, it will be quite time enough!' said Lord Arthur politely, 'if it is delivered tomorrow night or Thursday morning. For the moment of the explosion, say Friday at noon exactly. The Dean is always at home at that hour.'

'Friday, at noon,' repeated Herr Winckelkopf, and he made a note to that effect in a large ledger that was lying on a bureau near the fireplace.

'And now,' said Lord Arthur, rising from his seat, 'pray let me know how much I am in your debt.'

'It is such a small matter, Lord Arthur, that I do not care to make any charge. The dynamite comes to seven and sixpence, the clock will be three pounds ten, and the carriage about five shillings. I am only too pleased to oblige any friend of Count Rouvaloff's.'

'But your trouble, Herr Winckelkopf?'

'Oh, that is nothing! It is a pleasure to me. I do not work for money; I live entirely for my art.'

Lord Arthur laid down £4 2s. 6d. on the table, thanked the little German for his kindness, and, having succeeded in declining an invitation to meet some Anarchists at a meat-tea on the following Saturday, left the house and went off to the Park.'

For the next two days he was in a state of the greatest excitement, and on Friday at twelve o'clock he drove down to the Buckingham to wait for news. All the afternoon the stolid hall-porter kept posting up telegrams from various parts of the country giving the results of horse-races, the verdicts in divorce suits, the state of the weather, and the like, while the tape ticked out wearisome details about an all-night sitting in the House of Commons, and a small panic on the Stock Exchange. At four o'clock the evening papers came in, and Lord Arthur disappeared into the library with the *Pall Mall*, the *St. James's*, the *Globe*, and the *Echo*, to the immense indignation of Colonel Goodchild, who wanted to read the reports of a speech he had delivered that morning at the Mansion House, on the subject of South African Missions, and the advisability of having black Bishops in every province, and for some reason or other had a strong prejudice against the *Evening News*. None of the papers, however, contained even the slightest allusion to Chichester, and Lord Arthur felt that the attempt must have failed. It was a terrible blow to him, and for a time he was quite unnerved. Herr Winkelkopf, whom he went to see the next day, was full of elaborate apologies, and offered to supply him with another clock free of charge, or with a case of nitro-glycerine bombs at cost price. But he had lost all faith in explosives, and Herr Winckelkopf himself acknowledged that everything is so adulterated nowadays, that even dynamite can hardly be got in a pure condition. The little German, however, while admitting that something must have gone wrong with the machinery, was not without hope that the clock might still go off, and instanced the case of a barometer that he had once sent to the military Governor at Odessa, which, though timed to explode in ten days, had not done so for something like three months. It was quite true that when it did go off, it merely succeeded in blowing a housemaid to atoms, the Governor having gone out of town six weeks before, but at least it showed that dynamite, as a destructive force, was, when under the control of machinery, a powerful, though somewhat unpunctual agent. Lord Arthur was a little consoled by this reflection, but even here he was destined to disappointment, for two days afterwards, as he was going upstairs, the Duchess called him into her boudoir, and showed him a letter she had just received from the Deanery.

'Jane writes charming letters,' said the Duchess; 'you must really read her last. It is quite as good as the novels Mudie sends us.'

Lord Arthur seized the letter from her hand. It ran as follows:—

THE DEANERY, CHICHESTER,
27th May.

My dearest Aunt,

Thank you so much for the flannel for the Dorcas Society, and also for the gingham. I quite agree with you that it is nonsense their wanting to wear pretty things, but everybody is so Radical and irreligious nowadays, that it is difficult to make them see that they should not try and dress like the upper classes. I am sure I don't know what we are coming to. As papa has often said in his sermons, we live in an age of unbelief.

We have had great fun over a clock that an unknown admirer sent papa last Thursday. It arrived in a wooden box from London, carriage paid; and papa feels it must have been sent by some one who had read his remarkable sermon, 'Is Licence Liberty?' for on the top of the clock was a figure of a woman, with what papa said was the cap of Liberty on her head. I don't think it very becoming myself, but papa said it was historical, so I suppose it is all right. Parker unpacked it, and papa put it on the mantelpiece in the library, and we were all sitting there on Friday morning, when just as the clock struck twelve, we heard a whirring noise, a little puff of smoke came from the pedestal of the figure, and the goddess of Liberty fell off, and broke her nose on the fender! Maria was quite alarmed, but it looked so ridiculous, that James and I went off into fits of laughter, and even papa was amused. When we examined it, we found it was a sort of alarm clock, and that, if you set it to a particular hour, and put some gunpowder and a cap under a little hammer, it went off whenever you wanted. Papa said it must not remain in the library, as it made a noise, so Reggie carried it away to the schoolroom, and does nothing but have small explosions all day long. Do you think Arthur would like one for a wedding present? I suppose they are quite fashionable in London. Papa says they should do a great deal of good, as they show that Liberty can't last, but must fall down. Papa says Liberty was invented at the time of the French Revolution. How awful it seems!

I have now to go to the Dorcas, where I will read your most instructive letter. How true, dear aunt, your idea is, that in their rank of life they should wear what is unbecoming. I must say it is absurd, their anxiety about dress, when there are so many more important things in this world, and in the next. I am so glad your flowered poplin turned out so well, and that your lace was not torn. I am wearing my yellow satin, that you so kindly gave me, at the Bishop's on Wednesday, and think it will look all right. Would you have bows or not? Jennings says that every one wears bows now, and that the underskirt should be frilled. Reggie has just had another explosion, and papa has ordered the clock to be sent to the stables. I don't think papa likes it so much as he did at first, though he is very flattered at being sent such a pretty and ingenious toy. It shows that people read his sermons, and profit by them.

Papa sends his love, in which James, and Reggie, and Maria all unite, and, hoping that uncle Cecil's gout is better, believe me, dear aunt, ever your affectionate niece,

Jane Percy.

PS.—Do tell me about the bows. Jennings insists they are the fashion.

Lord Arthur looked so serious and unhappy over the letter, that the Duchess went into fits of laughter.

'My dear Arthur,' she cried, 'I shall never show you a young lady's letter again! But what shall I say about the clock? I think it is a capital invention, and I should like to have one myself.'

'I don't think much of them,' said Lord Arthur, with a sad smile, and, after kissing his mother, he left the room.

When he got upstairs, he flung himself on a sofa, and his eyes filled with tears. He had done his best to commit this murder, but on both occasions he had failed, and through no fault of his own. He had tried to do his duty, but it seemed as if Destiny herself had turned traitor. He was oppressed with the sense of the barrenness of good intentions, of the futility of trying to be fine. Perhaps it would be better to break off the marriage altogether. Sybil would suffer, it is true, but suffering could not really mar a nature so noble as hers. As for himself, what did it matter? There is always some war in which a man can die, some cause to which a man can give his life, and as life had no pleasure for him, so death had no terror. Let Destiny work out his doom. He would not stir to help her.

At half-past seven he dressed, and went down to the club. Surbiton was there with a party of young men, and he was obliged to dine with them. Their trivial conversation and idle jests did not interest him, and as soon as coffee was brought he left them, inventing some engagement in order to get away. As he was going out of the club, the hall-porter handed him a letter. It was from Herr Winckelkopf, asking him to call down the next evening, and look at an explosive umbrella, that went off as soon as it was opened. It was the very latest invention, and had just arrived from Geneva. He tore the letter up into fragments. He had made up his mind not to try any more experiments. Then he wandered down to the Thames Embankment, and sat for hours by the river. The moon peered through a mane of tawny clouds, as if it were a lion's eye, and innumerable stars spangled the hollow vault, like gold dust powdered on a purple dome. Now and then a barge swung out into the turbid stream, and floated away with the tide, and the railway signals changed from green to scarlet as the trains ran shrieking across the bridge. After some time, twelve o'clock boomed from the tall tower at Westminster, and at each stroke of the sonorous bell the night seemed to tremble. Then the railway lights went out, one solitary lamp left gleaming like a large ruby on a giant mast, and the roar of the city became fainter.

At two o'clock he got up, and strolled towards Blackfriars. How unreal everything looked! How like a strange dream! The houses on the other side of the river seemed built out of darkness. One would have said that silver and shadow had fashioned the world anew. The huge dome of St Paul's loomed like a bubble through the dusky air.

As he approached Cleopatra's Needle he saw a man leaning over the parapet, and as he came nearer the man looked up, the gas-light falling full upon his face.

It was Mr Podgers, the chiromantist! No one could mistake the fat, flabby face, the gold-rimmed spectacles, the sickly feeble smile, the sensual mouth.

Lord Arthur stopped. A brilliant idea flashed across him, and he stole softly up behind. In a moment he had seized Mr Podgers by the legs, and flung him into the Thames. There was a coarse oath, a heavy splash, and all was still. Lord Arthur looked anxiously over, but could see nothing of the chiromantist but a tall hat, pirouetting in an eddy of moonlit water. After a time it also sank, and no trace of Mr Podgers was visible. Once he thought that he caught sight of the bulky misshapen figure striking out for the staircase by the bridge, and a horrible feeling of failure came over him but it turned out to be merely a reflection, and when the moon shone out from behind a cloud it passed away. At last he seemed to have realized the decree of Destiny. He heaved a deep sigh of relief, and Sybil's name came to his lips.

'Have you dropped anything, sir?' said a voice behind him suddenly.

He turned round, and saw a policeman with a bull's-eye lantern.

'Nothing of importance, sergeant,' he answered, smiling, and hailing a passing hansom, he jumped in, and told the man to drive to Belgrave Square.

For the next few days he alternated between hope and fear. There were moments when he almost expected Mr Podgers to walk into the room, and yet at other times he felt that Fate could not be so unjust to him. Twice he went to the chiromantist's address in West Moon Street, but he could not bring himself to ring the bell. He longed for certainty, and was afraid of it.

Finally it came. He was sitting in the smoking-room of the club having tea, and listening rather wearily to Surbiton's account of the last comic song at the Gaiety, when the waiter came in with the evening papers. He took up the *St James's*, and was listlessly turning over its pages, when this strange heading caught his eye:

'SUICIDE OF A CHIROMANTIST.'

He turned pale with excitement, and began to read. The paragraph ran as follows:

'Yesterday morning, at seven o'clock, the body of Mr Septimus R. Podgers, the eminent chiromantist, was washed on shore at Greenwich, just in front of the Ship Hotel. The unfortunate gentleman had been missing for some days, and considerable anxiety for his safety had been felt in chiromantic circles. It is supposed that he committed suicide under the influence of a temporary mental derangement, caused by overwork, and a verdict to that effect was returned this afternoon by the coroner's jury. Mr Podgers had just completed an elaborate treatise on the subject of the Human Hand, that will shortly be published, when it will no doubt attract much attention. The deceased was sixty-five years of age, and does not seem to have left any relations.'

Lord Arthur rushed out of the club with the paper still in his hand, to the immense amazement of the hall-porter, who tried in vain to stop him, and drove at once to Park Lane. Sybil saw him from the window, and something told her that he was the bearer of good news. She ran down to meet him, and, when she saw his face, she knew that all was well.

'My dear Sybil,' cried Lord Arthur, 'let us be married tomorrow!'

'You foolish boy! Why, the cake is not even ordered!' said Sybil, laughing through her tears.

VI

When the wedding took place, some three weeks later, St Peter's was crowded with a perfect mob of smart people. The service was read in the most impressive manner by the Dean of Chichester, and everybody agreed that they had never seen a handsomer couple than the bride and bridegroom. They were more than handsome, however—they were happy. Never for a single moment did Lord Arthur regret all that he had suffered for Sybil's sake, while she, on her side, gave him the best things a woman can give any man—worship, tenderness, and love. For them romance was not killed by reality. They always felt young.

Some years afterwards, when two beautiful children had been born to them, Lady Windermere came down on a visit to Alton Priory, a lovely old place, that had been the Duke's wedding present to his son; and one afternoon as she was sitting with Lady Arthur under a lime-tree in the garden, watching the little boy and girl as they played up and down the rose-walk, like fitful sunbeams, she suddenly took her hostess's hand in hers, and said, 'Are you happy, Sybil?'

'Dear Lady Windermere, of course I am happy. Aren't you?'

'I have no time to be happy, Sybil. I always like the last person who is introduced to me; but, as a rule, as soon as I know people I get tired of them.'

'Don't your lions satisfy you, Lady Windermere?'

'Oh dear, no! lions are only good for one season. As soon as their manes are cut, they are the dullest creatures going. Besides, they behave very badly, if you are really nice to them. Do you remember that horrid Mr Podgers? He was a dreadful impostor. Of course, I didn't mind that at all, and even when he wanted to borrow money I forgave him, but I could not stand his making love to me. He has really made me hate chiromancy. I go in for telepathy now. It is much more amusing.'

'You mustn't say anything against chiromancy here, Lady Windermere; it is the only subject that Arthur does not like people to chaff about. I assure you he is quite serious over it.'

'You don't mean to say that he believes in it, Sybil?'

'Ask him, Lady Windermere, here he is'; and Lord Arthur came up the garden with a large bunch of yellow roses in his hand, and his two children dancing round him.

'Lord Arthur?'

'Yes, Lady Windermere,'

'You don't mean to say that you believe in chiromancy?'

'Of course I do,' said the young man, smiling.

'But why?'

'Because I owe to it all the happiness of my life,' he murmured, throwing himself into a wicker chair.

'My dear Lord Arthur, what do you owe to it?'

'Sybil,' he answered, handing his wife the roses, and looking into her violet eyes.

'What nonsense!' cried Lady Windermere. 'I never heard such nonsense in all my life.'

The Sorcerer of the White Lotus Lodge

Once upon a time there was a sorcerer who belonged to the White Lotus Lodge. He knew how to deceive the multitude with his black arts, and many who wished to learn the secret of his enchantments became his pupils.

One day the sorcerer wished to go out. He placed a bowl which he covered with another bowl in the hall of his house, and ordered his pupils to watch it. But he warned them against uncovering the bowl to see what might be in it.

No sooner had he gone than the pupils uncovered the bowl and saw that it was filled with clear water. And floating on the water was a little ship made of straw, with real masts and sails. They were surprised and pushed it with their fingers till it upset. Then they quickly righted it again and once more covered the bowl. By that time the sorcerer was already standing among them. He was angry and scolded them, saying: 'Why did you disobey my command?'

His pupils rose and denied that they had done so.

But the sorcerer answered: 'Did not my ship turn turtle at sea, and yet you try to deceive me?'

On another evening he lit a giant candle in his room, and ordered his pupils to watch it lest it be blown out by the wind. It must have been at the second watch of the night and the sorcerer had not yet come back. The pupils grew tired and sleepy, so they went to bed and gradually fell asleep. When they woke up again the candle had gone out. So they rose quickly and re-lit it. But the sorcerer was already in the room, and again he scolded them.

'Truly we did not sleep! How could the light have gone out?'

Angrily the sorcerer replied: 'You let me walk fifteen miles in the dark, and still you can talk such nonsense!'

—RICHARD WILHELM

The Celestial Stag

An unaccountable tale is told in the *Tzǔ Puh Yü* of the *Celestial stag*, which lives in underground mines, and guides the workmen to the veins of gold and silver. If these creatures are hauled up into the daylight, they change into an offensively-smelling liquid, which deals pestilence and death around. If the miners refuse to haul them up (apparently they can speak, and are anxious to get out), the 'stags' molest the miners, and have to be overpowered, immured in the mine, and firmly embedded in clay. Where the 'stags' outnumber the miners, they sometimes torment the men and cause their death.

—G. WILLOUGHBY-MEADE

Saved by the Book

The literate Wu, of Ch'iang Ling on a certain occasion insulted the magician. Expecting the latter to try some trick on him, Wu sat up the following night with his lamp alight and the I Ching before him. Suddenly a wind was heard, rushing round the outside of his house; and a man-at-arms came in at the door, brandishing a spear and threatening to strike him. Wu knocked him down with the book. When he stooped to look at him, he saw that he was merely a doll cut out in paper. He slipped the paper figure between the leaves of the sacred classic. Presently entered two little Kuei with black faces, armed with axes. These, when knocked down with the book, turned out to be paper figures also, and were slipped between the leaves. In the middle of the night, a woman, weeping and wailing, came knocking at the door. 'I am the wife of Chang the magician,' she said. 'My husband and sons came to attack you, and you have imprisoned them in your book. I beg you to set them free.' 'I have neither your husband nor your sons in my book,' replied Wu. 'I have only these little paper figures.' 'Their souls are in those figures,' said the woman. 'Unless they return by the morning, their bodies, lying at home, will not revive.'

'Cursed magicians!' cried Wu. 'What can you justly expect, after what you have done to other people? I shall certainly not set them free. Out of compassion, I will let you have one of your sons back, but do not ask more.' Whereupon he handed her one of the little paper Kuei.

The next day he had enquiries made at Chang's house and learned that he and his elder son had died in the night, leaving a widow and a younger son.

—G. WILLOUGHBY-MEADE

The Reanimated Englishman

Mary Wollstonecraft Shelley, *(1797-1851), born in London, was the only child of William Godwin and Mary Wollstonecraft. In 1814 she went to the Continent with Shelley, marrying him two years later, and at Byron's villa at Lake Geneva she conceived the idea for her famous* novel Frankenstein, or the Modern Prometheus.

Animation (I believe physiologists agree) can as easily be suspended for a hundred or two years, as for as many seconds. A body hermetically sealed up by the frost, is of necessity preserved in its pristine entireness. That which is totally secluded from the action of external agency, can neither have any thing added to nor taken away from it: no decay can take place, for something can never become nothing; under the influence of that state of being which we call death, change but not annihilation removes from our sight the corporeal atoms; the earth receives sustenance from them, the air is fed by them, each element takes its own, thus seizing forcible repayment of what it had lent. But the elements that hovered around Mr Dodsworth's icy shroud had no power to overcome the obstacle it presented. No zephyr could gather a hair from his head, nor could the influence of dewy night or genial morn penetrate his more than adamantine panoply. The story of the Seven Sleepers rests on a miraculous interposition—they slept. Mr Dodsworth did not sleep; his breast never heaved, his pulses were stopped; death had his finger pressed on his lips which no breath might pass. He has removed it now, the grim shadow is vanquished, and stands wondering . . .

The Sentence

That night, at the hour of the rat, the Emperor dreamt that he went out of his palace to walk under the blossoming trees by moonlight. Suddenly someone knelt before him saying, 'Save me, your Majesty, save me!' 'Who are you?' asked the Emperor. 'Of course I'll help you.' 'Your Majesty,' said the dragon king, 'is a True Dragon. I am but a dragon by karma. I have disobeyed Heaven's instructions and am to be executed by your minister Wei Chêng. I have come to ask you to help me.' 'If it is Wei Chêng who is to execute you,' said the Emperor, 'I can certainly put things right. You needn't worry.' The dragon thanked him profusely and went off.

Scanning the ranks of his ministers at Court next morning, the Emperor noticed that Wei Chêng was not in his usual place. 'You must get him to come here at once, and keep him occupied all day,' said one of the other ministers, when he heard the Emperor's dream. 'That is the only way to keep your promise and save the dragon.'

Meanwhile Wei Chêng, sitting in his house at night, surveying the constellations and burning rare incense, suddenly heard the cry of a crane high up in the sky, and in a moment there alighted a heavenly messenger, bearing instructions from the Jade Emperor that Wei Chêng was in dream to execute the dragon king of the Ching River at noon next day. Wei Chêng accordingly purified himself, tested the sword of his intelligence and the free fling of his soul, and kept away from Court. But when the Emperor's summons came he dared not delay, and hastily robing himself he went back to Court at once with the messenger, and apologized for his absence. 'I am not complaining,' said the Emperor, and when they had discussed State affairs for a while, he sent for a draughts board and invited Wei Chêng to a game of draughts. Just before noon, when there were still a good many pieces on the board, Wei Chêng's head suddenly nodded, he began to snore heavily, and was evidently fast asleep. The Emperor smiled. 'No wonder he is tired,' thought the Emperor, 'when one thinks of all the public business he has on his shoulders,' and he did not attempt to wake him.

When at last Wei Chêng woke up, he was appalled to find that he had dozed in the Imperial presence, and flung himself at the Emperor's feet, saying, 'I deserve death a thousand times, I suddenly felt tired; I don't know why it happened. I beg your Majesty to pardon me for this gross disrespect.' 'Get up,' said the Emperor, 'you've done nothing disrespectful.' Then emptying the remaining pieces off the board he suggested that they should start a new game. They were just setting the pieces, when in rushed two captains, carrying a dragon's head dripping with blood. They flung it at the Emperor's feet, crying, 'Your Majesty, we have heard of seas becoming shallow and rivers running dry. But of so strange a thing as this we have never heard tell.' 'Where does this thing come from?' Wei Chêng and the Emperor exclaimed in chorus. 'To the south of the Thousand Steps Gallery, at the top of Cross Street,' they said, 'it fell from the clouds, and we thought it right to inform you at once.' 'What does all this mean?' asked the Emperor, turning much perturbed to Wei Chêng. 'It is the head of the dragon that I killed in dream just now, when I fell asleep,' he said.

—WU CH'ENG EN

The Sorcerers

William Butler Yeats, *born near Dublin in 1865. Went to London in 1887, where he became associated with the 'decadent' writers and dabbled in occultism and magic. He published* The Wanderings of Oisin *(1889) and* The Celtic Twilight *(1893). After his return to Ireland he was involved with the Abbey Theatre, and many of his best poems come from this period, in* The Wild Swans at Coole *(1917),* The Tower *(1928), and* The Winding Stair *(1929). He died in 1939.*

In Ireland we hear but little of the darker powers, and come across any who have seen them even more rarely, for the imagination of the people dwells rather upon the fantastic and capricious, and fantasy and caprice would lose the freedom which is their breath of life, were they to unite them either with evil or with good. I have indeed come across very few persons in Ireland who try to communicate with evil powers, and the few I have keep their purpose and practice wholly hidden from those among whom they live. They are mainly small clerks, and meet for the purpose of their art in a room hung with black hangings, but in what town that room is I shall not say. They would not admit me into this room, but finding me not altogether ignorant of the arcane science, showed elsewhere what they could do. 'Come to us,' said their leader, 'and we will show you spirits who will talk to you face to face, and in shapes as solid and heavy as our own.'

I had been talking of the power of communicating in states of trance with the angelical and faery beings—the children of the day and of the twilight—and he had been contending that we should only believe in what we can see and feel when in our ordinary everyday state of mind. 'Yes,' I said, 'I will come to you,' or some such words; 'but I will not permit myself to become entranced, and will therefore know whether these shapes you talk of are any the more to be touched and felt by the ordinary senses than are these I talk of.' I was not denying the power of other beings to take upon themselves a clothing of mortal substance, but only that simple invocations, such as he spoke of, seemed unlikely to do more than cast the mind into trance.

'But,' he said, 'we have seen them move the furniture hither and thither, and they go at our bidding, and help or harm people who know nothing of them.' I am not giving the exact words, but as accurately as I can the substance of our talk.

On the night arranged I turned up about eight, and found the leader sitting alone in almost total darkness in a small back room. He was dressed in a black gown, like an inquisitor's dress in an old drawing, that left nothing of him visible except his eyes, which peered out through two small round holes. Upon the table in front of him was a brass dish of burning herbs, a large bowl, a skull covered with painted symbols, two crossed daggers, and certain implements, whose use I failed to discover, shaped like quern stones. I also put on a black gown, and remember that it did not fit perfectly, and that it interfered with my movements considerably. The sorcerer then took a black cock out of a basket, and cut its throat with one of the daggers, letting the blood fall into the large bowl. He opened a book and began an invocation, which was neither English nor Irish, and had a deep guttural sound. Before he had finished, another of the sorcerers, a man of about twenty-five, came in, and having put on a black gown also, seated himself at my left hand. I had the invoker directly in front of me, and soon began to find his eyes, which glittered through the small holes in his hood, affecting me in a curious way. I struggled hard against their influence, and my head began to ache. The invocation continued, and nothing happened for the first few minutes. Then the invoker got up and extinguished the light in the hall, so that no glimmer might come through the slit under the door. There was now no light except from the herbs on the brass dish, and no sound except from the deep guttural murmur of the invocation.

Presently the man at my left swayed himself about, and cried out, 'O God! O God!' I asked him what ailed him, but he did not know he had spoken. A moment after he could see a great serpent moving about the room, and became considerably excited. I saw nothing with any definite shape, but thought that black clouds were forming about me. I felt I must fall into a trance if I did not struggle against it, and that the influence which was causing this trance was out of harmony with itself, in other words, evil. After a struggle I got rid of the black clouds and was able to observe with my ordinary senses again. The two sorcerers now began to see black and white columns moving about the room, and finally a man in a monk's habit, and they became greatly puzzled because I did not see these things also, for to them they were as solid as the table before them. The invoker appeared to be gradually increasing in power, and I bagan to feel as if a tide of darkness was pouring from him and concentrating itself about me; and now too I noticed that the man on my left hand had passed into a death-like trance. With a last great effort I drove off the black clouds; but feeling them to be the only shapes I could see without passing into a trance, and having no great love for them, I asked for lights and after the needful exorcism returned to the ordinary world.

I said to the more powerful of the two sorcerers, 'What would happen if one of your spirits had overpowered me?' 'You would go out of this room' he answered, 'with his character added to your own.'

Fragment

José Zorrilla, *Spanish poet and dramatist. Born in Valladolid in 1817, died in Madrid in 1893. On 22nd January, 1889, the Granada Academy awarded him a laureate in the presence of 14,000 spectators. He is the author of* Juan Dandolo *(1833),* A la memoria desraciada del joven literato D. Mariano Jose de Larra *(1837),* A buen juez mejor testigo *(1838),* Mas vale llegar a tiempo que rondar un ano *(1838),* Vigilias del estio *(1842),* Cain prata *(1842),* El caballo del rey D. Sancho *(1842),* El alcalde Ronguillo *(1844),* Un testigo de bronce *(1845),* La calentura *(1845),* Ofrenda poetica al Liceo Artistico y Literario de Madrid *(1848),* Traidor inconfeso y martir *(1849),* La rosa de Alejandria *(1857),* Album de un loco *(1866),* La leyenda del Cid *(1882),* Gnomos y mujeres *(1886),* A escape y al vuelo *(1888), etc. As a poet, he contributed* El album religioso *to* La corona funebre del 2 de mayo de 1808, *and to* El album del Bardo.

D. JUAN: Tolling for me . . .?

STATUE: For you.

D. JUAN: And these funereal dirges that I hear?

STATUE: The penitential psalms they chant for you. (At the back, left, between the tombs, lighted candles are seen passing, and the sounds of the service for the dead.)

D. JUAN: But how for me? They bear a wreathéd hearse.

STATUE: Your hearse, that bears your body.

D. JUAN: I, dead . . .?

STATUE: The Captain killed you at your door.

SOURCES AND ACKNOWLEDGEMENTS

The publishers would like to thank Jim Shean, Sheila Brownlee and Alison Bailey for their help with the research for this book, and special thanks are due to Lucia Alvarez de Toledo for her invaluable assistance. Thanks are also due to the copyright-holders detailed below for granting permission to reprint material. Whilst every effort has been made to trace authors and copyright-holders, in some cases this has proved impossible, and Xanadu Publications would be glad to hear from any such parties so that any omissions can be rectified in future editions of the book.

'Sennin' by Ryunosuke Akutagawa is from *The Three Treasures* (1951), translation by S. Takamasa reprinted by permission of Hukuseido Press, Tokyo. 'A woman alone With Her Soul' by Thomas Bailey Aldrich is from his *Works, Vol. 9* (1912). 'Ben-Tobith' by Leonid Andreyev is from *A Treasury of Russian Literature* (n.d.), translation by Bernard Guilbert Guerney reprinted by permission of The Bodley Head Ltd. 'The Phantom Basket' is from John Aubrey's *Miscellanies* (1696). 'The Drowned Giant' by J.G. Ballard was originally published under the title 'Souvenir' in *Playboy*, Copyright © 1965 by HMH Publications, reprinted by permission of the author. 'Enoch Soames' by Sir Max Beerbohm is from *Seven Man* (1919), reprinted by permission of William Heinemann Ltd. 'The Tail of the Sphinx' by Ambrose Bierce is from *Fantastic Fables*. 'The Squid in its Own Ink' by Adolfo Bioy Casares is from *El Lado de la Sombra* (1962), Copyright © A. Bioy Casares 1962, reprinted by permission of the author and Emecé Editores; translated by Lucia Alvarez de Toledo and Alexandra Potts. 'Anything You Want! ...' by Léon Bloy is from *Histoires Désobligeantes* (1894), translated by Moira Banks. 'Tlön, Uqbar, Orbis Tertius' by Jorge Luis Borges, translated by James E. Irby, is from *Labyrinths* and reprinted by permission of New Directions Publishing Corp; Copyright © The Estate of Jorge Luis Borges 1941. 'The Golden Kite, The Silver Wind' by Ray Bradbury is from *The Golden Apples of the Sun*, Copyright © Ray Bradbury 1952, 1953, reprinted by permission of Don Condon Associates Inc. 'The Man Who Collected the First of September 1973' by Tor Åge Bringsvaerd is translated by Oddrun Grønvik; Copyright © Tor Åge Bringsvaerd 1973, reprinted by permission of the author. 'The Careless Rabbi' by Martin Buber, translated by Olga Marx, is from *Tales of the Hasidin, Vol. 1* (1956), reprinted by permission of Thames and Hudson Ltd. 'Fate is a Fool' by Arturo Cancela and Pilar di Lusarreta is translated by Lucia Alvarez de Toledo and Alexandra Potts and reprinted by permission of Editorial Sudamericana. 'An Actual Authentic Ghost' by Thomas Carlyle is from *Sartor Resartus* (1834). 'The Red King's Dream' by Lewis Carroll is from *Through the Looking-Glass* (1871). 'The Tree of Pride' and 'The Tower of Babel' by G.K. Chesterton are from *The Man who Knew Too Much (1922)*. 'The Look of Death' by Jean Cocteau is from *Le Grand Ecart*, Copyright © Editions Stock 1923, reprinted by permission of the publisher. 'House Taken Over' by Julio Cortàzar is from *End of Game, and Other Stories*, translated by Paul Blackburn, Copyright © Random House, Inc., 1967, 1963; reprinted by permission of Random House, Inc., ALIA and the Estate of the author. 'Being Dust' by Santiago Dabove is from *La Muerte y su Traje* (1961), translated by Lucia Alvarez de Toldo and Alexandra Potts, reprinted by permission of the Estate of the author. 'A Parable of Gluttony' and 'The Persecution of the Master' by Alexandra David-Neel are from *With Mystics and Magicians in Tibet* (1931), reprinted by permission of The Bodley Head Ltd. 'The Idle City' by Lord Dunsany is from *A Dreamer's Tales*; Copyright © The Estate of Lord Dunsany 1910, reprinted by permission of Curtis Brown, London. 'Tantalia' by Macedonio Fernández, translated by Lucia Alvarez de Toledo and Alexandra Potts, is reprinted by permission of Ediciones Corregidor, Buenos Aires. 'Eternal Life' by J.G. Frazer is from *The Golden Bough, Part 7; Baldur the Beautiful* (1913), reprinted by permission of Macmillan and Company Ltd. 'A Secure Home' by Elena Garro, translated by Lucia Alvarez de Toledo and Alexandra Potts, is reprinted by permission of Universidad Veracruzana. 'The Man Who Did Not Believe in Miracles' by Herbert A. Giles is from *Confucianism and its Rivals* (1915). 'Ending for a Ghost Story' by I.A. Ireland is from *Visitations* (1919). 'The Monkey's Paw' by W.W. Jacobs is from *The Lady of the Barge* (1902), Copyright © the Estate of W.W. Jacobs, reprinted by permission of the Society of Authors as the literary representatives of the Estate of W.W. Jacobs. 'What is a Ghost?' and 'May Goulding' by James Joyce are from *Ulysses* (1921), reprinted by permission of the Executors of the James Joyce Estate. 'The Wizard Passed Over' by Don Juan Manuel is from *Count Lucanor* (1575); this version by Jorge Luis Borges from *A Universal History of Infamy* is translated by Norman Thomas di Giovanni, 1970, 1971, reprinted by permission of the publishers, E.P. Dutton, Inc. 'Josephine the Singer' and 'Before the Law' by Franz Kafka are from *The Penguin Complete Short Stories of Franz Kafka*, both translated by Willa and Edwin Muir; Copyright © 1946 by Schocken Books, Inc., reprinted by permission of Schocken Books, Inc. and Secker and Warburg Ltd. 'The Return of Imray' by Rudyard Kipling is from *Life's Handicap* (1891), reprinted by permission of Doubleday and Company, Inc. 'The Horses of Abdera' by Leopoldo Lugones is from *Las Fuerzas Extranas* (1906), reprinted by permission of Editorial Huemul, Buenos Aires; translated by Janet Barber. 'The Ceremony' by Arthur Machen, Copyright © the Estate of Arthur